Deerbrook

Harriet Martineau

Alpha Editions

This edition published in 2021

ISBN : 9789354752957

Design and Setting By
Alpha Editions
www.alphaedis.com
Email - info@alphaedis.com

As per information held with us this book is in Public Domain.
This book is a reproduction of an important historical work. Alpha Editions uses the best technology to reproduce historical work in the same manner it was first published to preserve its original nature. Any marks or number seen are left intentionally to preserve its true form.

Contents

Chapter One	- 1 -
Chapter Two	- 12 -
Chapter Three	- 16 -
Chapter Four	- 23 -
Chapter Five	- 30 -
Chapter Six	- 50 -
Chapter Seven	- 63 -
Chapter Eight	- 69 -
Chapter Nine	- 81 -
Chapter Ten	- 88 -
Chapter Eleven	- 104 -
Chapter Twelve	- 114 -
Chapter Thirteen	- 124 -
Chapter Fourteen	- 131 -
Chapter Fifteen	- 143 -
Chapter Sixteen	- 160 -
Chapter Seventeen	- 169 -
Chapter Eighteen	- 179 -
Chapter Nineteen	- 188 -
Chapter Twenty	- 204 -

Chapter Twenty One	- 212 -
Chapter Twenty Two	- 223 -
Chapter Twenty Three	- 232 -
Chapter Twenty Four	- 240 -
Chapter Twenty Five	- 252 -
Chapter Twenty Six	- 258 -
Chapter Twenty Seven	- 273 -
Chapter Twenty Eight	- 284 -
Chapter Twenty Nine	- 310 -
Chapter Thirty	- 315 -
Chapter Thirty One	- 326 -
Chapter Thirty Two	- 335 -
Chapter Thirty Three	- 341 -
Chapter Thirty Four	- 350 -
Chapter Thirty Five	- 360 -
Chapter Thirty Six	- 381 -
Chapter Thirty Seven	- 396 -
Chapter Thirty Eight	- 401 -
Chapter Thirty Nine	- 414 -
Chapter Forty	- 430 -
Chapter Forty One	- 446 -
Chapter Forty Two	- 459 -

Chapter Forty Three	- 465 -
Chapter Forty Four	- 476 -
Chapter Forty Five	- 482 -
Chapter Forty Six	- 488 -

Chapter One

An Event.

Every town-bred person who travels in a rich country region, knows what it is to see a neat white house planted in a pretty situation,—in a shrubbery, or commanding a sunny common, or nestling between two hills,—and to say to himself, as the carriage sweeps past its gate, "I should like to live there,"—"I could be very happy in that pretty place." Transient visions pass before his mind's eye of dewy summer mornings, when the shadows are long on the grass, and of bright autumn afternoons, when it would be luxury to saunter in the neighbouring lanes; and of frosty winter days, when the sun shines in over the laurustinus at the window, while the fire burns with a different light from that which it gives in the dull parlours of a city.

Mr Grey's house had probably been the object of this kind of speculation to one or more persons, three times a week, ever since the stage-coach had begun to pass through Deerbrook. Deerbrook was a rather pretty village, dignified as it was with the woods of a fine park, which formed the background to its best points of view. Of this pretty village, Mr Grey's was the prettiest house, standing in a field, round which the road swept. There were trees enough about it to shade without darkening it, and the garden and shrubbery behind were evidently of no contemptible extent. The timber and coal yards, and granaries, which stretched down to the river side, were hidden by a nice management of the garden walls, and training of the shrubbery.

In the drawing-room of this tempting white house sat Mrs Grey and her eldest daughter, one spring evening. It was rather an unusual thing for them to be in the drawing-room. Sophia read history and practised her music every morning in the little blue parlour which looked towards the road; and her mother sat in the dining-room, which had the same aspect. The advantage of these rooms was, that they commanded the house of Mr Rowland, Mr Grey's partner in the corn, coal, and timber business, and also the dwelling of Mrs Enderby, Mrs Rowland's mother, who lived just opposite the Rowlands. The drawing-room looked merely into the garden. The only houses seen from it were the greenhouse and the summerhouse; the latter of which now served the purpose of a schoolroom for the children of both families, and stood on the boundary-line of the gardens of the two gentlemen of the firm. The drawing-room was so dull, that it was kept for company; that is, it was used about three times a-year, when the pictures were unveiled, the green baize removed, and the ground-windows, which opened upon the lawn, thrown wide, to afford to the rare guests of the family a welcome from birds and flowers.

The ground-windows were open now, and on one side sat Mrs Grey, working a rug, and on the other Sophia, working a collar. The ladies were evidently in a state of expectation—a state exceedingly trying to people who, living at ease in the country, have rarely anything to expect beyond the days of the week, the newspaper, and their dinners. Mrs Grey gave her needle a rest every few minutes, to listen! and rang the bell three times in a quarter of an hour, to make inquiries of her maid about the arrangements of the best bedroom. Sophia could not attend to her work, and presently gave information that Fanny and Mary were in the orchard. She was desired to call them, and presently Fanny and Mary appeared at the window,—twins of ten years old, and very pretty little girls.

"My dears," said Mrs Grey, "has Miss Young done with you for to-day?"

"Oh yes, mamma. It is just six o'clock. We have been out of school this hour almost."

"Then come in, and make yourselves neat, and sit down with us. I should not wonder if the Miss Ibbotsons should be here now before you are ready. But where is Sydney?"

"Oh, he is making a pond in his garden there. He dug it before school this morning, and he is filling it now."

"Yes," said the other; "and I don't know when he will have done, for as fast as he fills it, it empties again, and he says he cannot think how people keep their ponds filled."

"He must have done now, however," said his mother. "I suppose he is tearing his clothes to pieces with drawing the water-barrel, and wetting himself to the skin besides."

"And spoiling his garden," said Fanny. "He has dug up all his hepaticas and two rose-bushes to make his pond."

"Go to him, my dears, and tell him to come in directly, and dress himself for tea. Tell him I insist upon it. Do not run. Walk quietly. You will heat yourselves, and I do not like Mrs Rowland to see you running."

Mary informed her brother that he was to leave his pond and come in, and Fanny added that mamma insisted upon it. They had time to do this, to walk quietly, to have their hair made quite smooth, and to sit down with their two dolls on each side the common cradle, in a corner of the drawing-room, before the Miss Ibbotsons arrived.

The Miss Ibbotsons were daughters of a distant relation of Mr Grey's. Their mother had been dead many years; they had now just lost their father, and were left without any nearer relation than Mr Grey. He had invited them to visit his family while their father's affairs were in course of arrangement, and till it could be discovered what their means of living were likely to be. They had passed their lives in Birmingham, and had every inclination to return to it, when their visit to their Deerbrook relations should have been paid. Their old schoolfellows and friends all lived there: and they thought it would be easier and pleasanter to make the smallest income supply their wants in their native town, than to remove to any place where it might go further. They had taken leave of their friends as for a very short time, and when they entered Deerbrook, looked around them as upon a place in which they were to pass a summer.

All Deerbrook had been informed of their expected arrival—as it always was of everything which concerned the Greys. The little Rowlands were walking with their mother when the chaise came up the street; but being particularly desired not to look at it, they were not much benefited by the event. Their grandmamma, Mrs Enderby, was not at the moment under the same restriction; and her high cap might be seen above the green blind of her parlour as the chaise turned into Mr Grey's gate. The stationer, the parish clerk, and the milliner and her assistant, had obtained a passing view of sundry boxes, the face of an elderly woman, and the outline of two black bonnets,—all that they could boast of to repay them for the vigilance of a whole afternoon.

Sophia Grey might be pardoned for some anxiety about the reception of the young ladies. She was four years younger than the younger of them; and Hester, the elder, was one-and-twenty,—a venerable age to a girl of sixteen. Sophia began to think she had never been really afraid of anything before, though she remembered having cried bitterly when first left alone with her governess; and though she had always been remarkable for clinging to her mother's side on all social occasions, in the approaching trial her mother could give her little assistance. These cousins would be always with her. How she should read history, or practise music with them in the room, she could not imagine, nor what she should find to say to them all day long. If poor Elizabeth had but lived, what a comfort she would have been now; the elder one would have taken all the responsibility! And she heaved a sigh once more, as she thought, to the memory of poor Elizabeth.

Mr Grey was at a market some miles off; and Sydney was sent by his mother into the hall, to assist in the work of alighting, and causing the luggage to alight. As any other boy of thirteen would have done, he slunk behind the hall door, without venturing to speak to the strangers, and left the business to the guests and the maids. Mrs Grey and Sophia awaited them in the drawing-room, and were ready with information about how uneasy they had all been about the rain in the morning, till they remembered that it would lay the dust, and so make the journey pleasanter. The twins shouldered their dolls, and looked on from their stools, while Sydney stole in, and for want of some better way of covering his awkwardness, began rocking the cradle with his foot till he tilted it over.

Sophia found the first half-hour not at all difficult to surmount. She and Margaret Ibbotson informed each other of the precise number of miles between Deerbrook and Birmingham. She ascertained fully to her satisfaction that her guests had dined. She assisted them in the observation that the grass of the lawn looked very green after the streets of Birmingham; and she had to tell them that her father was obliged to attend the market some miles off, and would not be home for an hour or two. Then the time came when bonnets were to be taken off, and she could offer to show the way to the spare-room. There she took Hester and Margaret to the window, and explained to them what they saw thence; and, as it was necessary to talk, she poured out what was most familiar to her mind, experiencing a sudden relief from all the unwonted shyness which had tormented her.

"That is Mr Rowland's house—papa's partner, you know. Isn't it an ugly place, with that ridiculous porch to it? But Mrs Rowland can never be satisfied without altering her house once a year. She has made Mr Rowland spend more money upon that place than would have built a new one of twice the size.—That house opposite is Mrs Enderby's, Mrs Rowland's mother's. So near as she lives to the Rowlands, it is shocking how they neglect her. There could be no difficulty in being properly attentive to her, so near as she is, could there? But when she is ill we are obliged to go and see her sometimes, when it is very inconvenient, because Mrs Rowland has never been near her all day. Is not it shocking?"

"I rather wonder she should complain of her family," observed Margaret.

"Oh, she is not remarkable for keeping her feelings to herself, poor soul! But really it is wonderful how little she says about it, except when her heart is quite full,—just to us. She tries to excuse Mrs Rowland all she can; and she makes out that Mrs Rowland is such an excellent mother, and so busy with her children, and all that. But you know that is no excuse for not taking care of her own mother."

"Those are the Verdon woods, are they not?" said Hester, leaning out of the window to survey the whole of the sunny prospect. "I suppose you spend half your days in those woods in summer."

"No; mamma goes out very little, and I seldom walk beyond the garden. But now you are come, we shall go everywhere. Ours is considered a very pretty village."

The sisters thought it so beautiful, that they gazed as if they feared it would melt away if they withdrew their eyes. The one discovered the bridge, lying in shadow; the other the pointed roof of the building which surmounted the spring in the park woods. Sophia was well pleased at their pleasure; and their questions, and her descriptions, went on improving in rapidity, till a knock at the door of the room cut short the catechism. It was Morris, the Miss Ibbotsons' maid; and her appearance gave Sophia a hint to leave her guests to refresh themselves. She glanced over the room, to see that nothing was wanting; pointed out the bell, intimated that the washstands were mahogany, which showed every splash, and explained that the green blinds were meant to be always down when the sun shone in, lest it should fade the carpet. She then withdrew, telling the young ladies that they would find tea ready when they came down.

"How very handsome Hester is!" was the exclamation of both mother and daughter, when Sophia had shut the drawing-room door behind her.

"I wonder," said Mrs Grey, "that nobody ever told us how handsome we should find Hester. I should like to see what fault Mrs Rowland can find in her face."

"It is rather odd that one sister should have all the beauty," said Sophia. "I do not see anything striking in Margaret."

"Mrs Rowland will say she is plain; but, in my opinion, Margaret is better looking than any of the Rowlands are ever likely to be. Margaret would not be thought plain away from her sister.—I hope they are not fine ladies. I am rather surprised at their bringing a maid. She looks a very respectable person; but I did not suppose they would keep a maid till they knew better what to look forward to. I do not know what Mr Grey will think of it."

When Hester and Margaret came down, Mrs Grey was ready with an account of the society of the place.

"We are as well off for society," said she, "as most places of the size. If you were to ask the bookseller at Blickley, who supplies our club, he would tell you that we are rather intellectual people: and I hope you will see, when our friends have called on you, that though we seem to be living out of the world, we are not without our pleasures. I think, Sophia, the Levitts will certainly call."

"Oh, yes, mamma, to-morrow, I have no doubt."

"Dr Levitt is our rector," observed Mrs Grey to her guests. "We are dissenters, as you know, and our neighbour, Mrs Rowland, is very much scandalised at it. If Mr Rowland would have allowed it, she would have made a difficulty on that ground about having her children educated with mine. But the Levitts' conduct might teach her better. They make no difference on account of our being dissenters. They always call on our friends the first day after they arrive,—or the second, at furthest. I have no doubt we shall see the Levitts to-morrow."

"And Mrs Enderby, I am sure," said Sophia, "if she is at all able to stir out."

"Oh, yes, Mrs Enderby knows what is right, if her daughter does not. If she does not call to-morrow, I shall think that Mrs Rowland prevented her. She can keep her mother within doors, as we know, when it suits her purposes."

"But Mr Philip is here, mamma, and Mrs Enderby can do as she likes when she has her son with her.—I assure you he is here, mamma. I saw the cobbler's boy carry home a pair of boots there this morning."

Sydney had better evidence still to produce. Mr Enderby had been talking with him about fishing this afternoon. He said he had come down for a fortnight's fishing. Fanny also declared that Matilda Rowland had told Miss Young to-day, that uncle Philip was coming to see the new schoolroom. Mrs Grey was always glad, on poor Mrs Enderby's account, when she had her son with her: but otherwise she owned she did not care for his coming. He was too like his sister to please her.

"He is very high, to be sure," observed Sophia.

"And really there is no occasion for that with us," resumed Mrs Grey. "We should never think of mixing him up with his sister's proceedings, if he did not do it himself. No one would suppose him answerable for her rudeness; at least, I am sure such a thing would never enter my head. But he forces it upon one's mind by carrying himself so high."

"I don't think he can help being so tall," observed Sydney.

"But he buttons up, and makes the most of it," replied Sophia. "He stalks in like a Polish count."

The sisters could not help smiling at this proof that the incursions of the Poles into this place were confined to the book club. They happened to be well acquainted with a Polish count, who was short of stature and did not stalk. They were spared all necessity of exerting themselves in conversation, for it went on very well without the aid of more than a word or two from them.

"Do you think, mamma, the Andersons will come?" asked Sophia.

"Not before Sunday, my dear. The Andersons live three miles off," she explained, "and are much confined by their school. They may possibly call on Saturday afternoon, as Saturday is a half-holiday; but Sunday after church is a more likely time.—We do not much approve of Sunday visits; and I dare say you feel the same: but this is a particular case,—people living three miles off, you know, and keeping a school. And being dissenters, we do not like to appear illiberal to those who are not of our own way of thinking: so the Andersons sometimes come in after church; and I am sure you will accept their call just as if it was made in any other way."

Hester and Margaret could only say that they should be happy to see Mr and Mrs Anderson in any mode which was most convenient to themselves. A laugh went through the family, and a general exclamation of "Mr and Mrs Anderson!" "The Andersons" happened to be two maiden sisters, who kept a young ladies' school. It was some time before Mrs Grey herself could so far command her countenance as to frown with becoming severity at Fanny, who continued to giggle for some time, with intervals of convulsive stillness, at the idea that "the Andersons" could mean Mr and Mrs Anderson. In the midst of the struggle, Mr Grey entered. He laid a hand on the head of each twin, observed that they seemed very merry, and asked whether his cousins had been kind enough to make them laugh already. To these cousins he offered a brief and hearty welcome, remarking that he supposed they had been told what had prevented his being on the spot on their arrival, and that he need not trouble them with the story over again.

Sydney had slipped out as his father entered, for the chance of riding his horse to the stable,—a ride of any length being in his opinion better than none. When he returned in a few minutes, he tried to whisper to Sophia, over the back of her chair, but could not for laughing. After repeated attempts, Sophia pushed him away.

"Come, my boy, out with it!" said his father. "What you can tell your sister you can tell us. What is the joke?"

Sydney looked as if he had rather not explain before the strangers; but he never dared to trifle with his father. He had just heard from little George Rowland, that Mrs Rowland had said at home, that the young ladies at Mr Grey's, who had been made so much fuss about, were not *young* ladies, after all: she had seen the face of one, as they passed her in the chaise, and she was sure the person could not be less than fifty.

"She saw Morris, no doubt," said Hester, amidst the general laugh.

"I hope she will come to-morrow, and see some people who are very little like fifty," said Mrs Grey. "She will be surprised, I think," she added, looking at Hester, with a very meaning manner of admiration. "I really hope, for her own sake, she will come, though you need not mind if she does not. You will have no great loss. Mr Grey, I suppose you think she will call?"

"No doubt, my dear. Mrs Rowland never omits calling on our friends; and why should she now?" And Mr Grey applied himself to conversation with his cousins, while the rest of the family enjoyed further merriment about Mrs Rowland having mistaken Morris for one of the Miss Ibbotsons.

Mr Grey showed a sympathy with the sisters, which made them more at home than they had felt since they entered the house. He knew some of their Birmingham friends, and could speak of the institutions and interests of the town. For a whole hour he engaged them in brisk conversation, without having once alluded to their private affairs or his own, or said one word about Deerbrook society. At the end of that time, just as Mary and Fanny had received orders to go to bed, and were putting their dolls into the cradle in preparation, the scrambling of a horse's feet was heard on the gravel before the front door, and the house-bell rang.

"Who can be coming at this time of night?" said Mrs Grey.

"It is Hope, I have no doubt," replied her husband. "As I passed his door, I asked him to go out to old Mr Smithson, who seems to me to be rather worse than better, and to let me know whether anything can be done for the old gentleman. Hope has come to report of him, no doubt."

"Oh, mamma, don't send us to bed if it is Mr Hope!" cried the little girls. "Let us sit up a little longer if it is Mr Hope."

"Mr Hope is a great favourite with the children,—with us all," observed Mrs Grey to the sisters. "We have the greatest confidence in him as our medical man; as indeed every one has who employs him. Mr Grey brought him here, and we consider him the greatest acquisition our society ever had."

The sisters could not be surprised, at this when they saw Mr Hope. The only wonder was, that, in the description of the intellectual society of Deerbrook, Mr Hope had not been mentioned first. He was not handsome; but there was a gaiety of countenance and manner in him under which the very lamp seemed to burn brighter. He came, as Mr Grey had explained, on business; and, not having been aware of the arrival of the strangers, would have retreated when his errand was done; but, as opposition was made to this by both parents and children he sat down for a quarter of an hour, to be taken into consultation about how the Miss Ibbotsons were to be conducted through the process of seeing the sights of Deerbrook.

With all sincerity, the sisters declared that the woods of the park would fully satisfy them,—that they had been accustomed to a life so quiet, that excursions were not at all necessary to their enjoyment. Mr Grey was determined that they should visit every place worth seeing in the neighbourhood, while it was in its summer beauty. Mr Hope was exactly the right person to consult, as there was no nook, no hamlet, to which his tastes or his profession had not led him. Sophia put paper before him, on which he was to note distances, according to his and Mr Grey's computations. Now, it was one peculiarity of Mr Hope that he could never see a piece of paper before him without drawing upon it. Sophia's music-books, and any sheet of blotting-paper which might ever have come in his way, bore tokens of this: and now his fingers were as busy as usual while he was talking and computing and arranging. When, as he said, enough had been planned to occupy a month, he threw down his pencil, and took leave till the morning, when he intended to make a call which should be less involuntary.

The moment he was gone, the little girls laid hands on the sheet of paper on which he had been employed. As they expected, it was covered with scraps of sketches; and they exclaimed with delight, "Look here! Here is the spring. How fond Mr Hope is of drawing the spring! And here is the foot-bridge at Dingleford! And what is this? Here is a place we don't know, papa."

"I do not know how you should, my dears. It is the Abbey ruin down the river, which I rather think you have never seen."

"No, but we should like to see it. Are there no faces this time, Fanny? None anywhere? No funny faces this time! I like them the best of Mr Hope's drawings. Sophia, do let us show some of the faces that are on your music-books."

"If you will be sure and put them away again. But you know if Mr Hope is ever reminded of them, he will be sure to rub them out."

"He did old Owen fishing so that he can't rub it out if he would," said Sydney. "He did it in ink for me; and that is better than any of your sketches, that will rub out in a minute."

"Come, children," said their father, "it is an hour past your bedtime."

When the children were gone, and Sophia was attending the sisters to their apartment, Mrs Grey looked at her husband over her spectacles. "Well, my dear!" said she.

"Well, my dear!" responded Mr Grey.

"Do not you think Hester very handsome?"

"There is no doubt of it, my dear. She is very handsome."

"Do not you think Mr Hope thinks so too?"

It is a fact which few but the despisers of their race like to acknowledge, and which those despisers of their race are therefore apt to interpret wrongly, and are enabled to make too much of—that it is perfectly natural,—so natural as to appear necessary,—that when young people first meet, the possibility of their falling in love should occur to all the minds present. We have no doubt that it always is so; though we are perfectly aware that the idea speedily goes out again, as naturally as it came in: and in no case so speedily and naturally as in the minds of the parties most nearly concerned, from the moment that the concern becomes very near indeed. We have no doubt that the minds in Mr Grey's drawing-room underwent the common succession of ideas,—slight and transient imaginations, which pass into nothingness when unexpressed. Probably the sisters wondered whether Mr Hope was married, whether he was engaged, whether he was meant for Sophia, in the prospect of her growing old enough. Probably each speculated for half a moment, unconsciously, for her sister, and Sophia for both. Probably Mr Grey might reflect that when young people are in the way of meeting frequently in country excursions, a love affair is no very unnatural result. But Mrs Grey was the only one who fixed the idea in her own mind and another's by speaking of it.

"Do not you think Mr Hope thinks Hester very handsome, Mr Grey?"

"I really know nothing about it, my dear. He did not speak on the subject as he mounted his horse; and that is the only opportunity he has had of saying anything about the young ladies."

"It would have been strange if he had then, before Sydney and the servants."

"Very strange indeed."

"But do you not think he must have been struck with her? I should like very well to have her settled here; and the corner-house of Mr Rowland's might do nicely for them. I do not know what Mrs Rowland would think of Mr Hope's marrying into our connection so decidedly."

"My dear," said her husband, smiling, "just consider! For anything we know, these young ladies may both be attached and engaged. Hope may be attached elsewhere—."

"No; that I will answer for it he is not. I—"

"Well, you may have your reasons for being sure on that head. But he may not like the girls; they may not like him:—in short, the only thing that has happened is, that they have seen each other for one quarter of an hour."

"Well! there is no saying what may come of it."

"Very true: let us wait and see."

"But there is no harm in my telling you whatever comes into my head!"

"None in the world, unless you get it so fixed there that somebody else happens to know it too. Be careful, my dear. Let no one of these young people get a glimpse of your speculation. Think of the consequence to them and to yourself."

"Dear me, Mr Grey! you need not be afraid. What a serious matter you make of a word or two!"

"Because a good many ideas belong to that word or two, my dear."

Chapter Two

Moonlight to Townsfolk.

The moment the door closed behind Sophia, as she left the sisters in their apartment, Hester crossed the room with a step very like a dance, and threw up the window.

"I had rather look out than sleep," said she. "I shall be ashamed to close my eyes on such a prospect. Morris, if you are waiting for us, you may go. I shall sit up a long while yet."

Morris thought she had not seen Hester in such spirits since her father's death. She was unwilling to check them, but said something about the fatigues of the journey, and being fresh for the next day.

"No fear for to-morrow, Morris. We are in the country, you know, and I cannot fancy being tired in the fields, and in such a park as that. Good-night, Morris."

When she too was gone, Hester called Margaret to her, put her arm round her waist, and kissed her again and again.

"You seem happy to-night, Hester," said Margaret's gentle voice.

"Yes," sighed Hester; "more like being happy than for a long time past. How little we know what we shall feel! Here have I been dreading and dreading this evening, and shrinking from the idea of meeting the Greys, and wanting to write at the last moment to say that we would not come;—and it turns out—Oh, so differently! Think of day after day, week after week of pure country life! When they were planning for us to-night, and talking of the brook, and lanes, and meadows, it made my very heart dance."

"Thank God!" said Margaret. "When your heart dances, there is nothing left to wish."

"But did not yours? Had you ever such a prospect before,—such a prospect of delicious pleasure for weeks together,—except perhaps when we caught our first sight of the sea?"

"Nothing can ever equal that," replied Margaret. "Do not you hear now the shout we gave when we saw the sparkles on the horizon,—heaving sparkles,—when we were a mile off, and mamma held me up that I might see it better; and baby,—dear baby,—clapped his little hands? Does it not seem like yesterday?"

"Like yesterday: and yet, if baby had lived, he would now have been our companion, taking the place of all other friends to us. I thought of him when I saw Sydney Grey; but he would have been very unlike Sydney Grey. He would have been five years older, but still different from what Sydney will be at eighteen—graver, more manly."

"How strange is the idea of having a brother!" said Margaret. "I never see girls with their brothers but I watch them, and long to feel what it is, just for one hour. I wonder what difference it would have made between you and me, if we had had a brother."

"You and he would have been close friends—always together, and I should have been left alone," said Hester, with a sigh. "Oh, yes," she continued, interrupting Margaret's protest, "it would have been so. There can never be the same friendship between three as between two."

"And why should you have been the one left out?" asked Margaret. "But this is all nonsense—all a dream," she added. "The reality is that baby died—still a baby—and we know no more of what he would have been, than of what he is. The real truth is, that you and I are alone, to be each other's only friend."

"It makes me tremble to think of it, Margaret. It is not so long since our home seemed full. How we used all to sit round the fire, and laugh and play with papa, as if we were not to separate till we had all grown old: and now, young as we are, here we are alone! How do we know that we shall be left to each other?"

"There is only one thing we can do, Hester," said Margaret, resting her head on her sister's shoulder. "We must make the most of being together while we can. There must not be the shadow of a cloud between us for a moment. Our confidence must be as full and free, our whole minds as absolutely open, as—as I have read and heard that two minds can never be."

"Those who say so do not know what may be," exclaimed Hester. "I am sure there is not a thought, a feeling in me, that I could not tell you, though I know I never could to any one else."

"If I were to lose you, Hester, there are many, many things that would be shut up in me for ever. There will never be any one on earth to whom I could say the things that I can tell to you. Do you believe this, Hester?"

"I do. I know it."

"Then you will never again doubt me, as you certainly have done sometimes. You cannot imagine how my heart sinks when I see you are fancying that I care for somebody else more than for you; when you think that I am feeling differently from you. Oh, Hester, I know every change of your thoughts by your face; and indeed your thoughts have been mistaken sometimes."

"They have been wicked, often," said Hester, in a low voice. "I have sometimes thought that I must be hopelessly bad, when I have found that the strongest affection I have in the world has made me unjust and cruel to the person I love best. I have a jealous temper, Margaret; and a jealous temper is a wicked temper."

"Now you are unkind to yourself, Hester. I do believe you will never doubt me again."

"I never will. And if I find a thought of the kind rising in me, I will tell you the moment I am aware of it."

"Do, and I will tell you the moment I see a trace of such a thought in your face. So we shall be safe. We can never misunderstand each other for more than a moment."

By the gentle leave of Heaven, all human beings have visions. Not the lowest and dullest but has the coarseness of his life relieved at moments by some scenery of hope rising through the brooding fogs of his intellect and his heart. Such visitations of mercy are the privilege of the innocent, and the support of the infirm. Here were the lonely sisters sustained in bereavement and self-rebuke, by the vision of a friendship which should be unearthly in its depth and freedom; they were so happy for the hour, that nothing could disturb them.

"I do not see," observed Hester, "that it will be possible to enjoy any intimate intercourse with this family. Unless they are of a different order from what they seem, we cannot have much in common; but I am sure they mean to be kind, and they will let us be happy in our own way. Oh, what mornings you and I will have together in those woods! Did you ever see anything so soft as they look—in this light?"

"And the bend of the river glittering there! Here, a little more this way, and you will see it as I do. The moon is not at the full yet; the river will be like this for some nights to come."

"And these rides and drives,—I hope nothing will prevent our going through the whole list of them. What is the matter, Margaret? Why are you so cool about them?"

"I think all the pleasure depends upon the companionship, and I have some doubts about that. I had rather sit at work in a drawing-room all day, than go among mountains with people—"

"Like the Mansons; Oh, that spreading of shawls, and bustle about the sandwiches, before they could give a look at the waterfall! I am afraid we may find something of the same drawback here."

"I am afraid so."

"Well, only let us get out into the woods and lanes, and we will manage to enjoy ourselves there. We can contrive to digress here and there together without being missed. But I think we are judging rather hastily from what we saw this evening even about this family; and we have no right to suppose that all their acquaintance are like them."

"No, indeed; and I am sure Mr Hope, for one, is of a different order. He dropped one thing, one little saying, which proved this to my mind."

"I know what you mean—about the old man that is to be our guide over that heath they were talking of—about why that heath is a different and more beautiful place to him than to us, or to his former self. Is it not true, what he said?"

"I am sure it is true. I have little to say of my own experience, or wisdom, or goodness, whichever it was that he particularly meant as giving a new power of sight to the old man; but I know that no tree waves to my eye as it did ten years ago, and the music of running water is richer to my ear as every summer comes round."

"Yes; I almost wonder sometimes whether all things are not made at the moment by the mind that sees them, so wonderfully do they change with one's mood, and according to the store of thoughts they lay open in one's mind. If I lived in a desert island (supposing one's intellect could go on to grow there), I should feel sure of this."

"But not here, where it is quite clear that the village sot (if there be one), and Mr Hope, and the children, and we ourselves all see the same objects in sunlight and moonlight, and acknowledge them to be the same, though we cannot measure feelings upon them. I wish Mr Hope may say something more which may lead to the old man on the heath again. He is coming to-morrow morning."

"Yes; we shall see him again to-morrow."

Chapter Three

Making Acquaintance.

The sisters were not so fatigued with their journey but that they were early in the open air the next morning. In the shrubbery they met the twins, walking hand in hand, each with a doll on the disengaged arm.

"You are giving your dolls an airing before breakfast," said Hester, stopping them as they would have passed on.

"Yes; we carry out our dolls now because we must not run before breakfast. We have made arbours in our own gardens for our dolls, where they may sit when we are swinging."

"I should like to see your arbours and your gardens," said Margaret, looking round her. "Will you take me to them?"

"Not now," answered they; "we should have to cross the grass, and we must not go upon the grass before breakfast."

"Where is your swing? I am very fond of swinging."

"Oh! it is in the orchard there, under that large tree. But you cannot—"

"I see; we cannot get to it now, because we should have to cross the grass." And Margaret began to look round for any place where they might go beyond the gravel-walk on which they stood. She moved towards the greenhouse, but found it was never unlocked before breakfast. The summerhouse remained, and a most unexceptionable path led to it. The sisters turned that way.

"You cannot go there," cried the children; "Miss Young always has the schoolroom before breakfast."

"We are going to see Miss Young," explained Hester, smiling at the amazed faces with which the children stared from the end of the path. They were suddenly seen to turn, and walk as fast as they could, without its being called running, towards the house. They were gone to their mother's dressing-room door, to tell her that the Miss Ibbotsons were gone to see Miss Young before breakfast.

The path led for some little way under the hedge which separated Mr Grey's from Mr Rowland's garden. There were voices on the other side, and what was said was perfectly audible. Uneasy at hearing what was not meant for them, Hester and Margaret gave tokens of their presence. The conversation on the other side of the hedge proceeded; and in a very short time the sisters were persuaded that they had been mistaken in supposing that what was said was not meant for them.

"My own Matilda," said a voice, which evidently came from under a lady's bonnet which moved parallel with Hester's and Margaret's; "My own Matilda, I would not be so harsh as to prevent your playing where you please before breakfast. Run where you like, my love. I am sorry for little girls who are not allowed to do as they please in the cool of the morning. My children shall never suffer such restriction."

"Mother," cried a rough little person, "I'm going fishing with Uncle Philip to-day. Sydney Grey and I are going, I don't know how far up the river."

"On no account, my dear boy. You must not think of such a thing. I should not have a moment's peace while you are away. You would not be back till evening, perhaps; and I should be fancying all day that you were in the river. It is out of the question, my own George."

"But I must go, mother. Uncle Philip said I might; and Sydney Grey is going."

"That is only another reason, my dear boy. Your uncle will yield to my wishes, I am sure, as he always does. And if Mrs Grey allows her son to run such risks, I am sure I should not feel myself justified. You will stay with me, love, won't you? You will stay with your mother, my own boy."

George ran roaring away, screaming for Uncle Philip; who was not at hand, however, to plead his cause.

"My Matilda," resumed the fond mother, "you are making yourself a sad figure. You will not be fit to show yourself at breakfast. Do you suppose your papa ever saw such a frock as that? There! look—dripping wet! Pritchard, take Miss Matilda, and change all her clothes directly. So much for my allowing her to run on the grass while the dew is on! Lose no time, Pritchard, lest the child should catch cold. Leave Miss Anna with me. Walk beside me, my Anna. Ah! there is papa. Papa, we must find some amusement for George today, as I cannot think of letting him go out fishing. Suppose we take the children to spend the morning with their cousins at Dingleford?"

"To-morrow would suit me better, my love," replied the husband. "Indeed I don't see how I can go to-day, or you either." And Mr Rowland lowered his voice, so as to show that he was aware of his liability to be overheard.

"Oh, as to that, there is no hurry," replied the lady, aloud. "If I had nothing else to do, I should not make that call to-day. Any day will do as well."

As Hester and Margaret looked at each other, they heard the gentleman softly say "Hush!" But Mrs Rowland went on as audibly as ever.

"There is no reason why I should be in any hurry to call on Mrs Grey's friends, whoever and whatever they may be. Any day will do for that, my dear."

Not having been yet forbidden to run before breakfast, Hester and Margaret fled to the summer-house, to avoid hearing any more of the domestic dialogues of the Rowland family.

"What shall we do when that woman calls?" said Hester. "How will it be possible to speak to her?"

"As we should speak to any other indifferent person," replied Margaret. "Her rudeness is meant for Mrs Grey, not for us; for she knows nothing about us: and Mrs Grey will never hear from us what has passed.—Shall we knock?"

In answer to the knock, they were requested to enter. Miss Young rose in some confusion when she found her visitors were other than her pupils: but she was so lame that Hester made her sit down again, while they drew seats for themselves. They apologised for breaking in upon her with so little ceremony, but explained that they were come to be inmates at Mr Grey's for some months, and that they wished to lose no time in making themselves acquainted with every resort of the family of which they considered themselves a part. Miss Young was evidently pleased to see them. She closed her volume, and assured them they were welcome to her apartment; "For," said she, "everybody calls it my apartment, and why should not I?"

"Do you spend all your time here?" asked Hester.

"Almost the whole day. I have a lodging in the village; but I leave it early these fine mornings, and stay here till dark. I am so lame as to make it inconvenient to pass over the ground oftener than is necessary; and I find it pleasanter to see trees and grass through every window here, than to look out into the farrier's yard,—the only prospect from my lodging. The furnace and sparks are pretty enough on a winter's evening, especially when one is too ill or too dismal to do anything but watch them; but at this season one grows tired of old horse-shoes and cinders; and so I sit here."

To the sisters there seemed a world of desolation in these words. They were always mourning for having no brother. Here was one who appeared to be entirely alone. From not knowing exactly what to say, Margaret opened the book Miss Young had laid aside. It was German—Schiller's Thirty Years' War. Every one has something to say about German literature; those who do not understand it asking whether it is not very mystical, and wild, and obscure; and those who do understand it saying that it is not so at all. It would be a welcome novelty if the two parties were to set about finding out what it is to be mystical,—a point which, for aught that is known to the generality, is not yet ascertained. Miss Young and her visitors did not enter upon precise definitions this morning. These were left for a future occasion. Meantime it was ascertained that Miss Young had learned the German language by the aid of dictionary and grammar alone, and also that if she should happen to meet with any one who wished to enjoy what she was enjoying, she should be glad to afford any aid in her power. Hester was satisfied with thanking her. She was old enough to know that learning a new language is a serious undertaking. Margaret was somewhat younger, and ready for any enterprise. She thought she saw before her hours of long mornings, when she should be glad to escape from the work-table to Miss Young's companionship and to study. The bright field of German literature seemed to open before her to be explored. She warmly thanked Miss Young, and accepted her offered assistance.

"So you spend all your days alone here," said she, looking round upon the rather bare walls, the matted floor, the children's desks, and the single shelf which held Miss Young's books.

"Not exactly all the day alone," replied Miss Young; "the children are with me five hours a day, and a set of pupils from the village comes to me besides, for a spare hour of the afternoon. In this way I see a good many little faces every day."

"And some others too, I should hope; some besides little faces?"

Miss Young was silent. Margaret hastened on—

"I suppose most people would say here what is said everywhere else about the nobleness and privilege of the task of teaching children. But I do not envy those who have it to do. I am as fond of children as any one; but then it is having them out to play on the grass, or romping with them in the nursery, that I like. When it becomes a matter of desks and school-books, I had far rather study than teach."

"I believe everybody, except perhaps mothers, would agree with you," said Miss Young, who was now, without apology, plying her needle.

"Indeed! then I am very sorry for you."

"Thank you; but there's no need to be sorry for me. Do you suppose that one's comfort lies in having a choice of employments? My experience leads me to think the contrary."

"I do not think I could be happy," said Hester, "to be tied down to an employment I did not like."

"Not to a positively disgusting one. But I am disposed to think that the greatest number of happy people may be found busy in employments that they have not chosen for themselves, and never would have chosen."

"I am afraid these very happy people are haunted by longings to be doing something else."

"Yes: there is their great trouble. They think, till experience makes them wiser, that if they were only in another set of circumstances, if they only had a choice what they would do, a chance for the exercise of the powers they are conscious of, they would do such things as should be the wonder and the terror of the earth. But their powers may be doubted, if they do not appear in the conquest of circumstances."

"So you conquer these giddy children, when you had rather be conquering German metaphysicians, or —, or —, what else?"

"There is little to conquer in these children," said Miss Young; "they are very good with me. I assure you I have much more to conquer in myself, with regard to them. It is but little that I can do for them; and that little I am apt to despise, in the vain desire to do more."

"How more?"

"If I had them in a house by myself, to spend their whole time with me, so that I could educate, instead of merely teaching them. But here I am doing just what we were talking of just now,—laying out a pretty-looking field of duty, in which there would probably be as many thorns as in any other. Teaching has its pleasures,—its great occasional, and small daily pleasures, though they are not to be compared to the sublime delights of education."

"You must have some of these sublime delights mixed in with the humbler. You are, in some degree, educating these children while teaching them."

"Yes: but it is more a negative than a positive function, a very humble one. Governesses to children at home can do little more than stand between children and the faults of the people about them. I speak quite generally."

"Is such an occupation one in which anybody can be happy?"

"Why not, as well as in making pins' heads, or in nursing sick people, or in cutting square blocks out of a chalk pit for thirty years together, or in any other occupation which may be ordained to prove to us that happiness lies in the temper, and not in the object of a pursuit? Are there not free and happy pin-makers, and sick-nurses, and chalk-cutters?"

"Yes: but they know how much to expect. They have no idea of pin-making in itself being great happiness."

"Just so. Well: let a governess learn what to expect; set her free from a hankering after happiness in her work, and you have a happy governess."

"I thought such a thing was out of the order of nature."

"Not quite. There have been such, though there are strong influences against it. The expectations of all parties are unreasonable; and those who are too humble, or too amiable, to be dissatisfied with others, are discontented with themselves, when the inevitable disappointment comes. There is a great deal said about the evils of the position of a governess—between the family and the servants—a great deal said that is very true, and always will be true, while governesses have proud hearts, like other people: but these are slight evils in comparison with the grand one of the common failure of the relation.—There! do you hear that bell?"

"What is it? The breakfast bell?"

"Yes. You must go. I would not be understood as inviting you here; for it is not, except upon sufferance, my room; and I have no inducement to offer. But I may just say, that you will always be welcome."

"Always?" said Margaret. "In and out of school hours?"

"In and out of school hours, unless your presence should chance to turn my pupils' heads. In that case, you will not be offended if I ask you to go away."

Mary and Fanny had just reported in the breakfast-parlour, that the Miss Ibbotsons had been "such a time with Miss Young!" when Hester and Margaret entered. The testimony there was all in favour of Miss Young. Mr Grey called her a most estimable young woman; and Mrs Grey declared that, though she could not agree with her on all points, and decidedly thought that she overrated Matilda Rowland's talents, she was convinced that her children enjoyed great advantages under her care. Sophia added, that she was very superior,—quite learned. Mrs Grey further explained that, though now so much at ease on the subject of her daughters' education, no one could have an idea of the trouble she had had in getting the plan arranged. It had seemed a pity that the Rowlands and her children should not learn together: it was such an advantage for children to learn together!

But Mrs Rowland had made a thousand difficulties. After breakfast, she would show her young friends the room which she had proposed should be the schoolroom,—as airy and advantageous in every way as could be imagined: but Mrs Rowland had objected that she could not have Matilda and George come out in all weathers,—as if they would have had to walk a mile, instead of just the sweep of the gravel-walk! Mrs Rowland had proposed that her back-parlour should be the schoolroom: but really it was not to be thought of—so small and close, and such a dull room for Miss Young! The gentlemen had been obliged to take it up at last. Nobody could ever find out which of them it was that had thought of the summerhouse, though she was satisfied in her own mind that Mr Rowland was not in the habit of having such clever ideas; but, however, it was soon settled. The summer-house was so exactly on the boundary-line between the two gardens, that really no objection had been left for Mrs Rowland to make. She came as near to it as she could, however; for she had had the walk covered in at great expense from her garden door to the summer-house, when everybody knew she did not mind her children getting wet at other times on the grass before the dew was off.

"And the covered way is quite an eyesore from the drawing-room windows," added Sophia.

"Quite," said Mrs Grey; "and it can be seen from ours, as I dare say you observed last night. But I have no doubt that entered into her calculations when she had it made."

Mr Grey inquired about the arrangements for the morning, and whether he could be of any service. It happened to be a leisure morning with him, and he did not know when he might have another at command. Sophia reminded her father that it would be impossible for the ladies of the family to go out, when they were expecting the neighbours to call: and this brought on another speculation as to who would call,—and especially when the Rowlands might be looked for. Hester and Margaret believed they could have settled this matter; but they forbore to speak of what they had overheard. They began to wonder whether the subject of Mrs Rowland was to be served up with every meal, for a continuance; and Hester found her anticipations of delight in a country life somewhat damped, by the idea of the frowning ghost of the obnoxious lady being for ever present.

Chapter Four

Morning Calls.

The little girls had been dismissed to the schoolroom before Mr Grey had finally pushed away his tea-cup. Not being wanted by the ladies, he walked off to his timber-yard, and his wife followed to ask him some question not intended for the general ear. Sophia was struck with a sudden panic at being left alone with the strangers, and escaped by another door into the store-room. As the last traces of the breakfast things vanished, Hester exclaimed—

"So we may please ourselves, it seems, as to what we are to do with our morning!"

"I hope so," said Margaret. "Do let us get down to the meadow we see from our window—the meadow that looks so flat and green! We may very well take two hours' grace before we need sit down here in form and order."

Hester was willing, and the bonnets were soon on. As Margaret was passing down stairs again, she saw Mrs Grey and Sophia whispering in a room, the door of which stood open. She heard it shut instantly, and the result of the consultation soon appeared. Just as the sisters were turning out of the house, Sophia ran after them to say that mamma wished they would be so good as to defer their walk; mamma was afraid that if they were seen abroad in the village, it would be supposed that they did not wish to receive visitors: mamma would rather that they should stay within this morning. There was nothing for it but to turn back; and Hester threw down her bonnet with no very good grace, as she observed to her sister that, to all appearance, a town life was more free than a country one, after all.

"Let us do our duty fully this first morning," said Margaret. "Look, I am going to carry down my work-bag; and you shall see me sit on the same chair from this hour till dinner-time, unless I receive directions to the contrary."

The restraint did not amount to this. Hester's chair was placed opposite to Mrs Grey, who seemed to have pleasure in gazing at her, and in indulging in audible hints and visible winks and nods about her beauty, to every lady visitor who sat near her. Margaret might place herself where she pleased. In the intervals of the visits of the morning, she was treated with a diversity of entertainments by Sophia, who occasionally summoned her to the window to see how Matilda Rowland was allowed to run across the road to her grandmamma's, without so much as a hat upon her head,—to see Jim Bird, the oldest man in the parish (believed to be near a hundred), who was resting himself on the bank of the hedge,—to see the peacock which had been sent as a present from Sir William Hunter to Mr James, the lawyer, and which was a great nuisance from its screaming,—to say whether the two little Reeves, dropping their curtseys as they went home from school, were not little beauties,—and, in short, to witness all the village spectacles which present themselves before the windows of an acute observer on a fine spring morning. The young ladies had to return to their seats as often as wheels were heard, or the approach of parasols was discerned.

Among the earliest visitors were Mrs Enderby and her redoubtable son, Mr Philip. Mrs Enderby was a bright-eyed, brisk, little old lady, who was rather apt to talk herself quite out of breath, but who had evidently a stronger tendency still; and that was, to look on the bright side of everything and everybody. She smiled smiles full of meaning and assent in return for Mrs Grey's winks about Hester's beauty; and really cheered Hester with accounts of how good everybody was at Deerbrook. She was thankful that her maid Phoebe was better; she knew that Mrs Grey would not fail to inquire; really Phoebe was very much better; the influenza had left sad effects, but they were dispersing. It would be a pity the girl should not quite recover, for she was a most invaluable servant—such a servant as is very rarely to be met with. The credit of restoring her belonged to Mr Hope, who indeed had done everything. She supposed the ladies would soon be seeing Mr Hope. He was extremely busy, as everybody knew—had very large practice now; but he always contrived to find time for everything. It was exceedingly difficult to find time for everything. There was her dear daughter, Priscilla (Mrs Rowland, whose husband was Mr Grey's partner); Priscilla devoted her life to her children (and dear children they were); and no one who knew what she did for her children would expect anything more from her; but, indeed, those who knew best, she herself, for instance, were fully satisfied that her dear Priscilla did wonders. The apology for Mrs Rowland, in case she should not call, was made not without ingenuity. Hester fully understood it; and Mrs Grey showed by her bridling that it was not lost upon her either.

Mr Enderby, meanwhile, was behaving civilly to Margaret and Sophia; that is to say, he was somewhat more than merely civil to Margaret, and somewhat less to Sophia. It was obviously not without reason that Sophia had complained of his hauteur. He could not, as Sydney had pleaded, help being tall; but he might have helped the excessive frigidity with which he stood upright till invited to sit down. The fact was, that he had reason to believe that the ladies of Mr Grey's family made very free with his sister's name and affairs; and though he would have been sorry to have been obliged to defend all she said and did, he felt some very natural emotions of dislike towards those who were always putting the worst construction upon the whole of her conduct. He believed that Mr Grey's influence was exerted on behalf of peace and good understanding, and he thought he perceived that Sydney, with the shrewdness which some boys show very early, was more or less sensible of the absurdity of the feud between the partners' wives and daughters; and towards these members of the Grey family, Mr Enderby felt nothing but good-will; he talked politics with Mr Grey in the shrubbery after church on Sunday, executed commissions for him in London, and sent him game: and Sydney was under obligations to him for many a morning of sport, and many a service such as gentlemen who are not above five-and-twenty and its freaks can render to boys entering their teens. Whatever might be his opinion of women generally, from the particular specimens which had come in his way, he had too much sense and gentlemanly feeling to include Mrs Grey's guests in the dislike he felt towards herself, or to suppose that they must necessarily share her disposition towards his relations. Perhaps he felt, unknown to himself some inclination to prepossess them in favour of his connections; to stretch his complaisance a little, as a precaution against the prejudices with which he knew Mrs Grey would attempt to occupy their minds. However this might be, he was as amicable with Margaret as his mother was with her sister.

He soon found out that the strangers were more interested about the natural features of Deerbrook than about its gossip. He was amused at the earnestness of Margaret's inquiries about the scenery of the neighbourhood, and he laughingly promised that she should see every nook within twenty miles.

"People always care least about what they have just at hand," said he. "I dare say, if I were to ask you, you have never seen a glass-bottle blown, or a tea-tray painted?"

"If I have," said Margaret, "I know many ladies in Birmingham who have not."

"You will not be surprised, then, if you find some ladies in Deerbrook who do not ride, and who can tell you no more of the pretty places near than if they had been brought up in Whitechapel. They keep their best sights for strangers, and not for common use. I am, in reality, only a visitor at Deerbrook. I do not live here, and never did; yet I am better able to be your guide than almost any resident. The ladies, especially, are extremely domestic: they are far too busy to have ever looked about them. But I will speak to Mr Grey, and—"

"Oh, pray, do not trouble Mr Grey! He has too much business on his hands already; and he is so kind, he will be putting himself out of his way for us; and all we want is to be in the open air in the fields."

"'All you want!' very like starlings in a cage;" and he looked as if he was smiling at the well-known speech of the starling; but he did not quote it. "My mother is now saying that Mr Hope finds time for everything: and she is right. He will help us. You must see Hope, and you must like him. He is the great boast of the place, next to the new sign."

"Is the sign remarkable, or only new?"

"Very remarkable for ingenuity, if not for beauty. It is 'The Bonnet so Blue:'—a lady's bonnet of blue satin, with brown bows, or whatever you may call the trimming when you see it; and we are favoured besides with a portrait of the milliner, holding the bonnet so blue. We talk nearly as much of this sign as of Mr Hope; but you must see them both, and tell us which you like best."

"We have seen Mr Hope. He was here yesterday evening."

"Well, then, you must see him again; and you must not think the worse of him for his being praised by everybody you meet. It is no ordinary case of a village apothecary."

Margaret laughed; so little did Mr Hope look like the village apothecary of her imagination.

"Ah, I see you know something of the predilection of villagers for their apothecary,—how the young people wonder that he always cures everybody; and how the old people could not live without him; and how the poor folks take him for a sort of magician; and how he obtains more knowledge of human affairs than any other kind of man. But Hope is, though a very happy man, not this sort of privileged person. His friends are so attached to him that they confide to him all their own affairs; but they respect him too much to gossip at large to him of other people's. I see you do not know how to credit this; but I assure you, though the inhabitants of Deerbrook are as accomplished in the arts of gossip as any villagers in England, Hope knows little more than you do at this moment about who are upon terms and who are not."

"My sister and I must learn his art of ignorance," said Margaret. "If it be really true that the place is full of quarrels, we shall be afraid to stay, unless we can contrive to know nothing about them."

"Oh, do not suppose we are worse than others who live in villages. Since our present rector came, we have risen somewhat above the rural average of peace and quiet."

"And the country has always been identical with the idea of peace and quiet to us town-bred people!" said Margaret.

"And very properly, in one sense. But if you leave behind the din of streets for the sake of stepping forth from your work-table upon a soft lawn, or of looking out upon the old church steeple among the trees, while you hear nothing but bleating and chirping, you must expect some set-off against such advantages: and that set-off is the being among a small number of people, who are always busy looking into one another's small concerns."

"But this is not a necessary evil," said Margaret. "From what you were saying just now, it appears that it may be avoided."

"From what I was saying about Hope. Yes; such an one as Hope may get all the good out of every situation, without its evils; but—"

"But nobody else," said Margaret, smiling. "Well, Hester and I must try whether we cannot have to do with lawns and sheep for a few months, without quarrelling or having to do with quarrels."

"And what if you are made the subject of quarrels?" asked Mr Enderby. "How are you to help yourselves, in that case?"

"How does Mr Hope help himself in that case?"

"It remains to be seen. As far as I know, the whole place is agreed about him at present. Every one will tell you that never was society so blessed in a medical man before;—from the rector and my mother, who never quarrel with anybody, down to the village scold. I am not going to prepossess you against even our village scold, by telling her name. You will know it in time, though your first acquaintance will probably be with her voice."

"So we are to hear something besides bleating and chirping?"

A tremendous knock at the door occurred, as if in answer to this. All the conversation in the room suddenly stopped, and Mr and Mrs Rowland walked in.

"This is my sister, Mrs Rowland," observed Mr Enderby to Margaret.

"This is my daughter Priscilla, Mrs Rowland," said Mrs Enderby to Hester.

Both sisters were annoyed at feeling timid and nervous on being introduced to the lady. There is something imposing in hearing a mere name very often, in the proof that the person it belongs to fills a large space in people's minds: and when the person is thus frequently named with fear and dislike, an idea is originated of a command over powers of evil which makes the actual presence absolutely awful. This seemed now to be felt by all. Sophia had nothing to say: Mrs Grey's head twitched nervously, while she turned from one to another with slight remarks: Mrs Enderby ran on about their having all happened to call at once, and its being quite a family party in Mrs Grey's parlour; and Mr Philip's flow of conversation had stopped. Margaret thought he was trying to help laughing.

The call could not be an agreeable one. The partners' ladies quoted their own children's sayings about school and Miss Young, and Miss Young's praise of the children; and each vied with the other in eulogium on Miss Young, evidently on the ground of her hopes of Fanny and Mary on the one hand, and of Matilda, George, and Anna, on the other. Mrs Enderby interposed praises of all the children, while Mr Rowland engaged Hester's attention, calling off her observation and his own from the sparring of the rival mothers. Philip informed Margaret at length, that George was a fine little fellow, who would make a good sportsman. There was some pleasure in taking such a boy out fishing. But Mr Philip had lighted on a dangerous topic, as he soon found. His sister heard what he was saying, and began an earnest protest against little boys fishing, on account of the danger, and against any idea that she would allow her George to run any such risks. Of course, this made Mrs Grey fire up, as at an imputation upon her care of her son Sydney; and before the rest of the company could talk down the dispute, it bore too much of the appearance of a recrimination about the discharge of maternal duties. Margaret thought that, but for the relationship, Mrs Rowland might fairly be concluded to be the village scold alluded to by Mr Enderby. It was impossible that he could have been speaking of his sister; but Deerbrook was an unfortunate place if it contained a more unamiable person than she appeared at this moment. The faces of the two ladies were still flushed with excitement when Mr Hope came in. The sisters thought he appeared like a good genius, so amiable did the party grow on his entrance. It seemed as if he was as great a favourite with the Rowlands as with the other family; so friendly was the gentleman, and so gracious the lady; while Mr Hope was, to all appearance, unconscious of the existence of any unpleasant feelings among his neighbours. The talk flowed on about the concerns of personages of the village, about the aspect of public affairs, about the poets of the age, and what kind of poetry was most read in Deerbrook, and how the Book Society went on, till all had grown cordial, and some began to propose to be hospitable. Mrs Rowland hoped for the honour of seeing the Miss Ibbotsons one day the next week, when Mr Rowland should have returned from a little excursion of business. Mrs Enderby wondered whether she could prevail on all her young friends to spend an evening with her before her son left Deerbrook; and Mrs Grey gave notice that she should shortly issue her invitations to those with whom she wished her young cousins to become better acquainted.

All went right for the rest of the morning. When the Enderbys and Rowlands went away, the Levitts came. When Dr Levitt inquired about the schools of Birmingham, it could not but come out that Hester and Margaret were dissenters. Yet, as they were desired to observe, he did not seem in the least shocked, and his manner was just as kind to them after this disclosure as before. He was pronounced a very liberal man. Mr Hope was asked to stay to dinner, and Mrs Grey complacently related the events of the morning to her husband as he took his place at table. Deerbrook had done its duty to Hester and Margaret pretty well for the first day. Everybody of consequence had called but the Andersons, and they would no doubt come on Sunday.

Chapter Five

The Meadows.

The afternoon was the time when Miss Young's pupils practised the mysteries of the needle. Little girls are not usually fond of sewing. Till they become clever enough to have devices of their own, to cut out a doll's petticoat, or contrive a pin-cushion to surprise mamma, sewing is a mere galling of the fingers and strain upon the patience. Every wry stitch shows, and is pretty sure to be remarked upon: the seam or hem seems longer the oftener it is measured, till the little work-woman becomes capable of the enterprise of despatching a whole one at a sitting; after which the glory is found to ameliorate the toil, and there is a chance that the girl may become fond of sewing.

Miss Young's pupils had not arrived at this stage. It was a mystery to them that Miss Young could sit sewing, as fast as her needle could fly, for the whole afternoon, and during the intervals of their lessons in the morning. It was in vain that she told them that some of her pleasantest hours were those which she passed in this employment: and that she thought they would perhaps grow as fond of work as their sister Sophia before they were as old as she. With languid steps did the twins return to the house this afternoon for another pair of shirt-sleeves, and to show mamma the work they had finished. Hand in hand, as usual, and carrying up for judgment their last performance, they entered the house. In a very different mood did they return. Running, skipping, and jumping, they burst again into the summer-house.

"Miss Young, oh, Miss Young, we are to have a holiday!"

"Mamma sends her compliments to you, Miss Young, and she hopes you will give us a holiday. It is a fine afternoon, she thinks, and my cousins have never gathered cowslips; and we are all going into the meadow for a cowslip-gathering; and Mr Hope will come to us there. He has to go somewhere now, but he will come to us before we have half done."

Matilda Rowland looked fall of dismay till she was told that Mrs Grey hoped she would be of the party, and begged that she would, go directly and ask her mamma's leave.

"What a quantity of cowslips we shall get!" observed Mary, as she took down Fanny's basket from the nail on which it hung, and then her own.

"We are each to have a basket, mamma says, that we may not quarrel. What shall we do with such a quantity of cowslips?"

"Make tea of them, to be sure," replied Fanny. "We may dry them in this window, may not we, Miss Young? And we will give you some of our cowslip-tea."

Miss Young smiled and thanked them. She did not promise to drink any of the promised tea. She had a vivid remembrance of the cowslip-drying of her young days, when the picked flowers lay in a window till they were laced all over with cobwebs; and when they were at length popped into the teapot with all speed, to hide the fact that they were mouldy. She remembered the good-natured attempts of her father and mother to swallow a doll's cupful of her cowslip-tea, rather than discourage the spirit of enterprise which, now that she had lost those whom she loved, was all that she had to trust to.

"Fanny," said Mary, with eyes wide open, "cannot we have a feast here for my cousins, when we make our cowslip-tea?"

"A feast! Oh, that would be grand!" replied Fanny. "I have a shilling, and so have you; and we could buy a good many nice things for that: and Matilda Rowland will lend us her doll's dishes to put with ours. Miss Young, will you let us have our feast here, one afternoon? We will ask my cousins, without telling them anything; and they will be so surprised!"

Miss Young promised everything, engaged not to tell, smoothed their hair, tied their bonnets, and sent them away quite happy with their secret.

Such a holiday as this was one of Miss Young's few pleasures. There were several occasions in the year when she could make sure beforehand of some hours to herself. Her Sundays were much occupied with the Sunday-school, and with intercourse with poor neighbours whom she could not meet on any other day: but Christmas-day, the day of the annual fair of Deerbrook, and two or three more, were her own. These were, however, so appropriated, long before, to some object, that they lost much of their character of holidays. Her true holidays were such as the afternoon of this day,—hours suddenly set free, little gifts of leisure to be spent according to the fancy of the moment. Let none pretend to understand the value of such whose lives are all leisure; who take up a book to pass the time; who saunter in gardens because there are no morning visits to make; who exaggerate the writing of a family letter into important business. Such have their own enjoyments: but they know nothing of the paroxysm of pleasure of a really hardworking person on hearing the door shut which excludes the business of life, and leaves the delight of free thoughts and hands. The worst part of it is the having to decide how to make the most of liberty. Miss Young was not long in settling this point. She just glanced up at her shelf of books, and down upon her drawing-board, and abroad through the south window, and made up her mind. The acacia with its fresh bunches of blossoms was waving above the window, casting in flickering shadows upon the floor: the evergreens of the shrubbery twinkled in the sun, as the light breeze swept over them: the birds were chirruping all about, and a yellow butterfly alighted and trembled on the window-sill at the moment. It was one of the softest and gayest days of spring; and the best thing was to do nothing but enjoy it. She moved to the south window with her work, and sewed or let the wind blow upon her face as she looked out.

The landscape was a wide one. Far beyond, and somewhat below the garden and shrubberies in which the summerhouse stood, flat meadows stretched to the brink of the river, on the other side of which were the park woods. All was bathed in the afternoon sunshine, except where a tree here and there cast a flake of shadow upon the grass of the meadows.

"It is a luxury," thought the gazer, "for one who cannot move about to sit here and look abroad. I wonder whether I should have been with the party if I had not been lame. I dare say something would have taken off from the pleasure if I had. But how well I can remember what the pleasure is! the jumping stiles—the feel of the turf underfoot,—the running after every flower,—the going wherever one has a fancy to go,—how well I remember it all! And yet it gives me a sort of surprise to see the activity of these children, and how little they are aware of what their privilege is. I fancy, however, the pleasure is more in the recollection of all such natural enjoyments than at the moment. It is so with me, and I believe with everybody. This very landscape is more beautiful to me in the dark night when I cannot sleep, than at this very moment, when it looks its best and brightest: and surely this is the great difference between that sort of pleasures and those which come altogether from within. The delight of a happy mood of mind is beyond everything at the time; it sets one above all that can happen; it steeps one in heaven itself; but one cannot recall it: one can only remember that it was so. The delight of being in such a place as those woods is generally more or less spoiled at the time by trifles which are forgotten afterwards;—one is hungry, or tired, or a little vexed with somebody, or doubtful whether somebody else is not vexed; but then the remembrance is purely delicious,—brighter in sunshine, softer in shade,— wholly tempered to what is genial. The imagination is a better medium than the eye. This is surely the reason why Byron could not write poetry on Lake Leman, but found he must wait till he got within four walls. This is the reason why we are all more moved by the slightest glimpses of good descriptions in books than by the amplitude of the same objects before our eyes. I used to wonder how that was, when, as a child, I read the openings of scenes and books in 'Paradise Lost.' I saw plenty of summer sunrises; but none of them gave me a feeling like the two lines:—

> "'Now morn, her rosy steps in the eastern clime
> Advancing, sowed the earth with orient pearl.'

"If all this be so, our lot is more equalised than is commonly thought. Once having received pictures into our minds, and possessing a clear eye in the mind to see them with, the going about to obtain more is not of very great consequence. This comforts one for prisoners suffering *carcere duro*, and for townspeople who cannot often get out of the streets; and for lame people like me, who see others tripping over commons and through fields where we cannot go. I wish there was as much comfort the other way,— about such as suffer from unhappy moods of mind, and know little of the joy of the highest. It would be a small gain to them to fly like birds,—to see like the eagle itself.—Oh, there are the children! So that is their cowslip meadow! How like children they all look together, down on the grass!— gathering cowslips, I suppose. The two in black are more eager about it than Sophia. She sits on the stile while they are busy. The children are holding forth to their cousins,—teaching them something, evidently. How I love to overlook people,—to watch them acting unconsciously, and speculate for them! It is the most tempting thing in the world to contrast the little affairs one sees them busy about, with the very serious ones which await them,—which await every one. There are those two strangers busy gathering cowslips, and perhaps thinking of nothing beyond the fresh pleasure of the air and the grass, and the scent of their flowers,—their minds quite filled with the spirit of the spring, when who knows what may be awaiting them! Love may be just at hand. The tempest of passion may be brewing under this soft sunshine. They think themselves now as full of happiness as possible; and a little while hence, upon a few words spoken, a glance exchanged, they may be in such a heaven of bliss that they will smile at their own ignorance in being so well pleased to-day. Or—but I pray they may escape the other chance. Neither of them knows anything of that misery yet, I am confident. They both look too young, too open, too free to have really suffered.—I wonder whether it is foolish to fancy already that one of them may be settled here. It can hardly be foolish, when the thought occurs so naturally: and these great affairs of life lie distinctly under the eye of such as are themselves cut off from them. I am out of the game, and why should not I look upon its chances? I am quite alone; and why should I not watch for others? Every situation has its privileges and its obligations.— What is it to be alone, and to be let alone, as I am? It is to be put into a post of observation on others: but the knowledge so gained is anything but a good if it stops at mere knowledge,—if it does not make me feel and act. Women who have what I am not to have, a home, an intimate, a perpetual call out of themselves, may go on more safely, perhaps, without any thought for themselves, than I with all my best consideration: but I, with the blessing of a peremptory vocation, which is to stand me instead of sympathy, ties and spontaneous action,—I may find out that it is my proper business to keep an intent eye upon the possible events of other people's lives, that I may use slight occasions of action which might otherwise pass me by. If one were thoroughly wise and good, this would be a sort of divine lot. Without being at all wiser or better than others,—being even as weak in judgment and in faith as I am,—something may be made of it. Without daring to meddle, one may stand clear-sighted, ready to help.—How the children are flying over the meadow towards that gentleman who is fastening his horse to the gate! Mr Hope, no doubt. He is the oldest cowslip gatherer of them all, I fancy. If one could overhear the talk in every house along the village, I dare say some of it is about Mr Hope winning one of these young ladies. If so, it is only what I am thinking about myself. Every one wishes to see Mr Hope married,—every one, even to the servants here, who are always disputing whether he will not have Miss Sophia, or whether Miss Sophia is not to make a grander match. Sophia will not do for him; but it is very possible that one of these girls may. And the other—but I will not think about that to-day.—How yellow the glow is upon those woods! What heavenly hues hang about the world we live in! but how strange is the lot of some in it! One would wonder why, when all are so plainly made to feel and act together, there should be any one completely solitary. There must be a reason: I would fain know it; but I can wait till we may know all."

Such were some of Maria Young's natural and unchecked thoughts. There was not much of common holiday spirit in them: but to Maria, liberty and peace were holiday, and her mind was not otherwise than peaceful. She was serious, but not sad. Any one who could at the moment have seen her face, would have pronounced her cheerful at heart; and so she was. She had been so long and so far banished from ordinary happiness, that her own quiet speculations were material enough for cheerfulness. The subject on which she would not think to-day, was the possibility of one of the sisters attaching Mr Enderby. Maria Young had not always been solitary, and lame, and poor. Her father had not been very long dead; and while he lived, no one supposed that his only child would be poor. Her youth passed gaily, and her adversity came suddenly. Her father was wont to drive her out in his gig, almost every summer day. One evening, the horse took fright, and upset the gig on a heap of stones by the road-side. Mr Young was taken up dead, and Maria was lamed for life. She had always known the Enderbys very well; and there had been some gossip among their mutual acquaintance about the probability that Philip would prove to be Maria's lover, when he should be old enough to think of marrying. It never went further than this,—except in Maria's own heart. She had, indeed, hoped—even supposed—that in Philip's mind the affair had at least been entertained thus far. She could never settle to her own satisfaction whether she had been weak and mistaken, or whether she had really been in any degree wronged. There had been words, there had been looks,—but words and looks are so easily misinterpreted! The probability was that she had no one to blame but herself—if fault there was. Perhaps there was no fault anywhere: but there was misery, intense and long. During her illness, no tidings came of Philip. He was in another part of the country when the accident happened; and it was not till long after it had been made known that Mr Young had died insolvent,—not till after Maria had recovered, as far as recovery was possible,—not till she had fallen into the habit of earning her bread, that Philip reappeared, and shook hands with her, and told her with how much concern he had heard of her sufferings. This interview gave her entire possession of herself:— so she believed. She got through it calmly, and it left her with one subject at least of intense thankfulness,—that her mind was known only to herself. Whatever might be her solitary struggles, she might look without shame into the face of every human being. She could bear being pitied for her poverty, for her lameness, for her change of prospects, when the recollection of this came across any of her acquaintance. If it had been necessary, she could probably have borne to be pitied for having loved without return; but she could not be too thankful that it was not necessary.

Maria was right in her supposition that the village was speculating upon the newly-arrived young ladies. The parish clerk had for some years, indeed ever since the death of the late stationer and dispenser of letters, carried on a flirtation with the widow, notwithstanding the rumours which were current as to the cause to which her late husband owed his death. It was believed that poor Harry Plumstead died of exhaustion from his wife's voice; for she was no other than the village scold, of whose existence Margaret had been warned by Mr Enderby. Some thought that Owen was acting a politic part in protracting this flirtation,—keeping her temper in check by his hold upon her expectations; and such had little doubt that the affair would linger on to the end, without any other result than Owen's exemption meanwhile from the inflictions of her tongue, to which, in the discharge of his office, he might otherwise become frequently liable. Others wished to see them married, believing that in Owen, a Welshman sufficiently irascible, Mrs Plumstead would at last meet her match. This afternoon, an observer would have thought the affair was proceeding to this point. Mrs Plumstead, looking particularly comely and gracious, was putting up an unclaimed letter at the window for display, when Owen stopped to ask if she had seen the pretty young ladies who had come to Deerbrook. He remarked that, to be sure, they might have gone to some place where they were more wanted, for Deerbrook was not without pretty faces of its own before: and, as he said so, he smiled hard in the widow's face. He should not wonder if some work for the rector should rise up before long, for, where there were pretty faces, weddings might be looked for. He even asked Mrs Plumstead if she did not think so: and added something so ambiguous about his own share in the work for the rector which was to arise, that the widow could not make out whether he spoke as her admirer or as parish clerk. In the milliner's workroom there was a spirited conversation between Miss Nares and her assistant, on the past wedding dresses of Deerbrook, arising out of the topic of the day,—the Miss Ibbotsons. Mrs Howell, who, with her shopwoman, Miss Miskin, dispensed the haberdashery of the place, smiled winningly at every customer who entered her shop, and talked of delightful acquisitions, and what must be felt about Mr Hope, in the midst of such charming society, and what it must be hoped would be felt; and how gay the place was likely to be with riding parties, and boating parties, and some said, dances on the green at Mrs Enderby's; and how partners in a dance have been known to become partners for life, as she had been jocosely told when her poor dear Howell prevailed on her to stand up with him,—the first time for twenty years,—at his niece's wedding. Hester's beauty, and what Mrs Grey had said about it to her maid, were discussed, just at the moment when Hester, passing the shop, was entreated by Sophia to look at a new pattern of embroidery which had lately arrived from London, and was suspended at the window. Mrs Howell and her gossips caught a glimpse of the face of the young lady, through the drapery of prints and muslins, and the festoons of ribbons; and when the party proceeded down the street, there was a rush to the door, in order to obtain a view of her figure. She was pronounced beautiful; and it was hoped that some gentleman in the village would find her irresistible. It was only rather strange that no gentleman was in attendance on her now.

If the gossips could have followed the party with their eyes into the meadow, they would soon have been satisfied; for it was not long before Mr Hope joined them there. On leaving Mr Grey's table, he was as little disposed to go and visit his patient, as medical men are when they are called away from the merriest company, or at the most interesting moment of a conversation. The liability to this kind of interruption is one of the great drawbacks of the profession to which Mr Hope belonged; another is, the impossibility of travelling,—the being fixed to one place for life, without any but the shortest intervals of journeying. Mr Hope had been settled for five years at Deerbrook; and, during that time, he had scarcely been out of sight of its steeple. His own active and gladsome mind had kept him happy among his occupations. There was no one in the place with whom he could hold equal converse; but, while he had it not, he did not feel the pressing want of it. He loved his profession, and it kept him busy. His kind heart was ever full of interest for his poorer patients. Seeing the best side of everybody, he could be entertained, though sometimes vexed, by his intercourse with the Greys and Rowlands. Then there was the kindly-tempered and gentlemanly rector; and Philip Enderby often came down for a few weeks; and Mr Hope had the chief management of the Book Society, and could thus see the best new books; and his professional rides lay through a remarkably pretty country.

He kept up a punctual and copious correspondence with the members of his own family,—with his married sisters, and with his only brother, now with his regiment in India,—relating to them every important circumstance of his lot, and almost every interesting feeling of his heart. With this variety of resources, life had passed away cheerily, on the whole, with Mr Hope, for the five years of his residence at Deerbrook; though there were times when he wondered whether it was to be always thus,—whether he was to pass to his grave without any higher or deeper human intercourses than he had here. If it had been possible, he might, like other men as wise as himself, have invested some one of the young ladies of Deerbrook with imaginary attributes, and have fallen in love with a creature of his own fancy. But it really was not possible. There was no one of the young ladies of Deerbrook who was not so far inferior to the women of Hope's own family,—to the mother he had lost, and the sisters who were settled far away,—as to render this commonest of all delusions impossible to him.

To such a man, so circumstanced, it may be imagined how great an event was the meeting with Hester and Margaret. He could not be in their presence ten minutes without becoming aware of their superiority to every woman he had seen for five years past. The beauty of the one, the sincerity and unconsciousness of the other, and the general elevation of both, struck him forcibly the first evening. His earliest thought the next morning was of some great event having taken place; and when he left Mr Grey's door after dinner, it was with an unwillingness which made him spur himself and his horse on to their business, that he might the sooner return to his new-found pleasure. His thoughts already darted forward to the time when the Miss Ibbotsons would be leaving Deerbrook. It was already a heavy thought how dull Deerbrook would be without them. He was already unconsciously looking at every object in and around the familiar place with the eyes of the strangers, speculating on how the whole would appear to them. In short, his mind was full of them. There are, perhaps, none who do not know what this kind of impression is. All have felt it, at some time or other,—many have felt it often,—about strangers whom they have been predisposed to like, or with whom they have been struck at meeting. Nine times out of ten, perhaps, the impression is fleeting; and when it is gone, there is an unwillingness to return to it, from a sense of absurdity in having been so much interested about one who so soon became indifferent: but the fact is not the less real and general for this. When it happens between two young people who are previously fancy-free, and circumstances favour the impression till it sinks deeper than the fancy, it takes the name of love at first sight. Otherwise it passes away without a name, without a record:— for the hour it is a secret: in an after time it is forgotten.

Possessed unconsciously with this secret, Hope threw himself from his horse at the entrance of the meadow where the cowslip-gatherers were busy, fastened his steed to the gate, and joined the party. The children ran to him with the gleanings of intelligence which they had acquired since he saw them last, half an hour before:— that it was well they did not put off their gathering any longer, for some of the flowers were beginning to dry up already: that cousins had never tasted cowslip-tea;—(was not this *very* odd?)—that cousin Hester would not help to pick the flowers for drying,— she thought it such a pity to pull the blossom out of the calyx: that Sophia would not help either, because it was warm: that cousin Margaret had gathered a great many, but she had been ever so long watching a spider's nest,—a nasty large spider's nest that Matilda was just going to break into, when cousin Margaret asked her not to spoil it?

Margaret was indeed on her knees, prying into the spider's nest. When duly laughed at, she owned to having seen cobwebs before, but maintained that cobwebs in a closet were a very different affair from a spider's nest in a field.

"I rather think, however," said she, "the word 'nest' itself has something to do with my liking for what I have been looking at. Some of your commonest country words have a charm to the ear and imagination of townspeople that you could not understand."

"But," said Mr Hope, "I thought nests were very common in Birmingham. Have you not nests of boxes, and nests of work-tables?"

"Yes, and so we have stacks of chimneys; but yet we do not think of hay-making when we see the smoke of the town.—I rather think country words are only captivating as relating to the country; but then you cannot think how bewitching they are to people who live in streets."

"The children might have found you a prettier sort of nest to indulge your fancy with, I should think. There must be plenty of creatures besides spiders in this wide meadow."

Mr Hope called out to the little girls, that whoever should find any sort of a nest in the meadow, for Miss Margaret Ibbotson, should have a ride on his horse. Away flew the children; and Hester and Sophia came from the water-side to know what all the bustle was about. Fanny returned to inquire whether the nests must be *in* the meadow; whether just outside would not do. She knew there was an ants' nest in the bank, just on the other side of the hedge. The decision was that the ants' nest would do only in case of her not being able to find any other within bounds. Sophia looked on languidly, probably thinking all this very silly. It put her in mind of an old schoolfellow of hers who had been called very clever before she came to school at nine years old. Till she saw her, Sophia had believed that town children were always clever: but no later than the very first day, this little girl had got into disgrace with the governess. Her task was to learn by heart Goldsmith's Country Clergyman, in the 'Deserted Village.' She said it quite perfectly, but, when questioned about the meaning, stopped short at the first line,—"Near yonder copse where once a garden smiled." She persisted that she did not know what a copse was: the governess said she was obstinate, and shut her up in the play hours between morning and afternoon school. Sophia never could make out whether the girl was foolish or obstinate in persisting that she did not know what a copse was: but her cousin Margaret now put her in mind of this girl, with all her town feelings, and her fuss about spiders' nests.

"How is old Mr Smithson to-day?" Sophia inquired of Mr Hope, by way of introducing something more rational.

"Not better: it is scarcely possible that he should be," was the reply.

"Papa thought last night he must be dying."

"He is dying."

"Have you just come from a patient who is dying?" asked Hester, with a look of anxiety, with which was mixed some surprise.

"Yes: from one who cannot live many days."

Sophia observed that Mr James had been sent for early this morning—no doubt to put the finish to the will: but nobody seemed to know whether the old gentleman would leave his money to his nephew or his step-son, or whether he would divide it between them. Hester and Margaret showed no anxiety on this point, but seemed so ready to be interested about some others as to make Mr Hope think that they were only restrained by delicacy from asking all that he could tell about his patient's state. They knew enough of the profession, however, to be aware that this kind of inquiry is the last which should be addressed to a medical man.

"You are surprised," said he, "that I am come from a dying patient to play with the children in the fields. Come, acknowledge that this is in your minds."

"If it is, it is an unreasonable thought," said Margaret. "You must see so many dying people, it would be hard that in every case you should be put out of the reach of pleasure."

"Never mind the hardship, if it be fitting," said Hope. "Hard or not hard, is it natural,—is it possible?"

"I suppose witnessing death so often does lessen the feelings about it," observed Hester. "Yet I cannot fancy that one's mind could be at liberty for small concerns immediately after leaving a house full of mourners, and the sight of one in pain. There must be something distasteful in everything that meets one's eyes,—in the sunshine itself."

"True. That is the feeling in such cases: but such cases seldom occur. Yes: I mean what I say. Such cases are very rare. The dying person is commonly old, or so worn out by illness as to make death at last no evil. When the illness is shorter, it is usually found that a few hours in the sick room do the work of months of common life, in reconciling the minds of survivors."

"I am sure that is true," observed Margaret.

"It is so generally the case that I know no set of circumstances in which I should more confidently reckon on the calmness, forethought, and composure of the persons I have to deal with than in the family of a dying person. The news comes suddenly to the neighbours: all the circumstances rush at once into their imaginations: all their recollections and feelings about the sufferer agitate them in quick succession; and they naturally suppose the near friends must be more agitated, in proportion to their nearness."

"The watchers, meanwhile," said Hester, "have had time in the long night to go over the past and the future, again and again; and by morning all seems so familiar, that they think they can never be surprised into grief again."

"So familiar," said Mr Hope, "that their minds are at liberty for the smallest particulars of their duty. I usually find them ready for the minutest directions I may have to give."

"Yes: the time for surprise,—for consternation,—is long afterwards," said Hester, with some emotion. "When the whole has become settled and finished in other minds, the nearest mourners begin to wake up to their mourning."

"And thus," said Margaret, "the strongest agitation is happily not witnessed."

"Happily not," said Mr Hope. "I doubt whether anybody's strongest agitations ever are witnessed. I doubt whether the sufferer himself is often aware of what are really his greatest sufferings; and he is so ashamed of them that he hides them from himself when it is possible. I cannot but think that any grief which reveals itself is very endurable."

"Is not that rather hard?" asked Margaret.

"How does it seem to you hard? Is it not merciful that we can keep our worst sorrows,—that we are disposed, as it were forced, to keep them from afflicting our friends?"

"But is it not saying that bereavement of friends is not the greatest of sorrows, while all seem to agree that it is?"

"Is it, generally speaking, the greatest of sorrows? I think not, for my own part. There are cases in which the loss is too heavy to bear being the subject of any speculation, almost of observation; for instance, when the happiest married people are separated, or when a first or only child dies: but I think there are many sorrows greater than a separation by death of those who have faith enough to live independently of each other, and mutual love enough to deserve, as they hope, to meet again hereafter. I assure you I have sometimes come away from houses unvisited, and unlikely to be visited by death, with a heart so heavy as I have rarely or never brought from a deathbed."

"I should have thought that would be left for the rector to say," observed Hester. "I should have supposed you meant cases of guilt or remorse."

"Cases of guilt or remorse," continued Mr Hope, "and also of infirmity. People may say what they will, but I am persuaded that there is immeasurably more suffering endured, both in paroxysms and for a continuance, from infirmity, tendency to a particular fault, or the privation of a sense, than from the loss of any friend upon earth, except the very nearest and dearest; and even that case is no exception, when there is the faith of meeting again, which almost every mourner has, so natural and welcome as it is."

"Do you tell your infirm friends the high opinion you have of their sufferings?" asked Margaret.

"Why, not exactly; that would not be the kindest thing to do, would it? What they want is, to have their trouble lightened to them, not made the worst of;—lightened, not by using any deceit, of course, but by simply treating their case as a matter of fact."

"Then surely you should make light of the case of the dying too: make light of it even to the survivors. Do you do this?"

"In one sense I do; in another sense no one can do it. Not regarding death as a misfortune, I cannot affect to consider it so. Regarding the change of existence as a very serious one, I cannot, of course, make light of it."

"That way of looking at it regards only the dying person; you have not said how you speak of it to survivors."

"As I speak of it to you now, or to myself when I see any one die; with the added consideration of what the survivors are about to lose. That is a large consideration certainly; but should not one give them credit for viewing death as it is, and for being willing to bear their own loss cheerfully, as they would desire to bear any other kind of loss? especially if, as they say, they believe it to be only for a time."

"This as looking on the bright side," observed Hester, in a low voice; but she was overheard by Mr Hope.

"I trust you do not object to the bright side of things," said he, smiling, "as long as there is so much about us that is really very dark?"

"What can religion be for," said Margaret, "or reason, or philosophy, whichever name you may call your faith by, but to show us the bright side of everything—of death among the rest? I have often wondered why we seem to try to make the most of that evil (if evil it be), while we think it a duty to make the least of every other. I had some such feeling, I suppose, when I was surprised to hear that you had come hither straight from a deathbed: I do not wonder at all now."

"Mr Smithson will not be much missed," observed Sophia, who felt herself relieved from the solemnity of the occasion by what had passed, and at liberty to speak of him as freely as if he was no nearer death than ever. "He has never been a sociable neighbour. I always thought him an odd old man, from the earliest time I can remember."

"Some few will miss him," said Mr Hope. "He is a simple-hearted, shy man, who never did himself justice, except with two or three who saw most of him. Their affection has been enough for him—enough to make him think now that his life has been a very happy one. There!" cried Hope, as a lark sprang up almost from under the feet of the party—"There is another member of Deerbrook society, ladies, who is anxious to make your acquaintance." There were two or three larks hovering above the meadow at this moment, and others were soaring further off. The air was full of lark music. The party stood still and listened. Looking up into the sunny sky, they watched one little warbler, wheeling round, falling, rising again, still warbling, till it seemed as if it could never be exhausted. Sophia said it made her head ache to look up so long; and she seemed impatient for the bird to have done. It then struck her that she also might find a nest, like her sisters; and she examined the place whence the lark had sprung. Under a thick tuft of grass, in a little hollow, she found a family of infant larks huddled together, and pointed them out to her cousins.

The children came upon being called. They were damped in spirits. They did not see how they were to find any nests, if the ants' nest would not do; unless, indeed, Mr Hope would hold them up into the trees or hedges to look; but they could not climb trees, Mr Hope knew. They were somewhat further mortified by perceiving that they might have found a nest by examining the ground, if they had happened to think of it. Margaret begged they would not be distressed at not finding nests for her; and Mr Hope proposed to try his luck, saying, that if he succeeded, every one who wished should have a ride on his horse.

To the surprise of the children, he turned towards the water, and walked along the bank. The brimming river was smooth as glass; and where it stood in among the rushes, and in every tiny inlet, it was as clear as the air, and alive with small fish, which darted at the flies that dimpled the surface. A swan, which had been quietly sailing in the middle of the stream, changed its deportment as the party proceeded along the bank. It ruffled its breast feathers, arched back its neck till the head rested between the erect wings, and drove through the water with a speed which shivered the pictures in it as a sweeping gale would have done.

"What is the matter with the creature?" asked Margaret; "I never saw a swan behave so."

The children seemed rather afraid that the bird would come on shore and attack them. Mr Hope took the opportunity of its being at some little distance, to open the rushes, and show where a fine milk-white egg lay in a large round nest.

"Oh, Mr Hope, you knew!" cried the children, "you knew there was a swan's nest near."

"Yes; and did not you, when you saw how the swan behaved? But I was aware of this nest before. Tom Creach has the care of the park swans; he made this nest, and he told me where it was. Let your cousins have a peep; and then we will go, before the poor swan grows too much frightened. And now, who will have a ride on my horse?"

All the children chose to ride; and, while Mr Hope was coursing with them in turn, round and round the meadow, the young ladies proceeded along the bank. A quarter of a mile further on, they fell in with Sydney Grey and his friend Mr Philip. They had been successful in their sport. Mr Enderby had had enough of it, and was stretched on the grass reading, while Sydney stood on the roots of an old oak, casting his line into the pool beneath its shadow.

"So, here you are, quite safe!" said Sophia; "George Rowland might have come after all. Poor boy! I am glad he is not with us, he would be so mortified to see all the fish you have caught without him!"

"How many times have we been in the river, Sydney? Can you remember?" asked Mr Enderby.

"I have seen no fish big enough to pull us in," said Sydney; "and I do not know any other way of getting a wetting at this sport. Mrs Rowland should have seen George and me climbing the old oak at the two-mile turning. I dared George to it, and there he hung over the water, at the end of the branch, riding up and down like a see-saw. She would think nothing of letting him go fishing after that."

"If the branch had broken," said Mr Enderby, "what would you have done then?"

"Oh, it is not often that a branch breaks."

"Old oaks are apt to break, sooner or later; and, the next time you dare George to see-saw over the river, I would advise you to consider beforehand how you would get him out, in case of his dropping in."

"Oh, he is not afraid. One day lately, when the water was low, he offered to cross the weir at Dingleford. I did not persuade him to that; but he pulled off his shoes and stockings, and got over and back, safe enough."

"Indeed! and you tried it too, I suppose?"

"Yes; it would be a shame if I could not do what George can. It was almost as easy as walking along this bank."

"I shall talk to Master George, however, before he goes to Dingleford again, or he may chance to find it easier some day to miss his footing than to hold it."

"I wonder Mrs Rowland is afraid to let George go out with you," said Sophia, "considering what things he does when you are not with him."

"She does not know of these pranks, or she would feel as you do; and I hope every one here will be kind enough not to tell her. It would only be making her anxious to no purpose, whenever the boy is out of her sight. It would be a pity to make a coward of him; and I think I can teach him what is mischief and what is not, without disturbing her. Come, ladies, suppose you rest yourselves here; you will find a pleasant seat on this bank: at least, I fell asleep on it just now, as if I had been on a sofa."

"I wish you would all go to sleep, or else walk off," said Sydney. "You make so much noise I shall never catch any fish."

"Suppose you were to go somewhere else," said Mr Enderby. "Would not that be rather more civil than sending us all away?"

Sydney thought he would find another place: there were plenty along the bank. He gathered up bait and basket, and trudged off. There was an amusement, however, which he liked better even than fishing; and for which he now surrendered it. He was presently seen cantering round the meadow on Mr Hope's horse.

Mr Enderby hoped the Miss Ibbotsons were able to say "No" with decision. If not, he did not envy them their supper this evening; for Sydney would certainly ask them to eat all the fish he had caught—bream and dace and all. The first pleasure of young anglers is to catch these small fry; and the next is, to make their sisters and cousins eat them. Sophia solemnly assured her cousins that mamma never allowed Sydney's fish to come to table, at least in the house. If the children liked to get the cook to boil them for their dolls' feasts in the schoolroom, they might.

"And then Miss Young is favoured with a share, I suppose?" said Margaret.

"Have you made acquaintance with Miss Young yet?" inquired Mr Enderby.

"Oh, yes! I had the pleasure of knowing Miss Young long before I knew you."

"Long! how long? I was not aware that you had ever met. Where did you meet?"

"In the schoolroom, before breakfast,—full four hours before you called this morning."

"Oh, that is all you mean! I wondered how you should know her."

Sophia asked whether Margaret and Miss Young were not going to study together: Margaret assented. Miss Young was kind enough to promise to help her to read German.

"And you?" said Mr Enderby to Hester.

"Why, no; I am rather afraid of the undertaking."

"And you, Miss Grey?"

"No. Mamma says, I have enough to do with my history and my music; especially while my cousins are here. I began German once, but mamma thought I was growing awry, and so I left it off. I find Mrs Rowland means Matilda to learn German."

"We are all disposed to have my little nieces learn whatever Miss Young will be kind enough to teach them; they will gain nothing but good from her."

"She is very learned, to be sure," observed Sophia.

"And something more than learned, I should think," said Hester; "I fancy she is wise."

"How can you have discovered that already?" asked Mr Enderby, whose fingers were busy dissecting a stalk of flowering grass.

"I hardly know; I have nothing to quote for my opinion. Her conversation leaves a general impression of her being very sensible."

"Sensible, as she is a woman," observed Margaret; "if she were a man, she would be called philosophical."

"She *is* very superior," observed Sophia. "It was mamma's doing that she is the children's governess."

"Philosophical!" repeated Mr Enderby. "It is a happy thing that she is philosophical in her circumstances, poor thing!"

"As she happens to be unprosperous," said Margaret, smiling. "If she were rich, and strong, and admired, her philosophy would be laughed at; it would only be in the way."

Mr Enderby sighed, and made no answer. Before any one spoke again, Mr Hope and his little companions came up.

"How quiet you all are!" exclaimed Sydney. "I've a good mind to come and fish here again, if you will only go on to be so drowsy."

Sophia declared that they had been talking, up to the last minute, about Miss Young, and learning German, and being philosophical.

"And which of the party have you made out to be the most philosophical?" inquired Mr Hope.

"We have not so much as made out what philosophy is for," said Hester; "can you tell us?"

As she looked up at Mr Hope, who was standing behind her, Sydney thought her question was addressed to him. Swinging his fishing-rod round, he replied doubtfully that he thought philosophy was good to know how to do things. What sort of things? Why, to make phosphorus lights, and electrify people, as Dr Levitt did, when he made Sophia jump off the stool with glass legs. Sophia was sure that any one else would have jumped off the stool as she did. She should take good care never to jump on it again. But she wondered Sydney did not know any better than that what philosophy was for. Her cousins said Miss Young was philosophical, and she had nothing to do with phosphorus or electrical machines.

Mr Enderby explained to Mr Hope that he had said what he was ready to maintain; that it was a happy thing for any one who, like Miss Young, was not so prosperous as she had been, to be supported by philosophy.

"And, granting this," said Margaret, "it was next inquired whether this same philosophy would have been considered equally admirable, equally a matter of congratulation, if Miss Young had not wanted it for solace."

"A question as old as the brigg at Stirling," replied Mr Hope; "older, older than any bridges of man's making."

"Why Stirling brigg? What do you mean?"

"I mean—do not you know the story?—that an old woman wanted to cross the Forth, and some ferrymen would have persuaded her to go in their boat when she was confident that a tempest was coming on, which would have made the ferry unsafe. They told her at last that she must trust to Providence. 'Na, na,' said she, 'I will ne'er trust to Providence while there is a brigg at Stirling.' The common practice is, you know, with the old woman.—We will not trust to the highest support we profess to have, till nothing else is left us. We worship philosophy, but never think of making use of it while we have prosperity as well."

"The question is whether such practice is wise," said Margaret: "we all know it is common."

"For my part," said Mr Enderby, "I think the old Scotchwoman was right; Providence helps those that help themselves, and takes care of those who take care of themselves."

"Just so," said Hope. "Her error was in supposing that the one course was an alternative from the other,—that she would not be trusting in Providence as much in going by the bridge as in braving the tempest. I think we are in the same error when we set up philosophy and prosperity in opposition to each other, taking up with the one when we cannot get the other, as if philosophy were not over all, compassing our life as the blue sky overarches the earth, brightening, vivifying, harmonising all, whether we look up to see whence the light comes or not."

"You think it a mistake, then," said Margaret, "not to look up to it till all is night below, and there is no light to be seen but by gazing overhead?"

"I do not see why we should miss seeing the white clouds and blue depths at noon because we may reckon upon moon and stars at midnight. Then again, what is life at its best without philosophy?"

"I can tell you, as well as anybody," said Mr Enderby, "for I never had any philosophy,—no, neither wisdom, nor the love of wisdom, nor patience, nor any of the things that philosophy is understood to mean."

"Oh, Mr Enderby!" cried Sydney, "what pains you took to teach me to fish, and to make me wait patiently for a bite! *You* say you are not patient!"

"My account of life without philosophy," said Mr Enderby, proceeding as if he did not hear the children testifying to his patience with them,—"my account of life without philosophy is, that it slips away mighty easily, till it is gone, you scarcely know where or how."

"And when you call upon philosophy at last to give an account of it, what does she say?" asked Margaret.

"I do not understand how life can slip away so," said Hester. "Is there ever a day without its sting?—without doubt of somebody, disappointment in oneself or another, dread of some evil, or weariness of spirit? Prosperity is no more of a cure for these than for sickness and death. If philosophy is—"

"Well!" exclaimed Mr Hope, with strong interest, "if philosophy is—"

"Happy they that have her, for all need her."

"Hear a testimony at least as candid as your own, Enderby. If you really find life steal away as easily as you now fancy, depend upon it you are more of a philosopher than you are aware of."

"What is philosophy?" asked Matilda of Sydney in a loud whisper, which the boy was not in any hurry to take notice of, so little was there in the conversation which seemed to bear upon phosphorus and electricity.

"A good question," observed Mr Enderby. "Hope, will you tell us children what we are talking about,—what philosophy is all this while?"

"You gave us a few meanings just now, which I should put into one. Call it enlargement of views, and you have wisdom, and the love of wisdom, and patience, all at once: ay, Sydney, and your kind of philosophy too:— It was by looking far and deep into nature that men found electricity."

"Did Dr Levitt find it out?" asked Matilda: "he is so very short-sighted! I don't believe he would see those fish snapping up the flies, if he sat where I do. What was that that fell on my bonnet? Is it raining?"

Sydney, tired of fishing, had climbed into the oak, and was sending down twigs and leaves upon the heads of the party. Sophia desired him to come down, and even assured him that if he did not, she should be angry. He replied, that he would only stay to see whether she would be angry or not. The experiment was cut short by the whole party rising, and moving homewards. The sun was setting, and the picked cowslips must not have any dew upon them.

As the group passed up the street, Sydney in advance, with his rod and basket, on Mr Hope's horse, Mr Hope himself following with Hester, and the tall Mr Enderby, with Sophia and Margaret on either arm, all, like the little girls, laden with cowslips, the gossips of Deerbrook were satisfied that the stranger ladies must have enjoyed their walk in the meadows.

Chapter Six

The School-Room.

Mrs Rowland was mortified that the Greys had been beforehand with her in the idea of a cowslip-gathering. From the moment of Matilda's asking leave to accompany them, she resolved to have such an expedition from her house as her neighbours should not be able to eclipse. Like Lear, she did not yet know what her deed was to be; but it should be the wonder and terror of the place: she would do such things as should strike the strangers with admiration. When she heard an account of it from her little daughter, she found this had been a very poor beginning,—a mere walk in the meadows, and home again to tea;—no boiling the kettle in the woods,—not even a surprise of early strawberries. She could not call this being forestalled; it could not give the young ladies any idea of a proper country excursion, with four or five carriages, or a boat with an awning. As soon as Mr Rowland came home in the evening, she consulted him about the day, the place, the mode, and the numbers to be invited. Mr Rowland was so well pleased to find his lady in the mood to be civil to her neighbours, that he started no difficulties, and exerted himself to overcome such as could not be overlooked. All the planning prospered so well, that notes to the Grey family and to the Miss Ibbotsons lay on Mr Grey's breakfast-table the next morning, inviting the whole party to dine with Mrs Rowland in Dingleford woods, that day week—the carriages to be at the door at ten o'clock.

The whole village rang with the preparations for this excursion; and the village was destined to ring with other tidings before it took place. Mrs Rowland often said that she had the worst luck in the world; and it seemed as if all small events fell out so as to plague her. She had an unusual fertility in such sensible suppositions and reasonable complaints; and her whole diversity of expressions of this kind was called into play about this expedition to Dingleford woods. The hams were actually boiled, and the chicken-pies baked, when clouds began to gather in the sky; and on the appointed morning, pattens clinked in the village street, Miss Young's umbrella was wet through in the mere transit from the farrier's gate to the schoolroom; the gravel-walk before Mr Grey's house was full of yellow pools, and the gurgling of spouts or drips from the trees was heard on every side. The worst of it was, this rain came after a drought of many weeks, which had perilled the young crops, and almost destroyed the hopes of hay; the ladies and children had been far from sufficiently sorry to hear that some of the poorer wheat lands in the county had been ploughed up, and that there was no calculating what hay would be a ton the next winter. They were now to receive the retribution of their indifference; rain had set in, and the farmers hoped that it might continue for a month. It would not be wise to fix any country excursion for a few weeks to come. Let the young people enjoy any fine afternoon that they might be able to turn to the account of a walk, or a drive, or a sail on the river; but picnic parties must be deferred till settled weather came. There was every hope that the middle of the summer would be fine and seasonable, if the rains came down freely now.

This course of meteorological events involved two great vexations to Mrs Rowland. One was, that the neighbours, who could pretend to entertain the strangers only in a quiet way at home, took the opportunity of the rainy weather to do so, hoping, as they said, not to interfere with any more agreeable engagements. Mrs Rowland really never saw anything so dissipated as the Greys; they were out almost every evening when they had not company at home. It was impossible that Sophia's studies could go on as they ought to do. What with taking a quiet cup of tea with one acquaintance, and being at a merry reading party at another's, and Mrs Enderby's little dance, and dinner at the Levitts', there were few evenings left; and on those few evenings they were never content to be alone. They were always giving the young men encouragement to go in. Mr Hope made quite a home house of Mr Grey's; and as for Philip, he seemed now to be more at Mr Grey's than even at his own mother's or sister's. Mrs Grey ought to remember how bad all this was for a girl of Sophia's age. It would completely spoil the excursion to Dingleford woods. The young people knew one another so well by this time, that the novelty was all worn off, and they would have nothing left to say to each other. It was provoking that Mr Rowland had promised that the excursion should take place whenever the weather should be settled enough. It might so fairly have been given up! and now it must be gone on with, when every one was tired of the idea, and the young people must almost be weary of one another, from being always together!

The other vexation was, that there were frequent short intervals of fine weather, which were immediately taken advantage of for a drive, or a walk, or a sail; and it came out one day from the children, who had learned it in the schoolroom, that the Miss Ibbotsons had been in Dingleford woods. There had been no such intention when the party set out; they had not designed to go nearly so far; but they had been tempted on by the beauty of the evening and of the scenery, till they had found it the shortest way to come home through the Dingleford woods. Mrs Rowland pronounced this abominable; and she was not appeased by hearing that her brother had been the proposer of this mode of return, and the guide of the party. Philip forgot everything, she declared, in his fancy for these girls; it was always his fault that he was carried away by the people he was with: he had got the name of a flirt by it, and a flirt he was; but she had never known him so possessed as he seemed to be by these strangers. She must speak to Mr Rowland about it; the matter might really become serious; and if he should ever be entrapped into marrying into the Grey connections, among people so decidedly objectionable, it would be a terrible self-reproach to her as long as she lived, that she had not interfered in time. She should speak to Mr Rowland.

Meanwhile she kept a watchful eye on her brother's proceedings. She found from the children that their Uncle Philip had fulfilled his promise of going to see the schoolroom, and had been so much better than his word, that he had been there very often. When he went, it was always when the Miss Ibbotsons were there, learning German, or drawing, or talking with Miss Young. It was impossible to pick a quarrel with Miss Young about this; for she always sent her visitors away the moment the clock struck the school hour. The summer-house was Mr Grey's property, too; so that Mrs Rowland could only be angry at the studies which went on in it, and had no power to close the doors against any of the parties.

The rainy weather had indeed been very propitious to the study of German. For a fortnight Margaret had spent some hours of each day with Miss Young; and over their books they had learned so much of one another's heart and mind, that a strong regard had sprung up between them. This new friendship was a great event to Miss Young;—how great, she herself could scarcely have believed beforehand. Her pupils found that Miss Young was now very merry sometimes. Mr Grey observed to his wife that the warmer weather seemed to agree with the poor young woman, as she had some little colour in her cheeks at last; and Margaret herself observed a change in the tone of the philosophy she had admired from the beginning. There was somewhat less of reasoning in it, and more of impulse; it was as sound as ever, but more genial. While never forgetting the constancy of change in human affairs, she was heartily willing to enjoy the good that befell her, while it lasted. It was well that she could do so; for the good of this new friendship was presently alloyed.

She was not aware, and it was well that she was not, that Hester was jealous of her, almost from the hour of Margaret's learning what a vast number of irregular verbs there is in the German. Each sister remembered the conversation by the open window, on the night of their arrival at Deerbrook. Remembering it, Margaret made Hester a partaker in all her feelings about Maria Young; her admiration, her pity, her esteem. Reserving to herself any confidence which Maria placed in her (in which, however, no mention of Mr Enderby ever occurred), she kept not a thought or feeling of her own from her sister. The consequence was, that Hester found that Maria filled a large space in Margaret's mind, and that a new interest had risen up in which she had little share. She, too, remembered the conversation, but had not strength to act up to the spirit of it. She had then owned her weakness, and called it wickedness, and fancied that she could never mistrust her sister again. She was now so ashamed of her own consciousness of being once more jealous, that she strove to hide the fact from herself; and was not therefore likely to tell it to Margaret. She struggled hourly with herself, rebuking her own temper, and making appeals to her own generosity. She sat drawing in the little blue parlour, morning after morning, during Sophia's reading or practising, telling herself that Margaret and Miss Young had no secrets, no desire to be always *tête-à-tête*; that they had properly invited her to learn German; and that she had only to go at any moment, and offer to join them, to be joyfully received. She argued with herself,—how mean it would be to do so; to agree to study at last, in order to be a sort of spy upon them, to watch over her own interests; as if Margaret—the most sincere and faithful of living beings— were not to be trusted with them. She had often vowed that she would cure the jealousy of her temper; now was the occasion, and she would meet it; she would steadily sit beside Sophia or Mrs Grey every morning, when Margaret was not with her, and never let her sister know how selfish she could be.

This was all very well; but it could not make Margaret suppose her sister happy when she was not. She could not be certain what was the matter, but she saw that something was wrong. At times, Hester's manner was so unboundedly affectionate, that it was impossible to suppose that unkind feelings existed towards herself; though a few pettish words were at other times let drop. Hester's moods of magnanimity and jealousy were accounted for in other ways by her sister. Margaret believed, after a course of very close observation, that she had discovered, in investigating the cause of Hester's discomposure, a secret which was unknown to her sister herself. Margaret was not experienced in love, nor in watching the signs of it; but here was the mind she understood best, discomposed without apparent cause—more fond, more generous to herself than ever, yet not reposing its usual confidence in her—and subject to those starts of delight and disappointment which she had heard and could understand to be the moods of love. She was confirmed in her suspicion by observing that the merits of Mr Hope were becoming daily a less common subject of conversation between them, while it was certain that he had in no degree lost favour with either. They had been charmed with him from the beginning, and had expressed to each other the freest admiration of his truth, his gaiety, his accomplishments, and great superiority to the people amidst whom he lived. He was now spoken of less every day, while his visits grew more frequent, longer, and, Margaret could not but think, more welcome to her sister. The hours when he was sure not to come happened to be those which she spent with Miss Young—the hours in which gentlemen are devoted to their business. Margaret thus witnessed all that passed; and if her conjecture about Hester was right, she could have wished to see Mr Hope's manner rather different from what it was. He was evidently strongly attracted to the house; and there was some reason to think that Mrs Grey believed that Hester was the attraction. But Margaret had no such impression. She saw that Mr Hope admired her sister's beauty, listened to her conversation with interest, and was moved at times by the generosity of her tone of moral feeling; but this, though much, was not enough for the anxious sister's full satisfaction; and the one thing besides which she would fain have discerned she could not perceive. These were early days yet, however; so early that, in the case of any one whom she knew, except her sister, she should have supposed her own conjectures wild and almost improper; but Hester's was one of those natures to which time and circumstance minister more speedily and more abundantly than to the generality. By the strength of her feelings, and the activity of her affections, time was made more comprehensive, and circumstance more weighty than to others. A day would produce changes in her which the impressions of a week would not effect in less passionate natures; and what were trifling incidents to the minds about her, were great events to her.

Margaret began to consider what was to be done. The more she thought, the more plainly she perceived that there was nothing to be done but to occupy Hester, simply and naturally, with as many interests as possible. This was safe practice, be the cause of her occasional discomposure what it might. It was particularly desirable that she should not continue the habit of sitting in silence for a considerable part of every morning.

One day, just after the voices of the children had been heard in the hall, giving token that school was over, Hester, sitting in the little blue parlour alone, with her head on her hand, was apparently contemplating the drawing on her board, but really considering that Margaret was now beginning to be happy with her friend, and asking why Margaret should not be happy with her friend, when Margaret herself entered.

"Do you want Sophia?" said Hester. "She is up-stairs."

"No; I want you."

"Indeed!"

There was an ironical tone of surprise in the one word she spoke, which let fall a weight upon Margaret's heart;—an old feeling, but one to which she had made no progress towards being reconciled.

"I cannot help you with your German, you know. How can you pretend to want me?"

"It is not about the German at all that I want you. Maria has found a Spenser at last, and I am going to read her the 'Hymn of Heavenly Beauty,' I know you never can hear that often enough; so come!"

"Perhaps Miss Young had rather not. I should be sorry to intrude myself upon her. But, however," continued she, observing Margaret's look of surprise, "I will come. Do not wait for me, dear. I will come the moment I have put up my drawing."

Margaret did wait, running over the keys of the open piano meanwhile.

"Shall I call Sophia too?" asked Hester, as she took up her work-bag. "I dare say she never read any of Spenser."

"I dare say not," replied Margaret; "and she would not care about it now. If you think we ought, we will call her. If not—"

Hester smiled, nodded, and led the way to the schoolroom without calling Sophia. She had not been two minutes in the cordial presence of her sister and Maria, before she felt the full absurdity of the feelings which had occupied her so lately, and was angry with herself to her own satisfaction. Her companions looked at each other with a smile as they observed at the same moment the downcast attitude of her moistened eyes, the beautiful blush on her cheek, and the expression of meek emotion on her lips. They thought that it was the image of heavenly beauty which moved her thus.

Before they had quite finished the Hymn, the door was burst open, and the children entered, dragging in Mr Enderby. Mr Enderby rebuked them, good-naturedly, for introducing him with so little ceremony, and declared to the ladies that Matilda had promised to knock before she opened the door. Hester advised Mary and Fanny to be more quiet in their mode of entrance, observing that they had made Miss Young start with their hurry.

Matilda was glad her uncle remembered to come sometimes. He had promised it several weeks before he came at all; even when he said he was going away in a fortnight.

"And if I had gone away in a fortnight," said he, "I should not have seen your schoolroom. But this is not the first time I have seen it, as you remember very well. I have been here often lately."

"But you never attend to me here, uncle! And I want so to show you my desk, where I keep my copy-book, and the work-box you gave me on my birthday."

"Well, you can show me now, cannot you? So, this is your desk! It seems convenient enough, whatever we may think of its beauty. I suppose it will hold all the knowledge you will want to have put into your head for some time to come. Now show me which is George's desk, and which Fanny's; and now Mary's,—a nice row of desks! Now," whispering to her, "can you show me which is Miss Margaret's desk?"

The little girl giggled as she answered, that Miss Margaret was too old to be a school-girl.

"So she is: but she learns of Miss Young, and I know she keeps some of her books here. Can you show me where?"

There was a desk rather larger than the rest, the lid of which now happened to be standing open. Matilda slyly pointed to it. While the ladies were engaged with the other children, Mr Enderby cast a glance into this desk, saw a book which he knew to be Margaret's, laid something upon it from his pocket, and softly closed the lid; the whole passing, if it was observed at all, as a survey of the children's desks. He then pretended to look round for the rod.

"No rod!" said he to the laughing children. "Oh, I should like to learn here very much, if there is no rod. Miss Margaret, do you not find it very pleasant learning here?"

The children were shouting, "Miss Young, Miss Young, do let uncle Philip come and learn with us. He says he will be a very good boy,—won't you, uncle Philip? Miss Young, when may uncle Philip come and learn his lessons?"

Margaret saw that there was constraint in the smile with which Maria answered the children. Little as she knew, it struck her that in his fun with the children, Mr Enderby was relying quite sufficiently on the philosophy he had professed to admire in Miss Young. Mr Enderby drew a chair to the window round which the ladies were sitting, and took up the volume Margaret had just laid down.

"Go, go, children!" said he; "run away to your gardens! I cannot spare you any more play to-day."

"Oh, but uncle, we want to ask you a question."

"Well, ask it."

"But it is a secret. You must come into the corner with Fanny, and Mary, and me."

For peace and quiet he went into the corner with them, and they whispered into each ear a question, how many burnt almonds and gingerbread-buttons, and how much barley-sugar, two shillings and threepence halfpenny would buy? The cowslips were now ready to make tea of, and the feast on the dolls' dishes might be served any day. Mr Enderby promised to inquire at the confectioner's, and not to tell anybody else; and at last the children were got rid of.

"Now that we have done with mysteries," said he, as he resumed his seat by the window, "that is, with children's mysteries that we can see to the bottom of, let us look a little into the poet's mysteries. What were you reading? Show me, and I will be your reader. Who or what is this Heavenly Beauty? We have not done with mysteries yet, I see."

"I was wondering," said Margaret smiling, "whether you take up Spenser because you are tired of mysteries. In such a case, some other poet might suit you better."

"What other?"

"Some one less allegorical, at least."

"I do not know that," said Hester. "The most cunning allegory that ever was devised is plain and easy in comparison with the simplest true story,—fully told: and a man is a poet in proportion as he fully tells a simple true story."

"A story of the mind, you mean," said Mr Enderby, "not of the mere events of life?"

"Of the mind, of course, I mean. Without the mind the mere life is nothing."

"Is not allegory a very pretty way of telling such a story of the mind, under the appearance of telling a story of a life?"

"Yes," said Margaret; "and that is the reason why so many like allegory. There is a pleasure in making one's way about a grotto in a garden; but I think there is a much higher one in exploring a cave on the sea-shore, dim and winding, where you never know that you have come to the end,—a much higher pleasure in exploring a life than following out an allegory."

"You are a true lover of mystery, Miss Margaret. You should have lived a thousand years ago."

"Thank you: I am very glad I did not. But why so long ago? Are there not mysteries enough left?"

"And will there not be enough a thousand years hence?" said Hester.

"I am afraid not. You and I cannot venture to speak upon what the Germans may be doing. But these two ladies can tell us, perhaps, whether they are not clearing everything up very fast;—making windows in your cave, Miss Margaret, till nobody will be afraid to look into every cranny of it."

"And then our complaint," said Miss Young, "will be like Mrs Howell's, when somebody told her that we were to have the Drummond light on every church steeple. 'Oh dear, ma'am!' said she, 'we shall not know how in the world to get any darkness.'"

"You speak as if you agreed that the Germans really are the makers of windows that Mr Enderby supposes them," observed Margaret; "but you do not think we are any nearer the end of mysteries than ever, do you?"

"Oh, no; not till we have struck our stone to the bottom of the universe, and walked round it: and I am not aware that the Germans pretend to be able to do that, any more than other people. Indeed, I think there are as many makers of grottoes as explorers of caves among them. What do you want, my dear?"

This last was addressed to George, whose round face, red with exertion, appeared at a back window. The little girls were hoisting him up, that he might call out once more, "Uncle Philip, be sure you remember not to tell."

"It would be a pity that mysteries should come to an end," observed Mr Enderby, "when they seem to please our human tastes so well. See there, how early the love of mystery begins! and who can tell where it ends? Is there one of your pupils, Miss Young, in whom you do not find it?"

"Not one; but is there not a wide difference between the love of making mysteries, and a taste for finding them out?"

"Do you not find both in children, and up into old age?"

"In children, one usually finds both: but I think the love of mystery-making and surprises goes off as people grow wiser. Fanny and Mary were plotting all last week how to take their sister Sophia by surprise with a piece of India-rubber, a token of fraternal affection, as they were pleased to call it; and you see George has a secret to-day: but they will have fewer hidings and devices every year: and, if they grow really wise, they will find that, amidst the actual business of life, there is so much more safety, and ease, and blessing in perfect frankness than in any kind of concealment, that they will give themselves the liberty and peace of being open as the daylight. Such is my hope for them. But all this need not prevent their delighting in the mysteries which are not of man's making."

"They will be all the more at leisure for them," said Margaret, "from having their minds free from plots and secrets."

"Surely you are rather hard upon arts and devices," said Philip. "Without more or fewer of them, we should make our world into a Palace of Truth,—see the Veillées du Château, which Matilda is reading with Miss Young. Who ever read it, that did not think the Palace of Truth the most disagreeable place in the world?"

"And why?" asked Margaret. "Not because the people in it spoke truth; but because the truth which they spoke was hatred, and malice, and selfishness."

"And how much better," inquired Hester, "is the truth that we should speak, if we were as true as the daylight? I hope we shall always be allowed to make mysteries of our own selfish and unkind fancies. There would be little mutual respect left if these things were told."

"I think there would be more than ever," said Margaret, carefully avoiding to meet her sister's eye. "I think so many mistakes would be explained, so many false impressions set right, on the instant of their being made, that our mutual relations would go on more harmoniously than now."

"And what would you do with the affairs now dedicated to mystery?" asked Mr Enderby. "How would you deal with diplomacy, and government, and with courtship? You surely would not overthrow the whole art of wooing? You would not doom lovers' plots and devices?"

The ladies were all silent. Mr Enderby, however, was determined to have an answer. He addressed himself particularly to Margaret.

"You do not disapprove of the little hidden tokens with which a man may make his feelings secretly known where he wishes them to be understood;—tokens which may meet the eye of one alone, and carry no meaning to any other! You do not disapprove of a more gentle and mysterious way of saying, 'I love you,' than looking full in one another's face, and declaiming it like a Quaker upon affirmation? You do not disapprove—"

"As for disapproving," said Margaret, who chanced to perceive that Maria's hand shook so that she could not guide her needle, and that she was therefore apparently searching for something in her work-box,—"as for disapproving, I do not pretend to judge for other people—"

She stopped short, struck with the blunder she had made. Mr Enderby hastened to take advantage of it. He said, laughing:

"Well, then, speak for yourself. Never mind other people's case."

"What I mean," said Margaret, with grave simplicity, "is, that all depends upon the person whose regard is to be won. There are silly girls, and weak women, who, liking mysteries in other affairs, are best pleased to be wooed with small artifices;—with having their vanity and their curiosity piqued with sly compliments—"

"Sly compliments! What an expression!"

"Such women agree, as a matter of course, in the old notion,—suitable enough five centuries ago,—that the life of courtship should be as unlike as possible to married life. But I certainly think those much the wisest and the happiest, who look upon the whole affair as the solemn matter that it really is, and who desire to be treated, from the beginning, with the sincerity and seriousness which they will require after they are married."

"If the same simplicity and seriousness were common in this as are required in other grave transactions," said Hester, "there would be less of the treachery, delusion, and heart-breaking, which lie heavy upon the souls of many a man and many a woman."

Mr Enderby, happening to be looking out of the window here, as if for something to say, caught the eye of his sister, who was walking in her garden. She beckoned to him, but he took no notice, not desiring to be disturbed at present. Turning again to Margaret, he said:

"But you would destroy all the graces of courtship: you would—"

"Nay," said Hester, "what is so graceful as the simplicity of entire mutual trust?—the more entire the more graceful."

"I wish you had left out the word 'trust.' You have spoiled something that I was going on to say about the simplicity of drawing lots like the Moravians,—the most sincere courtship of all: but that word 'trust' puts my illustration aside. You need not protest. I assure you I am not so dull as not to understand that you think love necessary to the wooing which seems graceful in your eyes;—Oh, yes: love, and mutual knowledge, and mutual reverence, and perfect trust! Oh, yes, I understand it all."

"Philip!" cried a soft, sentimental voice under the window:

"Brother, I want your arm for a turn in the shrubbery."

Mrs Rowland's bonnet was visible as she looked up to the window. She saw the braids of the hair of the young ladies, and her voice was rather less soft as she called again, "Philip, do you hear? I want you."

It was impossible to seem not to hear. Mr Enderby was obliged to go: but he left his hat behind him, as a sort of pledge that he meant to limit himself to the single turn proposed.

For various reasons, the young ladies were all disinclined to speak after he had left them. Miss Young was the first to move. She rose to go to her desk for something,—the desk in which Margaret kept the books she used in this place. Ever on the watch to save Maria the trouble of moving about, which was actual pain to her, Margaret flew to see if she could not fetch what was wanted: but Miss Young was already looking into the desk. Her eye caught the pretty new little volume which lay there. She took it up, found it was a volume of Tieck, and saw on the fly-leaf, in the well-known handwriting, "From P.E." One warm beam of hope shot through her heart:— how could it be otherwise,—the book lying in her desk, and thus addressed? But it was only one moment's joy. The next instant's reflection, and the sight of Margaret's German exercise, on which the book had lain, revealed the real case to her. In sickness of heart, she would, upon impulse, have put back the book, and concealed the incident: but she was not sure but that Margaret had seen the volume, and she *was* sure of what her own duty was. With a smile and a steady voice she held out the book to Margaret, and said:

"Here is something for you, Margaret, which looks a little like one of the hidden, and gentle, and mysterious tokens Mr Enderby has been talking about. Here it is, lying among your books; and I think it was not with them when you last left your seat."

Margaret blushed with an emotion which seemed to the one who knew her best to be too strong to be mere surprise. She looked doubtful for a moment about the book being meant for her. Its German aspect was conclusive against its being designed for Hester: but Miss Young,—was it certain that the volume was not hers? She asked this; but Maria replied, as her head was bent over her desk:

"There is no doubt about it. I am sure. It is nobody's but yours."

Some one proposed to resume the reading. The 'Hymn to Heavenly Beauty' was finished, but no remark followed. Each was thinking of something else. More common subjects suited their present mood better. It was urged upon Hester that she should be one of the daily party; and, her lonely fancies being for the hour dispersed, she agreed.

"But," she observed, "other people's visits alter the case entirely. I do not see how study is to go on if any one may come in from either house, as Mr Enderby did to-day. It is depriving Miss Young of her leisure, too, and making use of her apartment in a way that she may well object to."

"I am here, out of school hours, only upon sufferance," replied Miss Young. "I never call the room mine without this explanation."

"Besides," said Margaret, "it is a mere accident Mr Enderby's coming in to-day. If he makes a habit of it, we have only to tell him that we want our time to ourselves."

Miss Young knew better. She made no reply; but she felt in her inmost soul that her new-born pleasures were, from this moment, to be turned into pains. She knew Mr Enderby; and knowing him, foresaw that she was to be a witness of his wooings of another, whom she had just begun to take to her heart. This was to be her fate if she was strong enough for it,—strong enough to be generous in allowing to Margaret opportunities which could not without her be enjoyed, of fixing the heart of one whom she could not pronounce to have been faulty towards herself. His conversation today had gone far to make her suppose him blameless, and herself alone in fault; so complete had seemed his unconsciousness with regard to her. Her duty then was clearly to give them up to each other, with such spirit of self-sacrifice as she might be capable of. If not strong enough for this, the alternative was a daily painful retreat to her lodging, whence she might look out on the heaps of cinders in the farrier's yard, her spirit abased the while with the experience of her own weakness. Neither alternative was very cheering.

Chapter Seven

Family Confidence.

"When do you leave us, Philip?" inquired Mrs Rowland, putting her arm within her brother's, and marching him up the gravel-walk.

"Do you wish me to go?" replied he, laughing. "Is this what you were so anxious to say?"

"Why, we understood, six weeks since, that you meant to leave Deerbrook in a fortnight: that is all."

"So I did: but my mother is kind enough to be pleased that I am staying longer; and since I am equally pleased myself, it is all very well. I rather think, too, that the children consider Uncle Philip a good boy, who deserves a holiday."

"My mother! Oh, she always supposes everything right that you do; and that is the reason why Mr Rowland and I—"

"The reason why Rowland and I agree so well," interrupted the brother. "Yes, that is one reason, among many. Rowland's wish is to see the old lady happy; and she is naturally happiest when she has both her children with her; and for every merry hour of hers, your good husband looks the more kindly upon me."

"Of course; all that is a matter of course; though you are not aware, perhaps, of the fatigue it is to my mother to have any one with her too long a time. She will not tell *you*; but you have no idea how low she is for some time after you go away, if you have stayed more than a few days, from exhaustion—from pure exhaustion. Ah! you do not perceive it, because the excitement keeps her up while you are here; and she naturally makes an effort, you know. But if you were to see her as we do after you are gone;— you cannot think how it sets the Greys talking about her low spirits."

"Poor soul! I wish I could be always with her. I will try whether I cannot; for some time to come, at least. But, sister, how does it happen that neither you nor Rowland ever told me this before?"

"Oh, we would not distress you unnecessarily. We knew it was an unavoidable evil. You cannot always be here, and you must—"

"Yes, I must sometimes come: that is an unavoidable evil; and always will be, sister, while I have a good old mother living here."

"My dear Philip, how you do misunderstand one! I never heard anything so odd."

"Why odd? Have you not been giving me to understand, all this time, that you do not wish to have me here,—that you want me to go away? If not this, I do not know what you have been talking about."

"What an idea! My only brother! What can you be thinking of? Why upon earth should I wish you anywhere else?"

"That you may manage my mother and her affairs all your own way, I imagine."

Mrs Rowland had nothing to oppose to this plain speech but exclamations. When she had exhausted all she could muster, she avowed that the only consideration which could reconcile her to the sacrifice of her dear brother's society was anxiety for his happiness.

"Then, supposing I am happiest here, we are all satisfied." And Uncle Philip would have made a diversion from the path to give George his favourite swing, quite up to the second branch of the great pear-tree.

"Pray let George swing himself for once, brother. Hold your tongue, George! You are a very troublesome boy, and your uncle and I are busy. It is about your own affairs, brother, that I want to open my mind to you. As for your always remaining here, as you kindly hinted just now—"

"I did not mean to hint," said Philip; "I thought I had spoken quite plainly."

"Well, well. We all know how to appreciate the kindness of your intentions, I am sure: but your happiness must not be sacrificed to the good of any of us here. We can take care of one another: but, as it is impossible that you should find a companion for life here, and as it is time you were thinking of settling, we must not be selfish, and detain you among us when you should be creating an interest elsewhere. Mr Rowland and I are extremely anxious to see you happily married, brother; and indeed we feel it is time you were thinking about it."

"I am glad of that, sister. I am somewhat of the same opinion myself."

"I rejoice to hear it," replied the lady, in a rather uneasy tone. "We have been delighted to hear of these frequent visits of yours to the Buchanans'. There is a strong attraction there, I fancy, Philip."

"Joe Buchanan is the attraction to me there. If you mean Caroline, she has been engaged these three years to her brother's friend, Annesley."

"You do not say so! But you did not know it?"

"I have known it these two years, under the seal of secrecy. Ah! sister, I have had many an hour's amusement at your schemes on my behalf about Caroline Buchanan."

"I have been quite out, I see. When do you go to the Bruces', to make the visit you were disappointed of at Christmas?"

"When they return from the Continent, where they are gone for three years. Miss Mary is out of reach for three years, sister."

"Out of reach! You speak as if Paris,—or Rome, if you will,—was in Australia. And even in Australia one can hardly speak of people being out of reach."

"If one wishes to overtake them," said Mr Enderby: "whereas, I can wait very well for the Bruces till they come home again. Now, no more, sister! I cannot stand and hear the young ladies of my acquaintance catalogued as a speculation for my advantage. I could not look them in the face again after having permitted it."

"There is somebody in the schoolroom, I declare!" cried the lady, as if astonished. And she stood looking from afar at the summer-house, in which three heads were distinctly visible.

"Were you not aware of that before? Did you suppose I was asleep there, or writing poetry all alone, or what? The Miss Ibbotsons are there, and Miss Young."

"You remind me," said the lady, "of something that I declared to Mr Rowland that I would speak to you about. My dear brother, you should have some compassion on the young ladies you fall in with."

"I thought your great anxiety just now was that the young ladies should have compassion upon me."

"One, Philip; the right one. But you really have no mercy. You are too modest to be aware of the mischief you may be doing. But let me entreat you not to turn the head of a girl whom you cannot possibly think seriously of."

"Whom do you mean?"

"You may be making even more mischief than flattering the poor girl with vain hopes. If you once let it get into the heads of the Greys that any one belonging to us could think of marrying into their connection, you do not know the trouble you will impose upon Mr Rowland and me."

"Does Rowland say so?"

"Does he say so? one would think—Dear me! brother, there is nothing one might not think from your manner. You terrify me."

"Have you a pocket-mirror about you?" asked Philip. "I should like to see what this terrible manner of mine is like."

"Now, pray, no joking, Philip. I declare my nerves will not bear it. But I tell you what, Philip: if you let your old admiration of beauty carry you away, and make you forget yourself so far as to dream of marrying into that connection, you will repent it as long as you live. I shall never forgive you; and you will kill our poor dear mother."

"I will ask her whether she thinks so," said Philip, "and I give you my word of honour that I will not kill my mother."

"Girls seem to think that beauty is everything," continued the angry lady, "and so do their connections for them. I declare Mrs Grey sits winking at my mother when Miss Ibbotson has a colour, as if nobody ever saw a good complexion before. I declare it makes me sick. Now, Philip, you have been fairly warned; and if you fall into the trap, you will not deserve any consideration from me."

"I have let you lay down the law to me, sister, in your own way, because I know your way. Say what you please to me of myself and my affairs, and a joke is the worst that will come of it. But I tell you gravely, that I will not hear of traps—I will not hear imputations like those you have just spoken against these young ladies or their connections, without rebuke. You can know nothing of the Miss Ibbotsons which can justify this conversation."

"I shall soon believe you are in love," cried the lady, in high resentment.

"Only take care what grounds you go upon before you speak and act, sister. In my turn, I give you fair warning how you take any measures against them, even in your own inmost mind, without being quite sure what you are about."

"You do not say now that you do not mean to have that girl?" cried Mrs Rowland, fixing her fiery eyes upon her brother's face.

"Why should I? You have not set about obtaining my confidence in any way which could succeed. If I am in love, it would not be easy to own it upon such unwarrantable pressure. If I am not in love—"

"Ah! If you are not—"

"In that case I am disinclined to make my not caring for them the condition on which those young ladies may receive your civilities. These civilities are due to them, whatever I may feel or intend; and my respect for them is such that I shall keep my mind to myself."

"At least," said the lady, somewhat humbled, "do not be so much with them. For my sake, do not go into the schoolroom again."

"I am sorry I cannot oblige you," said he, smiling, "but I must go at this moment:— not to sit down,—not to speak five words, however,—but only to get my hat. I have to go into the village, on an errand for the children. Can I do anything for you in the village?"

"She thinks only of Hester, it is plain," thought he. "If I am to have any more lectures and advice, I hope they will proceed on the same supposition: it will make my part easier, and save my being driven to assert my own will, and so plunging poor Priscilla into hysterics. I can bear her interference, as long as Margaret's name is not on her lips. The moment she casts an evil eye on her, I shall speak to Rowland; which I had much rather avoid. It would be delicious, too, to be *her* protector, without her knowing it,—to watch over her as she walks in her bright innocence,—to shield her—but from whom? From my own sister? No! no! better keep her out of suspicion: better let it pass that it is really Hester. Hester has plenty of friends to stand by her. The Greys are so proud of her beauty, they have no eyes or ears but for her. People who meddle with concerns they have no business with, are strangely blind,—they make odd mistakes, from running away with notions of their own, prepared beforehand. Here is everybody determined that we shall all fall in love with Hester. Priscilla has jumped to her conclusion at once,—perhaps in emulation of Mrs Grey. Mrs Grey has clearly given Hester to Hope, in her own mind. I rather think Hope would be obliged to her if she would not show so plainly what is in her thoughts. I fear so,—I may be jealous,—but I am afraid Hope and I are too much of the same mind about these girls. I will stand up for Mrs Grey, as long as I live, if she proves right here. She shall wink and nod for evermore, and I will justify her, if Hope turns out to be in love with Hester. I will be the first to congratulate him, if he succeeds with her: and really he would be a happy fellow. She is a lovely creature; and how she will love whenever she does love! She would be a devoted wife. Why cannot he see the matter so, and leave my Margaret to me? Now, how will she look up as I go in?"

His vision of Margaret's looks remained a vision. No one was in the schoolroom but Miss Young, writing a letter.

"They are not here!" said Mr Enderby.

"No; they are gone with Mrs Grey into the village, I believe."

"Oh, well, I only came for my hat. You are in the children's secret, of course, Miss Young?"

"About their feast. Yes, I believe I know all about it."

"I am going to ask some important questions for them at the confectioner's. You will not object to my bringing them a few good things?"

"I? Oh, no."

"I would not act in so serious a matter without asking you. Can I be of any use to you in the village? Or perhaps you may want some pens mended before I go?"

"No, I thank you."

"Then I will not interrupt your letter any longer. Good morning."

It was a wonder that the letter was written at all. When Maria had done leaning back in her chair, and had taken up her pen again, she was disturbed by painful sounds from Mrs Rowland's garden. The lady's own Matilda, and precious George, and darling Anna, were now pronounced to be naughty, wilful, mischievous, and, finally, to be combined together to break their mamma's heart. It was clear that they were receiving the discharge of the wrath which was caused by somebody else. Now a wail, now a scream of passion, went to Maria's heart. She hastened on with her letter, in the hope that Mrs Rowland would presently go into the house, when the little sufferers might be invited into the schoolroom, to hear a story, or have their ruffled tempers calmed by some other such simple means.

"What a life of discipline this is!" thought Maria. "We all have it, sooner or later. These poor children are beginning early. If one can but help them through it! There she goes in, and shuts the door behind her! Now I may call them hither, and tell them something or another about Una and her lion."

At the well-known sound of Miss Young's lame step, the little ones all came about her. One ashamed face was hid on her shoulder; another was relieved of its salt tears; and the boy's pout was first relaxed, and then forgotten.

Chapter Eight

Family Correspondence.

From the time of the great event of the arrival of the Miss Ibbotsons, Mr Hope had longed to communicate all connected with it to his family. As often as Hester looked eminently beautiful, he wished his sisters could see her. As often as he felt his spirit moved and animated by his conversations with Margaret, he thought of Frank, and wished that the poor fellow could for a day exchange the heats and fatigues, and vapid society, of which he complained as accompaniments of service in India, for some one of the wood and meadow rambles, or garden frolics, which were the summer pleasures of Deerbrook, now unspeakably enhanced by the addition lately made to its society. Frank wrote that the very names of meadows and kine, of cowslips, trout, and harriers, were a refreshment to a soldier's fancy, when the heats, and the solitude of spirit in which he was compelled to live, made him weary of the novelties which had at first pleased him in the East. He begged that Edward would go on to write as he did of everything that passed in the village—of everything which could make him for a whole evening fancy himself in Deerbrook, and repose himself in its shacks and quietness. Mr Hope had felt, for a month past, that such a letter was by this time due to Frank, and that he had, for once, failed in punctuality: but he now, for the first time, found it difficult to get time to write. He never dreamed of sending Frank letters, which would be esteemed by others of a moderate length. When he did write, it was an epistle indeed: and during this particular May and June, there was always something happening which prevented his having his hours to himself. In other words, he was always at the Greys' when not engaged in his professional duties. The arrival of a letter from Frank one day gave him the necessary stimulus, and he sat down on the instant to open his heart to his brother.

Frank was his younger and only brother, and the person in the world most deeply indebted to him. Their parents being dead, it was Edward who had been Frank's dependence as he grew up. It was Edward who had, at great cost and pains, gratified his wish to go into the army, and had procured him the best educational advantages in preparation for a military life. It was Edward who had always treated him with such familiar friendship, that he had scarcely felt as if he wanted any other intimate, and who seemed to forget the five years' difference of age between them at all times but when it afforded a reason for pressing kindness and assistance upon him. The confidence between them was as familiar and entire as if they had been twin-brothers. The epistle which Frank was to have the benefit of, on the present occasion, was even longer than usual, from the delay which had caused an accumulation of tidings and of thoughts.

"Deerbrook, *June 20th*, 18—.

"Dear Frank,—Your letter of December last has arrived to remind me how far I am past my time in writing to you. I make no apologies for my delay, however, and I do not pretend to feel any remorse about it. We never write to one another from a mere sense of duty; and long may it be before we do so! Unless we write because we cannot help it, pray let us let it alone. As for the reasons why my inclination to talk to you has not overpowered all impediments till now,—you shall have them by-and-by. Meanwhile, here, before your eyes, is the proof that I cannot but spend this June evening with you.

"You ask about your grandfather; and I have somewhat to say to you about him. He is still living,—very infirm, as you may suppose, but, I think, as clear in mind as I have ever known him. He sent for me two months ago, as you will have heard from the letter I find he caused to be written to you about the business which then occupied his mind. My share in that business he would represent to you as it appeared to him: but I must give you an account of it as it appears to myself. He sent for me to take leave of me, as he said; but, in my opinion, to receive my acknowledgments for his latest disposition of his property by will. The new arrangements did not please me at all; and I am confident that you would have liked them no better than I; and I wished not a little that you were nearer, that we might have acted together. I know that he once intended to divide his property equally among us four; but of late, from some unaccountable feeling of indifference about Emily and Anne, or, as is more likely, from some notion about women not wanting money, and not knowing how to manage it, he has changed his mind, and destined his money for you and me, leaving my sisters only a hundred pounds each as a remembrance. He informed me of this, as soon as I arrived. I thought him quite well enough to hear reason, and I spoke my mind plainly to him. I had no right to answer for you, any further than for your sense of justice, and your affection for your sisters. The way in which the matter was settled at last, therefore, with great pains and trouble, was, that you and our sisters share equally, and that I have the legacy of 100 pounds, which was destined for one of them. The reasons why I declined a fourth part of the property were sufficient to my mind, and will be so, I doubt not, to yours. Out of this property I have had my professional education, while you and my sisters have received nothing at all. This professional education has enabled me to provide sufficiently for myself, so far, and this provision will in all probability go on to increase; while my sisters want as much as can fairly be put into their hands. Their husbands are not likely ever to be rich men, and will probably be poor for some years to come. Their children have to be educated; and in short, there is every reason why Emily and Anne should have this money, and none why I should. I am afraid the old gentleman is not very well pleased with my way of receiving what he intended for kindness; but that cannot be helped. If he falls back into his previous state of mind, and leaves the whole, after all, to you and me, I shall set the matter right, as far as I can, by dividing my portion between my sisters: and I feel confident that you will do the same; but I earnestly hope this will not happen. It will be a very different thing to my sisters receiving this money by their grandfather's will as their due, and from our hands as a gift—(the way in which they will look at it). The letter to you was sent off without delay, in order that, in case of any dissatisfaction whatever on your part, your wishes might have the better chance of being made known to us during the old gentleman's life. I doubt not that your thoughts, whatever they may be, will be on the way to me before this reaches you; and I can have as little doubt what they are. You know Mr Blunt says, that men are created to rob their sisters,—a somewhat partial view of the objects and achievements of mortal existence, it must be owned, and a statement which I conceive the course of your life, for one, will not go to confirm; but a man must have had a good deal of experience of what he is talking of before he could make so sweeping a generalisation from the facts of life; and I am afraid Mr Blunt has some reason for what he says. Medical men receive many confidences in sick rooms, you know; and some, among others, which had better be reserved for the lawyer. What I have seen in this way leads me to imagine that my grandfather's notion is a very common one,—that women have little occasion for money, and do not know how to manage it; and that their property is to be drawn upon to the very last, to meet the difficulties and supply the purposes of their brothers. On the utter injustice and absurdity of such a notion there can be no disagreement between you and me; nor, I imagine, in our actions with regard to it.

"I heard from Emily yesterday. The letter is more than half full of stories about the children, and accounts of her principles and plans with regard to them. She writes on the same subjects to you, no doubt, for her heart is full of them. Her husband finds the post of consul at a little Spanish port rather a dull affair, as we anticipated, and groans at the mention of Bristol or Liverpool shipping, he says. But I like the tone of his postscript very well. He is thankful for the honest independence his office affords him, and says he can tolerate his Spanish neighbours (though they are as ignorant as Turkish ladies), for the sake of his family, and of the hope of returning, sooner or later, to live in his own country, after having discharged his duty to his children. Theirs must be an irksome life enough, as much of it as is passed out of their own doors: but they seem to be finding out that it is not so much the *where* and the *how*, as the *what* people are, that matters to their peace of mind; and I suppose those who love each other, and have settled what they are living for, can attain what they most want, nearly so well in one place as another.

"Poor Anne wrote to *you*, I know, after the death of her infant—her little Highlandman, as she proudly called him in her last letter before she lost him. Gilchrist talked last year of bringing her and his boy south this summer, and I had some hopes of seeing them all here: but I have not been able to get them to speak again of travelling, and I give it up for this year. I hope your letters and theirs fall due seasonably; that your reports of all your devices to cool yourself, reach them in the depth of their Caithness winter; and that all they say to you of their snow-drifts and freshets is acceptable when you are panting in the hottest of your noons. Anne writes more cheerfully than she did, and Gilchrist says she is exerting herself to overcome her sorrow. Their love must be passing strange in the eyes of all such as despised Anne's match. It is such as should make Anne's brothers feel very cordially towards Gilchrist. We have drifted asunder in life rather strangely, when one comes to think of it; and our anchorage grounds are pretty far apart. Who would have thought it, when we four used to climb the old apple-tree together, and drop down from the garden wall? I wonder whether we shall ever contrive to meet in one house once more, and whether I may be honoured by my house being the place? It is possible; and I spend certain of my dreams upon the project. Do you not find that one effect of this wide separation is, to make one fancy the world smaller than one used to think it? You, on the other side of it, probably waked up to this conviction long ago. It is just opening upon me, shut up in my nook of our little island. When I have a letter from you, like that which lies before me, spiced with an old family joke or two, and a good many new ones of your own, all exactly like yourself, I am persuaded you cannot be very far off; and I should certainly call you from my window to come in to tea, but from a disagreeable suspicion that I should get no answer. But do tell me in your next whether our globe has not been made far too much of its children, and whether its oceans do not look very like ponds, when you cast your eye over them to that small old apple-tree I mentioned just now.

"But you want news,—this being the place of all others to send to from the other side of the world for news. Deerbrook has rung with news and rumours of news since winter. The first report after the ice broke up in March was, that I was going to be married to Deborah Giles. 'Who is Deborah Giles?' you will ask. She is not going to be a relation of yours, in the first place. Secondly, she is the daughter of the boatman whose boats Enderby and I are wont to hire. The young lady may be all that ever woman was, for aught I know, for I never spoke to her in my life, except that I one day asked her for something to bale the boat with: but I heard that the astonishment of Deerbrook was, that I was engaged to a woman who could not read or write. So you see we of Deerbrook follow our old pastime of first inventing marvels, and then being scarcely able to believe them. I rather suspect that we have some wag among us who fabricates news, to see how much will be received and retailed: but perhaps these rumours, even the wildest of them, rise 'by natural exhalation' from the nooks and crevices of village life. My five years' residence has not qualified me to pronounce absolutely upon this.

"Old Smithson is dead. You could not have seen him half-a-dozen times when you were here; but you may chance to recollect him,—a short old man, with white hair, and deep-set grey eyes. He is less of a loss to the village than almost any other man would be. He was so shy and quiet, and kept so much within his own gate, that some fancied he must be a miser: but though he spent little on himself, his money made its way abroad, and his heirs are rather disappointed at finding the property no larger than when he came into it. He is much missed by his household, and, I own, by myself. I was not often with him: but it was something to feel that there was one among us who was free from ambition and worldly cares, content to live on in the enjoyment of humble duties and simple pleasures,—one who would not have changed colour at the news of a bequest of ten thousand pounds, but could be very eager about his grand-nephew's prize at school, and about the first forget-me-not of the season beside his pond, and the first mushroom in his meadow. During the fortnight of his illness, the village inquired about him; but when it was all over, there was not much to forget of one so little known, and we hear of him no more.

"The Greys and Rowlands go on much as usual, the gentlemen of the family agreeing very well, and the ladies rather the reverse. The great grievance this spring has been, that Mrs Rowland has seen fit to enlarge her hall, and make a porch to her door. Her neighbours are certain that, in the course of her alterations, every principal beam of her house has been cut through, and that the whole will fall in. No such catastrophe has yet occurred, however. I have not been called in to set any broken bones; and I have not much expectation of an accident, as Mr Rowland understands building too well to allow his house to be cut down over his head. As for the porch, I do not perceive what can be alleged to its disadvantage, but that some people think it ugly.

"Here I must cease my gossip. I regularly begin my letters with the intention of telling you all that I hear and see out of my profession but I invariably stop short, as I do now, from disgust at the nonsense I should have to write. It is endurable enough to witness; for one thing quickly dismisses another, and some relief occurs from the more amiable or intellectual qualities of the parties concerned: but I hate detail in writing; and I never do get through the whole list of particulars that I believe you would like to have. You must excuse me now, and take my word for it, in the large, that we are all pretty much what we were when you saw us three years ago, except of course, being three years older, and some few of us three years wiser. It will be a satisfaction to you also to know that my practice has made a very good growth for the time. You liked my last year's report of it. It has increased more since that time than even during the preceding year; and I have no further anxiety about my worldly prospects. I am as well satisfied with my choice of an occupation in life as ever. Mine has its anxieties, and *désagrémens*, as others have: but I am convinced I could not have chosen better. You saw, when you were with me, something of the anxiety of responsibility; what it is, for instance, to await the one or the other event of a desperate case: and I could tell you a good deal that you do not and cannot know of the perils, and troubles attendant upon being the depository of so much domestic and personal confidence as my function imposes upon me the necessity of receiving. I sometimes long to be able to see nothing but what is apparent to all in society; to perceive what is ostensible, and to dream of nothing more,—not exactly like children, but like the members of large and happy families, who carry about with them the purity and peace of their homes, and therefore take cognisance of the pure and peaceful only whom they meet abroad; but it is childish, or indolent, or cowardly, to desire this. While there is private vice and wretchedness, and domestic misunderstanding, one would desire to know it, if one can do anything to cure or alleviate it. Dr Levitt and I have the same feeling about this; and I sometimes hope that we mutually prepare for and aid each other's work. There is a bright side to our business, as I need not tell you. The mere exercise of our respective professions, the scientific as well as the moral interest of them, is as much to us as the theory of your business to you; and that is saying a great deal. You will not quarrel with the idea of the scientific interest of Dr Levitt's profession in his hands; for you know how learned he is in the complex science of Humanity. You remember the eternal wonder of the Greys at his liberality towards dissenters. Of that liberality he is unconscious: as it is the natural, the inevitable result of his knowledge of men,—of his having been 'hunting the waterfalls' from his youth up,—following up thought and prejudice to their fountains. When I see him bland and gay amongst us, I feel pretty confident that his greatest pleasure is the same as mine,—that of reposing in the society of the innocent, the single-hearted, the unburdened, after having seen what the dark corners of social life are. It is like coming out of a foetid cave into the evening sunshine. Of late, we have felt this in an extraordinary degree. But I must tell you in an orderly way what has happened to us. I have put off entering upon the grand subject, partly from the pleasure of keeping one's best news for the last, and partly from shyness in beginning to describe what it is impossible that you should enter into. I am well aware of your powers of imagination and sympathy: but you have not lived five years within five miles of a country village; and you can no more understand our present condition than we can appreciate your sherbet and your mountain summer-house.

"There are two ladies here from Birmingham, so far beyond any ladies that we have to boast of, that some of us begin to suspect that Deerbrook is not the Athens and Arcadia united that we have been accustomed to believe it. You can have no idea how our vanity is mortified, and our pride abased, by finding what the world can produce out of the bounds of Deerbrook. We bear our humiliation wonderfully, however. Our Verdon woods echo with laughter; and singing is heard beside the brook. The voices of children, grown and ungrown, go up from all the meadows around; and wit and wisdom are wafted over the surface of our river at eventide. The truth is, these girls have brought in a new life among us, and there is not one of us, except the children, that is not some years younger for their presence. Mr Grey deserts his business for them, like a school-boy; and Mr Rowland watches his opportunity to play truant in turn. Mrs Enderby gives dances, and looks quite disposed to lead off in person. Mrs

Plumstead has grown quite giddy about sorting the letters, and her voice has not been heard further than three doors off since the arrival of the strangers. Dr Levitt is preaching his old sermons. Mrs Grey is well-nigh intoxicated with being the hostess of these ladies, and has even reached the point of allowing her drawing-room to be used every afternoon. Enderby is a fixture while they are so. Neither mother, sister, friend, nor frolic, ever detained him here before for a month together. He was going away in a fortnight when these ladies came: they have been here six weeks, and Enderby has dropped all mention of the external world. If you ask, as you are at this moment doing in your own heart, how I stand under this influence, I really cannot tell you. I avoid inquiring too closely. I enjoy every passing day too much to question it, and I let it go; and so must you.

"'But who are they?' you want to know. They are distant cousins of Mr Grey's,—orphans, and in mourning for their father. They are just above twenty, and their name is Ibbotson. 'Are they handsome?' is your next question. The eldest, Hester, is beautiful as the evening star. Margaret is very different. It does not matter what she is as to beauty, for the question seems never to have entered her own mind. I doubt whether it has often occurred to her whether she can be this, or that, or the other. She *is*, and there is an end of the matter. Such pure *existence*, without question, without introspection, without hesitation or consciousness, I never saw in any one above eight years old. Yet she is wise; it becomes not me to estimate how wise. You will ask how I know this already. I knew it the first day I saw them; I knew it by her infinite simplicity, from which all selfishness is discharged, and into which no folly can enter. The airs of heaven must have been about her from her infancy, to nourish such health of the soul. What her struggle is to be in life I cannot conceive, for not a morbid tendency is to be discerned. I suppose she may be destined to make mistakes,—to find her faith deceived, her affections rebuked, her full repose delayed. If, like the rest of us, she be destined to struggle, it must be to conflict of this kind; for it is inconceivable that any should arise from herself. Yet is she as truly human as the weakest of us,—engrossed by affection, and susceptible of passion. Her affection for her sister is a sort of passion. It has some of the features of the serene guardianship of one from on high; but it is yet more like the passionate servitude—of the benefited to a benefactor, for instance—which is perhaps the most graceful attitude in which our humanity appears. Where are the words that can tell what it is to witness, day by day, the course of such a life as this?—to see, living and moving before one's eyes, the very spirit that one had caught glimpses of, wandering in the brightest vistas of one's imagination, in the holiest hours of thought! Yet is there nothing fearful, as in the presence of a spirit; there is scarcely even a sense of awe, so childlike is her deportment. I go, grave and longing to listen; I come away, and I find I have been talking more than any one; revealing, discussing, as if I were the teacher and not the learner,—you will say the worshipper. Say it if you will. Our whole little world worships the one or the other. Hester is also well worthy of worship. If there were nothing but her beauty, she would have a wider world than ours of Deerbrook at her feet. But she has much more. She is what you would call a true woman. She has a generous soul, strong affections, and a susceptibility which interferes with her serenity. She is not exempt from the trouble and snare into which the lot of women seems to drive them,—too close a contemplation of self, too nice a sensitiveness, which yet does not interfere with devotedness to others. She will be a devoted wife: but Margaret does not wait to be a wife to be devoted. Her life has been devotedness, and will be to the end. If she were left the last of her race, she would spend her life in worshipping the unseen that lay about her, and would be as unaware of herself as now.

"What a comfort it is to speak freely of them! This is the first relief of the kind I have had. Every one is praising them; every one is following them: but to whom but you can I speak of them? Even to you, I filled my first sheet with mere surface matter. I now wonder how I could. As for the 'general opinion' of Deerbrook on the engrossing subject of the summer, you will anticipate it in your own mind,—concluding that Hester is most worshipped, on account of her beauty, and that Margaret's influence must be too subtle and refined to operate on more than a few. This is partly, but not wholly the case. It has been taken for granted from the beginning, by the many, that Hester is to be exclusively the adored; and Enderby has, I fancy, as many broad hints as myself of this general conclusion. But I question whether Enderby assents, any more than myself. Margaret's influence may be received as unconsciously as it is exerted, but it is not, therefore, the less real, while it is the more potent. I see old Jem Bird raise himself up from the churchyard bench by his staff, and stand uncovered as Hester passes by; I see the children in the road touch one another, and look up at her; I see the admiration which diffuses itself like sunshine around her steps: all this homage to Hester is visible enough. But I also see Sydney Grey growing manly, and his sisters amiable, under Margaret's eye. I fancy I perceive Enderby— But that is his own affair. I am sure I daily witness one healing and renovating process which Margaret is unconsciously effecting. There is no one of us so worthy of her, so capable of appreciating her, as Maria Young: they are friends, and Maria Young is becoming a new creature. Health and spirit are returning to that poor girl's countenance: there is absolutely a new tone in her voice, and a joyous strain in her conversation, which I, for one, never recognised before. It is a sight on which angels might look down, to see Margaret, with her earnest face, listening humbly, and lovingly serving the infirm and much-tried friend whom she herself is daily lifting up into life and gladness. I have done with listening to abuse of life and the world. I will never sit still under it again. If there are two such as these sisters, springing out of the bosom of a busy town, and quietly passing along their path of life, casting sanctity around them as they go,—if there are two such, why not more? If God casts such seeds of goodness into our nook, how do we know but that he is sowing the whole earth with it? I will believe it henceforth.

"You will wonder, as I have wondered many a time within the last six weeks, what is to become of us when we lose these strangers. I can only say, 'God help us!' But that time is far off. They came for several months, and no one hints at their departure yet. They are the most unlearned creatures about country life that you can conceive, with a surpassing genius for country pleasures. Only imagine the charm of our excursions! They are never so happy as when in the fields or on the river; and we all feel ourselves only too blest in being able to indulge them. Our mornings are all activity and despatch, that our afternoons may be all mirth, and our evenings repose. I am afraid this will make you sigh with mingled envy and sympathy; but whatever is that can be told, you may rely upon it that I shall tell you, trusting to your feeling both pleasure and pain in virtuous moderation.

"I have done my story; and now I am going to look what o'clock it is—a thing I have refrained from, in my impulse to tell you all. The house is quite still, and I heard the church clock strike something very long just now; but I would not count. It is so. It was midnight that the clock struck. I shall seal this up directly. I dare not trust my morning—my broad daylight mood with it. Now, as soon as you have got thus far, just take up your pen, and answer me, telling me as copiously of your affairs as I have written of ours. Heaven bless you.

"Yours ever,

"Edward Hope."

It was not only Mr Hope's broad daylight mood which was not to be trusted with this letter. In this hour of midnight a misgiving seized upon him that it was extravagant. He became aware, when he laid down his pen, that he was agitated. The door of his room opened into the garden. He thought he would look out upon the night. It was the night of the full moon. As he stood in the doorway, the festoons of creepers that dangled from his little porch waved in the night breeze; long shadows from the shrubs lay on the grass; and in the depth of one of these shadows glimmered the green spark of a glow-worm. It was deliciously cool and serene. Mr Hope stood leaning against the door-post, with his arms folded, and was not long in settling the question whether the letter should go.

"Frank will think that I am in love," he considered. "He will not understand the real state of my feeling. He will think that I am in love. I should conclude so in his place. But what matters it what he infers and concludes? I have written exactly what I thought and felt at the moment, and it is not from such revelations that wrong inferences are usually drawn. What I have written is true; and truth carries safely over land and sea—more safely than confidence compounded with caution. Frank deserves the simplest and freshest confidence from me. I am glad that no hesitation occurred to me while I wrote. It shall go—every word of it."

He returned to his desk, sealed and addressed the letter, and placed it where it was sure to be seen in the morning, and carried to the post-office before he rose.

Chapter Nine

Child's Play.

The afternoon arrived when the children were to have their feast in the summer-house. From the hour of dinner the little people were as busy as aldermen's cooks, spreading their table. Sydney thought himself too old for such play. He was hard at work, filling up the pond he had dug in his garden, having tried experiments with it for several weeks, and found that it never held water but in a pouring rain. While he was occupied with his spade, his sisters and the little Rowlands were arranging their dishes, and brewing their cowslip-tea.

"Our mamma is coming," said Fanny to Matilda: "is yours?"

"No; she says she can't come—but papa will."

"So will our papa. It was so funny at dinner. Mr Paxton came in, and asked whether papa would ride with him; and papa said it was out of the question; it must be to-morrow; for he had an engagement this afternoon."

"A very particular engagement, he said," observed Mary: "and he smiled at me so, I could not help laughing. Fanny, do look at Matilda's dish of strawberries! How pretty!"

"There's somebody coming," observed little Anna, who, being too young to help, and liable to be tempted to put her fingers into the good things, was sent to amuse herself with jumping up and down the steps.

"There now! That is always the way, is not it, Miss Young?" cried Fanny. "Who is it, George? Mr Enderby? Oh, do not let him come in yet! Tell him he must not come this half-hour."

Mr Enderby chose to enter, however, and all opposition gave way before him.

"Pray don't send me back," said he, "till you know what I am come for. Now, who will pick my pockets?"

Little Anna was most on a level with the coat pocket. She almost buried her face in it as she dived, the whole length of her arm, to the very bottom. George attacked its fellow, while the waistcoat pockets were at the mercy of the taller children. A number of white parcels made their appearance, and the little girls screamed with delight.

"Miss Young!" cried Fanny, "do come and help us to pick Mr Enderby's pockets. See what I have got—the very largest of all!"

When every pocket had been thoroughly picked without Miss Young's assistance, the table did indeed show a goodly pile of white cornucopia,—that most agitating form of paper to children's eyes. When opened, there was found such a store of sweet things as the little girls had seldom before seen out of the confectioner's shop. Difficulties are apt to come with good fortune; and the anxious question was now asked, how all these dainties were to be dished up. Miss Young was, as usual, the friend in need. She had before lent two small china plates of her own; and she now supplied the further want. She knew how to make pretty square boxes out of writing-paper; and her nimble scissors and neat fingers now provided a sufficiency of these in a trice. Uncle Philip was called upon, as each was finished, to admire her skill; and admire he did, to the children's entire content.

"Is this *our* feast, Mr Enderby?" inquired Mary, finally, when Anna had been sent to summon the company. "May we say it is ours?"

"To be sure," cried Fanny. "Whose else should it be?"

"It is all your own, I assure you," said Mr Enderby. "Now, you two should stand at the head of the table, and Matilda at the foot."

"I think I had better take this place," said Sydney, who had made his appearance, and who thought much better of the affair now that he saw Mr Enderby so much interested in it. "There should always be a gentleman at the bottom of the table."

"No, no, Sydney," protested Mr Enderby; "not when he has had no cost nor trouble about the feast. March off. You are only one of the company. Stand there, Matilda, and remember you must look very polite. I shall hide behind the acacia there, and come in with the ladies."

A sudden and pelting shower was now falling, however; and instead of hiding behind a tree, Mr Enderby had to run between the house and the schoolroom, holding umbrellas over the ladies' heads, setting clogs for them, and assuring Mrs Grey at each return that the feast could not be deferred, and that nobody should catch cold. Mr Grey was on the spot; to give his arm to Mrs Enderby, who had luckily chanced to look in,—a thing which "she really never did after dinner." Mr Hope had been seen riding by, and Mrs Grey had sent after him to beg he would come in. Mr Rowland made a point of being present: and thus the summer-house was quite full,—really crowded.

"I am glad Mrs Rowland keeps away," whispered Mrs Grey to Sophia. "She would say it is insufferably hot."

"Yes; that she would. Do not you think we might have that window open? The rain does not come in on that side. Did you ever see such a feast as the children have got? I am sure poor Elizabeth and I never managed such a one. It is really a pity Mrs Rowland should not see it. Mr Rowland should have made her come. It looks so odd, her being the only one to stay away!"

The room resounded with exclamations, and admiration, and grave jokes upon the children. Notwithstanding all Uncle Philip could do, the ingenuous little girls answered to every compliment—that Mr Enderby brought his, and that that and the other came out of Uncle Philip's pocket. They stood in their places, blushing and laughing, and served out their dainties with hands trembling with delight.

Maria's pleasure was, as usual, in observing all that went on.

She could do this while replying, quite to the purpose, to Mrs Enderby's praise of her management of the dear children, and to George's pressing offers of cake; and to Mr Rowland's suspicions that the children would never have accomplished this achievement without her, as indeed he might say of all their achievements; and to Anna's entreaty that she would eat a pink comfit, and then a yellow one, and then a green one; and to Mrs Grey's wonder where she could have put away all her books and things, to make so much room for the children. She could see Mr Hope's look of delight when Margaret declined a cup of chocolate, and said she preferred tasting some of the cowslip-tea. She saw how he helped Mary to pour out the tea, and how quietly he took the opportunity of getting rid of it through the window behind Margaret, when she could not pretend to say that she liked it. She observed Mr Rowland's somewhat stiff politeness to Hester, and Mr Enderby's equal partition of his attentions between the two sisters. She could see Mrs Grey watching every strawberry and sugar-plum that went down the throats of the little Rowlands, and her care, seconded by Sophia's, that her own children should have an exactly equal portion of the good things. She believed, but was not quite sure, that she saw Hester's colour and manner change as Mr Hope came and went, in the course of his service about the table; and that once, upon receiving some slight attention from him, she threw a hasty glance towards her sister, and turned quite away upon meeting her eye.

The rain had not prevented the servants from trying to amuse themselves with witnessing the amusement of the family. They were clustered together under umbrellas at the window nearest the stables, where they thought they should be least observed. Some commotion took place among them, at the same moment that an extraordinary sound became audible, from a distance, above the clatter of plates, and the mingling of voices, in the summer-house.

"What in the world is that noise?" asked Margaret.

"Only somebody killing a pig," replied Sydney, decidedly.

"Do not believe him," said Mr Enderby. "The Deerbrook people have better manners than to kill their pigs in the hearing of ladies on summer afternoons."

"But what is it? It seems coming nearer."

"I once told you," said Mr Enderby, "that we possess an inhabitant, whose voice you might know before her name. I suspect it is that same voice which we hear now."

"A human voice! Impossible!"

"What is the matter, Alice?" Mrs Grey asked of her maid out of the window.

"Oh, ma'am, it is Mrs Plumstead! And she is coming this way, ma'am. She will be upon us before we can get to the house. Oh, ma'am, what shall we do?"

Mrs Grey entreated permission of the ladies to allow the maid-servants to come into the summer-house. Their caps might be torn from their heads before they could defend themselves, she said, if they remained outside. Of course, leave was given instantly, and the maids crowded in, with chattering teeth and many a tale of deeds done by Mrs Plumstead, in her paroxysms of rage.

The children shared the panic, more or less: and not only they. Mr Grey proposed to put up the shutters of the windows nearest to the scene of action; but it was thought that this might draw on an attack from the virago, who might let the party alone if she were left unnoticed by them. She was now full in sight, as, with half Deerbrook at her heels, she pursued the object of her rage through the falling shower, and amidst the puddles in front of the stables. Her widow's cap was at the back of her head, her hair hanging from beneath it, wet in the rain: her black gown was splashed to the shoulders; her hands were clenched; her face was white as her apron, and her vociferations were dreadful to hear. She was hunting a poor terrified young countrywoman, who, between fright and running, looked ready to sink.

"We must put a stop to this," cried Mr Grey and Mr Rowland, each speaking to the other. It ended with their issuing forth together, looking as dignified as they could, and placing themselves between the scold and her victim. It would not do. They could not make themselves heard; and when she shook her fist in their faces, they retired backwards, and took refuge among their party, bringing the victim in with them, however. Mr Enderby declared this retreat too bad, and was gone before the entreaties of his little nieces could stop him. He held his ground longer; and the dumb show he made was so energetic as to cause a laugh in the summer-house, in the midst of the uneasiness of his friends, and to call forth shouts of mirth from the crowd at the virago's heels.

"That will not do. It will only exasperate her the more," said Mr Hope, pressing his way to the door. "Let me pass, will you?"

"Oh, Mr Hope! Oh, sir!" said Alice, "don't go! Don't think of going, sir! She does not mind killing anybody, I assure you, sir."

"Oh, Mr Hope, don't go!" cried almost everybody. Maria was sure she heard Hester's voice among the rest. The young countrywoman and the children grasped the skirts of his coat; but he shook them off, laughing, and went. Little Mary loved Mr Hope very dearly. She shot out at the door with him, and clasped her hands before Mrs Plumstead, looking up piteously, as if to implore her to do Mr Hope no harm. Already, however, the vixen's mood had changed. At the first glimpse of Mr Hope, her voice sank from being a squall into some resemblance to human utterance. She pulled her cap forward, and a tinge of colour returned to her white lips. Mr Enderby caught up little Mary and carried her to her mamma, crying bitterly. Mr Hope might safely be left to finish his conquest of the otherwise unconquerable scold. He stood still till he could make himself heard, looking her full in the face; and it was not long before she would listen to his remonstrance, and even at length take his advice, to go home and compose herself. He went with her, to ensure the good behaviour of her neighbours, and had the satisfaction of seeing her lock herself into her house alone before he returned to his party.

"It is as you told me," said Margaret to Mr Enderby; "Mr Hope's power extends even to the temper of the Deerbrook scold. How she began to grow quiet directly! It was like magic."

Mr Enderby smiled; but there was some uneasiness in his smile.

The countrywoman was commended to the servants, to be refreshed, and dismissed another way. There was no further reason for detaining her when it appeared that she really could give no account of how she had offended Mrs Plumstead in selling her a pound of butter. It remained to console little Mary, who was still crying,—more from grief for Mrs Plumstead than from fear, Maria thought, though Mrs Grey was profuse in assurances to the child that Mrs Plumstead should not be allowed to frighten her any more. All the children seemed so depressed and confounded, that their guests exerted themselves to be merry again, and to efface, as far as was possible, the impression of the late scene. When Mr Hope returned, he found Mr Grey singing his single ditty, about Dame Dumshire and her crockery-ware, amidst great mirth and unbounded applause. Then Mrs Enderby was fluttered, and somewhat flattered, by an entreaty that she would favour the company with one of the ballads for which she had been famous in her time. She could not refuse on such an occasion,—if indeed she had ever been able to refuse what she was told would give pleasure. She made her son choose for her what she should sing; and then followed a wonderful story of Giles Collins, who loved a lady: Giles and the lady both died of true love; Giles was laid in the lower chancel, and the lady in the higher; from the one grave grew a milk-white rose, and from the other a briar, both of which climbed up to the church top, and there tied themselves into a true-lover's knot, which made all the parish admire. At this part, Anna was seen looking up at the ceiling; but the rest had no eyes but for Mrs Enderby, as she gazed full at the opposite wall, and the shrill, quavering notes of the monotonous air were poured out, and the words were as distinct as if they were spoken.

"Is that true, grandmamma?" asked Anna, when all was over.

"You had better ask the person who made the song, my dear. I did not make it."

"But did you ever see that church with the briar growing in it, before the sexton cut it down?"

"Do not let us talk any more about it," said Philip, solemnly. "I wonder grandmamma dares sing such a sad song."

"Why, you asked her, Uncle Philip."

"Oh, ay, so I did. Well, we are much obliged to her; and now we will have something that is not quite so terrible.—Miss Grey, you will favour us with a song?"

Sophia's music-books were all in the house, and she could not sing without. Mr Enderby would fetch some, if she would give him directions what to bring. No; she could not sing without the piano. As it was clearly impossible to bring that, Philip feared the company must wait for the pleasure of hearing Miss Grey till another time. Mr Grey would have Hester and Margaret sing; and sing they did, very simply and sweetly, and much to the satisfaction of all present. One thing led on to another; they sang together,—with Mr Grey,—with Mr Enderby; Mr Hope listening with an unlearned eagerness, which made Mrs Grey wink at her husband, and nod at Sophia, and exchange smiles with Mrs Enderby. They proceeded to catches at last; and when people really fond of music get to singing catches in a summer-house, who can foresee the end?

"'Fair Enslaver!'" cried Mr Enderby. "You must know 'Fair Enslaver:' there is not a sweeter catch than that. Come, Miss Ibbotson, begin; your sister will follow, and I—"

But it so happened that Miss Ibbotson had never heard 'Fair Enslaver.' Margaret knew it, she believed; but she did not. With a gay eagerness, Mr Enderby turned round to Maria, saying that he knew she could sing this catch; and everybody was aware that when she had the power of doing a kindness, she never wanted the will;—he remembered that she could sing 'Fair Enslaver.' He might well remember this, for often had they sung it together. While several of the company were saying they did not know Miss Young could sing, and the children were explaining that she often sang at her work, Mr Enderby observed some signs of agitation in Maria, and hastened to say,—"You had rather not, perhaps. Pray do not think of it. I will find something else in a moment. I beg your pardon: I was very inconsiderate."

But Maria thought she had rather not accept the consideration; and besides, the children were anxious that she should sing. She bore her part in a way which made Mr Rowland and Mrs Grey agree that she was a very superior young woman indeed; that they were singularly fortunate to have secured her for their children; and that she was much to be pitied.

"I think Miss Young has got a little cold, though," observed Sydney. "Her voice is not in the least husky when she sits singing here by herself.— Father! look there! there are all the servants huddled together under the window again, to listen to the singing."

This was true; and the rain was over. It was presently settled that the schoolroom should be evacuated by the present party; that the children should be allowed to invite the servants in, to dispense to them the remains of the feast; and that Miss Young must favour Mrs Grey with her company this evening.

Mr Rowland was obliged to return home to business; but, before his friends dispersed, he must just say that Mrs Rowland and he had never, for a moment, given up the hope of the pleasure of entertaining them at dinner in the Dingleford woods; and, as the rains were now daily abating, he might perhaps be allowed to name Wednesday of the next week as the day of the excursion. He hoped to see the whole of the present company, from the oldest to the youngest,—bowing, as he spoke, to Mrs Enderby and to his own little daughter Anna. This was one of Mr Rowland's pieces of independent action. His lady had given him no commission to bring the affair to an issue; and he returned home, involuntarily planning what kind of an unconcerned face and manner he should put on, while he told her what he had done.

Chapter Ten

A Party of Pleasure.

Mr Rowland hoped "to see the whole of the present company, from the oldest to the youngest." This was the best part of his speech to the ears of the children; it made an impression also upon some others. Two or three days afterwards, Sydney burst, laughing, into the dining-room, where his mother and her guests were at work, to tell them that he had seen Mr Hope riding a pony in the oddest way, in the lane behind his lodgings. He had a side-saddle, and a horse-cloth put on like a lady's riding-habit. He rode the pony in and out among the trees, and made it scramble up the hill behind, and it went as nicely as could be, wherever he wanted it to go. Mr Hope's new way of riding was easily explained, the next time he called. Miss Young was certainly included in the invitation to Dingleford woods: it was a pity she should not go; and she could not walk in wild places:— the pony was training for her. Mrs Grey quite agreed that Miss Young ought to go, but thought that Mr Hope was giving himself much needless trouble; there would be room made for her in some carriage, of course. No doubt; but no kind of carriage could make its way in the woods; and, but for this pony, Miss Young would have to sit in a carriage, or under a tree, the whole time that the rest of the party were rambling about; whereas, this quiet active little pony would take care that she was nowhere left behind. It could do everything but climb trees. It was to be taken over to Dingleford the evening before, and would be waiting for its rider on the verge of the woods, when the party should arrive.

Miss Young was touched, and extremely pleased with Mr Hope's attention. In the days of her prosperity she had been accustomed to ride much, and was very fond of it; but since her misfortunes she had never once been in the saddle—lame as she was, and debarred from other exercise. To be on a horse again, and among the woods, was a delicious prospect; and when a few misgivings had been reasoned away—misgivings about being troublesome, about being in the way of somebody's pleasure or convenience—Maria resigned herself to the full expectation of a most delightful day, if the weather would only be fine. The children would be there; and they were always willing to do anything for her. Sydney would guide her pony in case of need, or show her where she might stay behind by herself, if the others should exhibit a passion for impracticable places. She knew that Margaret would enjoy the day all the more for her being there;

and so would Mr Hope, as he had amply proved. Maria was really delighted to be going, and she and the children rejoiced together.

This great pleasure involved some minor enjoyments too, in the way of preparation. On Sunday Mr Hope told her, that he believed the pony was now fully trained; but he should like that she should try it, especially as she had been long out of the habit of riding. She must take a ride with him on Monday and Tuesday afternoons, for practice. The Monday's ride was charming; through Verdon woods, and home over the heath from Crossley End. The circuit, which was to have been three miles, had extended to ten. She must be moderate, she said to herself, the next day, and not let Mr Hope spend so much of his time upon her; and besides, the pony had to be sent over to Dingleford in the evening, after she had done with it, to be in readiness for her on Wednesday morning.

The ride on Tuesday was happily accomplished, as that of Monday: but it was much shorter. Mr Hope agreed that it should be short, as he had a patient to visit on the Dingleford road, so near the hamlet that he might as well take the pony there himself. It would trot along beside his horse. Sydney saved him part of the charge. Sydney would at all times walk back any distance for the sake of a ride out, on whatever kind of saddle, or almost any kind of quadruped. He was in waiting at the farrier's gate, when Miss Young returned from her ride; and having assisted her into the house, he threw himself upon her pony, and rode three miles and a half on the Dingleford road before he would dismount, and deliver his bridle into Mr Hope's hand. Tea was over, and the tea-things removed, before he appeared at home, heated and delighted with his expedition. He ran to the dairy for a basin of milk, and declared that his being hot and tired did not matter in the least, as he had no lessons to do—the next day being a holiday.

It was about two hours after this, when Hester and Margaret were singing to Sophia's playing, that Mr Grey put his head in at the door, and beckoned Mrs Grey out of the room. She remained absent a considerable time; and when she returned, the singers were in the middle of another duet. She wandered restlessly about the room till the piece was finished, and then made a sign to Sophia to follow her into the storeroom, the double door of which the sisters could hear carefully closed. They were too much accustomed to the appearance of mystery among the ladies of the Grey family, to be surprised at any number of secret conferences which might take place in the course of the day. But evening was not the usual time for these. The family practice was to transact all private consultations in the morning, and to assemble round the work-table or piano after tea. The sisters made no remark to each other on the present occasion, but continued their singing, each supposing that the store-room conference related to some preparation for the next day's excursion.

It was too dark to distinguish anything in the room before their hostess re-entered it. Margaret was playing quadrilles; Hester was standing at the window, watching the shadows which the risen moon was flinging across the field, and the lighting up of Mrs Enderby's parlour behind the blinds; and Sydney was teasing his twin sisters with rough play on the sofa, when Mrs Grey returned.

"You are all in the dark," said she, in a particularly grave tone. "Why, did you not ring for lights, my dears?" and she rang immediately. "Be quiet, children! I will not have you make so much noise."

The little girls seemed to wish to obey; but their brother still forced them to giggle; and their struggling entreaties were heard—"Now don't, Sydney; now pray, Sydney, don't!"

"Mary and Fanny, go to bed," said their mother, decidedly, when lights were brought. "Sydney, bid your cousins good-night, and then come with me; I want to ask you a question."

"Good-night already, mother! Why, it is not time yet this half-hour."

"It is enough that I choose you to go to bed. Wish your cousins goodnight, and come with me."

Mrs Grey led the way once more into the store-room, followed, rather sulkily, by Sydney.

"What can all this be about?" whispered Hester to Margaret. "There is always something going on which we are not to know."

"Some affair of fruit, or wine, or bonbons, perhaps, which are all the better for making their appearance unexpectedly."

At this moment Sophia and her mother entered by opposite doors. Sophia's eyes were red; and there was every promise in her face that the slightest word spoken to her would again open the sluices of her tears. Mrs Grey's countenance was to the last degree dismal: but she talked—talked industriously, of everything she could think of. This was the broadest possible hint to the sisters not to inquire what was the matter; and they therefore went on sewing and conversing very diligently till they thought they might relieve Mrs Grey by offering to retire. They hesitated only because Mr Grey had not come in; and he so regularly appeared at ten o'clock, that they had never yet retired without having enjoyed half an hour's chat with him.

"Sophia, my dear," said her mother, "are the night candles there? Light your cousins' candles.—I am sure they are wishing to go; and it is getting late. You will not see Mr Grey to-night, my dears. He has been sent for to a distance."

At this moment, the scrambling of a horse's feet was heard on the gravel before the front door. Sophia looked at her mother, and each lighted a candle precipitately, and thrust it into a hand of each cousin.

"There, go, my dears," said Mrs Grey. "Never mind stopping for Mr Grey. I will deliver your good-night to him. You will have to be rather early in the morning, you know. Good-night, good-night."

Thus Hester and Margaret were hurried up-stairs, while the front door was in the act of being unbarred for Mr Grey's entrance. Morris was despatched after them, with equal speed, by Mrs Grey's orders, and she reached their chamber-door at the same moment that they did.

Hester set down her candle, bade Morris shut the door, and threw herself into an armchair with wonderful decision of manner, declaring that she had never been so treated;—to be amused and sent to bed like a baby, in a house where she was a guest!

"I am afraid something is the matter," said Margaret.

"What then? they might have told us so, and said plainly that they had rather be alone."

"People must choose their own ways of managing their own affairs, you know: and what those ways are cannot matter to us, as long as we are not offended at them."

"Do you take your own way of viewing their behaviour, then, and leave me mine," said Hester hastily.

Morris feared there was something amiss; and she believed Alice knew what it was: but she had not told either cook or housemaid a syllable about it. By Morris's account, Alice had been playing the mysterious in the kitchen as her mistress had in the parlour. Mr Grey had been suddenly sent for, and had saddled his horse himself, as his people were all gone, and there was no one on the premises to do it for him. A wine-glass had also been called for, for Miss Sophia, whose weeping had been overheard. Master Sydney had gone to his room very cross, complaining of his mother's having questioned him overmuch about his ride, and then sent him to bed half an hour before his usual time.

A deadly fear seized upon Margaret's heart, when she heard of Sydney's complaint of being overmuch questioned about his ride,—a deadly fear for

Hester. If her suspicion should prove true, it was out of pure consideration that they had been "amused and sent to bed like babies." A glance at Hester showed that the same apprehension had crossed her mind. Her eyes were closed for a moment, and her face was white as ashes. It was not for long, however. She presently said, with decision, that whatever was the matter, it must be some entirely private affair of the Greys'. If any accident had happened to any one in the village,—if bad news had arrived of any common friend,—there would be no occasion for secrecy. In such a case, Mrs Grey would have given herself the comfort of speaking of it to her guests. It must certainly be some entirely private, some family affair.— Hester was sincere in what she said. She knew so little of the state of her own heart, that she could not conceive how some things in it could be divined or speculated upon by others. Still only on the brink of the discovery that she loved Mr Hope, she could never have imagined that any one else could dream of such a thing,—much less act upon it. She was angry with herself for letting her fears now point for a moment to Mr Hope; for, if this bad news had related to him, her sister and she would, of course, have heard of it the next moment after the Greys. Margaret caught her sister's meaning, and strove to the utmost to think as she did; but Sydney's complaint of being "overmuch questioned about his ride" was fatal to the attempt. It returned upon her incessantly during the night; and when, towards morning, she slept a little, these words seemed to be sounding in her ear all the while. Before undressing, both she and Hester had been unable to resist stepping out upon the stairs to watch for signs whether it was the intention of the family to sit up or go to rest. All had retired to their rooms some time before midnight; and then it was certain that nothing more could be learned before morning.

Each sister believed that the other slept; but neither could be sure. It was an utterly wretched night to both, and the first which they had ever passed in misery, without speaking to each other. Margaret's suffering was all from apprehension. Hester was little alarmed in comparison; but she this night underwent the discovery which her sister had made some little time ago. She discovered that nothing could happen to her so dreadful as any evil befalling Mr Hope. She discovered that he was more to her than the sister whom she could have declared, but a few hours before, to be the dearest on earth to her. She discovered that she was for ever humbled in her own eyes; that her self-respect had received an incurable wound: for Mr Hope had never given her reason to regard him as more than a friend. During the weary hours of this night, she revolved every conversation, every act of intercourse, which she could recall; and from all that she could remember, the same impression resulted—that Mr Hope was a friend, a kind and sympathising friend—interested in her views and opinions, in her tastes and feelings;—that he was this kind friend, and nothing more. He had in no case distinguished her from her sister. She had even thought, at times, that Margaret had been the more important of the two to him. That might be from her own jealous temper, which, she knew, was apt to make her fancy every one preferred to herself: but she *had* thought that he liked Margaret best, as she was sure Mr Enderby did. Whichever way she looked at the case, it was all wretchedness. She had lost her self-sufficiency and self-respect, and she was miserable.

The first rays of morning have a wonderful power of putting to flight the terrors of the darkness, whether their causes lie without us or within. When the first beam of the midsummer sunshine darted into the chamber, through the leafy limes which shaded one side of the apartment, Hester's mood transiently changed. There was a brief reaction in her spirits. She thought she had been making herself miserable far too readily. The mystery of the preceding evening might turn out a trifle: she had been thinking too seriously about her own fancies. If she had really been discovering a great and sad secret about herself, no one else knew it, nor need ever know it. She could command herself; and, in the strength of pride and duty, she would do so. All was not lost. Before this mood had passed away, she fell asleep, with prayer in her heart, and quiet tears upon her cheek. Both sisters were roused from their brief slumbers by a loud tapping at their door. All in readiness to be alarmed, Margaret sprang up, and was at the door to know who was there.

"It is us—it is we, Fanny and Mary, cousin Margaret," answered the twins, "come to call you. It is such a fine morning, you can't think. Papa does not believe we shall have a drop of rain to-day. The baker's boy has just carried the rolls,—such a basket-full!—to Mrs Rowland's: so you must get up. Mamma is getting up already."

The sisters were vexed to have been thrown into a terror for nothing; but it was a great relief to find Mr Grey prophesying fine weather for the excursion. Nothing could have happened to cast a doubt over it. Margaret, too, now began to think that the mystery might turn out a trifle; and she threw up the sash, to let in the fresh air, with a gaiety of spirits she had little expected to feel.

Another tap at the door. It was Morris, with the news that it was a fine morning, that the whole house was astir, and that she had no further news to tell.

Another tap before they were half-dressed. It was Mrs Grey, with a face quite as sorrowful as on the preceding evening, and the peculiar nervous expression about the mouth—which served her instead of tears.

"Have you done with Morris yet, my dears?"

"Morris, you may go," said Hester, steadily.

Mrs Grey gazed at her with a mournful inquisitiveness, while she spoke; and kept her eyes fixed on Hester throughout, though what she said seemed addressed to both sisters.

"There is something the matter, Mrs Grey," continued Hester, calmly. "Say what it is. You had better have told us last night."

"I thought it best not to break your sleep, my dears. We always think bad news is best told in the morning."

"Tell us," said Margaret. Hester quietly seated herself on the bed.

"It concerns our valued friend, Mr Hope," said Mrs Grey. Hester's colour had been going from the moment Mrs Grey entered the room: it was now quite gone; but she preserved her calmness.

"He was safe when Sydney lost sight of him, on the ridge of the hill, on the Dingleford road; but he afterwards had an accident."

"What kind of accident?" inquired Margaret.

"Is he killed?" asked Hester.

"No, not killed. He was found insensible in the road. The miller's boy observed his horse, without a rider, plunge into the river below the dam, and swim across; and another person saw the pony Sydney had been riding, grazing with a side-saddle on, on the common. This made them search, and they found Mr Hope lying in the road insensible, as I told you."

"What is thought of his state?" asked Margaret.

"Two medical men were called immediately from the nearest places, and Mr Grey saw them last night; for the news reached us while you were at the piano, and we thought—"

"Yes but what do the medical men say?"

"They do not speak very favourably. It is a concussion of the brain. They declare the case is not hopeless, and that is all they can say. He has not spoken yet; only just opened his eyes: but we are assured the case is not quite desperate; so we must hope for the best."

"I am glad the case is not desperate," said Hester. "He would be a great loss to you all."

Mrs Grey looked at her in amazement, and then at Margaret. Margaret's eyes were full of tears. She comprehended and respected the effort her sister was making.

"Oh, Mrs Grey!" said Margaret, "must we go to-day? Surely it is no time for an excursion of pleasure."

"That must be as you feel disposed, my dears. It would annoy Mrs Rowland very much to have the party broken up; so much so, that some of us must go: but my young people will do their best to fill your places, if you feel yourselves unequal to the exertion." She looked at Hester as she spoke.

"Oh, if anybody goes, we go, of course," said Hester. "I think you are quite right in supposing that the business of the day must proceed. If there was anything to be done by staying at home,—if you could make us of any use, Mrs Grey, it would be a different thing: but—"

"Well, if there is nothing in your feelings which—if you believe yourselves equal to the exertion—"

Margaret now interposed. "One had rather stay at home and be quiet, when one is anxious about one's friends: but other people must be considered, as we seem to be agreed,—Mr and Mrs Rowland, and all the children. So we will proceed with our dressing, Mrs Grey. But can you tell us, before you go, how soon—How soon we shall know;—when this case will probably be decided?"

It might be a few hours, or it might be many days, Mrs Grey said. She should stay at home to-day, in case of anything being sent for from the farmhouse where Mr Hope was lying. He was well attended—in the hands of good nurses—former patients of his own: but something might be wanted; and orders had been left by Mr Grey that application should be made to his house for whatever could be of service: so Mrs Grey could not think of leaving home. Mr Grey would make inquiry at the farmhouse as the party went by to the woods: and he would just turn his horse back in the middle of the day, to inquire again: and thus the Rowlands' party would know more of Mr Hope's state than those who remained at home. Having explained, Mrs Grey quitted the room, somewhat disappointed that Hester had received the disclosure so well.

The moment the door was closed, Hester sank forward on the bed, her face hidden, but her trembling betraying her emotion.

"I feared this," said Margaret, looking mournfully at her sister.

"You feared what?" asked Hester, quickly, looking up.

"I feared that some accident had happened to Mr Hope."

"So did I."

"And if," said Margaret, "I feared something else—Nay, Hester, you must let me speak. We must have no concealments, Hester. You and I are alone in the world, and we must comfort each other. We agreed to this. Why should you be ashamed of what you feel? I believe that you have a stronger interest in this misfortune than any one in the world; and why—"

"How do you mean, a stronger interest?" asked Hester, trying to command her voice. "Tell me what you mean, Margaret."

"I mean," said Margaret, steadily, "that no one is so much attached to Mr Hope as you are."

"I think," said Margaret, after a pause, "that Mr Hope has a high respect and strong regard for you." She paused again, and then added, "If I believed anything more, I would tell you."

When Hester could speak again, she said, gently and humbly, "I assure you, Margaret, I never knew the state of my own mind till this last night. If I had been aware—"

"If you had been aware, you would have been unlike all who ever really loved, if people say true. Now that you have become aware, you will act as you *can* act—nobly—righteously. You will struggle with your feelings till your mind grows calm. Peace will come in time."

"Do you think there is no hope?"

"Consider his state."

"But if he should recover? Oh, Margaret, how wicked all this is! While he lies there, we are grieving about me! What a selfish wretch I am!"

Margaret had nothing to reply, there seemed so much truth in this. Even she reproached herself with being exclusively anxious about her sister, when such a friend might be dying; when a life of such importance to many was in jeopardy.

"I could do anything, I could bear anything," said Hester, "if I could be sure that nobody knew. But you found me out, Margaret, and perhaps—"

"I assure you, I believe you are safe," said Margaret. "You can hide nothing from me. But, Mrs Grey—and nobody except myself, has watched you like Mrs Grey—has gone away, I am certain, completely deceived. But, Hester! my own precious sister, bear with one word from me! Do not trust too much to your pride."

"I do trust to *my* pride, and I will," replied Hester, her cheeks in a glow. "Do you suppose I will allow all in this house, all in the village, to be pitying me, to be watching how I suffer, when no one supposes that he gave me cause? It is not to be endured, even in the bare thought. No. If you do not betray me—"

"I betray you?"

"Well, well! I know you will not: and then I am safe. *My* pride I can trust to, and I will."

"It will betray you," sighed Margaret. "I do not want you to parade your sorrow, God knows! It will be better borne in quiet and secrecy. What I wish for you is, that you should receive this otherwise than as a punishment, a disgrace in your own eyes for something wrong. You have done nothing wrong, nothing that you may not appeal to God to help you to endure. Take it as a sorrow sent by Him, to be meekly borne, as what no earthly person has any concern with. Be superior to the opinions of the people about us, instead of defying them. Pride will give you no peace: resignation will."

"I am too selfish for this," sighed Hester. "I hate myself, Margaret. I have not even the grace to love *him*, except for my own sake; and while he is dying, I am planning to save my pride! I do not care what becomes of me. Come, Margaret, let us dress and go down. Do not trouble your kind heart about me: I am not worth it."

This mood gave way a little to Margaret's grief and endearments; but Hester issued from her chamber for the day in a state of towering pride, secretly alternating with the anguish of self-contempt.

It was a miserable day, as wretched a party of pleasure as could be imagined. Mrs Rowland was occupied in thinking, and occasionally saying, how strangely everything fell out to torment her, how something always occurred to cross every plan of hers. She talked about this to her mother, Sophia, and Hester, who were in the barouche with her, till the whole cavalcade stopped, just before reaching the farmhouse where Mr Hope lay, and to which Mr Grey rode on to make inquiries. Margaret was with Mr Rowland in his gig. It was a breathless three minutes till Mr Grey brought the news. Margaret wondered how Hester was bearing it: it would have pleased her to have known that Mrs Rowland was holding forth so strenuously upon her disappointment about a dress at the last Buckley ball, and about her children having had the measles on the only occasion when Mr Rowland could have taken her to the races in the next county, that Hester might sit in silence, and bear the suspense unobserved. Mr Grey reappeared, quite as soon as he could be looked for. There might have been worse news. Mr Hope was no longer in a stupor: he was delirious. His medical attendants could not pronounce any judgment upon the case further than that it was not hopeless. They had known recovery in similar cases. As Mr Grey bore his report from carriage to carriage, every one strove to speak cheerfully, and to make the best of the case; and those who were not the most interested really satisfied themselves with the truth that the tidings were better than they might have been.

The damp upon the spirits of the party was most evident, when all had descended from the carriages, and were collected in the woods. There was a general tremor about accidents. If one of the gentlemen had gone forward to explore, or the children had lagged behind for play, there was a shouting, and a general stop, till the missing party appeared. Miss Young would fain have declined her pony, which was duly in waiting for her. It was only because she felt that no individual could well be spared from the party that she mounted at all. Mr Hope was to have had the charge of her; and though she had requested Sydney to take his place, as far as was necessary, Mr Enderby insisted on doing so; a circumstance which did not add to her satisfaction. She was not altogether so heart-sick as her friends, the Ibbotsons; but even to her, everything was weariness of spirit:— the landscape seemed dull; the splendid dinner on the grass tiresome; the sunshine sickly; and even the children, with their laughter and practical jokes, fatiguing and troublesome. Even she could easily have spoken sharply to each and all of the little ones. If she felt so, what must the day have been to Hester? She bore up well under any observation that she might suppose herself the object of; but Margaret saw how laboriously she strove, and in vain, to eat; how welcome was the glass of wine; how mechanical her singing after dinner; and how impatient she was of sitting still. The strangest thing was to see her walking in a dim glade, in the afternoon, arm-in-arm with Mrs Rowland,—as if in the most confidential conversation,—Mrs Rowland apparently offering the confidence, and Hester receiving it.

"Look at them!" said Mr Enderby. "Who would believe that my sister prohibited solitary walks and *tête-à-têtes*, only three hours ago, on the ground that every one ought to be sociable to-day? I shall go and break up the conference."

"Pray do not," said Margaret. "Let them forget rules, and pass their time as they like best."

"Oh! but here is news of Hope. Mr Grey has now brought word that he is no worse. I begin to think he may get through, which, God knows I had no idea of this morning."

"Do you really think so? But do not tell other people, unless you are quite confident that you really mean what you say."

"I may be wrong, of course: but I do think the chances improve with every hour that he does not get worse; and he is certainly not worse. I have a strong presentiment that he will struggle through."

"Go, then; and tell as many people as you choose: only make them understand how much is presentiment."

The *tête-à-tête* between the ladies, being broken off by Mr Enderby with his tidings, was not renewed. Hester walked beside Miss Young's pony, her cheek flushed, and her eye bright. Margaret thought there was pride underneath, and not merely the excitement of renewed hope, so feeble as that hope must yet be, and so nearly crushed by suspense.

Before the hour fixed for the carriages to be in readiness, the party had given up all pretence of amusing themselves and each other. They sat on a ridge, watching the spot where the vehicles were to assemble; and message after message was sent to the servants, to desire them to make haste. The general wish seemed to be, to be getting home, though the sun was yet some way from its setting. When the first sound of wheels was heard, Hester whispered to her sister—"I cannot be in the same carriage with that woman. No; you must not either. I cannot now tell you why. I dare say Miss Young would take my place, and let me go with the children in the waggon."

"I will do that; and you shall return in Mr Rowland's gig. You can talk or not as you please with him; and he is very kind. He is no more to be blamed for his wife's behaviour, you know, than her mother or her brother. It shall be so. I will manage it."

Margaret could manage what she pleased, with Maria and Mr Enderby both devoted to her. Hester was off with Mr Rowland, and Margaret with one child on her lap, and the others rejoicing at having possession of her, before Mrs Rowland discovered the shifting of parties which had taken place. Often during the ride she wanted to speak to her brother: three times out of four he was not to be had, so busy was he joking with the children, as he trotted his horse beside the waggon; and when he did hear his sister's call he merely answered her questions, said something to make his mother laugh, and dropped into his place beside the waggon again. It struck Maria that the waggon had not been such an attraction in going, though the flowers with which it was canopied had then been fresh, and the children more merry and good-humoured than now.

The report to be carried home to Deerbrook was, that Mr Hope was still no worse: it was thought that his delirium was somewhat quieter. Mrs Grey was out on the steps to hear the news, when the carriage approached. As it happened, the gig arrived first, and Hester had to give the relation. She spoke even cheerfully, declaring Mr Enderby's opinion, that the case was going on favourably, and that recovery was very possible. Mrs Grey, who had had a wretchedly anxious day by herself, not having enjoyed even the satisfaction of being useful, nothing having been sent for from the farmhouse, was truly cheered by seeing her family about her again.

"I have been watching for you this hour," said she; "and yet I hardly expected you so soon. As it grew late, I began to fancy all manner of accidents that might befall you. When one accident happens, it makes one fancy so many more! I could not help thinking about Mr Grey's horse. Does that horse seem to you perfectly steady, Hester? Well, I am glad of it: but I once saw it shy from some linen on a hedge, and it was in my mind all this afternoon. Here you are, all safe, however: and I trust we may feel more cheerfully now about our good friend. If he goes on to grow better, I shall get Mr Grey to drive me over soon to see him. But, my dears, what will you have after your ride? Shall I order tea, or will you have something more substantial?"

"Tea, if you please," said Hester. Her tongue was parched: and when Margaret followed her up-stairs, she found her drinking water, as if she had been three days deep in the Great Desert.

"Can you tell me now," asked Margaret, "what Mrs Rowland has been saying to you?"

"No, not at present: better wait. Margaret! what do you think now?"

"I think that all looks brighter than it did this morning; but what a wretched day it has been!"

"You found it so, did you? Oh, Margaret, I have longed every hour to lie down to sleep in that wood, and never wake again!"

"I do not wonder: but you will soon feel better. The sleep from which you will wake to-morrow morning will do nearly as well. We must sleep to-night, and hope for good news in the morning."

"No good news will ever come to me again," sighed Hester. "No, no; I do not quite mean that. You need not look at me so. It is ungrateful to say such a thing at this moment. Come: I am ready to go down to tea. It is really getting dark. I thought this day never would come to an end."

The evening was wearisome enough. Mrs Grey asked how Mrs Rowland had behaved, and Sophia was beginning to tell, when her father checked her, reminding her that she had been enjoying Mrs Rowland's hospitality. This was all he said, but it was enough to bring on one of Sophia's interminable fits of crying. The children were cross with fatigue: Mrs Grey thought her husband hard upon Sophia; and, to complete the absurdity of the scene, Hester's and Margaret's tears proved uncontrollable. The sight of Sophia's set them flowing; and though they laughed at themselves for the folly of weeping from mere sympathy, this did not mend the matter. Mrs Grey seemed on the verge of tears herself, when she observed that she had expected a cheerful evening after a lonely and anxious day. A deep sob from the three answered to this observation, and they all rose to go to their apartments. Hester was struck by the peculiar tender pressure of the hand given her by Mr Grey, as she offered him her mute good-night. It caused her a fresh burst of grief when she reached her own room.

Margaret was determined not to go to rest without knowing what it was that Mrs Rowland had said to her sister. She pressed for it now, hoping that it would rouse Hester from more painful thoughts.

"Though I have been enjoying that woman's hospitality, as Mr Grey says," declared Hester, "I must speak of her as I think, to you. Oh, she has been so insolent!"

"Insolent to you! How? Why?"

"Nay: you had better ask her why. Her confidence was all about her brother. She seems to think,—she did not say so, or I should have known better how to answer her, but she seems to think that her brother is—(I can hardly speak it even to you, Margaret!)—is in some way in danger from me. Now, you and I know that he cares no more for me than for any one of the people who were there to-day; and yet she went on telling me, and I could not stop her, about the views of his family for him!"

"What views?"

"Views which, I imagine, it by no means follows that he has for himself. If she has been impertinent to me, she has been even more so to him. I wonder how she dares meddle in his concerns as she does."

"Well, but what views?" persisted Margaret.

"Oh, about his marrying:— that he is the darling of his family,—that large family interests hang upon his marrying,—that all his relations think it is time he was settling, and that he told her last week that he was of that opinion himself:— and then she went on to say that there was the most delightful accordance in their views for him;—that they did not much value beauty,—that they should require for him something of a far higher order than beauty, and which indeed was seldom found with it—"

"Insolent creature! Did she say that to you?"

"Indeed she did: and that her brother's wife must be of a good family, with a fortune worthy of his own; and, naturally, of a county family."

"A county family!" said Margaret, half laughing. "What matters county or city, when two people are watching over one another for life and death, and for hereafter?"

"With such people as Mrs Rowland," said Hester, "marriage is a very superficial affair. If family, fortune, and equipage are but right, the rest may be left to Providence. Temper, mind, heart—. The worst of all, however, was her ending—or what was made her ending by our being interrupted."

"Well! what was her finish?"

"She put her face almost under my bonnet, as she looked smiling at me, and said there was a young lady—she wished she could tell me all about it—the time would come when she might—there was a sweet girl, beloved by them all for many years, from her very childhood, whom they had hopes of receiving, at no very distant time, as Philip's wife."

"I do not believe it," cried Margaret. After a pause, she added, "Do you believe it, Hester?"

"I am sure I do not know. I should not rate Mrs Rowland's word very highly: but this would be such a prodigious falsehood! It is possible, however, that she may believe it without its being true. Or, such a woman might make the most, for the occasion, of a mere suspicion of her own."

"I do not believe it is true," repeated Margaret.

"At all events," concluded Hester, "nothing that Mrs Rowland says is worth regarding. I was foolish to let myself be ruffled by her."

Margaret tried to take the lesson home, but it was in vain. She was ruffled; and, in spite of every effort, she did believe in the existence of the nameless young lady. It had been a day of trouble; and thus was it ending in fresh sorrow and fear.

Morris came in, hesitated at the door, was told she might stay, and immediately busied herself in the brushing of hair and the folding of clothes. Many tears trickled down, and not a word was spoken, till all the offices of the toilet were finished. Morris then asked, with a glance at the book-shelf, whether she should go or stay.

"Stay, Morris," said Hester, gently. "You shall not suffer for our being unhappy to-night. Margaret, will you, can you read?"

Margaret took the volume in which it was the sisters' common practice to read together, and with Morris at night. While Morris took her seat, and reverently composed herself to hear, Margaret turned to the words which have stilled many a tempest of grief, from the moment when they were first uttered to mourners, through a long course of centuries, "Let not your heart be troubled." "Believe in God; believe in me." Morris sometimes spoke on these occasions. She loved to hear of the many mansions in the House of the Father of all; and she said that though it might seem to her young ladies that their parents had gone there full soon, leaving them to undergo trouble by themselves, yet she had no doubt they should all be at peace together, sooner or later, and their passing troubles seem as nothing. Even this simple and obvious remark roused courage in the sisters. They remembered what their father had said to them about his leaving them to encounter the serious business and trials of life, and how they had promised to strive to be wise and trustful, and to help each other. This day the serious business and trials of life had manifestly begun: they must strengthen themselves and each other to meet them. They agreed upon this, and in a mood of faith and resolution fell asleep.

Chapter Eleven

Mediation.

Mr Hope's case turned out more favourably than any of his attendants and friends had ventured to anticipate. For some days the symptoms continued as alarming as at first; but from the hour that he began to amend, his progress towards recovery was without drawback, and unusually rapid. Within a month, the news circulated through the village, that he had been safely brought home to his own lodgings; and the day after, the ladies at Mr Grey's were startled by seeing him alight from a gig at the door, and walk up the steps feebly, but without assistance. He could not stay away any longer, he declared. He had been above a month shut up in a dim room, without seeing any faces but of doctor, nurse, and Mrs Grey, and debarred from books; now he was well enough to prescribe for himself; and he was sure that a little society, and a gradual return to his usual habits of life, would do him more good than anything.

Mrs Grey kept all her own children out of sight during this first visit, that Mr Hope might not see too many faces at once. She admitted only Hester and Margaret, and Alice, who brought him some refreshment. The girl made him a low curtsey, and looked at him with an expression of awe and pleasure, which brought tears into the eyes of even her mistress. Mr Hope had been a benefactor to this girl. He had brought her through a fever. She had of late little expected ever to see him again. Mr Hope replied to her mute looks:

"Thank you, Alice, I am much better. I hope to be quite well soon. Did not you make some of the good things Mrs Grey has been kind enough to bring me?—I thought so. Well, I'm much obliged to you; and to everybody who has been taking pains to make me well. I do not know how it is," he continued, when Alice had left the room, "but things do not appear as they used to do. Perhaps my eyes are dim still; but the room does not seem bright, and none of you look well and merry."

Mrs Grey observed that she had drawn the blinds down, thinking he would find it a relief after the sunshine. Margaret said ingenuously—

"We are all well, I assure you; but you should not wonder if you find us rather grave. Much has happened since we met. We have been thinking of you with great anxiety for so long, that we cannot on a sudden talk as lightly as when you used to come in every day."

"Ah!" said he, "I little thought, at one time, that I should ever see any of you again in this world."

"We have thought of you as near death," said Margaret; "and since that, as having a sick-room experience, which we respect and stand in awe of; and that is reason enough for our looking grave."

"You feel as if you had to become acquainted with me over again. Well, we must lose no time; here is a month gone that I can give no account of."

Hester felt how differently the case stood with her. The last month had been the longest she had ever known,—tedious as to the state captive, serving his noviciate to prison life. She would have been thankful to say that she could give no account of the past month. She inquired how the accident happened; for this was still a mystery to everybody. Mr Hope could not clear up the matter: he remembered parting with Sydney, and trotting, with the bridle of the pony in his hand, to the top of the ascent,—the point where Sydney lost sight of him: he had no distinct remembrance of anything more,—only a sort of impression of his horse rearing bolt upright. He had never been thrown before; and his supposition was, that a stone cast from behind the hedge might have struck his horse: but he really knew no more of the affair than any one else. The ladies all trusted he would not ride the same horse again; but this he would not promise: his horse was an old friend; and he was not in a hurry to part with old friends. He was glad to find that Miss Young had not laid the blame on the pony, but had ridden it through the woods as if nothing had happened.

"Not exactly so," said Margaret, smiling.

"The young folks did not enjoy their excursion very much, I fancy," said Mrs Grey, smiling also. "Mrs Rowland was quite put out, poor soul! You know she thinks everything goes wrong, on purpose to plague her."

"I think she had some higher feelings on that occasion," said Mr Hope, gently, but gravely. "I am indebted to her for a very anxious concern on my account, and for kind offices in which perhaps none of my many generous friends have surpassed her."

Mrs Grey, somewhat abashed, said that Mrs Rowland had some good qualities: it was only a pity that her unhappy temper did not allow them fair play.

"It is a pity," observed Mr Hope; "and it is at the same time, an appeal to us to allow her the fair play she does not afford herself. That sofa looks delightfully comfortable, Mrs Grey."

"Oh, you are tired; you are faint, perhaps?"

"Shall I ring?" said Hester, moving to the bell.

"No, no," said he, laughing; "I am very well at present. I only mean that I should like to stay all day, if you will let me. I am sure that sofa is full as comfortable as my own. I may stay, may I not?"

"No, indeed you shall not, this first day. If you will go away now before you are tired, and if I find when I look in upon you this evening, that you are not the worse for this feat, you shall stay longer to-morrow. But I assure you it is time you were at home now. My dears, just see whether the gig is at the door."

"So I only get sent away by begging to stay," said Mr Hope. "Well, I have been giving orders to sick people for so many years, that I suppose it is fairly my turn to obey now. May I ask you to send to Widow Rye's to-day? I looked in as I came; and her child is in want of better food, better cooked, than she is able to give him."

"I will send him a dinner from our table. You are not going to see any more patients to-day, I hope?"

"Only two that lie quite in my road. If you send me away, you must take the consequences. Farewell, till tomorrow."

"Mr Grey and I shall look in upon you this evening. Now do not look about you out of doors, to catch anybody's eye, or you will be visiting a dozen patients between this house and your own."

There were, indeed, many people standing about, within sight of Mr Grey's door, to see Mr Hope come out. All Mr Grey's children and servants were peeping through the shrubbery. Mrs Enderby waved her hand from a lower, and her two maids looked out from an upper window. The old man of a hundred years, who was sunning himself on the bank, as usual, rose and took off his hat: and the little Reeves and their schoolfellows stood whispering to one another that Mr Hope looked rarely bad still. Mrs Plumstead dropped a low curtsey, as she stood taking in the letter-bag, at her distant door. Mrs Grey observed to Hester on the respect which was paid to Mr Hope all through the place, as if Hester was not feeling it in her heart of hearts at the moment.

Mrs Grey flattered herself that Mr Hope was thinking of Hester when he said his friends did not look well. She had been growing thinner and paler for the last month, and no doubt remained in Mrs Grey's mind about the cause. Hester had commanded herself, to her sister's admiration; but she could not command her health, and that was giving way under perpetual feelings of anxiety and humiliation. Mrs Grey thought all this had gone quite far enough. She was more fond and proud of Hester every day, and more impatient that she should be happy, the more she watched her. She spoke to Margaret about her. Margaret was prepared for this, having foreseen its probability; and her answers, while perfectly true and sincere, were so guarded, that Mrs Grey drew from them the comfortable inference that she alone penetrated the matter, and understood Hester's state of mind. She came to the resolution at last of making the young people happy a little sooner than they could have managed the affair for themselves. She would help them to an understanding, but it should be with all possible delicacy and regard to their feelings. Not even Mr Grey should know what she was about.

Opportunities were not wanting. When are opportunities wanting to match-makers? If such do not find means of carrying their points, they can construct them. Few match-makers go to work so innocently and securely as Mrs Grey; for few can be so certain of the inclinations of the parties as she believed herself. Her own admiration of Hester was so exclusive, and the superiority of Hester's beauty so unquestionable, that it never occurred to her that the attraction which drew Mr Hope to the house could be any other than this. About the state of Hester's affections she felt justly confident; and so, in her view, nothing remained to be done but to save her from further pining by bringing about an explanation. She was frequently with Mr Hope at his lodgings, during his recovery, seeing that he took his afternoon rest, and beguiling a part of his evenings; in short, watching over him as over a son, and declaring to Hester that he was no less dear to her.

One evening, when she was spending an hour in Mr Hope's parlour, where Mr Grey had deposited her till nine o'clock, when he was to call for her, she made the same affectionate declaration to Mr Hope himself,—that he was as dear to her as if he had been her own son; "and," she continued, "I shall speak to you with the same freedom as I should use with Sydney, and may, perhaps, ten years hence."

"Pray do," said Mr Hope. "I shall be glad to hear anything you have to say. Are you going to find fault with me?"

"Oh dear, no! What fault should I have to find with you? unless, indeed, it be a fault or a folly to leave your own happiness and that of another person in needless uncertainty."

Mr Hope changed colour, quite to the extent of her wishes.

"I know," continued she, "that your illness has put a stop to everything; and that it has left you little nerve for any explanation of the kind: but you are growing stronger every day now, and the case is becoming so serious on the other side that I own I dread the consequences of much further delay. You see I speak openly."

She had every encouragement to do so, for Mr Hope's countenance was flushed with what appeared to her to be delight. "You observed, yourself, you know, that Hester did not look well; and indeed the few weeks after your accident were so trying to her,—the exertions she made to conceal her feelings were so—. But I must spare her delicacy. I trust you are quite assured that she has not the most remote idea of my speaking to you thus. Indeed, no human being is in the least aware of it."

"Hester! Miss Ibbotson! Pray, Mrs Grey, do not say another word. Let us talk of something else."

"Presently; when I have finished. You must have seen that I love this dear girl as a daughter; and there is not a thought of her heart that she can conceal from me, though her delicacy is so great that I am confident she thinks me unaware of her state of mind at this moment. But I saw how the affair was going from the very beginning; and the failure of her health and looks since your accident have left me no doubt whatever, and have made me feel it my duty to give you the encouragement your modesty requires, and to confide to you how wholly her happiness lies in your hands."

"Hester! Miss Ibbotson! I assure you, Mrs Grey, you must be completely mistaken."

"I beg your pardon: I am not so easily mistaken as some people. There is Mrs Rowland, now! I am sure she fancies that her brother is in love with Hester, when it is plain to everybody but herself that he and my other young cousin are coming to a conclusion as fast as need be. However, I know you do not like to hear me find fault with Mrs Rowland; and, besides, I have no right to tell Margaret's secrets; so we will say no more about that."

Mr Hope sighed heavily. These remarks upon Enderby and Margaret accorded but too well with his own observations. He could not let Mrs Grey proceed without opposition; but all he was capable of was to repeat that she was entirely mistaken.

"Yes, that is what men like you always say,—in all sincerity, of course. Your modesty always stands in the way of your happiness for a while: but you are no losers by it. The happiness is all the sweeter when it comes at last."

"But that is not what I mean. You have made it difficult for me to explain myself. I hardly know how to say it; but it must be said. You have mistaken my intentions,—mistaken them altogether."

It was now Mrs Grey's turn to change colour. She asked in a trembling voice:

"Do you mean to say, Mr Hope, that you have not been paying attentions to Hester Ibbotson?"

"I do say so; that I have paid no attentions of the nature you suppose. You compel me to speak plainly."

"Then I must speak plainly too, Mr Hope. If any one had told me you would play the part you have played, I should have resented the imputation as I resent your conduct now. If you have not intended to win Hester's affections, you have behaved infamously. You have won her attachment by attentions which have never varied, from the very first evening that she entered our house, till this afternoon. You have amused yourself with her, it seems; and now you are going to break her heart."

"Stop, stop, Mrs Grey! I cannot hear this."

"There is not a soul in the place that does not think as I do. There is not a soul that will not say—."

"Let us put aside what people may say. If, by any imprudence of my own, I have brought blame upon myself, I must bear it. The important point is—. Surely, Mrs Grey, it is possible that you may be in error about Miss Ibbotson's—Miss Ibbotson's state of mind."

"No, Mr Hope, it is not possible." And being in for it, as she said, Mrs Grey gave such a detail of her observations, and of unquestionable facts, as left the truth indeed in little doubt.

"And Margaret," said Mr Hope, in a troubled voice: "do you know anything of her views of my conduct?"

"Margaret is not so easily seen through as Hester," said Mrs Grey: an assertion from which Mr Hope silently dissented; Margaret appearing to him the most simple-minded person he had ever known; lucid in her sincerity, transparent in her unconsciousness. He was aware that Mrs Grey had been so occupied with Hester as not to have been open to impression from Margaret.

"Margaret is not so easily seen through as Hester, you know; and she and I have never talked over your conduct confidentially: but if Margaret does not perceive the alteration in her sister, and the cause of it, it can only be because she is occupied with her own concerns."

"That is not like Margaret," thought Mr Hope.

"However, she does see it, I am sure; for she has proposed their return to Birmingham,—their immediate return, though their affairs are far from being settled yet, and they do not know what they will have to live upon. They promised to stay till October, too; and we are only half through

August yet. Margaret can hardly have any wish to leave us on her own account, considering whom she must leave behind. It is for Hester's sake, I am confident. There is no doubt of the fact, Mr Hope. Your honour is involved. I repeat, you have won this dear girl's affections; and now you must act as a man of conscience, which I have always supposed you to be."

Mr Hope was tempted to ask for further confirmation, from the opinions of the people who were about Hester; but he would not investigate the degree of exposure which might have taken place. Even if no one agreed with Mrs Grey, this would be no proof that her conviction was a wrong one; it might happen through Hester's successful concealment of what she must be striving to suppress.

Mrs Grey urged him about his honour and conscience more closely than he could bear. He faintly begged her to leave him. He obtained from her a promise that she would inform no person of what had been said; and she again assured him that neither Hester, nor any one else, had the remotest idea of her speaking as she had done this evening. On his part, Mr Hope declared that he should reflect on what had passed, and act with the strictest regard to duty. As, in Mrs Grey's eyes, his duty was perfectly clear, this declaration was completely satisfactory. She saw the young people, with her mind's eye, settled in the corner house which belonged to Mr Rowland, and was delighted that she had spoken. As soon as she was gone, Mr Hope would discover, she had little doubt, that he had loved Hester all this time without having been conscious what the attraction had really been; and in a little while he would be thankful to her for having smoothed his way for him. With these thoughts in her mind, she bade him good-night, just as Mr Grey drove up to the door. She whispered once more, that he was as dear to her as a son, and that this was the reason of her having spoken so plainly.

"How are you this evening, Hope?" said Mr Grey, from the doorway. "On the sofa, eh? don't rise for me, then. Rather done up, eh? Ah! I was afraid you were for getting on too fast. Bad economy in the end. You will be glad to be rid of us: so I shall not come in. Take care of yourself, I beg of you. Good-night."

In what a state of mind was Hope left! His plain-speaking motherly friend little guessed what a storm she had raised in a spirit usually as calm as a summer's morning. There was nothing to him so abhorrent as giving pain; nothing so intolerable in idea as injuring any human being: and he was now compelled to believe that through some conduct of his own, some imprudence, in a case where imprudence is guilt, he had broken up the peace of a woman whom, though he did not love, he respected and warmly regarded! His mind was in too tumultuous a state for him to attempt to settle with himself the degree of his culpability. He only knew that he was abased in his own sense of deep injury towards a fellow-creature. In the same breath came the destruction of his hopes,—hopes, of which, till the moment, he had been scarcely conscious,—with regard to the one on whom his thoughts had been really fixed. He had pledged himself to act strictly according to his sense of duty. His consolation, his refuge in every former trial of life, since the days of childhood, had been in resolving to abide faithfully by the decisions of duty. In this he had found freedom; in this he had met strength and repose, so that no evil had been intolerable to him. But what was his duty now? Amidst the contradictions of honour and conscience in the present case, where should he find his accustomed refuge? At one moment he saw clearly the obligation to devote himself to her whose affections he had gained,—thoughtlessly and carelessly, it is true, but to other eyes purposely. At the next moment, the sin of marrying without love,—if not while loving another,—rose vividly before him, and made him shrink from what, an instant before, seemed clear duty. The only hope was in the possibility of mistake, which might yet remain. The whole could not be mistake, about Hester, and Enderby, and Margaret, and all Mrs Grey's convictions. Some of all this must be true. The probability was that it was all true: and if so,—he could almost repine that he had not died when his death was expected. Then he should not have known of all this injury and woe; then he should not have had to witness Margaret's love for another: then Hester's quiet grief would have melted away with time, unembittered by reproach of him. No one had, till this hour, loved and relished life more than he; yet now this gladsome being caught himself mourning that he had survived his accident. He roused himself from this; but all was fearful and confused before him. He could see nothing as it was, and as it ought to be: he could decide upon nothing. He must take time: he must be deliberate upon this, the most important transaction of his life.

Thus he determined, as the last remains of twilight faded away in his apartment, and the night air blew in chill from the open window. He was so exhausted by his mental conflict as to be scarcely able to rise to close the window, and retire to rest. There was one hope, familiar as the sunshine to his eyes, but unusually feeble, still abiding in his mind for comfort,—that he should, sooner or later, clearly discern what it was his duty to do. All was at present dark; but this light might flow in. He would wait: he would not act till it did.

He did wait. For many days he was not seen in any of the haunts to which he had begun to return. The answer to inquiries was that Mr Hope was not so well, and wished for entire quiet. Everyone was anxious. Hester was wretched, and Mrs Grey extremely restless and uneasy. She made several attempts to see him; but in no instance did she succeed. She wrote him a private note, and received only a friendly verbal answer, such as all the world might hear.

Mr Hope did wait for his duty to grow clear in the accumulating light of thought. He decided at length how to act; and he decided wrong;—not for want of waiting long enough, but because some considerations intruded themselves which warped his judgment, and sophisticated his feelings. He decided upon making the great mistake of his life.

Nothing had ever been clearer to his mind than the guilt of marrying without love. No man could have spoken more strongly, more solemnly than he, on the presumption, the dishonourableness, the profligacy, of such an act: but he was unaware how a man may be betrayed into it while he has neither presumption, nor treachery, nor profligacy in his thoughts. Hope went through a world of meditation during the days of his close retirement; some of his thoughts were superficial, and some deceived him. He considered Margaret lost to him: he glanced forwards to his desolation when he should lose the society of both sisters—an event likely to happen almost immediately, unless he should so act as to retain them. He dwelt upon Hester's beauty, her superiority of mind to every woman but one whom he had known, her attachment to himself; her dependence upon him. He pondered these things till the tone of his mind was lowered, and too many superficial feelings mingled with the sacredness of the transaction, and impaired its integrity. Under their influence he decided what to do.

He had no intention, all this while, of taking Mrs Grey's word for the whole matter, without test or confirmation. From the beginning, he was aware that his first step must be to ascertain that she was not mistaken. And this was his first step.

There were two obvious methods of proceeding. One was to consult Mr Grey, who stood in the place of guardian to these girls, as to the probability of his success with Hester, in case of his proposing himself to her. The other was to ask the same question of Margaret. The advantage of speaking to Mr Grey was, that he might not be bound to proceed, in case of Mr Grey differing from his lady's view of the case; but then, Mr Grey was perhaps unaware of the real state of Hester's mind. From Margaret there was certainty of hearing nothing but the truth, however little of it her feelings for her sister might allow her to reveal; but such a conversation with her would compel him to proceed: all retreat would be cut off after it; and he naturally shrank from conversing with Margaret, of all people, on this subject. But Hope was equal to any effort which he thought a matter of duty; and he resolved not to flinch from this. He would speak first to Mr Grey; and if Mr Grey did not undertake to answer for Hester's indifference, he would seek an interview with Margaret. If Margaret should encourage his advances on her sister's behalf; the matter was decided. He should have a wife who might be the pride of any man,—whom it would be an honour to any man to have attached. If, as was still just possible, Margaret should believe that her sister felt no peculiar regard for him, he thought he might intimate so much of the truth as, without offending her feelings on her sister's account, would secure for him freedom to reconsider his purposes. No man disliked more than he so circuitous a method of acting in the most important affair of life. He had always believed that, in the case of a genuine and virtuous attachment, there can or ought to be nothing but the most entire simplicity of conduct in the parties,—no appeal to any but each other,—no seeking of an intervention, where no stranger ought to intermeddle with the joy: but the present affair, though perpetually brightening before Hope's fancy, could not for a moment be thought of as of this kind: and here the circuitous method, which had always appeared disgusting to his imagination, was a matter of necessity to his conscience.

Chapter Twelve

A Turn in the Shrubbery.

Mr Grey looked extremely pleased when asked whether he supposed Hester might be won. His reply was simple enough. He was not in his young cousin's confidence: he could not undertake to answer for the state of mind of young ladies; but he knew of no other attachment,—of nothing which need discourage his friend Hope, who would have his hearty good wishes if he should persevere in his project. Yes, yes; he fully understood: it was not to be spoken of;—it was to rest entirely between themselves till Hope should have felt his way a little. He knew it was the fashion in these days to feel the way a little more than was thought necessary or desirable in his time: but he liked that all should follow their own method in an affair which concerned themselves so much more than any one else: so the matter should be a perfect secret, as Mr Hope desired; though he did not fancy it would have to be kept so close for any great length of time.

This was over. Now for the interview with Margaret, which had become necessary.

His reappearance in the family party at Mr Grey's, under the inquisitive eyes of Mrs Grey herself, must be an awkward business at the best, while he remained in uncertainty. The only way was to put an end to the uncertainty as soon as possible. He would go this very afternoon, and ascertain his fate before the day was over. He went boldly up to the door and rang. "The family were all out in the garden after dinner," Alice said: "would Mr Hope join them there, or would he rest himself while she told them he had arrived?" Alice's anxiety about his looks was not yet satisfied.

"I will step in here," said he, the door of the blue parlour being open. "Send Morris to me," Morris at that moment crossing the hall. "Morris, I want to see Miss Margaret. Will you just tell her that some one wishes to speak with her? I know she will excuse my asking the favour of her to come in."

"Miss Margaret, sir?"

"Yes."

"I am sure, sir, you look more fit to sit here than to be gathering apples with them all in the orchard. Did you say Miss Margaret, sir?"

"Yes."

"Whatever else may be in Morris's mind," thought Hope, "it is clear that she is surprised at my wanting to see Margaret.—Here she comes."

He was not sorry that the step paused in the hall,—that there was a delay of some seconds before Margaret appeared. He felt as weak at the moment as on first rising from his bed after his accident; but he rallied his resolution before he met her eye,—now timid and shrinking as he had never seen it before. Margaret was very grave, and as nearly awkward as it was possible for her to be. She shook hands with him, however, and hoped that he was better again.

"I am better, thank you. Will you sit down, and let me speak to you for a few minutes?"

It was impossible to refuse. Margaret sank down, while he shut the door.

"I hear," said he, "that you are already thinking of returning to Birmingham. Is this true?"

"Yes: we shall go home in a few days."

"Then, before you leave us, will you allow me to ask your advice—?"

At the word "advice" a glow of pleasure passed over Margaret's face, and she could not quite suppress a sigh of relief. She now looked up freely and fearlessly. All this was good for Mr Hope: but it went to his heart, and for a moment checked his speech. He soon proceeded, however.

"I want your advice as a friend, and also some information which you alone can give me. What I have to say relates to your sister."

Margaret's ecstasy of hope was scarcely controllable. For her sister's sake she hung her head upon her bosom, the better to conceal her joy. It was a bitter moment for him who could not but note and rightly interpret the change in her countenance and manner.

"I wish to know, if you have no objection to tell me, whether your sister is disengaged."

"I have no objection to say," declared Margaret, looking up cheerfully, "that my sister is not engaged."

"That is the information I wished for. Now for the opinion which I venture to ask of you, as of the one to whom your sister's mind is best known. Do you believe that, if I attempt it, I am likely to win her?"

Margaret was silent. It was difficult to answer the question with perfect truth, and with due consideration to her sister.

"I see," said Hope, "that you do not approve my question: nor do I myself. Rather tell me whether you suppose that she prefers any one to me,—that she had rather I should not seek her,—whether, in short, you would advise me to withdraw."

"By no means," said Margaret. "I cannot say anything tending to deter you. I know of nothing which need discourage you; and I assure you, you have my best wishes that you may succeed."

She looked at him with the bright expression of sincerity and regard which had touched his heart oftener and more deeply than all Hester's beauty. He could not have offered to shake hands at the moment; but she held out hers, and he could not but take it. The door burst open at the same instant, and Mr Enderby entered. Both let drop the hand they held, and looked extremely awkward and grave. A single glance was enough to send Mr Enderby away, without having spoken his errand, which was to summon Margaret to the orchard, for the final shake of the apple-tree. When he was gone, each saw that the face of the other was crimson: but while Hope had a look of distress which Margaret wondered at, remembering how soon Mr Enderby would understand the nature of the interview, she was struggling to restrain a laugh.

"Thank you for your truth," said Mr Hope. "I knew I might depend upon it from you."

"I have told you all I can," said Margaret rising; "and it will be best to say no more at present. It is due to my sister to close our conversation here. If she should choose," continued she, gaily, "to give us leave to renew it hereafter, I shall have a great deal to say to you on my own part. You have done me the honour of calling me 'friend.' You have my friendship, I assure you, and my good wishes."

Hope grasped her hand with a fervour which absolved him from the use of words. He then opened the door for her.

"I must return to the orchard," said she. "Will you go? or will you repose yourself here till we come in to tea?"

Mr Hope preferred remaining where he was. The die was cast, and he must think. His hour of meditation was salutary. He had never seen Margaret so—he dared not dwell upon it: but then, never had her simplicity of feeling towards him, her ingenuous friendship, unmixed with a thought of love, been so clear. He had made no impression upon her, except through her sister, and for her sister. He recalled the stiffness and fear with which she had come when summoned to a *tête-à-tête*; her sudden relief on the mention of her sister; and her joyous encouragement of his project.

"I ought to rejoice—I do rejoice at this," thought he. "It seems as if everyone else would be made happy by this affair. It must have been my own doing; there must have been that in my manner and conduct which authorised all this expectation and satisfaction,—an expectation and satisfaction which prove to be no fancy of Mrs Grey's. I have brought upon myself the charge of Hester's happiness. She is a noble woman, bound to me by all that can engage my honour, my generosity, my affection. She shall be happy from this day, if my most entire devotion can make her so. Margaret loves Enderby: I am glad I know it. I made him dreadfully jealous just now; I must relieve him as soon as possible. I do not know how far matters may have gone between them; but Margaret is not at liberty to explain what he saw till I have spoken to Hester. There must be no delay: I will do it this evening. I cannot bring myself to communicate with Mrs Grey. If Mr Grey is at home, he will make the opportunity for me."

Mr Grey was at home, and on the alert to take a hint. "I guessed how it was," said he. "Margaret has been trying to keep down her spirits, but not a child among them all flew about the orchard as she did, when Mr Enderby had been to look for her, and she followed him back. I thought at first it was something on her own account; but Enderby looked too dull and sulky for that. I have no doubt he is jealous of you. He found you together, did he? Well, he will soon know why, I trust. Oh, you have a hearty well-wisher in Margaret, I am sure! Now, you see they are setting Sophia down to the piano; and I think I can find for you the opportunity you want, if you really wish to bring the business to a conclusion this evening. I will call Hester out to take a turn with me in the shrubbery, as she and I often do, these fine evenings; and then, if you choose, you can meet us there."

Hester was not at all sorry to be invited by Mr Grey to the turn in the shrubbery, which was one of the best of her quiet pleasures,—a solace which she enjoyed the more, the more she became attached to kind Mr Grey: and she did much respect and love him. This evening she was glad of any summons from the room. Margaret had fully intended not to speak to her of what had passed, thinking it best for her sister's dignity, and for Mr Hope's satisfaction, that he should not be anticipated. All this was very wise and undeniable while she was walking back to the orchard: but it so happened that Hester's hand hung by her side, as she stood looking up at the apple-tree, unaware that Margaret had left the party. Margaret could not resist seizing the hand, and pressing it with so much silent emotion, such a glance of joy, as threw Hester into a state of wonder and expectation. Not a syllable could she extort from Margaret, either on the spot or afterwards, when summoned to tea. Whether it was on account of Mr Hope's return to the house, she could not satisfy herself. She had sat, conscious and inwardly distressed, at the tea-table, where nothing remarkable had occurred; and was glad to escape from the circle where all that was said appeared to her excited spirit to be tiresome, or trifling, or vexatious.

How different was it all when she returned to the house! How she loved the whole world, and no one in it was dull, and nothing was trifling, and it was out of the power of circumstances to vex her! Life had become heaven: its doubts, its cares, its troubles, were gone, and all had given place to a soul-penetrating joy. She should grow perfect now, for she had one whom she believed perfect to lead her on. Her pride, her jealousy, would trouble her no more: it was for want of sympathy—perfect sympathy always at hand—that she had been a prey to them. She should pine no more, for there was one who was her own. A calm, nameless, all-pervading bliss had wrapped itself round her spirit, and brought her as near to her Maker as if she had been his favoured child. There needs no other proof that happiness is the most wholesome moral atmosphere, and that in which the immortality of man is destined ultimately to thrive, than the elevation of soul, the religious aspiration, which attends the first assurance, the first sober certainty, of true love. There is much of this religious aspiration amidst all warmth of virtuous affections. There is a vivid love of God in the child that lays its cheek against the cheek of its mother, and clasps its arms about her neck. God is thanked (perhaps unconsciously) for the brightness of his earth, on summer evenings, when a brother and sister, who have long been parted, pour out their heart stores to each other, and feel their course of thought brightening as it runs. When the aged parent hears of the honours his children have won, or looks round upon their innocent faces as the glory of his decline, his mind reverts to Him who in them prescribed the purpose of his life, and bestowed its grace. But, religious as is the mood of every good affection, none is so devotional as that of love, especially so called. The soul is then the very temple of adoration, of faith, of holy purity, of heroism, of charity. At such a moment the human creature shoots up into the angel: there is nothing on earth too defiled for its charity—nothing in hell too appalling for its heroism—nothing in heaven too glorious for its sympathy. Strengthened, sustained, vivified by that most mysterious power, union with another spirit, it feels itself set well forth on the way of victory over evil, sent out conquering and to conquer. There is no other such crisis in human life. The philosopher may experience uncontrollable agitation in verifying his principle of balancing systems of worlds, feeling, perhaps, as if he actually saw the creative hand in the act of sending the planets forth on their everlasting way; but this philosopher, solitary seraph, as he may be regarded, amidst a myriad of men, knows at such a moment no emotions so divine as those of the spirit becoming conscious that it is beloved—be it the peasant girl in the meadow, or the daughter of the sage, reposing in her father's confidence, or the artisan beside his loom, or the man of letters musing by his fireside. The warrior, about to strike the decisive blow for the liberties of a nation, however impressed with the solemnity of the hour, is not in a state of such lofty resolution as those who, by joining hearts, are laying their joint hands on the whole wide realm of futurity for their own. The statesman who, in the moment of success, feels that an entire class of social sins and woes is annihilated by his hand, is not conscious of so holy and so intimate a thankfulness as they who are aware that their redemption is come in the presence of a new and sovereign affection. And these are many—they are in all corners of every land. The statesman is the leader of a nation—the warrior is the grace of an age—the philosopher is the birth of a thousand years; but the lover—where is he not? Wherever parents look round upon their children, there he has been—wherever children are at play together, there he will soon be—wherever there are roofs under which men dwell—wherever there is an atmosphere vibrating with human voices, there is the lover, and there is his lofty worship going on, unspeakable, but revealed in the brightness of the eye, the majesty of the presence, and the high temper of the discourse. Men have been ungrateful and perverse; they have done what they could to counteract, to debase, this most heavenly influence of their life; but the laws of their Maker are too strong, the benignity of their Father is too patient and fervent, for their opposition to withstand: and true love continues, and will continue, to send up its homage amidst the meditations of every eventide, and the busy hum of noon, and the song of the morning stars.

Hester, when she re-entered the house, was full of the commonest feeling of all in happy lovers,—a wonder that such intense happiness should be permitted to her. Margaret was lingering about the stair-head in the dusk, and met her sister at the door of their own apartment.

"May I come in?" said she.

"May you come in? Oh, Margaret! I want you."

"All is right: all is well; is it, Hester? And I was quite wrong throughout. I grieve now that I helped to make you miserable: but, indeed, I was miserable myself. I saw no hope; I was completely mistaken."

"We were both mistaken," said Hester, resting her head at Margaret's shoulder. "Mistaken in judgment,—blinded by anxiety. But all that is over now. Margaret, what have I done that I should be so happy?"

"You have loved one who deserves such a love as yours," said Margaret, smiling. "That is what you have done: and you will have the blessings of all who know you both. You have mine, dearest."

"What an ungrateful wretch shall I be, if I do not make every one happy that is within my reach!" cried Hester. "Margaret, I will never grieve his heart as I have grieved yours. I will never grieve yours again."

"But how is it?" asked Margaret. "You have not told me yet. Is it all settled?"

A silent embrace told that it was.

"I may shake hands with you upon it, then. Oh, Hester, after all our longings for a brother, you are going to give me one! We are not alone in the world. My father,—our mother,—where are they? Do they know? Have they foreseen while we have been suffering so? Do they now foresee for us?"

"There was not one word of his," said Hester, "that I should not have gloried in their hearing. So gentle, Margaret! so noble! so calm!"

"And you?" said Margaret, softly. "Did you speak—speak openly?"

"Yes: it was no time for pride. With him I have no pride. I could not have believed how I should tell him all: but he was so noble,—spoke so gloriously,—that it would have been an insult to use any disguise. He knows all that you know, Margaret,—and I am not ashamed."

"I honour you," said Margaret. "Thank God, all is right! But where is Mr Hope all this time?"

"He went away when I came in. You will see him in the morning."

"Can you go down this evening? If you think you can—."

"Go down! Yes:— this moment. I feel as if I could face the whole world."

"Let me ask one thing. May I tell Maria in the morning? She will be so pleased! and no one but you understands my feelings so well. Everybody will rejoice with me; but I can say anything to her. May I tell her all in the morning?"

"Dear Maria! Oh, yes: tell her from me, with my love. I know I shall have her blessing. Now let us go down."

"But we must just settle how matters are to proceed," said Margaret. "Are the family to know or not?"

"Oh, let all that take its chance!" said Hester. "I am sure I do not care. Let it be as it happens, for to-night at least."

"For to-night at least," agreed Margaret.

All was going on as usual below-stairs. The working of collars and of rugs was proceeding, as the family sat round the lamp. On the appearance of Hester and Margaret, the book, with the Society's cover on it, was produced; and it was requested that some one would read aloud, as it was necessary that forty pages a day should be gone through, to get the volume done by the time it must be sent to Mrs Enderby. Sophia asked whether some one else would be so good as to read this evening, as she thought she could finish her collar by keeping steadily to it till bedtime.

Margaret took the book, and was surprised to find how easy a process it is to read aloud passably without taking in a word of the sense. Fortunately the Greys were not much given to make remarks on what they read. To have gone through the books that came from the Society was enough; and they could not have accomplished the forty pages an evening if they had stopped to talk. The only words spoken during the lecture, therefore, were occasional remarks that the reader seemed hoarse, and that some one else had better take the book; and whispered requests across the table for scissors, thread, or the adjustment of the light. Such being the method of literary exercise in the family, Hester and Margaret were able to think of anything they pleased with impunity.

"There! here comes papa!" said Sophia; "and I do not believe we have read nearly forty pages. Where did you begin, Margaret?"

Margaret resigned the volume to her to have the place found, and was told that she should not have shifted the marker till the evening reading was done, unless she at once set it forward forty pages: it made it so difficult to find the place. Sophia was detained only five minutes from her collar, however, before she discovered that they had read only eight-and-twenty pages. Mrs Grey observed that Mr Grey was coming in rather earlier than usual to-night; and Sophia added, that her cousins had been a good while in their own room.

Hester was conscious that Mr Grey cast a rapid, penetrating glance upon her as he drew his chair, and took his seat at her elbow.

"What a clever book this is!" said Mrs Grey.

"Very entertaining," added Sophia.

"What is your opinion of it?" asked Mr Grey of Hester.

She smiled, and said she must read more of it before she could judge.

"It is such a relief," said Mrs Grey, "to have a book like this in hand after the tiresome things Mr Rowland orders in! He consults Mrs Rowland's notions about books far too much; and she always takes a fancy to the dullest. One would almost think it was on purpose."

Sydney liked the sport of knocking on the head charges against the Rowlands. He showed, by a reference to the Society's list, that the book just laid down was ordered by the Rowlands.

"Dear me! Sophia," said her mother, "you made quite a mistake. You told us it was ordered in by Mr Hope. I am sure, I thought so all this time."

"Well, I dare say we shall not be able to finish it," said Sophia. "We have read only eight-and-twenty pages this evening. Papa! how shockingly Mr Hope looks still, does not he? I think he looks worse than when he was here last."

"And I trust he will look better when we see him next. I have the strongest hopes that he will now gain ground every day."

"I am sure he seems to have gained very little yet."

"Oh, yes, he has; as I trust you will soon see."

Sophia was about to bewail Mr Hope's sickly looks again, when her mother trod on her foot under the table; and, moreover, winked and frowned in a very awful way, so that Sophia felt silenced, she could not conceive for what reason. Not being able to think of anything else to say, to cover her confusion, she discovered that it was bedtime,—at least for people who had been gathering apples.

Once more Mrs Grey gazed over her spectacles at her husband, when the young people were gone.

"My dear," said she, "what makes you think that Mr Hope is gaining ground every day?"

"My dear, what made you tread on all our toes when I said so?"

"Dear me, I only gave Sophia a hint, to prevent her saying dismal things before people. One does not know what may be passing in their minds, you know."

"And so you kindly show what is passing in yours. However, these young ladies may soon be able, perhaps, to tell us more about Hope than we can tell them."

"My dear, what do you mean?"

"I saw a glance between them, a smile, when you were silencing Sophia. I believe you may prepare yourself for some news, my dear."

"I have no doubt of Hester's state of mind—"

"And I feel confident of Hope's; so here is the case, pretty well made out between us."

Mrs Grey was in raptures for a moment; but she then resumed her system of mysterious tokens. She shook her head, and owned that she had reason to think her husband was mistaken.

"Well, just observe them the next time they are together; that is all."

"And my poor Hester looks wretchedly, Mr Grey. It really makes my heart ache to see her."

"How differently people view things! I was just thinking that I never saw her so lovely, with such a sprightliness, such a glow in her face, as five minutes ago."

"Just this evening, she does not look so pale; but she is sadly altered—grievously changed indeed. Seeing this, is the only thing which reconciles me to parting with her. Now, Mr Grey, I should like to know what sets you smiling in that manner at the poor girl."

"I was smiling to think how, as young ladies have been known to change their minds, it may be possible that we may have the pleasure of seeing Hester pick up her good looks again here, in spite of all that Morris says about her native air. I should not wonder that we may persuade her to stay yet."

Mrs Grey shook her head decisively. She should have been very glad, a little while since, to hear her husband's opinion that Mr Hope's views were fixed upon Hester; but now—. But men were always so positive; and always the most positive where they knew the least! A deep sigh from the one party, and a broad smile from the other, closed the conversation.

Chapter Thirteen

Sophia in the Village.

Deerbrook was not a place where practical affairs could be long kept secret, even where the best reasons for secrecy existed. About Hester's engagement there was no reason whatever for concealment; and it was accordingly made known to every one in Deerbrook in the course of the next day.—Margaret shut herself up with Maria before breakfast, and enjoyed an hour of hearty sympathy from her, in the first place. As they were both aware that this communication was a little out of order,—Mr and Mrs Grey having a clear title to the earliest information,—Maria had to be discreet for nearly three hours—till she heard the news from another quarter.

Immediately after breakfast, Mr Hope called on Mr Grey at the office, and informed him. Mr Grey stepped home, and found Margaret enlightening his wife. Sophia was next called in, while Morris was closeted with her young ladies. Sophia burst breathless into the summer-house to tell Miss Young, which she did in whispers so loud as to be overheard by the children. Matilda immediately found she had left her slate-pencil behind her, and ran into the house to give her mamma the news, just at the moment that Mr Grey was relating it to his partner in the office. On returning, Sophia found her mother putting on her bonnet, having remembered that it was quite time she should be stepping across the way to hear how poor Mrs Enderby was, after the thunder-storm of three days ago. This reminded Sophia that she ought to be inquiring about the worsteds which Mrs Howell must have got down from London by this time, to finish Mrs Grey's rug. Mrs Grey could not trust her eyes to match shades of worsteds; and Sophia now set out with great alacrity to oblige her mother by doing it for her. On the way she met Dr Levitt, about to enter the house of a sick parishioner. Dr Levitt hoped all at home were well. All very well, indeed, Sophia was obliged to him. Her only fear was that the excitement of present circumstances might be too much for mamma. Mamma was so very much attached to cousin Hester, and it would be such a delightful thing to have her settled beside them! Perhaps Dr Levitt had not heard that Hester and Mr Hope were going to be married. No, indeed, he had not. He wondered his friend Hope had not told him of his good fortune, of which he heartily wished him joy. How long had this happy affair been settled? Not long, he fancied? Not very long; and perhaps Mr Hope did not consider that it was quite made public yet: but Sophia thought that Dr

Levitt ought to know. Dr Levitt thanked her, and said he would try and find Hope in the course of the morning, to congratulate him; and he and Mrs Levitt would give themselves the pleasure of calling on the ladies, very shortly.

"Ritson, how is your wife?" said Sophia, crossing over to speak to a labourer who was on his way up the street.

"A deal better, Miss. She's coming about right nicely!"

"Ah! that is Mr Hope's doing. He attends her, of course."

"Oh, yes, Miss; he's done her a sight o' good."

"Ah! so he always does: but Ritson, if he should not be able to attend to her quite so closely as usual, just now, you will excuse it, when you hear how it is."

"Lord, Miss! the wonder is that he has come at all, so ill as he has been hisself."

"I don't mean that: you will soon see him very well now. He is going to be married, Ritson—"

"What, is he? Well—"

"To my cousin, Miss Ibbotson. He will be more at our house, you know, than anywhere else." And with a wink which was a very good miniature of her mother's Sophia passed on, leaving Ritson to bless Mr Hope and the pretty young lady.

She cast a glance into the butcher's shop as she arrived opposite to it; and her heart leaped up when she saw Mrs James, the lawyer's wife, watching the weighing of a loin of veal.

"You will excuse my interrupting you, Mrs James," said she, from the threshold of the shop: "but we are anxious to know whether Mr James thinks Mrs Enderby really altered of late. We saw him go in last week, and we heard it was to make an alteration in her will."

"I often wonder how things get abroad," said Mrs James, "My husband makes such a particular point of never speaking of such affairs; and I am sure no one ever hears them from me."

"I believe Mrs Enderby told mamma that about the will herself."

"Well, that is as she pleases, of course," said Mrs James, smiling. "What is the weight with the kidney, Mr Jones?"

"We should like so to know," resumed Sophia, "whether Mr James considers Mrs Enderby much altered of late."

"I should think you would be better able to judge than he, Miss Grey; I believe you see her ten times to his once."

"That is the very reason: we see her so often, that a gradual change would be less likely to strike us."

"Mr Hope will give you satisfaction: he must be a better judge than any of us."

"Oh, yes; but we cannot expect him to have eyes for any person but one, at present, you know."

"Oh, so he is going to marry Deborah Giles, after all?"

"Deborah Giles!"

"Yes; was he not said to be engaged to her, some time ago?"

"Deborah Giles! the boatman's daughter! I declare I never heard of such a place as this for gossip! Why, Deborah Giles can barely read and write; and she is beneath Mr Hope in every way. I do not believe he ever spoke to her in his life."

"Oh, well; I do not pretend to know. I heard something about it. Eleven and threepence. Can you change a sovereign, Mr Jones? And, pray, send home the chops immediately."

"It is my cousin, Miss Ibbotson, that Mr Hope is engaged to," said Sophia, unable to refrain from disclosures which she yet saw were not cared for:— "the beautiful Miss Ibbotson, you know."

"Indeed: I am sure somebody said it was Deborah Giles. Then you think, Mr Jones, we may depend upon you for game when the season begins?"

Mr Jones seemed more interested in the news than his customer; he wished Mr Hope all good luck with his pretty lady.

Sophia thought herself fortunate when she saw Mr Enderby turn out of the toy-shop with his youngest nephew, a round-faced boy, still in petticoats, perched upon his shoulder. Mr Enderby bowed, but did not seem to heed her call: he jumped through the turnstile, and proceeded to canter along the church lane amidst the glee of the child so rapidly, that Sophia was obliged to give up the hope of being the first to tell him the news. It was very provoking: she should have liked to see how he would look.

She was sure of a delighted listener in Mrs Howell, to whom no communication ever came amiss: but there was a condition to Mrs Howell's listening—that she should be allowed to tell her own news first. When she found that Sophia wanted to match some worsteds, she and her shop-woman exchanged sympathetic glances—Mrs Howell sighing, with her head on the right side, and Miss Miskin groaning, with her head on the left side.

"Are you ill, Mrs Howell?" asked Sophia.

"It shook me a little, I confess, ma'am, hearing that you wanted worsteds. We have no relief, ma'am, from ladies wanting worsteds."

"No relief, day or night," added Miss Miskin.

"Day or night! Surely you do not sell worsteds in the night-time?" said Sophia.

"Not sell them, ma'am; only match them. The matching them is the trial, I assure you. If you could only hear my agent, ma'am—the things he has to tell about people in my situation—how they are going mad, all over the country, with incessantly matching of worsteds, now that that kind of work is all the fashion. And nothing more likely, ma'am, for there is no getting one's natural rest. I am for ever matching of worsteds in my dreams; and when I wake, I seem to have had no rest: and, as you see, directly after breakfast, ladies come for worsteds."

"And Miss Anderson's messenger left a whole bundle of skeins to be matched for her young ladies, as early as eight this morning," declared Miss Miskin: "and so we go on."

"It will not be for long, I dare say, Mrs Howell. It is a fashionable kind of work, that we may soon grow tired of."

"Dear me, ma'am, think how long former generations went on with it! Think of our grandmothers' work, ma'am, and how we are treading in their steps. We have the beautifulest patterns now, I assure you. Miss Miskin will confirm that we sold one, last week, the very day we had it—the interior of Abbotsford, with Sir Walter, and the furniture, and the dogs, just like life, I assure you."

"That was beautiful," said Miss Miskin, "but not to compare—"

"Oh, dear, no! not to compare, Miss Grey, with one that we were just allowed the sight of—not a mere pattern, but a finished specimen—and I never saw anything so pathetic.—I declare I was quite affected, and so was Miss Miskin. It was 'By the Rivers of Babylon,' most sweetly done! There were the harps all in cross-stitch, ma'am, and the willows all in tent-stitch—I never saw anything so touching."

"I don't think mamma will trouble you for many more worsteds for some time to come, Mrs Howell. When there is going to be a wedding in the family, there is not much time for fancy-work, you know."

"Dear me, a wedding!" smiled Mrs Howell.

"A wedding! Only think!" simpered Miss Miskin.

"Yes: Mr Hope and my cousin Hester are going to be married. I am sure they will have your best wishes, Mrs Howell?"

"That they will, ma'am, as I shall make a point of telling Mr Hope. But Miss Grey, I should think it probable that your mamma may think of working a drawing-room screen, or perhaps a set of rugs, for the young folks; and I assure you, she will see no such patterns anywhere as my agent sends down to me; as I have no doubt you will tell her. And pray, ma'am, where are Mr Hope and his lady to live? I hope they have pleased their fancy with a house?"

"That point is not settled yet. It is a thing which requires some consideration, you know."

"Oh, dear, ma'am! to be sure it does: but I did not mean to be impertinent in asking, I am sure. Only you mentioned making wedding-clothes, Miss Grey."

"I did not mean that we have exactly set about all that yet. I was only looking forward to it."

"And very right too, ma'am. My poor dear Howell used to say so to me, every time he found so much difficulty in inducing me to listen to future projects—about the happy day, you know, ma'am. He was always for looking forward upon principle, dear soul! as you say, ma'am. That is the very brown, ma'am—no doubt of it. Only two skeins, ma'am?"

Here ended Sophia's pleasures in this kind. She could not summon courage to face Mrs Plumstead, without knowing what was the mood of the day; and the half-door of the little stationery shop was closed, and no face was visible within. All her father's household, and all whom she had told, were as busy as herself; so that by the time she walked down the street again, nobody remained to be informed. She could only go home, put off her bonnet, and sit with her mother, watching who would call, and planning the external arrangements which constitute the whole interest of a wedding to narrow minds and apathetic hearts.

No one in Deerbrook enjoyed the news more than Mr Enderby. When he evaded Sophia in the street, he little knew what pleasure she had it in her power to afford him. It was only deferred for a few minutes, however; for, on his returning his little nephew to mamma's side, he found his mother and sister talking the matter over. Mrs Grey's visit to Mrs Enderby had been unusually short, as she could not, on so busy a day, spare much time to one person. The moment she was gone, the old lady rang for her calash and shawl, and prepared to cross the way, telling the news meanwhile to her maid Phoebe. It was a disappointment to find Mrs Rowland already informed: but then came Philip, ignorant and unconscious as could be desired.

The extreme graciousness of his sister guided him in his guess when he was desired to say who was going to be married; but there was a trembling heart beneath his light speech. It was more difficult to disguise his joy when he heard the truth. He carried it off by romping with the child, who owed several rides from corner to corner of the room to the fact that Mr Hope was going to be married to Hester.

"I am delighted to see Philip take it in this way," observed Mrs Rowland.

"I was just thinking the same thing," cried Mrs Enderby; "but I believe I should not have said so if you had not. I was afraid it might be a sad disappointment to poor Philip; and this prevented my saying quite so much as I should have done to Mrs Grey. Now I find it is all right, I shall just call in, and express myself more warmly on my way home."

"I beg Philip's pardon, I am sure," said Mrs Rowland, "for supposing for a moment that he would think of marrying into the Grey connexion. I did him great injustice, I own."

"By no means," said Philip. "Because I did not happen to wish to marry Miss Ibbotson, it does not follow that I should have been wrong if I had. It was feeling this, and a sense of justice to her and myself, which made me refuse to answer your questions, some weeks ago, or to make any promises."

"Well, well: let us keep clear of Mrs Grey's connexions, and then you may talk of them as you please," said the sister, in the complaisance of the hour.

Philip remembered his pledge to himself to uphold Mrs Grey as long as he lived, if she should prove right about Mr Hope and Hester. He began immediately to discharge his obligations to her, avowing that he did not see why her connexion was not as good as his own; that Mrs Grey had many excellent points; that she was a woman of a good deal of sagacity; that she had shown herself capable of strong family attachments; that she had been gracious and kind to himself of late in a degree which he felt he had not deserved; and that he considered that all his family were obliged to her for her neighbourly attentions to his mother. Mrs Enderby seized the occasion of her son's support to say some kind thing of the Greys. It gave her frequent pain to hear them spoken of after Mrs Rowland's usual fashion; but when she was alone with her daughter, she dared not object. Under cover of Mr Rowland's presence occasionally, and to-day of Philip's, she ventured to say that she thought the Greys a very fine family, and kind neighbours to her.

"And much looked up to in Deerbrook," added Philip.

"And a great blessing to their poor neighbours," said his mother.

"Dr Levitt respects them for their conscientious dissent," observed Philip.

"And Mr Hope, who knows them best, says they are a very united family among themselves," declared Mrs Enderby.

Mrs Rowland looked from one to the other as each spoke, and asked whether they were both out of their senses.

"By no means," said Philip; "I never was more in earnest in my life."

"I have always thought just what I now say," protested Mrs Enderby.

"Yes, my dear ma'am," said the daughter, scornfully, "we are all aware of your ways of thinking on some points—of your—"

"Of my mother's love of justice and neighbourly temper," said Philip, giving his little nephew a glorious somerset from his shoulder. "I believe, if we could find my mother's match, the two would be an excellent pair to put into Eddystone lighthouse. They would chat away for a twelvemonth together without ever quarrelling."

"Philip, do let that poor boy alone," said mamma. "You are shaking him to pieces."

"We have both had enough for the present, eh, Ned? Mother, I am at your service, if you are going to call at the Greys."

Mrs Enderby rose with great alacrity.

"Come to me, my pet," cried mamma. "Poor Ned shall rest his head in mamma's lap. There, there, my pet!"

Mamma's pet was not the most agreeable companion to her when they were left alone: he was crying lustily after uncle Philip, for all mamma could say about uncle Philip always tiring him to death.

Chapter Fourteen

Preparing for Home.

The affair proceeded rapidly, as such affairs should do where there is no reason for delay. There was no more talk of Birmingham. The journey which was to have been taken in a few days was not spoken of again. The external arrangements advanced well, so many as there were anxious about this part of the matter, and accomplished in habits of business. Mr Rowland was happy to let the corner-house to Mr Hope, not even taking advantage, as his lady advised, of its being peculiarly fit for a surgeon's residence, from its having a door round the corner (made to be a surgery-door!), to raise the rent. Mr Rowland behaved handsomely about everything, rent, alterations, painting, and papering, and laying out the garden anew. Mr Grey bestirred himself to get the affairs at Birmingham settled; and he was soon enabled to inform Mr Hope that Hester's fortune was ascertained, and that it was smaller than could have been wished. He believed his cousins would have seventy pounds a-year each, and no more. It was some compensation for the mortifying nature of this announcement, that Mr Hope evidently did not care at all about the matter. He was not an ambitious, nor yet a luxurious man: his practice supplied an income sufficient for the ease of young married people, and it was on the increase.

No one seemed to doubt for a moment that Margaret would live with her sister. There was no other home for her; she and Hester had never been parted; there seemed no reason for their parting now, and every inducement for their remaining together. Margaret did not dream of objecting to this: she only made it a condition that fifty pounds of her yearly income should go into the family-stock, thus saving her from obligation to any one for her maintenance. Living was so cheap in Deerbrook, that Margaret was assured that she would render herself quite independent by paying fifty pounds a-year for her share of the household expenses, and reserving twenty for her personal wants.

Both the sisters were surprised to find how much pleasure they took in the preparations for this marriage. They could not have believed it, and, but that they were too happy to feel any kind of contempt, they would have despised themselves for it. But such contempt would have been misplaced. All things are according to the ideas and feelings with which they are connected; and if, as old George Herbert says, dusting a room is an act of religious grace when it is done from a feeling of religious duty, furnishing a house is a process of high enjoyment when it is the preparation of a home for happy love. The dwelling is hung all round with bright anticipations, and crowded with blissful thoughts, spoken by none, perhaps, but present to all. On this table, and by this snug fireside, will the cheerful winter breakfast go forward, when each is about to enter on the gladsome business of the day; and that sofa will be drawn out, and those window-curtains will be closed, when the intellectual pleasures of the evening—the rewards of the laborious day—begin. Those ground-windows will stand open all the summer noon, and the flower stands will be gay and fragrant; and the shaded parlour will be the cool retreat of the wearied husband, when he comes in to rest from his professional toils. There will stand the books destined to refresh and refine his higher tastes; and there the music with which the wife will indulge him. Here will they first feel what it is to have a home of their own—where they will first enjoy the privacy of it, the security, the freedom, the consequence in the eyes of others, the sacredness in their own. Here they will first exercise the graces of hospitality, and the responsibility of control. Here will they feel that they have attained the great resting-place of their life—the resting-place of their individual lot, but only the starting-point of their activity. Such is the work of furnishing a house once in a lifetime. It may be a welcome task to the fine lady, decking her drawing-room anew, to gratify her ambition, or divert her *ennui*—it may be a satisfactory labour to the elderly couple, settling themselves afresh when their children are dispersed abroad, and it becomes necessary to discard the furniture that the boys have battered and spoiled—it may be a refined amusement to the selfish man of taste, wishing to prolong or recall the pleasures of foreign travel; but to none is it the conscious delight that it is to young lovers and their sympathising friends, whether the scene be the two rooms of the hopeful young artisan, about to bring home his bride from service; or the palace of a nobleman, enriched with intellectual luxuries for the lady of his adoration; or the quiet abode of an unambitious professional man, whose aim is privacy and comfort.

Margaret's delight in the process of preparation was the most intense of all that was felt, except perhaps by one person. Mrs Grey and Sophia enjoyed the bustle, and the consequence, and the exercise of their feminine talents, and the gossip of the village, and the spitefulness of Mrs Rowland's criticisms, when she had recovered from her delight at her brother's escape from Hester, and had leisure to be offended at Mr Hope's marrying into the Grey connexion so decidedly. The children relished the mystery of buying their presents secretly, and hiding them from their cousins, till the day before the wedding. Sydney was proud to help Margaret in training the chrysanthemums, putting the garden into winter trim, and in planting round the walls of the surgery with large evergreens. Mr Grey came down almost every evening to suggest and approve; and Morris left her needle (now busy from morning till night in Hester's service) to admire, and to speak her wishes, when desired, about the preparations in her department. Morris, another maid, and a foot-boy, were the only servants; and Morris was to have everything as she liked best for her own region. But Margaret was as eager and interested as all the rest together. Her heart was light for her sister; and for the first time since she was capable of thought, she believed that Hester was going to be happy. Her own gain was almost too great for gratitude: a home, a brother, and relief from the responsibility of her sister's peace—as often as she thought of these blessings, she looked almost as bright as Hester herself.

How was Mr Hope, all this while? Well, and growing happier every day. He believed himself a perfectly happy man, and looked back with wonder to the struggle which it had cost him to accept his present lot. He was not only entirely recovered from his accident before the rich month of October came in, but truly thankful for it as the means of bringing to his knowledge, sooner at least, the devoted affection which he had inspired. It cannot but be animating, flattering, delightful to a man of strong domestic tendencies, to know himself the object of the exclusive attachment of a strong-minded and noble-hearted woman: and when, in addition to this, her society affords the delight of mental accomplishment and personal beauty, such as Hester's, he must be a churl indeed if he does not greatly enjoy the present, and indulge in sweet anticipations for the future. Hope also brought the whole power of his will to bear upon his circumstances. He dwelt upon all the happiest features of his lot; and, in his admiration of Hester, thought as little as he could of Margaret. He had the daily delight of seeing how he constituted the new-born happiness of her whose life was to be devoted to him: he heard of nothing but rejoicings and blessings, and fully believed himself the happy man that every one declared him. He dwelt on the prospect of a home full of domestic attachment, of rational pursuit, of intellectual resource; and looked forward to a life of religious usefulness, of vigorous devotedness to others, of which he trusted that his first act of self-sacrifice and its consequences were the earnest and the pledge. He had never for a moment repented what he had done; and now, when he hastily recurred to the struggle it had cost him, it was chiefly to moralise on the short-sightedness of men in their wishes, and to be grateful for his own present satisfaction. A few cold misgivings had troubled him, and continued to trouble him, if Hester at any time looked at all less bright and serene than usual: but he concluded that these were merely the cloud-shadows which necessarily chequer all the sunshine of this world. He told himself that when two human beings become closely dependent on each other, their peace must hang upon the variations in one another's moods; and that moods must vary in all mortals. He persuaded himself that this was a necessary consequence of the relation, and to be received as a slight set-off against the unfathomable blessings of sympathy. He concluded that he had deceived himself about his feelings for Margaret: he must have been mistaken; for he could now receive from her the opening confidence of a sister; he could cordially agree to the arrangement of her living with them; he could co-operate with her in the preparation for the coming time, without any emotion which was inconsistent with his duty to Hester. With unconscious prudence, he merely said this to himself, and let it pass, reverting to his beautiful, his happy, his own Hester, and the future years over which her image spread its sunshine. The one person who relished the task of preparation more than Margaret herself was Hope. Every advance in the work seemed to bring him nearer to the source of the happiness he felt. Every day of which they marked the lapse appeared to open wider the portals of that home which he was now more than ever habituated to view as the sanctuary of duty, of holiness, and of peace. All remarked on Mr Hope's altered looks. The shyness and coldness with which he had seemed to receive the first congratulations on his engagement, and which excited wonder in many, and uneasiness in a few, had now given place to a gaiety only subdued by a more tender happiness. Even Mrs Grey need no longer watch his countenance and manner, and weigh his words with anxiety, and try to forget that there was a secret between them.

One ground of Mr Hope's confidence was Hester's candour. She had truly told her sister, she felt it was no time for pride when he offered himself to her. Her pride was strong; but there was something in her as much stronger in force than her pride as it was higher in its nature; and she had owned her love with a frankness which had commanded his esteem as much as it engaged his generosity. She had made a no less open avowal of her faults to him. She had acknowledged the imperfections of her temper (the sorest of her troubles) both at the outset of their engagement, and often since. At first, the confession was made in an undoubting confidence that she should be reasonable, and amiable, and serene henceforth for ever, while she had him by her side. Subsequent experience had moderated this confidence into a hope that, by his example, and under his guidance, she should be enabled to surmount her failings. He shared this hope with her; pledged himself to her and to himself to forbear as he would be forborne; to aid her, and to honour her efforts; and he frequently declared, for his own satisfaction and hers, that all must be safe between them while such generous candour was the foundation of their intercourse,—a generosity and candour in whose noble presence superficial failings of temper were as nothing. He admitted that her temper was not perfect; and he must ever remember his own foreknowledge of this: but he must also bear in mind whence this foreknowledge was derived, and pay everlasting honour to the greatness of soul to which he owed it.

An early day in December was fixed for the marriage, and no cause of delay occurred. There happened to be no patients so dangerously ill as to prevent Mr Hope's absence for his brief wedding trip; the work-people were as nearly punctual as could be expected, and the house was all but ready. The wedding was really to take place, therefore, though Mrs Rowland gave out that in her opinion the engagement had been a surprisingly short one; that she hoped the young people knew what they were about, while all their friends were in such a hurry; that it was a wretched time of year for a wedding; and that, in her opinion, it would have been much pleasanter to wait for fine spring weather.

As it happened, the weather was finer than it had been almost any day of the preceding spring. The day before the wedding was sunny and mild as an October morning, and the fires seemed to be blazing more for show than use. When Mr Hope dropped in at the Greys', at two o'clock, he found the family dining. It was a fancy of Mrs Grey's to dine early on what she considered busy days. An early dinner was, with her, a specific for the despatch of business. On this day, the arrangement was rather absurd; for the great evil of the time was, that everything was done, except what could not be transacted till the evening; and the hours were actually hanging heavy on the hands of some members of the family. Morris had packed Hester's clothes for her little journey, and put out of sight all the mourning of both sisters, except what they actually had on. Sophia's dress for the next morning was laid out, in readiness to be put on, and the preparations for the breakfast were as complete as they could be twenty hours beforehand. It only remained to take a final view of the house in the evening (when the children's presents were to be discovered), and to cut the wedding-cake. In the interval, there was nothing to be done. Conversation flagged; every one was dull; and it was a relief to the rest when Mr Hope proposed to Hester to take a walk.

Mrs Rowland would have laughed at the idea of a walk on a December afternoon, if she had happened to know of the circumstance; but others than lovers might have considered it pleasant. The sun was still an hour from its setting; and high in the pale heaven was the large moon, ready to shine upon the fields and woods, and shed a milder day. No frost had yet bound up the earth; it had only stripped the trees with a touch as gentle as that of the fruit-gatherer. No wintry gusts had yet swept through the woods; and all there was this day as still as in the autumn noon, when the nut is heard to drop upon the fallen leaves, and the light squirrel is startled at the rustle along its own path. As a matter of course, the lovers took their way to the Spring in the Vernon woods, the spot which had witnessed more of their confidence than any other. In the alcove above it they had taken shelter from the summer storm and the autumn shower; they had sat on its brink for many an hour, when the pure depths of its rocky basin seemed like coolness itself in the midst of heat, and when falling leaves fluttered down the wind, and dimpled the surface of the water. They now paused once more under shelter of the rock which overhung one side of the basin, and listened to the trickle of the spring. If "aside the devil turned for envy" in the presence of the pair in Paradise, it might be thought that he would take flight from this scene also; from the view of this resting of the lovers on their marriage eve, when the last sun of their separate lives was sinking, and the separate business of their existence was finished, and their paths had met before the gate of their paradise, and they were only waiting for the portal to open to them. But there was that on Hester's brow which would have made the devil look closer. She was discomposed, and her replies to what was said were brief, and not much to the purpose. After a few moments' silence, Mr Hope said gaily—

"There is something on our minds, Hester. Come, what is it?"

"Do not say 'our minds.' You know you never have anything on yours. I believe it is against your nature; and I know it is against your principles. Do not say 'our minds.'"

"I say it because it is true. I never see you look grave but my heart is as heavy—. But never mind that. What is the matter, love?"

"Nothing," sighed Hester. "Nothing that any one can help—. People may say what they will, Edward: but there can be no escape from living alone in this world, after all."

"What *do* you mean?"

"I mean what no one, not even you, can gainsay. I mean that 'the heart knoweth its own bitterness;' that we have disappointments, and anxieties, and remorse, and many, many kinds of trouble that we can never tell to any human being—that none have any concern with—that we should never dare to tell. We must be alone in the world, after all."

"Where is your faith, while you feel so?" asked Edward, smiling. "Do you really think that confidence proceeds only while people believe each other perfect,—while they have not anxieties, and disappointments, and remorse? Do you not feel that our faults, or rather our failures, bind us together?"

"Our faults bind us together!" exclaimed Hester. "Oh how happy I should be, if I could think that!"

"We cannot but think it. We shall find it so, love, every day. When our faith fails, when we are discouraged, instead of fighting the battle with our faithlessness alone, we shall come to one another for courage, for stimulus, for help to see the bright, the true side of everything."

"That supposes that we can do so," said Hester, sadly. "But I cannot. I have all my life intended to repose entire confidence, and I have never done it yet."

"Yes: you have in me. You cannot help it. You think that you cannot, only because you mean more by reposing confidence than others do. Your spirit is too noble, too ingenuous, too humble for concealment. You cannot help yourself, Hester: you have fully confided in me, and you will go on to do so."

Hester shook her head mournfully. "I have done it hitherto with you, and with you only," said she: "and the mason has been—you know the reason—the same which made me own all to you, that first evening in the shrubbery. Ah! I see you think that this is a lasting security; that, as you will never change, I never shall: but you do not understand me wholly yet. There is something that you do not know,—that I cannot make you believe: but you will find it true, when it is too late. No good influence is permanent with me; many, all have been tried; and the evil that is in me gets the better of them all at last."

She snatched her hand from her lover's, and covered her face to hide her tears.

"I shall not contradict you, Hester," said he, tenderly, "because you will only abase yourself the more in your own eyes. But tell me again—where is your faith, while you let spectres from the past glide over into the future, to terrify you? I say 'you' and not 'us,' because I am not terrified. I fear nothing. I trust you, and I trust Him who brought us together, and moved you to lay open your honest heart to me."

"My sick heart, Edward. It is sick with fear. I thought I had got over it. I thought you had cured it; and that now, on this day, of all days, I should have been full of your spirit—of the spirit which made me so happy a few weeks ago, that I was sure I should never fall back again. But I am disappointed in myself, Edward—wholly disappointed in myself. I have often been so before, but this time it is fatal. I shall never make you happy, Edward."

"Neither God nor man requires it of you, Hester. Dismiss it—."

"Oh, hear me!" cried Hester, in great agitation. "I vowed to devote myself to my father's happiness, when my mother died; I promised to place the most absolute confidence in him. I failed. I fancied miserable things. I fancied he loved Margaret better; and that I was not necessary to him; and I was too proud, too selfish, to tell him so: and when he was dying, and commended Margaret and me to each other—Oh, so solemnly!—I am sure it was in compassion to me—and I shrank from it, even at that moment. When we came here, and Margaret and I felt ourselves alone among strangers, we promised the same confidence I vowed to my father. The next thing was—perhaps you saw it—I grew jealous of Margaret's having another friend, though Maria was as ready to be my friend as hers, if I had only been worthy of it. Up to this hour—at this very moment, I believe I am jealous of Maria—and with Margaret before my eyes—Margaret, who loves me as her own soul, and yet has never felt one moment's jealousy of you, I am certain, if her heart was known."

"We will rejoice, then, in Margaret's peace of mind, the reward of her faith."

"Oh, so I do! I bless God that she is rewarded, better than by me. But you see how it is. You see how I poison every one's life. I never made anybody happy! I never shall make anyone happy!"

"Let us put the thought of making happiness out of our minds altogether," said Hope. "I am persuaded that half the misery in the world comes of straining after happiness."

"After our own," said Hester. "I could give up my own. But yours! I cannot put yours out of my thoughts."

"Yes, you can; and you will when you give your faith fair play. Why cannot you trust God with my happiness as well as your own? And why cannot you trust me to do without happiness, if it be necessary, as well as yourself?"

"I know," said Hester, "that you are as willing to forego all for me as I am for you; but I cannot, I dare not, consent to the risk. Oh, Edward! if ever you wished to give me ease, do what I ask now! Give me up! I shall make you wretched. Give me up, Edward!"

Hope's spirit was for one instant wrapped in storm. He recoiled from the future, and at the moment of recoil came this offer of release. One moment's thought of freedom, one moment's thought of Margaret convulsed his soul; but before he could speak the tempest had passed away. Hester's face, frightfully agitated, was upraised: his countenance seemed heavenly to her when he smiled upon her, and replied—

"I will not. You are mine; and, as I said before, all our failures, all our heart-sickness, must bind us the more to each other."

"Then you must sustain me—you must cure me—you must do what no one has ever yet been able to do. But above all, Edward, you must never, happen what may, cast me off."

"That is, as you say, what no one has ever been able to do," said he, smiling. "Your father's tenderness was greatest at the last; and Margaret loves you, you know, as her own soul. Let us avoid promises, but let us rest upon these truths. And now," continued he, as he drew nearer to her, and made his shoulder a resting-place for her throbbing head, "I have heard your thoughts for the future. Will you hear mine?"

Hester made an effort to still her weeping.

"I said just now, that I believe half the misery in our lives is owing to straining after happiness; and I think, too, that much of our sin is owing to our disturbing ourselves too much about our duty. Instead of yielding a glad obedience from hour to hour, it is the weakness of many of us to stretch far forward into the future, which is beyond our present reach, and torment ourselves with apprehensions of sin, which we should be ashamed of if they related to pain and danger."

"Oh, if you could prove to me that such is my weakness!" cried Hester.

"I believe that it is yours, and I know that it is my own, my Hester. We must watch over one another. Tell me, is it not faithless to let our hearts be troubled about *any* possible evil which we cannot, at the moment of the trouble, prevent? And are we not sacrificing, what is, at the time, of the most importance—our repose of mind, the holiness, the religion of the hour?"

"I know I have defiled the holiness of this hour," said Hester, humbly. "But as my thoughts were troubled, was it not better to speak them? I could not but speak them."

"You cannot but do and speak what is most honourable, and true, and generous, Hester; and that is the very reason why I would fain have you trust, for the future as well as the present, to the impulse of the hour. Surely, love, the probation of the hour is enough for the strength of every one of us."

"Far, far too much for me."

"At times, too much for all. Well, then, what have we to do? To rest the care of each other's happiness upon Him whose care it is: to be ready to do without it, as we would hold ourselves ready to do without this, or that, or the other comfort, or supposed means of happiness. Depend upon it, this happiness is too subtle and too divine a thing for our management. We have nothing to do with it but to enjoy it when it comes. Men say of it—

'Lo! it is here!'—'Lo! there!'—but never has man laid hold of it with a voluntary grasp."

"But we can banish it," said Hester.

"Alas! yes: and what else do we do at the very moment when we afflict ourselves about the future? Surely our business is to keep our hearts open for it—holy and at peace, from moment to moment, from day to day."

"And yet, is it not our privilege—said at least to be so—to look before and after? I am not sure, however, that I always think this a privilege. I long sometimes to be any bird of the air, that I might live for the present moment alone."

"Let us be so far birds of the air—free as they, neither toiling nor spinning out anxious thoughts for the future: but why, with all this, should we not use our human privilege of looking before and after, to enrich and sanctify the present? Should we enjoy the wheat-fields in June as we do if we knew nothing of seed-time, and had never heard of harvest? And how should you and I feel at this moment, sitting here, if we had no recollection of walks in shrubberies, and no prospect of a home, and a lifetime to spend in it, to make this moment sacred? Look at those red-breasts: shall we change lots with them?"

"No, no: let us look forward; but how? We cannot persuade ourselves that we are better than we are, for the sake of making the future bright."

"True: and therefore it must be God's future, and not our own, that we must look forward to."

"That is for confessors and martyrs," said Hester. "They can look peacefully before and after, when there is a bright life and a world of hopes lying behind; and nothing around and before them but ignominy and poverty, or prison, or torture, or death. They can do this: but not such as I. God's future is enough for them—the triumph of truth and holiness; but—."

"And I believe it would be enough for you in their situation, Hester. I believe you could be a martyr for opinion. Why cannot you and I brave the suffering of our own faults as we would meet sickness or bereavement from Heaven, and torture and death from men?"

"Is this the prospect in view of which you marry me?"

"It is the prospect in view of which all of us are ever living, since we are all faulty, and must all suffer. But marriage justifies a holier and happier anticipation. The faults of human beings are temporary features of their prospect: their virtues are the firm ground under their feet, and the bright arch over their heads. Is it not so?"

"If so, how selfish, how ungrateful have I been in making myself and you so miserable! But I do so fear myself!"

"Let us fear nothing, but give all our care to the day and the hour. I am confident that this is the true obedience, and the true wisdom. If the temper of the hour is right, nothing is wrong."

"And I am sure, if the temper of the hour is wrong, nothing is right. If one could always remember this——."

"If we could always remember this, we should perhaps find ourselves a little above the angels, instead of being, like the serene, the Fénélons of our race, a little below them. We shall not always remember it, love; but we must remind each other as faithfully as may be."

"You must bring me here, when I forget," said Hester. "This spring will always murmur the truth to me—'If the temper of the hour is right nothing is wrong.' How wrong has my temper been within this hour!"

"Let it pass, my Hester. We are all faithless at times, and without the excuse of meek and anxious love. Is it possible that the moon casts that shadow?"

"The dark, dark hour is gone," said Hester, smiling as she looked up, and the moon shone on her face. "Nothing is wrong. Who would have believed, an hour ago, that I should now say so?"

"When you would have given me up," said Hope, smiling. "Oh, let us forget it all! Let us go somewhere else. Who will say this is winter? Is it October, or 'the first mild day of March?' It might be either."

"There is not a breath to chill us; and these leaves—what a soft autumn carpet they make! They have no wintry crispness yet."

There was one inexhaustible subject to which they now recurred—Mr Hope's family. He told over again, what Hester was never weary of hearing, how his sisters would cherish her, whenever circumstances should allow them to meet—how Emily and she would suit best, but how Anne would look up to her. As for Frank—. But this representation of what Frank would say, and think, and do, was somewhat checked and impaired by the recollection that Frank was just about this time receiving the letter in which Margaret's superiority to Hester was pretty plainly set forth. The answer to that letter would arrive, some time or other, and the anticipated awkwardness of that circumstance caused some unpleasant feelings at this moment, as it had often done before, during the last few weeks. Nothing could be easier than to set the matter right with Frank, as was already done with Emily and Anne; the first letter might occasion some difficulty. Frank was passed over lightly, and the foreground of the picture of family welcome was occupied by Emily and Anne.

It was almost an hour from their leaving the Spring before the lovers reached home. They were neither cold nor tired; they were neither merry nor sad. The traces of tears were on Hester's face; but even Margaret was satisfied when she saw her leaning on Edward's arm, receiving the presents of the children where alone the children would present them—in the new house. There was no fancy about the arrangements, no ceremony about the cake and the ring, to which Hester did not submit with perfect grace. Notwithstanding the traces of her tears, she had never looked so beautiful.

The same opinion was repeated the next morning by all the many who saw her in church, or who caught a glimpse of her, in her way to and from it. No wedding was ever kept a secret in Deerbrook; and Mr Hope's was the one in which concealment was least of all possible. The church was half full, and the path to the church-door was lined with gazers. Those who were obliged to remain at home looked abroad from their doors; so that all were gratified more or less. Every one on Mr Grey's premises had a holiday—including Miss Young, though Mrs Rowland did not see why her children should lose a day's instruction, because a distant cousin of Mr Grey's was married. The marriage was made far too much a fuss of for her taste; and she vowed that whenever she parted with her own Matilda, there should be a much greater refinement in the mode. Every one else appeared satisfied. The sun shone; the bells rang; and the servants drank the health of the bride and bridegroom. Margaret succeeded in swallowing her tears, and was, in her inmost soul, thankful for Hester and herself. The letters to Mr Hope's sisters and brother, left open for the signatures of Edward and Hester Hope, were closed and despatched; and the news was communicated to two or three of the Ibbotsons' nearest friends at Birmingham. Mr and Mrs Grey agreed, at the end of the day, that a wedding was, to be sure, a most fatiguing affair for quiet people like themselves; but that nothing could have gone off better.

Chapter Fifteen

Maria and Margaret.

Mr Hope's professional duties would not permit him to be long absent, even on such an occasion as his wedding journey. The young couple went only to Oxford, and were to return in a week. Margaret thought that this week never would be over. It was not only that she longed for rest in a home once more, and was eager to repose upon her new privilege of having a brother: she was also anxious about Hester,—anxious to be convinced, by the observation of the eye and the hearing of the ear, that her sister was enjoying that peace of spirit which reason seemed to declare must be hers. It would be difficult to determine how much Margaret's attachment to her sister was deepened and strengthened by the incessant solicitude she had felt for her, ever since this attachment had grown out of the companionship of their childhood. She could scarcely remember the time when she had not been in a state of either hope or fear for Hester;—hope that, in some new circumstances, she would be happy at last; or dread lest these new circumstances should fail, as all preceding influences had failed. If Hester had been less candid and less generous than she was, her sister's affection might have given way under the repeated trials and disappointments it had had to sustain; and there were times when Margaret's patience *had* given way, and she had for a brief while wished, and almost resolved, that she could and would regard with indifference the state of mind of one who was not reasonable, and who seemed incapable of being contented. But such resolutions of indifference dissolved before her sister's next manifestations of generosity, or appeals to the forgiveness of those about her. Margaret always ended by supposing herself the cause of the evil; that she had been inconsiderate; that she could not allow sufficiently for a sensitiveness greater than her own; and above all, that she was not fully worthy of such affection as Hester's—not sufficient for such a mind and heart. She had looked forward, with ardent expectation when she was happiest, and with sickly dread when she was depressed, to the event of Hester's marriage, as that which must decide whether she could be happy, or whether her life was to be throughout the scene of conflict that its opening years had been. Hester's connexion was all that she could have desired, and far beyond her utmost hopes. This brother-in-law was one of a thousand—one whom she was ready to consider a good angel sent to shed peace over her sister's life: and during the months of her engagement, she had kept anxiety at bay, and resigned herself to the delights of gratitude and of sweet anticipations, and to the satisfaction of feeling that her own responsibilities might be considered at an end. She had delivered Hester's happiness over into the charge of one who would cherish it better and more successfully than she had done; and she could not but feel the relief of the freedom she had gained: but neither could she repress her anxiety to know, at the outset, whether all was indeed as well as she had till now undoubtingly supposed that it would be.

Margaret's attachment to her sister would have been in greater danger of being worn out but for the existence of a closer sympathy between them than any one but themselves, and perhaps Morris, was aware of. Margaret had a strong suspicion that in Hester's place her temper would have been exactly what Hester's was in its least happy characteristics. She had tendencies to jealousy; and if not to morbid self-study, and to dissatisfaction with present circumstances, she was indebted for this, she knew, to her being occupied with her sister, and yet more to the perpetual warning held up before her eyes. This conviction generated no sense of superiority in Margaret—interfered in no degree with the reverence she entertained for Hester, a reverence rather enhanced than impaired by the tender compassion with which she regarded her mental conflicts and sufferings. Every movement of irritability in herself (and she was conscious of many) alarmed and humbled her, but, at the same time, enabled her better to make allowance for her sister; and every harsh word and unreasonable mood of Hester's, by restoring her to her self-command and stimulating her magnanimity, made her sensible that she owed much of her power over herself to that circumstance which kept the necessity of it perpetually before her mind. For the same reason that men hate those whom they have injured, Margaret loved with unusual fervour the sister with whom she had to forbear. For the same reason that the children, even the affectionate children, of tyrannical or lax parents, love liberty and conscientiousness above all else, Margaret was in practice gentle, long-suffering, and forgetful of self. For the same reason that the afflicted are looked upon by the pure-minded as sacred, Margaret regarded her sister with a reverence which preserved her patience from being spent, and her attachment from wasting away.

The first letter from her brother and sister had been opened in great internal agitation. All was well, however. It was certain that all was well; for, while Hester said not one word about being happy, she was full of thought for others. She knew that Margaret meant to take possession of the corner-house, to "go home," a few days before the arrival of the travellers, in order to make all comfortable for them. Hester begged that she would take care to be well amused during these few days. Perhaps she might induce Maria Young to waive the ceremony of being first invited by the real housekeepers, and to spend as much time as she could with her friend. "Give my kind regards to Maria," said the letter, "and tell her I like to fancy you two passing a long evening by that fireside where we all hope we shall often have the pleasure of seeing her." Six months ago Hester would not have spoken so freely and so kindly of Maria: she would not have so sanctioned Margaret's intimacy with her. All was right, and Margaret was happy.

Maria came, and, thanks to the holiday spirit of a wedding week, for a long day. Delicious are the pleasures of those whose appetite for them is whetted by abstinence. Charming, wholly charming, was this day to Maria, spent in quiet, free from the children, free from the observation of other guests, passed in all external luxury, and in sister-like confidence with the friend to whom she had owed some of the best pleasures of the last year. Margaret was no less happy in indulging her, and in opening much more of her heart to her than she could to any one else since Hester married—which now, at the end of six days, seemed a long time ago.

Miss Young came early, that she might see the house, and everything in it, before dark; and the days were now at their shortest. She did not mind the fatigue of mounting to the very top of the house. She must see the view from the window of Morris's attic. Yesterday's fall of snow had made the meadows one sheet of white; and the river looked black, and the woods somewhat frowning and dismal; but those who knew the place so well could imagine what all this must be in summer; and Morris was assured that her room was the pleasantest in the house. Morris curtseyed and smiled, and did not say how cold and dreary a wide landscape appeared to her, and how much better she should have liked to look out upon a street, if only Mr Hope had happened to have been settled in Birmingham. She pointed out to Maria how good Miss Hester had been, in thinking about the furnishing of this attic. She had taken the trouble to have the pictures of Morris's father and mother, which had always hung opposite her bed at Birmingham, brought hither, and fixed up in the same place. The bed-hangings had come, too; so that, except for its being so much lighter, and the prospect from the window so different, it was almost like the same room she had slept in for three-and-twenty years before. When Maria looked at "the pictures"—silhouettes taken from shadows on the wall, with numerous little deformities and disproportions incident to that method of taking likenesses—she appreciated Hester's thoughtfulness; though she fully agreed in what Margaret said, that if Morris was willing to leave a place where she had lived so many years, for the sake of remaining with Hester and her, it was the least they could do to make her feel as much at home as possible in her new abode.

Margaret's own chamber was one of the prettiest rooms in the house, with its light green paper, its French bed and toilet at one end, and the book-case, table and writing-desk, footstool and armchair, at the other.

"I shall spend many hours alone here in the bright summer mornings," said Margaret. "Here I shall write my letters, and study, and think."

"And nod over your books, perhaps," said Maria. "These seem comfortable arrangements for an old or infirm person; but I should be afraid they would send you to sleep. You have had little experience of being alone: do you know the strong tendency that solitary people have to napping?"

Margaret laughed. She had never slept in the daytime in her life, except in illness. She could not conceive of it, in the case of a young person, full of occupation, with a hundred things to think about, and twenty books at a time that she wanted to read. She thought that regular daily solitude must be the most delightful, the most improving thing in the world. She had always envied the privilege of people who could command solitude; and now, for the first time in her life, she was going to enjoy it, and try to profit by it.

"You began yesterday, I think," said Maria. "How did you like it?"

"It was no fair trial. I felt restless at having the house in my charge; and I was thinking of Hester perpetually; and then I did not know but that some of the Greys might come in at any moment: and besides, I was so busy considering whether I was making the most of the precious hours, that I really did next to nothing all day."

"But you looked sadly tired at night, Miss Margaret," said Morris. "I never saw you more fit for bed after any party or ball."

Maria smiled. She knew something of the fatigues, as well as the pleasures, of solitude. Margaret smiled too; but she said it would be quite another thing when the family were settled, and when it should have become a habit to spend the morning hours alone; and to this Maria fully agreed.

Morris thought that people's liking or not liking to be alone depended much on their having easy or irksome thoughts in their minds. Margaret answered gaily, that in that case, she was pretty sure of liking solitude. She was made grave by a sigh and a shake of the head from Morris.

"Morris, what do you mean?" said Margaret, apprehensively. "Why do you sigh and shake your head? Why should not I have easy thoughts as often as I sit in that chair?"

"We never know, Miss Margaret, my dear, how things will turn out. Do you remember Miss Stevenson, that married a gentleman her family all thought a great deal of, and he turned out a swindler, and—?"

The girls burst out a-laughing, and Maria assured Morris that she could answer for no accident of that kind happening with regard to Mr Hope. Morris laughed too, and said she did not mean that, but only that she never saw anybody more confident of everything going right than Miss Stevenson and all her family; and within a month after the wedding, they were in the deepest distress. That was what she meant: but there were many other ways of distress happening.

"There is death, my dears," she said. "Remember death, Miss Margaret."

"Indeed, Morris, I do," said Margaret. "I never thought so much of death as I have done since Mr Hope's accident, when I believed death was coming to make us all miserable; and the more I have since recoiled from it, the oftener has the thought come back."

"That is all right, my dear: all very natural. It does not seem natural to undertake any great new thing in life, without reminding one's self of the end that must come to all our doings. However, I trust my master and mistress, and you, have many a happy year to live."

"I like those words, Morris. I like to hear you speak of your master and mistress, it has such a domestic sound! Does it not make one feel at home, Maria? Yes, Morris, there I shall sit, and feel so at ease! so at home, once more!"

"But there may be other—." Morris stopped, and changed her mood. She stepped to the closet, and opened the door, to show Miss Young the provision of shelves and pegs; and pointed out the part of the room where she had hoped there would be a sofa. She should have liked that Miss Margaret should have had a sofa to lie down on when she pleased. It seemed to her the only thing wanting. Margaret gaily declared that nothing was wanting. She had never seen a room more entirely to her taste, though she had inhabited some that were grander.

By the time the little breakfast-room had been duly visited, and it had been explained that the other small parlour must necessarily be kept for a waiting-room for Mr Hope's patients, and the young ladies had returned to the drawing-room, Maria was in full flow of sympathy with the housekeeping interests and ideas which occupied, or rather amused, her companion. Women do inevitably love housekeeping, unless educational or other impediments interfere with their natural tastes. Household management is to them the object of their talents, the subject of their interests, the vehicle of their hopes and fears, the medium through which their affections are manifested, and much of their benevolence gratified. If it be true, as has been said, that there is no good quality of a woman's heart and mind which is not necessary to perfect housekeeping, it follows that there is no power of the mind or affection of the heart which may not be gratified in the course of its discharge. As Margaret and her guest enjoyed their pheasant, their table drawn close to the sofa and the fire, that Maria might be saved the trouble of moving, their talk was of tradespeople, of shopping at Deerbrook, and the market at Birmingham; of the kitchen and store-room, and the winter and summer arrangements of the table. The foot-boy, whom Margaret was teaching to wait, often forgot his function, and stood still to listen, and at last left the room deeply impressed with the wisdom of his instructor and her guest. When the dinner and the wine were gone, they sang, they gossiped, they quizzed. The Greys were sacred, of course; but many an anecdote came out, told honestly and with good-nature, of dear old Mrs Enderby, and her talent for being pleased; of Mrs Rowland's transactions abroad and at home—all regulated by the principle of eclipsing the Greys; and of Mrs Howell's and Miss Miskin's fine sentiments, and extraordinary pieces of news. Margaret produced some of her brother-in-law's outlines, which she had picked up and preserved—sketches of the children, in the oddest attitudes of children—of Dr Levitt, resting his book on the end of his nose, as he read in his study-chair—of Mrs Plumstead, exasperated by the arrival of an illegible letter—of almost every oddity in the place. Then out came the pencils, and the girls supplied omissions. They sketched Mr Hope himself, listening to an old woman's theory of her own case; they sketched each other. Mr Enderby was almost the only person omitted altogether, in conversation and on paper.

"Where can I have hidden my work bag?" asked Maria, after tea.

"You laid it beside you, and I put it away," said Margaret. "I wanted to see whether you could spend a whole afternoon without the feel of your thimble. You shall have it again now, for you never once asked for it between dinner and tea."

"I forgot it: but now you must give it me. I must finish my collar, or I shall not duly honour your sister in my first call. We can talk as well working as idle."

"Cannot I help you? Our affairs are all in such dreadfully perfect order, that I have not a stitch of work to do. I see a hole in your glove: let me mend it."

"Do; and when you have done that, there is the other. Two years hence, how you will wonder that there ever was a time when you had not a stitch of work in the house! Wedding clothes last about two years, and then they all wear out together. I wish you joy of the work you will have to do then—if nothing should come between you and it."

"What should come between us and it?" said Margaret, struck by the tone in which Maria spoke the last words. "Are you following Morris's lead? Are you going to say,—'Remember death, Miss Margaret?'"

"Oh, no; but there are other things which happen sometimes besides death. I beg your pardon, Margaret, if I am impertinent—"

"How should you be impertinent? You, the most intimate friend but one that I have in the world! You mean marriage of course; that I may marry within these same two years? Any one may naturally say so, I suppose, to a girl whose sister is just married: and in another person's case it would seem to me probable enough, but I assure you, Maria, I do not feel as if it was at all likely that I should marry."

"I quite believe you, Margaret. I have no doubt you feel so, and that you will feel so till—. But, dear, you may one day find yourself feeling very differently without a moment's warning; and that day may happen within two years. Such things have been known."

"If there was any one—" said Margaret, simply—"if I had ever seen any one for whom I could fancy myself feeling as Hester did—"

"If there was any one!"—repeated Maria, looking up in some surprise. "My dear Margaret, do you mean to say there is no one?"

"Yes, I do; I think so. I know what you mean, Maria. I understand your face and your voice. But I do think it is very hard that one cannot enjoy a pleasant friendship with anybody without seeing people on the watch for something more. It is so very painful to have such ideas put into one's mind, to spoil all one's intercourse—to throw restraint over it—to mix up selfishness with it! It is so wrong to interfere between those who might and would be the most useful and delightful companions to each other, without having a thought which need put constraint between them! Those who so interfere have a great deal to answer for. They do not know what mischief they may be doing—what pain they may be giving while they are gossiping, and making remarks to one another about what they know nothing at all about. I have no patience with such meddling!"

"So I perceive, indeed," replied Maria, somewhat amused. "But, Margaret, you have been enlarging a good deal on what I said. Not a syllable was spoken about any remarks, any observations between any people; or even about reference to any particular person. I alone must be subject to all this displeasure, and even I did not throw out a single hint about any friend of yours."

"No, you did not; that is all very true," said Margaret, blushing: "but neither was I vexed with you;—at least, not so much as with some others. I was hasty."

"You were, indeed," said Maria, laughing. "I never witnessed such an outburst from you before."

"And you shall not see such another; but I was answering less what you said than what I have reason to suppose is in the minds of several other people."

"In their minds? They have not told you their thoughts, then. And *several* other people, too! Why, Margaret, I really think it is not very reasonable in you to find fault with others for thinking something which they have not troubled you to listen to, and which is so natural, that it has struck 'several' of them. Surely, Margaret, you must be a little, just a very little, touchy upon the matter."

"Touchy! What should make me touchy?"

"Ay, what?"

"I do assure you, Maria, nothing whatever has passed between that person and me which has anything more than the commonest— No, I will not say the commonest friendship, because I believe ours is a very warm and intimate friendship; but indeed it is nothing more. You may be sure that, if it had been otherwise, I should not have said a word upon the whole matter, even to you; and I would not have allowed even you to speak ten words to me about it. Are you satisfied now?"

"I am satisfied that you any what you think."

"Oh, Maria! what a sigh! If you have no objection, I should like to know the meaning of that sigh."

"I was thinking of 'the course of true love.'"

"But not that it 'never does run smooth.' That is not true. Witness Hester's."

"Dear Margaret, be not presumptuous! Consider how early the days of that love are yet."

"And that love in their case has only just leaped out of the fountain, and can hardly be said to have begun its course. Well! may Heaven smile on it! But tell me about that course of love which made you sigh as you did just now."

"What can I tell you about it? And yet, you shall know, if you like, how it appears to me."

"Oh, tell me! I shall see whether you would have understood Hester's case."

"The first strange thing is, that every woman approaches this crisis of her life as unawares as if she were the first that ever loved."

"And yet all girls are brought up to think of marriage as almost the only event in life. Their minds are stuffed with thoughts of it almost before they have had time to gain any other ideas."

"Merely as means to ends low enough for their comprehension. It is not marriage—wonderful, holy, mysterious marriage—that their minds are full of, but connection with somebody or something which will give them money, and ease, and station, and independence of their parents. This has nothing to do with love. I was speaking of love—the grand influence of a woman's life, but whose name is a mere empty sound to her till it becomes, suddenly, secretly, a voice which shakes her being to the very centre—more awful, more tremendous, than the crack of doom."

"But why? Why so tremendous?"

"From the struggle which it calls upon her to endure, silently and alone;—from the agony of a change of existence which must be wrought without any eye perceiving it. Depend upon it, Margaret, there is nothing in death to compare with this change; and there can be nothing in entrance upon another state which can transcend the experience I speak of. Our powers can but be taxed to the utmost. Our being can but be strained till not another effort can be made. This is all that we can conceive to happen in death; and it happens in love, with the additional burden of fearful secrecy. One may lie down and await death, with sympathy about one to the last, though the passage hence must be solitary; and it would be a small trouble if all the world looked on to see the parting of soul and body: but that other passage into a new state, that other process of becoming a new creature, must go on in the darkness of the spirit, while the body is up and abroad, and no one must know what is passing within. The spirit's leap from heaven to hell must be made while the smile is on the lips, and light words are upon the tongue. The struggles of shame, the pangs of despair, must be hidden in the depths of the prison-house. Every groan must be stifled before it is heard: and as for tears—they are a solace too gentle for the case. The agony is too strong for tears."

"Is this true love?" asked Margaret, in agitation.

"This is true love; but not the whole of it. As for what follows—"

"But is this what every woman has to undergo?"

"Do you suppose that every woman knows what love really is? No; not even every unmarried woman. There are some among them, though I believe but few, who know nothing of what love is; and there are, undoubtedly, a multitude of wives who have experienced liking, preference, affection, and taken it for love; and who reach their life's end without being aware that they have never loved. There are also, I trust, a multitude of wives who have really loved, and who have reaped the best fruits of it in regeneration of soul."

"But how dreadful is the process, if it be as you say!"

"I said I had alluded to only a part of it. As for what follows, according as it is prosperous or unreturned love, heaven ensues upon this purgatory, or one may attain a middle region, somewhat dim, but serene. You wish me to be plainer?"

"I wish to hear all you think—all you know. But do not let us go on with it if it makes you sigh so."

"What woman ever spoke of love without sighing?" said Maria, with a smile. "You sighed yourself, just now."

"I was thinking of Hester, I believe. How strange, if this process really awaits women—if it is a region through which their path of life must stretch—and no one gives warning, or preparation, or help!"

"It is not so strange as at first sight it seems. Every mother and friend hopes that no one else has suffered as she did—that her particular charge may escape entirely, or get off more easily. Then there is the shame of confession which is involved: some conclude, at a distance of time, that they must have exaggerated their own sufferings, or have been singularly rebellious and unreasonable. Some lose the sense of the anguish in the subsequent happiness; and there are not a few who, from constitution of mind, forget altogether 'the things that are behind.' When you remember, too, that it is the law of nature and providence that each should bear his and her own burden, and that no warning would be of any avail, it seems no longer so strange that while girls hear endlessly of marriage, they are kept wholly in the dark about love."

"Would warning really be of no avail?"

"Of no more avail than warning to a pilgrim in the middle of the desert that he will suffer from thirst, and be deluded by the mirage, before he gets into green fields again. He has no longer the choice whether to be a pilgrim in the desert or to stay at home. No one of us has the choice to be or not to be; and we must go through with our experience, under its natural conditions."

"'To be or not to be,'" said Margaret, with a grave smile. "You remind one that the choice of suicide remains: and I almost wonder— Surely suicide has been committed from dread of lighter woes than you have described."

"I believe so: but in this case there is no dread. We find ourselves in the midst of the struggle before we are aware. And then—"

"Ay, and then—"

"He, who appoints the struggles of the spirit, supplies aids and supports. I fully believe that this time of conflict is that in which religion first becomes to many the reality for which they ever afterwards live. It may have been hitherto a name, a fancy, a dim abstraction, or an intermitting though bright influence: and it may yet be resorted to merely as a refuge for the spirit which can find no other. But there is a strong probability that it may now be found to be a wonderful reality; not only a potent charm in sorrow, but the life of our life. This is with many the reason why, and the mode in which, the conflict is endured to the end."

"But the beginning," said Margaret; "what can be the beginning of this wonderful experience?"

"The same with that of all the most serious of our experiences—levity, unconsciousness, confidence. Upon what subject in the world is there a greater accumulation of jokes than upon love and marriage; and upon what subject are jokes so indefatigably current? A girl laughs at her companions, and blushes or pouts for herself; as girls have done for thousands of years before her. She finds, by degrees, new, and sweet, and elevated ideas of friendship stealing their way into her mind, and she laments and wonders that the range of friendship is not wider—that its action is not freer—that girls may not enjoy intimate friendship with the companions of their brothers, as well as with their own. There is a quick and strong resentment at any one who smiles at, or speculates upon, or even observes the existence of such a friendship."

"Oh, Maria!" exclaimed Margaret, throwing down her work, and covering her face with her hands.

"This goes on for a while," proceeded Maria, as if she did not observe her companion, "this goes on for a while, smoothly, innocently, serenely. Mankind are then true and noble, the world is passing fair, and God is tender and bountiful. All evil is seen to be tending to good; all tears are meant to be wiped away; the gloom of the gloomy is faithless; virtue is easy and charming; and the vice of the vicious is unaccountable. Thus does young life glide on for a time. Then there comes a day—it is often a mystery why it should be that day of all days—when the innocent, and gay, and confident young creature finds herself in sudden trouble. The film on which she lightly trod has burst and she is in an abyss. It seems a mere trifle that plunged her there. Her friend did not come when she looked for him, or he is gone somewhere, or he has said something that she did not expect. Some such trifle reveals to her that she depends wholly upon him—that she has for long been living only for him, and on the unconscious conclusion that he has been living only for her. At the image of his dwelling anywhere but by her side, of his having any interest apart from hers, the universe is, in a moment, shrouded in gloom. Her heart is sick, and there is no rest for it, for her self-respect is gone. She has been reared in a maidenly pride, and an innocent confidence: her confidence is wholly broken-down; her pride is wounded and the agony of the wound is intolerable. We are wont to say, Margaret, that everything is endurable but a sense of guilt. If there be an exception, this is it. This wounding of the spirit ought not perhaps to be, but it is very like the sting of guilt; and a 'wounded spirit who can bear?'"

"How is it borne—so many as are the sufferers, and of a class usually thought so weak?"

"That is a mistake. There is not on earth a being stronger than a woman in the concealment of her love. The soldier is called brave who cheerfully bears about the pain of a laceration to his dying day; and criminals, who, after years of struggle, unbosom themselves of their secret, give tremendous accounts of the sufferings of those years; but I question whether a woman whose existence has been burdened with an unrequited love, will not have to unfold in the next world a more harrowing tale than either of these."

"It ought not to be so."

"It ought not, where there is no guilt. But how noble is such power of self-restraint! Though the principle of society may be to cultivate our pride to excess, what fortitude grows out of it! There are no bounds to the horror, disgust, and astonishment expressed when a woman owns her love to its object unasked—even urges it upon him; but I acknowledge my surprise to be the other way—that the cases are so rare. Yet, fancying the case one's own—"

"Oh, dreadful!" cried Margaret.

"No woman can endure the bare thought of the case being her own; and this proves the strong natural and educational restraint under which we all lie: but I must think that the frequent and patient endurance proves a strength of soul, a vigour of moral power, which ought to console and animate us in the depth of our abasement, if we could but recall it then when we want support and solace most."

"It can be little estimated—little understood," said Margaret, "or it would not be sported with as it is."

"Do not let us speak of that, Margaret. You talk of my philosophy sometimes; I own that that part of the subject is too much for any philosophy I have."

"I see nothing philosophical," said Margaret, "in making light of the deepest cruelty and treachery which is transacted under the sun. A man who trifles with such affections, and abuses such moral power, and calls his cruelty flirtation—"

"Is such an one as we will not speak of now. Well! it cannot be but that good—moral and intellectual good—must issue from such exercise and discipline as this; and such good does issue often, perhaps generally. There are sad tales sung and told everywhere of brains crazed, and graves dug by hopeless love: and I fear that many more sink down into disease and death from this cause, than are at all suspected to be its victims: but not a few find themselves lifted up from their abyss, and set free from their bondage of pride and humiliation. They marry their loves and stand amazed at their own bliss, and are truly the happiest people upon earth, and in the broad road to be the wisest. In my belief, the happiest are ever so."

"Bless you for that, for Hester's sake! And what of those who are not thus released?"

"They get out of the abyss too; but they have to struggle out alone. Their condition must depend much on what they were before the conflict befell them. Some are soured, and live restlessly. Some are weak, and come out worldly, and sacrifice themselves, in marriage or otherwise, for low objects. Some strive to forget, and to become as like as possible to what they were before; and of this order are many of the women whom we meet, whose minds are in a state of perpetual and incurable infancy. It is difficult to see the purpose of their suffering, from any effects it appears to have produced: but then there is the hope that their griefs were not of the deepest."

"And what of those whose griefs are of the deepest?"

"They rise the highest above them. Some of these must be content with having learned more or less of what life is, and of what it is for, and with reconciling themselves to its objects and conditions."

"In short, with being philosophical," said Margaret, with an inquiring and affectionate glance at her friend.

"With being philosophical," Maria smilingly agreed. "Others, of a happier nature, to whom philosophy and religion come as one, and are welcomed by energies not wholly destroyed, and affections not altogether crushed, are strong in the new strength which they have found, with hearts as wide as the universe, and spirits the gayest of the gay."

"You never told me anything of all this before," said Margaret; "yet it is plain that you must have thought much about it—that it must have been long in your mind."

"It has; and I tell it to you, that you may share what I have learned, instead of going without the knowledge, or, alas! gathering it up for yourself."

"Oh, then, it is so—it is from your own—"

"It is from my own experience that I speak," said Maria, without looking up. "And now, there is some one in the world who knows it beside myself."

"I hope you do not—I hope you never will repent having told me," said Margaret, rising and taking her seat on the sofa, beside her friend.

"I do not, and I shall not repent," said Maria. "You are faithful: and it will be a relief to me to have sympathy—to be able to speak sometimes, instead of having to deny and repress my whole heart and soul. But I can tell you no more—not one word."

"Do not. Only show me how I can comfort—how I can gratify you."

"I need no special comfort now," said Maria, smiling. "I *have* sometimes grievously wanted a friend to love and speak with—and if I could, to serve. Now I have a friend." And the look with which she gazed at her companion brought the tears into Margaret's eyes.

"Come, let us speak of something else," said Maria, cheerfully. "When do you expect your friend, Mr Enderby, at Deerbrook again?"

"His sister says nobody knows; and I do not think he can tell himself. You know he does not live at Deerbrook."

"I am aware of that; but his last visit was such a long one—"

"Six days," said Margaret, laughing.

"Ah! I did not mean his last week's appearance, or any of his pop visits. I was thinking of his summer visitation. It was so long, that some people began to look upon him as a resident."

"If his mother does not grow much better soon, we shall see him again," said Margaret. "It is always her illness that brings him.—Do you not believe me, Maria?"

"I believe, as before, that you say what you think. Whether you are mistaken is another question, which I cannot pretend to answer."

"I hope, Maria, that as you have placed so much confidence in me, you will not stop short at the very point which is of the greatest importance to me."

"I will not, dear. What I think on the subject of Mr Enderby, in relation to you, is, that some of your friends believe that you are the cause of his stay having been so long in the summer, and of his coming so often since. I know no more than this. How should I?"

"Then I will tell you something more, that I might as well have mentioned before. When Mrs Rowland had an idea that Mr Enderby might think of Hester, she told Hester—that miserable day in Dingleford woods—that his family expected he would soon marry a young lady of family and fortune, who was a great favourite with all his connections."

"Who may this young lady be?"

"Oh, she did not say; some one too high for our acquaintance, if we are to believe what Mrs Rowland declared."

"And do you believe it?"

"Why—. Do you?"

"I dare say Mrs Rowland may believe it herself; but she may be mistaken."

"That is exactly what Hester said," observed Margaret, eagerly. "And that was more than five months ago, and we have not heard a syllable of the matter since."

"And so intimate a friendship as yours and Mr Enderby's is," said Maria, smiling,—"it is scarcely probable that his mind should be full of such an affair, and that he should be able to conceal it so perfectly from you."

"I am glad you think so," said Margaret, ingenuously. "You cannot imagine how strange it is to see Mrs Grey and others taking for granted that he is free, when Hester and I could tell them in a moment what Mrs Rowland said. But if you think Mrs Rowland is all wrong, what do you really suppose about his coming so much to Deerbrook?"

"I have little doubt that those friends of yours—Mrs Grey and the others—are right. But—."

"But what?"

"Just this. If I might warn you by myself; I would caution you, not only against dwelling much upon such a fact, but against interpreting it to mean more than it possibly may. This is my reason for speaking to you upon the matter at all. I do it because you will be pretty sure to hear how the fact itself is viewed by others, while no one else would be likely to give you the caution. Mr Enderby *may* come, as you suppose, entirely to see his mother. He may come to see you: but, supposing he does, if he is like other men, he may not know his own mind yet: and, there is another possible thing—a thing which is possible, Margaret, though he is such a dear and intimate friend—that he may not know yours—all its strength of affection, all its fidelity, all its trust and power of self-control."

"Oh, stop; pray stop," said Margaret. "You frighten me with the thoughts of all you have been saying this evening, though I could so entirely satisfy you as to what our intercourse has been—though I know Mr Enderby so much better than you do. You need warn me no more. I will think of what you have said, if I find myself doubting whether he comes to see his mother—if I find myself listening to what others may suppose about his reasons. Indeed, I will remember what you have said."

"Then I am glad I ventured to say it, particularly as you are not angry with me this time."

"I am not at all angry: how could I be so? But I do not agree with you about the fact."

"I know it, and I may be mistaken."

"Now tell me," said Margaret, "what you suppose Morris meant when she said what you heard about the pleasure of solitude depending on one's thoughts being happy or otherwise. I know it is a common old idea enough; but Morris does not know that; and I am sure she had some particular instance in view. Morris does not make general propositions, except with a particular case in her mind's eye; and she is a wise woman; and we think her sayings are weighty."

"It struck me that she had a real probability in her mind; but I did not think it related to Mr Enderby, or to anything so exclusively your own concern."

"No; I hope not: but what then?"

"I think that Morris knows more of life and the world than you, and that she does not anticipate quite so much happiness from Hester's marriage as you do. Do not be distressed or alarmed. She means no mistrust of anybody, I imagine; but only that there is no perfect happiness in this life, that nobody is faultless; and no home, not even where her young ladies live, is quite free from care and trouble. It would not hurt you, surely, if she was to say this outright to you?"

"Oh, no; nor a good deal more of the same tendency. She might come much nearer to the point, good soul! without hurting me. Suppose I ask her what it was she did mean, to-night or to-morrow, when she and I are alone?"

"Well! if she is such a wise woman——. But I doubt whether you could get her nearer to the point without danger of hurting her. Can she bring herself to own that either of you have faults?"

"Oh, yes: she has never spared us, from the time we were two feet high."

"What can make you so anxious as to what she meant?"

"I really hardly know, unless it be that where one loves very much, one fears—Oh, so faithlessly! I know I ought to fear less for Hester than ever; and yet—."

The door burst open, and the foot-boy entered with his jingling tray, and news that the sedan for Miss Young was at the door. What sedan? Margaret had asked Mrs Grey for hers, as the snow had fallen heavily, and the streets were not fit for Maria's walking. Maria was very thankful.

Here was an end of Maria's bright holiday. Mr Grey's porters must not be kept waiting. The friends assured each other that they should never forget this day. It was little likely that they should.

Chapter Sixteen

Home.

Margaret had an unconscious expectation of seeing her sister altered. This is an irresistible persuasion in almost every case where an intimate friend is absent, and is under new influences, and amidst new circumstances. These accessories alter the image of the beloved one in our minds; our fancy follows it, acting and being acted upon in ways in which we have no share. Our sympathy is at fault, or we conceive it to be so; and doubt and trouble creep over us, we scarcely know why. Though the letters which come may be natural and hearty, as of old, breathing the very spirit of our friend, we feel a sort of surprise at the handwriting being quite familiar. We look forward with a kind of timidity to meeting, and fear there may be some restraint in it. When the hour of meeting comes, there is the very same face, the line of the cheek, the trick of the lip, the glance of the eye; the rise and fall of the voice are the same; and the intense familiarity makes our very spirit swim in joy. We are amazed at our previous fancy—we laugh at the solemn stiffness in which our friend stood before our mind's eye, and to relieve which we had striven to recall the ludicrous situations and merry moods in which that form and that face had been seen; and perhaps we have no peace till we have acknowledged to the beloved one the ingenuity of our self-tormentings. Is there a girl whose heart is with her brother at college, who does not feel this regularly as the vacation comes round? Is there a parent whose child is reaping honours in the field of life, and returning childlike from time to time, to rest in the old country-home—is there such a parent who is not conscious of the misgiving and the re-assurance, as often as the absence and the re-union occur? Is there even the most trustful of wives, whose husband is on the other side of the globe, that is wholly undisturbed by the transmutation of the idol in her mind? When the husband is returning, and her hungry heart is feasting on the anticipation of his appearance, she may revel in the thought—

"And will I see his face again,
And will I hear him speak?"

But it is not till that vivid face and that piercing voice thrill her sight and her ear again that all misgiving vanishes. There is nothing in life that can compensate for long partings. There ought to be few or no insurmountable obstacles to the frequent meetings, however short, of those who love each other. No duties and no privileges can be of more importance than the preservation, in all their entireness, of domestic familiarity and faith.

A very short separation will afford the experience of a long one, if it be full of events, or if the image of the absent one be dwelt upon, from hour to hour, with laborious strivings of the fancy. It has been said that this week of Hester's absence was the longest that Margaret had ever known. Besides this, she felt that she had forgotten her sister further than she could have supposed possible after a ten years' separation. On the evening when she was expecting the travellers home, her heart was sick with expectation; and yet she was conscious of a timidity which made her feel as if alone in the world. Again and again she looked round her, to fancy what would be the aspect, of everything to Hester's eye. She wandered about the house to see once more that all was in its right place, and every arrangement in due order. She watched the bright drawing-room fire nervously, and made herself anxious about the tea-table, and sat upright on the sofa, listening for the sound of horses' feet in the snowy street, as if it had been a solemn stranger that she was expecting, instead of her own sister Hester, with whom she had shared all her heart, and spent all her days. But a small part of this anxiety was given to Mr Hope: she retained her image of him unperplexed, as a treasure of a brother, and a man with a mind so healthy that he was sure to receive all things rightly, and be pleased and satisfied, happen what might.

They came; and Hester's spring from the carriage, and her husband's way of rubbing his hands over the fire, put all Margaret's anxieties to flight. How sweet was the welcome! How delicious the contest about which was to give the welcome to this, the lasting home of the three—whether she who had put all in order for them, or they who claimed to have the charge of her! Margaret's eyes overflowed when Hester led her to Edward for his brotherly kiss. Mr Hope's mind was disturbed for one single moment that he had not given this kiss with all the heartiness and simplicity of a brother; but the feeling was gone almost before he was conscious of it.

The fire crackled, the kettle sang, Hester took her own place at once at the tea-board, and her husband threw himself on the sofa, after ascertaining that there were no family letters for him. He knew that it was impossible that there should be any in answer to the announcement of his marriage. Even Anne's could not arrive these four or five days yet. He desired Margaret not to tell him at present if there were any messages for him; for, if all Deerbrook had colds, he had no inclination to go out to-night to cure them. There was a long list of messages, Margaret said, but they were in the surgery; and the pupil there might bring them in, if he thought proper: they should not be sent for. This one evening might be stolen for home and comfort. Their journey had been delightful. Oxford was more splendid than Hester had had an idea of. Every facility had been afforded them for seeing it, and Mr Hope's acquaintants there had been as kind as possible. The fall of snow had not put them in any danger, and the inconveniences it had caused were rather stimulating to people who had travelled but little. Hester had had to get out of the carriage twice; and once she had walked a mile, when the driver had been uncertain about the road; but as Mrs Grey had had the foresight to cause a pair of snow boots to be put into the carriage at the last moment, no harm had happened,—not even to the wetting of feet; only enough inconvenience to make them glad to be now by their snug fireside. Hester was full of mirth and anecdote. She seemed to have been pleased with everybody and awake to everything. As her sister looked upon her brow, now open as a sleeping child's, upon the thick curl of glossy brown hair, and upon the bright smile which lighted up her exquisite face, she was amazed at herself for having perplexed such an image with apprehensive fancies.

How had Margaret spent her week? Above all, it was to be hoped she had not fatigued herself in their service. There were four days' grace yet for preparation, before they should receive their company. Margaret should not have worked so hard. Had Maria Young come yesterday? Dear Maria! she must often come. Should not the Greys be asked to dine in a quiet way, before any one else was admitted into the house? Was it not due to them? But could the footboy wait at table? Would it be possible to bring him into such training as would prevent Mrs Grey's being too much shocked at their way of getting through dinner? Or was there any one in Deerbrook who went out as a waiter? Morris must be consulted; but they must have the Greys to dinner before Monday. How was Mrs Enderby? Was her illness really thought serious, or was it only Mrs Rowland's way of talking, which was just the same, whether Mrs Enderby had a twinge of rheumatism or one of her frightful attacks? Was Mr Enderby coming?—that was the chief point. If he did not appear, it was certain that he could not be feeling uneasy about his mother. Margaret blushed when she replied that she had not heard of Mr Enderby's being expected. She could not but blush; for the conversation with Maria came full into her mind. Mr Hope saw the blush, and painfully wondered that it sent trouble through his soul.

How were Morris and the new maid likely to agree? Did Morris think the girl promising? Surely it was time to take some notice of the servants. Edward would ring the bell twice, the signal for Morris; and Morris should introduce the other two into the parlour. They came, Morris in her best gown, and with her wedding ribbon on. When she had shaken hands with her master and mistress, and spoken a good word for her fellow-servants, as she called them, the ruddy-faced girl appeared, her cheeks many shades deeper than usual, and her cap quillings standing off like the rays on a signpost picture of the sun. Following her came the boy, feeling awkward in his new clothes, and scraping with his left leg till the process was put a stop to by his master's entering into conversation with him. Hester's beauty was really so striking, as with a blushing bashfulness, she for the first time enacted the mistress before her husband's eyes, that it was impossible not to observe it. Margaret glanced towards her brother, and they exchanged smiles. But the effect of Margaret's smile was that Mr Hope's died away, and left him grave.

"Brother!" said Margaret; "what is the true story belonging to that great book about the Polar Sea, that you see lying there?"

"How do you mean? Is there any story belonging to it at all?"

"Three at least; and Deerbrook has been so hot about it—"

"You should send round the book to cool them. It is enough to freeze one to look at the plates of those polar books."

"Sending round the book is exactly the thing I wanted to do, and could not. Mrs Rowland insists that Mrs Enderby ordered it in; and Mrs Grey demands to have it first; and Mr Rowland is certain that you bespoke it before anybody else. I was afraid of the responsibility of acting in so nice a case. An everlasting quarrel might come out of it: so I covered it, and put in the list, all ready to be sent at a moment's warning; and then I amused myself with it while you were away. Now, brother, what will you do?"

"The truth of the matter is, that I ordered it in myself, as Mr Rowland says. But Mrs Enderby shall have it at once, because she is ill. It is a fine large type for her; and she will pore over the plates, and forget Deerbrook and all her own ailments, in wondering how the people will get out of the ice."

"Do you remember, Margaret," said Hester, "how she looked one summer day,—like a ghost from the grave,—when she came down from her books, and had even forgotten her shawl?"

"Oh, about the battle!" cried Margaret, laughing.

"What battle?" asked Hope. "An historical one, I suppose, and not that of the Rowlands and Greys. Mrs Enderby is of a higher order than the rest of us Deerbrook people: she gets most of her news, and all her battles, out of history."

"Yes: she alighted among us to tell us that such a great, such a wonderful battle had been fought, at a place called Blenheim, by the Duke of Marlborough, who really seemed a surprisingly clever man: it was such a good thought of his to have a swamp at one end of his line, and to put some of his soldiers behind some bushes, so that the enemy could not get at them! and he won the battle."

"This book will be the very thing for her," said Margaret. "It is only a pity that it did not come in at Midsummer instead of Christmas. I am afraid she will sympathise so thoroughly that Phoebe will never be able to put on coals enough to warm her."

"Nay," said Mr Hope, "it is better as it is. She must be told now, at all events: whereas, if this book came to her at Midsummer, it would chill her whole month of July. She would start every time she looked out of her window, and saw the meadows green."

"I hope she is not really very ill," said Hester.

"You were thinking the same thought that I was," said her husband, starting up from the sofa. "It is certainly my business to go and see her to-night, if she wishes it. I will step down into the surgery, and learn if there is any message from her."

"And if there is not from her, there will be from some one else," said Hester, sorrowfully. "What a cold night for you to go out, and leave this warm room!"

Mr Hope laughed as he observed what an innocent speech that was for a surgeon's wife. It was plain that her education in that capacity had not begun. And down he went.

"Here are some things for you, cards and notes," said Margaret to her sister, as she opened a drawer of the writing-table: "one from Mrs Grey, marked 'Private.' I do not suppose your husband may not see it; but that is your affair. My duty is to give it you privately."

"One of the Grey mysteries, I suppose," said Hester, colouring, and tearing open the letter with some vehemence: "These mysteries were foolish enough before; they are ridiculous now. So, you are going out?" cried she, as her husband came in with his hat on.

"Yes; the old lady will be the easier for my seeing her this evening; and I shall carry her the Polar Sea. Where is pen and ink, Margaret? We do not know the ways of our own house yet."

Margaret brought pen and ink; and while Mr Hope wrote down the dates in the Book Society's list, Hester exclaimed against Mrs Grey for having sent her a letter marked "Private," now that she was married.

"If you mean it not to be private, you shall tell me about it when I come back," said her husband. "If I see Mrs Enderby to-night, I must be gone."

It was not twenty minutes before he was seated by his own fireside again. His wife looked disturbed; and was so; she even forgot to inquire after Mrs Enderby.

"There is Mrs Grey's precious letter!" said she. "She may mean to be very kind to me: I dare say she does: but she might know that it is not kindness to write so of my husband."

"I do not see that she writes any harm of me, my dear," said he, laying the letter open upon the table. "She only wants to manage me a little: and that is her way, you know."

"So exceedingly impertinent!" cried Hester, turning to Margaret. "She wants me to use my influence, quietly, and without betraying her, to make my husband—," she glanced into her husband's face, and checked her communication. "In short," she said, "Mrs Grey wants to be meddling between my husband and one of his patients."

"Well, what then?" said Margaret.

"What then? Why, if she is to be interfering already in our affairs—if she is to be always fancying that she has anything to do with Edward,—and we living so near,—I shall never be able to bear it."

And Hester's eyes overflowed with tears.

"My dear! is it possible?" cried Edward. "Such a trifle—."

"It is no trifle," said Hester, trying to command her voice; "it can never be a trifle to me that any one shows disrespect to you. I shall never be able to keep terms with any one who does."

Margaret believed that nothing would be easier than to put a stop to any such attempts—if indeed they were serious. Mrs Grey was so fond of Hester that she would permit anything from her; and it would be easy for Hester to say that, not wishing to receive any exclusively private letters, she had shown Mrs Grey's to her husband, though to no one else: and that it was to be the principle of the family not to interfere, more or less, with Mr Hope's professional affairs.

"Or, better still, take no notice of the matter in any way whatever, this time," said Mr Hope. "We can let her have her way while we keep our own, cannot we? So, let us put the mysterious epistle into the fire—shall we? I wait your leave," said he, laughing, as he held the letter over the flame.

"It is your property."

Hester signed to have it burned; but she could not forget it. She recurred to Mrs Grey, again and again. "So near as they lived," she said—"so much as they must be together."

"The nearer we all live, and the more we must be with our neighbours," said her husband, "the more important it is that we should allow each other our own ways. You will soon find what it is to live in a village, my love; and then you will not mind these little trifles."

"If they would meddle only with me," said Hester, "I should not mind. I hope you do not think I should care so much for anything they could say or do about me. If they only would let you alone—"

"That is the last thing we can expect," said Margaret. "Do they let any public man alone? Dr Levitt, or Mr James?"

"Or the parish clerk?" added Mr Hope. "It was reported lately that steps were to be taken to intimate to Owen, that it was a constant habit of his to cough as he took his seat in the desk. I was told once myself, that it was remarked throughout Deerbrook that I seemed to be half whistling as I walked up the street in the mornings; and that it was considered a practice too undignified for my profession."

Hester's colour rose again. Margaret laughed, and asked:

"What did you do?"

"I made my best bow, and thought no more about the matter, till events brought it to mind again at this moment. So, Hester, suppose we think no more of Mrs Grey's hints?" Seeing that her brow did not entirely clear, he took his seat by her, saying:

"Supposing, love, that her letter does not show enough deference to my important self to satisfy you, still it remains that we owe respect to Mrs Grey. She is one of my oldest, and most hospitable, and faithful friends here; and I need say nothing of her attachment to you. Cannot we overlook in her one little error of judgment?"

"Oh, yes, certainly," said Hester, cheerfully. "Then I will say nothing to her unless she asks; and then tell her, as lightly as I may, what Margaret proposed just now. So be it."

And all was bright and smooth again—to all appearance. But this little cloud did not pass away without leaving its gloom in more hearts than one. As Margaret set down her lamp on her own writing-table, and sank into the chair of whose ease she had bidden Maria make trial, she might have decided, if she had happened at the moment to remember the conversation, that the pleasure of solitude does depend much on the ease of the thoughts. She sat long, wondering how she could have overlooked the obvious probability that Hester, instead of finding the habit of mind of a lifetime altered by the circumstances of love and marriage, would henceforth suffer from jealousy for her husband in addition to the burden she had borne for herself. Long did Margaret sit there, turning her voluntary musings on the joy of their meeting, and the perfect picture of comfort which their little party had presented; but perpetually recurring, against her will, to the trouble which had succeeded, and following back the track of this cloud, to see whether there were more in the wind—whether it did not come from a horizon of storm.

Yet hers was not the most troubled spirit in the house. Hester's vexation had passed away, and she was unconscious, as sufferers of her class usually are, of the disturbance she had caused. She presently slept and was at peace. Not so her husband. A strange trouble—a fearful suspicion had seized upon him. He was amazed at the return of his feelings about Margaret, and filled with horror when he thought of the days, and months, and years of close domestic companionship with her, from which there was no escape. There was no escape. The peace of his wife, of Margaret—his own peace in theirs—depended wholly on the deep secrecy in which he should preserve the mistake he had made. It was a mistake. He could scarcely endure the thought; but it was so. For some months, he had never had a doubt that he was absolutely in the road of duty; and, if some apprehension about his entire happiness had chilled him, from time to time, he had cast them off, as inconsistent with the resolution of his conscience. Now he feared, he felt he had mistaken his duty. As, in the stillness of the night, the apprehension assailed him, that he had thrown away the opportunity and the promise of his life—that he had desecrated his own home, and doomed to withering the best affections of his nature, he for the moment wished himself dead. But his was a soul never long thrown off its balance. He convinced himself, in the course of a long sleepless night, that whatever might have been his errors, his way was now clear, though difficult. He must devote himself wholly to her whose devotion to him had caused him his present struggles; and he must trust that, if Margaret did not ere long remove from the daily companionship which must be his sorest trial, he should grow perpetually stronger in his self-command. Of one thing he was certain—that no human being suspected the real state of his mind. This was a comfort and support. Of something else he felt nearly certain—that Margaret loved Philip. This was another comfort, if he could only feel it so; and he had little doubt that Philip loved her. He had also a deep conviction, which he now aroused for his support—that no consecration of a home is so holy as that of a kindly, self-denying, trustful spirit in him who is the head and life of his house. If there was in himself a love which must be denied, there was also one which might be indulged. Without trammelling himself with vows, he cheered his soul with the image of the life he might yet fulfil, shedding on all under his charge the blessings of his activity, patience, and love; and daily casting off the burden of the day, leaving all care for the morrow to such as, happier than himself, would have the future the image of the present.

Chapter Seventeen

First Hospitality.

The Greys needed only to be asked to come and dine before the rest of the world could have an opportunity of seeing the bride and bridegroom. They had previously settled among themselves that they should be invited, and the answer was given on the instant. The only doubt was how far down in the family the pleasure ought to extend. Sydney was full of anxiety about it. His mother decided that he ought to be asked, but that perhaps he had better not go, as he would be in the way; and Sophia was sure it would be very dull for him; a sentence which made Sydney rather sulky. But Hester insisted on having him, and pleaded that William Levitt would come and meet him, and if the lads should find the drawing-room dull, there was the surgery, with some very curious things in it, where they might be able to amuse themselves. So Sydney was to take up his lot with the elderly ones, and the little girls were to be somewhat differently entertained another day.

Oh, the anxieties of a young wife's first dinner-party! If remembered, they become laughable enough when looked back upon from future years; but they are no laughing matter at the time. The terror lest there should be too little on the table, and the consequent danger of there being too much: the fear at once of worrying the cook with too many directions, and leaving any necessary thing unsaid: the trembling doubt of any power of entertainment that may exist in the house; the anticipation of a yawn on the part of any guest, or of such a silence as may make the creaking of the footboy's shoes heard at dinner, or the striking of the hall clock in the evening—these are the apprehensions which make the young wife wish herself on the other side of her first dinner-party, and render alluring the prospect of sitting down next day to hash or cold fowl, followed by odd custards and tartlets, with a stray mince-pie. Where a guest so experienced and so vigilant as Mrs Grey is expected, the anxiety is redoubled, and the servants are sure to discover it by some means or other. Morris woke, this Saturday morning, with the feeling that something great was to happen that day; and Sally began to be sharp with the footboy as early as ten o'clock. Hester and Margaret were surprised to find how soon there was nothing more left for them to do. The wine was decanted, the dessert dished up in the little storeroom, and even the cake cut for tea, soon enough to leave almost the whole morning to be spent as usual. Margaret sat down to study German, and Hester to read. She had just observed that they could not expect to see Edward for some hours, as he had been sent for to the almshouses, and meant to pay a country visit which would cost him a circuit on his return. These almshouses were six miles off; and when Mr Hope was sent for by one of the inmates, nearly all the rest were wont to discover that they ailed more or less; so that their medical guardian found it no easy matter to get away, and his horse had learned, by practice, to stand longer there than anywhere else without fidgeting. Knowing this, Margaret fully agreed to her sister's proposition, that it must be some hours before Edward could appear. In a little while, however, Hester threw down her book, and took up her work, laying her watch just under her eyes upon the table.

"Do you mean to do that for life, when your husband takes a country ride?" said Margaret, laughing.

"I hate these everlasting country rides!" cried Hester. "I do wish he would give up those almshouses."

"Give them up!"

"Yes: they are nothing but trouble and anxiety. The old folks are never satisfied, and never would be, if he lived among them, and attended to nobody else. And as often as he goes there, he is sure to be more wanted here than at any other time. There is another knock. There have been two people wanting him within this hour; and a country gentleman has left word that he shall call with his daughter at one o'clock."

"Well, let them come. If he is home, well and good; if not, they must wait till he arrives."

Hester started up, and walked about the room.

"I know what is in your mind," said Margaret. "The truth is, you are afraid of another accident. I do not wonder at it; but, dearest Hester, you must control this fear. Consider; supposing it to be Heaven's pleasure that you and he should live for forty or fifty years together, what a world of anxiety you will inflict on yourself if you are to suffer in this way every time he rides six miles out and back again!"

"Perhaps I shall grow used to it: but I do wish he would give up those almshouses."

"Suppose we ask him to give up practice at once," said Margaret, "that we may have him always with us. No, no, Hester; we must consider him first, and ourselves next, and let him have his profession all to himself, and as much of it as he likes."

"Ourselves!" cried Hester, contemptuously.

"Well, yourself, then," said Margaret, smiling. "I only put myself in that I might lecture myself at the same time with you."

"Lecture away, dear," said Hester, "till you make me as reasonable as if I had no husband to care for."

Margaret might have asked whether Hester had been reasonable when she had had neither husband nor lover to care for; but, instead of this, she opened the piano, and tempted her sister away from her watch to practise a duet.

"I will tell you what I am thinking of," cried Hester, breaking off in the middle of a bar of the second page. "Perhaps you thought me hasty just now; but you do not know what I had in my head. You remember how late Edward was called out, the night before last?"

"To Mrs Marsh's child? Yes; it was quite dark when he went."

"There was no moon. Mr Marsh wanted to send a servant back with him as far as the high-road: but he was sure he knew the way. He was riding very fast, when his horse suddenly stopped, and almost threw him over its head. He spurred in vain; the animal only turned round and round, till a voice called from somewhere near, 'Stop there, for God's sake! Wait till I bring a light.' A man soon came with a lantern, and where do you think Edward found himself? On the brink of a mill-dam! Another step in the dark night, and he might have been heard of no more!"

Margaret was not at all surprised that Hester covered her face with her hands at the end of this very disagreeable anecdote.

"It is clear," said she, "that Edward is the person who wants lecturing. We must bid him not ride very fast on dark nights, on roads that he does not know. But I have a high opinion of this horse of his. One of the two is prudent; and that is a great comfort. And, for the present, there is the consolation that there are no mill-dams in the way to the almshouses, and that it is broad daylight. So let us go on with our duet,—or shall we begin again?"

Hester played through the duet, and then sighed over a new apprehension—that some of those old invalids would certainly be taking Mr Hope away from home on the two mornings when their neighbours were to pay the wedding visit. "And what shall we do then?" she inquired.

"We shall see when the time comes," replied Margaret. "Meanwhile we are sure of one good thing,—that Edward will not be called away from the dinner-table to-day by the almshouse people. Come! let us play this over once more, that it may be ready for Mr Grey in the evening."

Sooner than he was looked for—sooner than it was supposed possible that he could have come—Edward appeared.

"Safe!" cried he, laughing: "what should prevent my being safe? What sort of a soldier's or sailor's wife would you have made?" he asked, looking in Hester's happy face.

"She would be crazed with every gale, and die at 'rumours of wars,'" said Margaret: "mill-dams are horror enough for her—and, to say the truth, brother, for other people, too, while you ride as you do."

"That was an accident which cannot recur," observed Hope. "I am sorry Mr Marsh's man mentioned it. But Hester—."

"I see what you would say," sighed Hester; "your mention of soldiers' and sailors' wives reminds me. I have no faith, I know: and I thought I should when—. Oh, I wonder how those old crusaders' wives endured their lives! But, perhaps, seven years' suspense was easier to bear than seven hours'."

Hester joined in the laugh at this speech, and Edward went to see his patients in a place where there was really no danger—in the waiting-room. Yet Hester was a little ruffled when the Greys appeared. So many messages had arrived for Edward, that the country gentleman and his daughter had been kept waiting, and a livery servant had called twice, as if impatient. She was afraid that people would blame Edward—that he would never manage to satisfy them all. Her colour was raised, and her brow slightly bent, when her guests entered; but all was right when Edward followed, looking perfectly at leisure, and stood talking before the fire, as if he had been a man of no profession.

Mr Hope had caused his feelings to be so well understood on one important subject, that it was necessary to respect them; and no mention of the Rowlands was made, either before dinner or in the presence of the servants. Nor was there any need of the topic. There was abundance to be said, without having recourse to doubtful subjects; and Margaret became so far relieved from all apprehension on this account, by the time the cheese appeared, that she assured herself that the day was passing off extremely well. There had not been a single pause left to be filled up with the clatter of knives and forks. Mrs Grey pronounced the room delightfully warm; Sophia protested that she liked having the fire at her back; and Mr Grey inquired where Hope got his ale. The boys, who had looked for the first half-hour as if they could not speak for the stiffness of their collars, were now in a full career of jokes, to judge by their stifled laughter. Hester blushed beautifully at every little circumstance that occurred, and played the hostess very gracefully. The day was going off extremely well.

The approaching county election was the principal topic at dinner, as it was probably at every dinner-table in Deerbrook. Mrs Grey first told Hope, at the bottom of the table, all about her wonder at seeing seven or eight gentlemen on horseback entering their field. She was exceedingly surprised to observe such a troop approaching the door: and she hardly knew what to make of it when the servant came in to say that the gentlemen wished to see her, as Mr Grey was at a distance—at market that day. It was strange that she should so entirely forget that there was to be an election soon. To be sure, it might have occurred to her that the party came to canvass Mr Grey: but she did not happen to remember at first; and she thought the gentleman who was spokesman excessively complimentary, both about the place and about some other things, till he mentioned his name, and that he was candidate for the county. Such a highly complimentary strain was not to her taste, she acknowledged; and it lost all its value when it was made so common as in this instance. This gentleman had kissed the little Rowlands all round, she had since been assured:— not that she wished to enlarge on that subject; but it only showed what gentlemen will do when they are canvassing. The other candidate, Mr Lowry, seemed a very high personage indeed. When he found Mr Grey was not at home, he and all his party rode straight on, without inquiring for the ladies. Everyone seemed to think that Mr Lowry was not likely to carry his election, his manners were so extremely high.

Meanwhile, Mr Grey was observing to his hostess that he was sorry to find there was an election impending. People in a small place like Deerbrook were quite apt enough to quarrel, day by day;—an election threw the place into an uproar.

"'How delightful!' those boys are thinking," said Hester, laughing.

"I am sure," said Sophia, "it is anything but delightful to me. I remember, last time, Sydney brought some squibs into the garden, and let them off while mamma and I were in the shrubbery; and we could none of us get to sleep till after midnight for the light of the bonfire down the street."

"They should manage those things more quietly," observed Mr Grey. "This time, however, there will be only a little effusion of joy, and then an end; for they say Ballinger will carry every vote in the place."

"Why, father!" cried Sydney, "are you going to vote for Ballinger this time?"

"No, my boy. I did not say so. I shall not vote at all," he added, observing that he was expected to explain himself. No remark being made, he continued— "It will not be convenient to me to meddle in election matters this time; and it would be of no use, as Lowry has not the slightest chance. One gets nothing but ill-will and trouble by meddling. So, my dear," turning to Hester, "your husband and I will just keep quiet, and let Deerbrook have its own way."

"I believe you may speak for yourself," replied Hester, her eyes sparkling. "Edward has no idea—." Then, remembering that she was speaking to a guest, she cut short her assurance that Edward had no idea of neglecting his duty when it was wanted most, for such a reason as that it was then most irksome.

"There is no occasion in the world for your husband to come forward," observed Mr Grey, with kind anxiety. "I was saying, Hope, that you are quite absolved from interfering in politics. Nobody expects it from a medical man. Everyone knows the disadvantage to a professional man, circumstanced like you, of taking any side in a party matter. You might find the consequences very serious, I assure you."

"And nobody expects it of a medical man," echoed Mrs Grey.

Mr Hope did not reply, that he voted for other reasons than that it was expected of him. He had argued the subject with Mr Grey before, and knew that they must agree to differ. He quietly declared his intention of voting for Mr Lowry, and then asked Sophia to take wine. His manner left no resource to Mrs Grey but to express her feelings to his wife in the drawing-room, after dinner.

She there drew Hester's arm within her own, and kindly observed what pleasure it gave her to see her anticipations so fulfilled. She had had this home, fitted up and inhabited as it now was, in her mind's eye for a longer time than she should choose to tell. Elderly folks might be allowed to look forward, and Mr Grey could bear witness that she had done so. It was delightful to look round and see how all had come to pass.

"Everybody is so interested!" observed Sophia. "Mrs Howell says, some have observed to her what a pity it is that you are dissenters, so that you will not be at church on Sunday. Everybody would be sure to be there: and she says she is of opinion that, considering how many friends wish to see you make your first appearance, you ought to go, for once. She cannot imagine what harm it could do you to go for once. But, whatever you may think about that, it shows her interest, and I thought you would like to know it. Have you seen Mrs Howell's window?"

"My dear! how should they?" exclaimed her mother.

"I forgot they could not go out before Sunday. But, Margaret you must look at Mrs Howell's window the first thing when you can get out. It is so festooned with purple and white, that I told Miss Miskin I thought they would be obliged to light up in the daytime, they have made the shop so dark."

"And they have thrust all the green and orange into the little side window, where nobody can see it!" cried Sydney.

"You managed to see it, I perceive," said Hester; Sydney having at the moment mounted a cockade, and drawn out his green and orange watch-ribbon into the fullest view. William Levitt lost no time in going through the same process with his purple and white.

"You will be the ornaments of Deerbrook," said Margaret, "if you walk about in that gay style. I hope I shall have the pleasure of meeting you both in the street, that I may judge of the effect."

"They will have lost their finery by that time," said Sophia. "We had a terrible snatching of cockades last time."

"Snatching! let them try to snatch mine, and see what they'll get by it!" cried Sydney.

"What would they get but the ribbons?" asked Margaret. Sydney drew her to the light, opened the bows of his cockade, and displayed a corking-pin stuck upright under each bow.

"Isn't it horrid?" said Sophia.

"Horrid! It is not half so horrid as fish-hooks."

And Sydney related how fish-hooks had actually been used during the last election, to detain with their barbs the fingers of snatchers of cockades. "Which do you use?" he asked of William Levitt.

"Neither. My father won't let me do anything more than just wear a cockade and watch-ribbon. I have got a watch-guard too, you see, for fear of losing my watch. But you won't get my cockade off a bit the sooner for my having no spikes under it. I have a particular way of fastening it on. Only try, any day. I defy you to it."

"Hush, hush, boys! don't talk of defiance," said Mrs Grey. "I am sure, I wish there were no such things as elections—in country places, at least. They make nothing but mischief. And, indeed, Hester, my dear, it is a great pity that those should meddle who can keep out of them, as your husband fairly may. Whichever way he might vote, a great many disagreeable remarks would be made; and if he votes as he says, for Mr Lowry, I really think, and so does Mr Grey, that it will be a serious injury to him in his profession."

Hester replied, with some gravity, that people could never do their whole duty without causing disagreeable remarks; and seldom without suffering serious injury.

"But why should he vote?" persisted Mrs Grey.

"Because he considers it his duty, which is commonly his reason for whatever he does."

"An excellent reason too: but I rather thought—I always fancied he defended acting from impulse. But I beg your pardon, my dear:" and she nodded and winked towards the young people, who were trying the impression of a new seal at the centre table, heeding nothing about either duty or impulse. Margaret had fixed the attention of the boys upon this curious seal of hers, in order to obviate a snatching of cockades, or other political feud, upon the spot.

"It seems as if I could speak about nothing but your husband, my dear," continued Mrs Grey, in a whisper: "but you know I feel towards him as towards a son, as I have told him. Do you think he has quite, entirely, got over his accident?"

"Entirely, he thinks. He calls himself in perfect health."

"Well, he ought to know best; but—"

"But what?" asked Hester, anxiously.

"It has occurred to us, that he may still want watching and care. It has struck both Mr Grey and me, that he is not quite the same that he was before that accident. It is natural enough. And yet I thought in the autumn that he was entirely himself again: but there is still a little difference—a little flatness of spirits sometimes—a little more gravity than used to be natural to him."

"But you do not think he looks ill? Tell me just what you think."

"Oh, no, not ill; rather delicate, perhaps; but I am sure it is wonderful that he is so well after such an accident. He calls himself perfectly well, does he?"

"Perfectly."

"Oh, then, we may be quite easy; for he must know best. Do not let anything that I have said dwell upon your mind, my dear. I only just thought I would ask."

How common it is for one's friends to drop a heavy weight upon one's heart, and then desire one not to let it dwell there! Hester's spirits were irrecoverably damped for this evening. Her husband seemed to be an altered man, flat in spirits, and looking delicate, and she told not to be uneasy! She was most eager for the entrance of the gentlemen from the dining-room, that she might watch him and, till they came, she had not a word of amusement to furnish to her guests. Margaret perceived that something had gone wrong and talked industriously till reinforced from the dining-room.

Sophia whispered a hint to her mother to inquire particularly about Mrs Enderby's health. At the mention of her name Mr Hope took his seat on the sofa beside Mrs Grey, and replied gravely and fully—that he thought Mrs Enderby really very unwell—more so than he had ever known her. She was occasionally in a state of great suffering, and any attention that her old friends could show her in the way of a quiet call would be a true kindness. Had he alarmed her family? There was quite hint enough for alarm, he said, in the state in which her relations saw her at times. But Mrs Rowland was always trying to make out that nothing was the matter with her mother: was it not so? Not exactly so. Mrs Rowland knew that there was no immediate danger—that her mother might live many months, or even a few years; but Mr Hope believed neither Mrs Rowland, nor any one else, could deny her sufferings.

"They say Mr Philip is coming," observed Mr Grey.

"Oh, I hope he is!" cried Sydney, turning round to listen.

"Some people say that he is otherwise occupied," observed Sophia, "If all accounts be true—" She caught her mother's eye, and stopped suddenly and awkwardly.

Mr Hope involuntarily glanced at Margaret, as one or two others were doing at the same time. Nothing was to be discerned, for she was stooping over the volume of engravings that she was showing to William Levitt; and she remained stooping for a long while.

When the proper amount of playing and singing had been gone through, and Mrs Grey's sedan was announced the cloaked and muffled guest left behind a not very happy party. Margaret's gaiety seemed exhausted, and she asked if it was not late. Hester was gazing at her husband. She saw the perspiration on his brow. She put her arm within his, and anxiously inquired whether he was not unwell. She was sure he had never fully recovered his strength: she had not taken care enough of him: why did he not tell her when he was weary and wanted nursing?

Mr Hope looked at her with an unaffected surprise, which went far to console her, and assured her that he was perfectly well; and that, moreover, he was so fond of indulgence that she would be sure to hear of it, if ever he could find a pretence for getting upon the sofa.

Hester was comforted, but said that his spirits were not always what they had been: and she appealed to Margaret. Margaret declared that any failure of spirits in Edward was such a new idea, that she must consider before she gave an answer. She thought that he had been too busy to draw so many caricatures as usual lately; but she had observed no deeper signs of despondency than that.

"Do not let us get into the habit of talking about spirits," said Hope. "I hear quite enough about that away from home; and I can assure you, professionally, that it is a bad subject to dwell upon. Every one who lives has variations of spirits: they are like the sunshine, or like Dr Levitt's last sermon, of which Mrs Enderby says every Sunday in the church porch—'It is to be felt, not talked about.'"

"But, as a sign of health—" said Hester.

"As a sign of health, my dear, the spirits of all this household may be left to my professional discrimination. Will you trust me, my dear?"

"Oh, yes!" she uttered, with a sigh of relief.

Chapter Eighteen

Grandmamma in Retreat.

"I am better now, Phoebe," said Mrs Enderby, sinking back faintly in her easy-chair, after one of her attacks of spasms. "I am better now; and if you will fan me for a minute or two, I shall be quite fit to see the children—quite delighted to have them."

"I declare," said the maid, "here are the drops standing upon your face this cold day, as if it was August! But if the pain is cone, never mind anything else! And I, for one, won't say anything against your having the children in; for I'm sure the seeing your friends has done you no harm, and nothing but good."

"Pray, draw up the blind, Phoebe, and let me see something of the sunshine. Bless me! how frosty the field looks, while I have been stifled with heat for this hour past! I had better not go to the window, however, for I begin to feel almost chilly already. Thank you, Phoebe; you have fanned me enough. Now call the children, Phoebe."

Phoebe wrapped a cloak about her mistress's knees, pinned her shawl up closer around her throat, and went to call the children in from the parlour below. Matilda drew up her head and flattened her back, and then asked her grandmamma how she did. George looked up anxiously in the old lady's face.

"Ah, George," said she, smiling; "it is an odd face to look at, is not it? How would you like your face to look as mine does?"

"Not at all," said George.

Mrs Enderby laughed heartily, and then told him that her face was not unlike his once—as round, and as red, and as shining in frosty weather.

"Perhaps if you were to go out now into the frost, your face would look as it used to do."

"I am afraid not. When my face looked like yours, it was when I was a little girl, and used to slide and make snowballs as you do. That was a long time ago. My face is wrinkled now, because I am old; and it is pale, because I am ill."

George heard nothing after the word "snowballs." "I wish some more snow would come," he observed. "We have plenty of ice down in the meadows, but there has been only one fall of snow, and that melted almost directly."

"Papa thinks there will be more snow very soon," observed Matilda.

"If there is, you children can do something for me that I should like very much," said grandmamma. "Shall I tell you what it is?"

"Yes."

"You can make a snow-man in that field. I am sure Mr Grey will give you leave."

"What good will that do you?" asked Matilda.

"I can sit here and watch you; and I shall like that exceedingly. I shall see you gathering the snow, and building up your man: and if you will turn about and shake your hand this way now and then, I shall be sure to observe it, and I shall think you are saying something kind to me."

"I wish the snow would come," cried George, stamping with impatience.

"I do not believe mamma will let us," observed Matilda. "She prohibits our going into Mr Grey's field."

"But she shall let us, that one time," cried George. "I will ask papa, and Mr Grey, and Sydney, and Uncle Philip, and all. When will Uncle Philip come again?"

"Some time soon, I dare say. But, George, we must do as your mamma pleases about my plan, you know. If she does not wish you to go into Mr Grey's field, you can make your snow-man somewhere else."

"But then you won't see us. But I know what I will do. I will speak to Sydney, and he and Fanny and Mary shall make you a snow-man yonder, where we should have made him."

Mrs Enderby pressed the boy to her, and laughed while she thanked him, but said it was not the same thing seeing the Greys make a snow-man.

"Why, George!" said Matilda, contemptuously.

"When *will* Uncle Philip come?" asked the boy, who was of opinion that Uncle Philip could bring all things to pass.

"Why, I will tell you how it is, my dear. Uncle Philip is very busy learning his lessons."

The boy stared.

"Yes: grown-up people who mean to be great lawyers, as I believe Uncle Philip does, have to learn lessons like little boys, only much longer and much harder."

"When will he have done them?"

"Not for a long while yet: but he will make a holiday some time soon, and come to see us. I should like to get well before that. Sometimes I think I shall, and sometimes I think not."

"Does he expect you will?"

"He expects nothing about it. He does not know that I am ill. I do not wish that he should know it, my dears; so, when I feel particularly well, and when I have heard anything that pleases me, I ask Phoebe to bring me the pen and ink, and I write to Uncle Philip."

"And why does not mamma tell him how you are?"

"Ah! why, indeed," muttered Phoebe.

"She knows that I do not wish it. Uncle Philip writes charming long letters to me, as I will show you. Bring me my reticule. Here—here is a large sheet of paper, quite full, you see—under the seal and all. When will you write such long letters, I wonder?"

"I shall when I am married, I suppose," said Matilda, again drawing up her little head.

"You married, my love! And pray when are you to be married?"

"Mamma often talks of the time when she shall lose me, and of what things have to be done while she has me with her."

"There is a great deal to be done indeed, love, before that day, if it ever comes."

"There are more ways than one of losing a child," observed Phoebe, in her straightforward way. "If Mrs Rowland thinks so long beforehand of the one way, it is to be hoped she keeps Miss Matilda up to the thought of the other, which must happen sooner or later, while marrying may not."

"Well, Phoebe," said the old lady, "we will not put any dismal thoughts into this little head: time enough for that: we will leave all that to Miss Young." Then, stroking Matilda's round cheek, she inquired, "My love, did you ever in your life feel any pain?"

"Oh, dear, yes, grandmamma: to be sure I have; twice. Why, don't you remember, last spring, I had a dreadful pain in my head for nearly two hours, on George's birthday? And last week, after I went to bed, I had such a pain in my arm, I did not know how to bear it."

"And what became of it?"

"Oh, I found at last I could bear it no longer, and I began to think what I should do. I meant to ring the bell, but I fell asleep."

Phoebe laughed with very little ceremony, and grandmamma could not help joining. She supposed Matilda hoped it might be long enough before she had any more pain. In the night-time, certainly, Matilda said. And not in the daytime? Is not pain as bad in the daytime? Matilda acknowledged that she should like to be ill in the daytime. Mamma took her on her lap when she was ill; and Miss Young was so very sorry for her; and she had something nice to drink.

"Then I am afraid, my dear, you don't pity me at all," said grandmamma. "Perhaps you think you would like to live in a room like this, with a sofa and a screen, and Phoebe to wait upon you, and whatever you might fancy to eat and drink. Would you like to be ill as I am?"

"Not at present," said Matilda: "not till I am married. I shall enjoy doing as I like when I am married."

"How the child's head runs upon being married!" said Phoebe. "And to suppose that being ill is doing as one likes, of all odd things!"

"I should often like to fly all over the world," said Mrs Enderby, "and to get anywhere out of this room—I am so tired of it: but I know I cannot: so I get books, and read about all the strange places, far off, that Mungo Park tells us about, and Gulliver, and Captain Parry. And I should often like to sleep at night when I cannot; and then I get up softly, without waking Phoebe, and look out at the bright stars, and think over all we are told about them—about their being all full of men and women. Did you know that, George?" asked she—George being now at the window.

"Oh, yes," answered Matilda for him, "we know all about those things."

"Are falling stars all full of men and women?" asked George.

"There were none on a star that my father saw fall on the Dingleford road," observed Phoebe. "It wasn't big enough to hold men and women."

"Did it fall in the middle of the road?" asked George, turning from the window. "What was it like?"

"It was a round thing, as big as a house, and all bright and crystal like," said Phoebe, with absolute confidence. "It blocked up the road from the great oak that you may remember, close by the second milestone, to the ditch on the opposite side."

"Phoebe, are you sure of that?" asked Mrs Enderby, with a face full of anxious doubt.

"Ma'am, my father came straight home after seeing it fall, and he let my brother John and me go the next morning early, to bring home some of the splinters."

"Oh, well," said Mrs Enderby, who always preferred believing to doubting; "I have heard of stones falling from the moon."

"This was a falling star, ma'am."

"Can you show me any of the splinters?" asked George, eagerly.

"There was nothing whatsoever left of them," said Phoebe, "by the time John and I went. We could not find a piece of crystal so big as my thimble. My father has often laughed at John and me since, for not having been there in time, before it was all gone."

"It is a good thing, my dears, depend upon it, as I was saying," observed Mrs Enderby, "to know all such things about the stars, and so on, against the time when you cannot do as you like, and go where you please. Matilda, my jewel, when you are married, as you were talking about, and can please yourself, you will take great care to be kind to your mamma, my dear, if poor mamma should be old and ill. You will always wish to be tender to your mother, love, I am sure; and that will do her more good than anything."

"Perhaps mamma won't be ill," replied Matilda.

"Then if she is never ill, she will certainly be old, some day; and then you will be as kind to her as ever you can be,—promise me, my love. Your mamma loves you dearly, Matilda."

"She says I dance better than any girl in Miss Anderson's school, grandmamma. I heard her tell Mrs Levitt so, yesterday."

"Here comes mamma," said George, from the window.

"Your mamma, my dear? Phoebe, sweep up the hearth. Hang that curtain straight. Give me that letter,—no, not that,—the large letter. There! now put it into my knitting-basket. Make haste down, Phoebe, to be ready to open the door for Mrs Rowland. Don't keep her waiting a moment on the steps."

"She has not got to the steps yet," said George. "She is talking to Mrs Grey. Mrs Grey was coming here, and mamma went and spoke to her. Oh,

Matilda, come and look how they are nodding their bonnets at each other! I think Mrs Grey is very angry, she wags her head about so. There! now she is going away. There she goes across the road! and mamma is coming up the steps."

After a minute or two of silent expectation, Mrs Rowland entered her mother's room. She brought with her a draught of wintry air, which, as she jerked aside her ample silk cloak, on taking her seat on the sofa, seemed to chill the invalid, though there was now a patch of colour on each withered cheek.

"How much better you look, ma'am!" was the daughter's greeting. "I always thought it would be a pity to disturb Philip about you: and now, if he were to see you, he would not believe that you had been ill. Mr Rowland would be satisfied that I am right, I am sure, if he were to come in."

"My mistress is noways better," said Phoebe, bluntly. "She is not the better for that flush she has got now, but the worse."

"Never mind, Phoebe! I shall do very well, I dare say," said Mrs Enderby, with a sigh. "Well, my dear, how do you all go on at home?"

"Much as usual, ma'am. But that reminds me—Matilda, my own love, Miss Young must be wanting you for your lesson on objects. Go, my dear."

"I hoped Matilda was come for the day," said Mrs Enderby. "I quite expected she was to stay with me to-day. Do let me have her, my dear: it will do me so much good."

"You are very kind, ma'am, but it is quite impossible. It is totally out of the question, I assure you. Matilda, my love, go this instant. We make a great point of the lessons on objects. Pray, Phoebe, tie Miss Rowland's bonnet, and make haste."

Phoebe did so, taking leave to observe that little girls were likely to live long enough to know plenty of things after they had no grandmammas left to be a comfort to.

Mrs Enderby struggled to say, "Hush, Phoebe;" but she found she could not speak. George was desired to go with his sister, and was scarcely allowed time to kiss his grandmamma. While Phoebe was taking the children down stairs, Mrs Rowland wondered that some people allowed their servants to take such liberties as were taken; and gave notice that though she tolerated Phoebe, because Phoebe's mistress had taken a fancy to her, she could not allow her family plans to be made a subject of remark to her mother's domestics. Mrs Enderby had not quite decided upon her line of reply, when Phoebe came back, and occupied herself in supplying her mistress, first with a freshly-heated footstool, and then with a cup of arrowroot.

"Where do you get your arrowroot, ma'am?" asked Mrs Rowland. "I want some extremely for my poor dear Anna; and I can procure none that is at all to compare with yours."

"Mrs Grey was so kind as to send me some, my dear; and it really is excellent. Phoebe, how much of it is there left? I dare say there may be enough for a cup or two for dear little Anna."

Phoebe replied, that there was very little left—not any more than her mistress would require before she could grow stronger. Mrs Rowland would not take the rest of the arrowroot on any account: she was only wondering where Mrs Grey got it, and how it was that the Greys always contrived to help themselves to the best of everything. Phoebe was going to observe that they helped their neighbours to good things as well as themselves; but a look from her mistress stopped her. Mrs Enderby remarked that she had no doubt she could learn from Mrs Grey or Sophia, the next time she saw either of them, where they procured their arrowroot. "It is a long time since I saw Mrs Grey," she observed, timidly.

"My dear ma'am, how can you think of seeing any one in your present state?" inquired the daughter. "One need but see the flush in your face, to know that it would be highly improper for you to admit company. I could not take the responsibility of allowing it."

"But Mrs Grey is not company, my love."

"Any one is company to an invalid. I assure you I prevented Mr Rowland's coming for the reason I assign. He was coming yesterday, but I would not let him."

"I should like to see him, however. And I should like to see Mrs Grey too."

Under pretence of arranging her mistress's shawl, Phoebe touched the old lady's shoulder, in token of intelligence. Mrs Enderby was somewhat flurried at the liberty which she felt her maid had taken with her daughter; but she could not notice it now; and she introduced another subject. Had everybody done calling on the Hopes? Were the wedding visits all over? Oh, yes, Mrs Rowland was thankful to say; that fuss was at an end at last. One would think nobody had ever been married before, by the noise that had been made in Deerbrook about this young couple.

"Mr Hope is such a favourite!" observed Mrs Enderby.

"He has been so; but it won't last. I never saw a young man so gone off as he is. He has not been like the same man since he connected himself with the Greys so decidedly. Surely, ma'am, you must perceive that."

"It had not occurred to me, my dear. He comes very often, and he is always extremely kind and very entertaining. He brought his bride with him yesterday, which I thought very attentive, as I could not go and pay my respects to her. And really, Priscilla, whether it was that I had not seen her for some time, or that pretty young ladies look prettiest in an old woman's sick-room, I thought she was more beautiful than ever."

"She is handsome," admitted Mrs Rowland. "Poor thing! it makes one sorry for her, when one thinks what is before her."

"What is before her?" ask Mrs Enderby, alarmed.

"If she loves her husband at all, she must suffer cruelly in seeing him act as he persists in doing; and she must tremble in looking forward to the consequences. He is quite obstinate about voting for Mr Lowry, though there is not a soul in Deerbrook to keep him in countenance; and everybody knows how strongly Sir William Hunter has expressed himself in favour of Mr Ballinger. It is thought the consequences will be very serious to Mr Hope. There is his almshouse practice at stake, at all events; and I fancy a good many families will have no more to do with him if he defies the Hunters, and goes against the opinions of all his neighbours. His wife must see that he has nobody with him. I do pity the poor young thing!"

"Dear me!" said the old lady, "can nothing be done, I wonder. I declare I am quite concerned. I should hope something may be done. I would take the liberty of speaking to him myself, rather than that any harm should happen to him. He has always been so very kind to me, that I think I could venture to say anything to him. I will turn it over in my mind, and see what can be done."

"You will not prevail with him, ma'am, I am afraid. If Mr Grey speaks in vain (as I know he has done), it is not likely that any one else will have any influence over him. No, no; the wilful must be left to their own devices. Whatever you do, ma'am, do not speak to the bride about it, or there is no knowing what you may bring upon yourself."

"What could I bring upon myself, my dear?"

"Oh, those who do not see the vixen in that pretty face of hers, have not such good eyes as she has herself. For God's sake, ma'am, do not offend her!"

Mrs Enderby was now full of concern; and being as unhappy as she could be made for the present, her daughter took her leave. The old lady looked into the fire and sighed, for some minutes after she was left alone. When Phoebe re-entered, her mistress declared that she felt quite tired out, and must lie down. Before she closed her eyes, she raised her head again, and said—

"Phoebe, I am surprised at you—"

"Oh, ma'am, you mean about my taking the liberty to make a sign to you. But, ma'am, I trust you will excuse it, because I am sure Mr Hope would have no objection to your seeing Mrs Grey; and, to my thought, there is no occasion to consult with anybody else; and I have no doubt Mrs Grey will be calling again some day soon, just at a time when you are fit to see her. Is not there any book, or anything, ma'am, that I could be carrying over to Mrs Grey's while you are resting yourself, ma'am?"

"Ah! do so, Phoebe. Carry that book,—it is not quite due, but that does not signify; carry that book over, and give my regards, and beg to know how Mrs Grey and all the family are. And if Mrs Grey *should* come in this evening," she continued, in excuse to herself for her devices, "I shall be able to find out, in a quiet way, where she gets her arrowroot; and Priscilla will be glad to know."

Whatever it might be that Phoebe said to Alice, and that brought Mrs Grey out into the hall to speak herself to Phoebe, the result was that Mrs Grey's lantern was ordered as soon as it grew dark, and that she arrived in Mrs Enderby's apartment just as the old lady had waked from her doze, and while the few tears that had escaped from under her eyelids before she slept were yet scarcely dried upon her cheeks.

Chapter Nineteen

Home at "The Hopes'."

The evil consequences of Mr Hope's voting for Lowry had not been exaggerated in the anticipations of his friends and vigilant neighbours; and these consequences were rather aggravated than alleviated by the circumstance that Mr Lowry won the election. First, the inhabitants of Deerbrook were on the watch for any words which might fall from Sir William or Lady Hunter; and when it was reported that Sir William had frowned, and sworn an oath at Mr Hope, on hearing how he had voted, and that Lady Hunter had asked whether it was possible that Mr Hope had forgotten under whose interest he held his appointment to attend the almshouses and the neighbouring hamlet, several persons determined to be beforehand with their great neighbours, and to give the benefit of their family practice to some one of better politics than Mr Hope. In another set of minds, a real fear of Mr Hope, as a dangerous person, sprang up under the heat of the displeasure of the influential members of society. Such were slow to have recourse to another medical attendant, and undertook the management of the health of their own families till they could find an adviser in whom they could perfectly confide. When Mr Lowry gained the contest, the population of Deerbrook was electrified, and the unpleasantness of their surprise was visited upon the only supporter of Mr Lowry whom the place contained. Wise folks were not wanting who talked of the skill which some persons had in keeping on the winning side,—of reasons which time sometimes revealed for persons choosing to be singular,—and some remarkable incidents were reported of conversations between Mr Lowry and Mr Hope in the lanes, and of certain wonderful advantages which had lately fallen to one or another of Mr Hope's acquaintances, through some strong political interest. Mr Rowland doubted, at his own table, all the news he heard on the subject, and said everywhere that he did not see why a man should not vote as he pleased. Mr Grey was very sorry about the whole affair; he was sorry that there had been any contest at all for the county, as it disturbed the peace of Deerbrook; he was sorry that the candidate he preferred had won, as the fact exasperated the temper of Deerbrook; he was sorry that Hope had voted, to the detriment of his name and rising fortunes; and he was sorry that he himself had been unable at last to vote for Lowry, to keep his young friend in countenance: it was truly unlucky that he should have passed his promise early to Sir William Hunter not to vote. It was a sad business altogether. It was only to be hoped that it would pass out of people's minds; that things would soon get into their usual train; and that it might be seven years before there was another election.

Hester complained to her husband and sister of the manner in which she was treated by the tradespeople of the place. She had desired to put herself on a footing of acquaintanceship with them, as neighbours, and persons with whom there must be a constant transaction of business for life. She saw at once the difference in the relation between tradespeople and their customers in a large town like Birmingham, and in a village where there is but one baker, where the grocer and hatter are the same personage, and where you cannot fly from your butcher, be he ever so much your foe. Hester therefore made it her business to transact herself all affairs with the village tradesmen. She began her housekeeping energetically, and might be seen in Mr Jones's open shop in the coldest morning of January, selecting her joint of meat; or deciding among brown sugars at Tucker's, the grocer's. After the election, she found some difference in the manner of most of the shop-people towards her; and she fancied more than there was. With some of these persons, there was no more in their minds than the consciousness of having discussed the new family and Mr Hope's vote, and come to a conclusion against his "principles." With others, Mrs Rowland's influence had done deeper mischief. A few words dropped by herself, or reports of her sayings, circulated by her servants, occasioned dislike or alarm which Hester's sensitiveness apprehended at once, and forthwith exaggerated. She complained to her husband that she could not go to the shops with any comfort, and that she thought she must turn over the housekeeping to Morris. Margaret remonstrated against this; and, by being her sister's constant companion in her walks of business as well as pleasure, hoped to be able to keep the peace, and to preserve or restore, if need were, a good understanding between parties who could most materially promote or injure each other's comfort. The leisure hours to which she had looked forward with such transport were all chequered with anxiety on this subject, in the intervals of speculation on another matter, to which she found her mind constantly recurring, in spite of her oft-repeated conviction that it was no concern of hers,—where Mr Enderby was,—what he was doing,—and when he would come. Day by day, as she spread her books before her, or began to write, she wondered at her own listlessness about employments to which she had looked forward with so much eagerness; and when she detected herself gazing into the fire by the half-hour together, or allowing the ink to dry in her suspended pen, she found that she was as far as ever from deciding whether Hester was not now in the way to be less happy than ever, and how it was that, with all her close friendship with Philip Enderby, of which she had spoken so confidently to Maria, she was now in perfect ignorance of his movements and intentions. The whole was very strange, and, in the experience, somewhat dreary.

Her great comfort was Edward: this was a new support and a strong one: but even here she was compelled to own herself somewhat disappointed. This brotherly relation, for which she had longed all her life, did not bring the fulness of satisfaction which she had anticipated. She had not a fault to find with Edward: she was always called upon by his daily conduct for admiration, esteem, and affection; but all this was not of the profit to her which she had expected. He seemed altered: the flow of his spirits was much moderated; but perhaps this was no loss, as his calmness, his gentle seriousness, and domestic benevolence were brought out more strikingly than ever. Margaret's disappointment lay in the intercourse between themselves. That Edward was reserved—that beneath his remarkable frankness there lay an uncommunicativeness of disposition—no one could before his marriage have made her believe: yet it certainly was so. Though Hester and she never discussed Edward's character, more or less—though Hester's love for him, and Margaret's respect for that love, rendered all such conversation unpossible, Margaret was perfectly well aware that Hester's conviction on this particular point was the same as her own—that Hester had discovered that she had not fully understood her husband, and that there remained a region of his character into which she had not yet penetrated. Margaret was obliged to conclude that all this was natural and right, and that what she had heard said of men generally was true even of Edward Hope—that there are depths of character where there are not regions of experience, which defy the sympathy and sagacity of women. However natural and right all this might be, she could not but be sorry for it. It brought disappointment to herself, and, as she sadly suspected, to Hester. While continually and delightedly compelled to honour and regard him more and more, and to rely upon him as she had never before relied, she felt that he did not win, and even did not desire, any intimate confidence. She found that she could still say things to Maria which she could not say to him; and that, while their domestic conversation rarely flagged—while it embraced a boundless range of fact, and all that they could ascertain of morals, philosophy, and religion—the greatest psychological events, the most interesting experiences of her life might go forward without express recognition from Edward. Such was her view of the case; and this was the disappointment which, in the early days of her new mode of life, she had to acknowledge to herself, and to conceal from all others.

One fine bright morning towards the end of January, the sisters set out for their walk, willingly quitting the clear crackling fire within for the sharp air and sparkling pathways without.

"Which way shall we go?" asked Margaret.

"Oh, I suppose along the high-road, as usual. How provoking it is that we are prevented, day after day, from getting to the woods by my snow-boots not having arrived! We will go by Mrs Howell's for the chance of their having come."

Mrs Howell had two expressions of countenance—the gracious and the prim. Till lately, Hester had been favoured with the first exclusively. She was now to be amused with variety, and the prim was offered to her contemplation. Never did Mrs Howell look more inaccessible than to-day, when she scarcely rose from her stool behind the counter, to learn what was the errand of her customer.

"You guess what I am come for, Mrs Howell, I dare say. Have my boots arrived yet?"

"I am not aware of their having arrived, ma'am. But Miss Miskin is now occupied in that department."

"Only consider how the winter is getting on, Mrs Howell! and I can walk nowhere but in the high-road, for want of my boot."

Mrs Howell curtsied.

"Can you not hasten your agent, or help me to my boots, one way or another? Is there no one in Deerbrook whom you could employ to make me a pair?"

Mrs Howell cast up her hands and eyes.

"How do other ladies manage to obtain their boots before the snow comes, instead of after it has melted?"

"Perhaps you will ask them yourself ma'am: I conceive you know all the ladies in Deerbrook. You will find Miss Miskin in that department, ladies, if you wish to investigate."

Hester invaded the domain of Miss Miskin—the shoe-shop behind the other counter—in the hope of finding something to put on her feet, which should enable her to walk where she pleased. While engaged in turning over the stock, without any help from Miss Miskin, who was imitating Mrs Howell's distant manner with considerable success, a carriage drove up to the door, which could be no other than Sir William Hunter's; and Lady Hunter's voice was accordingly heard, the next minute, asking for green sewing-silk. The gentle drawl of Mrs Howell's tone conveyed that her countenance had resumed its primary expression. She observed upon the horrors of the fire which had happened at Blickley the night before. Lady Hunter had not heard of it; and the relation therefore followed of: the burning down of a house and shop in Blickley, when a nursemaid and baby were lost in the flames.

"I should hope it is not true," observed Lady Hunter. "Last night, did you say?—Early this morning? There has scarcely been time for the news to arrive of a fire at Blickley early this morning."

"It is certainly true, however, my lady. No doubt whatever of the catastrophe, I am grieved to say." And Mrs Howell's sighs were sympathetically responded to by Miss Miskin in the back shop.

"But how did you hear it?" asked Lady Hunter.

There was no audible answer. There were probably signs and intimations of something; for Lady Hunter made a circuit round the shop, on some pretence, and stared in at the door of the shoe-parlour, just at the right moment for perceiving, if she so pleased, the beautiful smallness of Hester's foot. Some low, murmuring, conversation then passed at Mrs Howell's counter, when the words "black servant" alone met Margaret's ear.

Hester found nothing that she could wear. The more she pressed for information and assistance about obtaining boots, the more provokingly cool Miss Miskin grew. At last Hester turned to her sister with a hasty inquiry what was to be done.

"We must hope for better fortune before next winter, I suppose," said Margaret, smiling.

"And wet my feet every day this winter," said Hester; "for I will not be confined to the high-road for any such reason as this."

"Dear me, ma'am, you are warm!" simpered Miss Miskin.

"I warm! What do you mean, Miss Miskin?"

"You are warm, ma'am:— not that it is of any consequence; but you are a little warm at present."

"Nobody can charge that upon you, Miss Miskin, I must say," observed Margaret, laughing.

"No, ma'am, that they cannot, nor ever will. I am not apt to be warm, and I hope I can excuse... Good morning, ladies."

Mrs Howell treated her customers with a swimming curtsey as they went out, glancing at her shop-woman the while. Lady Hunter favoured them with a full stare.

"What excessive impertinence!" exclaimed Hester. "To tell me that I was warm, and she hoped she could excuse! My husband will hardly believe it."

"Oh, yes, he will. He knows them for two ignorant, silly women; worth observing, perhaps, but not worth minding. Have you any other shop to go to?"

Yes, the tinman's, for a saucepan or two of a size not yet supplied, for which Morris had petitioned.

The tinman was either unable or not very anxious to understand Hester's requisitions. He brought out everything but what was wanted; and was so extremely interested in observing something that was going on over the way, that he was every moment casting glances abroad between the dutch-ovens and fenders that half-darkened his window. The ladies at last looked over the way too, and saw a gig containing a black footman standing before the opposite house.

"A stranger in Deerbrook!" observed Margaret, as they issued from the shop. "I do not wonder that Mr Hill had so little attention to spare for us."

The sisters had been so accustomed, during all the years of their Birmingham life, to see faces that they did not know, that they could not yet sympathise with the emotions caused in Deerbrook by the appearance of a stranger. They walked on, forgetting in conversation all about the gig and black servant. Hester had not been pleased by the insufficient attention she had met with in both the shops she had visited, and she did not enjoy her walk as was her wont. As they trod the crisp and glittering snow, Margaret hoped the little Rowlands and Greys were happy in making the snow-man which had been the vision of their imaginations since the winter set in: but Hester cast longing eyes on the dark woods which sprang from the sheeted meadows, and thought nothing could be so delightful as to wander among them, and gather icicles from the boughs, even though the paths should be ankle-deep in snow.

Just when they were proposing to turn back, a horseman appeared on the ridge of the rising ground over which the road passed. "It is Edward!" cried Hester. "I had no idea we should meet him on this road." And she quickened her pace, and her countenance brightened as if she had not seen him for a month. Before they met him, however, the gig with the black footman, now containing also a gentleman driving, overtook and slowly passed them—the gentleman looking round him, as if in search of some dwelling hereabouts. On approaching Hope, the stranger drew up, touched his hat, and asked a question; and on receiving the answer, bowed, turned round, and repassed Hester and Margaret. Hope joined his wife and sister, and walked his horse beside the path.

"Who is that gentleman, Edward?"

"I believe it is Mr Foster, the surgeon at Blickley."

"What did he want with you?"

"He wanted to know whether he was in the right road to the Russell Taylors."

"The Russell Taylors! Your patients!"

"Once my patients, but no longer so. It seems they are Mr Foster's patients now."

Hester made no reply.

"Can you see from your pathway what is going on below there in the meadow? I see the skaters very busy on the ponds. Why do not you go there, instead of walking here every day?"

Margaret had to explain the case about the snow-boots, for Hester's face was bathed in tears. Edward rallied her gently; but it would not do. She motioned to him to ride on, and he thought it best to do so. The sisters proceeded in silence, Hester's tears flowing faster and faster. Instead of walking through Deerbrook, she took a back road homewards, and drew down her veil. As ill luck would have it, however, they met Sophia Grey and her sisters, and Sophia would stop. She was about to turn back with them, when she saw that something was the matter, and then she checked herself awkwardly, and wished her cousins good morning, while Fanny and Mary were staring at Hester.

"One ought not to mind," said Margaret, half laughing: "there are so many causes for grown people's tears! but I always feel now as I did when I was a child—a shame at being seen in tears, and an excessive desire to tell people that I have not been naughty."

"You could not have told Sophia so of me, I am sure," said Hester.

"Yes, I could; you are not crying because you have been naughty, but you are naughty because you cry; and that may be cured presently."

It was not presently cured, however. During the whole of dinner-time, Hester's tears continued to flow; and she could not eat, though she made efforts to do so. Edward and Margaret talked a great deal about skating and snow-men, and about the fire at Blickley; but they came to a stand at last. The foot-boy went about on tiptoe, and shut the door as if he had been in a sick-room; and this made Hester's short sobs only the more audible. It was a relief when the oranges were on the table at last, and the door closed behind the dinner and the boy. Margaret began to peel an orange for her sister, and Edward poured out a glass of wine; he placed it before her, and then drew his chair to her side, saying—

"Now, my dear, let us get to the bottom of all this distress."

"No, do not try, Edward. Never mind me! I shall get the better of this, by-and-by: only let me alone."

"Thank you!" said Hope, smiling. "I like to see people reasonable! I am to see you sorrowing in this way, and for very sufficient cause, and I am neither to mind your troubles nor my own, but to be as merry as if nothing had happened! Is not this reasonable, Margaret?"

"For very sufficient cause!" said Hester, eagerly.

"Yes, indeed; for very sufficient cause. It must be a painful thing to you to find my neighbours beginning to dislike me; to have the tradespeople impertinent to you on my account; to see my patients leave me, and call in somebody from a distance, in the face of all Deerbrook. It must make you anxious to think what is to become of us, if the discontent continues and spreads: and it must be a bitter disappointment to you to find that to be my wife is not to be so happy as we expected. Here is cause enough for tears."

In the midst of her grief, Hester looked up at her husband with an expression of gratitude and tenderness which consoled him for her.

"I will not answer for it," he continued, "but that we may all three sit down to weep together, one of these days."

"And then," said Margaret, "Hester will be the first to cheer up and comfort us."

"I have no doubt of it," replied Hope. "Meantime, is there anything that you would have had done otherwise by me? Was I right or not to vote? and was there anything wrong in my manner of doing it? Is there any cause whatever for repentance?"

"None, none," cried Hester. "You have been right throughout. I glory in all you do."

"To me it seems that you could not have done otherwise," observed Margaret. "It was a simple, unavoidable act, done with the simplicity of affairs which happen in natural course. I neither repent it for you, nor glory in it."

"That is just my view of it, Margaret. And it follows that the consequences are to be taken as coming in natural course too. Does not this again simplify the affair, Hester?"

"It lights it up," replied Hester. "It reminds me how all would have been if you had acted otherwise than as you did. It is, to be sure, scarcely possible to conceive of such a thing,—but if you had not voted, I should have—not despised you in any degree,—but lost confidence in you a little."

"That is a very mild way of putting it," said Hope, laughing.

"Thank Heaven, we are spared that!" exclaimed Margaret. "But, brother, tell us the worst that you think can come of this displeasure against you. I rather suspect, however, that we have suffered the worst already, in discovering that people can be displeased with you."

"That being so extremely rare a lot in this world, and especially in the world of a village," replied Hope, "I really do not know what to expect as the last result of this affair, nor am I anxious to foresee. I never liked the sort of attachment that most of my neighbours have testified for me. It was to their honour in as far as it showed kindness of heart, but it was unreasonable: so unreasonable that I imagine the opposite feelings which are now succeeding may be just as much in excess. Suppose it should be so, Hester?"

"Well, what then?" she asked, sighing.

"Suppose our neighbours should send me to Coventry, and my patients should leave me so far as that we should not have enough to live on?"

"That would be persecution," cried Hester, brightening. "I could bear persecution,—downright persecution."

"You could bear seeing your husband torn by lions in the amphitheatre," said Margaret, smiling, "but..."

"But a toss of Mrs Howell's head is unendurable," said Hope, with solemnity.

Hester looked down, blushing like a chidden child.

"But about this persecution," said she. "What made you ask those questions just now?"

"I find my neighbours more angry with me than I could have supposed possible, my dear. I have been treated with great and growing rudeness for some days. In a place like this, you know, offences seldom come alone. If you do a thing which a village public does not approve, there will be offence in whatever else you say and do for some time after. And I suspect that is my case now. I may be mistaken, however; and whatever happens, I hope, my love, we shall all be to the last degree careful not to see offence where it is not intended."

"Not to do the very thing we are suffering under ourselves," observed Margaret.

"We will not watch our neighbours, and canvass their opinions of us by our own fireside," said Hope. "We will conclude them all to be our friends till they give us clear evidence to the contrary. Shall it not be so, love?"

"I know what you mean," said Hester, with some resentment in her voice and manner. "You cannot trust my temper in your affairs: and you are perfectly right. My temper is not to be trusted."

"Very few are, in the first agonies of unpopularity; and such faith in one's neighbours as shall supersede watching them ought hardly to be looked for in the atmosphere of Deerbrook. We must all look to ourselves."

"I understand you," said Hester. "I take the lesson home, I assure you. It is clear to me through your cautious phrase,—the 'we,' and 'all of us,' and 'ourselves.' But remember this,—that people are not made alike, and are not able, and not intended to feel alike; and if some have less power than others over their sorrow, at least over their tears, it does not follow that they cannot bear as well what they have to bear. If I cannot sit looking as Margaret does, peeling oranges and philosophising, it may not be that I have less strength at my heart, but that I have more at stake,—more—"

Hope started from her side, and leaned against the mantelpiece, covering his face with his hands. At this moment, the boy entered with a message from a patient in the next street, who wanted Mr Hope.

"Oh, do not leave me, Edward! Do not leave me at this moment!" cried Hester. "Come back for five minutes!"

Hope quietly said that he should return presently, and went out. When the hall door was heard to close behind him, Hester flung herself down on the sofa. Whatever momentary resentment Margaret might have felt at her sister's words, it vanished at the sight of Hester's attitude of wretchedness. She sat on a footstool beside the sofa, and took her sister's hand in hers.

"You are kinder to me than I deserve," murmured Hester: "but, Margaret, mind what I say! never marry, Margaret! Never love, and never marry, Margaret!"

Margaret laid her hand on her sister's shoulder, saying,—"Stop here, Hester! While I was the only friend you had, it was right and kind to tell me all that was in your heart. But now that there is one nearer and dearer, and far, far worthier than I, I can hear nothing like this. Nor are you fit just now to speak of these serious things: you are discomposed—"

"One would think you were echoing Miss Miskin, Margaret,—'You are warm, ma'am.' But you must hear this much. I insist upon it. If you would have heard me, you would have found that I was not going to say a word about my husband inconsistent with all the love and honour you would have him enjoy. I assure you, you might trust me not to complain of my husband. I have no words in which to say how noble he is. But, oh! it is all true about the wretchedness of married life! I am wretched, Margaret."

"So I see," said Margaret, in deep sorrow.

"Life is a blank to me. I have no hope left. I am neither wiser, nor better, nor happier for God having given me all that should make a woman what I meant to be. What can God give me more than I have?"

"I was just thinking so," replied Margaret, mournfully.

"What follows then?"

"Not that all married people are unhappy because you are."

"Yes, oh, yes! all who are capable of happiness: all who can love. The truth is, there is no perfect confidence in the world: there is no rest for one's heart. I believed there was, and I am disappointed: and if you believe there is, you will be disappointed too, I warn you."

"I shall not neglect your warning; but I do believe there is rest for rational affections—I am confident there is, if the primary condition is fulfilled—if there is repose in God together with human love."

"You think that trust in God is wanting in me?"

"Do let us speak of something else," said Margaret. "We are wrong to think and talk of ourselves as we do. There is something sickly about our state while we do so, and we deserve to be suffering as we are. Come! let us be up and doing. Let me read to you; or will you practise with me till Edward comes back?"

"Not till you have answered my question, Margaret. Do you believe that my wretchedness is from want of trust in God?"

"I believe," said Margaret, seriously, "that all restless and passionate suffering is from that cause. And now, Hester, no more."

Hester allowed Margaret to read to her; but it would not do. She was too highly wrought up for common interests. The reading was broken off by her hysterical sobs; and it was clear that the best thing to be done was to get her to bed, under Morris's care, that all agitating conversation might be avoided. When Mr Hope returned, he found Margaret sitting alone at the tea-table. If she had had no greater power of self-control than her sister, Edward might have been made wretched enough, for her heart was full of dismay: but she felt the importance of the duty of supporting him, and he found her, though serious, apparently cheerful.

"I have sent Hester to bed," said she, as he entered. "She was worn out. Yes: just go and speak to her; but do not give her the opportunity of any more conversation till she has slept. Tell her that I am going to send her some tea; and by that time yours will be ready."

"Just one word upon the events of to-day," said Hope, as he took his seat at the tea-table, after having reported that Hester was tolerably composed:— "just one word, and no more. We must avoid bringing emotions to a point—giving occasion for—"

"I entirely agree with you," said Margaret. "She requires to be drawn out of herself. She cannot bear that opening of the sluices, which is a benefit and comfort to some people. Let us keep them shut, and when it comes to acting, see how she will act!"

"Bless you for that!" was on Hope's lips; but he did not say it. Tea was soon dismissed, and he then took up the newspaper; and when that was finished, he found he could not read to Margaret—he must write:— he had a case to report for a medical journal.

"I hope I have not spoiled your evening," said Hester, languidly, when her sister went to bid her good-night. "I have been listening; but I could not hear you either laughing or talking."

"Because we have been neither laughing nor talking. My brother has been writing—"

"Writing! To whom? To Emily, or to Anne?"

"To a far more redoubtable person than either: to the editor of some one of those green and blue periodicals that he devours, as if they were poetry. And I have been copying music."

"How tired you look!"

"Well, then, good-night!"

Margaret might well look tired; but she did not go to rest for long. How should she rest, while her soul was sick with dismay, her heart weighed down with disappointment, her sister's sobs still sounding in her ear, her sister's agonised countenance rising up from moment to moment, as often as she closed her eyes? And all this within the sacred enclosure of home, in the very sanctuary of peace! All this where love had guided the suffering one to marriage—where there was present neither sickness, nor calamity, nor guilt, but the very opposites of all these! Could it then be true, that the only sanctuary of peace is in the heart? that while love is the master passion of humanity, the main-spring of human action, the crowning interest of human life—while it is ordained, natural, inevitable, it should issue as if it were discountenanced by Providence, unnatural, and to be repelled? Could it be so? Was Hester's warning against love, against marriage, reasonable, and to be regarded? That warning Margaret thought she could never put aside, so heavily had it sunk upon her heart, crushing—she knew not what there. If it was not a reasonable warning, whither should she turn for consolation for Hester? If this misery arose out of an incapacity in Hester herself for happiness in domestic life, then farewell sisterly comfort—farewell all the bright visions she had ever indulged on behalf of the one who had always been her nearest and dearest? Instead of these, there must be struggle and grief, far deeper than in the anxious years that were gone; struggle with an evil which must grow if it does not diminish, and grief for an added sufferer—for one who deserved blessing where he was destined to receive torture. This was not the first time by a hundred that Hester had kept Margaret from her pillow, and then driven rest from it; but never had the trial been so great as now. There had been anxiety formerly; now there was something like despair, after an interval of hope and comparative ease.

Mankind are ignorant enough, Heaven knows, both in the mass, about general interests, and individually, about the things which belong to their peace: but of all mortals, none perhaps are so awfully self-deluded as the unamiable. They do not, any more than others, sin for the sake of sinning; but the amount of woe caused by their selfish unconsciousness is such as may well make their weakness an equivalent for other men's gravest crimes. There is a great diversity of hiding-places for their consciences—many mansions in the dim prison of discontent: but it may be doubted whether, in the hour when all shall be uncovered to the eternal day, there will be revealed a lower deep than the hell which they have made. They, perhaps, are the only order of evil ones who suffer hell without seeing and knowing that it is hell. But they are under a heavier curse even than this; they inflict torments, second only to their own, with an unconsciousness almost worthy of spirits of light. While they complacently conclude themselves the victims of others, or pronounce, inwardly or aloud, that they are too singular, or too refined, for common appreciation, they are putting in motion an enginery of torture whose aspect will one day blast their minds' sight. The dumb groans of their victims will sooner or later return upon their ears from the depths of the heaven to which the sorrows of men daily ascend. The spirit sinks under the prospect of the retribution of the unamiable, if all that happens be indeed for eternity, if there be indeed a record—an impress on some one or other human spirit—of every chilling frown, of every querulous tone, of every bitter jest, of every insulting word—of all abuses of that tremendous power which mind has over mind. The throbbing pulses, the quivering nerves, the wrung hearts, that surround the unamiable—what a cloud of witnesses is here! and what plea shall avail against them? The terror of innocents who should know no fear—the vindictive emotions of dependants who dare not complain—the faintness of heart of life-long companions—the anguish of those who love—the unholy exultation of those who hate,—what an array of judges is here! and where can appeal be lodged against their sentence? Is pride of singularity a rational plea? Is super-refinement, or circumstance of God, or uncongeniality in man, a sufficient ground of appeal, when the refinement of one is a grace granted for the luxury of all, when circumstance is given to be conquered, and uncongeniality is appointed for discipline? The sensualist has brutified the seraphic nature with which he was endowed. The depredator has intercepted the rewards of toil, and marred the image of justice, and dimmed the lustre of faith in men's minds. The imperial tyrant has invoked a whirlwind, to lay waste, for an hour of God's eternal year, some region of society. But the unamiable—the domestic torturer—has heaped wrong upon wrong, and woe upon woe, through the whole portion of time which was given into his power, till it would be rash to say that any others are more guilty than he. If there be hope or solace for such, it is that there may have been tempers about him the opposite of his own. It is matter of humiliating gratitude that there were some which he could not ruin; and that he was the medium of discipline by which they were exercised in forbearance, in divine forgiveness and love. If there be solace in such an occasional result, let it be made the most of by those who need it; for it is the only possible alleviation to their remorse. Let them accept it as the free gift of a mercy which they have insulted, and a long-suffering which they have defied.

Not thus, however, did Margaret regard the case of her sister. She had but of late ceased to suppose herself in the wrong when Hester was unhappy: and though she was now relieved from the responsibility of her sister's peace, she was slow to blame—reluctant to class the case lower than as one of infirmity. Her last waking thoughts (and they were very late) were of pity and of prayer.

As the door closed behind Margaret, Hope had flung down his pen. In one moment she had returned for a book; and she found him by the fireside, leaning his head upon his arms against the wall. There was something in his attitude which startled her out of her wish for her book, and she quietly withdrew without it. He turned, and spoke, but she was gone.

"So this is home!" thought he, as he surveyed the room, filled as it was with tokens of occupation, and appliances of domestic life. "It is home to be more lonely than ever before—and yet never to be alone with my secret! At my own table, by my own hearth, I cannot look up into the faces around me, nor say what I am thinking. In every act and every word I am in danger of disturbing the innocent—even of sullying the pure, and of breaking the bruised reed. Would to God I had never seen them! How have I abhorred bondage all my life! and I am in bondage every hour that I spend at home. I have always insisted that there was no bondage but in guilt. Is it so? If it be so, then I am either guilty, or in reality free. I have settled this before. I am guilty; or rather, I have been guilty; and this is my retribution. Not guilty towards Margaret. Thank God, I have done her no wrong! Thank God, I have never been in her eyes—what I must not think of! Nor could I ever have been, if... She loves Enderby, I am certain, though she does not know it herself. It is a blessing that she loves him, if I could but always feel it so. I am not guilty towards her, nor towards Hester, except in the weakness of declining to inflict that suffering upon her which, fearful as it must have been, might perhaps have proved less than, with all my care, she must undergo now. There was my fault. I did not, I declare, seek to attach her. I did nothing wrong so far. But I dared to measure suffering—to calculate consequences presumptuously and vainly: and this is my retribution. How would it have been, if I had allowed them to go back to Birmingham, and had been haunted with the image of her there? But why go over this again, when my very soul is weary of it all? It lies behind, and let it be forgotten. The present is what I have to do with, and it is quite enough. I have injured, cruelly injured myself; and I must bear with myself. Here I am, charged with the duty of not casting my shadow over the innocent, and of strengthening the infirm. I have a clear duty before me—that is one blessing. The innocent will soon be taken from under my shadow—I trust so—for my duty there is almost too hard. How she would confide in me, and I must not let her, and must continually disappoint her, and suffer in her affection. I cannot even be to her what our relation warrants. And all the while her thoughts are my thoughts; her... But this will never do. It is enough that she trusts me, and that I deserve that she should. This is all that I can ever have or hope for; but I have won thus much; and I shall keep it. Not a doubt or fear, not a moment's ruffle of spirits, shall she ever experience from me. As for my own poor sufferer—what months and years are before us both! What a discipline before she can be at peace! If she were to look forward as I do, her heart would sink as mine does, and perhaps she would try... But we must not look forward: her heart must not sink. I must keep it up. She has strength under her weakness, and I must help her to bring it out and use it. There ought to be, there must be, peace in store for such generosity of spirit as lies under the jealousy, for such devotedness, for such power.

Margaret says, 'When it comes to acting, see how she will act.' Oh, that it might please Heaven to send such adversity as would prove to herself how nobly she can act! If some strong call on her power would come in aid of what I would fain do for her, I care not what it is. If I can only witness my own wrong repaired—if I can but see her blessed from within, let all other things be as they may! The very thought frees me, and I breathe again!"

Chapter Twenty

Enderby News.

"Mamma, what do you think Fanny and Mary Grey say?" asked Matilda of her mother.

"My dear, I wish you would not tease me with what the Greys say. They say very little that is worth repeating."

"Well, but you must hear this, mamma. Fanny and Mary were walking with Sophia yesterday, and they met Mrs Hope and Miss Ibbotson in Turnstile Lane; and Mrs Hope was crying so, you can't think."

"Indeed! Crying! What, in the middle of the day?"

"Yes; just before dinner. She had her veil down, and she did not want to stop, evidently, mamma. She—."

"I should wonder if she did," observed Mr Rowland from the other side of the newspaper he was reading. "If Dr and Mrs Levitt were to come in the next time you cry, Matilda, you would not want to stay in the parlour, evidently, I should think. For my part, I never show my face when I am crying."

"You cry, papa!" cried little Anna. "Do you ever cry?"

"Have you never found me behind the deals, or among the sacks in the granary, with my finger in my eye?"

"No, papa. Do show us how you look when you cry."

Mr Rowland's face, all dolefulness, emerged from behind the newspaper, and the children shouted.

"But," said Matilda, observing that her mother's brow began to lower, "I think it is very odd that Mrs Hope did not stay at home if she wanted to cry. It is so very odd to go crying about the streets!"

"I dare say Deerbrook is very much obliged to her," said papa. "It will be something to talk about for a week."

"But what could she be crying for, papa?"

"Suppose you ask her, my dear? Had you not better put on your bonnet, and go directly to Mr Hope's, and ask, with our compliments, what

Mrs Hope was crying for at four o'clock yesterday afternoon? Of course she can tell better than anybody else."

"Nonsense, Mr Rowland," observed his lady. "Go, children, it is very near school-time."

"No, mamma; not by—"

"Go, I insist upon it, Matilda. I will have you do as you are bid. Go, George: go, Anna.—Now, my love, did I not tell you so, long ago? Do not you remember my observing to you, how coldly Mr Hope took our congratulations on his engagement in the summer? I was sure there was something wrong. They are not happy, depend upon it."

"What a charming discovery that would be!"

"You are very provoking, Mr Rowland! I do believe you try to imitate Mr Grey's dry way of talking to his wife."

"I thought I had heard you admire that way, my dear."

"For her, yes: it does very well for a woman like her: but I beg you will not try it upon me, Mr Rowland."

"Well, then, Mrs Rowland, I am going to be as serious as ever I was in my life, when I warn you how you breathe such a suspicion as that the Hopes are not happy. Remember you have no evidence whatever about the matter. When you offered Mr Hope your congratulations, he was feeble from illness, and probably too much exhausted at the moment to show any feeling, one way or another. And as for this crying fit of Mrs Hope's, no one is better able than you, my dear, to tell how many causes there may be for ladies' tears besides being unhappily married."

"Pray, Mr Rowland, make yourself easy, I beg. Whom do you suppose I should mention such a thing to?"

"You have already mentioned it to yourself and me, my dear, which is just two persons too many. Not a word more on the subject, if you please."

Mrs Rowland saw that this was one of her husband's authority days;—rare days, when she could not have her own way, and her quiet husband was really formidable. She buckled on her armour, therefore, forthwith. That armour was—silence. Mr Rowland was sufficiently aware of the process now to be gone through, to avoid speaking, when he knew he should obtain no reply. He finished his newspaper without further remark, looked out a book from the shelves, half-whistling all the while, and left the room.

Meantime, the children had gone to the schoolroom, disturbing Miss Young nearly an hour too soon. Miss Young told them she was not at liberty; and when she heard that their mamma had sent them away from the drawing-room, she asked why they could not play as usual. It was so cold! How did George manage to play? George had not come in with the rest. If he could play, so could they. The little girls had no doubt George would present himself soon: they did not know where he had run; but he would soon have enough of the cold abroad, or of the dullness of the nursery. In another moment Miss Young was informed of the fact of Hester's tears of yesterday; and, much as she wanted the time she was deprived of, she was glad the children had come to her, that this piece of gossip might be stopped. She went somewhat at length with them into the subject of tears, showing that it is very hasty to conclude that any one has been doing wrong, even in the case of a child's weeping; and much more with regard to grown people. When they had arrived at wondering whether some poor person had been begging of Mrs Hope, or whether one of Mr Hope's patients that she cared about was very ill, or whether anybody had been telling her an affecting story, Miss Young brought them to see that they ought not to wish to know;—that they should no more desire to read Mrs Hope's thoughts than to look over her shoulder while she was writing a letter. She was just telling them a story of a friend of hers who called on an old gentleman, and found him in very low spirits, with his eyes all red and swollen; and how her friend did not know whether to take any notice; and how the truth came out,—that the old gentleman had been reading a touching story:— she was just coming to the end of this anecdote, when the door opened and Margaret entered, holding George by the hand. Margaret looked rather grave, and said—

"I thought I had better come to you first, Maria, for an explanation which you may be able to give. Do you know who sent little George with a message to my sister just now? I concluded you did not. George has been calling at my brother's door, with his papa's and mamma's compliments, and a request to know what Mrs Hope was crying for yesterday, at four o'clock."

Maria covered her face with her hands, with as much shame as if she had been in fault, while "Oh, George!" was reproachfully uttered by the little girls.

"Matilda," said Miss Young, "I trust you to go straight to your papa, without saying a word of this to any one else, and to ask him to come here this moment. I trust you, my dear."

Matilda discharged her trust. She peeped into the drawing-room, and popped out again without speaking, when she saw papa was no longer there. She found him in the office, and brought him, without giving any hint of what had happened. He was full of concern, of course; said that he could not blame George, though he was certainly much surprised; that it would be a lesson to him not to use irony with children, since even the broadest might be thus misunderstood; and that a little family scene had thus been laid open, which he should hardly regret if it duly impressed his children with the folly and unkindness of village gossip. He declared he could not be satisfied without apologising,—well, then, without explaining, to Mrs Hope how it had happened; and he would do it through the medium of Mr Hope; for, to say the truth, he was ashamed to face Mrs Hope till his peace was made. Margaret laughed at this, and begged him to go home with her; but he preferred stepping over to Mrs Enderby's, where Mr Hope had just been seen to enter. Mr Rowland concluded by saying, that he should accept it as a favour in Miss Ibbotson, as well as Miss Young, if she would steadily refuse to gratify any impertinent curiosity shown by his children, in whatever direction it might show itself. They were exposed to great danger from example in Deerbrook, like most children brought up in small villages, he supposed: and he owned he dreaded the idea of his children growing up the scourges to society that he considered foolish and malignant gossips to be.

"Do sit down, Margaret," said Maria. "I shall feel uncomfortable when you are gone, if you do not stay a minute to turn our thoughts to something pleasanter than this terrible mistake of poor George's."

"I cannot stay now, however," said Margaret, smiling. "You know I must go and turn my sister's thoughts to something pleasanter. There she is, sitting at home, waiting to know how all this has happened."

"Whether she has not been insulted? You are right, Margaret. Make haste back to her, and beg her pardon for us all. Shall she not, children, if she will be so kind?"

Margaret was overwhelmed with the petitions for pardon she had to carry; and not one of the children asked what Mrs Hope had been crying for, after all.

Hester looked up anxiously as Margaret entered the drawing-room at home.

"It is all a trifle," said Margaret, gaily.

"How can it be a trifle?"

"The little Greys told what they saw yesterday, of course; and one of the little Rowlands wondered what was the reason;—(children can never understand what grown people, who have no lessons to learn, can cry for, you know); and Mr Rowland, to make their gossip ridiculous to themselves, told them they had better come and ask; and poor George, who cannot take a joke, came without any one knowing where he was gone. They were all in great consternation when I told them, and there is an ample apology coming to you through Edward. That is the whole story, except that Mr Rowland would have come himself to you, instead of going to your husband, but that he was ashamed of his joke. So there is an end of that silly matter, unless it be to make George always ask henceforth whether people are in joke or in earnest."

"I think Mr Rowland might have come to me," observed Hester. "Are you sure Mrs Rowland had nothing to do with it?"

"I neither saw her nor heard of her. You had better not go out to-day, it is so like snow. I shall be back soon; but as I have my bonnet on, I shall go and see Johnny Rye and his mother. Can I do anything for you?"

"Oh, my snow-boots! But I would not have you go to Mrs Howell's while she is in such a mood as she was in yesterday. I would not go myself."

"Oh! I will go. I am not afraid of Mrs Howell; and we shall have to encounter her again, sooner or later. I will buy something, and then see what my diplomacy will effect about the boots."

Mr Hope presently came in, and found his wife prepared for the apology he brought from Mr Rowland. But it was obvious that Hope's mind was far more occupied with something else.

"Where is Margaret?"

"She is gone out to Widow Rye's, and to Mrs Howell's."

"No matter where, as long as she is out. I want to consult you about something." And he drew a chair to the fire, and told that he had visited Mrs Enderby, whom he found very poorly, apparently from agitation of spirits. She had shed a few tears on reporting her health, and had dropped something which he could not understand, about this being almost the last time she should be able to speak freely to him. Hester anxiously hoped that the good old lady was not really going to die. There was no near probability of this, her husband assured her. He thought Mrs Enderby referred to some other change than dying; but what, she did not explain. She had gone on talking in rather an excited way, and at last hinted that she supposed she should not see her son for some time, as Mrs Rowland had intimated that he was fully occupied with the young lady he was going to be married to. Mrs Enderby plainly said that she had not heard this from Philip himself; but she seemed to entertain no doubt of the truth of the information she had received. She appeared to be struggling to be glad at the news; but it was clear that the uppermost feeling was disappointment at having no immediate prospect of seeing her son.

"Now, what are we to think and do?" said Hope.

"This agrees with what Mrs Rowland told me in Dingleford woods, six months ago," said Hester; "and I suppose what she then said may have been true all this time."

"How does that agree with his conduct to Margaret? Or am I mistaken in what I have told you I thought about that? Seriously—very seriously—how do you suppose the case stands with Margaret?"

"I know no more than you. I think he went further than he ought, if he was thinking of another; and, but for his conduct since, I should have quite concluded, from some observations that I made, that he was attached to Margaret."

"And she—?"

"And she certainly likes him very well; but I can hardly fancy her happiness at stake. I have thought her spirit rather flat of late."

Hope sighed deeply.

"Ah! you may well sigh," said Hester, sighing herself, and sinking back in her chair. "You know what I am going to say. I thought I might be the cause of her being less gay than she should be. I have disappointed her expectations, I know. But let us talk only of her."

"Yes: let us talk only of her, till we have settled what is our duty to her. Ought we to tell her of this or not?"

Both considered long. At length Hester said—

"I think she ought to hear it quietly at home first (whether it be true or not), to prepare her for anything that may be reported abroad. Perhaps, if you were to drop, as we sit together here, what Mrs Enderby said—"

"No, no; not I," said Hope, quickly. He went on more calmly: "Her sister and bosom friend is the only person to do this—if, indeed, it ought to be done. But the news may be untrue; and then she need perhaps never hear it. Do not let us be in a hurry."

Hester thought that if Margaret felt nothing more than friendship for Enderby, she would still consider herself ill-used; for the friendship had been so close an one that she might reasonably expect that she should not be left to learn such an event as this from common report. But was it certain, Hope asked, that she had anything new to learn? Was it certain that she was not in his confidence all this time—that she had not known ten times as much as Mrs Rowland from the beginning? Certainly not from the beginning, Hester said; and she had a strong persuasion that Margaret was as ignorant as themselves of Enderby's present proceedings and intentions.

At this moment, a note was brought in. It was from Mrs Enderby to Mr Hope, written hurriedly, and blistered with tears. It told that she had been extremely wrong in mentioning to him prematurely what was uppermost in her mind about a certain family affair, and begged the great favour of him to keep to himself what she had divulged, and, if possible, to forget it. Once more, Mr Hope unconsciously sighed. It was at the idea that he could forget such a piece of intelligence.

"Poor old lady!" said Hester; "she has been taken to task, I suppose, for relieving her mind to you. But, Edward, this looks more and more as if the news were true. My darling Margaret! How will it be with her? Does it not look too like being true, love?"

"It looks as if Enderby's family all believed it, certainly. This note settles the matter of our duty, however. If the affair is so private that Mrs Enderby is to be punished for telling me, it is hardly likely that Margaret will hear it by out-door chance. You are spared the task for the present at least, my dear!"

"I should like to be sure that Margaret does not love—that she might pass through life without loving," said Hester, sighing, "But here she comes! Burn the note!"

The note curled in the flames, was consumed, and its ashes fluttered up the chimney, and Margaret did not enter. She had gone straight up-stairs. She did not come down till dinner was on the table. She was then prepared with the announcement that the snow-boots might be looked for very soon. She told of her visit to Widow Rye's, and had something to say of the probability of snow; but she was rather absent, and she took wine. These were all the circumstances that her anxious sister could fix upon, during dinner, for silent comment. After dinner, having eaten an orange with something like avidity, Margaret withdrew for a very few minutes. As the door closed behind her, Hester whispered—

"She has heard. She knows. Is it not so?"

"There is no question about it," replied Hope, examining the screen he held in his hand.

"I wonder who can have told her."

"Tellers of bad news are never wanting, especially in Deerbrook," said Hope, with a bitterness of tone which Hester had never heard from him before.

Margaret took up the other screen when she returned, and played with it till the table was cleared, so that she could have the use of her work-box. It was Morris who removed the dessert.

"Morris," said Mr Hope, as she was leaving the room, "I want Charles: pray send him."

"Charles is out, sir."

"Out! when will he be back?"

"He will be back presently," said Margaret. "I sent him with a note to Maria."

As she leant over her work again, Hester and her husband exchanged glances.

An answer from Maria soon arrived. Margaret read it as she sat, her brother and sister carefully withdrawing their observation from her. Whatever else might be in the note, she read aloud the latter part—two or three lines relating to the incident of the morning. Her voice was husky, but her manner was gay. During the whole evening she was gay. She insisted on making tea, and was too quick with the kettle for Edward to help her. She proposed music, and she sang—song after song. Hester was completely relieved about her; and even Edward gave himself up to the hope that all was well with her. From music they got to dancing. Margaret had learned, by sitting with Maria during the children's dancing-lesson, a new dance which had struck her fancy, and they must be ready with it next week at Dr Levitt's. Alternately playing the dance and teaching it, she ran from the piano to them, and from them to the piano, till they were perfect, and her face was as flushed as it could possibly be at Mrs Levitt's dance next week. But in the midst of this flush, Hope saw a shiver: and Hester remarked, that during the teaching, Margaret had, evidently without being aware of it, squeezed her hand with a force which could not have been supposed to be in her. These things made Hope still doubt.

Chapter Twenty One

Consciousness to the Unconscious.

Mr Hope might well doubt. Margaret was not gay but desperate. Yes, even the innocent may be desperate under circumstances of education and custom, by which feelings natural and inevitable are made occasions of shame; while others, which are wrong and against the better nature of man, bask in daylight and impunity. There was not a famishing wretch prowling about a baker's door, more desperate than Margaret this day. There was not a gambler setting his teeth while watching the last turn of the die, more desperate than Margaret this day. If there was a criminal standing above a sea of faces with the abominable executioner's hands about his throat, Margaret was, for the time, as wretched as he.

If any asked why—why it should be thus with one who has done no wrong, the answer is—Why is there pride in the human heart?—why is there a particular nurture of this pride into womanly reserve?—Why is it that love is the chief experience, and almost the only object, of a woman's life? Why is it that it is painful to beings who look before and after to have the one hope of existence dashed away—the generous faith outraged—all self-confidence overthrown—life in one moment made dreary as the desert—Heaven itself overclouded—and death all the while standing at such a weary distance that there is no refuge within the horizon of endurance? Be these things right or wrong, they are: and while they are, will the woman who loves, unrequited, feel desperate on the discovery of her loneliness—and, the more pure and proud, innocent and humble, the more lonely.

For some little time past, Margaret had been in a state of great tranquillity about Philip—a tranquillity which she now much wondered at—now that it was all over. She had had an unconscious faith in him; and, living in this faith, she had forgotten herself, she had not thought of the future, she had not felt impatient for any change. Often as she wished for his presence, irksome as she had sometimes felt it to know nothing of him from week to week, she had been tacitly satisfied that she was in his thoughts as he was in hers; and this had been enough for the time. What an awakening from this quiescent state was hers this day!

It was from no other than Dr Levitt that she had heard in the morning that Mr Enderby was shortly going to be married to Miss Mary Bruce. Dr Levitt was at Widow Rye's when Margaret went, and had walked part of the way home with her. During the walk, this piece of news had dropped out, while they were talking of Mrs Enderby's health. All that Dr Levitt knew of Miss Mary Bruce was, that she was of sufficiently good family and fortune to make the Rowlands extremely well satisfied with the match; that Mrs Enderby had never seen her, and that it would be some time before she could see her, as the whole family of the Bruces was at Rome for the winter. When Dr Levitt parted from Margaret at the gate of the churchyard, these last words contained the hope she clung to—a hope which might turn into the deepest reason for despair. Philip had certainly not been abroad. Was it likely that he should lately have become engaged to any young lady who had been some time in Rome? It was not likely: but then, if it was true, he must have been long engaged: he must have been engaged at the time of his last visit of six days, when he had talked over his views of life with Margaret, and been so anxious to obtain hers:— he must surely have been engaged in the summer, when she found Tieck in the desk, and when he used to spend so many evenings at the Greys'—certainly not on Hester's account. At one moment she was confident all this could not be; she was relieved; she stepped lightly. The next moment, a misgiving came that it was all too true; the weight fell again upon her heart, she lost breath, and it was intolerable to have to curtesy to Mrs James, and to answer the butcher's inquiry about the meat that had been ordered. If these people would only go on with their own business, and take no notice of her! Then, again, the thought occurred, that she knew Philip better than any,—than even his own family; and that, say what they might, he was all her own. In these changes of mood, she had got through dinner; the dominant idea was then that she must, by some means or other, obtain certainty. She thought of Maria. Maria was likely to know the facts, from her constant intercourse with the Rowlands, and besides, there was certainly a something in Maria's mind in relation to Philip,—a keen insight, which might be owing to the philosophical habit of her mind, or to something else,—but which issued in information about him, which it was surprising that she could obtain. She seldom spoke of him; but when she did, it was wonderfully to the purpose. Margaret thought she could learn from Maria, in a very simple and natural way, that which she so much wished to know: and when she left the room after dinner, it was to write the note which might bring certainty.

> "Dear Friend,—I saw Dr Levitt this morning while I was out, and he told me, with all possible assurance, that Mr Enderby is going to be married very shortly to a young lady at Rome,—Miss Mary Bruce. Now, this is true or it is not. If true, you are as well aware as we are that we are entitled to have known it otherwise and earlier than by common report. If not true, the rumour should not be

allowed to spread. If you know anything certainly, one way or the other, pray tell us.

"Yours affectionately,

"Margaret Ibbotson."

The "we" and "us" were not quite honest; but Margaret meant to make them as nearly so as possible by *ex-post-facto* communication with her brother and sister: a resolution so easily made, that it did not occur to her how difficult it might be to execute. While her messenger was gone, she wrought herself up to a resolution to bear the answer, whatever it might be, with the same quietness with which she must bear the whole of her future life, if Dr Levitt's news should prove to be founded in fact. The door opening seemed to prick the nerves of her ears: her heart heaved to her throat at the sight of the white paper: yet it was with neatness that she broke the seal, and with a steady hand that she held the note to read it. The handwriting was only too distinct: it seemed to burn itself in upon her brain. All was over.

"Dear Margaret,—I do not know where Dr Levitt got his news; but I believe it is true. Mrs Rowland pretends to absolute certainty about her brother's engagement to Miss Bruce; and it is from this that others speak so positively about it. Whatever are the grounds that Mrs R. goes upon, there are others which afford a strong presumption that she is right. Some of these may be known to you. They leave no doubt in my mind that the report is true. As to the failure of confidence in his friends,—what can be said?—unless by way of reminder of the old truth that, by the blessing of Heaven, wrongs—be they but deep enough—may chasten a human temper into something divine.

"George has been very grave for the last three hours, pandering, I fancy, what irony can be for. Your sister will not grudge him his lesson, though afforded at her expense.

"Yours affectionately,

"Maria Young."

"Wrongs!" thought she;—"Maria goes too far when she speaks of wrongs. There was nothing in my note to bring such an expression in answer. It is going too far."

This was but the irritability of a racked soul, needing to spend its agony somewhere. The remembrance of the conversation with Maria, held so lately, and of Maria's views of Philip's relation to her, returned upon her, and her soul melted within her. She, felt that Maria had understood her better than she did herself; and was justified in the words she had used. Under severe calamity, to be endured alone, evil thoughts sometimes come before good ones. Margaret was, for an hour or two, possessed with the bad spirit of defiance. Her mind sank back into what it had been in her childhood, when she had hidden herself in the lumber-room, or behind the water-tub, for many hours, to make the family uneasy, because she had been punished,—in the days when she bore every infliction that her father dared to try, with apparent unconcern, rather than show to watchful eyes that she was moved,—in the days when the slightest concession would dissolve her stubbornness in an instant, but when, to get rid of a life of contradiction, she had had serious thoughts of cutting her throat, had gone to the kitchen door to get the carving-knife, and had been much disappointed to find the servants at dinner, and the knife-tray out of reach. This spirit, so long ago driven out by the genial influences of family love, by the religion of an expanding intellect, and the solace of appreciation, now came back to inhabit the purified bosom which had been kept carefully swept and garnished. It was the motion of this spirit, uneasy in its unfit abode, that showed itself by the shiver, the flushed cheek, the clenching hand, and the flashing eye. It kept whispering wicked things,—"I will baffle and deceive Maria: she shall withdraw her pity, and laugh at it with me." "I defy Edward and Hester: they shall wonder how it is that my fancy alone is free, that my heart alone is untouched, that the storms of life pass high over my head, and dare not lower." "I will humble Philip, and convince him..." But, no; it would not do. The abode was too lowly and too pure for the evil spirit of defiance: the demon did not wait to be cast out; but as Margaret sat down in her chamber, alone with her lot, to face it as she might, the strange inmate escaped, and left her at least herself.

Margaret was in agonised amazement at the newness of the misery she was suffering. She really fancied she had sympathised with Hester that dreadful night of Hope's accident: she had then actually believed that she was entering into her sister's feelings. It had been as much like it as seeing a picture of one on the rack is like being racked. But Hester had not had so much cause for misery, for she never had to believe Edward unworthy. Her pride had been wounded at finding that her peace was no longer in her own power; but she had not been trifled with—duped. Here again Margaret refused to believe. The fault was all her own. She had been full of herself, full of vanity; fancying, without cause, that she was much to another when she was little. She was humbled now, and she no doubt deserved it. But how ineffably weak and mean did she appear in her own eyes! It was this which clouded Heaven to her at the moment that earth had become a desert. She felt so debased, that she durst not ask for strength where she was wont to find it. If she had done one single wrong thing, she thought she could bear the consequences cheerfully, and seek support, and vigorously set about repairing the causes of her fault; but here it seemed to her that her whole state of mind had been low and selfish. It must be this sort of blindness which had led her so far in so fearful a delusion. And if the whole condition of her mind had been low and selfish, while her conscience had given her no hint of anything being amiss, where was she to begin to rectify her being? She felt wholly degraded.

And then what a set of pictures rose up before her excited fancy! Philip going forth for a walk with her and Hester, after having just sealed a letter to Miss Bruce, carrying the consciousness of what he had been saying to the mistress of his heart, while she, Margaret, had supposed herself the chief object of his thought and care! Again, Philip discussing her mind and character with Miss Bruce, as those of a friend for whom he had a regard! or bestowing a passing imagination on how she would receive the intelligence of his engagement! Perhaps he reserved the news till he could come down to Deerbrook, and call and tell her himself, as one whose friendship deserved that he should be the bearer of his own tidings. That footstep, whose spring she had strangely considered her own signal of joy, was not hers but another's. That laugh, the recollection of which made her smile even in these dreadful moments, was to echo in another's home. She was stripped of all her heart's treasure, of his tones, his ways, his thoughts,—a treasure which she had lived upon without knowing it; she was stripped of it all—cast out—left alone—and he and all others would go on their ways, unaware that anything had happened! Let them do so. It was hard to bear up in solitude when self-respect was gone with all the rest; but it must be possible to live on—no matter how—if to live on was appointed. If not, there was death, which was better.

These thoughts were not beneath one like Margaret—one who was religious as she. It requires time for religion to avail anything when self-respect is utterly broken-down. A devout sufferer may surmount the pangs of persecution at the first onset, and wrestle with bodily pain, and calmly endure bereavement by death; but there is no power of faith by which a woman can attain resignation under the agony of unrequited passion otherwise than by conflict, long and terrible.

Margaret laid down at last, because her eyes were weary of seeing; and she would fain have shut out all sounds. The occasional flicker of a tiny blaze, however, and the fall of a cinder in the hearth, served to lull her senses, and it was not long before she slept. But, oh, the horrors of that sleep! The lines of Maria's note stared her in the face—glaring, glowing, gigantic. Sometimes she was trying to read them, and could not, though her life depended on them. Now Mrs Rowland had got hold of them; and now they were thrown into the flames, but would not burn, and the letters grew red-hot. Then came the image of Philip; and that horror was mixed up with whatever was most ludicrous. Once she was struggling for voice to speak to him, and he mocked her useless efforts. Oh, how she struggled! till some strong arm raised her, and some other voice murmured gently in her throbbing ear.

"Wake, my dear! Wake up, Margaret! What is it, dear? Wake!"

"Mother! is it you? Oh, mother! have you come at last?" murmured Margaret, sinking her head on Morris' shoulder.

It was some moments before Margaret felt a warm tear fall upon her cheek, and heard Morris say:

"No, my dear: not yet. Your mother is in a better place than this, where we shall all rest with her at last, Miss Margaret."

"What is all this?" said Margaret, raising herself, and looking round her. "What did I mean about my mother? Oh, Morris, my head is all confused, and I think I have been frightened. They were laughing at me, and when somebody came to help me, I thought it must be my mother. Oh, Morris, it is a long while—I wish I was with her."

Morris did not desire to hear what Margaret's dream had been. The immediate cause of Margaret's distress she did not know; but she had for some time suspected that which only one person in the world was aware of besides herself. The terrible secret of this household was no secret to her. She was experienced enough in love and its signs to know, without being told where love was absent, and where it rested. She had not doubted, up to the return from the wedding-trip, that all was right; but she had never been quite happy since. She had perceived no sign that either sister was aware of the truth; the continuance of their sisterly friendship was a proof that neither of them was: but she wished to avoid hearing the particulars of Margaret's dream, and all revelations which, in the weakness and confusion of an hour like this, she might be tempted to make. Morris withdrew from Margaret's clasp, moved softly across the room, gently put the red embers together in the grate, and lighted the lamp which stood on the table.

"I hope," whispered Margaret, trying to still her shivering, "that nobody heard me but you. How came you to think of coming to me?"

"My room being over this, you know, it was easy to hear the voice of a person in an uneasy sleep. I am glad I happened to be awake: so I put on my cloak and came."

Morris did not say that Edward had heard the stifled cry also, and that she had met him on the stairs coming to beg that she would see what could be done. Hester having slept through it, Margaret need never know that other ears than Morris' had heard her. Thus had Hope and Morris tacitly agreed.

"Now, my dear, when I have warmed this flannel, to put about your feet, you must go to sleep again. I will not leave you till daylight—till the house is near being astir: so you may sleep without being afraid of bad dreams. I will rouse you if I see you disturbed. Now, no more talking, or we shall have the house up; and all this had better be between you and me."

To satisfy Margaret, Morris lay down on the outside of the bed, warmly covered; and the nurse once more, as in old days, felt her favourite child breathing quietly against her shoulder: once more she wiped away the standing tears, and prayed in her heart for the object of her care. If her prayer had had words, it would have been this:—

"Thou hast been pleased to take to thyself the parents of these dear children; and surely thou wilt be therefore pleased to be to them as father and mother, or to raise up or spare to them such as may be so. This is what I would ask for myself; that I may be that comfort to them. Thou knowest that a strange trouble hath entered this house—thou knowest, for thine eye seeth beneath the face into the heart, as the sun shines into a locked chamber at noon. Thou knowest what these young creatures know not. Make holy to them what thou knowest. Let thy silence rest upon that which must not be spoken. Let thy strength be supplied where temptation is hardest. Let the innocence which has come forth from thine own hand be kept fit to appear in all the light of thy countenance. Oh! let them never be seen sinking with shame before thee. Father, if thou hast made thy children to love one another for their good, let not love be a grief and a snare to such as these. Thou canst turn the hearts even of the wicked: turn the hearts of these thy dutiful children to love, where love may be all honour and no shame, so that they may have no more mysteries from each other, as I am sure they have none from thee. All who know them have doubtless asked thy blessing on their house, their health, their basket and store: let me ask it also on the workings of their hearts, since, if their hearts be right, all is well—or will be in thine own best time."

When Margaret entered the breakfast-room in the morning, she found her brother sketching the skaters of Deerbrook, while the tea was brewing. Hester was looking over his shoulder, laughing, as she recognised one after another of her neighbours in the act of skating—this one by the stoop—that by the formality—and the other by the coat-flaps flying out behind. No inquiries were made—not a word was said of health or spirits. It seems strange that sufferers have not yet found means to stop the practice of such inquiries—a practice begun in kindness, and carried on in the spirit of hospitality, but productive of great annoyance to all but those who do not need such inquiries—the healthful and the happy. There are multitudes of invalids who can give no comfortable answer respecting their health, and who are averse from giving an uncomfortable one, and for whom nothing is therefore left but evasion. There are only too many sufferers to whom it is irksome to be questioned about their hours of sleeplessness, or who do not choose to have it known that they have not slept. The unpleasant old custom of pressing people to eat has gone out: the sooner the other observance of hospitality is allowed to follow it, the better. All who like to tell of illness and sleeplessness can do so; and those who have reasons for reserve upon such points, as Margaret had this morning, can keep their own counsel.

At the earliest possible hour that the etiquette of Deerbrook would allow, there was a knock at the door.

"That must be Mrs Rowland," exclaimed Hester. "One may know that woman's temper by her knock—so consequential, and yet so sharp. Margaret, love, you can run upstairs—there is time yet—if you do not wish to see her."

"Why should I?" said Margaret, looking up with a calmness which perplexed Hester.

"This is either ignorance," thought she, "or such patience as I wish I had."

It *was* Mrs Rowland, and she *was* come to tell what Hester feared Margaret might not be able to bear to hear. She was attended only by the little fellow who was so fond of riding on Uncle Philip's shoulder. It was rather lucky that Ned came, as Margaret was furnished with something to do in taking off his worsted gloves, and rubbing his little red hands between her own. And then she could say a great many things to him about learning to slide, and the difficulty of keeping on the snow-man's nose, and about her wonder that they had not thought of putting a pipe into his mouth. Before this subject was finished, Mrs Rowland turned full round to Margaret, and said that the purpose of her visit was to explain fully something that her poor mother had let drop yesterday to Mr Hope. Her mother was not what she had been—though, indeed, she had always been rather apt to let out things that she should not. She found that Mr Hope had been informed by her mother of her brother Philip's engagement to a charming young lady, who would indeed be a great ornament to the connexion.

"I assure you," said Margaret, "my brother is very careful, and always remembers that he is upon honour as to what he hears in a sick-room. He has not mentioned it."

"Oh! then it is safe. We are much obliged to Mr Hope, I am sure. I said to my mother—'My dear ma'am,'—"

"But I must mention," said Margaret, "that the news was abroad before... I must beg that you will not suppose my brother has spoken of it, if you should find that everybody knows it. I heard it from Dr Levitt yesterday, about the same time, I fancy, that Mr Hope was hearing it from Mrs Enderby."

Hester sat perfectly still, to avoid all danger of showing that this was news to her.

"How very strange!" exclaimed the lady. "I often say there is no keeping anything quiet in Deerbrook. Do you know where Dr Levitt got his information?"

"No," said Margaret, smiling. "Dr Levitt generally knows what he is talking about. I dare say he had it from some good authority. The young lady is at Rome, I find."

"Are you acquainted with Miss Bruce?" asked Hester, thinking it time to relieve Margaret of her share of the conversation.

Margaret started a little on finding that her sister had heard the news. Was it possible that her brother and sister had been afraid to tell her? No: it was a piece of Edward's professional discretion. His wife alone had a right to the news he heard among his patients.

"Oh, yes!" replied Mrs Rowland; "I have long loved Mary as a sister. Their early attachment made a sister of her to me an age ago."

"It has been a long engagement, then," said Hester, glad to say anything which might occupy Mrs Rowland, as Margaret's lips were now turning very white.

"Not now, my dear," Margaret was heard to say to little Ned, over whom she was bending her head as he stood by her side. "Stand still here," she continued, with wonderful cheerfulness of tone; "I want to hear your mamma tell us about Uncle Philip." With the effort her strength rallied, and the paleness was gone before Mrs Rowland had turned round.

"How long the engagement has existed," said the lady, "I cannot venture to say. I speak only of the attachment. Young people understand their own affairs, you know, and have their little mysteries, and laugh behind our backs, I dare say, at our ignorance of what they are about. Philip has been sly enough as to this, I own: but I must say I had my suspicions. I was pretty confident of his being engaged from the day that he told me in the summer, that he fully agreed with me that it was time he was settled."

"How differently some people understood that!" thought Hester and Margaret at the same moment.

"Is Mr Enderby at Rome now?" asked Hester.

"No: he is hard at work, studying law. He is really going to apply to a profession now. Not that it would be necessary, for Mary has a very good fortune. But Mary wishes so much that he should—like a sensible girl as she is."

"It is what I urged when he consulted me," thought Margaret. She had had little idea whose counsel she was following up.

"We shall soon hear of his setting off for the Continent, however, I have no doubt," said the lady.

"To bring home his bride," observed Margaret, calmly.

"Why, I do not know that. The Bruces will be returning early in the spring; and I should like the young people to marry in town, that we may have them here for their wedding trip."

"How you do hug me!" cried the laughing little boy, around whom Margaret's arm was passed.

"Have I made you warm at last?" asked Margaret. "If not, you may go and stand by the fire."

"No, indeed; we must be going," said mamma. "As I find this news is abroad, I must call on Mrs Grey. She will take offence at once, if she hears it from anybody but me. So much for people's husbands being partners in business!"

Margaret was now fully qualified to comprehend her sister's irritability. Every trifle annoyed her. The rustle of Mrs Rowland's handsome cloak almost made her sick; and she thought the hall clock would never have done striking twelve. When conscious of this, she put a strong check upon herself.

Hester stood by the mantelpiece, looking into the fire, and taking no notice of their mutual silence upon this piece of news. At last she muttered, in a soliloquising tone—

"Do not know—but I am not sure this news is true, after all."

After a moment's pause, Margaret replied—"I think that is not very reasonable. What must one suppose of everybody else, if it is not true?"

Hester was going to say, "What must we think of him, if it is?" but she checked herself. She should not have said what she had; she felt this, and only replied—

"Just so. Yes; it must be true."

Margaret's heart once more sank within her at this corroboration of her own remark.

Chapter Twenty Two

The Meadows in Winter.

Hester was tired of her snow-boots before she saw them. She had spent more trouble on them than they were worth; and it was three weeks yet before they came. It was now past the middle of February—rather late in the season for snow-boots to arrive: but then there was Margaret's consolatory idea, that they would be ready for next year's snow.

"It is not too late yet," said Mr Hope. "There is skating every day in the meadow. It will soon be over; so do not lose your opportunity. Come! let us go to-day."

"Not unless the sun shines out," said Hester, looking with a shiver up at the windows.

"Yes, to-day," said Edward, "because I have time to-day to go with you. You have seen me quiz other skaters: you must go and see other skaters quiz me."

"What points of your skating do they get hold of to quiz?" asked Margaret.

"Why, I hardly know. We shall see."

"Is it so very good, then?"

"No. I believe the worst of my skating is, that it is totally devoid of every sort of expression. That is just the true account of it," he continued, as his wife laughed. "I do not square my elbows, nor set my coat flying, nor stoop, nor rear; but neither is there any grace. I just go straight on; and, as far as I know, nobody ever bids any other body look at me."

"So you bid your own family come and look at you. But how are your neighbours to quiz you if they do not observe you?"

"Oh, that was only a bit of antithesis for effect. My last account is the true one, as you will see. I shall come in for you at twelve."

By twelve the sun had shone out, and the ladies, booted, furred, and veiled, were ready to encounter the risks and rigours of the ice and snow. As they opened the hall door they met on the steps a young woman, who was just raising her hand to the knocker. Her errand was soon told.

"Please, ma'am, I heard that you wanted a servant."

"That is true," said Hester. "Where do you come from?—from any place near, so that you can call again?"

"Surely," said Margaret, "it is Mrs Enderby's Susan."

"Yes, miss, I have been living with Mrs Enderby. Mrs Enderby will give me a good character, ma'am."

"Why are you leaving her, Susan?"

"Oh, ma'am, only because she is gone."

"Gone!—where?—what do you mean?"

"Gone to live at Mrs Rowland's, ma'am. You didn't know?—it *was* very sudden. But she moved yesterday, ma'am, and we were paid off—except Phoebe, who stays to wait upon her. I am left in charge of the house, ma'am: so I can step here again, if you wish it, some time when you are not going out."

"Do so; any time this evening, or before noon to-morrow."

"Did you know of this, Edward?" said his wife, as they turned the corner.

"Not I. I think Mrs Rowland is mistaken in saying that nothing can be kept secret in Deerbrook. I do not believe anybody has dreamed of the poor old lady giving up her house."

"Very likely Mrs Rowland never dreamed of it herself; till the day it was done," observed Margaret.

"Oh, yes, she did," said Mr Hope. "I understand now the old lady's agitation, and the expressions she dropped about 'last times' nearly a month ago."

"By-the-by, that was the last time you saw her—was it not?"

"Yes; the next day when I called I was told that she was better, and that she would send when she wished to see me again, to save me the trouble of calling when she might be asleep."

"She has been asleep or engaged every time I have inquired at the door of late," observed Margaret. "I hope she is doing nothing but what she likes in this change of plan."

"I believe she finds most peace and quiet in doing what her daughter likes," said Mr Hope. "Here, Margaret, where are you going? This is the gate. I believe you have not learned your way about yet."

"I will follow you immediately," said Margaret: "I will only go a few steps to see if this can really be true."

Before the Hopes had half crossed the meadow, Margaret joined them, perfectly convinced. The large bills in the closed windows of Mrs Enderby's house bore "To be Let or Sold" too plainly to leave any doubt.

As the skating season was nearly over, all the skaters in Deerbrook were eager to make use of their remaining opportunities, and the banks of the brook and of the river were full of their wives, sisters, and children. Sydney Grey was busy cutting figures-of-eight before the eyes of his sisters, and in defiance of his mother's careful warnings not to go here, and not to venture there, and not to attempt to cross the river. Mr Hope begged his wife to engage Mrs Grey in conversation, so that Sydney might be left free for a while, and promised to keep near the boy for half an hour, during which time Mrs Grey might amuse herself with watching other and better performers further on. As might have been foreseen, however, Mrs Grey could talk of nothing but Mrs Enderby's removal, of which she had not been informed till this morning, and which she had intended to discuss in Hester's house, on leaving the meadows.

It appeared that Mrs Enderby had been in agitated and variable spirits for some time, apparently wishing to say something that she did not say, and expressing a stronger regard than ever for her old friends—a regular sign that some act of tyranny or rudeness might speedily be expected from Mrs Rowland. The Greys were in the midst of their speculations as to what might be coming to pass, when Sydney burst in, with the news that Mrs Enderby's house was to be "Let or Sold." Mrs Grey had mounted her spectacles first, to verify the fact, and then sent Alice over to inquire, and had immediately put on her bonnet and cloak, and called on her old friend at Mrs Rowland's. She had been told at the door that Mrs Enderby was too much fatigued with her removal to see any visitors. "So I shall try again to-morrow," concluded Mrs Grey.

"How does Mr Hope think her spasms have been lately?" asked Sophia.

"He has not seen her for nearly a month; so I suppose they are better."

"I fear that does not follow, my dear," said Mrs Grey, winking. "Some people are afraid of your husband's politics, you are aware; and I know Mrs Rowland has been saying and doing things on that score which you had better not hear about. I have my reasons for thinking that the old lady's spasms are far from being better. But Mrs Rowland has been so busy crying up those drops of hers, that cure everything, and praising her maid, that I have a great idea your husband will not be admitted to see her till she is past cure, and her daughter thoroughly frightened. Mr Hope has never been forgiven, you know, for marrying into our connection so decidedly. And I really don't know what would have been the consequence, if, as we once fancied likely, Mr Philip and Margaret had thought of each other."

Margaret was happily out of hearing. A fresh blow had just been struck. She had looked to Mrs Enderby for information on the subject which for ever occupied her, and on which she felt that she must know more or sink. She had been much disappointed at being refused admission to the old lady, time after time. Now all hope of free access and private conversation was over. She had set it as an object before her to see Mrs Enderby, and learn as much of Philip's affair as his mother chose to offer: now this object was lost, and nothing remained to be done or hoped—for it was too certain that Mrs Enderby's friends would not be allowed unrestrained intercourse with her in her daughter's house.

For some little time Margaret had been practising the device, so familiar to the unhappy, of carrying off mental agitation by bodily exertion. She was now eager to be doing something more active than walking by Mrs Grey's side, listening to ideas which she knew just as well without their being spoken. Mrs Grey's thoughts about Mrs Rowland, and Mrs Rowland's ideas of Mrs Grey, might always be anticipated by those who knew the ladies. Hester and Margaret had learned to think of something else, while this sort of comment was proceeding, and to resume their attention when it came to an end. Margaret had withdrawn from it now, and was upon the ice with Sydney.

"Why, cousin Margaret, you don't mean that you are afraid of walking on the ice?" cried Sydney, balancing himself on his heels. "Mr Hope, what do you think of that?" he called out, as Hope skimmed past them. "Cousin Margaret is afraid of going on the ice!"

"What does she think can happen to her?" asked Mr Hope, his last words vanishing in the distance.

"It looks so grey, and clear, and dark, Sydney."

"Pooh! It is thick enough between you and the water. You would have to get down a good way, I can tell you, before you could get drowned."

"But it is so slippery!"

"What of that? What else did you expect with ice? If you tumble, you can get up again. I have been down three times this morning."

"Well, that is a great consolation, certainly. Which way do you want me to walk?"

"Oh, any way. Across the river to the other bank, if you like. You will remember next summer, when we come this way in a boat, that you have walked across the very place."

"That is true," said Margaret. "I will go if Sophia will go with me."

"There is no use in asking any of them," said Sydney. "They stand dawdling and looking, till their lips and noses are all blue and red, and they are never up to any fun."

"I will try as far as that pole first," said Margaret. "I should not care if they had not swept away all the snow here, so as to make the ice look so grey and slippery."

"That pole!" said Sydney. "Why, that pole is put up on purpose to show that you must not go there. Don't you see how the ice is broken all round it? Oh, I know how it is that you are so stupid and cowardly to-day. You've lived in Birmingham all your winters, and you've never been used to walk on the ice."

"I am glad you have found that out at last. Now, look—I am really going. What a horrid sensation!" she cried, as she cautiously put down one foot before the other on the transparent floor. She did better when she reached the middle of the river, where the ice had been ground by the skates.

"Now, you would get on beautifully," said Sydney, "if you would not look at your feet. Why can't you look at the people, and the trees opposite?"

"Suppose I should step into a hole."

"There are no holes. Trust me for the holes. What do you flinch so for? The ice always cracks so, in one part or another. I thought you had been shot."

"So did I," said she, laughing. "But, Sydney, we are a long way from both banks."

"To be sure: that is what we came for."

Margaret looked somewhat timidly about her. An indistinct idea flitted through her mind—how glad she should be to be accidentally, innocently drowned; and scarcely recognising it, she proceeded.

"You get on well," shouted Mr Hope, as he flew past, on his return up the river.

"There, now," said Sydney, presently; "it is a very little way to the bank. I will just take a trip up and down, and come for you again, to go back; and then we will try whether we can't get cousin Hester over, when she sees you have been safe there and back."

This was a sight which Hester was not destined to behold. Margaret had an ignorant partiality for the ice which was the least grey; and, when left to herself, she made for a part which looked less like glass. Nobody particularly heeded her. She slipped, and recovered herself: she slipped again, and fell, hearing the ice crack under her. Every time she attempted to rise, she found the place too slippery to keep her feet; next, there was a hole under her; she felt the cold water—she was sinking through; she caught at the surrounding edges—they broke away. There was a cry from the bank, just as the death-cold waters seemed to close all round her, and she felt the ice like a heavy weight above her. One thought of joy—"It will soon be all over now"—was the only experience she was conscious of.

In two minutes more, she was breathing the air again, sitting on the bank, and helping to wring out her clothes. How much may pass in two minutes! Mr Hope was coming up the river again, when he saw a bustle on the bank, and slipped off his skates, to be ready to be of service. He ran as others ran, and arrived just when a dark-blue dress was emerging from the water, and then a dripping fur tippet, and then the bonnet, making the gradual revelation to him who it was. For one instant he covered his face with his hands, half-hiding an expression of agony so intense that a bystander who saw it, said, "Take comfort, sir: she has been in but a very short time. She'll recover, I don't doubt." Hope leaped to the bank, and received her from the arms of the men who had drawn her out. The first thing she remembered was hearing, in the lowest tone she could conceive of—"Oh, God! my Margaret!" and a groan, which she felt rather than heard. Then there were many warm and busy hands about her head—removing her bonnet, shaking out her hair, and chafing her temples. She sighed out, "Oh, dear!" and she heard that soft groan again. In another moment she roused herself, sat up, saw Hope's convulsed countenance, and Sydney standing motionless and deadly pale.

"I shall never forgive myself," she heard her brother exclaim.

"Oh, I am very well," said she, remembering all about it. "The air feels quite warm. Give me my bonnet. I can walk home."

"Can you? The sooner the better, then," said Hope, raising her.

She could stand very well, but the water was everywhere dripping from her clothes. Many bystanders employed themselves in wringing them out; and in the meanwhile Margaret inquired for her sister, and hoped she did not know of the accident. Hester did not know of it, for Margaret happened to be the first to think of any one but herself.

Sydney was flying off to report, when he was stopped and recalled.

"You must go to her, Edward," said Margaret, "or she will be frightened. You can do me no good. Sydney will go home with me, or any one here, I am sure." Twenty people stepped forward at the word. Margaret parted with her heavy fur tippet, accepted a long cloth cloak from a poor woman, to throw over her wet clothes, selected Mr Jones, the butcher, for her escort, sent Sydney forward with directions to Morris to warm her bed, and then she set forth homeward. Mr Hope and half a dozen more would see her across the ice; and by the time she had reached the other bank, she was able to walk very much as if nothing had happened.

Mr Hope had perfectly recovered his composure before he reached the somewhat distant pond where Hester and the Greys were watching sliding as good as could be seen within twenty miles. It had reached perfection, like everything else, in Deerbrook.

"What! tired already?" said Hester to her husband. "What have you done with your skates?"

"Oh, I have left them somewhere there, I suppose." He drew her arm within his own. "Come, my dear, let us go home. Margaret is gone."

"Gone! Why? Is not she well? It is not so very cold."

"She has got wet, and she has gone home to warm herself." Hester did not wait to speak again to the Greys when she comprehended that her sister had been in the river. Her husband was obliged to forbid her walking so fast, and assured her all the way that there was nothing to fear. Hester reproached him for his coolness.

"You need not reproach me," said he. "I shall never cease to reproach myself for letting her go where she did." And yet his heart told him that he had only acted according to his deliberate design of keeping aloof from all Margaret's pursuits and amusements that were not shared with her sister. And as for the risk, he had seen fifty people walking across the ice this very morning. Judging by the event, however, he very sincerely declared that he should never forgive himself for having left her.

When they reached home, Margaret was quite warm and comfortable, and her hair drying rapidly under Morris's hands. Hester was convinced that everybody might dine as usual. Margaret herself came down-stairs to tea; and the only consequence of the accident seemed to be, that Charles was kept very busy opening the door to inquirers how Miss Ibbotson was this evening.

It made Hope uneasy to perceive how much Margaret remembered of what had passed around her in the midst of the bustle of the morning. If she was still aware of some circumstances that she mentioned, might she not retain others—the words extorted from him, the frantic action which he now blushed to remember?

"Brother," said she, "what *was* the meaning of something that I heard some one say, just as I sat up on the bank? 'There's a baulk for the doctor! He is baulked of a body in his own house.'"

"Oh, Margaret," cried her sister, who sat looking at her all the evening as if they had been parted for ten years, "you dreamed that. It was a fancy. Think what a state your poor head was in! It may have a few strange imaginations left in it still. May it not, Edward?"

"This is not one," he replied. "She heard very accurately."

"What did they mean?"

"There is a report abroad about me, arising out of the old prejudice about dissection. Some of my neighbours think that dissecting is the employment and the passion of my life, and that I rob the churchyard as often as anybody is buried."

"Oh, Edward! how frightful! how ridiculous!"

"It is very disagreeable, my dear. I am taunted with this wherever I go."

"What is to be done?"

"We must wait till the prejudices against me die out: but I see that we shall have to wait some time; for before one suspicion is given up, another rises."

"Since that unhappy election," said Hester, sighing. "What a strange thing it is that men like you should be no better treated! Here is Mrs Enderby taken out of your hands, and your neighbours suspecting and slandering you, whose commonest words they are not worthy to repeat."

"My dear Hester!" said he, in a tone of serious remonstrance. "That is rather a wife-like way of putting the case, to be sure," said Margaret, smiling: "but, in as far as it is true, the matter surely ceases to be strange. Good men do not come into the world to be what the world calls fortunate, but to be something far better. The best men do not use the means to be rich, to be praised by their neighbours, to be out of the way of trouble; and if they will not use the means, it does not become them—nor their wives— to be discouraged at losing their occupation, or being slandered, or suspected as dangerous people."

Edward's smile thanked her, and so did her sister's kiss. But Hester looked grave again when she said—"I suppose we shall know, sooner or later, why it is that good people are not to be happy here, and that the more they love one another, the more struggles and sorrows they have to undergo."

"Do we not know something of it already?" said Hope, after a pretty long pause. "Is it not to put us off from the too vehement desire of being what we commonly call happy? By the time higher things become more interesting to us than this, we begin to find that it is given to us to put our own happiness under our feet, in reaching forward to something better. We become, by natural consequence, practised in this (forgetful of the things that are behind); and if the practice be painful, what then? We shall not quarrel with it, surely, unless we are willing to exchange what we have gained for money, and praise, and animal spirits, shutting in an abject mind."

"Oh, no, no!" said Hester; "but yet there are troubles—" She stopped short on observing Margaret's quivering lip.

"There are troubles, I own, which it is difficult to classify and interpret," said her husband. "We can only struggle through them, taking the closest heed to our innocence. But these affairs of ours—these mistakes of my neighbours—are not of that sort. They are intelligible enough, and need not therefore trouble us much."

Hope was right in his suspicion of the accuracy of Margaret's memory. His tones, his words, had sunk deep into her heart—her innocent heart—in which everything that entered it became safe and pure as itself. "Oh God! my Margaret!" sounded there like music.

"What a heart he has!" she thought. "I was very selfish to fancy him reserved; and I am glad to know that my brother loves me so. If it is such a blessing to be his sister, how happy must Hester be—in spite of everything! God has preserved my life, and He has given these two to each other! And, oh, how He has shown me that they love me! I will rouse myself, and try to suffer less."

Chapter Twenty Three

Moods of the Mind.

Hester's sleeping as well as waking thoughts were this night full of solicitude as to her feelings and conduct towards her sister. A thousand times before the morning she had said to herself, in dreams and in meditation, that she had failed in this relation—the oldest, and, till of late, the dearest. She shuddered to think how nearly she had lost Margaret; and to imagine what her state of mind would have been, if her sister had now been beyond the reach of the voice, the eye, the hand, which she was resolved should henceforth dispense to her nothing but the love and the benefits she deserved. She reflected that to few was granted such a warning of the death of beloved ones: to few was it permitted to feel, while it was yet not too late, the agony of remorse for pain inflicted, for gratifications withheld; for selfish neglect, for insufficient love. She remembered vividly what her emotions had been as a child, on finding her canary dead in its cage;—how she had wept all day, not so much for its loss as from the recollection of the many times when she had failed to cheer it with sugar, and groundsel, and play, and of the number of hours when she had needlessly covered up its cage in impatience at its song, shutting out its sunshine, and changing the brightest seasons of its little life into dull night. If it had been thus with her sister! Many a hasty word, many an unjust thought, came back now to wring her heart, when she imagined Margaret sinking in the water,—the soft breathing on which our life so marvellously hangs, stopped without struggle or cry. How near—how very near, had Death, in his hovering, stooped towards their home! How strange, while treading thus precariously the film which covers the abyss into which all must some day drop, and which may crack under the feet of any one at any hour,—how strange to be engrossed with petty jealousies, with selfish cares, and to be unmindful of the great interests of existence, the exercises of mutual love and trust! Thank God! it was not too late. Margaret lived to be cherished, to be consoled for her private griefs, as far as consolation might be possible; to have her innocent affections redeemed from the waste to which they now seemed doomed,—gathered gradually up again, and knit into the interests of the home life in which she was externally bearing her part. Full of these thoughts, and forgetting how often her best feelings had melted away beneath the transient heats kindled by the little provocations of daily life, Hester now believed that Margaret would never have to suffer from her more,—that their love would be henceforth like that of angels,—

like that which it would have been if Margaret had really died yesterday. It was yet early, when, in the full enjoyment of these undoubting thoughts, Hester stood by her sister's bedside.

Margaret was still sleeping, but with that expression of weariness in her face which had of late become too common. Hester gazed long at the countenance, grieving at the languor and anxiety which it revealed. She had not taken Margaret's suffering to heart,—she had been unfeeling,— strangely forgetful. She would minister to her now with reverent care. As she thus resolved, she bent down, and kissed her forehead. Margaret started, shook off sleep, felt quite well, would rise;—there was no reason why she should not rise at once.

When she entered the breakfast-room, Hester was there, placing her chair by the fire, and inventing indulgences for her, as if she had been an invalid. It was in vain that Margaret protested that no effects of the accident remained,—not a single sensation of chill: she was to be taken care of; and she submitted. She was touched by her sister's gentle offices, and felt more like being free and at peace, more like being lifted up out of her woe, than she had yet done since the fatal hour which rendered her conscious and wretched. Breakfast went on cheerfully. The fire blazed bright: the rain pelting against the windows gave welcome promise of exemption from inquiries in person, and from having to relate, many times over, the particulars of the event of yesterday. Hester was beautiful in all the glow of her sensibilities, and Edward was for this morning in no hurry. No blue or yellow backed pamphlet lay beside his plate; and when his last cup was empty, he still sat talking as if he forgot that he should have to go out in the rain. In the midst of a laugh which had prevented their hearing a premonitory knock, the door opened, and Mrs Grey's twin daughters entered, looking half-shy, half-eager. Never before had they been known to come out in heavy rain: but they were so very desirous to see cousin Margaret after she had been in the water!—and Sydney had held the great gig umbrella over himself and them, as papa would not hear of Sydney not coming:— he was standing outside the door now, under the large umbrella, for he said nothing should make him come in and see cousin Margaret—he would never see her again if he could help it. Sydney had said another thing,—such a wicked thing! Mamma was quite ashamed of him. Mr Hope thought they had better not repeat anything wicked that any one had said: but Hester considered it possible that it might not appear so wicked if spoken as if left to the imagination. What Sydney had said was, that if cousin Margaret had been really drowned, he would have drowned himself before dinner-time. Mary added that she heard him mutter that he was almost ready to do it now. Mr Hope thought that must be the reason why he was standing out at present, to catch all this rain, which was very nearly enough to drown anybody; and he went to bring him in. But Sydney was not to be caught. He was on the watch; and the moment he saw Mr Hope's coat instead of his sisters' cloaks, he ran off with a speed which defied pursuit, and was soon out of sight with the large umbrella.

His cousins were sorry that he felt the event so painfully, and that he could not come in and confide his trouble of mind to them. Hope resolved not to let the morning pass without seeing him, and, if possible, bringing him home to dinner, with William Levitt to take off the awkwardness.

"What are we to do?" exclaimed Sydney's little sisters. "He has carried off the great umbrella."

"I cannot conveniently send you, just at present," said Hester; "so you had better put off your cloaks, and amuse yourselves here till the rain abates, or some one comes for you. We will speak to Miss Young to excuse your not being with her."

"Oh, cousin Margaret," said the children, "if you will speak to Miss Young, she will give us any sort of a holiday. She minds everything you say. She will let us stop all day, and dine here, if you ask her."

Hester said she could not have them stay all day,—she did not mean to have them to dinner: and the little girls both looked up in her face at once, to find out what made her speak so angrily. They saw cousin Margaret glancing the same way too.

"Do you know, Mary," said Fanny, "you have not said a word yet of what Miss Young bade you say?"

Mary told cousin Margaret, that Miss Young was wishing very much to see her, and would be pleased if Margaret would mention what evening she would spend with her,—a nice long evening, Mary added, to begin as soon as it grew dark, and on till—nobody knew when.

"Maria had better come here," observed Hester, quickly; "and then some one else besides Margaret may have the benefit of her conversation. She seems to forget that anybody cares for her besides Margaret. Tell Miss Young she had better fix an evening to come here."

"I do not think she will do that," said both the little girls.

"Why not?"

"She is very lame now," replied Mary, "and she cannot walk further than just to school and back again."

"And, besides," remarked Fanny, "she wants to talk with cousin Margaret alone, I am sure. They have such a great deal of talk to do whenever they are together! We watch them sometimes in the schoolroom, through the window, when we are at play in the garden; and their heads nod at one another in this way. I believe they never leave off for a minute. We often wonder what it can be all about."

"Ah, my dears, you and I had better not ask," said Hester. "I have no doubt it is better that we should not know."

Margaret looked beseechingly at her sister. Hester replied to her look:

"I mean what I say, Margaret. You cannot but be aware how much more you have to communicate to Maria than to me. Our conversation soon comes to a stand: and I must say I have had much occasion to admire your great talent for silence of late. Maria has still to learn your accomplishments in that direction, I fancy."

Margaret quietly told the little girls that she would write a note to Maria, with her answer.

"You must not do that," said Fanny. "Miss Young said you must not. That was the reason why she sent you a message instead of a note—that you might not have to write back again, when a message would do as well."

Margaret, nevertheless, sat down at the writing-table.

"You go to-day, of course," said Hester, in the voice of forced calmness which Margaret knew so well. "The little girls may as well stay and dine, after all, as I shall otherwise be alone in the evening."

"I shall not go to-day," said Margaret, without turning her head.

"You will not stay away on my account, of course."

"I have said that I shall go on Thursday."

"Thursday! that is almost a week hence. Now, Margaret, do not be pettish, and deny yourself what you know you like best. Do not be a baby, and quarrel with your supper. I had far rather you should go to-night, and have done with it, than that you should wait till Thursday, thinking all day long till then that you are obliging me by staying with me. I cannot bear that."

"I wish I knew what you could bear," said Margaret, in a voice which the children could not hear. "I wish I knew how I could save you pain."

The moment the words were out, Margaret was sorry for them. She was aware that the best kindness to her sister was to take as little notice as possible of her discontents—to turn the conversation—to avoid scenes, or any remarks which could bring them on. It was hard—sometimes it seemed impossible—to speak calmly and lightly, while every pulse was throbbing, and every fibre trembling with fear and wretchedness; but yet it was best to assume such calmness and lightness. Margaret now asked the little girls, while she sealed her note, how their patchwork was getting on—thus far the handsomest patchwork quilt she had ever seen.

"Oh, it will be far handsomer before it is done. Mrs Howell has found up some beautiful pieces of print for us—remnants of her first morning-gown after she was married, and of her poor dear Howell's last dressing-gown, as she says. We were quite sorry to take those; but she would put them up for us; and she is to see the quilt sometimes in return."

"But Miss Nares's parcel was the best, cousin Margaret. Such a quantity of nankeen for the ground, and the loveliest chintz for the centre medallion! Is not it, Mary?"

"Oh, lovely! Do you know, cousin Margaret, Miss Nares and Miss Flint both cried when they heard how nearly you were drowned! I am sure, I had no idea they would have cared so much."

"Nor I, my dear. But I dare say they feel kindly towards anyone saved from great danger."

"Not everybody," said Fanny; "only you, because you are a great favourite. Everybody says you are a great favourite. Papa cried last night—just a little tear or two, as gentlemen do—when he told mamma how sorry everybody in Deerbrook would have been if you had died."

"There! that will do," said Hester, struggling between her better and worse feelings—her remorse of this morning, and her present jealousy—and losing her temper between the two. "You have said quite enough about what you do not understand, my dears. I cannot have you make so free with your cousin's name, children."

The little girls looked at each other in wonder; and Hester thought she detected a lurking smile.

"I see what you are thinking, children. Yes, look, the rain is nearly over; and then you may go and tell Mrs Howell and Miss Nares, and all the people you see on your way home, that they had better attend to their own concerns than pretend to understand what would have been felt if your cousin had been drowned. I wonder at their impertinence."

"Are you in earnest, cousin Hester? Shall we go and tell them so?"

"No; she is not in earnest," said Margaret. "But before you go, Morris shall give you some pieces for your quilt—some very pretty ones, such as she knows I can spare."

Margaret rang, and Morris took the children up-stairs, to choose for themselves out of Margaret's drawer of pieces. When the door had closed behind them, Margaret said—"Sister, do not make me wish that I had died under the ice yesterday."

"Margaret, how dare you say anything so wicked?"

"If it be wicked, God forgive me! I was wretched enough before—I would fain have never come to life again: and now you almost make me believe that you would have been best pleased if I never had."

At this moment Hope entered. He had left them in a far different mood: it made him breathless to see his wife's face of passion, and Margaret's of woe.

"Hear her!" exclaimed Hester. "She says I should have been glad to have lost her yesterday!"

"Have mercy upon me!" cried Margaret, in excessive agitation. "You oppress me beyond what I can bear. I cannot bear on as I used to do. My strength is gone, and you give me none. You take away what I had!"

"Will you hear me spoken to in this way?" cried Hester, turning to her husband.

"I will."

Margaret's emotion prevented her hearing this, or caring who was by. She went on—"You leave me nothing—nothing but yourself—and you abuse my love for you. You warn me against love—against marriage—you chill my very soul with terror at it. I have found a friend in Maria; and you poison my comfort in my friendship, and insult my friend. There is not an infant in a neighbour's house but you become jealous of it the moment I take it in my arms. There is not a flower in your garden, not a book on my table, that you will let me love in peace. How ungenerous—while you have one to cherish and who cherishes you, that you will have me lonely!—that you quarrel with all who show regard to me!—that you refuse me the least solace, when my heart is breaking with its loneliness! Oh, it is cruel!"

"Will you hear this, Edward?"

"I will, because it is the truth. For once, Hester, you must hear another's mind; you have often told your own."

"God knows why I was saved yesterday," murmured Margaret; "for a more desolate creature does not breathe."

Hope leaned against the wall. Hester relieved her torment of mind with reproaches of Margaret.

"You do not trust me," she cried; "it is you who make me miserable. You go to others for the comfort you ought to seek in me. You place that confidence in others which ought to be mine alone. You are cheered when you learn that the commonest gossips in Deerbrook care about you, and you set no value on your own sister's feelings for you. You have faith and charity for people out of doors, and mistrust and misconstruction for those at home. I am the injured one, Margaret, not you."

"Margaret," said Hope, "your sister speaks for herself. I think that you are the injured one, as Hester herself will soon agree. So far from having anything to reproach you with, I honour your forbearance,—unremitting till this hour,—I mourn that we cannot, if we would, console you in return. But whatever I can do shall be done. Your friendships, your pursuits, shall be protected. If we persecute your affections at home, I will take care that you are allowed their exercise abroad. Rely upon me, and do not think yourself utterly lonely while you have a brother."

"I have been very selfish," said Margaret, recovering herself at the first word of kindness; "wretchedness makes me selfish, I think."

She raised herself up on the sofa, and timidly held out her hand to her sister. Hester thrust it away. Margaret uttered a cry of agony, such as had never been heard from her since her childhood. Hope fell on the floor—he had fainted at the sound.

Even now there was no one but Morris who understood it. Margaret reproached herself bitterly for her selfishness—for her loss of the power of self-control. Hester's remorse, however greater in degree, was of its usual kind, strong and brief. She repeated, as she had done before, that she made her husband wretched—that she should never have another happy moment—that she wished he had never seen her. For the rest of the day she was humbled, contrite, convinced that she should give way to her temper no more. Her eyes filled when her husband spoke tenderly to her, and her conduct to Margaret was one act of supplication. But a lesser degree of this same kind of penitence had produced no permanent good effect before; and there was no security that the present paroxysm would have a different result.

Morris had seen that the children were engaged up-stairs when she came down at Margaret's silent summons, to help to revive her master. When she saw that there had been distress before there was illness, she took her part. She resolved that no one but herself should hear his first words, and sent the ladies away when she saw that his consciousness was returning. All the world might have heard his first words. He recovered himself with a vigorous effort, swallowed a glass of wine, and within a few minutes was examining a patient in the waiting-room. There the little girls saw him as they passed the half-open door, on their way out with their treasure of chintz and print; and having heard some bustle below, they carried home word that they believed Mr Hope had been doing something to somebody which had made somebody faint; and Sophia, shuddering, observed how horrid it must be to be a surgeon's wife.

Chapter Twenty Four

Warnings.

Maria Young's lodging at the farrier's had one advantage over many better dwellings;—it was pleasanter in Winter than in Summer. There was little to find fault with in the tiny sitting-room after candles were lighted. The fire burned clear in the grate; and when the screen was up, there were no draughts. This screen was quite a modern improvement. When Fanny and Mary Grey had experienced the pleasure of surprising Sophia with a token of sisterly affection, in the shape of a piece of India-rubber, and their mother with a token of filial affection, in the form of a cotton-box, they were unwilling to stop, and looked round to see whether they could not present somebody with a token of some other sort of affection. Sophia was taken into their counsels; and she, being aware of how Miss Young's candle flared when the wind was high, devised this screen. The carpenter made the frame; Sydney covered it with canvas and black paper for a ground; and the little girls pasted on it all the drawings and prints they could muster. Here was the Dargle, an everlasting waterfall, that looked always the same in the sunny-coloured print. There was Morland's Woodcutter, with his tall figure, his pipe, his dog, and his faggot, with the snow lying all around him. Two or three cathedrals were interspersed; and, in the midst of them, and larger than any of them, a silhouette of Mr Grey, with the eyelash wonderfully like, and the wart upon his nose not to be mistaken. Then there was Charles the First taking leave of his family; and, on either side of this, an evening primrose in water-colours, by Mary, and a head of Terror, with a square mouth and starting eyes, in crayon, by Fanny. Mrs Grey produced some gay border which the paper-hanger had left over when the attics were last furnished; and Sydney cut out in white paper a huntsman with his whip in the air, a fox, a gate, and two hounds. Mr Grey pleaded, that, having contributed his face, he had done all that could be expected of him: nevertheless, he brought home one day, on his return from market, a beautiful Stream of Time, which made the children dance round their screen. It was settled at first that this would nobly ornament the whole of one side; but it popped into Sydney's head, just as he was falling asleep one night, how pretty it would be to stick it round with the planets. So the planets were cut out in white, and shaded with Indian ink. There was no mistaking Saturn with his ring, or Jupiter with his moons. At length, all was done, and the cook was glad to hear that no more paste would be wanted, and the little girls might soon leave off giggling when Miss Young asked them, in the schoolroom, why they were jogging one another's elbows. Mr Grey spared one of his men to deposit the precious piece of handiwork at Miss Young's lodging; and there, when she went home one cold afternoon, she found the screen standing between the fire and the door, and, pinned on it, a piece of paper, inscribed, "A Token of friendly Affection."

This was not, however, the only, nor the first, gift with which Maria's parlour was enriched. Amidst all the bustle of furnishing the Hopes' house, Margaret had found time to plan and execute a window-curtain for her friend's benefit; and another person—no other than Philip Enderby—had sent in a chaise-longue, just the right size to stand between the fire and the table. It had gone hard with Maria to accept this last gift; but his nephew and nieces were Philip's plea of excuse for the act; and this plea cut her off from refusing: though in her heart she believed that neither the children nor ancient regard were in his thoughts when he did it, but rather Margaret's affection for her. For some time, this chaise-longue was a couch of thorns; but now affairs had put on a newer aspect still, and Maria forgot her own perplexities and troubles in sympathy with her friend.

There was nothing to quarrel with in the look of the chaise-longue, when Margaret entered Maria's room in the twilight, in the afternoon of the appointed Thursday.

"Reading by fire-light?" said Margaret.

"I suppose I am: but it had not occurred to me—the daylight went away so softly. Six o'clock, I declare! The days *are* lengthening, as we say every year. But we will have something better than firelight, if you will be so kind as to set those candles on the table."

The time was long put when Maria thought of apologising for asking her friend to do what her lameness rendered painful to herself. Margaret laid aside her bonnet and cloak behind the screen, lighted the candles, put more coals on the fire, and took her seat—not beside Maria, but in a goodly armchair, which she drew forward from its recess.

"Now," said she, "we only want a cat to be purring on the rug to make us a complete winter picture. The kettle will be coming soon to sing on the hob: and that will do nearly as well. But, Maria, I wonder *you* have no cat. We have set up a cat. I think I will send you a kitten, some day, as a token of neighbourly affection."

"Thank you. Do you know, I was positively assured lately that I had a cat? I said all I could in proof that I had none; but Mrs Tucker persisted in her inquiries after its health, notwithstanding."

"What did she mean?"

"She said she saw a kitten run into the passage, and that it never came out again: so that it followed of course that it must be here still. One day, when I was in school, she came over to satisfy herself; and true enough, there had been a kitten. The poor thing jumped from the passage window into the yard, and went to see what they were about at the forge. A hot horse-shoe fell upon its back, and it mewed so dolefully that the people drowned it. So there you have the story of my cat, as it was told to me."

"Thank you, it is a good thing to know. But what does Mrs Grey say to your setting up a cat?"

"When she heard Mrs Tucker's first inquiries, she took them for an imputation, and was vexed accordingly. 'Miss Young!' said she, 'You must be mistaken, Mrs Tucker. Miss Young cannot afford to keep a kitten!'"

"Oh, for shame!" said Margaret, laughing. "But what is the annual expense of a kitten—can you tell us? I am afraid we never considered that."

"Why, there is the breast of a fowl, once a year or so, when your cook forgets to shut the larder-door behind her. Cats never take the drumsticks when there is a breast, you are aware. You know best how Mr Hope looks, when the drumsticks and side bones come to table, with an empty space in the middle of the dish where the breast ought to have been."

"I will tell you, the first time it happens." And Margaret sank into an absent fit, brought on by the bare suggestion of discontent at home. Hester had made her uncomfortable, the last thing before she left the house, by speaking sharply of Maria, without any fresh provocation. Undisciplined still by what had happened so lately, she had wished Maria Young a hundred miles off. Margaret meditated and sighed. It was some time before Maria spoke. When she did, she said:

"Margaret, do not you think people had better not persuade themselves and their very intimate friends that they are happy when they are not?"

"They had better not think, even in their own innermost minds, whether they are happy or not, if they can help it."

"True: but there are times when that is impossible—when it is far better to avoid the effort. Come—I suspect we may relieve each other just now, by allowing the truth. I will own, if you will, that I am very unhappy to-night. Never mind what it is about."

"I will, if you will," replied Margaret, faintly smiling.

"There now, that's right! We shall be all the better for it. We have quite enough of seeming happy, God knows, beyond these doors. We can talk there about kittens and cold fowl. Here we will not talk at all, unless we like; and we will each groan as much as we please."

"I am sorry to hear you speak so," said Margaret, tenderly. "Not that I do not agree with you. I think it is a terrible mistake to fancy that it is religious to charm away grief, which, after all, is rejecting it before it has done its work; and, as for concealing it, there must be very good reasons indeed for that, to save it from being hypocrisy. But the more I agree with you, the more sorry I am to hear you say just what I was thinking. I am afraid you must be very unhappy, Maria."

"I'm in great pain to-night; and I do not find that pain becomes less of an evil by one's being used to it. Indeed, I think the reverse happens; for the future comes into the consideration."

"Do you expect to go on to suffer this same pain? Can nothing cure it? Is there no help?"

"None, but in patience. There are intermissions, happily, and pretty long ones. I get through the summer very well; but the end of the winter—this same month of February—is a sad aching time; and so it must be for as many winters as I may have to live. But I am better off than I was. Last February I did not know you. Oh, Margaret, if they had not brought you up from under the ice, the other day, how different would all have been to-night!"

"How strange it seems to think of the difference that hung on that one act!" said Margaret, shivering again at the remembrance of her icy prison. "What, and where, should I have been now? And what would have been the change in this little world of ours? You would have missed me, I know; and on that account I am glad it ended as it did."

"And on no other?" asked Maria, looking earnestly at her friend.

"My sister would have grieved sadly at first—you do not know what care she takes of me—how often she is thinking of my comfort. And Edward is fond of me too: I know he is; but they live for each other, and could spare every one else. You and Morris would have been my mourners, and you two are enough to live for."

"To say nothing of others who may arise."

"I hope nothing more will arise in my life, Maria. I want no change. I have had enough of it."

"You think so now. I understand your feeling very well. But yet I can fancy that when you are twice as old as you are—when a few grey hairs peep out among all that brown—when this plump little hand grows thin, and that girlish figure of yours looks dignified and middle-aged, and people say that nobody thought when you were young that you would turn out a handsome woman—I can fancy that when all this has happened, you may be more disposed to look forward, and less disinclined to change, than you feel at this moment. But there is no use in saying so now. You shake your head, and I nod mine. You say, 'No,' and I say, 'Yes,' and there is an end of it."

"Where will you be then, I wonder?"

"I do not wish to know, nor even to inquire of my own judgment. My health is very bad—worse than you are aware of. I cannot expect to be able to work always; some of my present pupils are growing very tall; and no strangers will take me if I do not get much better; which is, I believe, impossible. The future, therefore, is all a mystery; and so let it remain. I am not anxious about that."

"But I am."

"Here comes tea. Now you will be doing a finer thing in making us a good cup of tea, than in settling my future ever so satisfactorily—seeing that you cannot touch it with so much as your little finger. The tea is wholly in your power."

"You look forward to other people's grey hair and sedateness of face, though you will not to your own."

"Mere grey hair is as certain as futurity itself; and I will allow you to prophesy that much for me or for anybody."

"Why should we not prophesy about your pupils too? They seem to be improving very much."

"They certainly are; and I am glad you have lighted upon the pleasantest subject I ever think about. Oh, Margaret, you do not know what encouragement I have about some of those children! Their lot is and will be a hard one, in many respects. It will be difficult for them to grow kindly, and liberal, and truthful, with such examples as they have before their eyes. They advance like the snail on the wall, creeping three inches on in the day, and falling back two at night. They get out of a pretty mood of mind in the morning, and expand and grow interested in things out of Deerbrook; and then, in the evening, the greater part of this is undone, and they go to bed with their heads full of small, vile notions about their neighbours."

"And when they grow too wise to have their heads so filled, their hearts will be heavy for those who are not rising like themselves."

"That is unavoidable, and they must bear the sorrow. We must hope that they will disperse from Deerbrook, and find their way into a more genial society than they can ever know here. I must keep the confidence of my children sacred even from you, Margaret: but you may believe me when I tell you, that if you knew all that we have to say to one another, you would find some of these children animated with really noble thoughts, and capable of really generous acts."

"'Some of them.' Mary, in particular, I venture to conjecture to be in your thoughts."

"Yes: Mary in particular; but she had always a more gentle and generous temper than her sisters. Fanny, however, is improving remarkably."

"I am delighted to hear it, and I had begun to suspect it. Fanny, I observe, lays fewer informations than she did; and there is more of thought, and less of a prying expression, in her face. She is really growing more like Mary in countenance. The little Rowlands—the younger ones—seem simple enough; but Matilda, what a disagreeable child she is!"

"The most that can be done with her is to leave her only a poor creature—to strip her of the conceit and malice with which her mother would overlay her feeble intellect. This sounds deplorably enough; but, as parents will not speak the plain truth to themselves about their charge, governesses must. There is, perhaps, little better material in Fanny: but I trust we may one day see her more lowly than she can at present relish the idea of being, and with energy enough to improve under the discipline of life, when she can no longer have that of school. She and Mary have been acknowledging to-day a fine piece of experience. Mr Grey is pleased with their great Improvement in Latin. He finds they can read, with ease and pleasure, some favourite classical scraps which he used to talk about without exciting any interest in them. They honestly denied having devoted any more time to Latin than before, or having taken any more pains; and no new methods have been tried. Here was a mystery. To-day they have solved it. They find that all is owing to their getting up earlier in the morning to teach those little orphans, the Woods, to read and sew."

"Not a very circuitous process," said Margaret; "love and kind interest, energy and improvement—whether in Latin or anything else. But what did you mean just now about truth? What should make the Greys otherwise than truthful?"

"Oh, not the Greys! I was thinking of the other family when I said that. But that is a large subject: let us leave it till after tea. Will you give me another cup?"

"Now; shall we begin upon our large subject?" said she, as the door closed behind the tea-tray and kettle, and Margaret handed her her work-bag.

"I am aware that I asked for it," replied Margaret; "but it is a disagreeable topic, and perhaps we had better avoid it."

"You will take me for a Deerbrook person, if I say we will go into it, will not you?"

"Oh, no: you have a reason, I see. So, why should not the little Rowlands be truthful?"

"Because they have so perpetual an example of falsehood before them at home. I have made some painful discoveries there lately."

"Is it possible you did not know that woman long ago?"

"I knew her obvious qualities, which there is no need to specify: but the depth of her untruth is a new fact to me."

"Are you sure of it, now?"

"Quite sure of it in some particulars, and strongly suspecting it in others. Do not tell your sister anything of what I am going to say, unless you find it necessary for the direction of her conduct. Let your disclosures be rather to Mr Hope. That is settled, is it? Well, Mrs Rowland's ruling passion just now is hatred to your household."

"I suspected as much. But—the untruth."

"Wait a little. She dislikes you, all and severally."

"What, my brother?"

"Oh, yes; for marrying into the Grey connection so decidedly. Did you ever hear that before?"

Margaret laughed; and her friend went on—

"This capture and imprisonment of her mother (for the poor old lady is not allowed to see whom she pleases) is chiefly to get her from under Mr Hope's care. I fancy, from her air, and from some things she has dropped, that she has some grand *coup-de-theâtre* in reserve about that matter; but this is merely suspicion: I will now speak only of what I know to exist. She is injuring your brother to an extent that he is not, but ought to be, aware of."

"What does she say? She shudders at his politics, I know."

"Yes; that might be ignorance merely, and even conscientious ignorance: so we will let that pass. She also hints, very plainly and extensively, that your brother and sister are not happy together."

"She is a wicked woman," said Margaret, with a deep sigh. "I half suspected what you tell me, from poor George's errand that unhappy day."

"Right. Mr Rowland's irony was intended to stop his wife's insinuations before the children. She says the most unwarrantable things about Mrs Grey's having made the match—and she intimates that Hester has several times gone to bed in hysterics, from Mr Hope having upbraided her with taking him in."

"What *is* to be done?" cried Margaret, throwing down her work.

"Your brother will decide for himself whether to speak to Mr Rowland, or to let the slander pass, and live it down. Our duty is to give him information; and I feel that it is a duty. And now, have you been told anything about Mr Hope's practice of dissection?"

Margaret related what she had heard on the bank of the river, and Hope's explanation of it.

"He knows more than he told you, I have no doubt," replied Maria. "The beginning of it was, your brother's surgery-pupil having sent a great toe, in a handsome-looking sealed packet, to some lad in the village, who happened to open it at table. You may imagine the conjectures as to where it came from, and the revival of stories about robbing churchyards, and of prejudices about dissection. Mrs Rowland could not let such an opportunity as this pass by; and her neighbours have been favoured with dark hints as to what has been heard under the churchyard wall, and what she herself has seen from her window in sleepless nights. Now, Mr Hope must take notice of this. It is too dangerous a subject to be left quietly to the ignorance and superstitions of such a set of people as those among whom his calling lies. No ignorance on earth exceeds that of the country folks whom he attends."

"But they worship him," cried Margaret.

"They have worshipped him; but you know, worship easily gives place to hatred among the extremely ignorant; and nothing is so likely to quicken the process as to talk about violating graves. Do not be frightened; I tell you this to prevent mischief, not to prophesy it. Mr Hope will take what measures he thinks fit: and I shall tell Mr Rowland, tomorrow morning, that I am the source of your information. I was just going to warn him to-day that I meant to speak to you in this way; but I left it till to-morrow, that I might not be prevented."

"Dear Maria, this will cost you your bread."

"I believe not; but this consideration belongs to that future of time on which, as I was saying, we cannot lay our little fingers. The present is clear enough—that Mr Hope ought to know his own case."

"He shall know it. But, Maria, do you mean that Mrs Rowland talks of all these affairs before her children?"

"When Mr Rowland is not present to check it. And this brings me to something which I think ought to be said, though I have no proof to bring. Having found of late what things Mrs Rowland can say for a purpose—how variously and how monstrously untrue—and seeing that all her enterprises are at present directed against the people who live in a pleasant little corner-house—"

"But why? You have not yet fully accounted for this enmity."

"I have not, but I will now. I think she joins your name with her brother's, and that she accordingly hates you now as she once hated Hester. But mind, I am not sure of this."

"But how—? Why—?"

"You will divine that I have changed my opinion about Mr Enderby's being engaged to Miss Bruce, since you asked me for my judgment upon it. I may very possibly be mistaken: but as Mr Enderby lies under censure for forming and carrying on such an arrangement in strange concealment from his most intimate friends, I think it due to him at least to put the supposition that he may not be guilty."

Margaret could not speak, though a thousand questions struggled in her heart.

"I am aware," continued Maria, "with what confidence she has everywhere stated the fact of this engagement, and that Mrs Enderby fully believes it. But I have been struck throughout with a failure of particularity in Mrs Rowland's knowledge. She cannot tell when her brother last saw Miss Bruce, nor whether he has any intention of going to Rome. She does not know, evidently, whether he was engaged when he was last here; and I cannot get rid of the impression, that his being engaged now is a matter of inference from a small set of facts, which will bear more than one interpretation."

"Surely she would not dare—." Margaret paused.

"It is a bold stroke (supposing me right), but she would strike boldly to make a quarrel between her brother and his friends in the corner-house: and if the device should fail at last, she has the intermediate satisfaction of making them uncomfortable."

"Horrid creature!" said Margaret, feeling, however, that she would forgive all the horridness for the sake of finding that Mrs Rowland had done this horrid thing.

"We must not forget," said Maria, "that there is another side to the question. Young men have been known to engage themselves mysteriously, and without sufficient respect to the confidence of intimate friends."

"This must be ascertained, Maria;" and again Margaret stopped short with a blush of shame.

"By time, Margaret; in no other way. I cannot, of course, speak to Mr Rowland, or any one, on so private an affair of the family; nor, under the circumstances, can Mr Hope stir in it. We must wait; but it cannot be for long. Some illumination must reach Deerbrook soon—either from Mr Enderby's going to Rome, or coming here to see his mother."

"Mrs Rowland said he would come here, she hoped, for his wedding journey."

"She did say so, I know. And she has told plenty of people that her brother is delighted that Mrs Enderby is settled with her; whereas some beautiful plants arrived this morning for Mrs Enderby's conservatory, by his orders (the Rowlands have no conservatory you know). The children were desired not to mention the arrival of these plants to grandmamma; and Mrs Rowland wrote by return of post—I imagine to inform him for the first time of his mother's removal."

Margaret thought these things were too bad to be true.

"I should have said so, too, some time ago: and as I cannot too earnestly repeat, I may be wrong now. But I have done my duty in giving you reason for suspending your judgment of Mr Enderby. This being done, we will talk of something else.—Now, do not you think there may be some difficulty in preserving my pupils from a habit of untruth?"

"Yes, indeed."

But the talking of something else did not operate so well as it sounded. The pauses were long after what had passed. At length, when Margaret detected herself in the midst of the speculation, "if he is not engaged to Miss Bruce, it does not follow—," she roused herself, and exclaimed—

"How very good it is of you, Maria, to have laid all this open to me!"

Maria hung her head over her work, and thought within herself that her friend could not judge of the deed. She replied—

"Thank you! I thought I should get some sympathy from you in the end, to repay me for the irksomeness of exposing such a piece of social vice as this poor lady's conduct."

"Yes, indeed, I ought to have acknowledged it before, as I feel it; but you know there is so much to think over! it is so wonderful—so almost inconceivable!"

"It is so."

"Is it quite necessary, Maria—yes, I see it is necessary that you should speak to Mr Rowland to-morrow? You are bound in honesty to do so; but it will be very painful. Can we not help you? Can we not in some way spare you?"

"No, you cannot, thank you. For Mr Rowland's sake, no one must be by; and none of you can testify to the facts. No; leave me alone. By this time to-morrow night it will be done. What knock is that? No one ever knocks on my account. Surely it cannot be your servant already. It is only now half-past eight."

"I promised Hester I would go home early."

"She cannot want you half so much as I do. Stay another hour."

Margaret could not. Hester made a point of her returning at this time. When the cloaking and final chat were done, and Margaret was at the door, Maria called her. Margaret came skipping back to hear her friend's whisper.

"How is your wretchedness, Margaret?"

"How is yours?" was Margaret's reply.

"Much better. The disburdening of it is a great comfort."

"And the pain—the aching?"

"Oh, never mind that!"

Margaret shook her head; she could not but mind it—but wish that she could take it upon herself sometimes. She had often thought lately, that she should rather enjoy a few weeks of Maria's pain, as an alternative to the woe under which she had been suffering; but this, if she could have tried the experiment, she would probably have found to be a mistake. When she saw her friend cover her eyes with her hand, as if for a listless hour of solitude, she felt that she had been wrong in yielding to her sister's jealousy of her being so much with Maria; and she resolved that, next time, Maria should appoint the hour for her return home.

When Maria was thus covering her eyes with her hand, she was thinking— "Now, half this task is over. The other half to-morrow—and then the consequences!"

When Margaret entered the drawing-room at home, where her brother was reading aloud to Hester, he exclaimed—

"We beat all Deerbrook for early visiting, I think. Here are you home; and I dare say Mr Tucker has still another pipe to smoke, and the wine is not mulled yet at the Jameses."

"It is quite time Margaret was giving us a little of her company, I am sure," said Hester. "You forget how early she went. If it was not for the school, I think she and Maria would spend all their time together. I have every wish not to interfere: but I cannot think that this friendship has made Maria less selfish."

"It would, I dare say, my dear, but that there was no selfishness to begin upon. I am afraid she is very unwell, Margaret?"

"In much pain, I fear."

"I will go and see if I can do her any good. You can glance over what we have read, and I shall be back in a quarter of an hour, to go on with it."

"I wonder you left Maria, if she is so poorly."

"I determined that I would not, another time; but this time I had promised."

"Pray, do not make out that I am any restraint upon your intercourse with Maria. And yet—it is not quite fair to say that, either."

"I do not think it is quite fair."

"But you should warn me—you should tell me, if I ask anything unreasonable. When are you going again? An old patient of my husband's has sent us a quarter of a chest of very fine oranges. We will carry Maria a basketful of oranges to-morrow."

Chapter Twenty Five

Long Walks.

The unhappy are indisposed to employment: all active occupations are wearisome and disgusting in prospect, at a time when everything, life itself, is full of weariness and disgust. Yet the unhappy must be employed, or they will go mad. Comparatively blessed are they, if they are set in families, where claims and duties abound, and cannot be escaped. In the pressure of business there is present safety and ultimate relief. Harder is the lot of those who have few necessary occupations, enforced by other claims than their own harmlessness and profitableness. Reading often fails. Now and then it may beguile; but much oftener the attention is languid, the thoughts wander, and associations with the subject of grief are awakened. Women who find that reading will not do, will obtain no relief from sewing. Sewing is pleasant enough in moderation to those whose minds are at ease the while; but it is an employment which is trying to the nerves when long continued, at the best; and nothing can be worse for the harassed, and for those who want to escape from themselves. Writing is bad. The pen hangs idly suspended over the paper, or the sad thoughts that are alive within write themselves down. The safest and best of all occupations for such sufferers as are fit for it, is intercourse with young children. An infant might beguile Satan and his peers the day after they were couched on the lake of fire, if the love of children chanced to linger amidst the ruins of their angelic nature. Next to this comes honest, genuine acquaintanceship among the poor; not mere charity-visiting, grounded on soup-tickets and blankets, but intercourse of mind, with real mutual interest between the parties. Gardening is excellent, because it unites bodily exertion with a sufficient engagement of the faculties, while sweet, compassionate Nature is ministering cure in every sprouting leaf and scented blossom, and beckoning sleep to draw nigh, and be ready to follow up her benignant work. Walking is good,—not stepping from shop to shop, or from neighbour to neighbour; but stretching out far into the country, to the freshest fields, and the highest ridges, and the quietest lanes. However sullen the imagination may have been among its griefs at home, here it cheers up and smiles. However listless the limbs may have been when sustaining a too heavy heart, here they are braced, and the lagging gait becomes buoyant again. However perverse the memory may have been in presenting all that was agonising, and insisting only on what cannot be retrieved, here it is first disregarded, and then it sleeps and the sleep of the memory is the day in Paradise to the unhappy. The mere breathing of the cool wind on the face in the commonest highway, is rest and comfort which must be felt at such times to be believed. It is disbelieved in the shortest intervals between its seasons of enjoyment: and every time the sufferer has resolution to go forth to meet it, it penetrates to the very heart in glad surprise. The fields are better still; for there is the lark to fill up the hours with mirthful music; or, at worst, the robin and flocks of fieldfares, to show that the hardest day has its life and hilarity. But the calmest region is the upland, where human life is spread out beneath the bodily eye, where the mind roves from the peasant's nest to the spiry town, from the schoolhouse to the churchyard, from the diminished team in the patch of fallow, or the fisherman's boat in the cove, to the viaduct that spans the valley, or the fleet that glides ghost-like on the horizon. This is the perch where the spirit plumes its ruffled and drooping wines, and makes ready to let itself down any wind that Heaven may send.

No doubt Margaret found the benefit of exercise, and the solitary enjoyment of the country; for, during the last few weeks, walking seemed to have become a passion with her. Hester was almost out of patience about it, when for a moment she lost sight of what she well knew must be the cause of this strong new interest. Every doubtful morning, Margaret was at the window exploring the clouds. Every fine day she laid her watch on the table before her, impatiently waiting the approach of the hour when her brother was to come in for Hester, and when she might set off by herself, not to return till dinner-time. She became renowned in Deerbrook for the length of her excursions. The grocer had met her far out in one direction, when returning from making his purchases at the market town. The butcher had seen her in the distant fields, when he paid a visit to his grazier in the pastures. Dr Levitt had walked his horse beside her in the lane which formed the limit of the longer of his two common rides; and many a neighbour or patient of Mr Hope's had been surprised at her declining a cast in a taxed-cart or gig, when there was only a long stretch of plain road before her, and the lanes and fields were too miry to enable her to seek any variety in them, in her way home.

These were, in fact, Margaret's times of refreshing—of practical worship. These were the times when she saw what at other moments she only repeated to herself—that all things are right, and that our personal trials derive their bitterness from our ignorance and spiritual inexperience. At these times she could not only pity all who suffered, but congratulate all who enjoyed, and could afford feelings of disinterested regard to Philip, and of complacency to Miss Bruce. She remembered that Miss Bruce was unconscious of having injured her—was possibly unaware even of her existence; and then she enjoyed the luxury of blessing her rival, and of longing for an opportunity to serve her secretly and silently, as the happy girl's innocence of all wrong towards her deserved.

Margaret's desire for a long solitary walk was as strong as ever, the day after she had visited Maria. No opportunity had occurred of speaking to her brother without alarming Hester; and she had almost determined merely to refer him to Maria, instead of telling the story herself. She should not see him again till dinner. He was gone into the country: the day was gloomy and cold, and Hester was not disposed to leave the fireside: so Margaret issued forth, with thick shoes, umbrella, and muff—guarded against everything that might occur overhead and under foot. She had generally found hope, or at least comfort, abroad; to-day, when she ought to have been much happier, she found anxiety and fear. The thought, the very words, would incessantly recur, 'If he is not engaged to Miss Bruce, it does not follow...' Then she seriously grieved for her brother, and the troubles which she feared awaited him; and then she reproached herself with not grieving enough—not having attention enough to spare from her own concerns. While she was walking along on the dry causeway, looking straight before her, but thinking of far other things than the high-road, she was startled by the stroke of a horse's foot against a stone close by her side, and a voice speaking almost in her ear. It was only Edward. He was going a couple of miles forward, and he brought his horse beside the raised causeway, so that they could converse as if walking together.

"There is nobody to overhear us, I think," said Margaret, looking round. "I have been wanting, since yesterday evening, to speak to you alone—about something very disagreeable, which I would not disturb Hester with. You, of course, can do as you please about telling her."

She related to him the whole story of Mrs Rowland's imputations and proceedings—her reports of the hysterics and their origin, the body-snatching, and the cause and mode of Mrs Enderby's removal. Margaret had always considered her brother as a man of uncommon nerve; and her surprise was therefore great at seeing him change colour as he did.

"We shall agree," said she, "that the worst of all this is, that there is some truth at the bottom part of it."

"Oh, Heavens!" thought Hope, "is it possible that Mrs Grey can have told the share she had in my marriage?" It was but a momentary fear. Margaret went on.

"I have never hoped—I never hoped at Birmingham, and much less here—that Hester could escape the observation of her neighbours—that her occasional agitation of spirits should not excite remark and speculation. As we are not quite whole and sound in our domestic peace—(I must speak plainly, brother, at such a time as this) I should think it would be better to take no notice of that set of imputations. I trust we shall live them down."

"You gave me great comfort in a few words once," said Hope. "Do you remember saying, 'When the time for acting comes, see how she will act!' You know her well, and you judge her rightly: and you will, perhaps, be the less sorry to hear that the time seems coming when we may all have to act—I scarcely see how—but against adversity."

"She will come out nobly then. I fear nothing for her but too much prosperity."

"There is no fear of that, I assure you," said Hope, smiling somewhat sadly.

"You find the effect of this woman's slanders?"

"My situation has, from one cause or more, totally changed since you first knew me. It would break Hester's heart to hear what I am subjected to in the discharge of my daily business. I tell her a trifle now and then, to prepare her for what may happen; but she and you do not know a tenth part of what is inflicted upon me."

"And what may happen?"

"I cannot see the extent of it myself: but I am losing my practice every day. No; not through any failure; not through any of the accidents which will happen in all medical practice. There are reports of such abroad, I believe; but nothing is commoner than those reports. The truth is, no patient of mine has died, or failed to do well, for an unusually long space of time. The discontent with me is from other causes."

"From Mrs Rowland's tongue, I doubt not, more than from your politics."

"The ignorance of the people about us is the great evil. Without this, neither Mrs Rowland, nor any one else, could persuade them that I rob the churchyard, and vaccinate children to get patients, and draw good teeth to sell again."

"Oh, monstrous!" said Margaret, who yet could not help laughing. "You never draw teeth, do you?"

"Sometimes; but not when I can get people to go to the dentist at Blickley. Mrs Grey used to boast to you of my popularity; but I never liked it much. I had to be perpetually on the watch to avoid confidences; and you see how fast the stream is at present running the contrary way. I can hardly get on my horse now, without being insulted at my own door."

"Must you submit to all this?"

"By no means. I have called two or three men to account, and shaken my whip over one or two more—with excellent effect. If there were none but bullies among my enemies, I could easily deal with them."

"But cannot we go away, and settle somewhere else?"

"Oh, no! Wherever I might go, it would soon be understood that I had been obliged to leave Deerbrook, from being detected in body-snatching and the like. I owe it to myself to stay. We must remain, and live down all imputations whatever, if we can."

"And if we cannot?"

"Then we shall see what to do when the time comes."

"And having managed the bullies, how do you propose to manage Mrs Rowland? What do you think of speaking to Mr Grey?"

"I shall not do that. The Greys have no concern with it; but they will think they have. Then there will be a partisan warfare, with me for the pretext, and the two families have had quite warfare enough for a lifetime already. No, I shall not bring the Greys into it. I am sorry enough for Mr Rowland, for I am sure he has no part in all this. I shall go to him to-day. I should confront the lady at once, and call her to account, but that Miss Young must be considered. The more courageous and disinterested she is, the more care we must take of her."

"Perhaps she is at this moment telling Mr Rowland what we talked about last night. How very painful! Do you know she thinks—(it is right to tell the whole for other people's sake)—she thinks that what Mrs Rowland says is not to be trusted, in any case where she feels enmity. Maria even doubts whether Mr Enderby has treated you and his other friends so very negligently—whether he is engaged to Miss Bruce, after all."

Mr Hope was so much engaged about one of his stirrups while Margaret said this, that he could not observe where and how she was looking.

"Very likely," replied Hope, at length. "Hester has thought all along that this was possible. We shall know the truth from Enderby himself, one of these days, by act or word. Meantime, I, for one, shall wait to hear his own story."

There was another pause, at the end of which Mr Hope clapped spurs to his horse, and said he must be riding on. Margaret called him back for a moment, to ask what he wished her to do about informing Hester of the state of affairs. Mr Hope was disposed to tell her the whole, if possible; but not till he should have come to some issue with Mr Rowland. He hated mysteries—any concealments in families; and it was due both to Hester and to himself that there should be no concealment of important affairs from her. The only cautions to be observed were, to save her from suspense, to avoid the appearance of a formal telling of bad news, and to choose an opportunity when she might have time, before seeing any of the Rowlands, to consider the principles which should regulate her conduct to them, that she might do herself honour by the consistency and temper of which she was capable under any circumstances, when she was only allowed time.

This was settled, and he rode off with almost his usual gaiety of air.

He saw Mr Rowland before night. The next day but one, a travelling-carriage from Blickley was seen standing at Mr Rowland's door; and before the clock struck nine, it was loaded with trunks and band-boxes, and crowded with people. As it drove down the village street, merry little faces appeared at each carriage window. Mr Rowland was on the box. He was going to take his family to Cheltenham for the spring months. Miss Rowland was rather delicate, and Deerbrook was cold in March. Mrs Enderby was left behind; but there was Phoebe to take care of her; and Mr Rowland was to return as soon as he had settled his family. It seemed rather a pity, to be sure, that the old lady had been moved out of her own house just before she was to be left alone in her new residence; but, between Mr Rowland and her maid, she would be taken good care of; and the family would return when the warm weather set in.

Chapter Twenty Six

Disclosures.

The whole village seemed relieved by the departure of the Rowlands. Mrs Grey, who had always been refused admission to her old friend on one pretence or another, was joyfully welcomed by Phoebe, and was plunged into all the delights of neighbourly chat before the clock struck twelve, on the very first morning, Fanny and Mary Grey voluntarily offered to go to Miss Young, now that they were her only pupils, to save her the trouble of the walk to the schoolroom. This was a great relief to Maria, and her little parlour held the three very nicely; and when the girls had sufficiently admired the screen over again,—their father's profile, the planets, and the Dargle, they settled quite as well as at home. There was still a corner left for cousin Margaret, when she chose to come with her German books, or her work, and her useful remarks on what they were doing. No immediate consequences had happened to Maria from her plain-dealing with Mr Rowland; and she was quite ready to enjoy the three months of freedom, without looking too anxiously towards the end of them. The very gardener at the Rowlands' seemed to bestir himself with unusual alacrity to put the garden into spring trim; and the cook and housemaid might be seen over the hedge, walking arm-in-arm on the gravel-walks, smelling at the mezereon, and admiring Miss Anna's border of yellow crocuses, as the gardener said, as much as if they had been fine plants out of a conservatory. The birds themselves seemed to begin their twittering in the trees, and the cows their lowing in the meadow, from the hour that Mrs Rowland went away. In other words, there were many whom that event left free and at ease to observe the harmonies of nature, who were usually compelled to observe only the lady, and the discords of her household.

It was only the second day after the departure of the family that Margaret took her seat in the offered corner of Maria's parlour. She laid down her book, and took up her work, when the question arose, which has probably interested all intelligent school-girls for many a year—What made so many Athenians,—so many, that there must have been some wise and good men among them,—treat such a person as Socrates in the way they did? Margaret was quite occupied in admiring the sort of Socratic method with which Maria drew out from the minds of her pupils some of the difficult philosophy of Opinion, and the liberality with which she allowed for the distress of heathen moralists at having the sanction of Custom broken up. Margaret was thus quite occupied with the delight of seeing a great subject skilfully let down into young minds, and the others were no less busy with the subject itself, when Mary started, and said it made her jump to see Sydney bring Fairy close up to the window. Fanny imperiously bade her mind what she was about, and let Sydney alone: but yet, in a minute or two, Fanny's own eyes were detected wandering into the yard where Sydney still remained. "He is getting Fairy shod," she said in a soliloquising tone. Every one laughed,—the idea of shoeing a fairy was so ridiculous!—and some witticisms, about Bottom the Weaver, and his ass's head, were sported. It was evident that Socrates had no more chance this day, and Maria changed the subject.

"Sydney looks very much as if he wanted to come in," observed Mary.

Sydney did particularly wish to come in; but he saw that cousin Margaret was there: and he had felt an unconquerable awe of cousin Margaret ever since the day of his conveying her over the ice. So he stood irresolutely watching, as nail after nail was driven into Fairy's hoof, casting glances every minute at the window.

"Shall I see what he wants?" asked Margaret, perceiving that lessons would not go on till Sydney had got out what he wished to say. "May I open the window for a moment, Maria, to speak to him?"

"What do you think?" cried Sydney, taking instant advantage of the movement, and carrying off his awkwardness by whipping the window-sill while he spoke. "What *do* you think? Mr Enderby is come by the coach this morning. I saw him myself; and you might have met our Ben carrying his portmanteau home from where he was put down, half an hour ago. We'll have rare sport, if he stays as long as he did last summer. I do believe," he continued, leaning into the room, and speaking with a touch of his mother's mystery, "he would have come long since if Mrs Rowland had not been here. I wish she had taken herself off two months ago, and then I might have had a run with the harriers with him, as he promised I should."

"Now you have said just a little too much, Sydney; so you may go," said Maria. "Shut down the window, will you?"

It was well for Margaret that there was the recess of the window to lean in. There she stood, not speaking a word. It was not in nature for Maria to refrain from casting a glance at her,—which glance grew into a look of intelligence.

"You do not quite wink as mamma does," observed Fanny, "but I know very well what you mean, Miss Young."

"So people always fancy when they observe upon nothing, or upon what they know nothing about, Fanny. But I thought you were convinced, some time ago, that you should not watch people's countenances, to find out what they are thinking, any more than—"

"I should read a letter they are writing," interrupted Fanny. "Well, I beg your pardon, Miss Young; but I really thought I saw you looking at cousin Margaret's face. However, I dare say everybody supposes the same,—that Mr Enderby would not have been here now if Mrs Rowland had not gone away. You need not mind Mary and me, Miss Young; you know we hear all about Mrs Rowland at home."

"I know you are apt to fancy that you understand all about Mrs Rowland, my dear; but perhaps Mrs Rowland herself might happen to differ from you, if she could look into your mind. It is for you to settle with yourself, whether you think she would be satisfied that you have done by her as you would have her do by you. This is your own affair, Fanny; so now, without any one trying to see in your face what you think of yourself, we will go to our business."

The scratching of pens in the exercise-books, and the turning over of the dictionary, now proceeded for some time in profound silence, in the midst of which Margaret stole back to her corner.

"There goes twelve!" softly exclaimed Mary. "Mamma said we might go with her to call at cousin Hester's, if we were home and ready by half-past twelve. We shall not have nearly done, Miss Young."

Miss Young did not take the hint. She only said—

"Is your mamma going to call on Mrs Hope? Then, Margaret, do not let us detain you here. You will wish to be at home, I am sure."

Never, as Maria supposed, had Margaret more impatiently desired to be at home. Though accustomed to go in and out of Maria's abode, with or without reason assigned, she had not now ventured to move, though the little room felt like a prison. An awkward consciousness had fixed her to her seat. Now, however, she made haste to depart, promising to visit her friend again very soon. The little girls wanted her to arrange to come every morning, and stay all the time of lessons: but Margaret declined making any such engagement.

As she went home, she scarcely raised her eyes, for fear of seeing *him*; and yet she lingered for an instant at her brother's door, from a feeling of disappointment at having met no one she knew.

She had fully and undoubtingly intended to tell Hester of Philip's arrival; but when she had taken off her bonnet, and settled herself beside her sister in the drawing-room, she found that it was quite impossible to open the subject. While she was meditating upon this, the entrance of the

Greys seemed to settle the matter. She supposed they would make the disclosure for her: but she soon perceived that they had not heard the news. Mrs Grey went on quoting Mrs Enderby and Phoebe, and Sophia remarked on the forsaken condition of the old lady, in a way which was quite incompatible with any knowledge of the new aspect which affairs had assumed this morning. It was a great relief to Margaret to be spared the discussion of a fact on which so much was to be said; but lo! in the midst of a flow of talk about fomentations, and the best kind of night-light for a sick room, there was a knock at the door, every stroke of which was recognised to a certainty by Margaret. While the other ladies were pushing back their chairs, to break up the appearance of a gossip, and make room for another party of visitors, Margaret was wholly occupied with contriving to sit upright, notwithstanding the dimness that came over her sight.

It was he. He entered the room quickly, looked taller than ever, as Sophia thought to herself, and more than ever like a Polish Count, now that his blue great-coat was buttoned up to the chin. He stopped for half a moment on seeing ladies in cloaks and bonnets, and then came forward, and shook hands with everybody. Hester observed that he looked full at Margaret as he held out his hand to her; but Margaret did not see this, for, though she commanded herself wonderfully, she could not meet his eye. Of course, he was asked when he arrived, and had to answer the question, and also the remarks which were made on the length of his absence, and on the expectations of everybody in Deerbrook that he would have visited the old place at Christmas or New Year. He was then pitied on account of the state of his mother's health. To this he made no reply whatever; but when Mrs Grey inquired how he found Mrs Enderby, he briefly—somewhat abruptly—answered that he thought her very ill. It was equally impossible for Margaret to sit totally silent while all this was going on, and to address herself to him: she therefore kept some conversation with Sophia on the greenhouse, and the fate of the evergreens in the shrubbery, in consequence of the severity of the frost in January—which laurestinus had been lost, and how the arbutus had suffered, and how long it would be before the laurels on the grass could grow up to their former size and beauty. While Sophia was telling that the greenhouse occupied a great deal of time, and that she had therefore turned over her interest in it to Sydney, and begged the little girls to divide her garden between them, Mr Enderby was seen to take Hester into the window, and after remarking upon the snowdrops beneath, to speak privately to her. Margaret was afraid Mrs Grey would take the hint, and go away. Her presence now appeared a sort of protection, which Margaret exerted herself to retain, by not allowing the conversation to flag. She need not have feared; Mrs Grey was turning over in her mind how she might best introduce her congratulations on Mr Enderby's engagement, and her inquiries after Miss Bruce's welfare—topics on which she conceived that good manners required her to enter. Meantime, Mr Enderby had been saying to Hester:

"You will excuse the offer of my good wishes on your settlement here being briefly and hastily made; but I am at this moment in great anxiety. Is Hope at home?"

"No: he is some miles off in the country."

"Then I must charge you with a message to him. I think my mother very ill; and I find it is some time since Hope has seen her. Will you beg him to come to her without loss of time, when he returns?"

"Certainly; he will be home within two or three hours, I have no doubt."

"And then ask him whether he will not prescribe a visit from you to my mother. It will do her good, I am confident. You know she is all alone now with her maid."

"I am aware of that. It is not from negligence or disinclination, I assure you, that we have seen so little of Mrs Enderby for some time past."

"I know it, I know it," said he, shaking his head. Then, after a pause—"Shall you be at home this evening?"

"Yes."

"And alone?"

"Yes. Will you come?"

"Thank you; I will come in for an hour. I shall then hear Hope's report of my mother; and—between ourselves—I want a few words with your sister. Can you manage this for me?"

"No doubt."

He was gone in another moment, with a bow to the whole party.

"Gone!" cried Mrs Grey; "and I have not said a word to him about his engagement and Miss Bruce! How very odd he must think us, Sophia!"

"There will be plenty of time for all we have to say," observed Hester. "He is so uneasy about his mother, I see, that he will not leave her yet awhile."

Margaret was sure she perceived in her sister's beautiful eye and lip the subtle expression of amusement that they bore when a gay thought was in her mind, or when her neighbours were setting off in speculation on a wrong scent.

"But half the grace of one's good wishes is in their being offered readily," said Mrs Grey, "as I was saying to Sophia, the other day, when we were considering whether Mr Grey should not write to Mr Enderby with our congratulations. *We* should not like to appear backward on such an occasion, for many reasons. Well now, my dears; one thing more. You must come to tea with us this evening. It will be a mild evening, I have no doubt; and I have sent to Miss Young, to say that my sedan will bring her at six o'clock. We have quite set our hearts upon having you for a sociable evening."

"Thank you," said Hester: "we would come with great pleasure, but that we are engaged."

"Engaged, my dear! Margaret has just told us that you have no engagement."

"So Margaret thought: but we are engaged. A friend of Mr Hope's is coming to spend the evening, and I promised that we would be at home."

"Dear!" said Sophia; "and we had quite set our hearts upon your coming."

"Cannot you bring the gentleman with you, my dear? I am sure Mr Grey will be happy to see any friend of Mr Hope's."

"Thank you; but he is coming on business."

"Oh, well! But Margaret can be spared, surely. I suppose you must stay and make tea, my dear. It would not do, I know, for you to appear to neglect your husband's country patients—particularly in the present state of affairs. But Margaret can come, surely. Sydney shall step for her, a little before six."

"Oh, yes," said Sophia; "Margaret can come. The gentleman can have no business with her, I suppose."

Margaret was again puzzled with the fun that lurked in the eye and lip. She had been passive till now; but seeing Hester's determination that she should not go, she said very decidedly that she should much prefer coming some evening when her brother and sister need not be left behind.

"Mrs Grey is not very well pleased," observed Margaret, when their visitors were gone. "Could not you have been a little more explicit as to this gentleman, whoever he may be?"

"I thought it better not to say more," said Hester, now unable to help stealing a glance at her sister. "Our visitor is to be Mr Enderby. He is so uneasy about his mother, that my husband is to see her this afternoon; and Mr Enderby offers to come in the evening, to discuss her case." After a slight pause, Hester continued— "Sophia was very positive about its being impossible that our visitor could have any business with you—was not she?"

"Oh, Hester!" said Margaret, imploringly, with her eyes full of tears.

"Well, well," said Hester, remembering how cruel this speech might appear to her sister, "I ought not to speak to you from my own habitual disbelief of Mrs Rowland's news. I will go away, dear; only just saying, first, that I like Philip's looks very well. He does not seem happier than he ought to be, while his mother is so ill: nor does he act as if he felt he had neglected us, his old friends. As my husband says, we must hear his own story before we judge him."

When she left the room, Margaret could not have settled with herself whether there was most pain or pleasure in the prospect of this evening. Five minutes before, she had believed that she should spend it at the Greys'—should hear the monotonous hiss of the urn, which seemed to take up its song, every time she went, where it had left off last—should see Mrs Grey's winks from behind it—should have the same sort of cake, cut by Sophia into pieces of exactly the same size—should hear Sydney told to be quiet, and the little girls to go to bed—should have to play Mrs Grey's favourite waltz, and sing Mr Grey's favourite song—and at last, to refuse a glass of sherry three times over, and come away, after hearing much wonder expressed that the evening was gone already. Now, instead of this, there was to be the fear and constraint of Philip's presence, so unlike what that had ever been before!—no longer gay, easy, and delightful, but all that was awkward. No one would be sure of what the others were feeling; or whether there was any sufficient reason for their mutual feelings being so changed. Who would find the conversation? What could be talked about which would not bring one or another into collision with Mrs Rowland or Miss Bruce? But yet, there would be his presence, and with it, bliss. There would be his very voice; and something of his thoughts could not but come out. She was better pleased than if his evening was to be spent anywhere else.

Dinner passed, she did not know how, except that her brother thought Mrs Enderby not materially worse than when he saw her last. The tea-tray came and stood an hour—Mr Hope being evidently restless and on the watch. He said at last that it would be better to get tea over before Enderby came; and Margaret repeated in her own mind that it *was* less awkward; and yet she was disappointed. The moment the table was cleared, *his* knock was heard. He would not have tea: he had been making his mother's tea, and had had a cup with her. And now, what was Hope's judgment on her state of health?

The gentlemen had scarcely entered upon the subject when a note was brought in for Margaret. Everything made her nervous; but the purport of this note was merely to ask for a book which she had promised to lend Mrs Levitt. As she went up to her room for it, she was vexed that the interruption had occurred now; and was heartily angry with herself that she could command herself no better, and be no more like other people than she fancied she had been this day. "There is Hester," thought she, "looking nothing less than merry, and talking about whatever occurs, as if nothing had happened since we met him last; while I sit, feeling like a fool, with not a word to say, and no courage to say it if I had. I wonder whether I have always been as insignificant and dull as I have seen myself to be to-day. I do not believe I ever thought about the matter before: I wish I could forget it now." Notwithstanding her feeling of insignificance in the drawing-room, however, she was so impatient to be there again that her hands trembled with eagerness in doing up the parcel for Mrs Levitt.

When she re-entered the drawing-room, Philip was there alone—standing by the fire. Margaret's first impulse was to retreat; but her better judgment prevailed in time to intercept the act. Philip said:

"Mr and Mrs Hope have, at my desire, given me the opportunity of speaking to you alone. You must not refuse to hear what I have to say, because it is necessary to the vindication of my honour;—and it is also due to another person."

Of course, Margaret sat down. She seemed to intend to speak, and Philip waited to hear her; but no words came, so he went on.

"You have been told, I find, that I have been for some time engaged to a lady who is now at Rome—Miss Bruce. How such a notion originated, we need not inquire. The truth is, that I am but slightly acquainted with Miss Bruce, and that nothing has ever occurred which could warrant such a use of that lady's name. I heard nothing of this till to-day, and—"

"Is it possible?" breathed Margaret.

"I was shocked to hear of it from my poor mother; but infinitely more shocked—grieved to the very soul, to find that you, Margaret, believed it."

"How could we help it? It was your sister who told us."

"What does my sister know of me compared with you? I thought—I hoped—but I see now that I was presumptuous—I thought that you knew me enough, and cared for me enough, to understand my mind, and trust my conduct through whatever you might hear of me from others. I have been deceived—I mean I have deceived myself, as to the relation in which we stand. I do not blame you, Margaret—that is, I will not if I can help it—for what you have given credit to about me; but I did not think you would have mortified me so deeply."

"You are partly wrong now; you are unjust at this moment," replied Margaret, looking up with some spirit. "I do not wish to speak of Mrs Rowland—but remember, your mother never doubted what your sister said; the information was given in such a way as left almost an impossibility of disbelief. There was nothing to set against the most positive assurances—nothing from you—not a word to any of your old friends—"

"And there was I, working away on a new and good plan of life, living for you, and counting the weeks and days between me and the time when I might come and show you what your power over me had enabled me to do—and you were all the while despising or forgetting me, allowing me no means of defending myself, yielding me up to dishonour with a mere shake of the head, as if I had been an acquaintance of two or three ball-nights. It is clear that you knew my mind no better than I now find I knew yours."

"What would you have had me do?" asked Margaret, with such voice as she had.

"I believe I had not thought of that," said Philip, half laughing. "I only felt that you ought to have trusted me—that you must have known that I loved neither Miss Bruce, nor any one but you; and that I could not be engaged to any one while I loved you.—Tell me at once, Margaret—did I not deserve this much from you?"

"You did," said Margaret, distinctly. "But there is another way of viewing the whole, which does not seem to have occurred to you. I have been to blame, perhaps; but if you had thought of the other possibility—"

"What other? Oh! do speak plainly."

"I must, at such a time as this. If I could not think you guilty, I might fancy myself to have been mistaken."

"And did you fancy so? Did you suppose I neither loved you, nor meant you to think that I did?"

"I did conclude myself mistaken."

"Oh, Margaret! I should say—if I dared—that such a thought—such humility, such generosity—could come of nothing but love."

Margaret made no reply. They understood one another too completely for words. Even in the first gush of joy, there was intense bitterness in the thought of what Margaret must have suffered; and Philip vowed, in the bottom of his soul, that his whole life should be devoted to make her forget it. He could have cursed his sister with equal energy.

There was no end to what had to be said. Philip was impatient to tell what he had been doing, and the reasons of the whole of his conduct. Margaret's views had become his own, as to the desultoriness of the life he had hitherto led. He had applied himself diligently to the study of the law, intending to prove to himself and to her, that he was capable of toil, and of a steady aim at an object in life, before he asked her to decide what their relation to each other was henceforth to be.

"Surely," said he, "you might have discovered this much from my letters to my mother."

"And how were we to know what was in your letters to your mother?"

"Do you mean that you have not read or heard them all this time?"

"Not a word for these three months. We have scarcely seen her for many weeks past; and then she merely showed us what long letters you wrote her."

"And they were all written for you! She told me, the last time I was here, that she could keep nothing from you: and, relying upon her words, I have supposed this to be a medium of communication between us throughout. I could have no other, you know. When did my mother leave off reading my letters to you?"

"From the week you went away last. Mrs Rowland came in while we were in the midst of one; and the consequence was—"

"That you have been in the dark about me ever since. You saw that I did write?"

"Yes. I have seen most of the post-marks—and the interiors—upside down. But Mrs Rowland was always there—or else Phoebe."

"And have you really known nothing about me whatever?"

"Little George told me that you had lessons to learn, very hard and very long, and, if possible, more difficult than his."

"And did not you see then that I was acting upon your views?"

"I supposed Miss Bruce might have had them first."

"Miss Bruce!" he cried, in a tone of annoyance. "I know nothing of Miss Bruce's views on any subject. I cannot conceive how my sister got such a notion into her head—why she selected her."

Margaret was going to mention the "sisterly affection" which had long subsisted between Miss Bruce and Mrs Rowland, according to the latter; but it occurred to her that it was just possible that Philip might not be altogether so indifferent to Miss Bruce as Miss Bruce was to him; and this thought sealed her lips.

"I wonder whether Rowland believed it all the time," said Philip: "and Hope? It was unworthy of Hope's judgment—of his faith—to view the case so wrongly."

"I am glad you are beginning to be angry with somebody else," said Margaret. "Your wrath seemed all to be for me: but your old friends, even to your mother, appear to have had no doubt about the matter."

"There is an excuse for them which I thought you had not. I am an altered man, Margaret—you cannot conceive how altered since I began to know you. They judged of me by what I was once... We will not say how lately."

"I assure you I do not forget the accounts you used to give of yourself."

"What accounts?"

"Of how you found life pleasant enough without philosophy and without anything to do... and other wise sayings of the kind."

"It is by such things that those who knew me long ago have judged me lately—a retribution which I ought not to complain of. If they believed me fickle, idle, selfish, it is all fair. Oh! Margaret, men know nothing of morals till they know women."

"Are you serious?"

"I am solemnly persuaded of it. Happy they who grow up beside mothers and sisters whom they can revere! But for this, almost all men would be without earnestness of heart—without a moral purpose—without generosity, while they are all the while talking of honour. It was so with me before I knew you. I am feeble enough, and selfish enough yet, God knows! but I hope still to prove that you have made a man of me, out of a light, selfish... But what right have I, you may think, to ask you to rely upon me, when I have so lately been what I tell you. I did not mean to ask you yet. This very morning, nothing could be further from my intentions. I do not know how long I should have waited before I should have dared. My sister has rendered me an inestimable service amidst all the mischief she did me. I thank her. Ah! Margaret, you smile!"

Margaret smiled again. The smile owned that she was thinking the same thing about their obligations to Mrs Rowland.

"Whatever you might have said to me this evening," continued Philip, "if your regard for me had proved to have been quite overthrown—if you had continued to despise me, as you must have done at times—I should still have blessed you, all my life—I should have worshipped you, as the being who opened a new world to me. You lifted me out of a life of trifling—of trifling which I thought very elegant at the time—trifling with my own time and faculties—trifling with other people's serious business—trifling with something more serious still, I fear—with their feelings. As far as I remember, I thought all this manly and refined enough: and but for you, I should have thought so still. You early opened my eyes to all the meanness and gross selfishness of such a life: and if you were never to let me see you again, I believe I could not fall back into the delusion. But if you will be the guide of my life—"

Margaret sighed deeply. Even at this moment of vital happiness, her thoughts rested on her sister. She remembered what Hester's anticipations had been, in prospect of having Edward for the guide of her life.

"I frighten you, I see," said Philip, "with my confessions; but, be the consequences what they may, I must speak, Margaret. If you despise me, I must do you the justice, and give myself the consolation, of acknowledging what I have been, and what I owe to you."

"It is not that," said Margaret. "Let the past go. Let it be forgotten in reaching forward to better things. But do not let us be confident about the future. I have seen too much of that. We must not provide for disappointment. Let us leave it till it comes. Surely," she added, with a gentle smile, "we have enough for the present. I cannot look forward yet."

"How you must have suffered!" cried Philip, in a tone of grief. "You have lost some of your confidence, love. You did not cling to the present, and shrink from the future when... Oh, it is bitter, even now, to think, that while I was working on, in hope and resolution, you were suffering here, making it a duty to extinguish your regard for me, I all the time toiling to deserve it—and there was no one to set us right, and the whole world in league to divide us."

"That is all over now."

"But not the consequences, Margaret. They have shaken you: they have made you know doubt and fear."

"We are both changed, Philip. We are older, and I trust it will appear that we are wiser than we were. Yes, older. There are times in one's life when days do the work of years and our days have been of that kind. You have discovered a new life, and my wishes and expectations are much altered. They may not be fewer, or less bright, but they are very different."

"If they were pure from fears—"

"They are pure from fears. At this moment I can fear nothing. We have been brought together by the unquestionable Providence which rules our lives; and this is enough. The present is all right; and the future, which is to come out of it, will be all right in its way. I have no fear—but I do not want to anticipate. This hour with its satisfactions, is all that I can bear."

Notwithstanding this, and Philip's transport in learning it, they did go back, again and again, into the past; and many a glance did they cast into the future. There was no end to their revelations of the circumstances of the last two months, and of the interior history which belonged to them. At last, the burning out of one of the candles startled them into a recollection of how long their conversation had lasted, and of the suspense in which Edward and Hester had been kept. Enderby offered to go and tell them the fact which they must be anticipating: and, after having agreed that no one else should know at present—that Miss Bruce's name should be allowed to die out of Deerbrook speculations, for Mrs Rowland's sake, before any other was put in its place, Philip left his Margaret, and went into the breakfast-room, where his presence was not wholly unexpected.

In five minutes, Margaret heard the hall door shut, and, in another moment, her brother and sister came to her. Hester's face was all smiles and tears: her mind all tumult with the vivid recollection of her own first hours of happy hopeful love, mingled with the griefs which always lay heavy within her, and with that warm attachment to her sister which circumstances occasionally exalted into a passion.

"We ought to rejoice with nothing but joy, Margaret," said she: "but I cannot see how we are to spare you. I do not believe I can live without you."

Her husband started at this echo of the thoughts for which he was at the moment painfully rebuking himself. He had nothing to say; but gave his greeting in a brotherly kiss, like that which he had offered on his marriage with her sister, and on his entrance upon his home.

"How quiet, how very quiet she is!" exclaimed Hester, an Margaret left the room, after a few words on the events of the evening, and a calm good-night. "I hope it is all right. I hope she is quite satisfied."

"Satisfied is the word," said her husband. "People are quiet when they are relieved—calm when they are satisfied—people like Margaret. It is only great minds, I believe, which feel real satisfaction."

Hester gave him pain by a deep sigh. She was thinking how seldom, and for how short a time, she had ever felt real satisfaction.

"And how often, and for how long," she asked, "do great minds find themselves in that heaven?"

"By the blessing of God, not seldom, I trust," replied he; "though not so often as, by obeying their nature, they might. Intellectual satisfaction is perhaps not for this world, except in a few of the inspired hours of the Newtons and the Bacons, who are sent to teach what the human intellect is. But as often as a great mind meets with full moral sympathy—as often as it is loved in return for love—as often as it confides itself unreservedly to the good Power which bestowed its existence, and appointed all its attributes, I imagine it must repose in satisfaction."

"Then satisfaction ought to be no new feeling to Margaret," said Hester. "She always loves every one: she meets with sympathy wherever she turns; and I believe she has faith enough for a martyr, without knowing it. Ought not she—must not she, have often felt real satisfaction?"

"Yes."

"I wonder you dole out your words so sparingly about such a being as Margaret," said Hester, resentfully. "I can tell you, Edward, though you take so coolly the privilege of having such a one so nearly connected with you, you might search the world in vain for her equal. You little know the wealth of her heart and soul, Edward. I ask you whether she does not deserve to feel full satisfaction of conscience and affections, and you just answer 'Yes,' with as much languor as if I had asked you whether the clock has struck eleven yet! I can tell you this—I have said in my own heart, and just to Morris, for years, that the happiest man of his generation will be he who has Margaret for a wife: and here you, who ought to know this, give me a grudging 'Yes,' in answer to the first question, arising out of my reverence for Margaret, that I ever asked you!"

"You mistake me," replied Hope, in a tone of gentleness which touched her very soul. "One's words may be restrained by reverence as well as by want of heart. I regard Margaret with a reverence which I should not have thought it necessary to put into words for your conviction."

"Oh, I am wrong—as I always am!" cried Hester. "You must forgive me again, as you do far, far too often. But tell me, Edward, ought not Margaret's husband to be the happiest man living?"

"Yes," said Edward, with a smile. "Will that do this time?"

"Oh, yes, yes," replied she—the thought passing through her mind, that, whether or not her husband excepted himself as a matter of course, she should not have asked a question to which she could not bear all possible answers. Even if he meant that Margaret's husband might be a happier man than himself, it was only too true. As quick as lightning these thoughts passed through her mind, and, apparently without a pause, she went on, "And now, as to Enderby—is he worthy to be this happy husband? Does he deserve her?"

Mr Hope did pause before he replied:

"I think we had better dwell as little as we can on that point of the story—not because I am afraid—(do not take fright and suppose I mean more than I say)—not because I am afraid, but because we can do nothing, discern nothing, about it. Time must show what Enderby is—or rather, what he has the power of becoming. Meanwhile, the thing is settled. They love and have promised, and are happy. Let us shun all comparison of the one with the other of them, and hope everything from him."

"There will be some amusement," said Hester, after a smiling reverie, "in having this secret to ourselves for a time, while all the rest of Deerbrook is so busy with a different idea and expectation. How *will* Mrs Rowland bear it?"

"Mrs Grey might have said that," said Hope, laughing.

"Well, but is it not true? Will it not be very amusing to see the circulation of stories about Miss Bruce, given 'from the best authority,' and to have all manner of news told us about Philip; and to watch how Mrs Rowland will get out of the scrape she is in? Surely, Edward, you are not above being amused with all this?"

"I shall be best pleased when it is all over. I have lived some years longer than you in Deerbrook, and have had more time to get tired of its mysteries and mistakes."

"For your comfort, then, it cannot be long before all is open and rightly understood. We need only leave Mrs Rowland time to extricate herself, I suppose. I wonder how she will manage it."

"We shall be taken by surprise with some clever device, I dare say. It is a pity so much ingenuity should be wasted on mischief."

Chapter Twenty Seven

A Morning in March.

Margaret was as calm as she appeared to be. To a nature like hers, blissful repose was congenial, and anxiety both appeared and felt unnatural. In her there was no weak wonder that Providence had blessed her as she felt she was blessed. While she suffered, she concluded with certainty that the suffering was for some good purpose; but no degree of happiness took her by surprise, or seemed other than a natural influence shed by the great Parent into the souls of his children. She had of late been fearfully shaken,—not in her faith, but in her serenity. In a moment this experience appeared like a sick dream, and her present certainty of being beloved spread its calm over her lately-troubled spirit, somewhat as her nightly devotions had done from her childhood upwards. Even now, it was little that she thought of herself: her recovered Philip filled her mind—he who had been a stranger—who had been living in a world of which she could conceive nothing—who had suddenly vanished from her companionship, as if an earthquake had swallowed him up—and who was now all her own again, by her side, and to be lived for. Amidst this security, this natural and delightful state of things, that restless uneasiness—now jealousy, and now self-abasement—which she had called her own vanity and selfishness, disappeared, and she felt like one who has escaped from the horrors of a feverish bed into the cool fragrant airs and mild sunshine of the early morning. Anxieties soon arose—gentle doubts expressing themselves in soft sighs, which were so endeared by the love from which they sprang that she would not have banished them if she could—anxieties lest she should be insufficient for Philip's happiness, lest he should overrate the peace of home, which she now knew was not to be looked for in full measure there, any more than in other scenes of human probation. Gentle questionings like these there were; but they tended rather to preserve than to disturb her calmness of spirit. Misery had broken her sleep by night, and constrained her conduct by day. Happy love restored her at once to her natural mood, lulling her to the deepest rest when she rested, and rendering her free and self-possessed in all the employments and intercourses of life.

There was one person who must not be kept waiting for this intelligence till Mrs Rowland's return—as Margaret told Philip—and that was Maria. Philip's heart was now overflowing with kindness towards all whom Margaret loved; and he spoke with strong interest of Maria, of her virtues, her misfortunes, and the grace and promise which once bloomed in her."

"You knew her before her misfortunes then?"

"To be sure I did:— that was the time when I did know her; for, as you may perceive, there is not much opportunity now. And, besides, she is so totally changed, that I do not feel sure that I understand her feelings—I am too much in awe of them to approach her very nearly. Oh yes, I knew Maria Young once, much better than I know her now."

"She never told me so. How very strange!"

"Does she ever speak of any other circumstance of her prosperous days?"

"That is true, only incidentally."

"Time was," said Philip, "when some boyish dreams connected themselves with Maria Young—only transiently, and quite at the bottom of my own fancy. I never spoke of them to any one before, nor fully acknowledged them to myself. She was the first sensible woman I ever knew—the first who conveyed to me any conception of what the moral nature of a woman may be, under favourable circumstances. For this I am under great obligations to her; and this is all the feeling that I brought out of our intercourse. It might possibly have come to more, but that I disliked her father excessively, and left off going there on that account. What a selfish wretch I was in those days! I can hardly believe it now; but I distinctly remember rejoicing, on hearing of her accident, that my esteem for her had not passed into a warmer feeling, as I should then have suffered so much on her account."

"Is it possible?" cried Margaret, who, in the midst of the unpleasant feeling excited by this fact, did not fail to remark to herself that there could have been no love in such a case.

"I ought, for my own sake, however, Margaret, to say that Maria Young had not the slightest knowledge of her influence over me—superficial and transient as it was. I never conveyed it to her by word or act; and I am thankful I did not—for this reason among many—that I am now perfectly free to show her all the kindness she deserves, both from her own merits, and from her being a beloved friend of yours."

Margaret had no doubt of Philip's full conviction of what he was saying; but she was far from certain that he was not mistaken—that looks and tones might not have communicated what words and acts had been forbidden to convey. She thought of Maria's silence about her former acquaintance with Philip, of her surprising knowledge of his thoughts and ways, betraying itself to a vigilant observer through the most trivial conversation, and of her confession that there had been an attachment to some one: and, thinking of these things, her heart melted within her for her friend. She silently resolved upon the only method she could think of, to spare her feelings. She would write the news of this engagement, instead of going to tell it, as she had intended. She was confident that it would be no surprise to Maria; but Maria should have time and solitude in which to reconcile herself to it.

What was to be done about Mrs Enderby? She had been told at once, on Philip's arrival, that it was all a mistake about Miss Bruce; and she had appeared relieved when freed from the image of an unknown daughter-in-law. Philip and Margaret agreed that they must deny themselves the pleasure of revealing the rest of the truth to her, till it had been inflicted upon Mrs Rowland. Mrs Enderby would never be able to keep it from the Greys; and she would be disturbed and alarmed in the expectation of the scenes which might ensue, when Mrs Rowland should discover that her brother meant to choose his wife for himself, instead of taking one of her selection. Margaret must go and see his mother as often as possible, but her new interest in her old friend must be concealed for the present. How Margaret—motherless for so many long years—felt her heart yearn towards the old lady, who seemed to be everybody's charge, but whom she felt now to be a sacred object of her care!

The lovers immediately experienced some of the evils attendant on concealment, in the difficulty of meeting as freely as they wished. There was the breakfast-room at Mr Hope's for them; and, by a little management on the part of brother and sister, a branching off in country walks, out of sight of the good people of Deerbrook. In company, too, they were always together, and without awkwardness. True lovers do not want to talk together in company; they had rather not. It is enough to be in mutual presence; and they have nothing to say at such times, and prefer joining in what everybody else is saying. When Philip had once put a stop to all congratulations about Miss Bruce, by earnestly and most respectfully, though gaily, releasing that lady's name from all connection with his own, no further awkwardness remained. He treated the affair as one of the false reports which are circulating every day, and left it for his sister to explain how she had been misled by it. It was amusing to the corner-house family to see that Mrs Grey and Sophia insisted on believing that either Mr Enderby was a rejected lover of Miss Bruce's, or that it had been an engagement which was now broken off, or that it would soon be an engagement. The gay state of Enderby's spirits accorded best with the latter supposition; but this gaiety might be assumed, to cover his mortification. Margaret was daily made a listener to one or other of these suppositions.

One bright, mild, March day, Hester and Margaret were accompanying Philip to Mr Rowland's to call on Mrs Enderby, when they met Mr Rowland in the street,—returned the evening before from Cheltenham.

"Ladies, your most obedient!" said he, stopping up the path before them. "I was on my way to call on you; but if you will step in to see Mrs Enderby, we can have our chat there." And he at once offered his arm to Margaret, bestowing a meaning smile on Hester. As soon as they were fairly on their way, he entered at once on the compliments it had been his errand to pay, but spoke for himself alone.

"I did not write," said he, "because I expected to deliver my good wishes in person so soon; but they are not the less hearty for being a little delayed. I find, however, that I am still beforehand with my neighbours—that even Mrs Enderby does not know, nor my partner's family. All in good time: but I am sorry for this mistake about the lady. It is rather awkward. I do not know where Mrs Rowland got her information, or what induced her to rely so implicitly upon it. All I can say is, that I duly warned her to be sure of her news before she regularly announced it. But I believe such reports—oftener unfounded than true—have been the annoyance of young people ever since there has been marriage and giving in marriage. We have all suffered in our turn, I dare say, though the case is not always so broad an one as this.—Come, Mr Philip, what are you about? Standing there, and keeping the ladies standing! and I do believe you have not knocked. Our doors do not open of themselves, though it be to let in the most welcome guests in the world. Now, ladies, will you walk in? Philip will prepare Mrs Enderby to expect you up-stairs; and, meanwhile, let me show you what a splendid jonquil we have in blow here."

The day was so mild, and the sun shone into the house so pleasantly, that Mrs Enderby had been permitted to leave her chamber, and establish herself for the day in the drawing-room. There she was found in a flutter of pleasure at the change of scene. Matilda's canary sang in the sunshine; Philip had filled the window with flowering plants for his mother, and the whole room was fragrant with his hyacinths. The little Greys had sent Mrs Enderby a bunch of violets; Phoebe had made bold, while the gardener was at breakfast, to abstract a bough from the almond tree on the grass; and its pink blossoms now decked the mantelpiece. These things were almost too much for the old lady. Her black eyes looked rather too bright, and her pale thin face twitched when she spoke. She talked a great deal about the goodness of everybody to her, and said it was almost worth while being ever so ill to find one's self so kindly regarded. It rejoiced her to see her friends around her again in this way. It was quite a meeting of friends again. If only her dear Priscilla, and the sweet children, had been here!—it was a great drawback, certainly, their being away, but she hoped they would soon be back; if they had been here, there would have been nothing left to wish. Hester asked if Mr Hope had visited her this morning. She had rather expected to meet him here, and had brought something for him which he had wished very much to have—a letter from his brother in India. She was impatient till it was in his hands. Had he made his call, or might she expect him presently? Mrs Enderby seemed to find difficulty in comprehending the question; and then she could not recollect whether Mr Hope had paid his visit this morning or not. She grew nervous at her own confusion of mind—talked faster than ever; and, at last, when the canary sang out a sudden loud strain, she burst into tears.

"We are too much for her," said Hester; "let us go, we have been very wrong."

"Yes, go," said Philip, "and send Phoebe. You will find your way into the garden, and I will join you there presently. Rowland, you will go with them."

Margaret cast a beseeching look at Philip, and he gratefully permitted her to stay. Hester carried off the canary. Margaret drew down the blinds, and then kneeled by Mrs Enderby, soothing and speaking cheerfully to her, while tears, called up by a strange mixture of emotions, were raining down her cheeks. Philip stood by the mantelpiece, weeping without restraint; the first time that Margaret had ever seen tears from him.

"I am a silly old woman," said Mrs Enderby, half laughing in the midst of her sobs. "Here comes Phoebe—Phoebe, I have been very silly, and I hardly know what about, I declare. My dear!" she exclaimed as she felt tears drop upon the hand which Margaret was chafing—"my dear Miss Ibbotson—"

"Oh! call me Margaret!"

"But, my dear, I am afraid there is something the matter, after all. Something has happened."

"Oh, dear, no, ma'am!" said Phoebe. "Only we don't like to see you in this way."

"There is nothing the matter, I assure you," said Margaret. "We were too much for you; we tired you; and we are very sorry—that is all. But the room will be kept quite quiet now, and you will soon feel better."

"I am better, my dear, thank you. How are you sitting so low? Bless me! you are kneeling. Pray, my dear, rise. To think of your kneeling to take care of me!"

"Give me one kiss, and I will rise," said Margaret, bending over her. It was a hearty kiss which Mrs Enderby gave her, for the old lady put all her energy into it. Margaret rose satisfied; she felt as if she had been accepted for a daughter.

As soon as Mrs Enderby appeared disposed to shut her eyes and lie quiet, Philip and Margaret withdrew, leaving her to Phoebe's care. Arm-in-arm they sauntered about the walks, till they came upon Hester and Mr Rowland, who were sitting in the sun, under the shelter of an evergreen hedge.

"Have you heard nothing of my husband yet?" asked Hester. "I do wish he would come, and read this letter from Frank."

"Her anxiety is purely disinterested," said Margaret to Philip. "There can be nothing about her in that letter. His greetings to her will come in the next."

"Edward enjoys Frank's letters above everything," observed Hester.

"Suppose you go in next door, and we will send Hope to you when he comes," said Philip, intending thus to set Mr Rowland free, to dismiss Hester, and have Margaret to himself for a garden walk.

"The Greys are all out for the day," observed Mr Rowland; "my partner and all; and this must be my excuse to you, ladies, for wishing you a good morning. There is a lighter at the wharf down there, whose lading waits for me."

"Ay, go," said Philip: "we have detained you long enough. We will find our way by some means into the Greys' grounds, and amuse ourselves there. If you will bid one of your people call us when Hope comes, we shall hear."

By the help of an overturned wheelbarrow, and some activity, and at the expense of a very little detriment to the hedge, the ladies were presently landed on Mr Grey's territories. By common consent, the three directed their steps towards the end of the green walk, whence might be seen the prospect of which the sisters were never tired. A purple and golden crocus peeped up here and there from the turf of this walk; there was a wilderness of daffodils on either side, the blossoms just bursting from their green sheaths; the periwinkle, with its starry flowers and dark shining sprays, overran the borders; and the hedge which bounded the walk was red with swollen buds. As the gazers leaned on this close-clipped, compact hedge, they overlooked a wide extent of country. They stood on a sort of terrace, and below them was the field where the Greys' pet animals were wont to range. The old pony trotted towards the terrace, as if expecting notice.

Fanny's and Mary's lambs approached and looked up, as awaiting something good. Philip amused himself and them with odd noises, but had nothing better for them; and so they soon scampered off, the pony throwing out his hind legs as if in indignation at his bad entertainment. Beyond this field, a few white cottages, in the rear of the village, peeped out from the lanes, and seemed to sit down to rest in the meadows, so profound was the repose which they seemed to express. The river wound quietly through the green level, filling its channel, and looking pearly under the light spring sky; and behind it the woods uprose, their softened masses and outlines prophesying of leafy summer shades. Near at hand the air was alive with twitterings: afar off, nature seemed asleep, and nothing was seen to move but the broad sail of a wherry, and a diminished figure of a man beside his horse, bush-harrowing in a distant green field.

Hester judged rightly that the lovers would like to have this scene to themselves; and having surveyed it with that sigh of delight with which Spring causes the heart to swell, she softly stole away, and sauntered down the green walk. She proceeded till she reached a bench, whence she could gaze upon the grey old church tower, rising between the intervening trees, and at the same time overlook Mr Rowland's garden. She had not sat many minutes before her husband leaped the hedge, and bounded over the grass towards her.

"What news?" cried he. "There is good news in your face."

"There is good news in my bag, I trust." And she produced the large square epistle, marked "Ship letter" in those red characters which have a peculiar power of making the heart beat. She did not wonder that her husband changed colour as she held up the letter. She knew that the arrival of news from Frank was a great event in life to Edward. She gloried in being, for the first time, the medium through which this rare pleasure reached him; and she longed to share, for the first time, the confidence of a brother. Margaret had for some months reposed upon the possession of a brother: she was now to have the same privilege. She made room upon the bench for her husband, and proposed to lose no time in reading the letter together. But Hope did not sit down, though, from his agitation, she would have supposed him glad of a seat. He said he would read in the shrubbery, and walked slowly away, breaking the seal as he went. Hester was rather disconcerted; but she suppressed her disappointment, begged him to take advantage of the bench, and herself retired into the orchard while he read his epistle. There, as she stood apparently amusing herself by the pond, wiping away a tear or two which would have way, she little imagined what agony her husband was enduring from this letter, which she was supposing must make his heart overflow with pleasure. The letter was half full of reply to Edward's account of Margaret, in his epistle of last June—of raillery about her, of intreaty that Edward would give him such a sister-in-law, and of intimations that nothing could be more apparent than that the whole rich treasure of his heart's love was Margaret's own. Hope's soul sickened as he read, with that deadly sickness which he had believed was past: but last June, with its delights and opening love, was too suddenly, and too vividly, re-awakened in his memory and imagination. The Margaret of yesterday, of last month, he trusted he had arrived at regarding as a sister: not so the Margaret of last summer. In vain he repeated, again and again, to himself, that he had expected this—that he always knew it must come—that this was the very thing, and no more, that he had been dreading for half a year past—that it was over now—that he ought to rejoice that he held in his hand the last witness and reminder of the mistake of his life. In vain did he repeat to himself these reasonable things—these satisfactory truths. They did not still the throbbing of his brain, or relieve the agony of his spirit;—an agony under which he could almost have cursed the hilarity of his brother as levity, and his hearty affection as cruel mockery. He recovered some breath and composure when he read the latter half of Frank's volume of communication, and, before he had finished it, the sound of distant footsteps fell upon his excited ear. He knew they were coming—the three who would be full of expectation as to what he should have to tell them from India. It was they, walking very slowly, as if waiting for the news.

"Come!" said he, starting up, and going to meet them. "Now, to the green walk—we shall be quiet there—and I will read you all about Frank."

He did read them all about Frank—all the last half of the letter—Hester hanging on his arm, and Philip and Margaret listening, as if they were taking in their share of family news. When it was done, and some one said it was time to be turning homewards, Hope disengaged his arm from Hester, and ran off, saying that he would report of Mrs Enderby to Mr Rowland in the office, and meet them before they should be out of the shrubbery. He did so: but he first took his way round by a fence which was undergoing the operation of tarring, thrust Frank's letter into the fire over which the tar was heating, and saw every inch of it consumed before he proceeded. When he regained his party, Hester took his arm, and turned once more towards the shrubbery, saying—

"We have plenty of time, and I am not at all tired: so now read me the rest."

"My love, I have read you all I can."

Hester stopped short, and with flashing eyes, whose fire was scarcely dimmed by her tears, cried—

"Do you mean to give me no more of your confidence than others? Is your wife—"

"My dear, it is not my confidence: it is Frank's."

"And is not Frank my brother? He is nothing to them."

"He was not your brother when this letter was written, nor did he know that he should ever be so. Consider this letter as one of old time—as belonging to the antiquity of our separate lives. I hope there will never be another letter from Frank, or anybody else (out of the range of my professional affairs) whose contents will not be as much yours as mine. This must satisfy you now, Hester; for I can tell you no more. This ought to satisfy you."

"It does not satisfy me. I never will be satisfied with giving all, and having nothing in return. I have given you all. Not a thought has there been in my heart about Margaret, from the day we married, that I have not imparted to you. Has it not been so?"

"I believe it, and I thank you for it."

"And what is it to you to have a sister—you who have always had sisters—what is it to you, in comparison with my longing to have a brother? And now you make him no more mine than he is Margaret's and Philip's. He himself, if he has the heart of a brother, would cry out upon you for disappointing me."

"I can allow for your feelings, Hester. I have known too well what disappointment is, not to feel for you. But here the fault is not mine."

"Whose is it then? It is to be charged upon Providence, I suppose, like most of our evils."

"No, Hester; I charge it upon you. The disappointment was unavoidable; but the sting of it lies in yourself. You are unreasonable. It is at your own request that I remind you to be reasonable."

"And when was that request made? When I believed that you would hold me your friend—that no others were to come near my place in your confidence—that all you cared for was to be equally mine—that your brother himself was to be my brother. It was when you promised me these things that I put my conscience and my feelings into your charge. But now all that is over. You are as much alone in your own soul as ever, and I am thrust out from it as if you were like other men... Oh!" she cried, covering her face with her hands, "call me your housekeeper at once—for I am not your wife—and breathe not upon my conscience—look not into my heart—for what are they to you? I reclaim from you, as your servant, the power I gave you over my soul, when I supposed I was to be your wife."

"Now you must hear me, Hester. Sit down; for you cannot stand under the tempest of your own feelings. Now, what are the facts out of which all this has arisen? I have had a letter, written before we were known to be engaged, containing something which is confided to my honour. We had both rather that such had not been the case. Would you now have me violate my honour? Let us have done. The supposition is too ridiculous."

"But the manner," pleaded Hester. "It is not curiosity about the letter. I care nothing if it contained the affairs of twenty nations. But, oh! your manner was cruel. If you loved me as you once did, you could not treat me exactly as you treat Margaret and Philip. You do not love me as you once did... You do not answer me," she continued in a tone of wretchedness. "Nay, do not answer me now. It will not satisfy me to hear you say upon compulsion that you love me. Ah! I had Margaret once; and once I had you. Philip has taken my Margaret from me; and if you despise me, I will lie down and die."

"Fear not!" said Hope, with great solemnity. "While I live you shall be honoured, and have such rest as you will allow to your own heart. But do you not see that you have now been distrusting me—not I you? Shall I begin to question whether you love me? Could you complain of injustice if I did, when you have been tempting my honour, insulting my trust in you, and wounding my soul? Is this the love you imagine I cannot estimate and return? This is madness, Hester. Rouse yourself from it. Waken up the most generous part of yourself. We shall both have need of it all."

"Oh, God! what do you intend? Consider again, before you break my heart, if you mean to say that we must... Edward! forgive me, Edward!"

"I mean to say that we must support each other under troubles of God's sending, instead of creating woes of our own."

"Support each other! Thank Heaven!"

"I see how your spirit rouses itself at the first sound of threatening from without. I knew it would. Rough and trying times are coming, love, and I must have your support. Trouble is coming—daily and hourly annoyance, and no end of it that I can see: and poverty, perhaps, instead of the ease to which we looked forward when you married me. I do not ask you whether you can bear these things, for I know you can. I shall look to you to help me to keep my temper."

"Are you not mocking me?" doubtfully whispered Hester.

"No, my love," her husband replied, looking calmly in her face. "I know you to be a friend made for adversity."

"Let it come, then!" exclaimed she. And she felt herself on the threshold of a new life, in which all the past might yet be redeemed.

They soon rejoined Margaret, and went home to relate and to hear what new threats the day had disclosed.

Chapter Twenty Eight

Deerbrook Commotions.

Among many vague threats, there was one pretty definite menace which had encountered Hope from various quarters of late. By whose agency, and by what means, he did not know, but he apprehended a design to supplant him in his practice. There was something more meant than that Mr Foster from Blickley appeared from time to time in the village. Hope imagined that there was a looking forward to somebody else, who was to cure all maladies as soon as they appeared, and keep death at a distance from Deerbrook. It seemed to be among the poor people chiefly that such an expectation prevailed. Philip was sure that Mr Rowland knew nothing of it, nor Mrs Enderby. Mr Grey, when spoken to, did not believe it, but would quietly and discreetly inquire. Mrs Grey was sure that the Deerbrook people would not venture to discountenance altogether any one who had married into their connection so decidedly. Her young folks were to hear nothing of the matter, as it would not do to propagate an idea which might bring about its own accomplishment.

At the almshouses to-day, the threat had been spoken plainly enough; and Hope had found his visit there a very unpleasant one. It had been wholly disagreeable. When within a mile and a half of the houses, a stone had been thrown at him from behind a hedge. It narrowly missed him. A little further on, there was another, from the opposite side of the road. This indication was not to be mistaken. Hope leaped his horse over a gate, and rode about the field, to discover who had attacked him. For some time he could see no one; but, on looking more closely to the fence, he saw signs in one part that hedging was going on. As he approached the spot, a labourer rose up from the ditch, and was suddenly very busy at his work. He looked stupid, and denied having thrown any stones, but admitted that there was nobody else in the field that he knew of. Further on, more stones were thrown: it was evidently a conspiracy; but Hope could find no one to call to account for it, but an old woman in one case, and two boys in another.—As he rode up to the almshouses, the aged inmates came out to their doors, or looked from their fanciful Gothic windows, with every indication of displeasure in their faces and manner. The old women shook their heads at him, and some their fists; the old men shook their sticks at him. He stopped to speak to one man of eighty-three, who was sitting in the sun at his door; but he could get no answer out of him, nothing but growls about the doctor being a pretty doctor not to have mended his patient's eye-sight yet. Not a bit better could he see now than he could a year ago, with all the doctoring he had had: and now the gentleman would not try anything more! A pretty doctor, indeed! But it would not be long before there would be another who would cure poor people's eyes as if they were rich: and poor people's eyes were as precious to them as rich people's.—He next went into a house where an aged woman was confined to bed with rheumatism; but her gossips stopped him in the middle of the room, and would not let him approach her, for fear he should be her death. As she had been lying awake the night before, she had heard her deceased husband's shoes dance of their own accord in the closet; and this was a sign that something was going to happen to somebody. She thought of the doctor at the time, and prayed that he might be kept from coming near her; for she knew he would be the death of her, somehow, as he had been of other folks. So Hope was obliged to leave her and her rheumatism to the gossips. The particular object of his visit to the place to-day, however, was a little girl, a grandchild of one of the pensioners, admitted by special favour into the establishment. This girl had small-pox, and her case was a severe one. Hope was admitted with unwillingness even to her, and was obliged to assume his ultimate degree of peremptoriness of manner with her nurses. He found her muffled up about the head with flannel, and with a slice of fat bacon, folded in flannel, tied about her throat,—a means considered a specific for small-pox in some regions. The discarding of the flannel and bacon, of course, caused great offence; and there was but too much reason to fear that all his directions as to the management of the girl would be observed by contraries, the moment his back was turned. He had long ago found explanation and argument to be useless. All that he could do was, to declare authoritatively, that if his directions were not followed, the girl would die, and her death would lie at the door of her nurses; that, in that case, he expected some of the people about her would be ill after her; but that if he was obeyed, he trusted she might get through, and nobody else be the worse. Almost before he was out of the house, another slice of fat bacon was cut, and the flannels put to the fire to heat again.

Hope mounted his horse to depart, just at the hour when the labourers were at their dinners in all the cottages around. They poured out to stare at him, some shouting that they should not have him long to look at, as they would get a better doctor soon. Some sent their dogs yelping at his horse's heels, and others vented wrath or jokes about churchyards. Soon after he had left the noise behind him, he met Sir William Hunter, riding, attended by his groom. Hope stopped him, making it his apology that Sir William might aid in saving the life of a patient in whom he was much interested. He told the story of the small-pox, of the rural method of treating it with which he had to contend, and proposed that Sir William should use his influence in securing for the patient a fair chance of her life. Sir William listened coolly, would certainly call at the almshouses and make inquiry; but did not like to interfere with the notions of the people there: made a point indeed of leaving them pretty much to their own ways; owned that it would be a pity the girl should die, if she really might be got through; would call, therefore, and inquire, and see whether Lady Hunter could not send down anything from the Hall. He smiled rather incredulously when assured that it was not anything that could be sent down from the Hall that was wanted by the patient, but only the use of the fresh air that was about her, and the observance of her doctor's simple directions. Sir William next began to make his horse fidget, and Hope took the hint.

"This has been my business with you at present," said he. "At some more convenient time, I should be glad of a little conversation with you on other matters connected with these almshouses."

Sir William Hunter bowed, put spurs to his horse, and galloped off, as if life or death depended on his reaching the Hall in three minutes and a half.

These hints of "another doctor"—"a better doctor"—"a new man"— met Hope in other directions. Mrs Howell was once quoted as a whisperer of the fact; and the milliner's young lady was known to have speculated on whether the new doctor would prove to be a single man. No one turned away from such gossip with more indifference than Hope; but it came to him in the form of inquiries which he was supposed best able to answer. He now told Hester of them all; warned her of the probable advent of a rival practitioner; and at the same time urged upon her a close economy in the management of the house, as his funds were rapidly failing. If his practice continued to fall off as it was now doing, he scarcely saw how they were to keep up their present mode of living. It grieved him extremely to have to say this to his wife in the very first year of their marriage. He had hoped to have put larger means in her power, from year to year; but at present he owned his way was far from being clear. They had already descended to having no prospect at all.

For all this Hester cared little. She had never known the pinchings of poverty, any more than the embarrassments of wealth. She could not conceive of such a thing as being very anxious about what they should eat, and what they should drink, and wherewith they should be clothed; though, if she had looked more narrowly at her own imaginations of poverty, she would perhaps have discovered on the visionary table always a delicate dish for her husband—in the wardrobe, always a sleek black coat—and in his waiting-room, a clear fire in winter; while the rest of the picture was made up of bread and vegetables, and shabby gowns for herself, and devices to keep herself warm without burning fuel. Her imagination was rather amused than alarmed with anticipations of this sort of poverty. It was certainly not poverty that she dreaded. A more serious question was, how she could bear to see her husband supplanted, and, in the eyes of others, disgraced. This question the husband and wife now often asked each other, and always concluded by agreeing that time must show.

The girl at the almshouses died in a fortnight. Some pains were taken to conceal from the doctor the time and the precise spot of her burial-points which the doctor never thought of inquiring about, and of which it was therefore easy to keep him in ignorance. A few of the neighbouring cottagers agreed to watch the grave for ten nights, to save the body from the designs of evil surgeons. One of the watchers reported, after the seventh night, that he had plainly heard a horse coming along the road, and that he rather thought it stopped opposite the churchyard. He had raised himself up, and coughed aloud, and that was no doubt the reason why nobody came: the horse must have turned back and gone away, whoever might be with it. This put people on the watch; and on the eighth night two men walked about the churchyard. They had to tell that they once thought they had caught the doctor in the fact. They had both heard a loud whistle, and had stood to see what would come of it (they could see very well, for it had dawned some time). A person came through the turnstile with a sack, which seemed to leave his intentions in no doubt. They hid themselves behind two opposite trees, and both sprang out upon him at once: but it was only the miller's boy on his way to the mill. On the ninth and tenth nights nothing happened; the neighbours began to feel the want of their regular sleep; and the querulous grandmother, who seemed more angry that they meant to leave the poor girl's body to itself now, than pleased that it had been watched at all, was compelled to put up with assurances that doctors were considered to wish to cut up bodies within the first ten days, if at all, and were not apt to meddle with them afterwards.

It was full three weeks from this time when Hope was sent for to the almshouses, after a longer interval than he had ever known to elapse without the old folks having some complaint to make. The inmate who was now ill was the least aged, and the least ignorant and unreasonable person, in the establishment. He was grateful to Hope for having restored him from a former illness; and, though now much shaken in confidence, had enough remaining to desire extremely to see his old friend, when he found himself ill and in pain. His neighbours wondered at him for wishing to court destruction by putting himself again into the hands of the suspicious doctor: but he said he could have no ease in his mind, and was sure he should never get well till he saw the gentleman's face again; and he engaged an acquaintance to go to Deerbrook and summon him. This acquaintance spread the fact of his errand along the road as he went; and therefore, though Hope took care to choose his time, so as not to ride past the cottage-doors while the labourers were at dinner, his visit was not more private or agreeable than on the preceding occasion.

The first symptom of his being expected on the road was, that Sir William Hunter, riding, as before, with his groom behind him, fell in with Hope, evidently by design.

Sir William Hunter's visit to the almshouses had produced the effect of making him acquainted with the discontents of the people, and had afforded him a good opportunity of listening to their complaints of their surgeon, without being troubled with the answers. Since the election, he had been eager to hear whatever could be said against Hope, whose vote, given contrary to Sir William's example and influence, was regarded by the baronet as an unpardonable impertinence.

"So you lost your patient down there, I find," said Sir William, rudely. "The girl slipped through your fingers, after all. However, I did my duty by you. I told the people they ought to allow you a fair chance."

"I requested your interference on the girl's account, and not on my own," said Hope. "But as you allude to my position among these people, you will allow me to ask, as I have for some time intended, whether you are aware of the treatment to which I am subjected, in your neighbourhood, and among your dependants?"

"I find you are not very popular hereabouts, indeed, sir," replied the baronet, with a half-smile, which was immediately reflected in the face of the groom.

"With your leave, we will have our conversation to ourselves," said Hope.

The baronet directed his groom to ride on slowly. Hope continued:

"The extreme ignorance of the country people has caused some absurd stories against me to be circulated and believed. If those who are not in this state of extreme ignorance will do me justice, and give me, as you say, a fair chance, I have no fear but that I shall live down calumnies, and, by perseverance in my professional duty, recover the station I lately held here. This justice, this fair chance, I claim, Sir William, from all who have the intelligence to understand the case, and rightly observe my conduct. I have done my best in the service of these pensioners of yours; and excuse my saying that I must be protected in the discharge of my duty."

"Ay, there's the thing, Mr Hope. That can't be done, you see. If the people do not like you, why then the only thing is for you to stay away."

"Then what is to become of the sick?"

"Ay, there's the thing, Mr Hope. If they do not like one, you see, why then they must try another. That is what we have been thinking. Now, if you take my advice, you will not go forward to-day. You will repent it if you do, depend upon it. They do not like you, Mr Hope."

"I need no convincing of that. You do not seem disposed to stir, Sir William, to improve the state of things; so I will go and try what I can do by myself."

"I advise you not, sir.—Mr Hope!" shouted Sir William, as Hope rode rapidly forward, "take care what you are about. They do not want to see you again. The consequences may be serious."

"And this man is a magistrate, and he fancies himself my patron!" thought Hope, as he rode on. "He wants me to throw up the appointment; but I will not, till I see that the poor old creatures can be consigned to care as good as my own. If he chooses to dismiss me, he may, though we can ill afford the loss just now."

For one moment he had thought of turning back, as Sir William's caution had seemed to foretell some personal risk in proceeding; but the remembrance of Hester's parting look inspired him afresh. Instead of the querulous anxiety which had formerly harassed him from its groundlessness and apparent selfishness, it was now an anxiety worthy of the occasion that flushed her cheek. So far from entreating him to remain with her, she had bidden him go where his duty led him. She had calculated the probable length of his absence, and the watch was laid on the table as formerly: but she had used the utmost expedition in sewing on the ring of his umbrella, and had kissed her hand to him from the window with a smile. He would not return to her without having fully discharged his errand. "She might be a soldier's or sailor's wife, after all," thought he.

The hours of his absence were indeed very anxious ones to the family at home. For nearly two hours, the sisters amused themselves and one another as well as they could: but it was a great relief when Philip came in. He would not believe anything they said, however, about their reasons for fear. It was nonsense—it was Deerbrook talk. What harm could a dozen old men and women, at almost a hundred years apiece, do to Hope?—and the country people, the labourers round, they had their own business to attend to: they would just swear an oath at him, and let him pass; and if they ventured to lay a finger on his bridle, Hope knew how to use his whip. He would come home, and get his dinner, and be very dull, they would see, from having nothing to tell.—Before Philip had finished his picture of the dull dining they might expect, Morris entered, and shut the door before she came forward to the table and spoke. She said she did not like to make mysteries, out of fear of frightening people; and she hoped there would be nothing to be really afraid of now: but if Mr Enderby thought he could contrive to meet her master out on the road, and get him to leave his horse somewhere, and come walking home by Turnstile Lane, she thought it would be best, and save some bad language, at least. Charles had brought in word that people—angry people—were gathering at the other end of the street, and her master could quite disappoint them by coming home on foot the back way.—How many angry people were there!—and what sort of people?—They were mostly countrymen out of the places round—more of those than of Deerbrook folks. There were a good many of them—so many as nearly to block up the street at one part. If the ladies would step up into the boy's attic, they would see something of what was going on, from the little window there, without being seen.

Philip snatched his hat, and said he would soon bring them news. He hoped they would go up to the attic, and amuse themselves with the show: for a mere show it would end in being, he was confident. He observed, however, that it would be as well to keep Charles at home, in case, as was possible, of a messenger being wanted. He himself would soon be back.

Charles was called up into the drawing-room, and questioned. Never before having been of so much importance, he was very grand in his statements, and made the most of all he had to say. Still, however, it was a story which no telling could have made other than an unpleasant one. Some of the people who had come in from the country had pitchforks. Two or three of the shopkeepers had put up their shutters. Many strangers were in the churchyard, peeping about the new graves: and others had set scouts on the road, to give notice when master was coming. Mrs Plumstead was very busy scolding the people all round; but it did not do any good, for they only laughed at her.

"You may go, Charles; but do not set foot out of the house till you are bid," said Hester, when she found the boy had told all he knew, and perhaps something more. Morris left the room with him, in order to keep her eye upon him.

"Oh, Margaret, this is very terrible!" said Hester.

"Most disagreeable. We must allow something for Charles's way of telling the story. But yet—is there anything we can do, Hester?"

"Mr Grey will surely be here, presently. Do not you think so?"

"Either he or Mr Rowland, no doubt."

"Dr Levitt is a magistrate: but this is Saturday, and he is so deep in his sermon, he could not be made to understand and believe till it would be too late.—Do you go up to the attic, Margaret, and I will keep the hall door. I shall hear his horse sooner than any one, and I shall stand ready to open to him in an instant. Hark now!"

It was only the boy with the post-bags, trotting slowly to Mrs Plumstead's, amusing himself by the way with observations on the unusual animation of Deerbrook.

"It is too soon yet, by half an hour," said Margaret. "He cannot possibly be here for this half-hour, I think. Do not wear yourself out with standing in the hall so long. I must just say one thing, love, I fear all kinds of danger less for Edward than for almost any one else in the world: he does always what is most simple and right; and I think he could melt anybody's heart if he tried."

"Thank you," said Hester, gratefully. "I agree and trust with you: but what hearts have these people? or, how can you get at them, through such heads? But yet he will triumph, I feel."

When Margaret went up-stairs to the attic window, Hester moved a chair into the hall, softly opened the window a little, to facilitate her hearing whatever passed outside, and took her seat by it, listening intently. There was soon but too much to listen to. Shuffling feet multiplied about the door; and some of the grumbling voices seemed to come from men who had stationed themselves on the steps. Hester rose, and, with the utmost care to avoid noise, put up the chain of the house door. While she was doing this, Morris came from the kitchen, for the same purpose. She feared there was an intention to surround the house: she wished her master would keep away, for a few hours at least; she could not think where all the gentlemen of the place were, that they did not come and see after her young ladies. Before the words were uttered, there was a loud rap at the door. Morris made her mistress keep back, while she found out who it was, before letting down the chain. Hester knew it was not her husband's knock; and it turned out to be Mr Grey's. Margaret came flying down, and they all exclaimed how glad they were to see him.

"I wish I could do you any good," said he; "but this is really a sad business, my dears."

"Have you heard anything, sir?"

"Nothing about your husband. Enderby bade me tell you that he is gone out to meet him, and to stir up Sir William Hunter, who may be said to be the cause of all this, inasmuch as he never attempted to stop the discontent when he might. But that unlucky vote, my dear, that was much to be deplored."

"No use casting that up now, surely," observed Morris.

"Yes, Morris, there is," said her mistress; "it gives me an opportunity of saying that I glory in the vote; and I would have my husband give it again to-day, if he had to pass through yonder crowd to go up to the poll."

"My dear," remonstrated Mr Grey, "be prudent. Do not urge your husband on into danger: he has quite enthusiasm enough without; and you see what comes of it.—But I am here to say that my wife hopes you and Margaret will retire to our house, if you can get round without bringing any of these troublesome people with you. We think you might slip out from the surgery, and along the lane, and through the Rowlands' garden door, and over the hedge which they tell me you managed to climb one day lately for pleasure. By this way, you might reach our house without any one being the wiser."

"On no account whatever," said Hester. "I shall not leave home, under any circumstances."

"You are very kind," said Margaret; "but we are expecting my brother every moment."

"But he will follow you by the same road."

Both wife and sister were sure he would do no such thing. They thought the kindest thing Mr Grey could do would be to go out the back way, and see that the constable was kept up to his duty. He promised to do so; and that he would speak to Dr Levitt, to have some of Grey and Rowlands men sworn in as special constables, if such a measure should appear to be desirable.

"I do not know how to believe all this now," said Margaret; "it seems so causeless and ridiculous! In Birmingham we could never have given credit to the story of such a riot about nothing."

Morris was not sure of this. In large towns there were riots sometimes for very small matters, or on account of entire mistakes. She had always heard that one of the worst things about living in a village is, that when the people once get a wrong idea into their heads, there is no getting it out again; and that they will even be violent upon it against all reason; but such things she knew to happen occasionally in towns.

Another knock. It was Mr Rowland, and Hester's heart turned sick at there being no news of her husband. Mr Rowland had every expectation, of course, that Mr Hope would be quite safe, and that this would turn out a disturbance of very slight consequence: but he would just ask whether it would not be advisable to close the window-shutters. If stones should find their way into the parlours, it might be disagreeable to the ladies.—There was no doubt of that: but would not closing the shutters be a hint to the people outside to throw stones?—Well, perhaps so. He only thought he would offer the suggestion, and see if he could be of any service to the ladies.

"Morris, go up to the attic and watch; and Margaret, do you stay here. Yes, Mr Rowland," said Hester, fixing her glorious eyes full on him; "you can be of service to us, if my husband outlives this day. You ought to pray that he may; for if not, it is your wife who has murdered him."

Mr Rowland turned as pale as ashes.

"We know well that you have no share in all this injury: we believe that you respect my husband, and have friendly feelings towards us all. I will spare you what I might say—what Mrs Rowland should sink to the earth to hear, if she were standing where you stand. I look upon you as no enemy—"

"You do me only justice," said Mr Rowland, leaning upon the chair which Hester had brought for herself.

"I wish to do you justice; and therefore I warn you that if you do not procure complete protection for my husband—not only for this day—but for the future;—if you do not cause your wife to retract her slanders—"

"Stop, Mrs Hope! this is going too far," said Mr Rowland, drawing himself up, and putting on an air of offended dignity.

"It is not going too far. You cannot, you dare not, pretend to be offended with what I say, when you know that my noble husband has been injured in his character and his prospects, attacked in his domestic peace, and now exposed to peril of his life, by the falsehoods your wife has told. I tell you that we do not impute her crimes to you. If this is justice, you will prove it by doing your full duty to my husband. If you decline any part of this duty—if you countenance her slanders—if you shrink from my husband's side in whatever we may have to go through—if you do not either compel your wife to do us right, or do it yourself in opposition to her—you are her partner in guilt, as well as in life and lot."

"Consider what a situation you place me in!—But what would you have me do?"

"I would have you see that every false charge she has brought is retracted—every vile insinuation recanted. You must make her say everywhere that my husband has not stolen dead bodies; that he is not a plotter against the peace and order of society; that he has not poisoned a child by mistake, or cut off a sound limb for the sake of practice and amusement. Your wife has said these things, and you know it; and you must make her contradict them all."

"Consider what a situation you place me in!" said Mr Rowland again.

"Be generous, Hester!" said Margaret.

"Do not trample on a wretched man!" cried Mr Rowland, covering his face with his hands.

"'Consider!' 'Be generous!'" exclaimed Hester in a softened tone. "I might well say, Consider what a situation my husband is placed in! and that I must see justice done to him before I can be generous to others; but I have such a husband that I can afford to spare the wretched, and be generous to the humbled. Go now and do *your* duty by us: and the next time you hear your wife say that we do not love and are not happy, tell her that if we forbear to crush her, it is because we are too strong for her—too strong in heart, however weak in fortunes:— because we are strong in a peace which she cannot poison, and a love which she will never understand."

Even at a moment like this, and while feeling that she could not have said the things that Hester said, Margaret's eyes swam in tears of joy. Here was her sister, in a moment of that high excitement when nothing but truth ventures upon utterance, acknowledging herself blessed in peace which could not be poisoned, and love which the vile could not understand. The day, whatever might be its events, was worth enduring for this.

Mr Rowland walked once or twice up and down the hall, wiped his brows, and then, evidently unable to endure Hester's presence, said he would let himself out, and there await Mr Hope's arrival, or anything else that might occur.

Oh! would he ever come? It seemed to Hester like a week since she had given him his umbrella, and seen him ride away.

Hark! Surely this must be—it certainly was his horse this time. Yes—there was Morris calling from the stairs that her master was fighting his way down the street! There was Charles giving notice that the crowd was running round from the back to the front of the house! There was the noise among the people outside, the groaning, the cries!

"Now, ma'am!" said Morris, breathless with the haste she had made down stairs. Morris supposed her mistress would softly let down the chain, open the door just wide enough for Hope to slip in, and shut, bolt, and chain it again. This was what Hester had intended; but her mood was changed. She bade the servants all step out of sight, and then threw the door wide open, going forth herself upon the steps. The people had closed round Hope's horse; but Philip was pushing his in between the mob and their object, and riding round and round him with a sort of ludicrous gravity, which lowered the tone of the whole affair to Margaret's mind, and gave her great relief. Mr Rowland was shaking hands with Hope with one hand, and holding the bridle of the uneasy horse with the other. Hope himself was bespattered with mud from head to foot, and his umbrella was broken to pieces. He nodded cheerfully to Hester when she threw open the door. When she held out her hand to him with a smile as he ascended the steps, the noise of the crowd was suddenly hushed. They understood rather more of what they saw than of anything that could be said to them. They allowed Charles to come out, and lead the horse away round the corner to the stable. They stood stock-still, gaping and staring, while Hope invited Mr Rowland in, and Mr Rowland declined entering; while that gentleman shook hands with the ladies, spoke with Mr Enderby, mounted Mr Enderby's horse, and rode off. They saw Philip turn slowly into the house with the family party, and the door closed, before they thought of giving another groan.

"Well, love!" said Hester, looking anxiously at her husband.

"You made good battle," said Philip.

"Yes, I had a pretty hard fight of it, from the toll-bar hither," said Hope, stretching vigorously. "They wrenched my whip out of my hand—five hands to one; but then I had my umbrella. I broke it to pieces with rapping their knuckles."

"Which are as hard as their pates," observed Philip. "What are we to do next?"

"If they do not disperse presently, I will go and speak to them; but I dare say they have had enough of the show for to-day: Mrs Plumstead must have satisfied them with oratory. That poor woman's face and voice will haunt me when I have forgotten all the rest. One had almost rather have her against one, than that such screaming should be on one's behalf. Now, my love, how has the morning gone with you?"

"Very pleasantly, I would answer for it from her looks," said Philip. And Hester's face was certainly full of the beauty of happiness.

"Thank God, the morning is over! That is all I have to say about it," replied she.

"Surely those people outside are growing more noisy!" observed Margaret.

"I must change my clothes, in case of its being necessary to speak to them," said Hope. "I look too like a victim at present."

While he and Hester were out of the room, Philip told Margaret how her brother had been treated at the almshouses. He had narrowly escaped being pulled from his horse and thrown into the pond. He had been followed half-way to Deerbrook by a crowd, throwing stones and shrieking; and just when he had got beyond their reach, he had met Philip, and learned that he had the same thing to go through, at the other extremity of his journey. Finding that both his doors were surrounded, he had judged it best to make for the front, coming home as nearly as possible in his usual manner. He had kept his temper admirably, joking with his detainers, while dealing his blows upon their hands.

"Where will all this end?" cried Margaret.

"With some going to dinner, and others to supper, I imagine," replied Philip, stepping to the window. "From what I see, that seems likely to be the upshot; for here is Sir William Hunter talking to the people. I had rather he should do it than Hope; and, Margaret, I had rather set my mischievous sister to do it than either. This uproar is all of her making, I am afraid."

"Hester has been telling Mr Rowland so, this morning."

"I am glad of it. He must help me to work upon her fears, if there is nothing better left to operate upon."

"You will not succeed," said Margaret. "Your sister is as strong a heroine in one direction as mine is in another."

"She shall yield, however. She may be thankful that she is not here to-day. If she was, I would have her out upon the steps, and make her retract everything; and if she should not be able to speak, I would stand by her and say it for her."

"Oh, Philip! what a horrible idea!"

"Not half so horrible as the mischief she has done. Why, Margaret, if you were one-tenth part as guilty as Priscilla is, I should require you to make reparation."

"Indeed, I hope you would: or rather, that—"

"But do not let us conjure up such dreadful images, my Margaret. You never wronged any one, and you never will."

"Edward never did, I am sure," said Margaret.

"Not even by poisoning children, nor cutting off limbs for sport? Are you quite sure, love? What is Sir William doing here, with only his groom?

He and the people look in high good-humour with each other, with all this shaking of hands, and nodding and laughing. I cannot conceive what he can be saying to them, for there are not three faces among the whole array that look as if they belonged to rational creatures."

"Never mind," said Margaret. "If what he says sends them away, I care for nothing else about it."

"Oh, but I do. One would like to be favoured with a specimen of this kind of rural oratory. I ought to benefit by all the oratory that comes in my way, you know: so I shall just open the window an inch or two, now he is drawing hitherward, and take a lesson."

It seemed as if Sir William Hunter desired that his powers of persuasion should be expended on none but the immediate objects of them: for whatever he said was spoken as he bent from his horse, and with the air of a mystery. Many a plump red face was thrust close up to his—many a pair of round staring eyes was puckered up with mirth as he spoke: the teamster in his olive-coloured smock, the hedger in his shirt-sleeves, and the little bumpkins who had snatched a holiday from scaring the crows, all seemed, by their delight, to be capable of entering into the baronet's method of argumentation. All this stimulated Philip's curiosity to learn what the speechifying tended to. He could catch only a few words, and those were about "a new man,"—"teach him to take himself off,"—"all bad things come to an end,"—"new state of things, soon." Philip was afraid there was treachery here. Margaret had no other expectation from the man—the tyrannical politician, who bore a grudge against a neighbour for having used his constitutional liberty according to his conscience.

Some spectacle now drew the attention of the crowd another way. It was Lady Hunter, in her chariot and greys, statelily pacing through the village. She had heard that there was some commotion in Deerbrook; and, as sights are rare in the country, she thought she would venture to come to the village to shop, rather than wait for Sir William's account of the affair in the evening, over their wine and oranges, and before he dropped off into his nap. She rightly confided in the people, that they would respect her chariot and greys, and allow her to pass amidst them in safety and honour. She had never seen a person mobbed. Here was a good opportunity. It was even possible that she might catch a glimpse of the ladies in their terrors. At all events, she should be a great person, and see and hear a great deal: so she would go. Orders were given that she should be driven quickly up to the milestone beyond the toll-bar, and then very slowly through Deerbrook to Mrs Howell's. Her servants were prompt, for they, too, longed to see what was going forward; and thus they arrived, finding a nice little mob ready-made to their expectations, and no cause of regret but that they arrived too late to see Mr Hope get home. There were no ladies in terror within sight: but then there was the affecting spectacle of Sir William's popularity. In full view of all the mob, Lady Hunter put a corner of her embroidered handkerchief to each eye, on witnessing the affection of his neighbours to her husband, shown by the final shaking of hands which was now gone through. Sir William then rode slowly up to the carriage-door, followed by his groom, who touched his hat. Orders were given to drive on; and then Lady Hunter's servants touched their hats. The carriage resumed its slow motion, and Sir William rode beside it, his hand on the door, and his countenance solemn as if he was on the bench, instead of on horseback. The great blessing of the arrangement was that everybody followed. Lady Hunter having come to see the mob, the mob now, in return, went to see Lady Hunter: and while they were cherishing their mutual interest, the family in the corner-house were left in peace to prosecute their dinners. Philip threw up the window which looked into the garden, and then ran down to bring Margaret some flowers to refresh her senses after the hurry of the morning. Margaret let down the chain of the hall door; and Morris laid the cloth, as she had sent Charles to sweep down the steps and pavement before the house, that all things might wear as much as possible their usual appearance. Hester ordered up a bottle of her husband's best ale, and the servants went about with something of the air peculiar to a day of frolic.

"Dear heart! Lady Hunter! Can it be your ladyship?" exclaimed Mrs Howell, venturing to show her face at the door of her darkened shop, and to make free entrance for her most exalted customer.

"Good heavens! your ladyship! Who would have thought of seeing your ladyship here on such a day?" cried Miss Miskin.

"Where's Bob, Miss Miskin? Do, Miss Miskin, send Bob to take down the shutters:— that is, if your ladyship thinks that Sir William would recommend it. If Sir William thinks it safe,—that is my criterion."

"I hope we are all safe, now, Mrs Howell," replied the lady. "Sir William's popularity is a most fortunate circumstance for us all, and for the place at large."

"Oh dear, your ladyship! what should we be, not to estimate Sir William? We have our faults, like other people: but really, if we did not know how to value Sir William—"

"Thank Heaven!" said Miss Miskin, "we have not fallen so low as that. Now your ladyship can see a little of our goings on—now the shutters are down: but, dear heart! your ladyship would not have wondered at our putting them up. I am sure I thought for my part, that that middle shutter never would have gone up. It stuck, your ladyship—"

"Oh!" cried Mrs Howell, putting her hands before her face, as if the recollection was even now too much for her, "the middle shutter stuck—Bob had got it awry, and jammed it between the other two, and there, nothing that Bob could do would move it! And there we heard the noise at a distance—the cries, your ladyship—and the shutter would not go up! And Miss Miskin ran out, and so did I—"

"Did you really? Well, I must say I admire your courage, Mrs Howell."

"Oh, your ladyship, in a moment of desperation, you know... If anybody had seen Miss Miskin's face, I'm sure, as she tugged at the shutter—it was as red... really scarlet!"

"And I'm sure so was yours, Mrs Howell, downright crimson."

"And after all," resumed Mrs Howell, "we should never have got the shutter up, if Mr Tucker had not had the politeness to come and help us. But we are talking all this time, and perhaps your ladyship may be almost fainting with the fright. Would not your ladyship step into my parlour, and have a little drop of something? Let me have the honour—a glass of mulled port wine, or a drop of cherry-bounce. Miss Miskin—you will oblige us—the cherry-bounce, you know."

Miss Miskin received the keys from the girdle with a smile of readiness; but Lady Hunter declined refreshment. She explained that she felt more collected than she might otherwise have done, from her not having been taken by surprise. She had been partly aware, before she left the Hall, of what she should have to encounter.

"Dear heart! what courage!"

"Goodness! how brave!"

"I could not be satisfied to remain safe at the Hall, you know, when I did not know what might be happening to Sir William; so I ordered the carriage, and came. It was a very anxious ride, I assure you, Mrs Howell. But I found, when I got here, that I need not have been under any alarm for Sir William. He has made himself so beloved, that I believe we have nothing to fear for him under any circumstances. But what can we think, Mrs Howell, of those who try to create such danger?"

"What, indeed, ma'am! Any one, I'm sure, who would so much as dream of hurting a hair of Sir William's head... As I said to Miss Miskin, when Mr Tucker told us Sir William was come among them—'that's the criterion,' said I."

"As it happens, Sir William is in no danger, I believe; but no thanks to those who are at the bottom of this disturbance. It is no merit of theirs that Sir William is so popular."

"No, indeed, your ladyship. We may thank Heaven for that, not them. But what *is* to be done, your ladyship? I declare it is not safe to go on in this way. It makes one think of being burnt in one's bed." And all the three shuddered.

"Sir William will take the right measures, you need not doubt, Mrs Howell. Sir William looks forward—Sir William is very cautious, though, from his intrepidity, some might doubt it. The safety of Deerbrook may very well be left to Sir William."

"No doubt, your ladyship, no doubt! We should be really afraid to go to our beds, if we had not Sir William to rely on, as Miss Miskin said to me only this morning. But, dear heart! what can Sir William, or an angel from heaven do, in some sorts of dangers? If one might ask, for one's confidential satisfaction, what does Sir William think of this affair of the church-door?"

Amidst shrugs and sighs, Miss Miskin drew quite near, to hear the fate of Deerbrook revealed by Lady Hunter. But Lady Hunter did not know the facts about the church-door, on which the inquiry was based. This only showed how secret some people could be in their designs. There was no saying what Lady Hunter might think of it; it really seemed as if Deerbrook, that had had such a good character hitherto, was going to be on a level with Popish places—a place of devastation and conflagration. Lady Hunter looked excessively grave when she heard this; and, if possible, graver than ever, when she was told that not only had a lantern been found in the churchyard with a bit of candle left in the socket, but that a piece of charred stick, full three inches long, had been picked up close by the church-door. After hearing this, Lady Hunter would not commit herself any further. She asked for some hair-pins, with a dignified and melancholy air. While she was selecting the article, she let Mrs Howell talk on about the lantern and the stick—that no one wondered about the lantern, knowing what practices went on in the churchyard when quiet people were asleep; but that the charred stick was too alarming: only that, to be sure, anybody might be aware that those who would go into churchyards for one bad purpose would be ready enough for another; and that Heaven only knew how long the churches of the land would be safe while Lowrys were sent to Parliament, and those that sent them there were all abroad. Lady Hunter sighed emphatically, whispered her desire that the hair-pins should be set down in her account, and went away, amidst deep and mournful curtseys from those whom she left behind.

Under certain circumstances, the mind becomes so rapidly possessed of an idea, is enabled to assimilate it so completely and speedily, that the possessor becomes unaware how very recently the notion was received, and deals with it as an old-established thought. This must be Lady Hunter's excuse (for no other can be found) for speaking of the plot for burning Deerbrook church as one of the signs of the times which had alarmed Sir William and herself of late. She had so digested Mrs Howell's fact by the time she had reached Mr Tucker's shop, that she thus represented the case of the charred stick to Mr Tucker without any immediate sting of conscience for telling a lie. She felt rather uncomfortable when Mr Jones, the butcher, who had stepped in at Tucker's to discuss the event of the morning, observed, with deference, but with much decision, that he was sorry to hear Sir William was made uneasy by the circumstance of the charred stick having been found, as it seemed to him a very simple matter to account for. Several of the boys of the village—his own son John for one—had lately taken to the old sport of whirling round a lighted stick at the end of a string, to make a circle of fire in the dark. Sometimes it happened that a spark caught the string; and then the stick was apt to fly off, nobody knew where. It was an unsafe sport, certainly; and as such he had forbidden it to his son John: but there was no doubt in his mind (without defending the sport), that the stick in question had jerked itself over the churchyard wall, and had not been put there by anybody;—to say nothing of its having lain so far from the door (and in the grass, too), that it was difficult to see what could be expected to catch fire from it. Jones took up his hat from the counter, saying, that as Sir William was close at hand, he would step and tell him what he thought would ease his mind about this affair. This movement laid open to Lady Hunter's mind the enormity of her fib: and remembering that, as far as she knew, her husband had never heard of the charred stick, she vigorously interfered to keep Mr Jones where he was, averring that Sir William had rather hear the explanation from her than from any person actually resident in Deerbrook. He had his reasons, and she must insist. Mr Jones bowed; her alarm ceased, and her compunction gradually died away.

When Mr Tucker had received his orders about the fire-guard (which occasioned his whispering that there had never been so much need in Deerbrook of guards against fire as now), Lady Hunter's footman came into the shop to say that his master was in the carriage. Sir William had sent his horse home, and would return in the chariot with his lady. She hastened away, to prevent any chat between Sir William and Mr Jones. But, once in the carriage, in all the glory of being surrounded and watched by a number of gaping clowns and shouting boys, she could not resolve to bury herself in the seclusion of the Hall, without enjoying the bustle a little longer. She therefore suddenly discovered that she wanted to order a morning cap at

Miss Nares'; and the carriage drew up in state before the milliner's door. Miss Flint, whose hair had come out of curl, from her having leaned out of an upper window to watch the commotion, now flew to the glass to pull off her curl-papers; Miss Nares herself hastily drew out of drawers and cupboards the smart things which had been huddled away under the alarm about the sacking of Deerbrook; and then threw a silk handkerchief over the tray, on which stood the elder wine and toast with which she and her assistant had been comforting themselves after the panic of the morning. All the caps were tried on with mysterious melancholy, but with some haste. Sir William must not be kept long waiting: in times like these, a magistrate's moments were valuable. Sir William was reading the newspaper, in order to convey the impression that he considered the affair of this morning a trifling one; but—

"These are strange times, Miss Nares."

"Very alarming, my lady. I am sure I don't know when we shall recover from the fright. And no further back than six weeks, I had that person in, my lady, to attend Miss Flint in a sore throat. So little were we aware!"

"I am thankful enough it was not for a broken arm," observed Miss Flint, in accents of devout gratitude.

"Yes, indeed, my dear," observed Miss Nares, "it would have ruined all your prospects in life if he had done by you as he did by the Russell Taylors' nursemaid. Have you never heard that, my lady? Well! I am astonished! I find the story is in everybody's mouth. Mrs Russell Taylor's nursemaid was crossing the court, with the baby in her arms, when she tripped over the string of Master Hampden Taylor's kite. Well, my lady, she fell; and her first thought, you know, was to save the baby; so she let all her weight go on the other arm—the right—and, as you may suppose, broke it. It snapped below the elbow. The gentleman in the corner-house was sent for immediately, to set it. Now they say (you, my lady, know all about it, of course,) that there are two bones in that part of one's arm, below the elbow."

"There are so. Quite correct. There are two bones."

"Well, my lady, all the story depends upon that. The gentleman in question did set the bones; but he set them across, you see,—as it might be so." And Miss Nares arranged four pieces of whalebone on the table in the shape of a long, narrow letter X; there could not have been a better exemplification. "The consequence was, my lady, that the poor girl's hand was found, when she had got well, to be turned completely round: and, in fact, it is all but useless."

"When her hands are in her lap," observed Miss Flint, "the palm of the right lies uppermost. Ugh!"

"When she beckons the children with that hand," observed Miss Nares, "they think she means them to go further off. A girl who has to earn her bread, my lady! It is in everybody's mouth, I assure you."

"What has become of the girl?" asked Lady Hunter.

"Oh, she was got rid of—sent away—to save the credit of the gentleman in the corner-house. But these things will come out, my lady. You are aware that the Russell Taylors have for some time been employing Mr Foster, from Blickley?"

"Ah, true! I had heard of that."

With unrelaxed gravity, Lady Hunter returned to her equipage, carrying with her Miss Nares's newest cap and story.

As the carriage drew near the corner-house, the driver, as if sympathising with his lady's thoughts, made his horses go their very slowest. Lady Hunter raised herself, and leaned forward, that she might see what she could see in this dangerous abode. The spring evening sunshine was streaming in at the garden window at the back of the house; so that the party in the room was perfectly visible, in the thorough light, to any one who could surmount the obstacle of the blind. Lady Hunter saw four people sitting at dinner, and somebody was waiting on them. She could scarcely have told what it was that surprised her; but she exclaimed to Sir William—

"Good heavens! they are at dinner!"

Sir William called out angrily to the coachman to drive faster, and asked whether he meant to keep everybody out till midnight.

The Hopes were far less moved by seeing the baronet and his lady driving by, than the baronet and his lady were by seeing the Hopes dining. They had not the slightest objection to the great folks from the Hall deriving all the excitement and amusement they could from an airing through the village; and they were happily ignorant of the most atrocious stories about Hope which were now circulating from mouth to mouth, all round Deerbrook.

It was not long, however, before they found that they had been indebted to the great folks from the Hall for a certain degree of protection, partly from the equipage having drawn off the attention of some of the idlers, and partly from the people having been unwilling to indulge all their anger and impertinence in the presence of a magistrate. Scarcely half an hour had elapsed after the sound of the carriage wheels had died away, before a face was seen surmounting the blind of the windows towards the street. Presently another appeared, and another. Men below were hoisting up boys, to make grimaces at the family, and see what was going on. The shutters were closed rather earlier than usual. Philip went out to make a survey. He and Mr Grey soon returned, to advise that the ladies should quit the house, and that a guard should enter it. The first proposition was refused; the second accepted. Mr Grey carried off all the money and small valuables. Hester and Margaret bestirred themselves to provide refreshments for Messrs Grey and Rowland's men, who were to be ready to act in their defence. They scarcely knew what to expect; but they resolved to remain where Edward was, and to fear nothing from which he did not shrink.

There was much noise round the house—a multitude of feet and of voices. Messengers were sent off to the Hall and to Dr Levitt, who must now be disturbed, whatever might become of his sermon. Philip brought in Mr Rowland's men, and declared he should not leave the premises again if the ladies would not be persuaded to go. He took up his station in the hall, whence he thought he could learn most of what it was that the people had intended to do, and be most ready to act as occasion might require. No one could imagine what was designed, or whether there was any design at all on foot. The only fact at present apparent was, that the crowd was every moment increasing.

Hester was stooping over the cellaret in the room where they had dined, when a tremendous crash startled her, and a stone struck down the light which stood beside her, leaving her in total darkness. Philip came to her in a moment. No one had thought of closing the shutters of the back windows; and now the garden was full of people. The house was besieged back and front; and, in ten minutes from the entrance of this first stone, not a pane of glass was left unbroken in any of the lower windows. Hope ran out, his spirit thoroughly roused by these insults; and he was the first to seize and detain one of the offenders; but the feat was rather too dangerous to bear repetition. He was recognised, surrounded, and had some heavy blows inflicted upon him. He succeeded in bringing off his man; but it was by the help of a sally of his friends from the house; and having locked up his prisoner in his dressing-room, he found it best to await the arrival of a magistrate before he went forth again.

The surgery was the most open to attack; and this being the place where the people expected to find the greatest number of dead bodies, their energies were directed towards the professional part of the premises. The pupil took flight, and left the intruders to work their pleasure. They found no bodies, and were angry accordingly. When the crashing of all the glass was over, the shelves and cases were torn down, and, with the table and chairs, carried out into the street, and cast into a heap. Other wood was brought; and it was owing to the pertinacity of the mob in front of the house, in attacking the shutters, that the rioters met with no opposition in the surgery. Hope, Enderby, and their assistants, had more on their hands than they could well manage, in beating off the assailants in front. If the shutters were destroyed, the whole furniture of the house would go, and no protection would remain to anybody in it. The surgery must be left to take its chance, rather than this barrier between the women and the mob be thrown down. Whatever offensive warfare was offered from the house was from the servants, from the upper window. The women poured down a quick succession of pails of water; and Charles returned, with good aim, such stones as had found their way in. The gentlemen were little aware, for some time, that the cries of vexation or ridicule, which were uttered now and then, were caused by the feats of their own coadjutors overhead: and it was in consequence of seeing Hester and Margaret laughing in the midst of their panic that the fact became known to them.

Soon after, a bright light was visible between the crevices of the shutters, and a prodigious shout arose outside. The bonfire was kindled. Hester and Margaret went to the upper windows to see it; and when the attacks upon the shutters seemed to have ceased, Enderby joined them. There were very few faces among the crowd that were known even to Charles, whose business it was, in his own opinion, to know everybody. Mr Tucker was evidently only looking on from a distance. Mrs Plumstead had been on the spot, but was gone—terrified into quietness by the fire, into which the rioters had threatened to throw her, if she disturbed their proceedings. She had professed to despise the idea of a ducking in the brook; but a scorching in the fire was not to be braved; so no more was heard of her this night. Three or four of the frequenters of the public-house were on the spot; but though they lent a hand to throw fresh loads of fuel on the fire, they did not take their pipes from their mouths, nor seem to be prime movers in the riot. The yellow blaze lighted up a hundred faces, scowling with anger or grinning with mirth, but they were all strange—strange as the incidents of the day. A little retired from the glare of the fire, was a figure, revealed only when the flame shot up from being freshly fed—Sir William Hunter on horseback with his immovable groom behind him. How long he had been there, nobody in the house could tell; nor whether he had attempted to do anything in behalf of peace and quiet. There he sat, as if looking on for his amusement, and forgetting that he had any business with the scene.

It was no wonder that Dr Levitt was not yet visible. If he should arrive by dawn, that was all that could be expected. But where were Mr Grey and

Sydney? Where was Mr Rowland? Like some of Mr Hope's other neighbours, who ought to have come to his aid on such an occasion, these gentlemen were detained at home by the emotions of their families. Sydney Grey was locked up by his tender mother as securely as Mr Hope's prisoner; and all the boy's efforts to break the door availed only to bruise him full as seriously as the mob would have done. His father was detained by the tremors of his wife, the palpitations of Sophia, and the tears and sobs of the twins, all of which began with the certainty of the first stone having been thrown, and were by no means abated by the sight of the reflection of the flames on the sky. Mr Grey found it really impossible to leave his family, as he afterwards said. He consoled himself with the thought that he had done the best he could, by sending his men. These things were exactly what his partner said. He, too, had done the best he could, in sending his men. He, too, found it impossible to leave his family. In the dusk of the evening, when the first stones had begun to fly, the carriage which was heard, in the intervals of the crashes, to roll by, contained Mrs Rowland and her children, and some one else. It may easily be imagined that it was made impossible to Mr Rowland to leave his family, to go to the assistance of the people in the corner-house.

A fresh shout soon announced some new device. A kind of procession appeared to be advancing up the street, and some notes of rude music were heard. A party was bringing an effigy of Mr Hope to burn on the pile. There was the odious thing—plain enough in the light of the fire—with the halter round its neck, a knife in the right hand, and a phial—a real phial out of Hope's own surgery, in the left!

"This is too bad to be borne," cried Enderby; while Hope, who had come up to see what others were seeing, laughed heartily at the representative of himself. "This is not to be endured. Morris, quick! Fetch me half a dozen candles!"

"Candles, sir?"

"Yes, candles. I will put this rabble to flight. I wish I had thought of it before."

"Oh, Philip!" said Margaret, apprehensively.

"Fear nothing, Margaret. I am going to do something most eminently safe, as you will see."

He would not let any one go with him but Charles and Morris. It was some minutes before any effect from his absence was perceived; but, at length, just when the effigy had been sufficiently insulted, and was about to be cast into the flames, and Hester had begged her husband not to laugh at it any more, a roar of anguish and terror was heard from the crowd, which began to disperse in all directions. The ladies ventured to lean out of the window, to see what was the cause of the uproar. They understood it in a moment. Mr Enderby had possessed himself of the skeleton which hung in the mahogany case in the waiting-room, had lighted it up behind the eyes and the ribs, and was carrying it aloft before him, approaching round the corner, and thus confronting the effigy. The spectre moved steadily on, while the people fled. It made straight for Sir William Hunter, who now seemed for the first time disposed to shift his place. He did so with as much slowness and dignity as were compatible with the urgency of the circumstances, edging his horse further and further into the shade. When he found, however, that the spectre continued to light its own path towards him, there was something rather piteous in the tone of his appeal:— "I am Sir William Hunter! I am—I am Sir William Hunter!" The spectre disregarding even this information, there was nothing for the baronet to do but to gallop off—his groom for once in advance of him. When they were out of sight, the spectre turned sharp round, and encountered Dr Levitt, who was now arriving just when every one else was departing. He started, as might have been expected, spoke angrily to the "idle boy" whom he supposed to be behind the case of bones, and laughed heartily when he learned who was the perpetrator, and what the purpose of the joke. He entered Hope's house, to learn the particulars of the outrage, and order off the prisoner into confinement elsewhere, his ideas being too extensively discomposed to admit of any more sermon-writing this night. Charles had already captured the effigy, and set it up in the hall: a few more pailsful of water extinguished the fire in the street; and in a quarter of an hour the neighbourhood seemed to be as quiet as usual.

"Where are you to sleep after all this fatigue?" said Hope to his wife and sister, when Dr Levitt and Philip were gone, and the men were at their supper below. "I do not believe they have left you a room which is not open to the night air. What a strange home to have put you in! Who would have thought it a year ago?"

Hester smiled, and said she was never less sleepy. Morris believed that not a pane of glass was broken in the attics, and her ladies could sleep there, if they preferred remaining at home to stepping to Mr Grey's. They much preferred remaining where they were: and, on examination, it was found that Margaret's room was also entire. Hope proposed to take possession of Charles's attic, for once; and Charles enjoyed the novelty of having a mattress laid down for him in a corner of the upper landing. Morris tempted the ladies and her master to refresh themselves with tea. She piled up the fire to a Christmas height, to compensate for the draughts which blew in from the broken windows. Hope soon grew discontented with her plan.

"This will never do," said he, shivering. "You will all be ill: and nobody must be ill now, for I have no medicines left."

Morris murmured a wish that the physic had been forced down the people's throats.

"It is better where it is, Morris," said her master; "and we will forgive these poor people; shall we not? They are lamentably ignorant, you see."

Morris thought forgiveness was always pretty sure to come in time but it was not very easy at the moment. She thought she could get over their robbing her master of any amount of property; but she could not excuse their making him ridiculous before his lady's own eyes.

"They cannot make him ridiculous, Morris," said Hester, cheerfully.

"People who are persecuted are considered great, you know, Morris," said Margaret.

"Bravo, ladies!" cried Hope. "You keep up your own spirits, and my complacency, bravely. But seriously, Morris," he continued, perceiving that the vulgarity of the present affliction weighed down the good woman's heart; "is it not true that few of our trials—none of those which are most truly trials—seem dignified at the time? If they did, patience would be easier than it is. The death of martyrs to their faith is grand to look back upon; but it did not appear so to the best of the martyrs at the time. This little trial of ours looks provoking, and foolish, and mean, to us to-night; but whether it really is so, will depend on how we bear it; and whatever it may bring after it, grand or mean, all we have to do is to be good-humoured with it, Morris."

Morris curtsied low.

"And now, to your rooms," resumed Hope: "this place is growing too chilly for you, notwithstanding Morris's capital fire."

"One thing more," said Margaret. "I am a little uneasy about Maria. Has any one thought of her? She must be anxious about us."

"I will go this moment," said Hope. "Nay, my love, it is early yet; no one in Deerbrook is gone to rest yet, but the children. I can be back in ten minutes, and the street is empty."

"Let him go," said Margaret. "It will be a great kindness; and surely there is no danger now."

Hope was gone. He did not come back in ten minutes, nor in half an hour. Even Margaret heartily repented having urged him to leave home. During his absence she thus repented, but no longer when he returned. He brought news which made her hasten to dress herself for the open air, when she was quite ready to retire to rest. It was well that her brother had gone. Maria had been thrown down by the crowd, which had overtaken her as she was walking homewards, and she had broken her leg. The limb was set, the case was a simple and promising one; but she was in pain, and Margaret must go and pass the night with her. How thankful were they all now, that some one had thought of Maria! She had been in extreme anxiety for them; and she would not certainly have sent for aid before the morning. It was indeed a blessing that some one had thought of Maria.

Chapter Twenty Nine

Coming to an Understanding.

Mr Enderby was too angry with his sister to see her that night. He went straight to his room, at his mother's old house, and did not breakfast with the Rowlands. He knocked at their door when breakfast was finished, and sent to request Mrs Rowland's presence in the drawing-room. All this had given the lady time to prepare her mood, and some very clever and bold sayings but when the interview was over, she was surprised to find how some of these sayings had gone out of her mind, and how others had remained there, for want of opportunity to speak them; so that she had not made nearly so good a figure as she had intended.

There was all due politeness in Enderby's way of inducing his sister to sit down, and of asking after the health of herself and her children.

"We are all wonderfully improved, thank you, brother. Indeed I have hopes that we shall all enjoy better health henceforward than we have ever known. Mr Walcot's care will be new life to us."

"Whose care?"

"Mr Walcot's. We brought him with us last night; and he is to go at once into my mother's house. He is a surgeon of the first degree of eminence. I think myself extremely fortunate in having secured him. The chief reason, however, of my inviting him here was, that my poor mother might be properly taken care of. Now I shall be at peace on her account, which I really never was before. Now that she will be in good hands, I shall feel that I have done my duty."

"And, pray, does Rowland know of your having brought this stranger here?"

"Of course. Mr Walcot is our guest till his own house can be prepared for him. As I tell you, he arrived with me, last night."

"And now let me tell you, sister, that either Mr Walcot is not a man of honour, or you have misinformed him of the true state of affairs here: I suspect the latter to be the case. It is of a piece with the whole of your conduct, towards Mr Hope—conduct unpardonable for its untruthfulness, and hateful for its malice."

Not one of Mrs Rowland's prepared answers would suit in this place. Before she could think of anything to say, Enderby proceeded:—

"It is a dreadful thing for a brother to have to speak to a sister as I now speak to you; but it is your own doing. Mr Hope must have justice, and you have no one to blame but yourself that justice must be done at your expense. I give you fair notice that I shall discharge my duty fully, in the painful circumstances in which you have contrived to place all your family."

"Do what you will, Philip. My first duty is to take care of the health of my parent and my children; and if, by the same means, Deerbrook is provided with a medical man worthy of its confidence, all Deerbrook will thank me."

"Ignorant and stupid as Deerbrook is about many things, Priscilla, it is not so wicked as to thank any one for waging a cowardly war against the good, for disparaging the able and accomplished, and fabricating and circulating injurious stories against people too magnanimous for the slanderer to understand."

"I do not know what you mean, Philip."

"I mean that you have done all this towards the Hopes. You do not know that he and his wife are not happy. You know that Hope is an able and most humane man in his profession, and that he does not steal dead bodies. You know the falsehood of the whole set of vulgar stories that you have put into circulation against him. You know, also, that my mother has entire confidence in him, and that it will go near to break her heart to have him dismissed for any one else. This is the meaning of what I say. As for what I mean to do—it is this. I shall speak to Mr Walcot at once, before his intention to settle here is known."

"You are too late, my dear sir. Every one in Deerbrook knows it as well as if Dr Levitt was to give notice of it from the pulpit to-day."

"So much the worse for you, Priscilla. I shall explain the whole of Hope's case to Mr Walcot, avoiding, if possible, all exposure of you—."

"Oh, pray do not disturb yourself about that. Mr Walcot knows me very well. I am not afraid."

"Avoiding, if possible, all exposure of you," resumed Enderby, "but not shrinking from the full statement of the facts, if that should prove necessary to Hope's justification. If this gentleman be honourable, he will decline attending my mother, and go away more willingly than he came. I shall bear testimony to my friend with equal freedom everywhere else; and I will never rest till the wrongs you have done him are repaired—as far as reparation is possible."

"You take the tone of defiance, I see, Philip. I have not the slightest objection. We defy each other, then."

"I cannot but take that tone for a purpose which, I conceive, is the kindest which, under the circumstances, can be entertained towards you, sister. I do it in the hope that, before it is too late, you will yourself do the justice which I vow shall be done. I give you peremptory warning, leaving you opportunity to retrieve yourself, to repair the mischief you have done, and to alleviate the misery which I see is coming upon you."

"You are very good: but I know what I am about, and I shall proceed in my own way. I mean to get rid of these Hopes; and, perhaps, you may be surprised to see how soon I succeed."

"The Hopes shall remain as long as they wish to stay, if truth can prevail against falsehood. I am sorry for you, if you cannot endure the presence of neighbours whose whole minds and conduct are noble and humane, and known by you to be so. This desire to get rid of them is a bad symptom, Priscilla—a symptom of a malady which neither Hope nor Mr Walcot, nor any one but yourself, can cure. I would have you look to it."

"Is your sermon ended? It is time I was getting ready to hear Dr Levitt's."

"What I have to say is not finished. I desire to know what you mean by telling everybody that I am engaged to Miss Mary Bruce."

"I said so, because it is true."

The cool assurance with which she said this was too much for Enderby's gravity. He burst out a-laughing.

"If not precisely true when I said it, it was sure to be so soon; which is just the same thing. I mean that it shall be true. I have set my heart upon your marrying, and upon your marrying Mary Bruce. I know she would like it, and—"

"Stop there! Not another word about Miss Bruce! I will not have you take liberties with her name to me; and this is not the first time I have told you so. It is not true that she would like it—no more true than many other things that you have said: and if you were to repeat it till night, it would make no sort of impression upon me. Miss Bruce knows little, and cares less, about me; and beware how you say to the contrary!—And now for the plain fact. I am engaged elsewhere."

"No; you are not."

"Yes; I am."

"You will marry no one but Mary Bruce at last, you will see, whatever you may think now."

"For Heaven's sake, Priscilla, if you have any of the regard you profess to have for Miss Bruce, treat her name with some respect!—I am accepted by Margaret Ibbotson!"

"I dare say you are? Margaret Ibbotson! So this is at the bottom of all your energy about the Hopes!"

"I admired Hope before I ever saw Margaret, with sufficient energy to prompt me to anything I mean to do in his support. But Margaret has certainly exalted my feelings towards him, as she has towards everything morally great and beautiful."

"I hope you will all make yourselves happy with your greatness and your beauty: for these friends of yours seem likely to have little else left to comfort themselves with."

"They will be happy with their greatness and loveliness, sister; for it is Heaven's decree that they should. Why will you not let yourself be happy in witnessing it, Priscilla? Why will you not throw off the restraint of bad feelings, and do magnanimous justice to this family, and, having thus opened and freed your mind, glory in their goodness—the next best thing to being as good as they? You have power of mind to do this: the very force with which you persist in persecuting them shows that you have power for better things. Believe me, they are full of the spirit of forgiveness. Do but try—"

"Thank you. I am glad you are aware of my power. If they forgive me for anything, it shall be for my power."

"That is not for you to determine, happily. To what extent they forgive is between God and themselves. You lie under their forgiveness, whether you will or not. I own, Priscilla, I would fain bestow on Margaret a sister whom she might respect rather than forgive."

"Pray how many persons have you persuaded that Margaret Ibbotson is to be my sister-in-law?"

"Very few; for your sake, scarcely any. We have been willing to allow you your own time and methods for extricating yourself from the difficulties you have made for yourself by your inconsiderate talk about Miss Bruce. I own I cannot conceive how you could originate and carry on such a device. You must now get out of the scrape in your own way."

"I am glad you have told so few people of your entanglement. It makes it an easier matter to help you. I shall deny the engagement everywhere."

"That will hardly avail against my testimony."

"It will, when you are gone. The Deerbrook people always attend to the last speaker. Indeed, I think I have the majority with me now, as the events of last night pretty plainly show."

"Hope is not the first good man who has been slandered and suffered violence. Oh, Priscilla, I am unwilling to give you up! Let me hope, that the pride, the insane pride of this morning, is but the reaction of your internal suffering from witnessing the results of your influence in the outrages of last night. Confide this to me now, and give yourself such ease as you yet can."

"Thank you: but you are quite mistaken. I was extremely glad to arrive when I did. It satisfied me as to the necessity of getting rid of these people; and it proved to Mr Walcot, as I observed to him at the time, how much he was wanted here. Now, if you have nothing more to say to me, I must go. I shall deny your engagement everywhere."

Philip fixed his eyes upon her with an earnestness from which, for one moment, she shrank; but she instantly rallied, and returned him a stare which lasted till she reached the door.

"There is something almost sublime in audacity like this," thought he. "But it cannot last. It comes from internal torture—a thing as necessarily temporary as faith (the source of the other kind of strength) is durable. Not the slightest compunction has she for having caused the misery she knows of: and not a whit would she relent if she could become aware (which she never shall) of what she made Margaret suffer. I fear my Margaret has still much to endure from her. I will watch and struggle to ward off from her every evil word and thought. This is the only comfort under the misery of her being exposed to the malice of any one belonging to me. No; not the only comfort. She does not suffer from these things as she did. She says she has a new strength; and, thank God! I believe it. Now for Mr Walcot! I must catch him as he comes out of church, and see what I can make of him. If he is an honourable man, all may turn out well. If not—Rowland and I must see what can be done next."

Chapter Thirty

Condolence.

The family in the corner-house thought this the strangest Sunday morning they had ever looked upon. Outside their premises, all was like a May sabbath. The gardens sent up their fragrance into the warm, still air: the cottage windows were open, and early roses and late hyacinths appeared within the casements. The swallows were skimming and dipping about the meadows; and the swans steered their majestic course along the river, rippling its otherwise unbroken surface. The men of the village sat on the thresholds of their doors, smoking an early pipe! and their tidy children, the boys with hair combed straight, and the girls with clean pinafores, came abroad; some to carry the Sunday dinner to the baker's, and others to nurse the baby in the sunshine, or to snatch a bit of play behind a neighbour's dwelling. The contrast within the corner-house was strange. Morris and the boy had been up early to gather the stones, and sweep up the fragments of glass from the floors, to put the effigy out of sight, and efface the marks of feet in the hall and parlours. The supper had been cleared away in the kitchen, and the smell of spirits and tobacco got rid of: but this was all that the most zealous servants could do. The front shutters must remain closed, and the garden windows empty of glass. The garden itself was a mournful spectacle,—the pretty garden, which had been the pride and pleasure of the family all this spring; part of the wall was thrown down; the ivy trailed on the earth. Of the shrubs, some were pulled up, and others cut off at the roots. The beds were trodden into clay, and the grass, so green and sunny yesterday, was now trampled black where it was not hidden with fragments of the wood-work of the surgery, and with the refuse of the broken glasses and spilled drugs. Hope had also risen early. He had found his scared pupil returned, and wandering about the ruins of his abode,—the surgery. They set to work together, to put out of sight whatever was least seemly of the scattered contents of the professional apartment; but, with all their pains, the garden looked forlorn and disagreeable enough when Hester came down, shawled, to make breakfast in the open air of the parlour, and her husband thought it time to go and see how Maria had passed the night, and to bring Margaret home.

Hester received from her husband and sister a favourable report of Maria. She had slept, and Margaret had slept beside her. Maria carried her philosophy into all the circumstances of her lot, and she had been long used to pain and interruption of her plans. These things, and the hurry of an accident in the street, might dismay one inexperienced in suffering, but not her. When not kept awake by actual pain, she slept; and when assured that her case was perfectly simple, and that there was every probability of her being as well as usual in a few weeks, all her anxieties were for the Hopes. No report of them could have satisfied her so well as Mr Hope's early visit,—as his serene countenance and cheerful voice. She saw that he was not sad at heart; and warmly as she honoured his temper, she could hardly understand this. No wonder for she did not know what his sufferings had previously been from other causes, nor how vivid was his delight at the spirit in which Hester received their present misfortunes. Margaret saw at once that all was well at home, and made no inquiries about her sister.

"Here is a letter for you, with a magnificent seal," said Hester, as they entered. "And here is tea as hot, I believe, as if we were still blessed with glass windows."

The letter had just been left by Sir William Hunter's groom. It was from the Baronet, and its contents informed Mr Hope that his attendance would not be required at the almshouses in future, as their inmates were placed under the medical superintendence of Mr Walcot.

"I am glad," said Hester. "No more danger and insult from that quarter!"

"Nor funds either, my dear. It is pleasant enough to have no insult and danger to apprehend; but what will you say to having no funds?"

"We shall see when that time comes, love. Meantime, here is breakfast, and the sweet Sunday all before us?"

The pressure of her hand by her husband effaced all woes, present and future.

"Who is Mr Walcot?" asked Margaret.

"Somebody from Blickley, I suppose," said Hester.

"No," replied Hope. "Mr Walcot is a surgeon, last from Cheltenham, who settled in Deerbrook at seven o'clock yesterday evening, and who has already swept the greater part of the practice of the place, I suspect. He is, no doubt, the 'better doctor,' 'the new man,' of whom we have heard so much of late."

Hester changed colour, and Margaret too, while Hope related the arrival of Mrs Rowland and her party, as he had heard it from his pupil early this morning.—What sort of man was Mr Walcot? Time must show. His coming to settle in this manner, at such a conjuncture of circumstances, did not look very well, Hope said; but it should be remembered that he must necessarily be extremely prejudiced against the family in the corner-house, if his information about Deerbrook was derived from Mrs Rowland. He ought not to be judged till he had had time and opportunity to learn for himself what was the real state of affairs in the place. He must have fair play; and it was very possible that he might turn out a man who would give others fair play.

At the next knock, Hester started, thereby showing that she was moved. Mr Jones had called to know how the family were; and, after satisfying himself on this point, had left a delicate sweetbread, with his respects, and wishes that Mrs Hope might relish it after her fright. This incident gave the little family more pleasure than Mr Walcot had yet caused them pain. Here was sympathy,—the most acceptable offering they could receive.

Next came a message of inquiry from Dr and Mrs Levitt, with an intimation that they would call, if not inconvenient to the family, after church. This was pleasant too.

While it was being agreed that a nurse must be found immediately for Maria, and that the glazier at Blickley must have notice to send people to mend the windows as early as possible to-morrow morning, a letter was brought in, which looked longer, but less grand, than Sir William Hunter's. It was from Mr Rowland.

"(Private.)

"My Dear Sir, *Sunday Morning, 7 o'clock.*

"During the greater part of an anxious night, my mind was full of the intention of calling on you this morning, for some conversation on a topic which must be discussed between us; but the more I dwell upon what must be said, the more I shrink from an interview which cannot but be extremely painful to each party; and I have at length come to the conclusion that, for both our sakes, it is best to write what I have to say. It is painful enough, God knows, to write it!

"Your position here, my dear sir, must have been anything but pleasant for some time past. I regret that its uneasiness should have been augmented, as I fear it has, by the influence of any one connected with myself. My respect for you has been as undeviating as it is sincere; and I have not to reproach myself with having uttered a word concerning you or your family which I should be unwilling to repeat to yourselves: but I am aware that the same cannot be said with regard to every one for whom I am in a manner answerable. In relation to this unpleasant fact I can only say, that I entreat you to accept the assurance of my deep regret and mortification.

"A new aspect of affairs has presented itself,—to me very suddenly, as I trust you will believe, on my word of honour. A gentleman of your profession, named Walcot, arrived last night, with a view to settling in Deerbrook. The first inducement held out to him was the medical charge of Mrs Enderby, and of the whole of my family: but, of course, it is not probable that his expectations of practice among your patients stop here; and the present unfortunate state of the public mind of Deerbrook regarding yourself, makes it too probable that his most sanguine expectations will be realised. I write this with extreme pain; but I owe it to you not to disguise the truth, however distasteful may be its nature.

"These being the circumstances of the case, it appears to me hopeless to press the departure of Mr Walcot. And if he went away to-day, I should fear that some one would arrive to-morrow to occupy his position. Yet, my dear sir, justice must be done to you. After protracted and anxious consideration, one mode of action has occurred to me by which atonement may be made to you for what has passed. Let me recommend it to your earnest and favourable consideration.

"Some other place of residence would, I should hope, yield you and your family the consideration and comfort of which you have here been most unjustly deprived. Elsewhere you might ensure the due reward of that professional ability and humanity which we have shown ourselves unworthy to appreciate. If you could reconcile yourself to removing, with your family, I believe that the peace of our society would be promoted, that unpleasant collisions of opinions and interests would be avoided, and that that reparation would be made to you which I fear would be impracticable here. All difficulty about the process of removal might and should be obviated. To speak frankly, I should, in that case, consider myself your debtor to such an amount as, by a comparison of your losses and my means, should appear to us both to be just. I believe I might venture to make myself answerable for so much as would settle you in some more favourable locality, and enable you to wait a moderate time for that appreciation of your professional merits which would be certain to ensue.

"I need not add that, in case of your acceding to my proposition, all idea of *obligation* would be misplaced. I offer no more than I consider actually your due. The circumstance of the father of a large and rising family offering to become responsible to such an extent, indicates that my sense of your claim upon me is very strong. I should be glad to be relieved from it: and I therefore, once more, beseech your best attention to my proposal,—*the latter particulars of which have been confided to no person whatever*,—nor shall they be, under any circumstances, unless you desire it.

"I shall await your reply with anxiety—yet with patience, as I am aware that such a step as I propose cannot be decided on without some reflection.

"I rejoice to find that your family have not suffered materially from the outrages of last night. It was matter of sincere regret to me that the unexpected arrival of my family at the very time prevented my hastening to offer my best services to you and yours. The magistracy will, of course, repair all damages; and then I trust no evil consequences will survive.

"I beg my best compliments to Mrs Hope and Miss Ibbotson, and entreat you to believe me, my dear sir,

"With the highest respect,

"Your obedient servant,

"H. Rowland."

For one moment Hester looked up in her husband's face, as he read this letter in a subdued voice—for one moment she hoped he would make haste to live elsewhere—in some place where he would again be honoured as he once was here, and where all might be bright and promising as ever: but that moment's gaze at her husband changed her thoughts and wishes. Her colour rose with the same feelings which drew a deep seriousness over his countenance.

"Mr Rowland means well," said Margaret; "but surely this will never do."

"I hardly know what you would consider meaning well," replied Hope. "Rowland would buy himself out of an affair which he has not the courage to manage by nobler means. He would give hush-money for the concealment of his wife's offences. He would bribe me from the assertion of my own character, and would, for his private ends, stop the working out of the question between Deerbrook and me. This is, to my mind, the real aspect of his proposal, however persuaded he himself may be that he intends peace to his neighbours, and justice to me. This letter," he continued, waving it before him, "is worthy only of the fire, where I would put it this moment, but that I suppose prudence requires that we should retain in our own hands all evidence whatever relating to the present state of our affairs."

"I do not exactly see what is to become of us," said Hester, cheerfully.

"Nor do I, love: but is not all the world in the same condition? How much does the millionaire know of what is to intervene between to-day and his death?"

"And the labouring classes," observed Margaret—"that prodigious multitude of toiling, thinking, loving, trusting beings! How many of them see further than the week which is coming round? And who spends life to more purpose than some of them? They toil, they think, they love, they obey, they trust; and who will say that the most secure in worldly fortune are making a better start for eternity than they? They see duty around them and God above them; and what more need they see?"

"You are right," said Hester. "What I said was cowardly. I wish I had your faith."

"You have it," said her husband. "There was faith in your voice, and nothing faithless in what you said. It is a simple truth, that we cannot see our way before us. We must be satisfied to discern the duty of the day, and for the future to do what we ought always to be doing—'to walk by faith and not by sight.' Now, as to this present duty, it seems to me very clear. It is my duty to offer moral resistance to oppression, and to make a stand for my reputation. When it pleases God that men should be overwhelmed by calumny, it is a dreadful evil which must be borne as well as it may; but not without a struggle. We must not too hastily conclude that this is to be the issue in our case. We must stay and struggle for right and justice—struggle for it, by living on with firm, patient, and gentle minds. This is surely what we ought to do, rather than go away for the sake of ease, leaving the prejudices of our neighbours in all their virulence, because we have not strength to combat them, and letting the right succumb to the wrong, for want of faith and constancy to vindicate it."

"Oh, we will stay!" cried Hester. "I will try to bear everything, and be thankful to have to bear, for such reasons. It is all easy, love, when you lay open your views of our life—when you give us your insight into the providence of it. I believe I should have looked at it in this way before, if you had been suffering in any great cause—any cause manifestly great, because the welfare of many others was involved in it. I see now that the principle of endurance and the duty of steadfastness are the same, though—." And yet she paused, and bit her lip.

"Though the occasion looks insignificant enough," said her husband. "True. Some might laugh at our having to appeal to our faith because we have been mobbed on pretences which make us blush to think what nonsense they are, and because a rival has come to supplant me in my profession. But with all this we have nothing to do. The truth to us is, that we are living in the midst of malice and hatred, and that poverty stares us in the face. If these things are quite enough for our strength (and I imagine we shall find they are so), we have no business to quarrel with our trial because it is not of a grander kind. Well! wife and sister, we stay. Is it not so? Then I will go and write to Mr Rowland."

The sisters were silent for some moments after he had left them. Margaret was refreshing her flowers—the flowers which Philip had brought in from the garden the day before. How precious were they now, even above other flowers brought by the same hand—for not another blossom was left in the desolate garden! Margaret was resolving silently that she would keep these alive as long as she could, and then dry them in memory of the place they came from, in its wedding trim. Hester presently showed the direction her thoughts had taken, by saying—

"I should think that it must be always possible for able and industrious people, in health, to obtain bread."

"Almost always possible, provided they can cast pride behind them."

"Ah! I suspect that pride is the real evil of poverty—of gentlefolks' poverty. I could not promise for my own part, to cast pride behind me: but then, you know, it has pleased God to give me something to be proud of, far different from rank and money. I could go to jail or the workhouse with my husband without a blush. The agony of it would not be from pride."

"Happily, we are sure of bread, mere bread," said Margaret, "for the present, and for what we call certainty. What you and I have is enough for bread."

"What I have can hardly be called sufficient for even that," said Hester: "and you—I must speak my thankfulness for that—you will soon be out of the reach of such considerations."

"Not soon: and I cannot separate my life from yours—I cannot fancy it. Do not let us fancy it just now."

"Well, we will not. I am glad Susan has warning from me to go. It is well that we began retrenching so soon. We must come to some full explanation with Morris, that we may see what can best be done for her."

"She will never leave you while you will let her stay."

"It may be necessary to dismiss Charles. But we will wait to talk that over with my husband. He will tell us what we ought to do. Was that a knock at the door?"

"I rather think it was a feeble knock."

It was Mrs Grey, accompanied by Sydney. Mrs Grey's countenance wore an expression of solemn misery, with a little of the complacency of excitement under it. The occasion was too great for winks: mute grief was the mood of the hour. Sydney was evidently full of awe. He seemed hardly to like to come into the parlour. Margaret had to go to the door, and laugh at him for his shyness. His mother's ideas were as much deranged as his own by the gaiety with which Hester received them, boasting of the thorough ventilation of the room, and asking whether Sophia did not think their bonfire surpassed the famous one at the last election but one. Sophia had not seen anything of the fire of last night. She had been so much agitated, that the whole family, Mr Grey and all, had been obliged to exert themselves to compose her spirits. Much as she had wished to come this morning, to make her inquiries in person, she had been unable to summon courage to appear in the streets; and indeed her parents could not press it—she had been so extremely agitated! She was now left in Alice's charge.

Hester and Margaret hoped that when Sophia found there was nothing more to fear, and that her cousins were perfectly well, she would be able to spare Alice for some hours, to wait upon Miss Young. Maria's hostess was with her now, and Margaret would spend the night with her again, if a nurse could not be procured before that time. Mrs Grey had not neglected Maria in her anxiety for her cousins. She was just going to propose that Alice should be the nurse to-night, and had left word at Miss Young's door that she herself would visit her for the hour and half that people were in church. Her time this morning was therefore short. She was rejoiced to see her young friends look so much like themselves—so differently from what she had dared to expect. And Mr Hope—it was not fair perhaps to ask where he was;—he had probably rather not have it known where he might be found: (and here the countenance relaxed into a winking frame). Not afraid to show himself abroad! Had been out twice! and without any bad consequences! It would be a cordial to Sophia to hear this, and a great relief to Mr Grey. But what courage! It was a fine lesson for Sydney. If Mr Hope was really only writing, and could spare a minute, it would be a comfort to see him. Hester went for him. He had just finished his letter. She read and approved it, and sat down to take a copy of it while her husband occupied her seat beside Mrs Grey.

The wife let fall a few tears—tears of gentle sorrow and proud love, not on her husband's letter (for not for the world would she have had that letter bear a trace of tears), but on the paper on which she wrote. The letter appeared to her very touching; but others might not think so: there was so much in it which she alone could see! It took her only a few minutes to copy it; but the copying gave her strength for all the day. The letter was as follows:—

"My Dear Sir—Your letter expresses, both in its matter and phrase, the personal regard which I have always believed you to entertain towards me and mine. I cannot agree with you, however, in thinking that the proceeding you propose involves real good to any of the parties concerned in it. The peace of society in Deerbrook is not likely to be permanently secured by such deference to ignorant prejudice as would be expressed by the act of my departure; nor would my wrongs be repaired by my merely leaving them behind me. I cannot take money from your hands as the price of your tranquillity, and as a commutation for my good name, and the just rewards of my professional labours. My wife and I will not remove from Deerbrook. We shall stay, and endeavour to discharge our duty, and to bear our wrongs, till our neighbours learn to understand us better than they do.

"You will permit to say, with the respect which I feel, that we sympathise fully in the distress of mind which you must be experiencing. If you should find comfort in doing us manful justice, we shall congratulate you yet more than ourselves: if not, we shall grieve for you only the more deeply.

"My wife joins me in what I have said, and in kindly regards.

"Yours sincerely,

"Edward Hope."

Edward had left his seal with Hester. She sealed the letter, rang for Charles, and charged him to deliver it into Mr Rowland's own hands, placed the copy in her bosom to show to Margaret, and returned to the parlour. Mrs Grey, who was alone with Hope, stopped short in what she was saying.

"Go on," said Hope. "We have no secrets here, and no fears of being frightened—for one another any more than for ourselves. Mrs Grey was saying, my dear, that Mr Walcot is very popular here already; and that everybody is going to church to see him."

Mrs Grey had half-a-dozen faults or oddities of Mr Walcot's to tell of already; but she was quietly checked in the middle of her list by Mr Hope, who observed that he was bound to exercise the same justice towards Mr Walcot that he hoped to receive from him—to listen to no evil of him which could not be substantiated: and it was certainly too early yet for anything to be known about him by strangers, beyond what he looked like.

"To go no deeper than his looks, then," continued Mrs Grey, "nobody can pretend to admire them. He is extremely short. Have you heard how short he is?"

"Yes; that inspired me with some respect for him, to begin with. I have heard so much of my being too tall, all my life, that I am apt to feel a profound veneration for men who have made the furthest escape from that evil. By the way, my dear, I should not wonder if Enderby is disposed in Walcot's favour by this, for he is even taller than I."

"I am surprised that you can joke on such a subject, Mr Hope. I assure you, you are not the only sufferers by this extraordinary circumstance of Mr Walcot's arrival. It is very hard upon us, that we are to have him for an opposite neighbour—in Mrs Enderby's house, you know. Sophia and I have been in the habit of observing that house, for the old lady's sake, many times in a day. We scarcely ever looked out, but we saw her cap over the blind, or some one or another was at the door, about one little affair or another. It has been a great blank since she was removed—the shutters shut, and the bills up, and nobody going and coming. But now we can never look that way."

"I am afraid you will have to get Paxton to put up a weathercock for you on his barn, so that you may look in the opposite direction for the wind."

"Nay, Edward, it is really an evil," said Hester, "to have an unwelcome stranger settled in an opposite house, where an old friend has long lived. I can sympathise with Mrs Grey."

"So can I, my dear. It is an evil: but I should, under any circumstances, hold myself free to look out of my window in any direction—that is all. Do, Mrs Grey, indulge yourself so far."

"We cannot possibly notice him, you know. It must be distinctly understood, that we can have nothing to say to an interloper like Mr Walcot. Mr Grey is quite of my opinion. You will have our support in every way, my dear sir; for it is perfectly plain to our minds, that all this would not have happened but for your having married into our connection so decidedly. But this intruder has been thought, and talked about, by us more than he is worth. I want to hear all you can tell me about the riot, Hester, love. Your husband has been giving me some idea of it, but... Bless me! there is the first bell for church; and I ought to have been at Miss Young's by this time. We must have the whole story, some day soon; and, indeed, Sophia would quarrel with me for hearing it when she is not by. Where is Sydney?"

Sydney and Margaret were in the garden, consulting about its restoration. Sydney declared he would come and work at it every day till it was cleared and planted. He would begin to-morrow with the cairn for the rock-plants.

"I am glad the Levitts are to call after church," observed Mrs Grey. "They always do what is proper, I must say; and not less towards dissenters than their own people. I suppose Dr Levitt will consult with you about the damages."

"Sooner or later, I have no doubt."

"Come, Sydney, we must be gone. You hear the bell. Sophia will be quite revived by what I shall tell her, my dears. No—do not come out to the door—I will not allow it, on my account. There is no knowing what I might have to answer for, if you let yourself be seen at the door on my account. I am sorry you will not come in this evening. Are you quite determined? Well, perhaps Mr Grey will say you are right not to leave your premises in the evening, at present. No; you must not say anything about *our* coming just now. We have not courage, really, for that. Now hold your tongue, Sydney. It is out of the question—your being out of our sight after dark. Good morning, my love."

As soon as Charles returned home, after having delivered the letter into Mr Rowland's own hands, Mr Hope gathered his family together, for their Sunday worship. The servants entered the room with countenances full of the melancholy which they concluded, notwithstanding all evidence to the contrary, that their master and mistress must be experiencing: but, when service was over, they retired with the feeling that the family-worship had never been more gladsome.

Chapter Thirty One

Keeping Sunday.

Mr Enderby was in the churchyard when the congregation poured out from the porch. Group after group walked away, and he saw no signs of the party he was waiting for. Mrs Rowland lingered in the aisle, with the intention of allowing all Deerbrook time to look at Mr Walcot. When none but the Levitts remained, the lady issued forth from the porch, leaning on Mr Walcot's arm, and followed by four of her children, who were walking two and two, holding up their heads, and glancing round to see how many people were observing the new gentleman they had brought with them from Cheltenham. Mr Enderby approached the family party, and said—

"Sister, will you introduce me to Mr Walcot?"

"With the greatest pleasure, my dear brother. Mr Walcot, my brother, Mr Enderby. Brother, my friend, Mr Walcot."

Mr Walcot blushed with delight, looked as if he longed to shake hands if he dared, and said something of his joy at becoming acquainted with the brother of so kind a friend as Mrs Rowland.

"There is not much to be apprehended here," thought Mr Enderby. "How perfectly unlike what I had fancied! This dragon, which was to devour the Hopes, seems a pretty harmless creature. Why he looks a mere boy, and with hair so light, one can't see it without spectacles. What will he do with himself in my mother's good house? Fanny Grey's bird-cage would suit him better;—and then he might hang in Rowland's hall, and be always ready for use when the children are ill. I must have out what I mean to say to him, however; and, from his looks, I should fancy I may do what I please with him. He will go away before dinner, if I ask him, I have little doubt. I wonder that, while she was about it, Priscilla did not find out somebody who had the outside of a professional man at least. This youth looks as if he would not draw one's tooth for the world, because it would hurt one so! How he admires the rooks and the green grass on the graves, because the children do!—Sister," he continued aloud, "I am sorry to deprive you of your companion; but it is absolutely necessary that Mr Walcot and I should have some conversation together immediately. The children will go home with you; and we will follow presently."

Mrs Rowland looked thunder and lightning at her brother; but Mr Walcot appeared so highly pleased, that she considered it safest to acquiesce in the present arrangement, trusting to undo Philip's work in the course of the afternoon. So she sailed away with the children.

"This is no time for ceremony," observed Enderby, as he led the way to the walk under the trees. "I have used none with my sister, as you perceive; and I shall use none with you."

"Thank you, sir. My dear parents have always taught me that there could be no occasion for ceremony where people feel kindly, and mean only what is right. They will be pleased to hear that you do not think ceremony necessary between us."

"The circumstances are too urgent for it in the present case;—that is what I mean," said Philip. "I am confident, Mr Walcot, from what you say about feeling kindly and meaning rightly, that you cannot be aware what is the real state of affairs in Deerbrook, or you could not have been induced to think of settling here."

"Oh, I assure you, sir, you are mistaken. Mrs Rowland herself was the person who told me all about it; and I repeated all she said to my parents. They strongly advised my coming; and I am sure they would never recommend me to do anything that was not right."

"Then, if I tell you what I know to be the true state of the case here, will you represent it fully to your parents, and see what they will say then?"

"Certainly. I can have no objection to that. They will be very sorry, however, if any difficulty should arise. I had a letter from them this very morning, in which they say that they consider me a fortunate youth to have fallen in with such a friend as Mrs Rowland, who promises she will be a mother, or rather, I should say, a sister to me, and to have stepped at once into such practice as Mrs Rowland says I shall certainly have here. They say what is very true, that it is a singular and happy chance to befall a youth who has only just finished his education."

"That is so true, that you ought not to be surprised if it should turn out that there is something wrong at the bottom of the affair. I am going to show you what this wrong is, that you may take warning in time, and not discover, when it is too late, that you have been injuring an honourable man, who has been too hardly treated already."

"I should be sorry to do that: but I cannot think what you can mean."

"I dare say not. Pray have you been told of a Mr Hope who lives here?"

"Oh, yes; we saw the people breaking his windows as we drove past, yesterday evening. He must be a very improper, disagreeable man. And it is very hard upon the ladies and gentlemen here to have no one to attend them but that sort of person."

"That is one account of Mr Hope: now you must hear the other." And Mr Enderby gave a full statement of Hope's character, past services, and present position, in terms which he conceived to be level with the capacity of the young man. He kept his sister out of the story, as far as it was possible, but did not soften the statement of her calumnies, though refraining from exhibiting their origin. "Now," said he, at the end of his story, "have I not shown cause for consideration, as to whether you should settle here or not?"

"For consideration, certainly. But, you see, it is so difficult to know what to think. Here is Mrs Rowland telling me one set of things about Mr Hope, and you tell me something quite different."

"Well, what do you propose to do?"

"I shall consult my parents, of course."

"Had not you better set off by the coach to-morrow morning, and tell your parents all about it before you commit yourself?"

"I do not see how I could do that very well, as I have engaged to go over and see these people in Sir William Hunter's almshouses, that I am to have the charge of. No; I think my best way will be this. I will write fully to my parents first. I will do that this afternoon. Then, considering that I have said I shall stay here, and that the house is going to be got ready for me,— and considering how hard it is upon the ladies and gentlemen here to have nobody to attend them but a person they do not like,—and considering, too, that I cannot tell for myself what Mr Hope really is, while people differ so about him, I think I had better wait here (just as I should have done if you had not told me all this) till Mrs Rowland, and you, and Sir William Hunter, and everybody, have settled whether Mr Hope is really a good man or not: and then, you know, I can go away, after all, if I please."

Philip thought that Dr Levitt must have been preaching to his new parishioner to join the wisdom of the serpent with the harmlessness of the dove. Mr Walcot himself seemed quietly satisfied with his own decision, for he adhered to it, repeating it in answer to every appeal that Philip could devise.

"I think it right to warn you," said Philip, "that if the prospect of being my mother's medical attendant has been part of your inducement to settle here, you have been misled in relying on it. My mother is much attached to Mr Hope and his family; she prefers him to every other medical attendant; and I shall take care that she has her own way in this particular."

"While I am in Mrs Rowland's house, I shall, of course, attend Mrs Rowland's family," replied Mr Walcot.

"Her children, if she pleases; but not necessarily her mother."

"Yes; her mother too, as I dare say you will see."

"You will allow Mrs Enderby to choose her own medical attendant, I presume?"

"Oh, yes: and I have no doubt she will choose me. Mrs Rowland says so."

"Here comes a gentleman with whom I want to speak," said Philip, seeing Mr Grey approaching from a distance. "He is as warm a friend and admirer of Mr Hope as I am; and—"

"Mr Hope married into his family,—did not he?"

"Yes; but Mr Grey and Mr Hope were friends long before either of them was acquainted with Mrs Hope. The friendship between the gentlemen was more likely to have caused the marriage than the marriage the friendship."

"Ah! that does happen sometimes, I know."

"What I was going to say is this, Mr Walcot, that Mr Hope's friends have determined to see justice done him; and that if, in the prosecution of this design, you should imagine that you are remarkably coolly treated,—by myself, for instance,—you must remember that I fairly warned you from the beginning that I shall give no countenance to any one who comes knowingly to establish himself on the ruins of a traduced man's reputation. You will remember this, Mr Walcot."

"Oh, certainly. I am sure I shall expect nothing from anybody; for nobody here knows me. It is only through Mrs Rowland's kindness that I have any prospect here at all."

"I will just give you one more warning, as you seem a very young man. The Deerbrook people are apt to be extremely angry when they are angry at all. What would you think of it, if they should break your windows, as they broke Mr Hope's last night, when they find that you have been thriving upon his practice, while they were under a mistake concerning him which you were fully informed of?"

"I do not think I should mind it. I might get over it, you know, as Mr Hope would then have done. Or I might go away, after all, if I pleased. But you want to speak to that gentleman; so I will wish you good morning."

"You will represent to your parents all I have said? Then, pray, do not omit the last,—about what dreadful people the Deerbrook people are when they are angry; and how likely it is that they may be very angry with you some day. I advise you by all means to mention this."

"Yes, certainly; thank you. I shall write this afternoon."

"I wish Mrs Rowland joy of her fledgling," said Enderby, as he joined Mr Grey.

"I was just thinking, as you and he came up, that a few lessons from the drill-sergeant at Blickley would do him no harm. Perhaps, however, your sister will teach him to hold up his head better. I rather think he is a little scared with the rooks, is not he? What in the world is your sister to do with him, now she has got him here?"

"I hope little Anna will lend him her cup and ball on rainy days."

"Do you find him a simpleton?"

"I hardly know. One must see him more than once to be quite sure. But enough of him for the present. I have just come from the corner-house; but I am not going to talk about the Hopes either: and yet I have something out of the common way to say to you, my good friend."

"I am glad you call me by that name," observed Mr Grey, kindly. "I never could see, for the life of me, why men should look askance upon one another, because their relations, (no matter on which side, or perhaps on both), happen to be more or less in the wrong."

"And there are other reasons why you and I should beware of being affected by the faults and weaknesses of our connections, Mr Grey,—and that is what I have now to say. I mean, because we may become connected ourselves. How will you like me for a relation, I wonder."

"It is so, then?"

"It is so: and it is by Margaret's desire that I inform you of it now, before the circumstance becomes generally known. If you think Mrs Grey will be gratified by early information, I believe I must beg that you will go home and tell her directly. We are as fully aware as you can be, of the absurdity of this way of talking: but circumstances compel us to—"

"I know, I understand. People here have been persuaded that you were engaged to some other lady; and you will have no help in contradicting this from your own family, who may not like your marrying into our connection so decidedly—as I have heard the ladies say about our friend Hope."

"Just so."

"Well, my opinion is, that it is of little consequence what your friends may say now, when time is so sure to justify your choice. There is no need for me to tell you that you are a happy man, Mr Enderby. There is not a more amiable girl living than that cousin Margaret of mine. I charge you to make her happy, Enderby. I do not mean that I have any doubt of it: but I charge you to make her happy."

Philip did not like to speak (any more than to do other things) without being pretty sure of doing it well. He was silent now because he could not well speak. He was anything but ashamed of his attachment to Margaret; but he could not open his lips upon it.

"I trust there is the better chance of her being happy," continued Mr Grey, "that she is going to marry a man of somewhat less enthusiasm than her sister has chosen, Mr Enderby."

"Do not speak of that, Mr Grey. We might not agree. I can only say that I am so fully sensible of my immeasurable inferiority to Hope, I know I am hardly worthy to appreciate him... I cannot give you an idea of my sense of his superiority... And to hear him set below me...

"Do not mistake me, my dear friend. No one can value Mr Hope more than I do, as indeed I have every reason to do. Only you see the effects of that unfortunate vote of his. That is just what I mean, now. If you had been in his place, I rather think you would have done what was prudent—you would not have run into anything so useless as giving that vote, when there was not another person in Deerbrook to vote the same way. You would not, Enderby."

"I trust I should, if I had had Margaret to keep me up to my duty."

"Well, well; I may be wrong; but it vexes me to see anxiety and sorrow in my cousin Hester's beautiful face; and that is the truth of it. But, indeed, her husband is a fine fellow, and I respect him from the bottom of my soul; and it makes me extremely happy to hear that Margaret has met with one whom I can as cordially approve. You have my hearty good wishes, I assure you. Now, when may I see my cousin, to wish her joy? I must go home now, and let my family know about it, you say?"

"If you please; for I must tell Margaret how kindly you have received what I had to communicate. She will be waiting anxiously."

"Why, she could not doubt my good will, surely? How should I be otherwise than pleased? Nor have I any doubt of my wife's feeling. You stand very high in her good graces, Enderby, I can assure you. I was not fully aware of this myself, till I saw how vexed she was at hearing that you were engaged to that lady abroad. She never could make out what Margaret was feeling about that; but she used to say to me when we were by ourselves, that if Margaret was not hurt and angry, she was. But I suppose the little gipsy was laughing at us and all Deerbrook all the time; though she kept her gravity wonderfully."

Philip was not disposed to throw any light on this part of the affair; and the gentlemen parted at the turnstile. After a few steps, Philip heard himself called. Mr Grey was hastening after him, to know whether this matter was to be spoken of, or to remain quiet, after Mrs Grey had been informed. He had perfectly understood that all Deerbrook was soon to know it; but it was a different question whether his family were to be authorised to tell it. Mr Enderby desired they would follow their own inclinations entirely. Margaret's only wish was, that her kind relations should be informed directly from herself before anybody else but her friend, Miss Young: and his own only desire was, that, on Margaret's account, every one should understand that his engagement was to her, and not to any lady at Rome or elsewhere. Virtual provision having thus been made for the enlightenment of all Deerbrook in the course of the day, the gentlemen once more went their respective ways.

In her present mood of amiability, Mrs Rowland determined on giving the Greys the pleasure of a call from Mr Walcot. In the afternoon, when Fanny was saying her catechism to her mamma, and Mary was repeating a hymn to Sophia, Mrs Rowland's well-known knock was heard, and any religious feelings which might have been aroused in the minds of the little girls were put to flight by the sound. Sophia turned her feet off the sofa, where she had been lying all day, that Mrs Rowland might not suspect that she had suffered from the mobbing of the Hopes. The children were enjoined not to refer to it, and were recommended to avoid the subject of Miss Young also, if possible.

The amazement and wrath of the party at hearing Mr Walcot announced was beyond expression. Mrs Grey was sufficiently afraid of her neighbour to confine herself to negative rudeness. She did the most she dared in not looking at Mr Walcot, or asking him to sit down. He did not appear to miss her attentions, but seated himself beside her daughter, and offered remarks on the difference between Deerbrook and Cheltenham. Sophia made no intelligible replies, and looked impenetrably reserved; he therefore tried another subject, enlarged upon Mrs Rowland's extreme kindness to him, and said that his parents wrote that they considered him a fortunate youth in having met with a friend who would be a mother or sister to him, now that he was no longer under the parental wing. Sophia had intended to be quite distant and silent, but his long-winded praises of all the Rowlands were too much for her. She observed that it was generally considered that there was nobody in Deerbrook to compare with the family in the corner-house—the Hopes and Miss Ibbotson. From this moment, the *tête-à-tête* became animated; the speakers alternated rapidly and regularly; for every virtue in a Rowland there was a noble quality in a Hope; for every accomplishment in Matilda and Anna, there was a grace in "our dear Mr Hope" or "our sweet Hester." Fanny and Mary listened with some amusement to what they heard on either side of their pair of low stools. As sure as they were desired particularly to avoid any subject with the Rowlands, they knew that their mother would presently be in the midst of it. The prohibition showed that her mind was full of it: and whatever her mind was full of was poured out upon Mrs Rowland. The two ladies were presently deep in the riot, and almost at high words about Miss Young. The girls looked at each other, and strove to keep the corners of their mouths in order. In the midst of the conflict of sentiment on these two subjects, Mrs Rowland's ear caught what Sophia was saying—that there was one person in the same house with Mr Walcot who properly estimated the Hopes—Mr Enderby, who was engaged to Margaret Ibbotson. While Mr Walcot was carefully explaining that Mr Enderby was not in the same house, Mr Enderby having a bed at his mother's house still, though that house was already preparing for the reception of himself, its new tenant, Mrs Rowland leaned forward with her most satirical air, and begged to assure Miss Grey that she had been misinformed—that what she had just been saying was a mistake.

Sophia looked at her mother in absolute terror, lest they should have adopted a joke of her father's for earnest. But Mrs Grey was positive. Mrs Rowland laughed more and more provokingly: Mrs Grey grew more and more angry; and at last sent the little girls to see whether their father was at home, that he might bear his testimony. He came; and in reply to his astonishment about what she could mean, Mrs Rowland said that she did not deny that there was some present entanglement; but that she warned Margaret's connections not to suppose that her brother would ever be married to Miss Ibbotson. Mr Grey observed that time would show, and inquired after Mrs Enderby. The report of her was very flattering indeed. She was to be quite well now soon. Mr Walcot's opinion of her case was precisely what Mrs Rowland had always held. Mrs Enderby's complaints were nervous—nervous altogether. With retirement from common acquaintances, and the society of the dear children, and the attendance of a servant (most highly recommended) who would not humour her fancies as Phoebe had done; and, above all, with a medical attendant under the same roof for the present, she was to be quite well immediately. Mr Walcot's countenance wore an expression of perfect delight at the prospect, and Mr Grey's of the blackest displeasure.

When the visitors were gone, Mr Walcot being allowed to find his way out as he could, the little girls heard them discussed in the way which might be expected, and were then desired to finish their catechism and hymn. Mamma and Sophia were still flushed and agitated with what they had been hearing and saying, when the low serious voices of Fanny and Mary recited—the one an abjuration of all envy, malice, hatred, and uncharitableness; and the other—

> "Teach me to feel for others' woe,
> To hide the faults I see;
> The mercy I to others show,
> That mercy show to me."

"You have a warning, my dear," said Mrs Grey to Fanny, "in the lady who was here just now—a terrible warning against malice and all those faults. You see how unhappy she makes every one about her, by her having indulged her temper to such a degree. You see—"

"Mary, my darling," said Mr Grey, "repeat that hymn to me again:—

> "'Teach me to feel for others' woe,
> To hide the faults I see.'

"Let us have that hymn over again, my dear child."

Chapter Thirty Two

Going to Rest.

Mr Walcot had arrived nearly at the end of his letter to his parents, when summoned to attend Mrs Rowland to call on the Greys. He was afterwards glad that he had left room to put in that perhaps what Mr Enderby had said about Deerbrook ought to be the less regarded, from its having come out that he was in an entanglement with the sister-in-law of this Mr Hope, when he had rather have been engaged to another person—being actually, indeed, attached to a lady now abroad. He represented that Mrs Rowland evidently paid very little regard to her brother's views of Deerbrook affairs, now that his mind was in a state of distraction between his proper attachment and his new entanglement. So Mr Enderby's opinion ought not to go for more than it was worth.

The letter was still not quite finished when he was called to Mrs Enderby. She was very ill, and Mr Rowland and Phoebe were alarmed. Philip was at the corner-house. Mrs Rowland was gone to see Miss Young, to convince her that she must put herself into Mr Walcot's hands immediately—to declare, indeed, that she should send her own medical man to attend her dear children's governess. The argument occupied some time, and Mrs Rowland's absence was protracted. Mrs Enderby had been extremely terrified, the evening before, at the noises she had heard, and the light of the bonfire upon the sky. The children were permitted to carry to her all the extravagant reports that were afloat about Mr Hope being roasted in the fire, the ladies being in the hands of the mob, and so forth; and though her son-in-law had seen her before she settled for the night, and had assured her that everybody was safe, she could not be tranquillised. She thought he was deceiving her for her good, and that the children were probably nearest the truth. She was unable to close her eyes, and in the middle of the night told Phoebe that she could not be satisfied—she should not have a moment's peace—till she had seen some one of the dear people from the corner-house, to know from themselves that they were quite safe. Phoebe had found it difficult to persuade her that it was now two o'clock in the morning, and that they were all, no doubt, sleeping in their beds. She passed a wretched night; and the next day, after Philip had succeeded in composing her, a strange gentleman was brought to her to prescribe for her. This revived her terrors. She said she would ask no more questions, for all were in league to deceive her. Then she cried because, she had said so harsh a thing, and begged that Phoebe would not expose it. Her weeping continued till Phoebe's heart was almost broken. The infallible drops failed; arrowroot was in vain; the children were sent away as soon as they came in, as it would hurt their spirits, their mother thought, to see distress of this kind. In the afternoon quiet was prescribed by the authorities, and the old lady was left alone with Phoebe. To the weeping succeeded the spasms, so violent that little George was despatched with all speed to summon his uncle, and Mr Walcot was called away from crossing the ends of his letter. No one but he proposed sending for Mrs Rowland; and his hint to that effect was not taken.

Philip arrived in a shorter time than could have been supposed possible. Mr Rowland then immediately disappeared. He had formed the heroic resolution of bringing Margaret into the house, on his own responsibility, for Mrs Enderby's relief and gratification and he was gone to tell Margaret that he considered her now as Mrs Enderby's daughter, and was come to summon her to the sick bed. Philip presently discovered that the presence of some one from the Hopes would be the best cordial that could be administered; and he set forth on the same errand—to bring Margaret, that she might have his protection in case of his sister returning before her arrival. Mrs Rowland did return: and the two gentlemen, having taken different roads to the corner-house (it being a matter of old dispute which was the shortest) missed each other. Margaret was gone with Mr Rowland before Philip arrived.

"Here I will leave you," said Mr Rowland to Margaret, on the steps of his own house. "You will find Philip and Phoebe upstairs, and Mr Walcot. I must go in search of Mr Hope, and beg the favour of him to tell me whether we are proceeding rightly with our patient. She is too ill for ceremony."

Margaret wondered why, if this was the case, Mr Rowland did not bring Edward to the patient at once; but she had her wonder to herself, for her escort was gone. The servant did not more than half-open the door, and seemed unwilling to let Margaret enter; but she passed in, saying that she must see Phoebe for a moment. She soon found that she was to be left standing on the mat; for no person appeared, though she thought she heard whispers upstairs. Ned coming to peep from the study-door, she beckoned him to her, and asked to be shown to where Phoebe was. The child took her hand, and led her upstairs. At the top of the first flight she met the lady of the house, who asked her, with an air of astonishment, what she wanted there? Margaret replied that Mr Rowland had brought her to see Mrs Enderby. That was impossible, the lady replied. Mr Rowland knew that Mrs Enderby was too ill to receive visitors. She herself would send for Miss Ibbotson whenever it should be proper for Mrs Enderby to admit strangers. Margaret replied that she must see Phoebe—that she should not retire till she had spoken to her, or till Mr Rowland's return. Mrs Rowland sent Ned to desire the servant to open the door for Miss Ibbotson; and Margaret took her seat on a chair on the landing, saying that, relying on her title to be admitted to Mrs Enderby, at the desire of her old friend herself, and of all the family but Mrs Rowland, she should wait till she could obtain admittance.

How rejoiced was she, at this moment, to hear the house door open, to hear the step she knew so well, to see Philip, and to have her arm drawn within his!

"Let us pass," said he to his sister, who stopped the way.

"Rest a moment," said Margaret. "Recover your breath a little, or we shall flurry her."

"She is flurried to death already," said Philip, in his deepest tone of emotion. "Priscilla, our mother is dying; it is my belief that she is dying. If you have any humanity,—if you have any regard for your own future peace of mind, conduct yourself decently now. Govern your own family as you will, when you have lost your mother; but hold off your hand from her last hours."

"Your own last hours are to come," said Margaret. "As you would have Matilda be to you then, be you to your mother now."

"I must ascertain one thing, Philip," said Mrs Rowland. "Does my mother know of what you call your engagement to Miss Ibbotson?"

"She does not; and the sole reason is, that I would not subject her to what you might say and do. I wished, for her own sake, to keep the whole affair out of her thoughts, when once I had removed the false impressions you had given her. But Margaret and I may see fit to tell her now. I may see fit to give her the comfort of a daughter who will be to her what you ought to have been."

He gently drew his sister aside, to make way for Margaret to pass.

"In my own house!" exclaimed Mrs Rowland, in a tone of subdued rage.

"We should have been in the house over the way," replied her brother; "and we act as if we were there. Come, my Margaret, we are doing right."

"We are," replied Margaret; but yet she trembled.

"I must go in first, and tell her that I have brought you," said Philip. "And yet I do not like to leave you, even for a moment."

"Oh, never mind! I am not to be shaken now."

Mrs Rowland did not appear during the two long minutes that Margaret was left by herself in the dressing-room. When Philip came for her, he said:

"You must not leave her again. You will stay, will not you? You shall be protected: but you must stay. I shall tell her how we stand to each other,—we will tell her,—carefully, for she cannot bear much emotion.—You are tired,—you must be tired," he continued, looking at her with anxiety: "but—"

"Do not speak of it. I did sleep last night, and there will be time enough for sleep when duty is done,—the duty for which I have longed ever since I knew what duty was." And her eyes swam in tears.

Phoebe's face was a dismal sight,—too dismal for the sickroom, for so many hours had she been in tears. She was dismissed to refresh herself with a turn in the garden. It was Philip's doing that she was at hand at all. Mrs Rowland had ordained that she should go; but Philip had supported the girl in her resolution to bear anything, rather than leave her mistress while it was essential to her mistress's comfort that she should stay.

Mrs Enderby was in great pain; but yet not suffering too much to be comforted by finding that all were safe and well in the corner-house. She even smiled when the others laughed at the ridiculous stories with which the children had assaulted her imagination. She thought it was very wrong for people to fabricate such things, and tell them to children:—they might chance to put some extremely old ladies into a terrible fright.—She was soothed in the very midst of a spasm, by hearing that Margaret would stay with her as long as she liked, if it would be of any comfort to her. In answer to her surprise and almost alarm at such a blessing, Philip said that Margaret wished it as a pleasure, and asked it as a sort of right. Now, could she not guess any reason why it was a sort of right of Margaret's to attend upon her like a daughter? Yes,—it was so indeed! Margaret was to be her daughter—some time or other,—when her big boy should have learned all his lessons, as little George would say.

"I am thankful! Indeed I *am* thankful, my dears, to hear this. But, my loves, that will be too late for me. I rejoice indeed; but it will be too late for me."

"Well, then, let me be your daughter now."

The old lady clasped her arms about Margaret, and endured her next paroxysm with her head upon her young friend's shoulder.

"I have a daughter already," said she, when she revived a little: "but I have room in my heart for another: and I always had you in my heart, my love, from the first moment I saw you."

"You hold all the world in your heart, I think."

"Ah! my love, you flatter me. I mean I took to you particularly from the very hour I saw you. You have always been so kind and gentle with me!"

Margaret's heart swelled at the thought that any one could ever have been otherwise than kind and gentle to one so lowly and so loving.

Nothing more could be done than was done for the sufferer. Hope saw her, at Mr Rowland's desire, and said this. He left directions with Margaret, and then declined staying where his presence could be of no use, and caused much annoyance. Mrs Enderby was sinking rapidly. The probability was, that a few hours would end the struggle. Mrs Rowland was much alarmed and shocked. She went and came between the drawing-room and her mother's chamber, but talked of the claims of her children at such a time, and persuaded herself that her duty lay chiefly with them. Others wanted no persuasion about the matter. They were too glad to have her dispose herself where she would be out of her mother's way. Mrs Enderby looked round now and then, and seemed as if on the point of asking for her, but that her courage failed. At last, about eight in the evening, when Mrs Rowland had come in softly, and Phoebe had met her at the door, to say something very unceremonious, Mrs Enderby's voice was heard.

"Phoebe, I hope you are not preventing any person from coming in. I should wish to see my daughter. Priscilla, my dear, let me see you. Come to me, my dear."

Mrs Rowland's face was very pale, and her brow told of a dreadful headache. There was a dark expression in her countenance, but the traces of irritability were gone. She was subdued for the hour.

"My dear daughter," said Mrs Enderby, "I may not be able at another time to thank you as I should like for all the care you have taken of me:— nor can I now do it as I could wish: but I thank you, my love."

Mrs Rowland involuntarily cast a glance at her brother and Margaret, to see how they took this: but their eyes were fixed on her mother.

"And I can only say," continued Mrs Enderby, "that I am aware that you must have had many things to bear from me. I must have been much in your way, and often—"

Margaret and Philip implored her to say nothing of this kind; they could not bear it from one who was all patience herself, and gave no cause for forbearance in others. Mrs Rowland did not speak—perhaps because she could not.

"Well, well; I will not dwell upon these things. You are all very kind. I only wanted to say that I was sensible of—of many things. Priscilla—"

"Mother!" said she, starting.

"This dear young friend of ours,—she calls herself my daughter, bless her!—is to be your sister, my love. Philip has been telling me—. Let me see—. Give me the pleasure of seeing—"

Margaret could have opened her arms to any spectre from the pale kingdoms at a moment like this, and under the imploring eye of Mrs Enderby. She disengaged her hand from that of her old friend, and took Mrs Rowland's, offering to kiss her cheek. Mrs Rowland returned the kiss, with some little visible agitation.

"Thank you, my dears!" said Mrs Enderby, in a strong voice of satisfaction. She had made a great effort. Her speech now failed her; but they thought she would have said something about the children.

"The children—" said Mrs Rowland, rather eagerly. She turned, and went slowly out of the room. The moment the door was shut, there was a heavy fall. She had fainted on the outside.

Her mother heard it not. When Mrs Rowland was found to be reviving, the children were brought to their grandmamma's room. They quietly visited the bed, one by one, and with solemnity kissed the wasted cheek,— the first time they had ever kissed grandmamma without return. The baby made its remark upon this in its own way. As it had often done before, it patted the cheek rather roughly: several hands were instantly stretched out to stop its play; it set up a cry, and was hurried out of the room.

By the middle of the night, Margaret was longing to be at home and alone. It was all over. She was ashamed to think of her own share of the loss while witnessing Philip's manly grief, or even while seeing how Phoebe lamented, and how Mr Rowland himself was broken-down; but not the less for this was her heart repeating, till it was sick of itself, "I have lost another mother."

She did not see Mrs Rowland again.

In the earliest grey of the morning, Mr Rowland took Margaret home. As they stood on the steps, waiting to be let in, she observed that the morning star was yellow and bright in the sky. As soon as the sun had risen, the toll of the church bell conveyed to every ear in Deerbrook the news that Mrs Enderby was dead. Perhaps there might have been compunction in the breasts of some who had been abroad on Saturday night, on hearing the universal remark that it must have been rather sudden at last.

Chapter Thirty Three

Moving Onward.

The world rolls on, let what may be happening to the individuals who occupy it. The sun rises and sets, seed-time and harvest come and go, generations arise and pass away, law and authority hold on their course, while hundreds of millions of human hearts have stirring within them struggles and emotions eternally new,—an experience so diversified as that no two days appear alike to any one, and to no two does any one day appear the same. There is something so striking in this perpetual contrast between the external uniformity and internal variety of the procedure of existence, that it is no wonder that multitudes have formed a conception of Fate,—of a mighty unchanging power, blind to the differences of spirits, and deaf to the appeals of human delight and misery; a huge insensible force, beneath which all that is spiritual is sooner or later wounded, and is ever liable to be crushed. This conception of Fate is grand, is natural, and fully warranted to minds too lofty to be satisfied with the details of human life, but which have not risen to the far higher conception of a Providence to whom this uniformity and variety are but means to a higher end than they apparently involve. There is infinite blessing in having reached the nobler conception; the feeling of helplessness is relieved; the craving for sympathy from the ruling power is satisfied; there is a hold for veneration; there is room for hope: there is, above all, the stimulus and support of an end perceived or anticipated; a purpose which steeps in sanctity all human experience. Yet even where this blessing is the most fully felt and recognised, the spirit cannot but be at times overwhelmed by the vast regularity of aggregate existence,—thrown back upon its faith for support, when it reflects how all things go on as they did before it became conscious of existence, and how all would go on as now, if it were to die to-day. On it rolls,—not only the great globe itself, but the life which stirs and hums on its surface, enveloping it like an atmosphere;—on it rolls; and the vastest tumult that may take place among its inhabitants can no more make itself seen and heard above the general stir and hum of life, than Chimborazo or the loftiest Himalaya can lift its peak into space above the atmosphere. On, on it rolls; and the strong arm of the united race could not turn from its course one planetary mote of the myriads that swim in space: no shriek of passion nor shrill song of joy, sent up from a group of nations on a continent, could attain the ear of the eternal Silence, as she sits throned among the stars. Death is less dreary than life in this view—a view which at times, perhaps, presents itself to every mind, but which speedily vanishes before the faith of those who, with the heart, believe that they are not the accidents of Fate, but the children of a Father. In the house of every wise parent may then be seen an epitome of life,—a sight whose consolation is needed at times, perhaps, by all. Which of the little children of a virtuous household can conceive of his entering into his parent's pursuits, or interfering with them? How sacred are the study and the office, the apparatus of a knowledge and a power which he can only venerate! Which of these little ones dreams of disturbing the course of his parent's thought or achievement? Which of them conceives of the daily routine of the household—its going forth and coming in, its rising and its rest—having been different before his birth, or that it would be altered by his absence? It is even a matter of surprise to him when it now and then occurs to him that there is anything set apart for him,—that he has clothes and couch, and that his mother thinks and cares for him. If he lags behind in a walk, or finds himself alone among the trees, he does not dream of being missed; but home rises up before him as he has always seen it—his father thoughtful, his mother occupied, and the rest gay, with the one difference of his not being there. Thus he believes, and has no other trust than in his shrieks of terror, for being ever remembered more. Yet, all the while, from day to day, from year to year, without one moment's intermission, is the providence of his parent around him, brooding over the workings of his infant spirit, chastening its passions, nourishing its affections,—now troubling it with salutary pain, now animating it with even more wholesome delight. All the while is the order of household affairs regulated for the comfort and profit of these lowly little ones, though they regard it reverently because they cannot comprehend it. They may not know of all this,—how their guardian bends over their pillow nightly, and lets no word of their careless talk drop unheeded, hails every brightening gleam of reason, and records every sob of infant grief; and every chirp of childish glee,—they may not know this, because they could not understand it aright, and each little heart would be inflated with pride, each little mind would lose the grace and purity of its unconsciousness: but the guardianship is not the less real, constant, and tender, for its being unrecognised by its objects. As the spirit expands, and perceives that it is one of an innumerable family, it would be in danger of sinking into the despair of loneliness if it were not capable of:—

> "Belief
> In mercy carried infinite degrees
> Beyond the tenderness of human hearts,"

while the very circumstance of multitude obviates the danger of undue elation. But, though it is good to be lowly, it behoves every one to be sensible of the guardianship of which so many evidences are around all who breathe. While the world and life roll on and on, the feeble reason of the child of Providence may be at times overpowered with the vastness of the system amidst which he lives; but his faith will smile upon his fear, rebuke him for averting his eyes, and inspire him with the thought, "Nothing can crush me, for I am made for eternity. I will do, suffer and enjoy, as my Father wills and let the world and life roll on!"

Such is the faith which supports, which alone can support, the many who, having been whirled in the eddying stream of social affairs, are withdrawn, by one cause or another, to abide, in some still little creek, the passage of the mighty tide. The broken-down statesman, who knows himself to be spoken of as politically dead, and sees his successors at work building on his foundations, without more than a passing thought on who had laboured before them, has need of this faith. The aged who find affairs proceeding at the will of the young and hardy, whatever the grey-haired may think and say, have need of this faith. So have the sick, when they find none but themselves disposed to look on life in the light which comes from beyond the grave. So have the persecuted, when, with or without cause, they see themselves pointed at in the streets; and the despised, who find themselves neglected, whichever way they turn. So have the prosperous, during those moments which must occur to all, when sympathy fails, and means to much desired ends are wanting, or when satiety makes the spirit roam abroad in search of something better than it has found. This universal, eternal, filial relation is the only universal and eternal refuge. It is the solace of royalty weeping in the inner chambers of its palaces, and of poverty drooping beside its cold hearth. It is the glad tidings preached to the poor, and in which all must be poor in spirit to have part. If they be poor in spirit, it matters little what is their external state, or whether the world which rolls on beside or over them be the world of a solar system, or of a conquering empire, or of a small-souled village.

It now and then seemed strange to Hope, his wife and sister—now and then, and for a passing moment—that while their hearts were full of motion and their hands occupied with the vicissitudes of their lot, the little world around them, which was wont to busy itself so strenuously with their affairs, should work its yearly round as if it heeded them not. As often as they detected themselves in this thought, they smiled at it; for might not each neighbour say the same of them as constituting a part of the surrounding world? there a cottage where some engrossing interest did not defy sympathy; where there was not some secret joy, some heart-sore, hidden from every eye; some important change, while all looked as familiar as the thatch and paling, and the faces which appeared within them? Yet there seemed something wonderful in the regularity with which affairs proceeded. The hawthorn hedges blossomed, and the corn was green in the furrows: the saw of the carpenter was heard from day to day, and the anvil of the blacksmith rang. The letter-carrier blew his horn as the times came round; the children shouted in the road; and their parents bought and sold, planted and delved, ate and slept, as they had ever done, and as if existence were as mechanical as the clock which told the hours without fail from the grey steeple. Amidst all this, how great were the changes in the corner-house!

In the early spring, the hearts of the dwellers in that house had been, though far less dreary than in the winter, still heavy at times with care. Hester thought that she should never again look upon the palm boughs of the willow, swelling with sap, and full of the hum of the early bees, or upon the bright green sprouts of the gooseberry in the cottage gardens, or upon the earliest primrose of the season on its moist bank, without a vivid recollection of the anxieties of this first spring season of her married life. The balmy month of May, rich in its tulips, and lilacs, and guelder roses, was sacred to Margaret, from the sorrow which it brought in the death of Mrs Enderby. She wandered under the hedgerows with Philip, during the short remainder of his stay, and alone when he was gone; and grew into better acquaintance with her own state of heart and mind, and into higher hope for the future of all whom she loved most. When the mowers were in the field, and the chirping fledgelings had become birds of the air, and the days were at the longest, her country rambles became more precious, for they must henceforth be restricted;—they must be scarcer and shorter. In the place of the leisure and solitude for books in her own room and for meditation in the field—leisure and solitude which had been to this day more dreamed of than enjoyed, she must now betake herself to more active duty. The maid Susan was discharged at Midsummer: and not only Susan. After ample consultation with Morris, it was decided that Charles must go too, his place being in part supplied by a boy of yet humbler pretensions out of the house, who should carry out the medicines from the surgery, and do the errands of the family. Morris spoke cheerfully enough of these changes, smiled as if amused at the idea of her leaving her young ladies; and did not doubt but that, if Miss Margaret would lend her a helping hand sometimes, she should be able to preserve the credit of the family.

There was something more to be done than to lend this helping hand in the lighter domestic offices. Their Midsummer remittance had been eagerly looked for by the sisters, not only because it was exceedingly wanted for the current expenses of the household, but because it was high time that preparations were begun for the great event of the autumn—the birth of Hester's little one. During this summer, Margaret was up early, and was busy as Morris herself about the house till breakfast, and for some time after Hope had gone forth on his daily round—now so small that he soon returned to his books and his pen in the study. The morning hours passed pleasantly away, while Hester and Margaret sat at work by the window which looked into their garden, now, by Sydney's care, trimmed up into a state of promise once more. Hester was so much happier, so reasonable, so brave, amidst her sinking fortunes, that Margaret could scarcely have been gayer than in plying her needle by her side. Their cares lay chiefly out of doors now: the villagers behaved rudely to Edward, and cherished Mr Walcot; Mrs Rowland took every opportunity of insulting Margaret, and throwing discredit on her engagement; and the Greys caused their cousins much uneasiness by the spirit in which they conducted their share of the great controversy of the place. These troubles awaited the corner-house family abroad; but their peace was perpetually on the increase at home. Morris and they were so completely in one interest, Edward was so easily pleased, and they were so free from jealous dependants, that they could carry their economy to any extent that suited their conscience and convenience. One superfluity after another vanished from the table; every day something which had always been a want was discovered to be a fancy; and with every new act of frugality, each fresh exertion of industry, their spirits rose with a sense of achievement, and the complacency proper to cheerful sacrifice. In the evenings of their busy days, the sisters went out with Edward into their garden, or into the meadows, or spent an hour in the Greys' pretty shrubbery. Maria often saw them thus, and thought how happy are they who can ramble abroad, and find their cares dispersed by the breeze, or dissolved in the sunshine of the fields. The little Rowlands sometimes met them in the lanes: and the younger ones would thrust upon them the wild flowers which Mr Walcot had helped them to gather, while Mrs Rowland and Matilda would draw down their black crape veils, and walk on with scarcely a passing salutation. Every such meeting with the lady, every civil bow from Mr Walcot, every tale which Mrs Grey and Sophia had to tell against the new surgeon, seemed to do Hester good, and make her happier. These things were appeals to her magnanimity; and she could bear for Edward's sake many a trial which she could not otherwise have endured. All this told upon the intercourse at home; and Morris's heart was often cheered, as she pursued her labours in kitchen or chamber, with the sound of such merry laughter as had seldom been heard in the family, during the anxious winter that had gone by. It seemed as if nothing depressed her young ladies now. There was frequent intelligence of the going over of another patient to Mr Walcot; the summer was not a favourable one, and everybody else was complaining of unseasonable weather, of the certainty of storms in the autumn, of blight, and the prospect of scarcity; yet, though Mr Grey shook his head, and the parish clerk could never be seen but with a doleful prophecy in his mouth, Morris's young master and mistresses were gay as she could desire. She was piously thankful for Margaret's engagement; for she concluded that it was by means of this that other hearts were working round into their true relation, and into a peace which the world, with all its wealth and favours, can neither make nor mar.

In one of Margaret's hedgerow rambles with Philip, a few days after his mother's funeral, she had been strongly urged to leave Deerbrook and its troubles behind her—to marry at once, and be free from the trials from which he could not protect her, if she remained in the same place with Mrs Rowland. But Margaret steadily refused.

"You will be wretched," said Philip; "you will be wretched—I know you will—the moment I am gone."

"I never was less likely to be wretched. Mrs Rowland cannot make me so, and other people will not. I have every expectation of a happy summer, which I mention for your sake; for I do not like to indulge in that sort of anticipation without some such good reason as comforting you."

"You cannot be happy here. Priscilla will never let you have an easy day, while she fancies she can separate us. When I think of the pertinacity with which she disowns you, the scorn with which she speaks about you, even in my presence, I see that nothing will do but your being mine at once."

"That would not mend the matter. Our haste and imprudence would go to countenance the scandal she spreads. Why cannot we rather live it down?"

"Because your spirit will be broken in the mean time. Margaret, I must be your guardian. This is my first duty, and an absolute necessity. If you will not go with me, I will not leave this place: and if my plan of life is broken up, you will be answerable for it. It was your plan, and you may demolish it if you choose."

"I have a plan of life, too," said Margaret. "It is to do the duty that lies nearest at hand; and the duty that lies nearest at hand is, to keep you up to yours. After this, there is one which lies almost as close, I cannot leave Hester and Edward till this crisis in their fortunes is past. I am bound to them for the present."

"What are their claims to mine?"

"Nothing, if they were fortunate, as I trust they yet may be;—nothing, if you had followed your plan of life up to the point when we may carry it out together. We are wrong, Philip, in even thinking of what you say. You must go and study law, and you must go without me. Indeed, I could not be happy to join you yet. Your good name would suffer from what Mrs

Rowland might then say. Your future prospects would suffer from the interruption of your preparation for your profession. I should feel that I had injured you, and deserted my own duty. Indeed, Philip, I could not be happy."

"And how happy do you imagine we shall be apart?"

Margaret gave him a look which said what words could not—what it was to be assured of his love. What, it seemed to ask, could all the evil tongues in the world do to poison this joy?

"Besides," said she, "I have the idea that I could not be spared; and there is great pleasure in that vanity. Edward and Hester cannot do without me at present."

"You may say so at any future time."

"No: when the right time comes, they will not want me. Oh, Philip! you are grieved for them, and you long to see them prosperous. Do not tempt me to desert them now. They want my help; they want the little money I have; they want my hands and head. Let this be your share of the penalty Mrs Rowland imposes upon us all—to spare me to them while their adversity lasts."

"I would not be selfish, Margaret—I would not trespass upon your wishes and your duty, but the truth is, I sometimes fear that I may have some heavier penalty even than this to pay for Priscilla's temper. Ah! you wonder what can be heavier. Remember she has put misunderstanding between us before."

"But she never can again. Ours was then merely a tacit understanding. Now, supposing me ever to hear what she may hint or say, do you imagine I should give the slightest heed to it? I would not believe her news of a person I had never seen; and do you think she can make the slightest impression on me with regard to you."

"It seems unreasonable at this moment; but yet, I have a superstitious dread of the power of spirits of evil."

"Superstitious, indeed! I defy them all, now that we have once understood each other. If she were able to do far more than she can—if she could load the winds with accusations against you—if she could haunt my dreams, and raise you up in visions mocking at me—I believe she could not move me now. Before, I blamed myself—I thought I was lost in vanity and error: now that I have once had certainty, we are safe."

"You are right, I trust—I believe it. But there is a long hard battle to be fought yet. It fills me with shame to think how she treats you in every relation you have. She is cruel to Maria Young. She hopes to reach you through her. Ah! you will hear nothing of it from Maria, I dare say; but she spoke infamously to her this morning, before Mrs Levitt. Mrs Levitt happened to be sitting with Maria, when Priscilla and one or two of the children went in. Mrs Levitt spoke of us: Priscilla denied our engagement: Maria asserted it—very gently, but quite decidedly. Priscilla reminded her of her poverty and infirmities, spoke of the gratitude she owed to those from whom she derived her subsistence, and reproached her with having purposes of her own to answer, in making matches in the families of her employers."

"And Maria?"

"Maria trembled excessively, the children say, weak and reduced by pain as she is. One can hardly conceive of temper carrying any woman into such cruelty! Mrs Levitt rose, in great concern and displeasure, to go: but Maria begged her to sit down again, sent one of the children for me, and appealed to me to declare what share she had had in my engagement with you. I set her right with Mrs Levitt, who, I am convinced, sees how the matter stands. But it was really a distressing scene."

"And before the children, too!"

"That was the worst part of it. They stood looking from the furthest corner of the room in utter dismay. It would have moved any one but Priscilla to see the torrent of tears Maria shed over them, when they came timidly to wish her good morning, after Mrs Levitt was gone. She said she could do nothing more for them: they had been taught to despise her, and her relation to them was at an end."

"It is; it must be," exclaimed Margaret. "Is there no way of stopping a career of vice like this? While Mrs Plumstead gets a parish boy whipped for picking up her hens' eggs from among the nettles, is Maria to have no redress for slander which takes away her peace and her bread?"

"She shall have redress. For the children's sake, as well as her own, her connection with them must go on. I do not exactly see how; but the thing must be done. I dread speaking to poor Rowland about any of these things; I know it makes him so wretched: but the good and the innocent must not be sacrificed. If these poor children must despise somebody, their contempt must be made to fall in the right place, even though it be upon their mother."

"Let us go and see Maria," said Margaret, turning back. "If there is a just and merciful way of proceeding in this case, she will point it out. I wish you had told me all this before. Here have we been rambling over the grass and among the wild-flowers, where, at the best, Maria can never go; and she lies weeping all alone, looking for me, I dare say, every moment! Let us make haste."

Philip made all the haste that was compatible with gathering a handful of wild hyacinth and meadow narcissus for poor Maria. He found himself farther from success than ever, when he would have again urged Margaret to marry at once. A new duty seemed to have sprung up to keep her at Deerbrook. Maria wanted her. Her summer work lay clear before her. She must nurse and cheer Maria, she must ply her needle for Hester, and play the housewife, spending many of her hours in the business of living; a business which is often supposed to transact itself, but, which in reality requires all the faculties which can be brought to it, and all the good moral habits which conscience can originate. The most that Philip could obtain was, permission to come when his duties would fairly allow it, and a promise that he should be summoned, if Margaret found herself placed in any difficulty by Mrs Rowland.

Maria was not now literally alone; nor did she depend on her hostess or on Margaret for nursing and companionship. It occurred to all the kindest of her friends, immediately after Mrs Enderby's death, that Phoebe might be her attendant. Phoebe was not, just then, the most cheerful of nurses, so truly did she mourn her good old mistress; but she was glad of occupation, glad to be out of Mrs Rowland's way, glad to be useful: and she was an inestimable comfort to Maria.

Nothing could be done about placing the children again under Maria's care, when she had recovered. Mr Rowland was naturally unwilling to stir in the business, and saw that the best chance for his children was to send them to school at a distance from Deerbrook: and Maria had been too grossly insulted in the presence of her pupils to choose to resume her authority. The Greys took her up with double zeal, as the Rowlands let her down. They assured her that her little income should not suffer for her being able to devote all her time to Fanny and Mary. The money, indeed, was nothing to Mrs Grey, in comparison with the pleasure it procured her. It put her upon equal terms with Mrs Rowland, at last. She did not know how it was, but it was very difficult to patronise Mr Hope. He always contrived to baffle her praise. But here was an unconnected person thrown upon her care: and if Mrs Rowland had a young surgeon to push, Mrs Grey had an incomparable governess, now all to herself.

Chapter Thirty Four

Old and Young.

One of the characteristics of this summer at Deerbrook was the rival parties of pleasure with which the village was entertained. There had been rival parties of pleasure the preceding year; but from what a different cause! Then, all were anxious to do honour to Hester and Margaret, or to show off in their eyes: now, the efforts made were, on the one hand, to mortify, and on the other, to sustain them. The Rowlands had a carriage party to the woods one week, and the Greys a cavalcade to the flower-show at Blickley the next. The Rowlands gave a dinner to introduce Mr Walcot to more and more of their country neighbours; and the Greys had a dance in the green walk for the young people of the village. The Rowlands went to a strawberry gathering at Sir William Hunter's; and the Greys, with all their faction, as Mrs Rowland called it, were invited to a syllabub under the cow, at the Miss Andersons' breaking-up for the holidays.

All pretence of a good understanding between the two families was now at an end. They ceased to invite each other, and scrambled for their mutual acquaintances. The best of their mutual acquaintances saw no reason for taking part in the quarrel, and preserved a strict neutrality; and the worst enjoyed being scrambled for. The Levitts visited both families, and entertained everybody in return, as if nothing was happening. Sir William and Lady Hunter ate their annual dinner with each, and condescended to pay two or three extra visits to Mrs Rowland, without making a point of a full moon. Every circumstance that happened afforded occasion for comment, of course. Mrs Grey thought it very improper in the Rowlands to indulge in all this gaiety while they were in deep mourning. It was painful to her feelings, she owned, to hear the children shouting with laughter, while they were all bombazine and crape from head to foot: she had hoped to see the memory of her dear old friend treated with more respect. In vain did Mr Hope plead Mrs Enderby's delight in the mirth of children, and that their innocent gaiety would cheer her in her grave, if it could reach her there. In vain did Hester urge the danger and sin of training the little creatures to hypocrisy—a probable result, if they were to be kept solemn and unamused to the day when they might put off their mourning. Mrs Grey felt herself only the more called upon by all this to furnish the amount of sighs and tears which she believed to be due to Mrs Enderby's memory. Margaret rather sided with her—it was so sweet to her to hear Philip's mother mourned.

Mrs Grey's tears were, however, interspersed with smiles. On the day of the Rowlands' great dinner-party, when all was to be so stately for the Hunters, when the new dessert service was procured from Staffordshire, the fish had not arrived from London. This was certainly a fact; the fish had come by the coach the next morning. And what was still more remarkable, it had not occurred to Mrs Rowland that such an accident might happen— was very likely to happen; and, as if she had been an inexperienced housekeeper, she had not any dish in reserve, in case of the non-arrival of the fish. It was said that Mrs Rowland had sat down to table with a face perfectly crimson with anxiety and vexation. To such a temper as hers, what a vexation it must have been! There was a counterpart to this story for Mrs Rowland. She fancied that Mrs Grey's friends, the Andersons, must have looked rather foolish on occasion of their great syllabub party. She hoped the Miss Andersons trained their pupils better than their cows: they had a sad obstreperous cow, she understood. Some of the young ladies had lured it up the lawn with a potato, and got it to stand still to be milked; but, when somebody began to sing (she had no doubt it was Miss Ibbotson who sang) the poor animal found the music was not to its taste, and, of course, it kicked away the china bowl, and pranced down the lawn again. There was a dirge sung over the syllabub, no doubt. The poor Miss Andersons must have been terribly annoyed.

The good understanding of the gentlemen seemed all this time to be uninterrupted. They had much to put up with at home on this account; but their good-humour towards each other remained unbroken. Mr Rowland's anxious face, and his retirement within the enclosure of his own business, told his neighbours something of what he had to go through at home. Mrs Grey was vexed with her husband that he did not visit Hope's misfortunes upon Mr Rowland, and call the husband to account for the mischief the wife had caused; and Hester more than once expressed some resentment against her relation for not espousing Edward's cause more warmly. Hope told her this was not reasonable.

"Remember," said he, as they sauntered in their garden, one evening, "that these gentlemen must be more weary than we are (which is saying a great deal) of these perpetual squabbles; and they must earnestly desire to have peace in the counting-house. God forbid that their dominions should be invaded for our sake!"

"Not for our sake only, but for the sake of justice."

"Everything depends on the sort of men you have to deal with, in such cases as this. You must not expect too much. Here are two kind-hearted men, bound to each other by mutual good will and mutual interest. There is no other resemblance between them, except that they are both overpowered—made rather cowardly by the circumstances of their environment. Once departing from their plan of keeping the peace, they would be plunged into quarrel. They view things so differently, from the differences of their minds, that their only safety is in avoiding altogether all subjects of Deerbrook contention. If you expect the heroism of devoted friendship, or of an enthusiastic sense of justice from such men, you will not find it. We must take them as they are."

"And humbly accept such countenance as they choose to bestow?"

"Take it or leave it, as you will. There is no use in quarrelling with them for not being what they are not—that is all. Be generous with them; and do not expect from them the conduct which they have a right to expect from you."

"I rather wonder," observed Margaret, "that they have had the courage to go so far as they do, in bearing testimony in your favour."

"They have been very handsome in their conduct on the whole; and it would grieve me sincerely if they were to suffer further than they have already done on my account. I am afraid Mr Rowland is wretched now, because I will accept no assistance from him. He told me, the other day, that he should receive no rent for this house while Walcot occupies the other. He was beyond measure mortified when I positively declined being under any such obligation to any landlord. If Mr Rowland steadily refuses to turn us out of our house, and goes on offering favours that I cannot accept, that is all we can expect from him."

"It never occurred to me that he can turn us out," said Hester, "that we are tenants at will. Oh! how sorry I should be to go!" she continued, as she surveyed the place. "I should grieve to quit our first home."

"There is no danger I believe: Mr Rowland will be firm on that head."

"And there is no danger, I should think," said Margaret, "but that the Greys would find us something better the next day. Oh, I do not know where or how; but it would be such a splendid opportunity for patronage, that they would work miracles rather than let it slip. How far this ivy has trailed over the wall already! I should be sorry to leave this garden now that it promises to look like itself so soon again. Sydney despises me for my admiration of it at present. He looks melancholy about the blight. It is a pity certainly. Look at this rose-bush, how curled and withered it is!"

"Sydney is doing like every one else in looking grave about the blight," observed Hope. "So bad a season has not been known since I came to Deerbrook. I see care in the face of many an one who does not stand anything like our chance of want. Here comes Sydney, with news of every ill-looking field for five miles round, I doubt not."

"And Mr and Mrs Grey, and Sophia," said Hester, quitting her husband's arm, and hastening to meet her friends.

The Greys pronounced it so pleasant an evening, that they had no wish to sit down within doors; they preferred walking in the garden. They seemed to come for two purposes—to offer an invitation, and to relate that Mr Walcot was gone to dine at Sir William Hunter's to-day, and that Sir William had sent the carriage for him. Mr Walcot had not been ready for full five minutes after the carriage had driven up to the door. This delay was no doubt intended to give all Deerbrook time to observe the peculiar consideration with which Mr Walcot was treated by Sir William and Lady Hunter, who were by no means in the habit of sending their carriage for their Deerbrook guests.

"Did you ever hear of such a thing," said Sophia, "as sending a carriage for a young man? I have no doubt it is because he cannot ride."

"There you are out, Sophy," cried Sydney. "Mr Walcot rides as well as Mr Hope, every bit."

"I cannot think what has happened to Sydney," observed his mother. "He does nothing but stand up for Mr Walcot in the most unaccountable way! I hope you will forgive it, Mr Hope. Boys take strange fancies, you know. You must forgive it, my dears, in consideration of the rest of us."

"Instead of forgiving it," said Hope, "I shall take leave rather to admire it. There is a fine chivalrous spirit shown in fighting Mr Walcot's battles with our friends and relations."

"There, now!" cried Sydney, triumphantly. "But I can't help it, you see. Mr Walcot can ride, and he does ride well; and he is very civil to me, and asks me to go fishing with him; and I am sure he always inquires very respectfully after the rest of them. I never said any more than that in praise of him; and I can't say less, can I, when they are all abusing him for whatever he does?"

"I think not. I believe we may spare him that much credit without grudging."

"But, Sydney, you know it is not pleasant to us to hear you speak in praise of Mr Walcot under present circumstances; and you should have a little consideration for us."

"Well, mother, if you will not speak of him at all, no more will I." And he glanced up into his mother's face, to see how the proposition was taken. "That is fair, is not it?" he inquired of Mr Hope.

"Excellent in theory, Sydney; but who likes to be tied down not to speak on any subject, especially one which is turning up every hour? Your plan will not answer."

"I will ask you because I said I would—and all the more because you are not cross about Mr Walcot—"

"Hold your tongue, Sydney!" said the mother.

"Do not be ridiculous, Sydney," advised the sister.

"Mr Hope will say whether it is ridiculous, Sophy. Now, Mr Hope, would not you, and cousin Hester, and Margaret, go down the water with us to the abbey, just the same if Mr Walcot was with us?"

"With any guest of your father's and mother's, Sydney. We have no quarrel with Mr Walcot. The truth is, we feel, after all we have heard, that we know very little about him. We have not the slightest objection to meet Mr Walcot."

"Neither wish nor objection," said Hester, calmly. "We are perfectly indifferent about him."

Sydney vehemently beckoned his father, who left the apricot he and Margaret were examining by the surgery wall, and came to see what he was wanted for.

"You see," said he to Hope, when the matter was explained, "I have naturally been rather anxious to bring this about this meeting between you and the young man. In a small place like this, it is painful to have everybody quarrelling, and not to be able to get one's friends about one, for fear they should brawl in one's very drawing-room. Mr Rowland is of my mind there; and I know it would gratify him if I were to take some notice of this young man. I really could hardly refuse, knowing how handsomely Mr Rowland always speaks of you and yours, and believing Mr Walcot to be a very respectable, harmless young man. If I thought it would injure your interests in the least, I would see him at Cape Horn before I would invite him, of course: you must be aware of that. And I should not think of asking you to meet Mrs Rowland; that would be going too far. But Mrs Grey wishes that your wife and Margaret should visit these ruins that we were always prevented from getting to last year: and Mr Walcot is anxious to see them too; and he has been civil to Sydney; and, in short, I believe that Sydney half promised that he should go with us."

"Say no more," replied Hope. "You will have no difficulty with us. I really know nothing against Mr Walcot. He had a perfect right to settle where he pleased. Whether the manner of doing it was handsome or otherwise, is of far more consequence to himself than to me, or to any one else."

"I wish we all viewed the matter as you do. If the ladies had your temper, we should have a heaven upon earth. But they take things up so warmly, you see, when their feelings are interested for anybody; Mrs Rowland for one, and my wife for another. I hardly know what she will say to the idea of our having Walcot with us. Let us go and see."

"I have a word to say to you first. Do you know of any one who wants a horse? I am going to dispose of mine."

"Mr Walcot wants a horse," said Sydney, delighted at the idea of solving a difficulty.

Hope smiled, and told Mr Grey that he had rather sell his horse at a distance. Mr Walcot had already hired the boy Charles, whom Hope had just dismissed; and if he obtained the horse too, the old servant who knew his way to every patient's door, all the country round—it really would look too like the unpopular man patronising his opponent. Besides, it would be needlessly publishing in Deerbrook that the horse was given up.

"What is the fault of your horse?" asked Mr Grey, rousing himself from an absent fit.

"Merely that he eats, and therefore is expensive. I cannot afford now to keep a horse," he declared, in answer to Mr Grey's stare of amazement. "I have so few patients now out of walking reach, that I have no right to keep a horse. I can always hire, you know, from Reeves."

"Upon my soul, I am sorry to hear this—extremely sorry to hear it. Matters must have gone further than I had any idea of. My dear fellow, we must see how we can serve you. You must let me accommodate you—indeed you must—rather than give up your horse."

"Do not speak of it. You are very kind; but we need no help, I do assure you. My mind is quite made up about the horse. It would only be an incumbrance now. And, to satisfy you, I will mention that I have declined repeated offers of accommodation—offers very strongly urged. All I need ask of you is, to help me to dispose of my horse, somewhere out of Deerbrook."

"I will manage that for you, the next time I go to market; and—" In the emotion of the moment, Mr Grey was on the point of offering the use of his own horse when it should be at home: but he stopped short on the verge of his rash generosity. He was very particular about no one riding his horse but himself and the man who groomed it: he remembered his friend Hope's rapid riding and 'enthusiasm' and suspected that he should sooner or later repent the offer: so he changed it into, "I will get your horse disposed of to the best advantage, you may depend upon it. But I am very sorry—very sorry, indeed."

It is probable that nothing could have reconciled the ladies of Mr Grey's family to the idea of admitting Mr Walcot into their party, but the fact that they had of late cut rather a poor figure in contrast to Mrs Rowland. That lady had the advantage of novelty in the person of Mr Walcot, and her 'faction' was by far the larger of the two. The Greys found fault with all its elements; but there was no denying its superiority of numbers. It was a great hardship to have Mr Walcot forced upon them; but they reflected that his presence might bring a reinforcement—that some neighbours would perhaps come to meet him who would be otherwise engaged to the Rowlands for the very day on which they were wanted; for Mrs Rowland had the art of pre-engaging just the people the Greys intended to have. Sophia observed that Mr Walcot's presence would be less of a restraint in a boat, and at tea among the ruins, than in the drawing-room: there was always something to be said about the banks and the woods; and there was singing; and in a boat people were not obliged to talk unless they liked. She should not wonder if he would rather relish a little neglect; he had been made much of lately at such a ridiculous rate.

"If we do our part, my love," said Mrs Grey to Hester, in a mysterious low voice, "I think you should exert yourselves a little. Nothing can be done without a little exertion in this world, you know. Sophia and I were agreeing that it is a long time since you had any of your friends about you."

"Very few since your wedding company," observed Sophia.

"We remember you had all your acquaintance in the winter, my dear. It was very proper, I am sure, all you did then: but it is now the middle of July, you know; and our neighbours if Deerbrook always expect to be invited twice a year."

"I should be happy to see them, I assure you," said Hester, "but it happens to be not convenient."

"Not convenient, my dear!"

"Just so. We shall always be glad to see you and yours; but we have no hospitality to spare for the common world just now. We have no servants, you know, but Morris; and we are spending as little as we can."

"Tea company costs so very little!" said Sophia. "At this time of the year, when you need not light candles till people are going away, and when fruit is cheap and plentiful—"

"And we will take care of the cake," interposed Mrs Grey. "Sophia will make you some of her vicarage-cake, and a batch of almond biscuits; and Alice shall come and wait. We can manage it very easily."

"You are extremely kind: but if our acquaintance are to eat your cake, it had better be at your house. It does not suit our present circumstances to entertain company."

"But it costs so very little!" persisted Sophia. "Mr Russell Taylor's father used to give a general invitation to all his friends to come to tea in the summer, because, as he said, they then cost him only twopence-halfpenny a-head."

"I am afraid we are not such good managers as Mr Russell Taylor's father," replied Hester, laughing. "And if we were, it is not convenient to spend even twopence-halfpenny a-head upon our common acquaintance at present. If we grow richer, we will get our friends about us, without counting the cost so closely as that."

"That time will soon come, Sophia, my dear," said her mother, winking at Hester. "In every profession, you know, there are little ups and downs, and particularly in the medical. I dare say, if the truth were told, there is scarcely any professional man, without private fortune, who has not, at some time of his life, broken into his last guinea without knowing where he is to get another. But professional people generally keep their difficulties to themselves, I fancy, Hester: they are not often so frank as you. Mind that, Sophia. You will be discreet, Sophia."

"We have no intention of proclaiming in the streets that we are poor," said Hester. "But we owe it to you, dear Mrs Grey, to give our reasons for not doing all that we and you might wish. We are not dissatisfied: we want no help or pity: but we must live as we think right—that is all."

"Indeed, my dear, I must say you do not look as if anything was amiss. You look charmingly, indeed."

"Charmingly, indeed," echoed Sophia. "And Mrs Levitt was saying, that Margaret seems to have grown quite handsome, this summer. I fancy Mrs Rowland gets very few to agree with her as to Margaret being so very plain."

"No, indeed. Margaret's countenance is so intelligent and pleasant that I always said, from the beginning, that nobody but Mrs Rowland could call her plain. I suppose we shall soon be losing her, Hester."

"Oh, no; not soon. She has no thought of leaving us at present. She would not go in the spring, and sit beside Philip while he was learning his lessons; and now, they will wait, I believe, till the lessons are finished."

"She would not! Well, that shows what love will do. That shows what her power over Mr Enderby is. We used to think—indeed, everybody used to say it of Mr Enderby, that he always managed to do as he liked—he carried all his points. Yet even he is obliged to yield."

"Margaret has a way of carrying her points too," said Hester: "the best way in the world—by being always right."

"Mind that, Sophia. But, my dear Hester, I am really anxious about you. I had no idea, I am sure—. I hope you get your natural rest."

"Perfectly, I assure you. Mrs Howell might envy me, if she still 'cannot sleep for matching of worsteds.' The simple truth is, Mrs Grey, we never were so happy in our lives. This may seem rather perverse; but so it is."

Mrs Grey sighed that Mrs Rowland could not be aware of this. Hester thought it was no business of Mrs Rowland's; but Mrs Grey could not but feel that it would be a great satisfaction that she should know that those whom she hated, slept. She heard Margaret and Sydney saying something in the middle of the grass-plot about the Milky Way: looking up, she was surprised to perceive how plain it was, and how many stars were twinkling in the sky. She was sure Hester must be dreadfully tired with sauntering about so long. They had been very inconsiderate, and must go away directly. Sydney must call his father.

"They are delightful young people, really," observed Mrs Grey to her husband, during their walk home. "One never knows how to get away. Lady Hunter little supposes what she loses in not cultivating them. Go on before us, Sophia. Make haste home with your sister, Sydney. But, my dear, they speak in a very poor way of their affairs."

"Oh, Hester spoke to you, did she? Hope told me he must part with his horse. So Hester spoke to you?"

"Yes: not at all in a melancholy way, however. She keeps up her spirits wonderfully, poor girl! We really must push them, Mr Grey. I see nothing but ruin before them, if we do not push them."

"Ah! there is the difficulty: that is where that little enthusiasm of Hope's comes in. I have a great respect for him; but I own I should like to see him a little more practical."

"I really am pleased to hear you say so. It is just what I think; and I always fancied you did not agree with me. It really puts me almost out of patience to hear him speak of Mr Walcot—encouraging Sydney in his notions! It is unnatural: it looks a little like affectation—all that sort of feeling about Mr Walcot."

"I do not object to that, I confess. His thinking fairly of Walcot can do no harm, and may save mischief, and it looks honourable and well. I do not regret that, I own. But I think he is clearly wrong in selling his horse in such a hurry. All Deerbrook will know it directly, and it will not look well. I offered him such accommodation as would enable him to keep it; but he is quite obstinate. Some enthusiastic notion of honour, I suppose—. But I told them that there is no profession or business in the world that has not its ups and downs."

"Exactly what I told Hester, when she declined having any parties at present—in the very crisis, in my opinion, when it is of great consequence that they should get their friends about them. Sophia would have made the cake, and Alice would have waited at tea. But the fact is, Mr Hope has put some of his spirit into his wife, and they must take their own way, I suppose."

"He gave me his reasons, however," observed Mr Grey. "He regards this as something more than one of the slack times common in his profession. He will not accept obligation, while he sees no clear prospect of being able to discharge it. I could not prevail upon him. However, they must have enough: they cannot be actually pinched. I never saw him in better spirits. There can be no occasion for our doing anything more than just being on the look-out to serve them."

"We must push them—that is all we can do. They cannot really be wanting anything, as you say, such fine spirits as they are in. Hester looks sweetly. The first game that we have to spare this season shall go to them: and I shall bear them in mind when we gather our apples."

"If you find we have any apples to gather, my dear. I doubt it."

"Do you really? It will be unfortunate for our young friends, if prices rise next winter, as you seem to expect. There goes ten o'clock, I declare; and there are the children looking out for us, as well they may. But those are really delightful young people. There is no getting away from them."

Chapter Thirty Five

Boating.

Mr Walcot was delighted with the invitation to the water-party, but was fully engaged for the next three weeks. Mr Grey decreed that he was to be waited for. Then the lady moon had to be waited for another ten days; so that it was past the middle of August before Mrs Grey and Sophia were called upon to endure Mr Walcot's society for six hours. The weather was somewhat dubious when the day arrived: but in so bad a season as the present, it would never do to let a doubt put a stop to an excursion which had been planned above a month. One of Mr Grey's men was sent round among the ladies in the morning, to request to be the bearer of their cloaks, as it was thought they would be cold on the water without all the wraps they had. Hester sent as many warm things as she thought Margaret could possibly wear. She was not going herself. She wished it much; but it was decided on all hands that it would be imprudent, as there was no calculating the amount of fatigue which each might have to incur.

At three o'clock the party assembled on the wharf on Messrs Grey and Rowland's premises, everyone having dined at home. Mrs Rowland had tried to persuade Mr Walcot that he ought not to be out of the way, after what Lady Hunter had said in a note about her terrible headache of yesterday. It might be the beginning of a feverish attack; and it would be unfortunate if he should be six miles down the river—not expected home till nine or ten at night, when a messenger should arrive from the Hall. But Mr Walcot had seen few water-parties in the course of his life, and he was resolved to go.

Margaret and her brother repaired in gay spirits to the water-side. In the days of poverty, trifles become great events, and ease is luxury. Hope felt himself clear of the world to-day. He had received the money from the sale of his horse; and after paying for its corn, there was fifteen pounds left to be put by for his rent. Hester had bidden adieu to the horse with a sort of glee, as she had never been able to overcome her panic during her husband's long country rides; and Hope found that he hung more and more upon Hester's smiles: they cheered him, from whatever cause they arose. Margaret was gay from discourse with Philip. She had just despatched a letter to him—a letter which had acknowledged that it was, indeed, long since they had met—that it was almost time that he was coming to Deerbrook again.

The party they joined looked less merry than themselves. The two boats which lay at the wharf were gay enough—the one with crimson cushions, and the other with blue. A servant-maid was to go in each, to take care of the provisions, and provide tea at the ruins; and Alice and her companion were alert and smiling. But Mrs Grey wore a countenance of extraordinary anxiety; and the twitching of her face showed that something had gone very seriously wrong. Sophia nearly turned her back upon Mr Walcot, who continued to address her with patient diligence. Maria was sitting on some deals, waiting to be called to enter the boat; and some of the people of the village were staring at her from a little distance. Margaret immediately joined her.

"What are those people looking at you for?"

"I cannot conceive. I fancied that while I was sitting I looked pretty much like other people."

"To be sure you do. I will ask Mr Grey. I am sure there is some meaning in their gaze—so ridiculously compassionate."

"Do not you know?" said Mr Grey. "Do not you know the story they have got up about Miss Young's case. They say Mr Hope set her limb so badly that he had to break it again twice. I have been asked several times whether he did not get me to help him: and they will not believe me when I deny the whole."

Maria laughed; and Margaret observed that they would presently see how much better Maria could walk now than she did before her last accident, such being the effect of the long and complete rest which had been enforced upon her.

"Nothing like seeing for themselves," observed Mr Grey, surveying the company. "All come but Dr Levitt now, I think. It really goes to my heart not to take some of my partner's children. There they are, peeping at us, one head behind another, from that gate. There is room for two or three, from the Jameses failing us at the last. The little things might as well go; but I suppose there would be no use in saying anything about it. I must have a word with my daughter before we embark. Sophia, my dear! Sophia!"

Sophia came, and Margaret overheard her father say to her, that every person present was his guest, and to be treated with the civility and attention due to him as such. Sophia looked rather sulky at hearing this, and walked far away from Mr Walcot to devote herself to Miss Anderson.

By dint of sending a messenger to Dr Levitt's a quarter of an hour before the time, his presence was secured a quarter of an hour after it. He made his usual approach—looking bland and gentlemanly, and fearing he was late.

The party were ordered into the boats as if they had been going to dinner. Mr Walcot was appointed to hand Margaret in; but he showed, amidst great simplicity, an entire determination to be Sophia's companion. Hope was approaching Maria's seat, to give her his arm, when some bustle was heard at the gate where the little Rowlands were clustered.

"There is my partner! He will go with us, after all," said Mr Grey. "Come, my dear sir, we have plenty of room."

"So much the better for my brother-in-law. You have room for Enderby, have you? He will be delighted to join you, I have no doubt. Room for me too? I really think I must indulge myself. Yes; Enderby took us quite by surprise this morning: but that is his way, you know."

Philip here, and without notice! Margaret thought she was dreaming the words she heard. She felt much oppressed—as if there must be something wrong in so sudden and strange a proceeding. At the very moment of suspense, she caught Mrs Grey's eye fixed upon her with the saddest expression she thought she had ever seen.

Philip was come—it was no dream. He was presently in the midst of the party, making his compliments—compliments paid to Margaret in a manner scarcely different in the eyes of others from those which were shared by all: but to her, a world of wonder and of horror was revealed by the glance of the eye and the quiver of the lip, too slight to be detected by any eye less intently fixed than hers. Margaret stood alone, as the others were stepping into the boats; but Philip did not approach her. He interfered between Hope and Maria Young. Maria looked agitated and uncertain; but she thought she had no right to cause any delay or difficulty; and she took his arm, though she felt herself unable to conceal her trembling. Hope saw that Margaret was scarcely able to support herself.

"I cannot go," she said, as he drew her arm within his. "Leave me behind. They will not miss me. Nobody will miss me."

The agonised tone of these last words brought back the colour which Hope had lost in the tempest of emotions, in which anger was uppermost. He was no longer deadly pale when he said:

"Impossible. I cannot leave you. You must not stay behind. It is of the utmost consequence that you should go. Cannot you? Do try. I will place you beside Mrs Grey. Cannot you make the effort?"

She did make the effort. With desperate steadiness she stepped into the boat where Mrs Grey was seated. She was conscious that Philip watched to see what she would do, and then seated Maria and himself in the other boat. Hope followed Margaret. If he had been in the same boat with Enderby, the temptation to throw him overboard would have been too strong.

Till they were past the weir and the lock, and all the erections belonging to the village, and to the great firm which dignified it, the boats were rowed. Conversation went on. The grey church steeple was pronounced picturesque, as it rose above the trees; and the children looked up at Dr Levitt, as if the credit of it by some means belonged to him, the rector. Sydney desired his younger sisters not to trail their hands through the water, as it retarded the passage of the boat. The precise distance of the ruins from Deerbrook ferry was argued, and Dr Levitt gave some curious traditions about the old abbey they were going to see. Then towing took the place of rowing, and the party became very quiet. The boat cut steadily through the still waters, the slight ripple at the bows being the only sound which marked its progress. Dr Levitt pointed with his stick to the "verdurous wall" which sprang up from the brink of the river, every spray of the beech, every pyramid of the larch, every leaf of the oak, and the tall column of the occasional poplar, reflected true as the natural magic of light and waters could make them. Some then wished the sun would come out, without which it could scarcely be called seeing the woods. Others tried to recognise the person who stood fishing under the great ash; and it took a minute or two to settle whether it was a man or a boy; and two minutes more to decide that it was nobody belonging to Deerbrook. Margaret almost wondered that Edward could talk on about these things as he did—so much in his common tone and manner. But for his ease and steadiness in small talk, she should suppose he was striving to have her left unnoticed, to look down into the water as strenuously as she pleased. She little knew what a training he had had in wearing his usual manner while his heart was wretched.

"There, now!" cried Fanny, "we have passed the place—the place where cousin Margaret fell in last winter. We wanted to have gone directly over it."

Margaret looked up, and caught Sydney's awe-struck glance. He had not yet recovered from that day.

"If you had mentioned it sooner," said Margaret, "I could have shown you the very place. We did pass directly over it."

"Oh, why did you not tell us? You should have told us."

Dr Levitt smiled as he remarked that he thought Miss Ibbotson was likely to be the last person to point out that spot to other people, as well as to forget it herself. Margaret had indeed been far from forgetting it. She had looked down into its depths, and had brought thence something that had been useful to her—something on which she was meditating when Fanny spoke. She had been saved, and doubtless for a purpose. If it was only to suffer for her own part, and to find no rest and peace but in devoting herself to others—this was a high purpose. Maria could live, and was thankful to live, without home, or family, or prospect. But it was not certain that this was all that was to be done and enjoyed in life. Something dreadful had happened: but Philip loved her: he still loved her—for nothing but agonised love could have inspired the glance which yet thrilled through her. There was some mistake—some fearful mistake; and the want of confidence in her which it revealed—the fault of temper in him—opened a long perspective of misery; but yet, he loved her, and all was not over. At times she felt certain that Mrs Rowland was at the bottom of this new injury: but it was inconceivable that Philip should be deluded by her, after his warnings, and his jealous fears lest his Margaret should give heed to any of his sister's misrepresentations. No light shone upon the question, from the cloudy sky above, or the clear waters beneath; but both yielded comfort through that gentle law by which things eminently real—Providence, the mercy of death, and the blessing of godlike life, are presented or prophesied to the spirit by the shadows amidst which we live. When Margaret spoke, there was a calmness in her voice, so like an echo of comfort in her heart, that it almost made Edward start.

The party in the other boat were noisier, whether or not they were happier, than those in whose wake they followed. Mr Walcot had begun to be inspired as soon as the oars had made their first splash, and was now reciting to Sophia some "Lines to the Setting Sun," which he had learned when a little boy, and had never forgotten. He asked her whether it was not a sweet idea—that of the declining sun being like a good man going to his rest, to rise again to-morrow morning. Sophia was fond of poetry that was not too difficult; and she found little disinclination in herself now to observe her father's directions about being civil to Mr Walcot. The gentleman perceived that he had won some advantage; and he persevered. He next spoke of the amiable poet, Cowper, and was delighted to find that Miss Grey was acquainted with some of his writings; that she had at one time been able to repeat his piece on a Poplar Field, and those sweet lines beginning—

"The rose had been washed, just washed in a shower."

But she had never heard the passage about "the twanging horn o'er yonder bridge," and "the wheeling the sofa round," and "the cups that cheer but not inebriate;" so Mr Walcot repeated them, not, as before, in a high key, and with his face turned up towards the sky, but almost in a whisper, and inclining towards her ear. Sophia sighed, and thought it very beautiful, and was sorry for people who were not fond of poetry. A pause of excited feeling followed, during which they found that the gentlemen were questioning a boatman, who was awaiting his turn to tow, about the swans in the river.

"The swans have much increased in number this season, surely. Those are all of one family, I suppose—those about the island," observed Mr Grey.

"Yes, sir; they can't abide neighbours. They won't suffer a nest within a mile."

"They fight it out, if they approach too near, eh?" said Enderby.

"Yes, sir; they leave one another for dead. I have lost some of the finest swans under my charge in that way."

"Do you not part them when they fight?" asked Walcot.

"I would. I always part little boys whom I see fighting in the streets, and tell them they should not quarrel."

"You would repent meddling with the swans, sir, if you tried. When I knew no better, I meddled once, and I thought I should hardly get away alive. One of the creatures flapped my arm so hard, that I thought more than once it was broken. I would advise you, sir, never to go near swans when they are angry."

"You will find ample employment for your peace-making talents among the Deerbrook people, Mr Walcot," said Philip. "They may break your windows, and perhaps your heart; but they will leave you your eyes and your right arm. For my part, I do not know but I had rather do battle with the swans."

"Better not, sir," said the boatman. "I would advise you never to go near swans when they are angry."

"Look!" said Sophia, anxiously. "Is not this one angry? Yes, it is: I am sure it is! Did you ever see anything like its feathers? and it is coming this way, it is just upon us! Oh, Mr Walcot!"

Sophia threw herself over to the other side of the boat, and Mr Walcot started up, looking very pale.

"Sit down!" cried Mr Grey, in his loudest voice. Mr Walcot sat down as if shot; and Sophia crept back to her place, with an anxious glance at the retreating bird. Of course, the two young people were plentifully lectured about shifting their places in a boat without leave, and were asked the question, more easily put than answered, how they should have felt if they had been the means of precipitating the whole party into the water. Then there was a calling out from the other boat to know what was the matter, and an explanation; so that Sophia and Mr Walcot had to take refuge in mutual sympathy from universal censure.

"The birds always quarrel with the boats—boats of this make," explained the boatman; "because their enemies go out in skiffs to take them. They let a lighter pass without taking any notice, while they always scour the water near a skiff; but I never heard of their flying at a pleasure party in any sort of boat."

"Where are the black swans that a sea-captain brought to Lady Hunter?" asked Philip. "I see nothing of them."

"The male died; choked, sir,—with a crust of bread a stranger gave him. But for that, he would have been now in sight, I don't doubt; for he prospered very well till that day."

"Of a crust of bread! What a death!" exclaimed Philip. "And the other?"

"She died, sir, by the visitation of God," replied the boatman, solemnly.

It was obviously so far from the man's intention that any one should laugh, that nobody did laugh. Maria observed to her next neighbour that, to a keeper of swans, his birds were more companionable, and quite as important, as their human charge to coroners and jurymen.

The boat got aground amongst the flags, at a point where the tow-rope had to be carried over a foot-bridge at some little distance inland. One of the men, in attempting to leap the ditch, had fallen in, and emerged dripping with mud. Ben jumped ashore to take his turn at the rope, and Enderby pushed the boat off again with an oar, with some little effort. Mr Walcot had squeezed Sophia's parasol so hard, during the crisis, as to break its ivory ring. The accident, mortifying as it was to him, did not prevent his exclaiming in a fervour of gratitude, when the vibration of the boat was over, and they were once more afloat—

"What an exceedingly clever man Mr Enderby is!"

"Extremely clever. I really think he can do everything."

"Ah! he would not have managed to break the ring of your parasol, as I have been so awkward as to do. But I will see about getting it mended to-morrow. If I were as clever as Mr Enderby now, I might be able to mend it myself."

"You will not be able to get another ring in Deerbrook. But never mind. I beg you will not feel uncomfortable about it. I can fasten it with a loop of green ribbon and a button till the next time I go to Blickley. Pray do not feel uncomfortable."

"How can I help it? You say there is no ring in Deerbrook. Not any sort of ring? My dear Miss Grey, if I cannot repair this sort of ring—"

Sophia was a good deal flurried. She begged he would think no more of the parasol; it was no manner of consequence.

"Do not be too good to me," whispered he. "I trust. I know my duty better than to take you at your word. From my earliest years, my parents have instilled into me the duty of making reparation for the injuries we cause to others."

Sophia gave him an affecting look of approbation, and asked with much interest where his parents lived, and how many brothers and sisters he had; and assured him, at last, that she saw he belonged to a charming family.

"It does not become me to speak proudly of such near relations," said he; "and one who has so lately left the parental roof is, perhaps, scarcely to be trusted to be impartial; but I will say for my family that, though not perhaps so clever as Mrs Rowland and Mr Enderby—"

"Oh, for Heaven's sake, do not name them together!"

Mr Walcot saw that he had broken the charm: he hastened to repair the mischief which one unhappy name had caused.

"It is natural, I know, that you should take the most interest in that member of the family who is to be your relation. You consider him in that light, I believe?"

"Of course. He is to be our cousin."

"The parties wish it to be kept a secret, I conclude," said he, glancing at Enderby, and then stretching back as far as he thought safe, to look at the other boat.

"Oh dear, no! There is no secret about the matter."

"I should not have supposed them to be engaged, by their manner to each other. Perhaps it is off," said he, quickly, fixing his eyes upon her.

"Off! What an odd idea! Who ever thought of such a thing?"

"Such things have been heard of as engagements going off, you know."

Both had raised their voices during the last few eager sentences. Sophia became aware that they had been overheard, by seeing the deep flush which overspread Miss Young's pale face. Philip looked at Mr Walcot as if he would have knocked him down, if they had only been on land. The young man took off his hat, and ran his fingers through his white hair, for the sake of something to do: replaced his hat, and shook his head manfully, as if to settle his heart in his breast, as well as his beaver on his crown. He glanced down the river, in hopes that the abbey was not yet too near. It was important to him that the wrath of so extremely clever a man as Mr Enderby should have subsided before the party went on shore.

It would have been a strange thing to have known how many of that company were dreading to reach the object of their excursion. A thrill passed through many hearts when the ruins, with their overshadowing ivy, were at length discerned, seated in the meadow to which the boats seemed approaching far too rapidly. In the bustle of landing, however, it was easy for those who wished to avoid one another to do so.

Most of the guests walked straight up to the abbey walls, to examine all that was left of them. Mrs Grey and her maids went to the little farmhouse which was at one corner of the old building, and chiefly constructed out of its ruins; and while the parties on whom the cares of hospitality devolved were consulting with the farmer's wife about preparations for tea, any stray guest might search for wood-plants in the skirts of the copse on the hill behind, or talk with the children who were jumping in and out of an old saw-pit in the wood, or if contemplative, might watch the minnows in the brook, which was here running parallel with the river.

Mrs Grey obviously considered that Margaret was her peculiar charge. She spoke little to her; but when Philip was off somewhere, she took her arm, and seemed to insist on her company when she proceeded to her treaty with the dame of the farm. Margaret stood for some time patiently, while they discussed whether it should be tea in the farmhouse parlour, which was too small—or tea in the meadow, which might be damp—or tea in the ruins, where there might be draughts, and the water could not be supplied hot. Before this matter was settled, Margaret saw that her friend Maria was seated on a log beside the brook, and gazing wistfully at her. Margaret tried to disengage her arm from Mrs Grey; Mrs Grey objected.

"Wait a moment, my dear. I will not detain you five minutes. You must not go anywhere without me, my dear child."

Never before had Mrs Grey spoken to Margaret with tenderness like this. Margaret was resolved to know why now; but she would first speak to Maria. She said she would return presently: she wished to return: but she must speak to Maria.

"Margaret, what is all this?" said Maria, in a voice whose agitation she could not control. "Have I been doing wrong? Am I now thinking what is wrong? I did not know whether to be angry with him or not. I was afraid to speak to him, and afraid not to speak to him. How is it? tell me, Margaret."

"I wish I could," said Margaret, in a tone calmer than her friend's. "I am in a miserable dream. I wrote to him this morning."

"To London?"

"Yes, to London. He must have been in Deerbrook while I was writing it. I heard from him, as usual, three days ago; and since then, I have never had a line or a word to prepare me for this. There is some dreadful mistake."

"The mistake is not his, I fear," said Maria, her eyes filling as she spoke. "The mistake is yours, Margaret, and mine, and everybody's who took a selfish man of the world for a being with a heart and a conscience."

"You are wrong, Maria. You go too far. You will find that you are unjust. He is as wretched as I am. There is some mistake which may be explained: for he... he loves me, I am certain. But I wish I was anywhere but here—it is so wretched!"

"I am afraid I have done wrong in speaking with him at all," said Maria. "I longed for three words with you; for I did not know what I ought to do. We must learn something before we return. Your friends must act for you. Where is Mr Hope?"

"I do not know. Everybody deserts me, I think."

"I will not. It is little I can do; but stay by me: do not leave me. I will watch for you."

Margaret fell into the common error of the wretched, when she said these last words. Her brother was at work on her behalf. Hope had gone towards the ruins with the rest of the party, to keep his eye on Enderby. Sophia hung on his arm, which she had taken that she might relieve herself of some thoughts which she could not so well speak to any one of the strangers of the party.

"Oh, Mr Hope!" cried she, "how very much mistaken we have been in Mr Walcot all this time! He is a most delightful young man—so refined! and so domestic!"

"Indeed! You will trust Sydney's judgment more readily another time."

"Yes, indeed. But I could not help telling you. I know you will not be offended; though some people, perhaps, would not venture to speak so to you; but I know you will excuse it, and not be offended."

"So far from being offended, I like what you now say far better than the way I have heard you sometimes speak of Mr Walcot. I have thought before that you did not allow him fair play. Now, in my turn, I must ask you not to be offended with me."

"Oh, I never could be offended with you; you are always so good and amiable. Mamma seemed a little vexed when you encouraged Sydney to praise Mr Walcot: but she will be delighted at your opinion of him, when she finds how accomplished he is—and so refined!"

"You speak of my opinion. I have no opinion about Mr Walcot yet, because I do not know him. You must remember that, though all Deerbrook has been busy about him since May, I have scarcely heard him say five words. I do not speak as having any opinion of him, one way or another. How dark this place looks to-day!—that aisle—how gloomy!"

"I think it is the weather. There is no sun; and the ivy tosses about strangely. What do you think of the weather?"

"I think we shall have the least possible benefit of the moon. How like a solid wall those clouds look, low down in the sky!—Here comes Mr Walcot. Suppose you let him take you after the rest of the party? You will not like the gloom of that aisle where I am going."

Both Sophia and Mr Walcot much preferred each other's company to the damp and shadow of the interior of the abbey. They walked off together, and gathered meadow flowers, and admired poetry and poets till all were summoned, and they were compelled to join the groups who were converging from copse, brook, poultry-yard, and cloister, towards the green before the farmhouse, where, after all, the long tea-table was spread.

The reason of Hope's anxiety to consign Sophia to Mr Walcot's charge was, that he saw Enderby pacing the aisle alone with rapid steps, his face hung with gloom as deep as darkened the walls about him.

"Enderby, are you mad?" cried Hope, hastening in to him.

"I believe I am. As you are aware, no man has better cause."

"I wait your explanation. Till I have it, your conduct is a perfect mystery. To Margaret, or to me for her, you must explain yourself, and that immediately. In the mean time, I do not know how to address you—how to judge you."

"Then Mrs Grey has not told you of our conversation of this morning?"

"No," said Hope, his heart suddenly failing him.

"The whole dreadful story has become known to me; and I am thankful that it is revealed before it is too late. My sister is sometimes right, however she may be often wrong. She has done me a cruel kindness now. I know all, Hope;—how you loved Margaret;—how, when it was too late, you discovered that Margaret loved you;—how, when I burst in upon you and her, she was (Oh, why did I ever see her again?) she was learning from you the absurd resolution which Mrs Grey had been urging upon you, by working upon your false sense of honour—a sense of honour of which I am to have none of the benefit, since, after marrying the one sister out of compassion and to please Mrs Grey, you turn the other over to me—innocent in soul and conscience, I know, but no longer with virgin affections—you give her to me for your mutual security and consolation."

"Enderby! you *are* mad," cried Hope, his strength being roused by this extent of accusation from the depression caused by the mixture of truth in the dreadful words Philip had just spoken. "But mad, deluded, or wicked—however you may have been wrought into this state of mind, there are two things which must be said on the instant, and regarded by you in all coming time. These charges, as they relate to myself, had better be spoken of at another opportunity, and when you are in a calmer state of mind: but meanwhile I, as a husband, forbid you to speak lightly of my beloved and honoured wife: and I also charge you, as you revere the purity of Margaret's soul—of the innocent soul and conscience of which you speak—that you do not convey to her, by the remotest intimation, any conception of the horrible tale with which some wretch has been deluding you. She never loved any one but you. If you pollute and agonise her imagination with these vile fancies of your sister's, (for from whom else can such inventions come?) remember that you peril the peace of an innocent family; you poison the friendship of sisters whom bereavement has bound to each other; and deprive Margaret of all that life contains for her. You will not impair my wife's faith in me, I am confident; but you may turn Margaret's brain, if you say to her anything like what passed your lips just now. It seems but a short time, Enderby, since we committed Margaret's happiness to your care; and now I have to appeal on her behalf to your honour and conscience."

"Mrs Grey, Mrs Grey," Enderby repeated, fixing his eyes upon Hope's countenance.

"The quarrel between you and me shall be attended to in its turn, Enderby. I must first secure my wife and Margaret from any rashness on your part. If you put distrust between them, and pollute their home by the wildest of fancies, it would be better for you that these walls should fall upon us, and bury us both."

"Oh, that they would!" cried Philip. "I am sick of living in the midst of treachery. Life is a waste to a man treated as I have been."

"Answer me, Enderby—answer me this instant," Hope cried, advancing to place himself between Enderby and Margaret, whom he saw now entering the ruin, and rapidly approaching them.

"You are right," said Enderby, aloud. "You may trust me."

"Philip, what am I to think?" said Margaret, walking quite up to him, and looking intently in his face. "I hardly know whether we are living, and in our common world." Hope shuddered to see the glance she cast round the dreary place. Philip half turned away and did not speak.

"Why will not you speak? What reason can there be for this silence? When you last left me, you feared your sister might make mischief between us; and then I promised that if such a thing could happen as that I should doubt you, I would tell you my doubt as soon as I was aware of it myself; and now you are angry with me—you would strike me dead this moment, if you dared—and you will not speak."

"Go now, Margaret," said Hope, gently. "He cannot speak to you now: take my word for it that he cannot."

"I will not go. I will take nobody's word. What are you, Edward, between me and him? It is my right to know how I have offended him. I require no more than my right. I do not ask him to love me; nor need I, for he loves me still—I know it and feel it."

"It is true," said Enderby, mournfully gazing upon her agitated countenance, but retreating as he gazed.

"I do not ask to be yours, any farther than I am now—now when our affections are true, and our word is broken. But I do insist upon your esteem, as far as I have ever possessed it. I have done nothing to forfeit it; and I demand your reasons for supposing that I have."

"Not now," said Philip, faintly, shrinking in the presence of the two concerning whom he entertained so painful a complexity of feelings. There stood Hope, firm as the pillar behind him. There stood Margaret, agitated, but unabashed as the angels that come in dreams. Was it possible that these two had loved? Could they then stand before him thus? But Mrs Grey—what she admitted!—this, in confirmation with other evidence, could not be cast aside. Yet Philip dared not speak, fearing to injure beyond reparation.

"Oh, Margaret, not now!" he faintly repeated. "My heart is almost broken! Give me time."

"You have given me none. Let that pass, however. But I cannot give you time. I cannot hold out—who can hold out, under injurious secrecy—under mocking injustice—under torturing doubt from the one who is pledged to the extreme of confidence? Let us once understand one another, and we will never meet more, and I will endure whatever must be endured, and we shall have time—Oh, what a weary time!—to learn to submit. But not till you have given me the confidence you owe—the last I shall ever ask from you—will I endure one moment's suspense. I will not give you time."

"Yes, Margaret, you will—you must," said Hope. "It is hard, very hard; but Enderby is so far right."

"God help me, for every one is against me!" cried Margaret, sinking down among the long grass, and laying her throbbing head upon the cold stone. "He comes without notice to terrify me by his anger—me whom he loves above all the world; he leaves my heart to break with his unkindness in the midst of all these indifferent people; he denies me the explanation I demand; and you—you of all others, tell me he is right! I will do without protection, since the two who owe it forsake me: but God is my witness how you wrong me."

"Enderby, why do not you go?" said Hope, sternly. Almost before the words were spoken, Enderby had disappeared at the further end of the aisle.

"Patience, Margaret! A little patience, my dear sister. All may be well; all must be well for such as you; but I mean that I trust all may be repaired. He has been wrought upon by some bad influence—"

"Then all is over. If, knowing me as he did—. But, Edward, do not speak to me. Go: leave me! I cannot speak another word now—"

"I cannot leave you here. This is no place for you. Think of your sister, Margaret. You will do nothing to alarm her. If she were to see you now—."

Margaret raised herself; took her brother's arm, and went out into the air. No one was near.

"Now leave me, brother. I must be alone. I will walk here, and think what I must do. But how can I know, when all is made such a mystery? Oh, brother, tell me what I ought to do!"

"Calm yourself now. Command yourself; for this day. You, innocent as you are, may well do so. If I had such a conscience as yours—if I were only in your place, Margaret—if I had nothing to bear but wrongs, I would thank Heaven as Heaven was never yet thanked."

"You, Edward!"

"If the universe heaped injuries upon me, they should not crush me. If I had a self-respect like yours, I would lift my head to the stars."

"You, Edward!"

"Margaret, wretched as you are, your misery is nothing to mine. Have pity upon me, and command yourself. For my sake and your sister's, look and act like yourself, and hope peacefully, trust steadily, that all will yet be right."

"It cannot be that you have wronged me, brother. You sent him from me, I know; and that was unkind: but you could never really wrong any one."

"I never meant it. I honour you, and would protect you—I will protect you as a brother should. Only do not say again that you are forsaken. It would break our hearts to hear you say that again."

"I will not. And I will try to be for to-day as if nothing had happened: but I promise no more than to endeavour—I am so bewildered!"

"Then I will leave you. I shall not be far off. No one shall come to disturb you."

There is, perhaps, no mood of mind in which it is impossible for the sweet ministrations of nature to be accepted. Even now, as Margaret stood on the river-bank, the influences of the scene flowed in upon her. The operations of thought were quickened, and she was presently convinced that the next time she saw Philip she should learn all—she might even find him repentant for having been weak and credulous. Edward's self-reproach was the most inexplicable mystery of all. In his brotherly grief he had no doubt exaggerated some slight carelessness of speech, some deficiency of watchfulness and zeal. Hester must never know of these sorrowful things that Edward had said. There was substantial comfort in other of his words. It was true that she was only wronged. In her former season of wretchedness, it had been far worse: there was not only disappointment, but humiliation; loss, not only of hope, but of self-respect. Now, she was innocent of any wrong towards Philip and herself; and, in this consciousness, any lot must be supportable. While thus musing, she walked slowly along, sighing away some of her oppression. Her heart and head throbbed less. Her eye was caught by the little fish that leaped out of the water after the evening flies: she stood to watch them. The splash of a water-rat roused her ear, and she turned to track him across the stream. Then she saw a fine yellow iris, growing among the flags on the very brink, and she must have it for Maria. To reach it without a wetting required some skill and time. She tried this way—she tried that; but the flower was just out of reach. She went to the next alder-bush for a bough, which answered her purpose; and she had drawn the tuft of flags towards her, and laid hold of the iris, when Sydney shouted her name from a distance, and summoned her to tea.

Maria was seated at the table, amidst the greater proportion of the party, when Margaret arrived, escorted by Sydney, and followed at a little distance by Mr Hope. Never had flower been more welcome to Maria than this iris, offered to her with a smile. Pale as the face was, and heavy as were the eyes, there was a genuine smile. Maria had kept a place for Margaret, which she took, though Mrs Grey kept gazing at her, and assured her that she must sit beside her. Mr Enderby was not to be seen. Frequent proclamation was made for him; but he did not appear; and it was settled that if he preferred wood-ranging to good cheer, he must have his own way.

Tea passed off well enough. Dr Levitt and Mr Hope went over the subject of the abbey again, for the benefit of the rearward portion of the company, who had not heard it before. Mr Rowland and the farmer discussed the bad crops. Sophia spilled her tea, from Mr Walcot having made her laugh when she was carrying the cup to her lips; and Sydney collected a portion of every good thing that was on the table for Mr Enderby to enjoy on his return.

Mr Enderby did not return till it was quite time to be gone. Mr Grey had long been hurrying the servants in their business of packing up plates and spoons. He even offered help, and repeated his cautions to his guests not to stray beyond call. The farmer shook his head as he looked up at the leaden-coloured sky, across which black masses of cloud, like condensed smoke, were whirled, and prophesied a stormy night. There was no time to be lost. The boatmen came bustling out of the farm-kitchen, still munching; and they put the boats in trim with all speed, while the ladies stood on the bank quite ready to step in. Mrs Grey assorted the two parties, still claiming Margaret for her own boat, but allowing Maria to enter instead of Sydney. Hope chose to remain with them; so Dr Levitt exchanged with Sophia. Mr Walcot thought there was a lion in his path either way—Mr Hope, his professional rival, in one boat, and Mr Enderby, whom he fancied he had offended, in the other. He adhered to Sophia, as a sure ally.

"Mr Enderby! Where can he be?" was the exclamation, when all were seated, and the boatmen stood ready to start, with the tow-rope about their shoulders; when the dame of the farm had made her parting curtsey, and had stepped a few paces backward, after her swimming obeisance. The farmer was running over the meadow towards the copse in search of the missing gentleman, and Sydney would have sprung out of the boat to join in the chase, when his father laid a strong hand on him, and said that one stray member of a party on a threatening evening was enough. He could not have people running after one another till the storm came on. Mr Rowland was full of concern, and would have had Sydney throw away the basketful of good things he had hoarded for his friend. If Enderby chose to absent himself for his own enjoyments, Mr Rowland said, he could not expect to share other people's. Hope was standing up in the first boat, gazing anxiously round, and Margaret's eyes were fixed on his face, when every body cried out at once, "Here he is! here he comes!" and Enderby was seen leaping through a gap in the farthest hedge, and bounding over the meadow. He sprang into the boat with a force which set it rocking, and made the ladies catch at whatever could be grasped.

"Your hat!" exclaimed several voices.

"Why, Mr Enderby, where is your hat?" cried Sydney, laughing. Enderby clapped his hand on the top of his head, and declared he did not know. He had not missed his hat till this moment.

Hope called from the first boat to the farmer, and asked him to look in the aisle of the abbey for the gentleman's hat. It was brought thence; and Fanny and Mary laughed at Mr Hope for being such a good guesser as to fancy where Mr Enderby's hat might be, when Mr Enderby did not know himself. The moment the hat was tossed into the lap of its owner, Mr Grey's voice was heard shouting to the men—

"Start off, and get us home as soon as you can."

The men gave a glance at the sky, and set forth at a smart pace. Mr Grey saw that the umbrellas lay at his hand, ready for distribution, and advised each lady to draw her cloak about her, as the air felt to him damp and chill.

A general flatness being perceptible, some one proposed that somebody else should sing. All declined at first, however, except Maria, whose voice was always most ready when it was most difficult to sing— when the party was dull, or when no one else would begin. She wanted to prevent Margaret's being applied to, and she sang, once and again, on the slightest hint. Sophia had no music-books, and could not sing without the piano, as every one knew beforehand she would say. Mrs Grey dropped a tear to the memory of Mrs Enderby, whose ballad was never wanting on such occasions as these. Sydney concluded that it was the same thought which made Mr Enderby bury his head in his hat between his knees while Miss Young was singing. It could not surely be all from shame at having kept the party waiting.

It was with some uncertainty and awe that he whispered in his friend's ear—

"Don't you think you could sing your new song that cousin Margaret is so fond of? Do: we are all as flat as flounders, and everybody will be asleep presently if we don't do something. Can't you get over a thing or two, and sing for us?"

"I am sure I would if I only could."

Enderby shook his head without raising it from his knees.

Mr Walcot had no idea of refusing when he was asked. He could sing the Canadian Boat Song; but he was afraid they might have heard it before.

"Never mind that. Let us have it," said everybody.

"But there should be two: it is a duet, properly, you know."

Sophia believed she could sing that—just that—without the piano. She would try the first part, if he would take the second. Mr Grey thought to himself that his daughter seemed to have adopted his hint about civility to his guests very dutifully. But Mr Walcot could sing only the first part, because he had a brother at home who always took the second. He could soon learn it, he had no doubt, but he did not know it at present: so he had the duet all to himself; uplifting a slender voice in a very odd key, which Fanny and Mary did not quite know what to make of. They looked round into all the faces in their boat to see whether anyone was going to laugh: but everybody was immoveable, except that Sophia whispered softly to Miss Young, that Mr Walcot was a most delightful young man, after all—so accomplished and so refined!

Mr Walcot's song ended with a quaver, from a large, cold, startling drop of rain falling on his nose, as he closed his eyes to draw out his last note. He blushed at having started and flinched from a drop of rain, and so spoiled his conclusion. Some of his hearers supposed he had broken-down, till assured by others that he had finished. Then everybody thanked him, and agreed that the rain was really coming on.

There were now odd fleeces of white cloud between the lead colour and the black. They were hurried about in the sky, evidently by counter currents. The river was almost inky in its hue, and every large drop made its own splash and circle. Up went the umbrellas in both boats; but almost before they were raised, some were turned inside out, and all were dragged down again. The gust had come, and brought with it a pelt of hail—large hailstones, which fell in at Fanny's collar behind, while she put down her head to save her face, and which almost took away Mary's breath, by coming sharp and fast against her cheeks. Then somebody descried a gleam of lightning quivering in the grey roof of the sky; and next, every one saw the tremendous flash which blazed over the surface of the water, all round about. How Mr Walcot would have quavered if he had been singing still. But a very different voice was now to be heard—the hoarse thunder rolling up, like advancing artillery; first growling, then roaring, and presently crashing and rattling overhead. The boatmen's thoughts were for the ladies, exposed as they were, without the possibility of putting up umbrellas. It felt almost dark to those in the boats, as they cut rapidly—more and more rapidly—through the water which seethed about the bows. The men were trotting, running. Presently it was darker still: the bent heads were raised, and it appeared that the boats were brought to, under the wide branches of two oaks which overhung the water. The woods were reached already.

"Shelter for the ladies, sir," said the panting boatmen, touching their hats, and then taking them off to wipe their brows. Mr Grey looked doubtful, stood up to survey, and then asked if there was no farm, no sort of house anywhere near. None nearer than yon village where the spire was, and that was very little nearer than Deerbrook itself. The ladies who were disposed to say anything, observed that they were very well as they were: the tree kept off a great deal of the hail, and the wind was not felt quite so much as on the open river. Should they sit still, or step on shore? Sit still, by all means. Packed closely as they were, they would be warmer and drier than standing on shore; and they were now ready to start homewards as soon as the storm should abate. It did not appear that there was any abatement of the storm in five minutes, nor in a quarter of an hour. The young people looked up at the elder ones, as if asking what to expect. Several of the party happened to be glancing in the same direction with the boatmen, when they saw a shaft of lightning strike perpendicularly from the upper range of cloud upon the village spire, and light it up.

"Lord bless us!" exclaimed Mr Grey, as the spire sent its smoke up like a little volcano.

Fanny burst out a-crying, but was called a silly child, and desired not to make a noise. Everyone was silent enough now; most hiding their faces, that they might not see what happened next. Half way between the river and the smoking church, in the farther part of the opposite meadow, was a fine spreading oak, under which, as might just be seen, a flock of sheep were huddled together for shelter. Another fiery dart shot down from the dark canopy, upon the crown of this oak. The tree quivered and fell asunder, its fragments lying in a circle. There was a rush forth of such of the sheep as escaped, and a rattle of thunder which would have overpowered any ordinary voices, but in the midst of which a scream was heard from the first boat. It was a singular thing that, in talking over this storm in after-days at home, no lady would own this scream.

"I'm thinking, sir," said Ben, as soon as he could make himself heard, "we are in a bad place here, as the storm seems thickening this way. We had best get from under the trees, for all the hail."

"Do so, Ben; and make haste."

When the first boat was brought a little out into the stream, in order to clear it of the flags, Margaret became aware that Philip was gazing earnestly at her from the other boat. She alone of the ladies had sat with face upraised, watching the advance of the storm. She alone, perhaps, of all the company, had enjoyed it with pure relish. It had animated her mind, and restored her to herself. When she saw Philip leaning back on his elbow, almost over the edge of the boat, to contemplate her, she returned his gaze with such an expression of mournful wonder and composed sorrow, as moved him to draw his hat over his eyes, and resolve to look no more.

The storm abated, but did not cease. Rain succeeded to hail, lightning still hovered in the air, and thunder continued to growl afar off. But the umbrellas could now be kept up, and the ladies escaped with a slight wetting.

Before the party dispersed from the wharf Hope sought Philip, and had a few moments' conversation with him, the object of which was to agree upon further discourse on the morrow. Hope and Margaret then accompanied Maria to her lodging, and walked thence silently home.

Hester was on the watch for them—a little anxious lest they should have suffered from the storm, and ready with some reflections on the liabilities of parties of pleasure; but yet blithe and beaming. Her countenance fell when she saw her sister's pale face.

"Margaret! how you look!" cried she. "Cold, wet, and weary: and ill, too, I am sure."

"Cold, wet, and weary," Margaret admitted. "Let me make haste to bed. And do you make tea for Edward, and send some up to me. Good-night! I cannot talk now. Edward will tell you."

"Tell me what?" Hester asked her husband, when she found that Margaret had really rather have no attendance.

"That Margaret is unhappy, love, from some misunderstanding with Enderby. Some busy devil—I have no doubt the same that has caused so much mischief already—has come between him and Margaret."

He then told the story of Philip's sudden appearance, and his conduct throughout the day, omitting all hint that any conversation with himself had taken place. He hoped, in conclusion, that all would be cleared up, and the mutual faith of the lovers restored.

Hester thought this impossible. If Philip could be prejudiced against Margaret by any man or woman on earth, or any devil in hell, there must be an instability in his character to which Margaret's happiness must not be committed. Hope was not sure of this. There were circumstances of temptation, modes of delusion, under which the faith of a seraph might sink. But worse still, Hester said, was his conduct of to-day, torturing Margaret's affection, wounding her pride, insulting her cruelly, in the presence of all those among whom she lived. Hope was disposed to suspend his judgment even upon this. Enderby was evidently half-frantic. His love was undiminished, it was clear. It was the soul of all the madness of to-day. Margaret had conducted herself nobly. Her innocence, her faith, must triumph at last. They might bring her lover to her side again, Hester had little doubt: but she did not see what could now render Philip worthy of Margaret. This had always been her apprehension. How, after the passions of this day, could they ever again be as they had been? And tears, as gentle and sorrowful as Margaret had ever shed for her, now rained from Hester's eyes.

"Be comforted, my Hester—my generous wife, be comforted. You live for us—you are our best blessing, my love, and we can never bear to see you suffer for her. Be comforted, and wait. Trust that the retribution of this will fall where it ought; and that will never be upon our Margaret. Pray that the retribution may fall where it ought, and that its bitterness may be intense as the joy which Margaret and you deserve."

"I never knew you so revengeful, Edward," said his wife, taking the hand he held before his eyes. "Shall I admonish you for once? Shall I give you a reproof for wishing woe to our enemies? Shall I remind you to forgive—fully, freely, as you hope to be forgiven?"

"Yes, love; anything for the hope of being forgiven."

"Ah! how deep your sorrow for Margaret is! Grief always humbles us in our own eyes. Such humiliation is the test of sorrow. Bless you, love, that you grieve so for Margaret!"

Chapter Thirty Six

The Next Day.

The hours of a sleepless night were not too long for Hope to revolve what he must say and do on the morrow. He must meet Enderby; and the day would probably decide Margaret's fate. That this decision would implicate his own happiness or misery was a subordinate thought. It was not till after he had viewed Margaret's case in every light in which apprehension could place it, that he dwelt upon what the suffering to himself must be of seeing Margaret, day by day, living on, in meek patience, amidst the destruction of hope and happiness which his attachment had caused. When he did dwell upon it, his heart sank within him. All that had made him unhappy seemed of late to have passed away. For many months he had seen Margaret satisfied in her attachment to another; he had seen Hester coming out nobly from the trial of adversity, in which all her fine qualities had been exercised, and her weaknesses almost subdued. She had been not only the devoted wife, but patient and generous towards her foes, full of faith and cheerfulness in her temper, and capable of any degree of self-denial in the conduct of her daily life. She had been of late all that in the days of their engagement—in the days when he had dealt falsely with his own mind—he had trusted she would be. A friendship, whose tenderness was life enough for them both, had grown up in his soul, and he had been at peace. It had been a subject of incessant thankfulness to him, that the evil of what he could now hardly consider as a false step had been confined to himself—that his struggles, his strivings, the dreadful solitary conflicts of a few months, had not been in vain; that he had fulfilled the claims of both relations, and marred no one's peace. Now, he was plunged into the struggle again. The cause was at an end; but consequences, of perhaps endless wretchedness, remained to be borne. His secret was known, and made the basis of untruths to which the whole happiness of his household, so victoriously struggled for, so carefully cherished by him, and so lately secured, must be sacrificed. Again and again he turned from the fearful visions of Margaret cast off, of the estrangement of the sisters, of the possible loss of some of their fair fame—from these harrowing thoughts he turned again and again to consider what must be done.—The most certain thing was, that he must not by word, look, pause, or admission, countenance to Enderby himself the supposition that he had not preferred Hester at the time she became his wife. In the present state of their attachment, this was the merest justice to her. Nothing that it was in

Mrs Grey's power to reveal bore a relation to any time later than his early, and, it might be assumed, superficial, intercourse with the sisters and, as far as he knew, no one else, unless it were Frank (by this time in possession of the facts), had ever conceived of the true state of the case. He must decline all question about his domestic relations, except as far as Margaret was concerned. Beyond this, he would allow of no inquisition, and would forbid all speculation. For Margaret's sake, no less than Hester's, this was necessary. If she should ever be Enderby's wife, it was of the utmost importance that Enderby should not, in his most secret soul, hold this information, however strongly he might be convinced that Margaret was in ignorance of it, and had never loved any but himself. There must be no admission to Enderby of that which had been truth, but which would become untruth by being first admitted now. There must be entire silence upon the whole subject of himself.—As to Margaret, he did not see what could be done, but to declare his true and perfect belief that she had never loved any but Enderby. But alas! what chance was there of this testimony being received; the very point of Enderby's accusation being, that they both looked, perhaps in self-delusion, at the connection with him as their security from the consequences of Hope's weakness in marrying Hester? It was all confused—all wretched—all nearly hopeless. Margaret would be sacrificed without knowing why—would have her heart wrung with the sense of injury in addition to her woe.

From reflections and anticipations, Hope rose early to the great duty of the day. He told Hester that he was going to meet Enderby in the meadows, to receive a full explanation of his conduct of the preceding day; and that it was probable that he should bring home whatever tidings it might be Margaret's lot to hear.

He found, during the long and anxious conversation in the meadow, that he had need of all the courage, calmness, and discretion he could command. It was a cruel trial to one whose wont it had been from his childhood to converse in "simplicity and godly sincerity,"—it was a cruel trial to hear evidence upon evidence brought of what he knew to have been fact, and to find connected with this, revolting falsehoods, against which he could only utter the indignation of his soul. When he afterwards reflected how artfully the facts and falsehoods were connected, he could no longer wonder at Enderby's convictions, nor at the conduct which proceeded from them. There was in Enderby this morning no undue anger, no contempt which could excite anger in another;—no doubt cast by him upon Hope's honour, or Margaret's purity of mind, as the world esteems purity. However this might have been before their meeting of yesterday, it was now clear that, though immoveably convinced of their mutual attachment, he supposed it to have been entertained as innocently as it was formed;—that

Hope had been wrought upon by Mrs Grey, and by a consciousness of Hester's love; that he had married from a false sense of honour, and then discovered his mistake;—that he had striven naturally, and with success, to persuade himself that Margaret loved his friend, while Margaret had made the same effort, and would have married that friend for security and with the hope of rest in a home of her own, with one whom she might possibly love and to whom she was bound by his love of herself.

As for the evidence on which his belief was founded, there seemed to be no end to it. Hope could do little but listen to the detail. If he had been sitting in judgment on the conduct of an imputed criminal, he would have wrestled with the evidence obstinately and long; but what could he do, when it was the lover of his sister-in-law who was declaring why his confidence in her was gone, and he must resume his plighted faith? None but those who had done the mischief could repair it; and least of all, Hope himself. He could only make one single, solemn protestation of his belief that Margaret had loved none but Enderby, and deny the truth of every statement that was inconsistent with this.

The exhibition of the evidence showed how penetrating, how sagacious, as well as how industrious, malice can be. There seemed to be no circumstance connected with the sisters and their relation to Mr Hope, that Mrs Rowland had not laid hold of. Mrs Grey's visit to Hope during his convalescence; his subsequent seclusion, and his depression when he reappeared—all these were noted; and it was these which sent Enderby to Mrs Grey for an explanation, which she had not had courage or judgment to withhold—which, indeed, she had been hurried into giving. She had admitted all that had passed between herself and Mr Hope—his consternation at finding that it was Hester who loved him, and whom he must marry, and the force with which Mrs Grey had felt herself obliged to urge that duty upon him. Enderby connected with this his own observations and feelings at the time; his last summer's conviction that it was Margaret whom Hope loved; his rapturous surprise on hearing of the engagement being to Hester; and his wonder at the coldness with which his friend received his congratulations. He now thought that he must have been doomed to blindness not to have discerned the truth through all this.— Then there was his own intrusion during the interview which Hope had with Margaret;—their countenances had haunted him ever since. Hope's was full of constraint and anxiety;—he was telling his intentions:— Margaret's face was downcast, and her attitude motionless; she was hearing her doom.—Then, after Hope was married, all Deerbrook was aware of his failure of spirits; and of Margaret's no less. It was a matter of common remark, that there must be something amiss—that all was not right at home. They had, then, doubtless discovered that the attachment was mutual; and they might well be wretched.—Those who ought to know best had been convinced of this at an earlier stage of the intercourse. Mrs Rowland had met at Cheltenham a young officer, an intimate friend of Mr Hope's family, who would not be persuaded that it was not to the younger sister that Mr Hope was married. He declared that he knew, from the highest authority, that Hope was attached to Margaret, and that the attachment was returned. It was not till Mrs Rowland had shown him the announcement of the marriage in an old Blickley newspaper, which she happened to have used in packing her trunk, that he would believe that it was the elder sister who was Hope's wife.—There was one person, however, who had known the whole, Enderby said; perhaps she was the only person who had been aware of it all: and that was his mother.

In answer to Hope's exclamations upon the absurdity of this, Enderby said, that a thousand circumstances rose up to confirm Mrs Rowland's statement that her mother had known all, and had learned it from Margaret herself. Margaret had confided in her old friend as in a mother; and nothing could be more natural—nothing probably more necessary to an overburdened heart. This explained his mother's never having shown his letters to Margaret—the person for whom, as she knew, they were chiefly written. This explained the words of concern about the domestic troubles of the Hopes, which, now and then during her long confinement, she had dropped in Phoebe's hearing, and even in her letters to her son. She had repeatedly regretted that Margaret would not leave her sister's house, and return to Birmingham—saying that income and convenience were not to be thought of for a moment, in comparison with some other considerations. In fact she had—it was weakness, perhaps, but one not to be too hardly judged under the circumstances—she had revealed the whole to her daughter under injunctions to secrecy, which had been strictly observed while she lived, and broken now only for a brother's sake, and after a long conflict between obligations apparently contradictory. When, from her deathbed, she had welcomed Margaret as a daughter-in-law, it was in the gratitude which it was natural for a mother to feel, on finding the attachment of an only son at length appreciated and rewarded. When she had implored Mrs Rowland to receive Margaret as a sister, and had seen them embrace, her generous spirit had rejoiced in her young friend's conquest of an unhappy passion; and she had meant to convey to Priscilla an admonition to bury in oblivion what had become known to her, and to forgive Margaret for having loved any one but Philip. Priscilla could not make a difficulty at such a time, and in such a presence; she had submitted to the embrace, but her soul had recoiled from it; she had actually fainted under the shock: and ever since, she had declared to her brother, with a pertinacity which he had been unable to understand—which, indeed, had looked like sheer audacity, that he would never marry Margaret Ibbotson.

Philip was now convinced that he had done his sister much wrong. Her temper and conduct were in some instances indefensible; but since he had learned all this, and become aware how much of what he had censured had been said and done out of affection for himself, he had been disposed rather to blame her for the lateness of her explanations, than for any excess of zeal on his account,—zeal which he admitted had carried her a point or two beyond the truth in some of her aims. These statements about the condition of Margaret's mind were borne out by circumstances known to others. When Margaret had been rescued from drowning, Hope was heard to breathe, as he bent over her, "Oh God! my Margaret!" and it was observed that she rallied instantly on hearing the exclamation, and repaid him with a look worthy of his words. This had been admitted to Enderby himself by the one who heard it, and who might be trusted to speak of it to no one else. Then, it was known that when Margaret was in the habit of taking long walks alone, towards the end of the winter, she was met occasionally by her brother-in-law in his rides—naturally enough. Their conversation had been overheard, once at least, when they consulted about the peace of their home—how much of a certain set of circumstances they should communicate to Mrs Hope, and whether or not Mr Enderby was engaged to a lady abroad. Without these testimonies, Enderby felt that he had only to recur to his own experience to be convinced that Margaret had never loved him, though striving to persuade herself, as well as him, that she did. The calmness with which she had received his avowals that first evening last winter, struck him with admiration at the time: he now understood it better. He wondered he had felt so little till now the coldness of the tone of her correspondence. The first thing which awakened him to an admission of it, was her refusal to marry him in the spring. She shrank, as she avowed, from leaving her present residence—she might have said, from quitting those she loved best.

It was clear that in marrying she was to make a sacrifice to duty—to secure innocence and safety for herself and those who were dearest to her; and that, when the time drew near, she recoiled from the effort. Enderby was thankful that all had become clear in time for her release and his own.

The horror with which Hope listened to this was beyond what he had prepared himself for—beyond all that he had yet endured. Enderby seemed quite willing to hear him; but what could be said? Only that which he had planned. His protest against the truth of certain of the statements, and the justice of some of the constructions of facts, was strong. He declared that, in his perfect satisfaction with his domestic state, his happiness with his beloved and honoured wife, he would admit of no question about his family affairs, as far as he and Hester were concerned. He denied at once and for ever, all that went to show that Margaret had for a moment regarded him otherwise than as a friend and a brother; and declared that the bare mention to her of the idea which was uppermost in Enderby's mind would be a cruelty and insult which could never be retrieved. He was not going to plead for her. Bitterly as she must suffer, it was from a cause which lay too deep for cure—from a want of faith in her in one who ought to know her best, but from whom she would be henceforth best separated, if what he had been saying was his deliberate belief and judgment.—Enderby declaring that it was so, and that it was his intention to release Margaret from her engagement, gently and carefully, without useless explanation and without reproach, there was nothing more to be said or done. Hope prophesied, in parting, that, of all the days of Enderby's life, this was perhaps that of which he would one day most heartily repent; and while he spoke, he felt that this same day was the one which he might himself find the most difficult to endure. He left Enderby still pacing the meadow, and walked homewards with a heart weighed down with grief—a grief which yet he would fain have increased to any degree of intensity by taking Margaret's upon himself.

Margaret was at the breakfast-table with her sister when he entered. Her eyes were swollen, but her manner was gentle and composed. She looked up at Edward, when he appeared, with an expression of timid expectation in her face, which went to his soul. A few words passed—a very few, and then no more was said.

"Yes; I have seen him. He is very wretched. He will not come, but we shall hear something, I have no doubt. A strange persuasion which I cannot remove, of a prior attachment—of a want of frankness and confidence. He will explain himself presently. But his persuasion is irremoveable."

Hester had much to say of him out of her throbbing heart; but she looked at Margaret, and restrained herself. What must there be in *that* heart? To utter one word would be irreverent. The breakfast passed in an almost unbroken silence.

It had not been long over when the expected letter came. Hope never saw it; but there was no need: he perfectly anticipated its contents, while to her for whom they were written they were incomprehensible.

> "I spare you and myself the misery of an interview. It must be agonising to you, and there would be dishonour as well as pain to me, in witnessing that agony. If, as I fully believe, you have been hitherto blind to the injustice of your connecting yourself with me, from a sense of duty and expediency, when you had not a first genuine love to give, I think you will see it now; and I pity your suffering in the discovery. There is only one point on which I wish

or intend to hang any reproach. Why did you not, when I had become entitled to your confidence, lay your heart fully open to me? Did I not do so by you? Did I not reveal to you even the transient fancy which I entertained long ago, and which I showed my faith in you, her friend, by revealing? If you had only done the same—if you had only let me know, without a hint as to the object, that you had been attached, and that you believed I might succeed to your affections in time—if you had done this, I do not say that we should then have been what I so lately trusted we were to be, for my soul is jealous—has been made so by what I thought you—and will bear none but a first, and an entire, and an exclusive love: but in that case I should have cherished you in my inmost heart, as all that I have believed you to be, though not destined for me.

"But I do not blame you. You have done what you meant to be right; though, from too great regard to one set of considerations, you have mistaken the right, and have sacrificed me. I make allowance for your difficulty, and, for my own part, pardon you, and testify most sincerely and earnestly to the purity of your mind and intentions. Do not reject this parting testimony. I offer it because I would not have you think me harsh, or suppose that passion has made me unjust. I love you too deeply to do more than mourn. I have no heart to blame, except for your want of confidence. Of that I have a right to complain: but, for the rest, spare yourself the effort of self-justification. It is not needed. I do not accuse you. You were right in saying yesterday that I love you still. I shall ever love you, be our separate lives what they may. God bless you!

"P.E."

"Will you not wait, my dearest Margaret?" said Hester, when, within half an hour of the arrival of Enderby's letter, she met her sister on the stairs, with the reply in her hand, sealed, and ready to be sent. "Why such haste? The events of your life may hang on this day, on this one letter. Can it be right to be so rapid in what you think and do?"

"The event of my life is decided," she replied, "unless—No—the event of my life *is* decided. I have nothing more to wait for. I have written what I think, and it must go."

It was as follows:—

"I have nothing to say in reply to your letter, for I cannot understand it. Yet I wonder less at your letter than at your having written it instead of coming to me, to say all that is in your mind. At some moments I still think that you will—I feel that you are on your way hither, and I fancy that this dreadful dream of your displeasure will pass away. It is the first time in my life that any one has been seriously and lastingly displeased with me; and, though I feel that I have not deserved it, I am very wretched that you, of all others, should blame me, and cease to trust me. There ought to be some comfort in the thought that your anger is without cause: but I cannot find such comfort; for I feel that though I could endure your loss by long absence or death, I cannot live in the spirit in which I should wish to live, without your esteem.

"It is useless, alas! to entreat of you to come and explain yourself, or in some other way to put me in possession of the cause of your anger. If you could resist the claims I had upon you for confidence before I knew what was going to befall me—if you could resist the demand I made yesterday, I fear there is little use in imploring you to do me justice. If I thought there was any chance, I would submit to entreat, though I would not have you, any more than myself, forget that I have a right to demand. But indeed I would yield everything that I dare forego, to have you awakened from this strange delusion which makes us both wretched. It is no time for pride now. I care not how fully you know what I feel. I only wish that you could see into my soul as into your own; for then you would not misjudge me as you do. I care not what any one may think of my throwing myself upon the love which I am certain you feel for me, if I can only persuade you to tell me what you mean, and to hear what I shall then have to say. What can I now say? I will not reproach you, for I know you must be even, if possible, more miserable than I: but yet, how can I help feeling that you have been unjust and harsh with me? Yes; though the tone of your letter seems to be gentle, and you clearly mean it to be so, I feel that you have been very harsh to me. Nothing that you can do shall ever make me so cruel to you. You may rest satisfied that, if we should not meet again, I will never be unjust to you. To every one about me it will appear that you are fickle and dishonourable—that you have acted towards me as it is in the nature of some men to act towards the women whose affections they possess; in the nature of some men, but not in yours. I know you to be incapable of anything worse than error and mistrust (and, till yesterday, I could not have believed you capable of this much wrong): and you may trust me to impute to you nothing worse than this. Suffering as I now am, as we both are, under this error and mistrust, may I not implore you, for your own sake (for mine it is too late), to nourish the weak part of yourself, to question your own unworthy doubts, and to study the best parts of the minds you meet, till you grow assured (as a religious man ought to be) that there can be no self-interest, and much less falsehood, mixed up with any real affection—with any such affection as has existed between us two?

"I must not write more; for I do not know, I cannot conjecture, how you may receive what I have written, thinking of me as you now do. It seems strange to remember that at this time yesterday, in this very chair, I was writing to you. Oh how differently! Is it possible that it was only yesterday—such a world of misery as we have lived through since? But I can write no more. It may be that you will despise me in every line as you read: after what has happened, I cannot tell. Notwithstanding all I have said about trusting, I feel at this moment as if I could never depend on anything in this world again. If you should come within this hour and explain all, how could I be sure that the same thing might not happen again? But do not let this weigh a moment with you, if indeed you think of coming. If I do not see you to-day, I shall never see you. I will then bear in mind, as you desire, and as I cannot help, that you love me still; but how little comfort is there in such love, when trust is gone! God comfort us both!

"Margaret Ibbotson."

Mrs Rowland was crossing the hall at the moment that her maid Betsy opened the door to Mr Hope's errand-boy, and took in this letter.

"Where are you carrying that letter?" said she, as Betsy passed her.

"To the study, ma'am, against Mr Enderby comes in. It is for Mr Enderby, ma'am."

"Very well."

The letter was placed on the study mantelpiece; the place of deposit for letters for absent members of the family. Mrs Rowland meantime resumed her seat in the drawing-room, where the nursemaid was amusing the baby. Mamma took the baby, and sent the maid away. She had a strong belief that her brother might be found somewhere in the shrubbery, though some feeling had prevented her telling the servant so when the letter was taken in. She went, with the baby in her arms, into the study, to see whether Philip was visible in any part of the garden that could be seen thence. But she stopped short of the window. The handwriting on the address of the letter troubled her sight. More than half-persuaded, as she was, of the truth of much that she had told her brother, strenuously as she had nourished the few facts she was in possession of, till she had made them yield a double crop of inferences, she was yet conscious of large exaggerations of what she knew, and of huge additions to what she believed to be probabilities, and had delivered as facts. There was in that handwriting a prophecy of detection: and, like other cowards, she began to tamper with her reason and conscience.

"There is great mischief in letters at such times," she thought. "They are so difficult to answer! and it is so possible to produce any effect that may be wished by them! As my husband was reading the other day—'It is so easy to be virtuous, to be perfect, upon paper!' Nothing that the girl can say ought to alter the state of the case: it can only harass Philip's feelings, and perhaps cause all the work to be gone over again. His letter was meant to be final, I am confident, from his intending to go away this evening. There should have been no answer. This letter is a pure impertinence, and ought to be treated as such. It is a sort of duty to use it as it deserves. Many parents (at least I know old Mr Boyle did) burn letters which they know to contain offers to daughters whom they do not wish to part with. Mr Boyle had no scruple; and I am sure this is a stronger case. Better end the whole affair at once; and then Philip will be free to form a better connection. He will thank me one day for having broken off this."

She carried the letter into the drawing-room, slowly contemplating it as she went. She thought, for one fleeting instant, of reading it. She was not withheld by honour, but by fear. She shrank from encountering its contents. She glanced over the mantelpiece, and saw that the lucifer-matches were at hand. To make the letter burn quickly, it was necessary to unfold it. She put the child down upon the rug—a favourite play-place, for the sake of the gay pink and green shavings which, at this time of the year, curtained the grate. While baby crawled, and gazed quietly and contentedly there, Mrs Rowland broke the seal of Margaret's letter, turning her eyes from the writing, laid the blistered sheet in the hearth, and set fire to it. The child set up a loud crow of delight at the flame. At that moment, even this simple and familiar sound startled its mother out of all power of self-control. She snatched up the child with a vehemence which frightened it into a shrill cry. She feared the nursemaid would come before all the sparks were out; and she tried to quiet the baby by dancing it before the mirror over the mantelpiece. She met her own face there, white as ashes; and the child saw nothing that could amuse it, while its eyes were blinded with tears. She opened the window to let it hearken to the church clock; and the device was effectual. Baby composed its face to serious listening, before the long succession of strokes was finished, and allowed the tears to be wiped from its cheeks.

One thing more remained to be done. Mrs Rowland heard a step in the hall, and looked out: it was Betsy's.

"I thought it was you. Pray desire cook to send up a cup of broth for Miss Rowland's lunch; and be sure and let Miss Rowland know, the moment it is ready. Mr Enderby is in the shrubbery, I think."

"Yes, ma'am; seeing he was there, I was coming to ask about the letter, ma'am, to carry it to him."

"Oh, that letter—I sent it to him. He has got it. Tell cook directly about the broth."

At lunch-time, one of the children was desired to summon Uncle Philip. Mrs Rowland took care to meet him at the garden door. She saw him cast a wistful eye towards the study mantelpiece, as he passed the open door. His sister observed that she believed it was past post time for this half-week. He sighed deeply; and she felt that no sigh of his had ever so gone to her heart before.

"Why, mamma! do look!" cried George, as well as a mouthful of bread would allow. "Look at the chimney! Where are all the shavings gone? There is the knot at the top that they were tied together with, but not a bit of shaving left. Have they blown up the chimney?"

"What will poor baby say?" exclaimed Matilda. "All the pretty pink and green gone!"

"There is some tinder blowing about," observed George. "I do believe they have been burnt."

"Shut the window, George, will you? There is no bearing this draught. There is no bearing Betsy's waste either. She has burned those shavings somehow in cleaning the grate. Her carelessness is past endurance."

"Make her buy some new shavings, mamma, for baby's sake."

"Do be quiet, and get your lunch. Hand your uncle the dish of currants."

Philip languidly picked a few bunches. He had noticed nothing that had passed, as his sister was glad to observe. Besides being too much accustomed, to hear complaints of the servants to give any heed to them, he was now engrossed with his own wretched thoughts. Every five minutes that passed without bringing a reply from Margaret, went to confirm his most painful impressions.

Margaret meantime was sitting alone in her chamber, enduring the long morning as she best might. Now plying her needle as if life depended on her industry, and now throwing up her employment in disgust, she listened for the one sound she needed to hear, till her soul was sick of every other. "I must live wholly within myself now," she thought, "as far as he is concerned. I can never speak of him, or allow Hester and Maria to speak of him to me; for they will blame him. Every one will blame him: Maria did yesterday. No one will do him justice. I cannot ask Mrs Grey, as I intended, anything of what she may have seen and heard about all this. I have had my joy to myself: I have carried about my solitary glory and bliss in his being mine; and now I must live alone upon my grief for him; for no one person in the world will pity and justify him but myself. He has done me no wrong that he could help. His staying away to-day is to save me pain, as he thinks. I wish I had not said in my letter that he has been harsh to me. Perhaps he would have been here by this time if I had not said that. How afraid he was, that day in the spring when he urged me so to marry at once—(Oh! if I had, all this would have been saved! and yet I thought, and I still think, I was right.) But how afraid he was of our parting, lest evil should come between us! I promised him it should not, for my own part: but who could have thought that the mistrust would be on his side? He had a superstitious feeling, he said, that something would happen—that we should be parted: and I would not hear of it. How presumptuous I was! How did I dare to make so light of what has come so dreadfully true?—Oh! why are we so made that we cannot see into one another's hearts? If we are made to depend on one another so absolutely as we are, so that we hold one another's peace to cherish or to crush, why is it such a blind dependence? Why are we left so helpless? Why, with so many powers as are given us, have we not that one other, worth all the rest, of mutual insight? If God would bestow this power for this one day, I would give up all else for it for ever after. Philip would trust me again then, and I should understand him; and I could rest afterwards, happen what might—though then nothing would happen but what was good. But now, shut in, each into ourselves, with anger and sorrow all about us, from some mistake which a moment's insight might remove—it is the dreariest, the most tormenting state! What are all the locks, and bars, and fetters in the world to it? So near each other too! When one look, one tone, might perhaps lead to the clearing up of it all! There is no occasion to bear this, however. So near as we are, nothing should prevent our meeting—nothing shall prevent it."

She started up, and hastily put on her bonnet and gloves: but when her hand was on the lock of her door, her heart misgave her. "If it should fail!" she thought. "If he should neither look at me nor speak to me—if he should leave me as he did yesterday! I should never get over the shame. I dare not store up such a wretched remembrance, to make me miserable as often as I think of it, for as long as I live. If he will not come after reading my letter, neither would he hear me if I went to him. Oh! he is very unjust! After all his feats of my being influenced against him, he might have distrusted himself. After making me promise to write, on the first doubt that any one might try to put into my mind, he might have remembered to do the same by me, instead of coming down in this way, not to explain, but to overwhelm me with his displeasure, without giving me a moment's time to justify myself. Edward seems strangely unkind too," she sighed, as she slowly untied her bonnet and put it away, as if to avoid tempting herself with the sight of it again. "I never knew Edward unjust or unkind before; but I heard him ask Philip why he staid to hear me in the abbey yesterday; and though he has been with Philip this morning, he does not seem to have made the slightest attempt to bring us together. When such as Edward and Philip do so wrong, one does not know where to trust, or what to hope. There is nothing to trust, but God and the right. I will live for these, and no one shall henceforth hear me complain, or see me droop, or know anything of what lies deepest in my heart. This must be possible; it has been done. Many nuns in their convents have carried it through: and missionaries in heathen countries, and all the wisest who have been before their age; and some say—Maria would say—almost every person who has loved as I have: but I do not believe this: I do not believe that many—that any can have felt as I do now. It is not natural and right that any should live as I mean to do. We are made for confidence, not for such solitude and concealment. But it may be done when circumstances press as they do upon me; and, if God gives me strength, I will do it. I will live for Him and his; and my heart, let it suffer as it may, shall never complain to human ear. It shall be as silent as the grave."

The resolution held for some hours. Margaret was quiet and composed through dinner, though her expectation, instead of dying out, grew more intense with every hour. After dinner, Hope urged his wife to walk with him. It had been a fine day, and she had not been out. There was still another hour before dark. Would not Margaret go too? No; Margaret could not leave home.

When Hester came down, equipped for her walk, she sat beside her sister on the sofa for a minute or two, while waiting for Edward.

"Margaret," said she, "will you let me say one word to you?"

"Anything, Hester, if you will not be hard upon any one whom you cannot fully understand."

"I would not for the world be hard, love. But there was once a time, above a year ago, when you warned me, kindly warned me, though I did not receive it kindly, against pride as a support. You said it could not support me; and you said truly. May I say the same to you now?"

"Thank you. It is kind of you. I will consider; but I do not think that I have any pride in me to-day. I feel humbled enough."

"It is not for you to feel humbled, love. Reverence yourself; for you may. Nothing has happened to impair your self-respect. Admit freely to your own mind, and to us, that you have been cruelly injured, and that you suffer as you must and ought. Admit this freely, and then rely on yourself and us."

Margaret shook her head. She did not say it, but she felt that she could not rely on Edward, while he seemed to stand between her and Philip. He came in at the moment, and she averted her eyes from him. He felt her displeasure in his heart's core.

When they returned, sooner than she had expected, from their walk, they had bad news for her, which they had agreed it was most merciful not to delay. They had seen Enderby in Mr Rowland's gig on the Blickley road. He had his carpet-bag with him; and Mr Rowland's man was undoubtedly driving him to Blickley, to meet the night coach for London.

"It is better to save you all further useless expectation," observed Edward. "We keep nothing from you."

"You keep nothing from me!" said Margaret, now fixing her eyes upon him. "Then what is your reason for not having brought us together, if indeed you have not kept us apart? Do you suppose I did not hear you send him from me yesterday? And how do I know that you have not kept him away to-day?"

"My dear Margaret!" exclaimed Hester: but a look from her husband, and the recollection of Margaret's misery, silenced her. For the first time Hester forgave on the instant the act of blaming her husband.

"Whatever I have done, whether it appears clear to you or not," replied Hope, "it is from the most tender respect for your feelings. I shall always respect them most tenderly; and not the less for their being hurt with me."

"I have no doubt of your meaning all that is kind, Edward: but surely when two people misunderstand each other, it is best that they should meet. If you have acted from a regard to what you consider my dignity, I could wish that you had left the charge of it to myself."

"You are right: quite right."

"Then why——. Oh! Edward, if you repent what you have done, it may not yet be too late!"

"I do not repent. I have done you no wrong to-day, Margaret. I grieve for you, but I could not have helped you."

"Let us never speak on this subject again," said Margaret, stung by the consciousness of having so soon broken the resolution of the morning, that her suffering heart should be as silent as the grave. "It is not from pride, Hester, that I say so; but let us never again speak of all this."

"Let us know but one thing, Margaret," said Edward;—"that yours is the generous silence of forgiveness. I do not mean with regard to him—for I fear you will forgive him sooner than we can do. I do not mean him particularly, nor those who have poisoned his ear; but all. Only tell us that your silence is the oblivion of mercy, so mourning for the erring that, for its own sake, it remembers their transgressions no more."

Margaret looked up at them both. Though her eyes swam in tears, there was a smile upon her lips as she held out her hand to her brother, and yielded herself to Hester's kiss.

Chapter Thirty Seven

The Conqueror.

Mrs Rowland did not find herself much the happier for being borne out by the whole world in her assertions, that Philip and Margaret were not engaged. She knew that, with regard to this, she now stood justified in the eyes of all Deerbrook, that almost everyone there now believed that it had been an entanglement from which she had released her brother. From selfish fear, from dread of the consequences of going so far as to be again sent by her husband to Cheltenham, or by the Levitts to Coventry; from foresight of the results which would ensue from her provoking an inquiry into the domestic concerns of the Hopes—an inquiry which might end in the reconciliation of Philip and Margaret, and in some unpleasant discoveries about herself—she was very guarded respecting the grand accusation by which she had wrought on her brother. No hint of it got abroad in Deerbrook: nothing was added to the ancient gossip about the Hopes not being very happy together. Mrs Rowland knew that affairs stood in this satisfactory state. She knew that Margaret was exposed to as much observation and inquiry as a country village affords, respecting her disappointed attachment—that the Greys were very angry, and praised Margaret to every person they met—that Mr Walcot eulogised Mrs Rowland's discernment to all Mrs Rowland's party—that Mrs Howell and Miss Miskin lifted up their eyes in thankfulness at Mr Enderby's escape from such a connection—that Mr Hope was reported to be rather flat in spirits—and that Margaret was certainly looking thin: she knew of all this success, and yet she was not happier than six months ago. The drawback on such successes is, that they are never complete. There is always some Mordecai sitting at the gate to mar the enjoyment. Mrs Rowland was aware of Mrs James having dropped that she and her husband had nothing to do with anybody's family quarrels; that there was always a great deal to be said on both sides in such cases; and that they had never seen anything but what was amiable and pleasant in Miss Ibbotson and her connections. She knew that Dr Levitt called on the Hopes full as often as at any house in Deerbrook; and that Mrs Levitt had offered to take some of Margaret's plants into her greenhouse, to be nursed through the winter. She was always hearing that Miss Young and Margaret were much together, and that they were happy in each other's society; and she alternately fancied them talking about her, exposing to each other the injuries she had wrought to both, and enjoying an oblivion of their cares in her despite. She could never see Maria taking an airing in the Greys' shrubbery, leaning on Margaret's arm, or Margaret turning in at the farrier's gate, without feeling her colour rise. She knew that Mr Jones was apt to accommodate Miss Ibbotson with a choice of meat, in preference to his other customers; and that Mrs Jones had spoken indignantly to a neighbour about fine gentlemen from London that think little of breaking one young heart after another, to please their own vanity, and never come back to look upon the eyes that they have made dim, and the cheeks that grow pale for them.

All these things Mrs Rowland knew; and they ate into her heart. In these days of her triumph she moved about in fear; and no hour passed without troubling her victory. She felt that she could not rest till the corner-house family was got rid of. They did not seem disposed to move of their own accord. She incessantly expressed her scorn of the want of spirit of a professional man who would live on in a place where he had lost his practice, and where a rival was daily rising upon his ruins: but the Hopes staid on still. Week after week they were to be met in the lanes and meadows—now gleaning in the wake of the harvest-wain, with Fanny and Mary, for the benefit of widow Rye; now blackberry gathering in the fields; now nutting in the hedgerows. The quarterly term came round, and no notice that he might look out for another tenant reached Mr Rowland. If they would not go of their own accord, they must be dislodged; for she felt, though she did not fully admit the truth to herself, that she could not much longer endure their presence. She looked out for an opportunity of opening the subject advantageously with Mr Rowland.

The wine and walnuts were on the table, and the gentleman and lady were amusing themselves with letting Anna and Ned try to crack walnuts (the three elder children being by this time at school at Blickley), when Mrs Rowland began her attack.

"My dear," said she, "is the corner-house in perfectly good repair at present?"

"I believe so. It was thoroughly set to rights when Mr Hope went into it, and again after the riot; and I have heard no complaint since."

"Ah! after the riot; that is what I wanted to know. The surgery is well fitted up, is it?"

"No doubt. The magistrates took care that everything should be done handsomely. Mr Hope was fully satisfied."

"He was: then there seems no doubt that Mr Walcot had better remove to the corner-house when the Hopes go away. It is made to be a surgeon's residence: and I own I do not like to see those blinds of Mr Walcot's, with that staring word 'Surgery,' upon them, in the windows of my poor mother's breakfast-room."

"Nor I: but the Hopes are not going to remove."

"I believe they will be leaving Deerbrook before long."

"I believe not."

"My dear Mr Rowland, I have reason for what I say."

"So have I. Take care of that little thumb of yours, my darling, or you will be cracking it instead of the walnut."

"What is your reason for thinking that the Hopes will not leave Deerbrook, Mr Rowland?"

"Mr Hope told me so himself."

"Ah! that is nothing. You will be about the last person he will inform of his plans. Mr Walcot's nearest friends will be the last to know, of course."

"Pray, do not make me out one of Mr Walcot's nearest friends, my dear. I have a very slight acquaintance with the young gentleman, and do not intend to have more."

"You say so now to annoy me, my love: but you may change your mind. If you should see Mr Walcot your son-in-law at some future day, you will not go on to call him a slight acquaintance, I suppose?"

"My son-in-law! Have you been asking him to marry Matilda?"

"I wait, Mr Rowland, till he asks it himself; which I foresee he will do as soon as our dear girl is old enough to warrant his introducing the subject. Her accomplishments are not lost upon him. He has the prophetic eye which sees what a wonderful creature she must become. And if we are permitted to witness such an attachment as theirs will be, and our dear girl settled beside us here, we shall have nothing left to wish."

"To speak of something more nearly at hand, I beg, my dear, that you will hold out no expectation of the corner-house to Mr Walcot, as it is not likely to be vacated."

"Has the rent been regularly paid, so far?"

"To be sure it has."

"By Mr Grey's help, I have no doubt. My dear, I know what I am saying. The Hopes are as poor as the rats in your granary; and it is not to be supposed that Mr Grey will long go on paying their rent for them, just for the frolic of sustaining Mr Hope against Mr Walcot. It is paying too dear for the fancy. The Hopes are wretchedly pinched for money. They have dropped their subscription to the book club."

"I am very sorry to hear it. I would give half I am worth that it were otherwise."

"Give it them at once, then, and it will be otherwise."

"I would, gladly; but they will not take it."

"I advise you to try, however; it would make such a pretty romantic story!—Well, Mr Grey is extremely mortified at their withdrawing from the book club. He remonstrated very strongly indeed."

"That does not agree very well with his paying their rent for them."

"Perfectly well. He thinks that if he undertakes the large thing, for the sake of their credit, they might have managed the small. This is his way of viewing the matter, no doubt. He sees how their credit will suffer by their giving up the book club. He sees how everybody will remark upon it."

"So do they, I have no doubt."

"And the matter will not be mended by Sophia Grey's nonsense. What absurd things that girl does! I wonder her mother allows it,—only that, to be sure, she is not much wiser herself. Sophia has told some of her acquaintance, and all Deerbrook will hear it before long, that her cousins have withdrawn from the book club on account of Hester's situation; that they are to be so busy with the baby that is coming, that they will have no time to read."

"As long as the Hopes are above false pretences, they need not care for such as are made for them. There! show mamma what a nice plump walnut you have cracked for her."

"Nicely done, my pet. But, Mr Rowland, the Hopes cannot hold out. They cannot possibly stay here. You will not get their rent at Christmas, depend upon it."

"I shall not press them for it, I assure you."

"Then you will be unjust to your family. You owe it to your children, to say nothing of myself, to look after your property."

"I owe it to them not to show myself a harsh landlord to excellent tenants. But we need not trouble ourselves about what will happen at Christmas. It may be that the rent will make its appearance on the morning of quarter-day."

"Then, if not, you will give them notice that the house is let from the next quarter, will you not?"

"By no means, my dear."

"If you do not like to undertake the office yourself, perhaps you will let me do it. I have a good deal of courage about doing disagreeable things, on occasion."

"You have, my dear; but I do not wish that this should be done. I mean, I desire that it be not done. The Hopes shall live in that house of mine as long as they please. And if," continued Mr Rowland, not liking the expression of his lady's eye,—"if any one disturbs them in their present abode—the consequence will be that I shall be compelled to invite them here. I shall establish them in this very house, sooner than that they shall be obliged to leave Deerbrook against their will; and then, my dear, you will have to be off to Cheltenham again."

"What nonsense you talk, Mr Rowland! Who should disturb them, if you won't be open to reason, so as to do it yourself? I thought you knew enough of what it is to be ridden by poor tenants, to wish to avoid the plague, if warned in time. But some people can never take warning."

"Let us see that you can, my love. You will remember what I have said about the Hopes being disturbed, I have no doubt. And now we have done with that, I want to tell you—"

"Presently, when we have really done with this subject, my dear. I have other reasons—"

"Which you will spare me the hearing. My dear Priscilla, there are no reasons on earth which can justify me in turning this family out of their house, or you in asking me to do it. Let us hear no more about it."

"But you must hear. I will be heard on a subject in which I have such an interest, Mr Rowland."

"Ring the bell, my little fellow. Pull hard. That's it—Candles in the office immediately."

And Mr Rowland tossed off the last half of his glass of port, kissed the little ones, and was gone. The lady remained to compassionate herself; which she did very deeply, that she could find no means of ridding herself of the great plague of her life. These people were always in her way, and no one would help her to dislodge them. Her own husband was against her—quite unmanageable and perverse.

Chapter Thirty Eight

The Victims.

If Mrs Rowland was dissatisfied with her success, while seeing that some resources of comfort remained to the Hopes and Margaret, a view of the interior of the corner-house would probably have affected her deeply, and set her moralising on the incompleteness of all human triumphs. There was peace there which even she could not invade—could only, if she had known it, envy. Her power was now exhausted, and her work was unfinished. For many weeks, she had made Margaret as miserable as she had intended to make her. Margaret had suffered from an exasperating sense of injury; but that was only for a few hours. Hers was not a nature which could retain personal resentment for any length of time. She needed the relief of compassionate and forgiving feelings; and she cast herself into them for solace, as the traveller, emerging from the glaring desert, throws himself down beside the gushing spring in the shade. From the moment that she did this, it became her chief trouble that Philip was blamed by others. Her friends said as little as they could in reference to him, out of regard for her feelings; but she could not help seeing that Maria's indignation was strong, and that Hester considered that her sister had had a happy escape from a man capable of treating her as Philip had done. If it had been possible to undertake his defence, Margaret would have done so. As there were no means of working upon others to forgive her wrongs, she made it her consolation to forgive them doubly herself; to cheer up under them; to live for the aim of being more worthy of Philip's love, the less he believed her to be so. Her lot was far easier now than it had been in the winter. She had been his; and she believed that she still occupied his whole soul. She was not now the solitary, self-despising being she had felt herself before. Though cut off from intercourse with him as if the grave lay between them, she knew that sympathy with her heart and mind existed. She experienced the struggles, the moaning efforts, of affections doomed to solitude and silence; the shrinking from a whole long life of self-reliance, of exclusion from domestic life; the occasional horror of contemplating the waste and withering of some of the noblest parts of the immortal nature,— a waste and withering which are the almost certain consequence of violence done to its instincts and its laws. From these pains and terrors she suffered; and from some of smaller account,—from the petty insults, or speculations of the more coarse-minded of her neighbours, and the being too suddenly reminded by passing circumstances of the change which had come over her expectations and prospects; but her love, her forgiveness, her conviction of being beloved, bore her through all these, and saved her from that fever of the heart, in the paroxysms of which she had, in her former and severer trial, longed for death, even for non-existence.

She could enjoy but little of what had been her favourite solace at that time. She had but few opportunities now for long solitary walks. She saw the autumn fading away, melting in rain and cold fog, without its having been made use of. It had been as unfavourable a season as the summer,—dreary, unproductive, disappointing in every way; but there had been days in the latter autumn when the sun had shown his dim face, when the dank hedges had looked fresh, and the fallen leaves in the wood-paths had rustled under the tread of the squirrel; and Margaret would on such days have liked to spend the whole morning in rambles by herself. But there were reasons why she should not. Almost before the chilliness of the coming season began to be felt, hardship was complained of throughout the country. The prices of provisions were inordinately high; and the evil consequences which, in the rural districts, follow upon a scarcity, began to make themselves felt. The poachers were daring beyond belief; and deep was the enmity between the large proprietors and the labourers around them. The oldest men and women, and children scarcely able to walk, were found trespassing day by day in all plantations, with bags, aprons, or pinafores, full of fir-cones, and wood snapped off from the trees, or plucked out of the hedges. There was no end to repairing the fences. There were unpleasant rumours, too, of its being no longer safe to walk singly in the more retired places. No such thing as highway robbery had ever before been heard of at Deerbrook, within the memory of the oldest inhabitant; the oldest of the inhabitants being Jim Bird, the man of a hundred years. But there was reason now for the caution. Mr Jones's meat-cart had been stopped on the high-road, by two men who came out of the hedge, and helped themselves to what the cart contained. An ill-looking fellow had crossed the path of Mrs James and her young sister in the Verdon woods, evidently with the intention of stopping the ladies; but luckily the jingling of a timber-wain was heard below, and the man had retreated. Mr Grey had desired that the ladies of his family would not go further without his escort than a mile out and back again on the high-road. They were not to attempt the lanes. The Miss Andersons no longer came into Deerbrook in their pony-chaise; and Mrs Howell reported to all her customers that Lady Hunter never walked in her own grounds without a footman behind her, two dogs before her, and the game-keeper within hearing of a scream. Mr Walcot was advised to leave his watch and purse at home when he set forth to visit his country patients; and it did not comfort him much to perceive that his neighbours were always vigilant to note the hour and minute of his setting forth, and to learn the precise time when he might be looked for at home again. It was observed, that he was generally back half-an-hour sooner than he was expected, with a very red face, and his horse all in a foam.

In addition to these grounds of objection to solitary walks, Margaret had strong domestic reasons for denying herself the rambles she delighted in. As the months rolled on, poverty pressed closer and closer. When the rent was secured, and some of the comforts provided which Hester must have in her confinement, so little was left that it became necessary to limit the weekly expenses of the family to a sum small enough to require the nicest management, and the most strenuous domestic industry, to make it suffice. Hope would not pledge his credit while he saw so little prospect of redeeming it. His family were of one mind as to purchasing nothing which they were not certainly able to pay for. This being his principle, he made every effort to increase his funds. A guinea or two dropped in now and then, in return for contributions to medical periodicals. Money was due to him from some of his patients. To these he sent in his bills again, and even made personal application. From several he obtained promises; from two or three the amount of whose debt was very small, he got his money, disgraced by smiles of wonder and contempt. From the greater number he received nothing but excuses on account of the pressure of the times. The small sums he did recover were of a value which none of the three had ever imagined that money could be to them. Every little extra comfort thus obtained,—the dinner of meat once oftener in the week, the fire in the evening, the new gloves for Hope, when the old ones could no longer, by any mending, be made to look fit for him,—what a luxury it was! And all the more for being secretly enjoyed. No one out of the house had a suspicion how far their poverty had gone. Mr Grey had really been vexed at them for withdrawing from the book club; had attributed this instance of economy to the "enthusiasm" which was, in his eyes, the fault of the family; and never dreamed of their not dining on meat, vegetables, and pudding, with their glass of wine, every day. The Greys little knew what a blessing they were conferring on their cousins, when they insisted on having them for a long day once more before Hester's confinement, and set them down to steaming soup, and a plentiful joint, and accompaniments without stint. The guests laughed, when they were at home again, over the new sort of pleasure they had felt, the delight at the sight of a good dinner, to which nothing was wanting but that Morris should have had her share. Morris, for her part, had been very happy at home. She had put aside for her mistress's luncheon next day, the broth which she had been told was for her, and had feasted on potatoes and water, and the idea of the good dinner her young ladies were to enjoy. While their affairs were in this state, it was a great luxury in the family to have any unusual comfort which betokened that Hope had been successful in some of his errands,—had received a fee, or recovered the amount of a bill. One day, Morris brought in a goose and giblets, which had been bought and paid for by Mr Hope, the messenger said. Another morning, came a sack of apples, from the orchard of a country patient who was willing to pay in kind. At another time Edward emptied his pockets of knitted worsted stockings and mittens, the handiwork of a farmer's dame, who was flattered by his taking the produce of her evening industry instead of money, which she could not well spare at the present season. There was more mirth, more real gladness in the house, on the arrival of windfalls like these, than if Hope had daily exhibited a purse full of gold. There was no sting in their poverty; no adventitious misery belonging to it. They suffered its genuine force, and that was all.

What is Poverty? Not destitution, but poverty? It has many shapes,—aspects almost as various as the minds and circumstances of those whom it visits. It is famine to the savage in the wilds; it is hardship to the labourer in the cottage; it is disgrace to the proud; and to the miser despair. It is a spectre which "with dread of change perplexes" him who lives at ease. Such are its aspects: but what is it? It is a deficiency of the comforts of life,—a deficiency present and to come. It involves many other things; but this is what it is. Is it then worth all the apprehension and grief it occasions? Is it an adequate cause for the gloom of the merchant, the discontent of the artisan, the foreboding sighs of the mother, the ghastly dreams which haunt the avaricious, the conscious debasement of the subservient, the humiliation of the proud? These are severe sufferings; are they authorised by the nature of poverty? Certainly not, if poverty induced no adventitious evils, involved nothing but a deficiency of the comforts of life, leaving life itself unimpaired. "The life is more than food, and the body than raiment;" and the untimely extinction of the life itself would not be worth the pangs which apprehended poverty excites. But poverty involves woes which, in their sum, are far greater than itself. To a multitude it is the loss of a pursuit which they have yet to learn will be certainly supplied. For such, alleviation or compensation is in store, in the rising up of objects new, and the creation of fresh hopes. The impoverished merchant, who may no longer look out for his argosies, may yet be in glee when he finds it "a rare dropping morning for the early colewort." To another multitude, poverty involves loss of rank,—a letting down among strangers whose manners are ungenial, and their thoughts unfamiliar. For these there may be solace in retirement, or the evil may fall short of its threats. The reduced gentlewoman may live in patient solitude, or may grow into sympathy with her neighbours, by raising some of them up to herself, and by warming her heart at the great central fire of Humanity, which burns on under the crust of manners as rough as the storms of the tropics, or as frigid as polar snows. The avaricious are out of the pale of peace already, and at all events. Poverty is most seriously an evil to sons and daughters, who see their parents stripped of comfort, at an age when comfort is almost one with life itself: and to parents who watch the narrowing of the capacities of their children by the pressure of poverty,—the impairing of their promise, the blotting out of their prospects. To such mourning children there is little comfort, but in contemplating the easier life which lies behind, and (it may be hoped) the happier one which stretches before their parents, on the other side the postern of life. If there is sunshine on the two grand reaches of their path, the shadow which lies in the midst is necessarily but a temporary gloom. To grieving parents it should be a consoling truth, that as the life is more than food, so is the soul more than instruction and opportunity, and such accomplishments as man can administer: that as the fowls are fed and the lilies clothed by Him whose hand made the air musical with the one, and dressed the fields with the other, so is the human spirit nourished and adorned by airs from heaven, which blow over the whole earth, and light from the skies, which no hand is permitted to intercept. Parents know not but that Providence may be substituting the noblest education for the misteaching of intermediate guardians. It may possibly be so; but if not, still there is appointed to every human being much training, many privileges, which capricious fortune can neither give nor take away. The father may sigh to see his boy condemned to the toil of the loom, or the gossip and drudgery of the shop, when he would fain have beheld him the ornament of a university; but he knows not whether a more simple integrity, a loftier disinterestedness, may not come out of the humbler discipline than the higher privilege. The mother's eyes may swim as she hears her little daughter sing her baby brother to sleep on the cottage threshold,—her eyes may swim at the thought how those wild and moving tones might have been exalted by art. Such art would have been in itself a good; but would this child then have been, as now, about her Father's business, which, in ministering to one of his little ones, she is as surely as the archangel who suspends new systems of worlds in the furthest void? Her occupation is now earnest and holy; and what need the true mother wish for more?

What is poverty to those who are not thus set in families? What is it to the solitary, or to the husband and wife who have faith in each other's strength? If they have the higher faith which usually originates mutual trust, mere poverty is scarcely worth a passing fear. If they have plucked out the stings of pride and selfishness, and purified their vision by faith, what is there to dread? What is their case? They have life, without certainty how it is to be nourished. They do without certainty, like "the young ravens which cry," and work for and enjoy the subsistence of the day, leaving the morrow to take care of what concerns it. If living in the dreariest abodes of a town, the light from within shines in the dark place, and, dispelling the mists of worldly care, guides to the blessing of tending the sick, and sharing the food of to-day with the orphan, and him who has no help but in them. If the philosopher goes into such retreats with his lantern, there may he best find the generous and the brave. If, instead of the alleys of a city, they live under the open sky, they are yet lighter under their poverty. There, however blank the future may lie before them, they have to-day the living reality of lawns and woods, and flocks in "the green pasture and beside the still waters," which silently remind them of the Shepherd, under whom they shall not want any real good thing. The quiet of the shady lane is theirs, and the beauty of the blossoming thorn above the pool. Delight steals through them with the scent of the violet, or the new mown hay. If they have hushed the voices of complaint and fear within them, there is the music of the merry lark for them, or of the leaping waterfall, or of a whole orchestra of harps, when the breeze sweeps through a grove of pines. While it is not for fortune to "rob them of free nature's grace," and while she leaves them life and strength of limb and soul, the certainty of a future, though they cannot see what, and the assurance of progression, though they cannot see how,—is poverty worth, for themselves, more than a passing doubt? Can it ever be worth the torment of fear, the bondage of subservience?—the compromise of free thought,—the sacrifice of free speech,—the bending of the erect head, the veiling of the open brow, the repression of the salient soul? If, instead of this, poverty should act as the liberator of the spirit, awakening it to trust in God and sympathy for man, and placing it aloft, fresh and free, like morning on the hill-top, to survey the expanse of life, and recognise its realities from beneath its mists, it should be greeted with that holy joy before which all sorrow and sighing flee away.

Their poverty, which had never afflicted them very grievously, was almost lost sight of by the corner-house family, when Hester's infant was born. They were all happy and satisfied then, though there were people in Deerbrook who found fault with their arrangements, and were extremely scandalised when it was found that no nurse had arrived from Blickley, and that Morris took the charge of her mistress upon herself. The Greys pronounced by their own fireside that it was a strange fancy—carrying an affection for an old servant to a rather romantic extreme—that it was a fresh instance of the "enthusiasm" which adversity had not yet moderated in their cousins, as might have been wished. Out-of-doors, however, Sophia vaunted the attachment of Morris to her young mistress—an attachment so strong, as that she would have been really hurt if any one else had been allowed to sit up with Hester; and indeed no one could have filled her place half so much to the satisfaction of the family—Morris had had so much experience, and was as fond of her charge as a mother could be. No one knew what a treasure her cousins had in Morris. All of which was true in its separate particulars, though altogether it did not constitute the reason why Hester had no nurse from Buckley.

They were happy and satisfied. Yes, even Margaret. This infant opened up a spring of consolation in her heart, which she could not have believed existed there. On this child she could pour out some of her repressed affections, and on him did she rest her baffled hopes. He beguiled her into the future, from which she had hitherto recoiled. That helpless, unconscious little creature, cradled on her arm, and knowing nothing of its resting-place, was more powerful than sister, brother, or friend—than self-interest, philosophy, or religion, in luring her imagination onward into future years of honour and peace. Holy and sweet was the calm of her mind, as, forgetting herself and her griefs, she watched the first efforts of this infant to acquaint himself with his own powers, and with the world about him; when she smiled at the ungainly stretching of the little limbs, and the unpractised movement of his eyes seeking the light. Holy and sweet were the tears which swelled into her eyes when she saw him at his mother's breast, and could not but gaze at the fresh and divine beauty now mantling on that mother's face, amidst the joy of this new relation. It was a delicious moment when Hope came in, the first day that Hester sat by the fireside, when he stopped short for a brief instant, as if arrested by the beauty of what he saw; and then glanced towards Margaret for sympathy. It was a delicious moment to her—the moment of that full, free, unembarrassed glance, which she had scarcely met since the first days of their acquaintance.

It was a pleasure to them all to see Hester well provided with luxuries. Maria, knowing that her surgeon would not accept money from her, took this opportunity of sending in wine. Oh, the pleasure of finding the neglected corkscrew, and making Morris take a glass with them! The Greys brought game, and Hester's little table was well served every day. With what zeal did Margaret apply herself, under Morris's teaching, to cook Hester's choice little dinners! Yes, to cook them. Margaret was learning all Morris's arts from her; for, of two troubles which somewhat disturbed this season of comfort, one was that it appeared too certain that Morris must go, as Susan and Charles had gone before her. No one had expressly declared this: it was left undiscussed, apparently by common consent, till it should be ascertained that baby was healthy and Hester getting strong; but the thought was in the minds of them all, and their plans involved preparation for this.

The other trouble was, that with peace and comfort, some slight, very slight symptoms recurred of Hester's propensity to self-torment. It could not be otherwise. The wonder was, that for weeks and months she had been relieved from her old enemy to the extent she had been. The reverence with which her husband and sister regarded the temper in which she had borne unbounded provocation and most unmerited adversity, sometimes beguiled them into a hope that her troubles from within were over for ever; but a little reflection, and some slight experience, taught them that this was unreasonable. They remembered that the infirmity of a lifetime was not to be wholly cured in half-a-year; and that they must expect some recurrence of her old malady at times when there was no immediate appeal to her magnanimity, and no present cause for anxiety for those in whom she forgot herself.

The first time that Hester was in the drawing-room for the whole day, Morris was laying the cloth for dinner, and Margaret was walking up and down the room with the baby on her arm, when Hope came in. Hester forgot everybody and everything else when her husband appeared—a fact which Morris's benevolence was never weary of noting and commenting upon to herself. She often wondered if ever lady loved her husband as her young mistress did; and she smiled to herself to see the welcome that beamed upon Hester's whole face when Hope came to take his seat beside her on the sofa. This was in her mind to-day, when her master presently said:

"Where is my boy? I have not seen him for hours. Why do you put him out of his father's way? Oh, Margaret has him! Come, Margaret, yield him up. You can have him all the hours that I am away. You do not grudge him to me, do you?"

"My master won't have to complain, as many gentlemen do," said Morris, "or as many gentlemen feel, if they don't complain, that he is neglected for the sake of his baby."

"If you enjoy your dinner to-day, love," said Hester, "you must not give me the credit of it. You and I are to sit down to our pheasant together, they tell me. Margaret and Morris will have it that they have both dined."

"There is little in getting a comfortable dinner ready," said Morris, "whether it is the lady herself, or another, that looks to a trifle like that. It is the seeing his wife so full of care and thought about her baby as to have none to spare for him, that frets many an one who does not like to say anything about it. Fathers cannot be so taken with a very young baby as the mothers are, and it is mortifying to feel themselves neglected for a newcomer. I have often seen that, my dears; but I shall never see it here, I find."

"I do not know how you should, Morris," said Hester, in something of the old tone, which made her sister's heart throb almost before it reached her ear. "Margaret will save me from any such danger. Margaret takes care that nobody shall be engrossed with the baby but herself. She has not a thought to spare for any of us while she has baby in her arms. The little fellow has cut us all out."

Margaret quickly transferred the infant to her brother's arm, and left the room. She thought it best; for her heart was very full, and she could not speak. She restrained her tears, and went into the kitchen to busy herself about the dinner she had cooked.

"'Tis a fine pheasant, indeed, Miss Margaret, my dear, and beautifully roasted, I am sure: and I hope you will go up and see them enjoy it. I am so sorry, my dear, for what I said just now. I merely spoke what came up in my mind when I felt pleased, and never thought of its bringing on any remark. Nor was anything intended, I am sure, that should make you look so sad: so do you go up, and take the baby again, when they sit down to dinner, as if nothing had been said. Do, my dear, if I may venture to say so. I will follow you with the dinner in a minute."

"I wonder how it is, my love," said Hope, in a voice which spoke all the tenderness of his heart; "I wonder how it is that you can endure wrong so nobly, and that you cannot bear the natural course of events. Tell me how it is, Hester, that you have sustained magnanimously all the injuries and misfortunes of many months, and that you now quarrel with Margaret's affection for our child."

"Ah why, indeed, Edward?" she replied, humbly. "Why, but that I am unworthy that such an one as Margaret should love me and my child."

"Enough, enough. I only want to show you how I regard the case about this new love of Margaret's. Do you not see how much happier she has been since this little fellow was born?"

"Oh, yes."

"One may now fancy that she may be gay again. Let us remember what an oppressed heart she had, and what it must be to her to have a new object, so innocent and unconscious as this child, to lavish her affection upon. Do not let us grudge her the consolation, or poison the pleasure of this fresh interest."

"I am afraid it is done," cried Hester, in great distress. "I was wicked— I was more cruel than any of our enemies, when I said what I did. I may well bear with them; for, God knows, I am at times no better than they. I have robbed my Margaret of her only comfort—spoiled her only pleasure."

"No, no. Here she comes. Look at her."

Margaret's face was indeed serene, and she made as light of the matter as she could, when Hester implored that she would pardon her hasty and cruel words, and that she would show her forgiveness by continuing to cherish the child. He must not begin to suffer already for his mother's faults, Hester said. There could be no doubt of Margaret's forgiveness, nor of her forgetfulness of what had been said, as far as forgetfulness was possible. But the worst of such sayings is, that they carry in them that which prevents their being ever quite forgotten. Hester had effectually established a constraint in her sister's intercourse with the baby, and imposed upon Margaret the incessant care of scrupulously adjusting the claims of the mother and the child. The evils arising from faulty temper may be borne, may be concealed, but can never be fully repaired. Happy they whose part it is to endure and to conceal, rather than to inflict, and to strive uselessly to repair!

Margaret's part was the easiest of the three, as they sat at the table—she with the baby in her arms, and all agreeing that the time was come for an explanation with Morris—for depending on themselves for almost all the work of the house.

"Come, Morris," said Hester, when the cloth was removed; "you must spare us half-an-hour. We want to consult with you. Come and sit down."

Morris came, with a foreboding heart.

"It will be no news to you," said Hope, "that we are very poor. You know nearly as much of our affairs as we do ourselves, as it is right that you should. We have not wished to make any further change in our domestic plans till this little fellow was born. But now that he is beginning to make his way in the world, and that his mother is well and strong, we feel that we must consider of some further effort to spend still less than we do now."

"There are two ways in which this may be done, we think, Morris," said Hester. "We may either keep the comfort of having you with us, and pinch ourselves more as to dress and the table—"

"Oh! ma'am, I hope you will not carry that any further."

"Well, if we do not carry that any further, the only thing to be done, I fear, is to part with you."

"Is there no other way, I wonder," said Morris, as if thinking aloud. "If it must be one of these ways, it certainly seems to me to be better for ladies to work hard with good food, than to have a servant, and stint themselves in health and strength. But who would have thought of my young ladies coming to this?"

"It is a situation in which hundreds and thousands are placed, Morris; and why not we, as well as they?"

"May be so, ma'am: but it grieves one, too."

"Do not grieve. I believe we all think that this parting with you is the first real grief that our change of fortune has caused us. Somehow or other, we have been exceedingly comfortable in our poverty. If that had been all, we should have had a very happy year of it."

"One would desire to say nothing against what is God's will, ma'am; but one may be allowed, perhaps, to hope that better times will come."

"I do hope it, and believe it," said her master.

"And if better times come, Morris, you will return to us. Will you not?"

"My dear, you know nothing would make me leave you now (as you say I am a comfort to you) if I had any right to say I would stay. I could live upon as little as anybody, and could do almost without any wages. But there is my poor sister, you know, ladies. She depends upon me for everything, now that she cannot work herself: and I must earn money for her."

"We are quite aware of that," said Margaret. "It is for your sake and hers, quite as much as for our own, that we think we must part."

"We wish to know what you would like to do," said Hester. "Shall we try to find a situation for you near us, or would you be happier to go down among your old friends?"

"I had better go where I am sure of employment, ma'am. Better go down to Birmingham at once. I should never have left it but for my young ladies' sakes. But I should be right glad, my dears, to leave it again for you, if you can at any time write to say you wish for me back. There is another way I have thought of sometimes; but, of course, you cannot have overlooked anything that could occur to me. If you would all go to Birmingham, you have so many friends there, and my master would be valued as he ought to be; which there is no sign of his being in this place. I do not like this place, my dears. It is not good enough for you."

"We think any place good enough for us where there are men and women living," said Hope, kindly but gravely. "Others have thought as you do, Morris, and have offered us temptations to go away; but we do not think it right. If we go, we shall leave behind us a bad character, which we do not deserve. If we stay, I have very little doubt of recovering my professional character, and winning over our neighbours to think better of us, and be kind to us again. We mean to try for it, if I should have to hire myself out as a porter in Mr Grey's yards."

"Pray, don't say that, sir. But, indeed, I believe you are so far right as that the good always conquers at last."

"Just so, Morris: that is what we trust. And for the sake of this little fellow, if for nothing else, we must stand by our good name. Who knows but that I may leave him a fine flourishing practice in this very place, when I retire or die?—always supposing he means to follow his father's profession."

"Sir, that is looking forward very far."

"So it is, Morris. But however people may disapprove of looking forward too far, it is difficult to help it when they become parents. Your mistress could tell you, if she would own the truth, that she sees her son's manly beauty already under that little wry mouth, and that odd button of a nose. Why may not I just as well fancy him a young surgeon?"

"Morris would say, as she once said to me," observed Margaret, "'Remember death, my dear; remember death.'"

"We will remember it," said Morris, "but we must remember at the same time God's mercy in giving life. He who gave life can preserve it: and this shall be my trust for you all, my dears, when I am far away from you. There is a knock! I must go. Oh! Miss Margaret, who will there be to go to the door when I am gone, but you?"

Mr Jones had knocked at the door, and left a letter. These were its contents:—

> "Sir,—I hope you will excuse the liberty I take in applying to you for my own satisfaction. My wife and I have perceived with much concern that we have lost much of your custom of late. We mind little the mere falling off of custom in any quarter, in comparison with failing to give satisfaction. We have always tried, I am sure, to give satisfaction in our dealings with your family, sir; and if there has been any offence, I can assure you it is unintentional, and shall feel obliged by knowing what it is. We cannot conceive, sir, where you get your meat, if not from us; and if you have the trouble of buying it from a distance, I can only say we should be happy to save you the trouble, if we knew how to serve you to your liking; for, sir, we have a great respect for you and yours.
>
> "Your obedient servants,
>
> "John Jones,
>
> "Mary Jones."

"The kind soul!" cried Hester. "What must we say to them?"

"We must set their minds at ease about our good-will to them. How that little fellow stares about him, like a child of double his age! I do believe I could make him look wise at my watch already. Yes, we must set the Joneses at ease, at all events."

"But how? We must not tell them that we cannot afford to buy of them as we did."

"No; that would be begging. We must trust to their delicacy not to press too closely for a reason, when once assured that we respect them as highly as they possibly can us."

"You may trust them," said Margaret, "I am convinced. They will look in your face, and be satisfied without further question; and my advice, therefore, is, that you do not write, but go."

"I will; and now. They shall not suffer a moment's pain that I can save them. Good-night, my boy! What! you have not learned to kiss yet. Well, among us all, you will soon know how, if teaching will do it. What a spirit he has! I fancy he will turn out like Frank."

Chapter Thirty Nine

The Long Nights.

Almost as soon as Hope had left the house, Sydney Grey arrived, looking full of importance. He took care to shut the door before he would tell his errand. His mother had been obliged to trust him for want of another messenger; and he delivered his message with a little of the parade of mystery he had derived from her. Mr Grey's family had become uneasy about his returning from the markets in the evening, since robberies had become so frequent as they now were, and the days so short; and had at length persuaded him to sleep at the more distant market-towns he had to visit, and return the next morning. From Blickley he could get home before the evening closed in; but on two days in the week he was to remain out all night. When he had agreed to this, his family had applauded him and felt satisfied: but as the evening drew on, on occasion of this his first absence, Mrs Grey and Sophia had grown nervous on their own account. They recalled story after story, which they had lately heard, of robberies at several solitary houses in the country round; and, though their house was not solitary, they could not reconcile themselves to going to rest without the comfort of knowing that there was, as usual, a strong man on their premises. If they had been aware how many strong men there were sometimes on their premises at night, they would not have been satisfied with having one within their walls. Not having been informed, however, how cleverly their dogs were silenced, how much poached game was divided under the shelter of their stacks of deals, and what dextrous abstractions were at such times made from the store of corn in their granaries, and coal in their lighters, they proposed nothing further than to beg the favour of Mr Hope that he would take a bed in their house for this one night. They dared not engage any of the men from the yards to defend them; they had not Mr Grey's leave, and he might not be pleased if they showed any fear to their own servants: but it would be the greatest comfort if Mr Hope would come, as if to supper, and stay the night. The spare room was ready; and Mrs Grey hoped he would not object to leaving his family just for once. Mr Grey intended to do the same thing twice a week, till the days should lengthen, and the roads become safer.

Though Sydney made the most of his message, he declared himself not thoroughly pleased with it.

"They might have trusted me to take care of them," said he. "If they had just let me have my father's pistols——."

"Come, come, Sydney, do not talk of pistols," said Hester, who did not relish any part of the affair.

"He would not talk of them if he thought they were likely to be wanted," observed Margaret.

"Likely! when were they ever more likely to be wanted, I should like to know! Did you hear what happened at the Russell Taylors' last night?"

"No; and we do not wish to hear. Do not tell us any horrible stories, unless you mean my husband to stay at home to-night."

"Oh, you must just hear this, because it ended well; that is, nobody was killed. Mr Walcot told Sophia all about it this morning; and it was partly that which made her so anxious to have some one sleep in the house to-night."

"Well, then, do not tell us, or you will make us anxious for the same thing."

"What would your mother say if you were to carry home word that Mr Hope could not come—that his family dare not part with him?"

"Oh, then she must let me have my father's pistols, and watch for the fellows. If they came about our windows as they did about the Russell Taylors', how I would let fly among them! They came rapping at the shutters, at two this morning; and when Mr Taylor looked out from his bedroom above, they said they would not trouble themselves to get in, if he would throw out his money!"

"And did he?"

"Yes. They raised a hat upon a pole, and he put in four or five pounds—all he had in the house, he told them. So they went away; but none of the family thought of going to bed again."

"I dare say not. And what sort of thieves are these supposed to be? They set about their business very oddly."

"Not like London thieves," said Sydney, consequentially, as if he knew all about London thieves. "They are the distressed country people, no doubt—such as would no more think of standing a second shot from my pistol, than of keeping the straits of Thermopylae. Look here," he continued, showing the end of a pistol, which peeped from a pocket inside his coat; "here's a thing that will put such gentry into a fine taking."

"Pray, is that pistol loaded?" inquired Hester, pressing her infant to her.

"To be sure. What is the use of a pistol if it is not loaded? It might as well be in the shop as in my pocket, then. Look at her, cousin Margaret! If she is not in as great a fright as the cowardly thieves! Why, cousin Hester, don't you see, if this pistol went off, it would not shoot you or the baby. It would go straight through me."

"That is a great comfort. But I had rather you would go away, you and your pistol. Pray, does your mother know that you carry one?"

"No. Mind you don't tell her. I trust you not to tell her. Remember, I would not have told you if I had not felt sure of you."

"You had better not have felt sure of us. However, we will not tell your mother; but my husband will tell Mr Grey to-morrow, when he comes home. If he chooses that you should carry loaded pistols about, there will be no harm done."

"I have a great mind to say I will shoot you if you tell," cried Sydney, presenting the pistol with a grand air. But he saw that he made his cousins really uneasy, and he laid it down on the table, offering to leave it with them for the night, if they thought it would make them feel any safer. There were plenty more at home.

"Thank you," said Margaret, "but I believe we are more afraid of loaded pistols than of thieves. The sooner you take it away the better. You can go now, presently, for here comes my brother."

Sydney quickly pocketed his pistol. Hope agreed to go, and promised to be at Mr Grey's to supper by nine o'clock.

Margaret was incessantly thinking of Maria in these long evenings, when alarms of one kind or another were all abroad. She now thought she would go with Sydney, and spend an hour or two with Maria, returning by the time her brother would be going to the Greys'. Maria's landlord would see her home, no doubt.

She found her friend busy with book and needle, and as well in health as usual, but obviously somewhat moved by the dismal stories which had travelled from mouth to mouth through Deerbrook during the day. It seemed hardly right that any person in delicate health should be lonely at such a time; and it occurred to Margaret that her friend might like to go home with her, and occupy the bed which was this night to spare. Maria thankfully accepted the offer, and let Margaret put up her little bundle for her. The farrier escorted them to the steps of the corner-house, and then left them.

The door was half-open, as Morris was talking with some one on the mat in the hall. An extremely tall woman, with a crying baby in her arms, made way for the ladies, not by going out of the house, but by stepping further into the hall.

"Morris, had you not better shut the door?" said Margaret; "the wind blows in so, it is enough to chill the whole house."

But Morris held the door open, rather wider than before.

"So the gentleman is not at home," said the tall woman, gruffly. "If I come again in an hour with my poor baby, will he be at home then?"

"Is my brother gone, Morris?"

"Yes, Miss, three minutes ago."

"Then he will not be back in an hour. We do not expect him—."

"This good woman had better go to Mr Walcot, ma'am, as I have been telling her. There's no doubt he is at home."

"I could wait here till the gentleman comes home," said the tall woman; "and so get the first advice for my poor baby. 'Tis very ill, ma'am."

"Better go to Mr Walcot," persisted Morris.

"Or to my brother at Mr Grey's," said Margaret, unwilling to lose the chance of a new patient for Edward, and thinking his advice better, for the child's sake, than Mr Walcot's.

"It is far the readiest way to go to Mr Walcot's," declared Maria, whose arm Margaret felt to tremble within her own.

"I believe you are right," said Margaret. "You had better not waste any more time here, good woman. It may make all the difference to your child."

"If you would let me wait till the gentleman comes home," said the tall woman.

"Impossible. It is too late to-night for patients to wait. This lady's landlord, without there, will show you the way to Mr Walcot's. Call him, Morris."

Morris went out upon the steps, but the tall woman passed her, and was gone. Morris stepped in briskly, and put up the chain.

"You were very ready to send a new patient to Mr Walcot, Morris," said Margaret, smiling.

"I had a fancy that it was a sort of patient that my master would not be the better for," replied Morris. "I did not like the looks of the person."

"Nor I," said Maria.

The drawing-room door was heard to open, and Morris put her finger on her lips. Hester had been alone nearly ten minutes; she was growing nervous, and wanted to know what all this talking in the hall was about. She was told that Mr Hope had been inquired for, about a sick baby; and the rest of the discourse went to the account of Maria's unexpected arrival. Hester welcomed Maria kindly, ordered up the cold pheasant and the wine, and then, leaving the friends to enjoy themselves over the fire, retired to rest. Morris was desired to go too, as she still slept in her mistress's room, and ought to keep early hours, since, in addition to her labours of the day, she was at the baby's call in the night. Margaret would see her friend to her room. Morris must not remain up on their account.

"How comfortable this is!" cried Maria, in a gleeful tone, as she looked round upon the crackling fire, the tray, the wine, and her companion. "How unlooked for, to pass a whole evening and night without being afraid of anything!"

"What an admission from you!—that you are afraid of something every night."

"That is just the plain truth. When I used to read about the horrors of living in a solitary house in the country, I little thought how much of the same terror I should feel from living solitary in a house in a village. You wonder what could happen to me, I dare say; and perhaps it would not be very easy to suppose any peril which would stand examination."

"I was going to say that you and we are particularly safe, from being so poor that there is no inducement to rob us. We and you have neither money nor jewels, nor plate, that can tempt thieves!—for our few forks and spoons are hardly worth breaking into a house for."

"People who want bread, however, may think it worth while to break in for that: and while our thieves are this sort of people, and not the London gentry whom Sydney is so fond of talking of, it may be enough that gentlemen and ladies live in houses to make the starving suppose that they shall find something valuable there."

"They would soon learn better if they came here. I doubt whether, when you and I have done our supper, they would find anything to eat. But how do you show your terrors, I should like to know? Do you scream?"

"I never screamed in my life, as far as I remember. Screaming appears to me the most unnatural of human sounds. I never felt the slightest inclination to express myself in that manner."

"Nor I: but I never said so, because I thought no one would believe me."

"No: the true mood for these doleful winter nights is, to sit trying to read, but never able to fix your attention for five minutes, for some odd noise or another. And yet it is almost worse to hear nothing but a cinder falling on the hearth now and then, startling you like a pistol-shot. Then it seems as if somebody was opening the shutter outside, and then tapping at the window. I have got so into the habit of looking at the window at night, expecting to see a face squeezed flat against the pane, that I have yielded up my credit to myself, and actually have the blinds drawn down when the outside shutters are closed."

"How glad I am to find you are no braver than the rest of us!"

"No; do not be glad. It is very painful, night after night. Every step clinks or craunches in the farrier's yard, you know. This ought to be a comfort: but sometimes I cannot clearly tell where the sound comes from. More than once lately I have fancied it was behind me, and have turned round in a greater hurry than you would think I could use. My rooms are a good way from the rest of the house; you remember the length of the passage between. I do not like disturbing the family in the evenings; but I have been selfish enough to ring, once or twice this week, without any sufficient reason, just for the sake of a sight of my landlady."

"A very sufficient reason. But I had no idea of all this from you."

"You have heard me say some fine things about the value of time to me—about the blessings of my long evenings. For all that (true as it is), I have got into the way of going to bed soon after ten, just because I know every one else in the house is in bed, and I do not like to be the only person up."

"That is the reason why you are looking so well, notwithstanding all these terrors. But, Maria, what has become of your bravery?"

"It is just where it was. I am no more afraid than I used to be of evils which may be met with a mature mind: and just as much afraid as ever of those which terrified my childhood."

"Our baby shall never be afraid of anything," asserted Margaret. "But Maria, something must be done for your relief."

"That is just what I hoped and expected you would say, and the reason why I exposed myself to you."

"Why do not the Greys offer you a room there for the winter? That seems the simplest and most obvious plan."

"It is not convenient."

"How should that be?"

"The bed would have to be uncovered, you know; and the mahogany wash-stand might be splashed."

"They can get a room ready for a guest, to relieve their own fears, but not yours. Can nothing be done about it?"

"Not unless the Rowlands should take in Mr Walcot, because he is afraid to live alone: in such case, the Greys would take me in for the same reason. But that will not be so, Margaret, I will ask you plainly, and you will answer as plainly—could you, without too much pain, trouble, and inconvenience, spend an evening or two a week with me, just till this panic is passed? If you could put it in my power to be always looking forward to an evening of relief, it would break the sense of solitude, and make all the difference to me. I see the selfishness of this; but I really think it is better to own my weakness than to struggle uselessly against it any longer."

"I could do that—should like of all things to do it till Morris goes: but that will be so soon—."

"Morris! where is she going?"

Margaret related this piece of domestic news, too private to be told to any one else till the last moment. Maria forgot her own troubles, or despised them as she listened, so grieved was she for her friends, including Morris. Margaret was not very sorry on Morris's own account. Morris wanted rest—an easier place. She had had too much upon her for some time past.

"What then will you have, when she is gone?"

"If I have work enough to drive all thought out of my head, I shall be thankful. Meantime, I will bestow my best wit upon your case."

"I am ashamed of my case already. While sitting in all this comfort here, I can hardly believe in my own tremors, of no earlier date than last night. Come, let us draw to the fire. I hope we shall not end with sitting up all night; but I feel as if I should like it very much."

Margaret stirred up a blaze, and put out the candles. No economy was now beneath her care. As she took her seat beside her friend, she said:

"Maria, did you ever know any place so dull and dismal as Deerbrook is now? Is it not enough to make any heart as heavy as the fortunes of the place?"

"Even the little that I see of it, in going to and from the Greys, looks sad enough. You see the outskirts, which I suppose are worse still."

"The very air feels too heavy to breathe. The cottages, and even the better houses, appear to my eyes damp and weather-stained on the outside, and silent within. The children sit shivering on the thresholds—do not they?—instead of shouting at their play as they did. Every one looks discontented, and complains—the poor of want of bread, and every one else of hard times, and all manner of woes, that one never hears of in prosperous seasons. Mr James says the actions for trespass are beyond all example; Mr Tucker declares his dog, that died the other day, was poisoned; and I never pass the Green but the women are even quarrelling for precedence at the pump."

"I have witnessed some of this, but not all: and neither, I suspect, have you, Margaret, though you think you have. We see the affairs of the world in shadow, you know, when our own hearts are sad."

"My heart is not so sad as you think. You do not believe me: but that is because you do not believe what I am sure of—that he is not to blame for anything that has happened—that, at least, he has only been mistaken,—that there his been no fickleness, no selfishness, in him. I could not speak of this, even to you, Maria, if it were not a duty to him. You must not be left to suppose from my silence that he is to blame, as you think he is. I suffer from no sense of injury from him. I got over that, long ago."

Maria would not say, as she thought, "You had to get over it, then?"

"It makes me very unhappy to think how he is suffering,—how much more he has to bear than I; so much more than the separation and the blank. He cannot trust me as I trusted him; and that is, indeed, to be without consolation."

"Do men ever trust as women do?"

"Yes, Edward does. If he were to go to India for twenty years, he would know, as certainly as I should, that Hester would be widowed in every thought till his return. And the time will come when Philip will know this as certainly of me. It is but a little while yet that I have waited, Maria; but it does sometimes seem a weary waiting."

Maria took her friend's hand, in token of the sympathy she could not speak,—so much of hopelessness was there mingled with it.

"I know you and others think that this waiting is to go on for ever."

"No, love; not so."

"Or that a certainty which is even worse will come some day. But it will be otherwise. His love can no more be quenched or alienated by the slanders of a wicked woman, than the sun can be put out by an eclipse, or sent to enlighten another world, leaving us mourning."

"You judge by your own soul, Margaret; and that should be a faithful guide. You judge him by your own soul,—and how much by this?" she added, with a smile, fixing her eyes on the turquoise ring, which was Philip's gift, and which, safely guarded, was on a finger of the hand she held.

Margaret blushed. She could not have denied, if closely pressed, that some little tinge of the Eastern superstition had entered into this sacred ring, and lay there, like the fire in the opal. She could not have denied, that, when she drew it on every morning, she noted with satisfaction that its blue was as clear and bright as ever.

"How is it that this ring is still here?" asked Maria. "Is it possible that he retains gifts of yours? Yet, I think, if he did not, this ring would not be on your finger."

"He does keep whatever I gave him. Thank God! he keeps them. This is one of my greatest comforts: it is the only way I have left of speaking to him. But if it were not so, this ring would still be where it is. I would not give it up. I am not altered. I am not angry with him. His love is as precious to me as it ever was, and I will not give up the tokens of it. Why, Maria, you surely cannot suppose that these things have any other value or use but as given by him! You cannot suppose that I dread the imputation of keeping them for their own sakes!"

"No: but—"

"But what?"

"Is any proof of his former regard of value now? That is the question. It has only very lately become a question with me. I have only lately learned to think him in fault. I excused him before... I excused him as long as I could."

"You will unlearn your present opinion of him. Yes; everything that was ever valuable from him is more precious than ever now,—now that he is under a spell, and cannot speak his soul. If it were, as you think, if he loved me no longer, they would be still more precious, as a relic of the dead. But it is not so."

"If faith can remove mountains, we may have to rejoice for you still, Margaret; for there can be no mass of calumnies between you and him which you have not faith enough to overthrow."

"Thank you for that. It is the best word of comfort that has come to me from without for many a day. Now there is one thing more in which you can perhaps help me. I have heard nothing about him for so long! You see Mr Rowland sometimes (I know he feels a great friendship for you); and you meet the younger children. Do you hear nothing whatever about *him*?"

"Nothing: nor do they. Mr Rowland told me, a fortnight ago, that Mrs Rowland and he are seriously uneasy at obtaining no answers to their repeated letters to Mr Enderby. Mrs Rowland is more disturbed, I believe, than she chooses to show. She must feel herself responsible. She has tried various means of accounting for his silence, all the autumn. Now she gives that up, and is silent in her turn. If it were not for the impossibility of leaving home at such a time as this, Mr Rowland would go to London to satisfy himself. Margaret, I believe you are the only person who has smiled at this."

"Perhaps I am the only one who understands him. I had rather know of this silence than of all the letters he could have written to Mrs Rowland. If he had been ill, they would certainly have heard."

"Yes; they say so."

"Then that is enough. Let us say no more now."

"You have said that which has cheered me for you, Margaret, though, as we poor irreligious human beings often say to each other, 'I wish I had your faith.' You have given me more than I had, however. But are we to say no more about anything? Must we leave this comfortable fire, and go to sleep?"

"Not unless you wish it. I have more to ask, if you are not tired."

"Come, ask me."

"Cannot you tell me of some way in which a woman may earn money?"

"A woman? What rate of woman? Do you mean yourself? That question is easily answered. A woman from the uneducated classes can get a subsistence by washing and cooking, by milking cows and going to service, and, in some parts of the kingdom, by working in a cotton mill, or burnishing plate, as you have no doubt seen for yourself at Birmingham. But, for an educated woman, a woman with the powers which God gave her, religiously improved, with a reason which lays life open before her, an understanding which surveys science as its appropriate task, and a conscience which would make every species of responsibility safe,—for such a woman there is in all England no chance of subsistence but by teaching—that almost ineffectual teaching, which can never countervail the education of circumstances, and for which not one in a thousand is fit—or by being a superior Miss Nares—the feminine gender of the tailor and the hatter."

"The tutor, the tailor, and the hatter. Is this all?"

"All; except that there are departments of art and literature from which it is impossible to shut women out. These are not, however, to be regarded as resources for bread. Besides the number who succeed in art and literature being necessarily extremely small, it seems pretty certain that no great achievements, in the domains of art and imagination, can be looked for from either men or women who labour there to supply their lower wants, or for any other reason than the pure love of their work. While they toil in any one of the arts of expression, if they are not engrossed by some loftier meaning, the highest which they will end with expressing will be, the need of bread."

"True—quite true. I must not think of any of those higher departments of labour, because, even if I were qualified, what I want is not employment, but money. I am anxious to earn some money, Maria. We are very poor. Edward is trying, one way and another, to earn money to live upon, till his practice comes back to him, as he is for ever trusting it will. I wish to earn something too, if it be ever so little. Can you tell me of no way?"

"I believe I should not if I could. Why? Because I think you have quite enough to do already, and will soon have too much. Just consider. When Morris goes, what hour of the day will you have to spare? Let us see;—do you mean to sweep the rooms with your own hands?"

"Yes," said Margaret, smiling.

"And to scour them too?"

"No; not quite that. We shall hire a neighbour to come two or three times a week to do the rougher parts of the work. But I mean to light the fire in the morning (and we shall have but one), and get breakfast ready; and Hester will help me to make the beds. That is nearly all I shall let her do besides the sewing; for baby will give her employment enough."

"Indeed, I think so; and that will leave you too much. Do not think, dear, of earning money. You are doing all you ought in saving it."

"I must think about it, because earning is so much nobler and more effectual than saving. I cannot help seeing that it would be far better to earn the amount of Morris's maintenance, than to save it by doing her work badly myself. Not that I shrink from the labour: I am rather enjoying the prospect of it, as I told you. Hark! what footstep is that?"

"I heard it a minute or two ago," whispered Maria, "but I did not like to mention it."

They listened in the deepest silence for a while. At first they were not sure whether they heard anything above the beating of their own hearts; but they were soon certain that there were feet moving outside the room door.

"The church clock has but lately gone twelve," said Maria, in the faint hope that it might be some one of the household yet stirring.

Margaret shook her head. She rose softly from her seat, and took a candle from the table to light it, saying she would go and see. Her hand trembled a little as she held the match, and the candle would not immediately light. Meantime, the door opened without noise, and some one walked in and quite up to the gazing ladies. It was the tall woman. Maria made an effort to reach the bell, but the tall woman seized her arm, and made her sit down. A capricious jet of flame from a coal in the fire at this moment lighted up the face of the stranger for a moment, and enabled Maria to "spy a creat peard under the muffler."

"What do you want at this time?" said Margaret.

"I want money, and what else I can get," said the intruder, in the no longer disguised voice of a man. "I have been into your larder, but you seem to have nothing there."

"That is true," said Margaret, firmly; "nor have we any money. We are very poor. You could not have come to a worse place, if you are in want."

"Here is something, however," said the man, turning to the tray. "With your leave, I'll see what you have left us to eat."

He thrust one of the candles between the bars of the grate to light it, telling the ladies they had better start no difficulty, lest they should have reason to repent it. There were others with him in the house, who would show themselves in an instant, if any noise were made.

"Then do you make none—I beg it as a favour," said Margaret. "There is a lady asleep up-stairs, with a very young infant. If you respect her life you will be quiet."

The man did not answer, but he was quiet. He cut slices from the loaf, and carried them to the door, and they were taken by somebody outside. He quickly devoured the remains of the pheasant, tearing the meat from the bones with his teeth. He drank from the decanter of wine, and then carried it where he had taken the bread. Two men put their heads in at the door, nodded to the ladies before they drank, and again withdrew. The girls cast a look at each other—a glance of agreement that resistance was not to be thought of: yet each was conscious of a feeling of rather pleasant surprise that she was not more alarmed.

"Now for it!" said the man, striding oddly about in his petticoats, and evidently out of patience with them. "Now for your money!" As he spoke, he put the spoons from the tray into the bosom of his gown, proceeding to murmur at his deficiency of pockets.

Margaret held out her purse to him. It contained one single shilling.

"You don't mean this is all you are going to give me?"

"It is all I have: and I believe there is not another shilling in the house. I told you we have no money."

"And you?" said he, turning to Maria.

"I have not my purse about me; and if I had there is nothing in it worth your taking. I assure you I have not got my purse. I am only a visitor here for this one night—and an odd night it is to have chosen, as it turns out."

"Give me your watches."

"I have no watch. I have not had a watch these five years," said Maria.

"I have no watch," said Margaret. "I sold mine a month ago. I told you we were very poor."

The man muttered something about the plague of gentlefolks being so poor, and about wondering that gentlefolks were not ashamed of being so poor. "You have got something, however," he continued, fixing his eye on the ring on Margaret's finger. "Give me that ring. Give it me, or else I'll take it."

Margaret's heart sank with a self-reproach worse than her grief, when she remembered how easily she might have saved this ring—how easily she might have thrust it under the fender, or dropped it into her shoe, into her hair, anywhere, while the intruder was gone to the room door to his companions. She felt that she could never forgive herself for this neglect of the most precious thing she had in the world—of that which most belonged to Philip.

"She cannot part with that ring," said Maria. "Look! you may see she had rather part with any money she is ever likely to have than with that ring."

She pointed to Margaret, who was sitting with her hands clasped as if they were never to be disjoined, and with a face of the deepest distress.

"I can't help that," said the man. "I must have what I can get."

He seized her hands, and, with one gripe of his, made hers fly open. Margaret could no longer endure to expose any of her feelings to the notice of a stranger of this character. "Be patient a moment," said she; and she drew off the ring after its guard, made of Hester's hair, and put them into the large hand which was held out to receive them; feeling, at the moment, as if her heart was breaking. The man threw the hair ring back into her lap, and tied the turquoise in the corner of the shawl he wore.

"The lady up-stairs has got a watch, I suppose."

"Yes, she has: let me go and fetch it. Do let me go. I am afraid of nothing so much as her being terrified. If you have any humanity, let me go. Indeed I will bring the watch."

"Well, there is no man in the house, I know, for you to call. You may go, Miss: but I must step behind you to the room door; no further—she shan't see me, nor know any one is there, unless you tell her. This young lady will sit as still as a mouse till we come back."

"Never mind me," said Maria, to her friend. While they were gone, she sat as she was desired, as still as a mouse, enforced thereto by the certainty that a man stood in the shadow by the door, with his eye upon her the whole time.

Margaret lighted a chamber candle, in order, as she said, to look as usual if her sister should see her. The robber did tread very softly on the stairs, and stop outside the chamber-door. Morris was sitting up in her truckle-bed, evidently listening, and was on the point of starting out of it on seeing that Margaret's face was pale, when Margaret put her finger on her lips, and motioned to her to lie down. Hester was asleep, with her sleeping infant on her arm. Margaret set down the light, and leaned over her, to take the watch from its hook at the head of the bed.

"Are you still up?" said Hester, drowsily, and just opening her eyes. "What do you want? It must be very late."

"Nearly half-past twelve, by your watch. I am sorry I disturbed you. Good-night."

As she withdrew with the watch in her hand, she whispered to Morris:

"Lie still. Don't be uneasy. I will come again presently." So, in a few minutes, as seemed to intently listening ears, the house was clear of the intruders. Within a quarter of an hour Margaret had beckoned Morris out of Hester's room, and had explained the case to her. They went round the house, and found that all the little plate they had was gone, and the cheese from the pantry. Morris's cloth cloak was left hanging on its pin, and even Edward's old hat. From these circumstances, and from the dialect of the only speaker, Margaret thought the thieves must be country people from the neighbourhood, who could not wear the old clothes of the gentry without danger of detection. They had come in from the surgery, whose outer door was sufficiently distant from the inhabited rooms of the house to be forced without the noise being heard. Morris and Margaret barricaded this door as well as they could, with such chests and benches as they were able to move without making themselves heard up-stairs: and then Morris, at Margaret's earnest desire, stole back to bed. Anything rather than alarm Hester.

While they were below, Maria had put on more coals, and restored some order and comfort to the table and the fireside. She concluded that sleep was out of the question for this night. For some moments after Margaret came and sat down by her, neither of them spoke. At length Margaret said, half laughing:

"That you should have come here for rest this night, of all nights in the year!"

"I am glad it happened so. Yes; indeed, I am. I know it must have been a comfort to you to have some one with you, though only poor lame me. And I am glad on my own account too, I assure you. Such a visitation is not half so dreadful as I had fancied—not worth half the fear I have spent upon it all my life. I am sure you felt as I did while he was here; you felt quite yourself, did not you? If it had not been for the woman's clothes, it would really have been scarcely terrifying at all. There is something much more human about a housebreaker than I had fancied. But yet it was very inhuman of him to take your ring."

Margaret wept more bitterly than any one had seen her weep since her unhappy days began, and her friend could not comfort her. It was a case in which there was no comfort to be given, unless in the very faint and unreasonable hope that the ring might be offered for sale to some jeweller in some market town in the county; a hope sadly faint and unreasonable; since country people who would take plate and ornaments must, in all probability, be in communication with London rogues, who would turn the property into money in the great city. Still, there was a possibility of recovering the lost treasure; and on this possibility Maria dwelt perseveringly.

"But, Margaret," she went on to ask, "what is this about your watch? Have you indeed sold it?"

"Yes. Morris managed that for me while Hester was confined. I am glad now that I parted with it as I did. It has paid some bills which I know made Edward anxious; and that is far better than its being in a housebreaker's hands."

"Yes, indeed: but I am sorry you all have such a struggle to live. Not a shilling in the house but the one you gave up!"

"So much for Edward's being out. It happened very well; for he could not have helped us, if he had been here. You saw there were three of them. What I meant was, that Edward has about him the little money that is to last us till Christmas. The rent is safe enough. It is in Mr Grey's strong box or the bank at Blickley. The rent is too important a matter to be put to any hazard, considering that Mr Rowland is our landlord. It is all ready and safe."

"That is well. Now, Margaret, could you swear to this visitor of ours?"

"No," said Margaret, softly, looking round, as if to convince herself that he was not there still. "No: his bonnet was so large, and he kept the shadow of it so carefully upon his face, that I should not know him again—at least, not in any other dress; and we shall never see him again in this. It is very disagreeable," she continued, shuddering slightly, "to think that we may pass him any day or every day, and that he may say to himself as we go by, 'There go the ladies that sat with their feet on the fender so comfortably when I went in, without leave!'"

"Poor wretch! he will rather say, 'There goes the young lady that I made so unhappy about her ring. I wish I had choked with the wine I drank, before I took that ring!' The first man you meet that cannot look you in the face is the thief, depend upon it, Margaret."

"I must not depend upon that. But, Maria, could you swear to him?"

"I am not quite sure at this moment, but I believe I could. The light from the fire shone brightly upon his black chin, and a bit of lank hair that came from under his mob cap. I could swear to the shawl."

"So could I: but that will be burned to-morrow morning. Now, Maria, do go to bed."

"Well, if you had rather—. Cannot we be together? Must I be treated as a guest, and have a room to myself?"

"Not if you think we can make room in mine. We shall be most comfortable there, shall not we—near to Morris and Hester?"

Rather than separate, they both betook themselves to the bed in Margaret's room. Maria lay still, as if asleep, but wide awake and listening. Margaret mourned her turquoise with silent tears all the rest of the night.

Chapter Forty

Lightsome Days.

Before he returned home in the morning, Hope went to Dr Levitt's, to report of what he had seen and heard on Mr Grey's premises in the course of the night. He was persuaded that several persons had been about the yards; and he had seen a light appearing and disappearing among the shrubs which grew thick in the rear of the house. Sydney and he had examined the premises this morning, in company with Mr Grey's clerk; and they had found the flower-beds trampled, and drops of tallow from a candle which had probably been taken out of a lantern, and ashes from tobacco-pipes, scattered under the lee of a pile of logs. Nothing was missed from the yards: it was probable that they were the resort of persons who had been plundering elsewhere: but the danger from fire was so great, and the unpleasantness of having such night neighbours so extreme, that the gentlemen agreed that no time must be lost in providing a watch, which would keep the premises clear of intruders. The dog, which had by some means been cajoled out of his duty, must be replaced by a more faithful one; and Dr Levitt was disposed to establish a patrol in the village.

The astonishment of both was great when Margaret appeared, early as it was, with her story. It was the faint hope of recovering her ring which brought her thus early to the magistrate's. Her brother was satisfied to stay and listen, when he found that Hester knew as yet nothing of the matter. It was a clear case that the Greys must find some other guardian for the nights that Mr Grey spent from home; and Dr Levitt said that no man was justified in leaving his family unprotected for a single night in such times as these. He spoke with the deepest concern of the state of the neighbourhood this winter, and of his own inability to preserve security, by his influence either as clergyman or magistrate. The fact was, he said, that neither law nor gospel could deter men from crime, when pressed by want, and hardened against all other claims by those of their starving families. Such times had never been known within his remembrance; and the guardians of the public peace and safety were almost as much at their wits' end as the sickly and savage population they had to control. He must to-day consult with as many of his brother magistrates as he could reach, as to what could be done for the general security and relief.

As Hope and Margaret returned home to breakfast, they agreed that their little household was more free to discharge the duties of such a time than most of their neighbours of their own rank could possibly be. They had now little or nothing of which they could be robbed. It was difficult to conceive how they could be further injured. They might now, wholly free from fear and self-regards, devote themselves to forgive and serve their neighbours. Such emancipation from care as is the blessing of poverty, even more than of wealth, was theirs; and, as a great blessing in the midst of very tolerable evil, they felt it. Margaret laughed, as she asked Edward if he could spare a few pence to buy horn spoons in the village, as all the silver ones were gone.

Hester was not at all too much alarmed or disturbed, when she missed her watch, and heard what had happened. She was chiefly vexed that she had slept through it all. It seemed so ridiculous that the master of the house should be safe at a distance, and the mistress comfortably asleep, during such an event, leaving it to sister, maid, and guest, to bear all the terror of it!

Dr Levitt's absence of mind did not interfere with the activity of his heart, or with his penetration in cases where the hearts of others were concerned. He perceived that the lost turquoise was, from some cause, inestimable to Margaret, and he spared no pains to recover it: but weeks passed on without any tidings of it. Margaret told herself that she must give up this, as she had given up so much else, with as much cheerfulness as she could; but she missed her ring every hour of the day.

Christmas came; and the expected contest took, place about the rent of the corner-house. Mr Rowland showed his lady the bank-notes on the morning of quarter-day, and then immediately and secretly sent them back. Mrs Rowland had never been so sorry to see bank-notes; yet she would have been so angry at their being returned, that her husband concealed the fact from her. Within an hour the money was in Mr Rowland's hands again, with a request that he would desist from pressing favours upon those who could not but consider them as pecuniary obligation, and not as justice. Mr Rowland sighed, turned the key of his desk upon the money, and set forth to the corner-house, to see whether no repairs were wanted—whether there was nothing that he could do as landlord to promote the comfort and security of his excellent tenants.

Christmas came; and Morris found she could not leave her young ladies while the days were so very short. She would receive no wages after Christmas, and she would take care that she cost them next to nothing; but she could not be easy to go till brighter days—days externally brighter, at least—were at hand, nor till the baby was a little less tender, and had shown beyond dispute that he was likely to be a stout little fellow. She could not think of Miss Margaret getting up quite in the dark, to light the fire; it was a dismal time to begin such a new sort of work. Margaret privately explained to her that these little circumstances brought no discouragement to persons who undertake such labour with sufficient motive; and Morris admitted this. She saw the difference between the case of a poor girl first going to service, who trembles half the night at the idea of her mistress's displeasure if she should not happen to wake in time; such poor girl undertaking service for a maintenance, and by no means from love in either party towards the other—Morris saw the difference between the morning waking to such a service and Margaret's being called from her bed by love of those whom she was going to serve through the day, and by an exhilarating sense of honour and duty. Morris saw that, while to the solitary dependant every accessory of cheerfulness is necessary to make her willingly leave her rest— the early sunshine through her window, and the morning songs of birds—it mattered little to Margaret under what circumstances she went about her business—whether in darkness or in light, in keen frost or genial warmth. She had the strength of will, in whose glow all the disgust, all the meanness, all the hardship of the most sordid occupations is consumed, leaving unimpaired the dignity and delight of toil. Morris saw and fully admitted all this; and yet she stayed on till the end of January.

By that time her friends were not satisfied to have her remain any longer. It was necessary that she should earn money; and she had an opportunity now of earning what she needed at Birmingham. The time was come when Morris must go.

The family had their sorrow all to themselves that dismal evening; for not a soul in Deerbrook, except Maria, knew that Morris was going at all. Maria had known all along; and it had been settled that Maria should occupy Morris's room, after it was vacated, as often as she felt nervous and lonely in her lodging. But she was not aware of the precise day when the separation of these old and dear friends was to take place. So they mourned Morris as privately as she had long grieved over their adversity.

Mr Hope meant to drive Morris to Buckley himself, and to see her into the coach for Birmingham; and he had borrowed Mr Grey's gig for the purpose. He had been urged by Mr Grey not to think of returning that night, had desired his wife and sister not to expect him, and had engaged a neighbour to sleep in the house. The sisters might well look forward to a sad evening; and their hearts were heavy when the gig came to the door, when they were fortifying Morris with a parting glass of wine, and wrapping her up with warm things which were to come back with her master, and expressing their heart-sorrow by the tenderness with which they melted the very soul of poor Morris. She could not speak; she could resist nothing. She took all they offered her to comfort herself with, from having neither heart nor voice to refuse. Morris never gave way to tears; but she was as solemn as if she were going to execution. The baby alone was insensible to her gravity; he laughed in her face when she took him into her arms for the last time;—a seasonable laugh it was, for it relieved his mother of some slight superstitious dread which was stealing upon her, as she witnessed the solemnity of Morris's farewell to him. They all spoke of her return to them; but no one felt that there was any comfort in so vague a hope, amidst the sadness of the present certainty.

As Hester and Margaret stood out on the steps to watch the gig till the last moment, a few flakes of snow were driven against their faces. They feared Morris would have a dreary journey; and this was not the pleasantest thought to carry with them into the house.

While Hester nursed her infant by the fire, Margaret went round the house, to see what there was for her to do to-night. It moved her to find how thoughtfully everything was done. Busy as Morris had been with a thousand little affairs and preparations, every part of the house was left in the completest order. The very blinds of the chambers were drawn down, and a fire was laid in every grate, in case of its being wanted. The tea-tray was set in the pantry, and not a plate left from dinner unwashed. Margaret felt and said how badly she should supply the place of Morris's hands, to say nothing of their loss of her head and heart. She sighed her thankfulness to her old friend, that she was already at liberty to sit down beside her sister, with actually nothing on her hands to be done before tea-time.

It was always a holiday to Margaret when she could sit by at leisure, as the morning and evening dressing and undressing of the baby went on. Hester would never entrust the business to her or to any one: but it was the next best thing to watch the pranks of the little fellow, and the play between him and his mother; and then to see the fun subside into drowsiness, and be lost in that exquisite spectacle, the quiet sleep of an infant. When he was this evening laid in his basket, and all was unusually still, from there being no one but themselves in the house, and the snow having by this time fallen thickly outside, Margaret said to her sister—"If I remember rightly, it is just a twelvemonth since you warned me how wretched marriage was. Just a year, is it not?"

"Is it possible?" said Hester, withdrawing her eyes from her infant.

"I wish I could have foreseen then how soon I might remind you of this."

"Is it possible that I said so?—and of all marriage?"

"Of all love, and all marriage. I remember it distinctly."

"You have but too much reason to remember it, love. But how thankless, how wicked of me ever to say so."

"We all, perhaps, say some wretched things which dwell on other people's minds, long after we have forgotten them ourselves. It is one of the acts we shall waken up to as sins—perhaps every one of us—whenever we become qualified to review our lives dispassionately;—as sins, no doubt, for the pain does not die with the utterance; and to give pain needlessly, and to give lasting pain, is surely a sin. We are none of us guiltless; but I am glad you said this particular thing—dreadful as it was to hear it. It has caused me a great deal of thought within the year; and it now makes us both aware how much happier we are than we were then."

"We!"

"Yes; all of us. I rather shrink from measuring states of fortune and of mind, as they are at one time against those of another; but it is impossible to recall that warning of yours, and be unaware how differently we have cause to think and speak now. I felt at the time that it was too late for us to complain of love and of marriage. The die was then cast for us all. It is much better to feel now that those complaints were the expression of passing pain, long since over."

"I rejoice to hear you say this for yourself, Margaret; though I own I should scarcely have expected it. And yet no one is more aware than I that it is a blessing to love—a blessing still, whatever may be the woe that must come with the love. It is a blessing to live for another, to feel far more deeply than the most selfish being on earth ever felt for himself. I know that it is better to have felt this disinterested attachment to another, even in the midst of storms of passion hidden in the heart, and of pangs from disappointment, than to live on in the very best peace of those who have never loved. Yet, knowing this, I have been cowardly for you, Margaret, and at one time sank under my own troubles. Any one who loved as I did should have been braver. I should have been more willing, both for you and for myself, to meet the suffering which belongs to the exercise of all the highest and best part of our nature: but I was unworthy then of the benignant discipline appointed to me: and at the moment, I doubt not I should have preferred, if the choice had been offered to me, the safety and quiet of a passionless existence to the glorious exercise which has been graciously appointed me against my will. I do try now, Margaret, to be thankful that you have had some of this exercise and discipline; but I have not faith enough. My thanks are all up in grief before I have done—grief that you have the struggle and the sorrow, without the support and the full return which have been granted to me."

"You need not grieve much for me. I have not only had the full return you speak of, but I have it still. It cannot be spoken, or written, or even indulged; but I know it exists; and therefore am I happier than I was last year. How foolish it is," she continued, as if thinking aloud, "how perfectly childish to set our hearts on what we call happiness,—on any arrangement of circumstances, either in our minds or our fortunes—so little as we know! How you and I should have dreaded this night and to-morrow, if they could have been foreshown to us a while ago! How we should have shrunk from sitting down under the cloud of sorrow which appears to have settled upon this house! And now this evening has come—"

"The evening of Morris's going away, and everything else so dreary! No servant, no money, no prospect! Careful economy at home, ill-will abroad; the times bad, the future all blank—we two sitting here alone, with the snow falling without!"

"And our hearts aching with parting with Morris (we must come back to that principal grief). How dismal all this would have looked, if we could have seen it in a fairy-glass at Birmingham long ago!—and yet I would not change this very evening for any we ever spent in Birmingham, when we were exceedingly proud of being very happy."

"Nor I. This is life: and to live—to live with the whole soul, and mind, and strength, is enough. It is not often that I have strength to feel this, and courage to say it; but to-night I have both."

"And in time we may be strong enough to pray that this child may truly and wholly live—may live in every capacity of his being, whatever suffering may be the condition of such life: but it requires some courage to pray so for him, he looks so unfit for anything but ease at present!"

"For anything but feeding and sleeping, and laughing in our faces. Did you ever see an infant sleep so softly? Are not those wheels passing? Yes; surely I heard wheels rolling over the snow."

She was right. In five minutes more, Margaret had to open the door to her brother.

Hope had arrived at Blickley only just in time to drive Morris up to the door of the Birmingham coach, and put her in as the guard was blowing his horn. Mr Grey's horse had gone badly, and they had been full late in setting off. He had not liked the prospect of staying where he was till morning, and had resolved to bid defiance to footpads, and return: so he stepped into the coffee-room, and read the papers while the horse was feeding, and came home as quickly after as he could. As he was safe, all the three were glad he had done so; and the more that, for once, Edward seemed sad. They made a bright fire, and gave him tea; but their household offices did not seem to cheer him as usual. Hester asked, at length, whether he had heard any bad news.

"Only public news. The papers are full of everything that is dismal. The epidemic is spreading frightfully. It is a most serious affair. The people you meet in the streets at Blickley look as if they had the plague raging in the town. They say the funerals have never ceased passing through the streets, all this week; and really the churchyard I saw seemed full of new graves. I believe the case is little better in any town in the kingdom."

"And in the villages?"

"The villages follow, of course, with differences according to their circumstances. None will be worse than this place, when once the fever appears among us. I would not say so anywhere but by our own fireside, because everything should be done to encourage the people instead of frightening them; but indeed it is difficult to imagine a place better prepared for destruction than our pretty village is just now, from the extreme poverty of most of the people, and their ignorance, which renders them unfit to take any rational care of themselves."

"You say, 'whenever the fever comes.' Do you think it must certainly come?"

"Yes: and I have had some suspicions, within a day or two, that it is here already. I must see Walcot to-morrow; and learn what he has discovered in his practice."

"Mr Walcot! Will not Dr Levitt do as well?"

"I must see Dr Levitt too, to consult about some means of cleansing and drying the worst of the houses in the village. But it is quite necessary that I should have some conversation with Walcot about the methods of treatment of this dreadful disease. If he is not glad of an opportunity of consulting with a brother in the profession, he ought to be—and I have no doubt he will be; for he will very soon have as much upon him as any head and hands in the world could manage."

"Cannot you let him come to you for advice and assistance when he wants it?"

"I must not wait for that. He is young, and, as we all imagine, not over wise: and a dozen of our poor neighbours might die before he became aware of as much as I know to-night about this epidemic. No, love; my dignity must give way to the safety of our neighbours. Depend upon it, Walcot will be glad enough to hear what I have to say—if not to-morrow, by next week at furthest."

"So soon? What makes you say next week?"

"I judge partly from the rate of progress of the fever elsewhere, and partly from the present state of health in Deerbrook. There are other reasons too. I have seen some birds of ill omen on the wing hitherward this evening."

"What can you mean?"

"I mean fortune-tellers. Are you not aware that in seasons of plague—of the epidemics of our times, as well as the plagues of former days—conjurors, and fortune-tellers, and quacks appear, as a sort of heralds of the disease? They are not really so, for the disease in fact precedes them; but they show themselves so immediately on its arrival, and usually before its presence is acknowledged, that they have often been thought to bring it. They have early information of its existence in any place; and they come to take advantage of the first panic of the inhabitants, where there are enough who are ignorant to make the speculation a good one. I saw two parties of these people trooping hither; and we shall have heard something of their prophecies, and of a fever case or two, before this time to-morrow, I have little doubt."

"It is this prospect which has made you sad," said Hester.

"No, my dear—not that alone. But do not let us talk about being sad. What does it matter?"

"Yes; do let us talk about it," said Margaret, "if, as I suspect, you are sad for us. It is about Morris's going away, is it not?"

"About many things. It is impossible to be at all times unaffected by such changes as have come upon us; I cannot always forget what my profession once was to me, for honour, for occupation, and for income. I confidently reckoned on bringing you both to a home full of comfort. Never were women so cherished as I meant that you should be. And now it has ended in your little incomes being almost our only resource, and in your being deprived of your old friend Morris, some years before her time. I can hardly endure to think of to-morrow."

"And do you really call this the end?" asked Margaret. "Do you consider our destiny fixed for evermore?"

"As far as you and I are concerned, love," said Hester to him, "I could almost wish that this were the end. I feel as if almost any change would be for the worse; I mean supposing you not to look as you do now, but as you have always been till now. Oh, Edward, I am so happy!"

Her husband could not speak for astonishment and delight. "You remember that evening in Verdon woods, Edward—the evening before we were married?"

"Remember it!"

"Well. How infinitely happier are we now than then! Oh! that fear—that mistrust of myself! You reproved me for my fear and mistrust then; and I must beg leave to remind you of what you then said. It is not often that I can have the honour of preaching to you, my dear husband, as it is rather difficult to find an occasion; but now I have caught you tripping. What is there for you to be uneasy about now, that can at all be compared with what I troubled myself about then?—Since that time I have caused you much misery, I know—misery which I partly foresaw I should cause you: but that is over, I trust. It is over at least for the time that we are poor and persecuted. I dare not and do not wish for anything otherwise than as we have it flow. Persecution seems to have made us wiser, and poverty happier; and how, if only Margaret were altogether as we would see her, how could we be better than we are?"

"You are right, my dear wife." These few tender words, and her husband's brightened looks, sufficed—Hester had no cares. She forgot even the fever, in seeing Edward look as gay as usual again, and in feeling that she was everything to that feeling, that conviction, for which she had sighed in vain, for long after her marriage. She had then fancied that his profession, his family, his own thoughts, were as important to him as herself. She now knew that she was supreme; and this was supreme satisfaction.

When Margaret sprang up to her new labours in the chill dusk of the next morning, she flattered herself that she was the first awake; but it was not so. When she went down, she found her brother busy shovelling the snow away, and making a clear path from the kitchen door to the coal-house. He declared it delightfully warm work, by the time he had brought in coals enough for the day, and wanted more employment of the same sort. He went round to the front of the house, and cleared the steps and pavement there; caring nothing for the fact, that two or three neighbours gazed from their doors, and that some children stood blowing upon their fingers, and stamping with their feet, enduring the cold, for the sake of seeing the gentleman clearing his own steps.

"What would the Greys say?" asked Margaret, laughing; as, duster in hand, she looked from the open window, and spoke to her brother outside.

"I am sure they ought to say I have done my work well."

"That is just what Hester is observing within here. You are almost ready for breakfast, are you not? She is setting the table."

"Quite ready. What warm work this is! Really I do not believe there is such a bit of pavement in all Deerbrook as this of ours."

"Come—come in to breakfast. You have admired your work quite enough for this morning."

The three who sat down to breakfast were as reasonable and philosophical as most people; but even they were taken by surprise with the sweetness of comforts provided by their own immediate toil. There was something in the novelty, perhaps; but Hope threw on the fire with remarkable energy the coals he had himself brought in from the coal-house, and ate with great relish the toast toasted by his wife's own hands. Margaret, too, looked round the room more than once, with a new sort of pride in there being not a particle of dust on table, chair, or book. It was scarcely possible to persuade Edward that there was nothing more for him to do about the house till the next morning; that the errand-boy would come in an hour, and clean the shoes; and that the only assistance the master of the house could render, would be to take charge of the baby for a quarter of an hour, while Hester helped her sister to make the beds.

After breakfast, when Hester was dressing her infant, and Margaret washing up the tea-cups and saucers, the postman's knock was heard. Margaret went to the door, and paid for the letter from the "emergency purse," as they called the little sum of money they had put aside for unforeseen expenses. The letter was for Edward, and so brief that it must be on business.

It was on business. It was from the lawyer of Mr Hope's aged grandfather; and it told that the old gentleman had at last sunk rather suddenly under his many infirmities. Mr Hope was invited to go—not to the funeral, for it must be over before he could arrive, but to see the will, in which he had a large beneficial interest, the property being divided between himself and his brother, subject to legacies of one hundred pounds to each of his sisters, and a few smaller bequests to the servants.

"This is as you always feared," said Hester to her husband, observing the expression of concern in his face, on reading the letter.

"Indeed, I always feared it would be so," he replied. "I did what I could to prevent this act of posthumous injustice; and I am grieved that I failed; for nothing can repair it. My sisters will have their money—the same in amount, but how different in value! They will receive it as a gift from their brothers, instead of as their due from their grandfather. I am very sorry his last act was of this character."

"Will you go? Must you go?"

"No, I shall not go—at least, not at present. The funeral would be over, you see, before I could get there; and I doubt not the rest of the business may be managed quietly and easily by letter. I have no inclination to travel just now, and no money to do it with, and strong reasons of another kind for staying at home. No, I shall not go."

"I am very glad. Now, the first duty is to write to Emily and Anne, I suppose: and to Frank?"

"Not to Frank just yet. He knows what I meant to do, in case of my grandfather recurring to this disposition of his property; and, further than this, I must not influence Frank. He must be left entirely free to do as he thinks proper, and I shall not communicate with him till he has had ample time to decide on his course. I shall write to Emily and Anne to-day."

"I am sorry for them."

"So am I. What a pity it is, when the aged, whom one would wish to honour after they are gone to their graves, impair one's respect, by an unjust arrangement of their affairs! How easily might my grandfather have satisfied us all, and secured our due reverence at the last, by merely being just! Now, after admitting what was just, he has gone back into his prejudices, and placed us all in a painful position, from which it will be difficult to every one of us to regard his memory as we should wish."

"He little thought you would look upon his rich legacy in this way," said Margaret, smiling.

"I gave him warning that I should. It was impossible to refuse it more peremptorily than I did."

"That must be your satisfaction now, love. You have done everything that was right; so we will not discompose ourselves because another has done a wrong which you can partly repair."

"My dear wife, what comfort you give! What a blessing it is, that you think, and feel, and will act, with me—making my duty easy instead of difficult!"

"I was going to ask," observed Margaret, "whether you have no misgiving—no doubt whatever that you are right in refusing all this money."

"Not the slightest doubt, Margaret. The case is not in any degree altered by my change of fortune. The facts remain, that my sisters have received nothing yet from the property, while I have had my professional education out of it. That my profession does not at present supply us with bread does not affect the question at all: nor can you think that it does, I am sure. But Hester, my love, what think you of our prospect of a hundred pounds?"

"A hundred pounds!"

"Yes; that is the sum set down for me when the honest will was made; and that sum I shall of course retain."

"Oh, delightful! What a quantity of comfort we may get out of a hundred pounds! How rich we shall be!"

"She is thinking already," said Margaret, "what sort of a pretty cloak baby is to have for the summer."

"And Margaret must have something out of it, must not she, love?" asked Hester.

"We will all enjoy it, with many thanks to my poor grandfather. Surely this hundred pounds will set us on through the year."

"That will be very pleasant, really," observed Margaret. "To be sure of bread for all the rest of the year! Oh, the value of a hundred pounds to some people!"

"What a pity that Morris did not stay this one other day!" exclaimed Hester. "And yet, perhaps, not so. It might have perplexed her mind about leaving us, and induced her to give up her new place; and there is nothing in a chance hundred pounds to justify that. It is better as it is."

"All things are very well as they are," said Hope, "as long as we think so. Now, I am going to call on Walcot. Good-bye."

"Stop, stop one moment! Stay, and see what I have found!" cried his wife, in a tone of glee. "Look! Feel! Tell me—is not this our boy's first tooth?"

"It is—it certainly is. I give you joy, my little fellow!"

"Worth all the hundreds of pounds in the world," observed Margaret, coming in her turn to see and feel the little pearly edge, whose value its owner was far from appreciating, while worried with the inquisition which was made into the mysteries of his mouth. "Now it *is* a pity that Morris is not here!" all exclaimed.

"We must write to her. Perhaps we might have found it yesterday, if we had had any idea it would come so soon."

No: Hester was quite positive there was no tooth to be seen or felt last night.

"Well, we must write to Morris."

"You must leave me a corner," said Hope. "We must all try our skill in describing a first tooth. I will consider my part as I walk. Bite my finger once more before I go, my boy."

The sisters busied themselves in putting the parlour in order, for the reception of any visitors who might chance to call, though the streets were so deep in snow as to render the chance a remote one. Margaret believed that, when the time should come, she might set the potatoes over the parlour fire to boil, and thus, without detection, save the lighting another fire. But before she had taken off her apron, while she was in the act of sweeping up the hearth, there was a loud knock, which she recognised as proceeding from the hand of a Grey. The family resemblance extended to their knocks at the door.

As if no snow had fallen, Mrs Grey and Sophia entered.

"You are surprised to see us, my dears, I have no doubt. But I could not be satisfied without knowing what Mr Hope thinks of this epidemic, this terrible fever, which every one is speaking about so frightfully."

"Why, what can he think?"

"I mean, my dear, does he suppose that it will come here? Are we likely to have it?"

"He tells us, what I suppose you hear from Mr Grey, that the fever seems to be spreading everywhere, and is just now very destructive at Buckley. Does not Mr Grey tell you so?"

"No, indeed; there is no learning anything from Mr Grey that he does not like to tell. Sophia, I think we must take in a newspaper again, that we may stand a chance of knowing something."

Sophia agreed.

"Sophia and I found that we really had no time to read the newspaper. There it lay, and nobody touched it; for Mr Grey reads the news in the office always. I told Mr Grey it was just paying so much a-week for no good to anybody, and I begged he would countermand the paper. But we must take it in again, really, to know how this fever goes on. Does Mr Hope think, my dears, as many people are saying here this morning, that it is a sort of plague?"

"Oh, mamma," exclaimed Sophia, "how can you say anything so dreadful?"

"I have not heard my husband speak of it so," said Hester. "He thinks it a very serious affair, happening as it does in the midst of a scarcity, when the poor are already depressed and sickly."

"Ah! that is always the way, Mr Grey tells me. After a scarcity comes the fever, he says. The poor are much to be pitied indeed. But what should those do who are not poor, have you heard Mr Hope say?"

"He thinks they should help their poor neighbours to the very utmost."

"Oh, yes; of course: but what I mean is, what precautions would be advise?"

"We will ask him. I have not heard him speak particularly of this on the present occasion."

"Then he has not established any regulations in his own family?"

"No. But I know his opinion on such cases in general to be, that the safest way is to go on as usual, taking rational care of health, and avoiding all unnecessary terror. This common way of living, and a particularly diligent care of those who want the good offices of the rich, are what he would recommend, I believe, at this time: but when he comes in, we will ask him. You had better stay till he returns. He may bring some news. Meantime, I am sorry my baby is asleep. I should like to show you his first tooth."

"His first tooth? Indeed! He is a forward little fellow. But, Hester, do you happen to have heard your husband say what sort of fumigation he would recommend in case of such a fever as this showing itself in the house?"

"Indeed I have not heard him speak of fumigations at all. Have you, Margaret?"

"I should just like to know; for Mrs Jones told me of a very good one; and Mrs Howell thinks ill of it. Mrs Jones recommended me to pour some sulphuric acid upon salt—common salt—in a saucer; but Mrs Howell says there is nothing half so good as hot vinegar."

"Somebody has come and put up a stall," said Sophia, "where he sells fumigating powders, and some pills, which he says are an infallible remedy against the fever."

"Preventive, my dear."

"Well, mamma, 'tis just the same thing. Does Mr Hope know anything of the people who have set up that stall?"

Hester thought she might venture to answer that question without waiting for her husband's return. She laughed as she said, that medical men avoided acquaintance with quacks.

"Does Mr Hope think that medical men are in any particular danger?" asked Sophia, bashfully, but with great anxiety. "I think they must be, going among so many people who are ill. If there is a whole family in the fever in a cottage at Crossly End, as Mrs Howell says there is, how very dangerous it must be to attend them!"

Sophia was checked by a wink from her mother, and then first remembered that she was speaking to a surgeon's wife. She tried to explain away what she had said; but there was no need. Hester calmly remarked that it was the duty of many to expose themselves at such times in an equal degree with the medical men; and that she believed that few were more secure than those who did so without selfish thoughts and ignorant panic. Sophia believed that every one did not think so. Some of Mr Walcot's friends had been remonstrating with him about going so much among the poor sick people, just at this time; and Mr Walcot had been consulting her as to whether his duty to his parents did not require that he should have some regard to his own safety. He had not known what to do about going to a house in Turnstile-lane, where some people were ill.

A dead silence followed this explanation. Mrs Grey broke it by asking Margaret if she might speak plainly to her—the common preface to a lecture. As usual, Margaret replied, "Oh! certainly."

"I would only just hint, my dear, that it would be as well if you did not open the door yourself. You cannot think how strangely it looks: and some very unpleasant remarks might be made upon it. It is of no consequence such a thing happening when Sophia and I come to your door. I would not have you think we regard it for ourselves in the least—the not being properly shown in by a servant."

"Oh! not in the least," protested Sophia.

"But you know it might have been the Levitts. I suppose it would have been just the same if the Levitts had called?"

"It certainly would."

"It might have been the Levitts certainly," observed Hester: "but I must just explain that it was to oblige me that Margaret went to the door."

"Then, my dear, I hope you will point out some other way in which Margaret may oblige you; for really you have no idea how oddly it looks for young ladies to answer knocks at the door. It is not proper self-respect, proper regard to appearance. And was it to oblige you that Margaret carried a basket all through Deerbrook on Wednesday, with the small end of a carrot peeping out from under the lid? Fie, my dears! I must say fie! It grieves me to find fault with you: but really this is folly. It is really neglecting appearances too far."

Mr Hope did not return in time to see Mrs Grey. When she could wait no longer, Hester promised to send her husband to solve Mrs Grey's difficulties.

"What would she have said," exclaimed Hester, "if she had seen my husband's doings of this morning?"

"Ah! what indeed?"

"Actually shovelling snow from his own steps!"

"Oh, I thought you meant giving away a competence. Which act would she have thought the least self-respectful?"

"She would have had a great deal to say on his duty to his family in both cases. But it is all out of kindness that she grieves so much over his 'enthusiasm,' and lectures us for our disregard of appearances. If she loved us less, we should hear less of her concern, and it would be told to others behind our backs. So we will not mind it. You do not mind it, Margaret?"

"I rather enjoy it."

"That is right. Now I wish my husband would come in. He has been gone very long; and I want to hear the whole truth about this fever."

Chapter Forty One

Deerbrook in Shadow.

It was some hours before Hope appeared at home again; and when he did, he was very grave. Mr Walcot had been truly glad to see him, and, it was plain, would have applied to him for aid and co-operation some days before, if Mrs Rowland had not interfered, to prevent any consultation of the kind. The state of health of Deerbrook was bad,—much worse than Hope had had any suspicion of. Whole families were prostrated by the fever in the labourers' cottages, and it was creeping into the better sort of houses. Mr Walcot had requested Hope to visit some of his patients with him: and what he had seen had convinced him that the disease was of a most formidable character, and that a great mortality must be expected in Deerbrook. Walcot appeared to be doing his duty with more energy than might have been expected: and it seemed as if whatever talent he had, was exercised in his profession. Hope's opinion of him was raised by what he had seen this morning. Walcot had complained that his skill and knowledge could have no fair play among a set of people so ignorant as the families of his Deerbrook patients. They put more faith in charms than in medicines or care; and were running out in the cold and damp to have their fortunes told by night, or in the grey of the morning. If a fortune-teller promised long life, all the warnings of the doctor went for nothing. Then, again, the people mistook the oppression which was one of the first symptoms of the fever, for debility; and before the doctor was sent for, or in defiance of his directions, the patient was plied with strong drinks, and his case rendered desperate from the beginning. Mr Walcot had complained that the odds were really too much against him, and that he believed himself likely to lose almost every fever patient he had. It may be imagined how welcome to him were Mr Hope's countenance, suggestions, and influence,—such as the prejudices of the people had left it.

Dr Levitt's influence was of little more avail than Mr Hope's. From this day, he was as busily engaged among the sick as the medical gentlemen themselves; laying aside his books, and spending all his time among his parishioners; not neglecting the rich, but especially devoting himself to the poor. He co-operated with Hope in every way; raising money to cleanse, air, and dry the most cheerless of the cottages, and to supply the indigent sick with warmth and food. But all appeared to be of little avail. The disease stole on through the village, as if it had been left to work its own way; from day to day tidings came abroad of another and another who was down in the fever,—the Tuckers' maidservant, Mr Hill's shop-boy, poor Mrs Paxton, always sure to be ill when anybody else was, and all John Ringworth's five children. In a fortnight, the church bell began to give token how fatal the sickness was becoming. It tolled till those who lived very near the church were weary of hearing it.

On the afternoon of a day when its sound had scarcely ceased since sunrise, Dr Levitt and Hope met at the door of the corner-house.

"You are the man I wanted to meet," said Dr Levitt. "I have been inquiring for you, but your household could give me no account of you. Could you just step home with me? Or come to me in the evening, will you? But stay! There is no time like the present, after all; so, if you will allow me, I will walk in with you now; and, if you are going to dinner, I will make one. I have nobody to sit down with me at home at present, you know,—or perhaps you do not know."

"Indeed I was not aware of the absence of your family," said Hope, leading the way into the parlour, where Margaret at the moment was laying the cloth.

"You must have wondered that you had seen nothing of my wife all this week, if you did not know where she was. I thought it best, all things considered, to send them every one away. I hope we have done right. I find I am more free for the discharge of my own duty, now that I am unchecked by their fears for me, and untroubled by my own anxiety for them. I have sent them all abroad, and shall go for them when this epidemic has run its course; and not till then. I little thought what satisfaction I could feel in walking about my own house, to see how deserted it looks. I never hear that bell but I rejoice that all that belong to me are so far off."

"I wanted to ask you about that bell," said Hope. "My question may seem to you to savour strongly of dissent; but I must inquire whether it is absolutely necessary for bad news to be announced to all Deerbrook every day, and almost all day long. However far we may be from objecting to hear it in ordinary times, should not our first consideration now be for the living? Is not the case altered by the number of deaths that takes place at a season like this?"

"I am quite of your opinion, Mr Hope; and I have talked with Owen, and many others, about that matter, within this week. I have proposed to dispense, for the present, with a custom which I own myself to be attached to in ordinary times, but which I now see may be pernicious. But it cannot be done. We must yield the point."

"I will not engage to cure any sick, or to keep any well, who live within sound of that bell."

"I am not surprised to hear you say so. But this practice has so become a part of people's religion, that it seems as if worse effects would follow from discontinuing it than from pursuing the usual course. Owen says there is scarcely a person in Deerbrook who would not talk of a heathen death and burial if the bell were silenced; and, if once the people's repose in their religion is shaken, I really know not what will become of them."

"I agree with you there. Their religious feelings must be left untouched, or all is over; but I am sorry that this particular observance is implicated with them so completely as you say. It will be well if it does not soon become an impossibility to toll the bell for all who die."

"It would be well, too," said Dr Levitt, "if this were the only superstition the people entertained. They are more terrified with some others than with this bell. I am afraid they are more depressed by their superstitions than sustained by their religion. Have you observed, Hope, how many of them stand looking at the sky every night?"

"Yes; and we hear, wherever we go, of fiery swords, and dreadful angels, seen in the clouds; and the old prophecies have all come up again—at least, all of them that are dismal. As for the death-watches, they are out of number; and there is never a fire lighted but a coffin flies out."

"And this story of a ghost of a coffin, with four ghosts to bear it, that goes up and down in the village all night long," said Hester, "I really do not wonder that it shakes the nerves of the sick to hear of it. They say that no one can stop those bearers, or get any answer from them: but on they glide, let what will be in their way."

"Come, tell me," said Dr Levitt, "have not you yourself looked out for that sight?"

Hester acknowledged that she had seen a real substantial coffin, carried by human bearers, pass down the middle of the street, at an hour past midnight; the removal of a body from a house where it had died, she supposed, to another whence it was to be buried. This coffin and the ghostly one she took to be one and the same.

Dr Levitt mentioned instances of superstition, which could scarcely have been believed by him, if related by another.

"Do you know the Platts?" he inquired of Hope. "Have you seen the poor woman that lies ill there with her child?"

"Yes: what a state of destitution they are in!"

"At the very time that that woman and her child are lying on shavings, begged from the carpenter's yard, her mother finds means to fee the fortune-teller in the lane for reading a dream. The fortune-teller dooms the child, and speaks doubtfully of the mother."

"I could not conceive the reason why no one of the family would do anything for the boy. I used what authority I could, while I was there; but I fear he has been left to his fate since. The neighbours will not enter the house."

"What neighbours?" said Margaret. "You have never so much as asked me."

"You are our main stay at home, Margaret. I could ask no more of you than you do here."

Margaret was now putting the dinner on the table. It consisted of a bowl of potatoes, salt, the loaf and butter, and a pitcher of water. Dr Levitt said grace, and they sat down, without one word of apology from host or hostess. Though Dr Levitt had not been prepared for an evidence like this of the state of affairs in the family, he had known enough of their adversity to understand the case now at a glance. No one ate more heartily than he; and the conversation went on as if a sumptuous feast had been spread before the party.

"I own myself disappointed," said Hope, "in finding among our neighbours so little disposition to help each other. I hardly understand it, trusting as I have ever done in the generosity of the poor, and having always before seen my faith justified. The apathy of some, and the selfish terrors of others, are worse to witness than the disease itself."

"How can you wonder," said Dr Levitt, "when they have such an example before their eyes in certain of their neighbours, to whom they are accustomed to look up? Sir William Hunter and his lady are enough to paralyse the morals of the whole parish at a time like this. Do not you know the plan they go upon? They keep their outer gates locked, lest any one from the village should set foot within their grounds; every article left at the lodge for the use of the family is fumigated before it is admitted into the house: and it is generally understood that neither the gentleman nor the lady will leave the estate, in any emergency whatever, till the disease has entirely passed away. Our poor are not to have the solace of their presence even in church, during this time of peril, when the face of the prosperous is like light in a dark place. Sir William makes it no secret that they would have left home altogether, if they could have hoped to be safer anywhere else—if they could have gone anywhere without danger of meeting the fever."

"If the fact had not been," said Hester, "as Mrs Howell states it, that the epidemic prevails partially everywhere."

"There is a case where Lady Hunter's example immediately operates," observed Dr Levitt. "If Lady Hunter had not forgotten herself in her duty, Mrs Howell would have given the benefit of her good offices to some whom she might have served; for she is really a kind-hearted woman: but she is struck with a panic because Lady Hunter is, and one cannot get a word with her or Miss Miskin."

"I saw that her shutters were nearly closed," observed Margaret. "I supposed she had lost some relation."

"No: she is only trying to shut out the fever. She and Miss Miskin are afraid of the milkman, and each tries to put upon the other the peril of serving a customer. This panic will destroy us if it spreads."

The sisters looked at each other, and in one glance exchanged agreement that the time was fully come for them to act abroad, let what would become of their home comforts.

"I ought to add, however," said Dr Levitt, "that Sir William Hunter has supplied my poor's purse with money very liberally. I spend his money as freely as my own at a time like this; but I tell him that one hour of his presence among us would do more good than all the gold he can send. His answer comes in the shape of a handsome draft on his banker, smelling strongly of aromatic vinegar. They fumigate even their blotting-paper, it seems to me. I did hope my last letter would have brought him to call."

"Our friends are very ready with their money," said Hope. "I should have begged of you before this, but that Mr Grey has been liberal in that way. He concludes it to be impossible that he should look himself into the wants of the village; but he permits me to use his purse pretty freely. Is there anything that you can suggest that can be done by me, Dr Levitt? Is there any case unknown to me where I can be of service?"

"Or I?" said Margaret. "My brother and sister will spare me, and put up with some hardship at home, I know, if you can point out any place where I can be more useful."

"To be sure I can. Much as I like to come to your house, to witness and feel the thorough comfort which I always find in it, I own I shall care little to see everything at sixes and sevens here for a few weeks, if you will give me your time and talents for such services as we gentlemen cannot perform, and as we cannot at present hire persons to undertake. You see I take you at your word, my dear young lady. If you had not offered, I should not have asked you: as you have, I snatch at the good you hold out. I mean to preach a very plain sermon next Sunday on the duties of neighbours in a season of distress like this: and I shall do it with the better hope, if I have, meanwhile, a fellow-labourer of your sex, no less valuable in her way than my friend Hope in his."

"I shall come and hear your sermon," said Hester, "if Margaret will take charge of my boy for the hour. I want to see clearly what is my duty at a time when claims conflict as they do now."

There was at present no time for the conscientious and charitable to lose in daylight loiterings over the table, or chat by the fireside. In a few minutes the table was cleared, and Margaret ready to proceed with Dr Levitt to the Platts' Cottage.

As soon as Margaret saw what was the real state of affairs in the cottage, she sent away Dr Levitt, who could be of no use till some degree of decency was instituted in the miserable abode. What to set about first was Margaret's difficulty. There was no one to help her but Mrs Platt's mother, who was sitting down to wait the result of the fortune-teller's predictions. Her daughter lay moaning on a bedstead spread with shavings only, and she had no covering whatever but a blanket worn into a large hole in the middle. The poor woman's long hair, unconfined by any cap, strayed about her bare and emaciated shoulders, and her shrunken bands picked at the blanket incessantly, everything appearing to her diseased vision covered with black spots. Never before had so squalid an object met Margaret's eyes. The husband sat by the empty grate, stooping and shrinking, and looking at the floor with an idiotic expression of countenance, as appeared through the handkerchief which was tied over his head. He was just sinking into the fever. His boy lay on a heap of rags in the corner, his head also tied up, but the handkerchief stiff with the black blood which was still oozing from his nose, ears, and mouth. It was inconceivable to Margaret that her brother, with Mr Grey's money in his pocket, could have left the family in this state. He had not. There were cinders in the hearth which showed that there had been a fire; and the old woman acknowledged that a pair of sheets and a rug had been pawned to the fortune-teller in the lane since the morning. There had been food; but nobody had any appetite but herself, and she had eaten it up. The fortune-teller had charmed the pail of fresh water that stood under the bed, and had promised a new spell in the morning.

In a case of such extremity, Margaret had no fears. She set forth alone for the fortune-teller's, not far off, and redeemed the sheets and blanket, which were quite clean. As she went, she was sorry she had dismissed Dr Levitt so soon. As a magistrate, he could have immediately compelled the restoration of the bedding. The use of his name, however, answered the purpose, and the conjurer even offered to carry the articles for her to Platt's house. She so earnestly desired to keep him and her charge apart, that she preferred loading herself with the package. Then the shavings were found to be in such a state that every shred of them must be removed before the sick man could be allowed to lie down. No time was to be lost. In the face of the old woman's protestations that her daughter should not stir, Margaret spread the bedding on the floor, wrapped the sick woman in a sheet, and laid her upon it, finding the poor creature so light from emaciation that she was as easy to lift as a child. The only thing that the old woman would consent to do, was to go with a pencil note to Mr Grey, and bring back the clean dry straw which would be given her in his yard. She went, in hopes of receiving something else with the straw; and while she was gone, Margaret was quite alone with the sick family.

Struggling to surmount her disgust at the task, she resolved to employ the interval in removing the shavings. The pail containing the charmed water was the only thing in the cottage which would hold them; and she made bold to empty it in the ditch close at hand. Platt was capable of watching all she did; and he made a frightful gesture of rage at her as she re-entered. She saw in the shadow of the handkerchief his quivering lips move in the act of speaking, and her ear caught the words of an oath. Her situation now was far from pleasant; but it was still a relief that no one was by to witness what she saw and was doing. She conveyed pailful after pailful of the noisome shavings to the dunghill at the back of the cottage, wondering the while that the inhabitants of the dwelling were not all dead of the fever long ago. She almost gave over her task when a huge toad crawled upon her foot from its resting-place among the shavings. She shrunk from it, and was glad to see it make for the door of its own accord. Platt again growled, and clenched his fist at her. He probably thought that she had again broken a charm for which he had paid money. She spoke kindly and cheerfully, again and again; but he was either deaf or too ill to understand. To relieve the sense of dreariness, she went to work again. She thoroughly cleansed the pail, and filled it afresh from the brook, looking anxiously down the lane for the approach of some human creature, and then applied herself to rubbing the bedstead as dry and clean as she could, with an apron of the old woman's.

In due time her messenger returned; and with her Ben, carrying a truss of straw. His face was the face of a friend.

"We must have some warm water, Ben, to clean these poor creatures; and there seems to be nothing to make a fire with."

"And it would take a long time, Miss, to get the coals, and heat the water; and the poor soul lying there all the time. Could not I bring you a pail of hot water from the 'Bonnet-so-Blue' quicker than that?"

"Do; and soap and towels from home."

Ben was gone with the pail. During the whole time of spreading the straw on the bedstead, the old woman remonstrated against anything being done to her daughter, beyond laying her where she was before, and giving her a little warm spirits; but when she discovered that the charmed water had been thrown out into the ditch, all to her seemed over. Her last hope was gone; and she sat down in sulky silence, eyeing Margaret's proceedings without any offer to help.

When the warm water arrived, and the sick woman seemed to like the sponging and drying of her fevered limbs, the mother began to relent, and at last approached to give her assistance, holding her poor daughter in her arms while Margaret spread the blanket and sheet on the straw, and then lifting the patient into the now clean bed. She was still unwilling to waste any time and trouble on the child in the corner; but Margaret was peremptory. She saw that he was dying; but not the less for this must he be made as comfortable as circumstances would permit. In half an hour he, too, was laid on his bed of clean straw; and the filthy rags with which he had been surrounded were deposited out of doors till some one who would wash them could come for them. By a promise of fire and food, Margaret bribed the old woman to let things remain as they were while she went for her brother, whose skill and care she hoped might now have some chance of saving his patients. She recommended that Platt himself should not attempt to sit up any longer, and engaged to return in half an hour.

She paused on the threshold a minute, to see how far Platt was able to walk; so great seemed to be the difficulty with which he raised himself from his chair, with the old woman's assistance. Once he stumbled, and would have fallen, if Margaret had not sprung to his side. On recovering himself, he wrenched his arm from her, and pushed her backwards with more force than she had supposed he possessed. There was a half-smile on the old woman's face as he did this, which made Margaret shudder; but she was more troubled by a look from the man, which she caught from beneath the handkerchief that bound his head; a look which she could not but fancy she had met before with the same feeling of uneasiness.

When she had seen him safely seated on the bedside, she hastened away for her brother. They lost no more time in returning than just to step to Widow Rye's, to ask whether she would sit up with this miserable family this night. The widow would have done anything else in the world for Mr Hope; and she did not positively refuse to do this; but the fear of her neighbours had so infected her, and her terror of a sick-room was so extreme, that it was evident her presence there would do more harm than good. She was glad to compound for a less hazardous service, and agreed to wash for the sick with all diligence, if she was not required to enter the houses, but might fetch the linen from tubs of water placed outside the doors. After setting on plenty of water to heat, she now followed Hope and Margaret to the cottage in the lane.

It was nearly dark, and they walked rapidly, Margaret describing as they went what she had done, and what she thought remained to be done, to give Mrs Platt a chance of recovery.

"What now? Why do you start so?" cried Hope, as she stopped short in the middle of a sentence.

Margaret even stood still for one moment. Hope looked the way she was looking, and saw, in the little twilight that remained, the figure of some one who had been walking on the opposite side of the road, but whose walk was now quickened to a run.

"It is—it is he," said Hope, as Philip disappeared in the darkness. Answering to what he knew must be in Margaret's thoughts, he continued—

"He knows the state the village is in—the danger that we are all in, and he cannot stay away."

"'We!' 'All?'"

"When I say 'we,' I mean you particularly."

"If you think so—" murmured Margaret, and stopped for breath.

"I think so; but it does not follow that there is any change. He has always loved you. Margaret, do not deceive yourself. Do not afflict yourself with expectations—"

"Do not speak to me, brother. I cannot bear a word from you about him."

Hope sighed deeply, but he could not remonstrate. He knew that Margaret had only too much reason for saying this. They walked on in entire silence to the lane.

A fire was now kindled, and a light dimly burned in Platt's cottage. As Margaret stood by the bedside, watching her brother's examination of his patient, and anxious to understand rightly the directions he was giving, the poor woman half raised her head from her pillow, and fixed her dull eyes on Margaret's face, saying, as if thinking aloud:

"The lady has heard some good news, sure. She looks cheerful-like."

The mother herself turned round to stare, and, for the first time, dropped a curtsey.

"I hope we shall see you look cheerful too, one day soon, if we nurse you well," said Margaret.

"Then, Miss, don't let them move me, to take the blankets away again."

"You shall not be moved unless you wish it. I am going to stay with you to-night."

Her brother did not oppose this, for he did not know of the unpleasant glances and mutterings with which Platt rewarded all Margaret's good offices. Hope believed he should himself be out all night among his patients. He would come early in the morning, and now fairly warned Margaret that it was very possible that the child might die in the course of the night. She was not deterred by this, nor by her dread of the sick man. She had gained a new strength of soul, and this night she feared nothing. During the long hours there was much to do—three sufferers at once requiring her cares; and amidst all that she did, she was sustained by the thought that she had seen Philip, and that he was near. The abyss of nothingness was passed, and she now trod the ground of certainty of his existence, and of his remembrance. When her brother entered, letting in the first grey of the morning as he opened the cottage door, he found her almost untired, almost gay. Platt was worse, his wife much the same, and the child still living. The old woman's heart was so far touched with the unwonted comfort of the past night, and with her having been allowed, and even encouraged, to take her rest, that she now offered her bundle of clothes for the lady to lie down upon; and when that favour was declined, readily promised not to part with any article to the fortune-teller, till she should see some of Mr Hope's family again.

Hope thought Mrs Platt might possibly get through: and this was all that was said on the way home. Margaret lay down to rest, to sweet sleep, for a couple of hours: and when she appeared below, her brother and sister had half done breakfast, and Mr Grey and his twin daughters were with them.

Mr Grey came to say that he and all his family were to leave Deerbrook in two hours. Where they should settle for the present, they had not yet made up their minds. The first object was to get away, the epidemic being now really too frightful to be encountered any longer. They should proceed immediately to Brighton, and there determine whether to go to the Continent, or seek some healthy place nearer home, to stay in, till Deerbrook should again be habitable. They were extremely anxious to carry Hester, Margaret, and the baby, with them. They knew Mr Hope could not desert his posts: but they thought he would feel as Dr Levitt did, far happier to know that his family were out of danger, than to have them with him. Hester had firmly refused to go, from the first mention of the plan; and now Margaret was equally decided in expressing her determination to stay. Mr Grey urged the extreme danger: Fanny and Mary hung about her, and implored her to go, and to carry the baby with her. They should so like to have the baby with them for a great many weeks! and they would take care of him, and play with him all day long. Their father once more interposed for the child's sake. Hester might go to Brighton, there wean her infant, and return to her husband; so that the little helpless creature might at least be safe. Mr Grey would not conceal that he considered this a positive duty—that the parents would have much to answer for, if anything should happen to the boy at home. The parents' hearts swelled. They looked at each other, and felt that this was not a moment in which to perplex themselves with calculations of incalculable things—with comparisons of the dangers which threatened their infant abroad and at home. This was a decision for their hearts to make. Their hearts decided that their child's right place was in his parents' arms; and that their best hope now, as at all other times, was to live and die together.

Hester had heard from her husband of the apparition of the preceding evening, and she therefore knew that there was less of 'enthusiasm,' as Mr Grey called what some others would have named virtue, in Margaret's determination to stay, than might appear. If Philip was here, how vain must be all attempts to remove her! Mr Grey might as well set about persuading the old church tower to go with him: and so he found.

"Oh, cousin Margaret," said Mary, in a whisper, with a face of much sorrow, "mamma will not ask Miss Young to go with us! If she should be ill while we are gone! If she should die!"

"Nonsense, Mary," cried Fanny, partly overhearing, and partly guessing what her sister had said; "you know mamma says it is not convenient: and Miss Young is not like my cousins, as mamma says, a member of a family, with people depending upon her. It is quite a different case, Mary, as you must know very well. Only think, cousin Margaret! what an odd thing it will be, to be so many weeks without saying any lessons! How we shall enjoy ourselves!"

"But if Miss Young should be ill, and die!" persisted Mary.

"Pooh! why should she be ill and die, more than Dr Levitt, and Ben, and our cook, and my cousins, and all that are going to stay behind? Margaret, I do wish cousin Hester would let us carry the baby with us. We shall have no lessons to do, you know; and we could play with him all day long."

"Yes, I wish he might go," said Mary. "But, Margaret, do you not think, if you spoke a word to papa and mamma, they would let me stay with Miss

Young? I know she would make room for me; for she did for Phoebe, when Phoebe nursed her; and I should like to stay and help her, and read to her, even if she should not be ill. I think papa and mamma might let me stay, if you asked them."

"I do not think they would, Mary: and I had rather not ask them. But I promise you that we will all take the best care we can of Maria. We will try to help and amuse her as well as you could wish."

"Come, Mary, we must go!" cried Fanny. "There is papa giving Mr Hope some money for the poor; people always go away quick after giving money. Good bye, cousin Margaret. We shall bring you some shells, or something, I dare say, when we come back. Now let me kiss the baby once more. I can't think why you won't let him go with us: we should like so to have him!"

"So do we," said Hester, laughing.

As the door closed behind the Greys, the three looked in each other's faces. That glance assured each other that they had done right. In that glance was a mutual promise of cheerful fidelity through whatever might be impending. There was no sadness in the tone of their conversation; and when, within two hours, the Greys went by, driven slowly, because there was a funeral train on each side of the way, there was full as much happiness in the faces that smiled a farewell from the windows, as in the gestures of the young people, who started up in the carriage to kiss their hands, and who were being borne away from the abode of danger and death, to spend several weeks without doing any lessons. Often, during this day, was the voice of mirth even heard in this dwelling. It was not like the mirth of the well-known company of prisoners in the first French revolution—men who knew that they should leave their prison only to lose their heads, and who, once mutually acknowledging this, agreed vainly and pusillanimously to banish from that hour all sad, all grave thoughts, and laugh till they died. It was not this mirth of despair; nor yet that of carelessness; nor yet that of defiance. Nor were theirs the spirits of the patriot in the hour of struggle, nor of the hero in the crisis of danger. In a peril like theirs, there is nothing imposing to the imagination, or flattering to the pride, or immediately appealing to the energies of the soul. There were no resources for them in emotions of valour or patriotism. Theirs was the gaiety of simple faith and innocence. They had acted from pure inclination, from affection, unconscious of pride, of difficulty, of merit; and they were satisfied, and gay as the innocent ought to be, enjoying what there was to enjoy, and questioning and fearing nothing beyond.

From a distant point of time or place, such a state of spirits in the midst of a pestilence may appear unnatural and wrong; but experience proves that it is neither. Whatever observers may think, it is natural and it is right that minds strong enough to be settled, either in a good or evil frame, should preserve their usual character amidst any changes of circumstance. To those involved in new events, they appear less strange than in prospect or in review. Habitual thoughts are present, familiarising wonderful incidents; and the fears of the selfish, the repose of the religious, the speculations of the thoughtful, and the gaiety of the innocent, pervade the life of each, let what will be happening.

Yet to the prevailing mood the circumstances of the time will interpose an occasional check. This very evening, when Margaret was absent at the cottage in the lane, and Hope, wearied with his toils among the sick all the night, and all this day, was apparently sleeping for an hour on the sofa, Hester's heart grew heavy, as she lulled her infant to rest by the fire. As she thought on what was passing in the houses of her neighbours, death seemed to close around the little being she held in her arms. As she gazed in his face, watching the slumber stealing on, she murmured over him—

"Oh, my child, my child! if I should lose you, what *should* I do?"

"Hester! my love!" said her husband, in a tone of tender remonstrance, "what *do* you mean?"

"I did not think you would hear me, love; but I thank you. What did I mean? Not exactly what I said; for God knows, I would strive to part willingly with whatever he might see fit to take away. But, oh, Edward! what a struggle it would be! and how near it comes to us! How many mothers are now parting from their children!"

"God's will be done!" cried Hope, starting up, and standing over his babe.

"Are you sure, Edward may we feel quite certain that we have done rightly by our boy in keeping him here?"

"I am satisfied, my love."

"Then I am prepared. How still he is now! How like death it looks!"

"What, that warm, breathing sleep! No more like death than his laugh is like sin."

And Hope looked about him for pencil and paper, and hastily sketched his boy in all the beauty of repose, before he went forth again among the sick and wretched. It was very like; and Hester placed it before her as she plied her needle, all that long solitary evening.

Chapter Forty Two

Church-Going.

Hester went to church the next Sunday, as she wished, to hear Dr Levitt's promised plain sermon on the duties of the times. Margaret gladly staid at home with the baby, thankful for the relief from the sight of sickness, and for the quiet of solitude while the infant slept. Edward was busy among those who wanted his good offices, as he now was, almost without intermission. Hester had to go alone.

Everything abroad looked very strange—quite unlike the common Sunday aspect of the place. The streets were empty, except that a party of mourners were returning from a funeral. Either people were already all in church, or nobody was going. She quickened her pace in the fear that she might be late, though the bell seemed to assure her that she was not. Widow Rye's little garden-plot was all covered with linen put out to dry, and Mrs Rye might be seen through the window, at the wash-tub. The want of fresh linen was so pressing, that the sick must not be kept waiting, though it was Sunday. Miss Nares and Miss Flint were in curl-papers, plying their needles. They had been up all night, and were now putting the last stitches to a suit of family mourning, which was to enable the bereaved to attend afternoon church. Miss Nares looked quite haggard, as she well might, having scarcely left her seat for the last fortnight, except to take orders for mourning, and to snatch a scanty portion of rest. She had endeavoured to procure an additional work-woman or two from among her neighbours, and then from Blickley: but her neighbours were busy with their domestic troubles, and the Blickley people wanted more mourning than the hands there could supply; so Miss Nares and Miss Flint had been compelled to work night and day, till they both looked as if they had had the sickness, and were justified in saying that no money could pay them for what they were undergoing. They began earnestly to wish what they had till now deprecated—that Dr Levitt might succeed in inducing some of his flock to forego the practice of wearing mourning. But of this there was little prospect: the people were as determined upon wearing black, as upon having the bell tolled for the dead; and Miss Nares's heart sank at the prospect before her, if the epidemic should continue, and she should be able to get no help.

Almost every second house in the place was shut up. The blank windows of the cottages, where plants or smiling faces were usually to be seen on a Sunday morning, looked dreary. The inhabitants of many of the better dwellings were absent. There were no voices of children about the little courts; no groups of boys under the churchyard wall. Of those who had frequented this spot, several were under the sod; some were laid low in fever within the houses; and others were with their parents, forming a larger congregation round the fortune-tellers' tents in the lanes, than Dr Levitt could assemble in the church.

Hester heard the strokes of the hammer and the saw as she passed the closed shop of the carpenter, who was also the undertaker. She knew that people were making coffins by candlelight within. Happening to look round after she had passed, she saw a woman come out, wan in countenance, and carrying under her cloak something which a puff of wind showed to be an infant's coffin—a sight from which every young mother averts her eyes. As Hester approached a cottage whose thatch had not been weeded for long, she was startled by a howl and whine from within; and a dog, emaciated to the last degree, sprang upon the sill of an open window. A neighbour who perceived her shrink back, and hesitate to pass, assured her that she need not be afraid of the dog. The poor animal would not leave the place, whose inmates were all dead of the fever. The window was left open for the dog's escape; but he never came out, though he looked famished. Some persons had thrown in food at first; but now no one had time or thought to spare for dogs.

Mr Walcot issued from a house near the church as Hester passed, and he stopped her. He was roused or frightened out of his usual simplicity of manner, and observed, with an air of deep anxiety, that he trusted Mr Hope had better success with his patients than he could boast of. The disease was most terrific: and the saving of a life was a chance now seemingly too rare to be reckoned on. It really required more strength than most men had to stand by their duty at such a time, when they could do little more than see their patients die. Hester thought him so much moved, that he was at this moment hardly fit for business. She said:

"We all have need of all our strength. I do not know whether worship gives it to you as it does to me. Will it not be an hour, or even half an hour, well spent, if you go with me there?" pointing to the church. "You will say you are wanted elsewhere; but will you not be stronger and calmer for the comfort you may find there?"

"I should like it... I have always been in the habit of going to church... It would do me good, I know. But, Mrs Hope, how is this? I thought you had been a dissenter. I always said so. I have been very wrong—very ill-natured."

"I am a dissenter," said Hester, smiling, "but you are not; and therefore I may urge you to go to church. As for the rest of the mystery, I will explain it when we have more time. Meanwhile, I hope you do not suppose that dissenters do not worship and need and love worship as other people do!"

Mr Walcot replied by timidly offering his arm, which Hester accepted, and they entered the church together.

The Rowlands were already in their pew. There was a general commotion among the children when they saw Mrs Hope and Mr Walcot walking up the aisle arm-in-arm. Matilda called her mother's attention to the remarkable fact, and the little heads all whispered together. The church looked really almost empty. There were no Hunters, with their train of servants: there were no Levitts. The Miss Andersons had not entered Deerbrook for weeks; and Maria Young sat alone in the large double pew commonly occupied by her scholars. There was a sprinkling of poor; but Hester observed that every one in the church was in mourning but Maria and herself. It looked sadly chill and dreary. The sights and sounds she had met, and the aspect of the place she was in, disposed her to welcome every thought of comfort that the voice of the preacher could convey.

There were others to whom consolation appeared even more necessary than to herself. Philip Enderby had certainly seen her, and was distressed at it. He could not have expected to meet her here; and his discomposure was obvious. He looked thin, and grave,—not to say subdued. Hester was surprised to find how she relented towards him, the moment she saw he was not gay and careless, and how her feelings grew softer and softer under the religious emotions of the hour. She was so near forgiving him, that she was very glad Margaret was not by her side. If she could forgive, how would it be with Margaret?

The next most melancholy person present, perhaps, was Mr Walcot. He knew that the whole family of the Rowlands remained in Deerbrook from Mrs Rowland's ostentation of confidence in his skill. He knew that Mr Rowland would have removed his family when the Greys departed, but that the lady had refused to go; and he felt how groundless was her confidence: not that he had pretended to more professional merit than he had believed himself to possess; but that, amidst this disease, he was like a willow-twig in the stream. He became so impressed with his responsibilities now, in the presence of the small and sad-faced congregation, that he could not refrain from whispering to Hester, that he could never be thankful enough that Mr Hope had not left Deerbrook long ago, and that he hoped they should be friends henceforth,—that Mr Hope would take his proper place again, and forgive and forget all that had passed. He thought he might trust Mr Hope not to desert him and Deerbrook now. Hester smiled gently, but made no reply, and did not appear to notice the proffered hand. It was no time or place to ratify a compact for her husband in his absence. All this time, Mr Walcot's countenance and manner were sufficiently subdued: but his agitation increased when the solemn voice of Dr Levitt uttered the prayer—

"Have pity upon us, miserable sinners, who now are visited with great sickness and mortality."

Here the voice of weeping became so audible from the lower part of the church, that the preacher stopped for a moment, to give other people, and possibly himself, time to recover composure. He then went on—

"That, like as Thou didst then accept of an atonement, and didst command the destroying angel to cease from punishing, so it may now please thee to withdraw from us this plague and grievous sickness; through Jesus Christ, our Lord."

Every voice in the church uttered 'Amen,' except Mr Walcot's. He was struggling with his sobs. Unexpected and excessive as were the tokens of his grief, Hester could not but respect it. It was so much better than gross selfishness and carelessness, that she could pity and almost honour it. She felt that Mr Walcot was as far superior to the quacks who were making a market of the credulity of the suffering people, as her husband, with his professional decision, his manly composure, and his forgetfulness of the injuries of his foes in their hour of suffering, was above Mr Walcot. The poor young man drank in, as if they were direct from Heaven, the suggestions contained in the preacher's plain sermon on the duties of the time. Plain it was indeed,—familiarly practical to an unexampled degree; so that most of his hearers quitted the church with a far clearer notion of their business as nurses and neighbours than they had ever before had. The effect was visible as they left their seats, in the brightening of their countenances, and the increased activity of their step as they walked.

"There, go," said Hester, kindly, to her companion. "Many must be wanting you: but you have lost no time by coming here."

"No, indeed. But Mr Hope—"

"Rely upon him. He will do his duty. Go and do yours."

"God bless you!" cried Walcot, squeezing her hand affectionately.

Mrs Rowland saw this, as she always saw everything. She beckoned to Mr Walcot, with her most engaging smile, and whispered him with an air of the most intimate confidence, till she saw that her presence was wanted elsewhere, when she let him go.

Mr Rowland, followed by Philip, slipped out of his pew as Hester passed, and walked down the aisle with her. He was glad to see her there; he hoped it was a proof that all her household were well in this sickly time. Philip bent forward to hear the answer. Mr Rowland went on to say how still and dull the village was. The shutters up, or the blinds down, at all the Greys' windows, looked quite sad; and he never saw any of his friends from the corner-house in the shrubbery now. They had too many painful duties, he feared, to allow of their permitting themselves such pleasures: but his friends must take care not to overstrain their powers. They and he must be very thankful that their respective households were thus far unvisited by the disease; and they should all, in his opinion, favour their health by the indulgence of a little rational cheerfulness. Hester smiled, aware that never had their household been more cheerful than now.

Whether it was that Hester's smile was irresistible, or that other influences were combined with it, it had an extraordinary effect upon Philip. He started forward in front of her, and offered his hand, saying, so as to be heard by her alone—

"Will you not?—I have no quarrel with you."

"And can you suppose," she replied, in a tone more of compassion than of anger, "that I have none with you?—How strangely you must forget!" she added, as he precipitately withdrew his offered hand, and turned from her.

"Forget! I forget!" he murmured, turning his face of woe towards her for one instant. "How little you know me!"

"How little we all know each other!" said Hester, for the moment careless what construction might be put upon her words.

"Even in this place," said Dr Levitt, who had now joined them, and had heard the last words: "even in this place, where all hearts should be open, and all resentments forgotten. Are there any here who refuse to shake hands—at such a time as this?"

"It is not for myself," said Hester, distressed: "but how can I?"

"It is true; she cannot. Do not blame her, Dr Levitt," said Philip; and he was gone.

It was this meeting which had cut short Mrs Rowland's whispers with Mr Walcot, and brought her down the aisle in all her stateliness, with her train of children behind her.

When Hester went home, she thought it right to tell Margaret exactly what had happened.

"I knew it?" was all that Margaret said; but her heightened colour during the day told what unspeakable things were in her heart.

Hester was occupied with speculations as to what might have been the event if Margaret had been to church instead of herself. Her husband would only shake his head, and look hopeless: but she still thought all might have come right, under the influences of the hour. Whether it were to be wished that Philip and Margaret should understand each other again, was another question. Yesterday Hester would have earnestly desired that Margaret should never see Enderby again. To-day she did not know what to wish. She and Margaret came silently to the same conclusion; "there is nothing for it but waiting." If he had heard this, Hope would have shaken his head again.

Chapter Forty Three

Working Round.

Several days passed, and there was no direct news of Enderby. Maria never spoke of him, though many little intervals in Margaret's busy life occurred when the friends were together, and Maria ought have taken occasion to say anything she wished. It was clear that she chose to avoid the subject. Her talk was almost entirely about the sick, for whom she laboured as strenuously as her strength would permit. She could not go about among them, nor sit up with the sufferers: but she cooked good things over her fire for them, all day long; and she took to her home many children who were too young to be useful, and old enough to be troublesome in a sick house. Between her cooking, teaching, and playing with the children, she was as fully occupied as her friends in the corner-house, and perhaps might not really know anything about Mr Enderby.

Each one of the family had caught glimpses of him at one time or another. There was reason to think that he was active among Mr Walcot's poor patients; and Hope had encountered him more than once in the course of his rounds, when a few words on the business of the moment were exchanged, and nothing more happened. Margaret saw him twice: once on horseback, when he turned suddenly down a lane to avoid her; and at the Rowlands' dining-room window, with Ned in his arms. She never now passed that house when she could help it: but this once it was necessary; and she was glad that Philip had certainly not seen her. His back was half-turned to the window at the moment, as if some one within was speaking to him. Each time, his image was so stamped in upon her mind, that, amidst all the trials of such near neighbourhood without intercourse, his presence in Deerbrook was, on the whole, certainly a luxury. She had gained something to compensate for all her restlessness, in the three glimpses of him with which she had now been favoured. A thought sometimes occurred to her, of which she was so ashamed that she made every endeavour to banish it. She asked herself now and then, whether, if she had been able to sit at home, or take her accustomed walks, she should not have beheld Philip oftener:—whether she was not sadly out of the way of seeing him at the cottage in the lane, and the other sordid places where her presence was necessary. Not for this occasional question did she stay away one moment longer than she would otherwise have done from the cottage in the lane; but while she was there, it was apt to recur.

There she sat one afternoon, somewhat weary, but not dreaming of going home. There lay the three sick creatures still. The woman was likely to recover; the boy lingered, and seemed waiting for his father to go with him. Platt had sunk very rapidly, and this day had made a great change. Margaret had taken the moaning and restless child on her lap, for the ease of change of posture: and she was now shading from his eyes with her shawl, the last level rays of the sun which shone in upon her from the window. She was unwilling to change her seat, for it seemed as if the slightest movement would quench the lingering life of the child: and there was no one to draw the window-curtain, the old woman having gone to buy food in the village. Mrs Platt slept almost all the day and night through, and she was asleep now: so Margaret sat quite still, holding up her shawl before the pallid face which looked already dead. Nothing broke the silence but the twitter of the young birds in the thatch, and the mutterings of the sick man, whom Margaret imagined to be somewhat disturbed by the unusual light that was in the room. It had not been the custom of the sun to shine into any houses of late; and the place full of yellow light, did not look like itself. She knew that in a few minutes the sun would have set; and she hoped that then poor Platt would be still. Meantime she appeared to take no notice, but sat with her eyes fixed on the boy's face, marking that each sigh was fainter than the last. At length a louder sound than she had yet heard from the sick man, made her look towards him; and the instant throb of her heart seemed to be felt by the child, for he moved his head slightly. Platt was trying to support himself upon his elbow, while in the other shaking hand, he held towards her her turquoise ring. She remembered her charge, and did not spring to seize it; but there was something in her countenance that strongly excited the sick man. He struggled to rise from his bed, and his face was fierce. Margaret spoke gently—as calmly as she could—told him she would come presently—that there was no hurry, and urged him to lie down till she could put the child off her lap; but her voice failed her, in spite of herself; for now, at last, she recognised in Platt the tall woman. This was the look which had perplexed her more than once.

"Patience! a little further patience!" she said to herself, as she saw the ring still trembling in the sick man's hand, and felt one more sigh from the little fellow on her lap. No more patience was needed. This was the boy's last breath. His head fell back, and the sunlight, which streamed in upon his half-closed eyes, could now disturb them no more. Margaret gently closed them and laid the body on its little bed in the corner, straightening and covering the limbs before she turned away.

She then gently approached the bed, and took her ring into a hand which trembled little less than the sick man's own. She spoke calmly, however. She strove earnestly to learn something of the facts: she tried to understand the mutterings amidst which only a word here and there sounded like speech. She thought, from the earnestness with which Platt seized and pressed her hand, that he was seeking pardon from her; and she spoke as if it were so. It grew very distressing—the earnestness of the man, and the uncertainty whether his mind was wandering or not. She wished the old woman would come back. She went to the door to look for her. The old woman was coming down the lane. Margaret put on her ring, and drew on her gloves, and determined to say nothing about it at present.

"Mr Platt has been talking almost ever since you went," said Margaret; "and I can make out nothing that he says. Do try if you can understand him. I am sure there is something he wishes me to hear. There is no time to lose, I am afraid. Do try."

The woman coaxed him to lie down, and then turning round, said she thought he wanted to know what o'clock it was.

"Is that all? Tell him that the sun is now setting. But if you have a watch, that will show more exactly. Are you sure you have no watch in the house?"

The old woman looked suspiciously at her, and asked her what made her suppose that poor folks had watches, when some gentlefolks had none? Margaret inquired whether a watch was not a possession handed down from father to son, and sometimes found in the poorest cottages. She believed she had seen such at Deerbrook. The old woman replied by saying, she believed Margaret might have understood some few things among the many the poor sick creature had been saying. Not one, Margaret declared; but it was so plain that she was not believed, that she had little doubt of Hester's watch having been harboured in this very house, if it was not there still.

The poor boy, who had had little care from his natural guardians while alive from the hour of his being doomed by the fortune-teller, was now loudly mourned as dead. Yet the mourning was strangely mixed with exultation at the fortune-teller having been right in the end. The mother, suddenly awakened, groaned and screamed, so that it was fearful to hear her. All efforts to restore quiet were in vain. Margaret was moved, shocked, terrified. She could not keep her own calmness in such a scene of confusion: but, while her cheeks were covered with tears, while her voice trembled as she implored silence, she never took off her glove. In the midst of the tumult, Platt sank back and died. The renewed cries had the effect of bringing some neighbours from the end of the lane. While they were there, Margaret could be of no further use. She promised to send coffins immediately—that stage of pestilence being now reached when coffins were the first consideration—and then slipped out from the door into the darkness, and ran till she had turned the corner of the long lane. She usually considered herself safe abroad, even in times like these, as she carried no property of value about with her: but now that she was wearing her precious ring again, she felt too rich to be walking alone in the dark.

She did not slacken her pace till she approached lights and people; and then she was glad to stop for breath. She could not resist going first to Maria, to show her the recovered treasure; and this caused her to direct her steps through the churchyard. It was there that she came in view of lights and people; and under the limes it was that she stopped for breath. The churchyard was now the most frequented spot in the village. The path by the turnstile was indeed grown over with grass: but the great gate was almost always open, and the ground near it was trodden bare by the feet of many mourners. Funeral trains—trains which daily grew shorter, till each coffin was now followed only by two or by three—were passing in from early morning, at intervals, till sunset, and now might be often seen by torchlight far into the night. The villager passing the churchyard wall might hear, in the night air, the deep voice of the clergyman announcing the farewell to some brother or sister, committing "ashes to ashes, and dust to dust." There was no disturbance now from boys leaping over the graves, or from little children, eager to renew their noisy play. Such of the young villagers as remained above ground appeared to be silenced and subdued by the privation, the dreariness, the neglect, of these awful days: they looked on from afar, or avoided the spot. Instead of such, the observer of the two funerals which were now in the churchyard, was a person quite at the other extremity of life. Margaret saw the man of a hundred years, Jem Bird, the pride of the village in his way, seated on the bench under the spreading tree, which was youthful in comparison with himself. He was listlessly watching the black figures which moved about in the light of a solitary torch, by an open grave, while waiting for the clergyman who was engaged with the group beyond.

"You are late abroad, Mr Bird," said Margaret. "I should not have looked for you here so far on in the evening."

"What's your will?" said the old man.

"Grandfather won't go home ever, till they have done here," said a great-grandchild of the old man, running up from his amusement of hooting to the owls in the church tower. "They'll soon have done with these two, and then grandfather and I shall go home. Won't we, granny?"

"Does it not make you sad to see so many funerals?" said Margaret, sitting down on the bench beside him.

"Ay."

"Had you not better stay at home than see so many that you knew laid in the ground?"

"Does he understand?" she asked aside of the boy. "Does he never answer but in this way?"

"Oh! he talks fast enough sometimes. It is just as you happen to take him."

Margaret was curious to know what were the meditations among the tombs of one so aged as this man: so she spoke again.

"I have heard that you knew this place before anybody lived in it: and now you seem likely to see it empty again."

"It was a wild place enough in my young time," said Jem, speaking now very fluently. "There was nothing of it but the church; and that was never used, because it had had its roof pulled off in the wars. There was only a footpath to it through the fields then, and few people went nigh it—except a few gentry that came a-pleasuring here, into the woods. The owls and I knew it as well then as we do to-day, and nobody else that is now living. The owls and I."

And the old man laughed the chuckling laugh which was all he had strength for.

"The woods!" said Margaret. "Did the Verdon woods spread as far as this church in those days? And were they not private property then?"

"It was all forest hereabouts, except a clear space round the church tower. It might be thin sprinkled, but it was called forest. The place where I was born had thorns all about it; and when I could scarce walk alone, I used to scramble among the blossoms that made the ground white all under those thorns. The birds that lived by the haws in winter were prodigious. That cottage stood, as near as I can tell, where Grey and Rowland's great granary is now. There used to be much swine in the woods then; and many's the time they have thrown me down when I was a young thing getting acorns. That was about the time of my hearing the first music I ever heard—unless you call the singing of the birds music (we had plenty of that), and the bells on the breeze from a distance, when the wind was south. The first music (so to call it) that I heard was from a blind fiddler that came to us. What brought him, I don't know—whether he lost his way, or what; but he lost his way after he left us. His dog seems to have been in fault: but he got into a pool in the middle of the wood, and there he lay drowned, with one foot up on the bank, when I went to see what the harking of the dog could be about. He clutched his fiddle in drowning; and I remember I tried to get the music out of it as it lay wet and broken on the bank, while father was saying the poor soul must have been under the water now two days. So I have reason to remember the first music I heard."

"You have got him talking now," said the grandchild, running off; and presently the owls were heard hooting again.

"Whereabouts was this pool?" asked Margaret.

"It is a deep part of the brook, that in hot summers is left a pond. It is there that the chief of the sliding goes on in winter now, in the meadow. It is meadow now; but then the deer used to come down through the wood to drink at the brook there. That is how the village got its name."

"So you remember the time when the deer came down to drink at the brook! How many things have happened since then! You have heard a great deal of music since those days."

"Ay, there has been a good deal of fiddling at our weddings since that. And we have had recruiting parties through in war times."

"And many a mother singing to her baby; and the psalm in the church for so many years! Yes, the place has been full of music for long; but it seems likely to be silent enough now."

"I began to think I should be left the last, as I was the first," said the old man: "but they say the sickness is abating now, and that several are beginning to recover. Pray God it may be so! First, after the wood was somewhat cleared, there was a labourer's cottage or two—now standing empty, and the folk that lived in them lying yonder. Then there was the farmhouse; and then a carpenter came, and a wheeler. Then there was a shop wanted; and the church was roofed in and used: and some gentry came and sat down by the river side; and the place grew to what it is. They say now, it is not near its end yet: but it is strange to me to see the churchyard the fullest place near, so that I have to come here for company."

And the old man chuckled again. As she rose to go, Margaret asked whether he knew the Platts, who lived in the cottage in the lane.

"I know him to see to. Is he down?"

"He is dead and his child: but his wife is recovering."

"Ay, there's many recovering now, they say."

"Indeed! who?"

"Why, a many. But the fever has got into Rowland's house, they say." Margaret's heart turned sick at hearing these words, and she hastily pursued her way. It was not Philip, however, who was seized. He was in the churchyard at this moment. She saw him walking quickly along the turnstile path, slackening his pace only for a moment, as he passed the funeral group. The light from the torch shone full upon his face—the face settled and composed, as she knew it would not be if he were aware who was within a few paces of him. She felt the strongest impulse to show him her ring—the strongest desire for his sympathy in its recovery: but an instant showed her the absurdity of the thought, and she hung down her blushing head in the darkness.

From Maria she had sympathy, such as it was—sympathy without any faith in Philip. She had from her also good news of the state of the village. There were recoveries talked of; and there would be more, now that those who were seized would no longer consider death inevitable. Mrs Howell was ill; and poor Miss Nares was down with the fever, which no one could wonder at: but Mr Jones and his son John were both out of danger, and the little Tuckers were likely to do well. Mr James was already talking of sending for his wife and sister-in-law home again, as the worst days of the disease seemed to be past, and so many families had not been attacked at all. It was too true that Matilda Rowland was unwell to-day; but Mr Walcot hoped it was only a slight feverish attack, which would be thought nothing of under any other circumstances.—On the whole, Maria thought the neighbours she had seen to-day in better spirits than at any time since the fever made its appearance.

Margaret found more good news at home. In the first place, the door was opened to her by Morris. Hester stood behind to witness the meeting. She had her bonnet on: she was going with her husband to see Mrs Howell, and make some provision for her comfort: but she had waited a little while, in hopes that Margaret would return, and be duly astonished to see Morris.

"You must make tea for each other, and be comfortable while we are away," said Hester. "We will go now directly, that we may be back as early as we can."

"I have several things to tell you," said Margaret, "when you return: and one now, brother, which must not be delayed. Platt and his child are dead, and coffins must be sent. The sooner the better, or we shall lose the poor woman too."

Hope promised to speak to the undertaker as he went by.

"We have become very familiar with death, Morris, since you went away," said Margaret, as she obliged her old friend to sit down by the fire, and prepared to make tea for both.

"That is why you see me here, Miss Margaret. Every piece of news I could get of this place was worse than the last; and I could perceive from your last letter, that you had sickness all about you; and I could not persuade myself but that it was my duty to come and be useful, and to take care of you, my dear, if I may say so."

"And now you are here, I trust you may stay—I trust we may be justified in keeping you. We have meat every day now, Morris,—at least when we have time to cook it. Since my brother has been attending so many of Mr Jones's family, we have had meat almost every day."

"Indeed, my dear, I don't know how you could keep up without it, so busy as I find you are among the sick;—busy night and day, my mistress tells me, till the people have got to call you 'the good lady.' You do not look as if you had lost much of your natural rest: but I know how the mind keeps the body up. Yours is an earnest mind, Margaret, that will always keep you up: but, my dear, I do hope it has been an easy mind too. You will excuse my saying so."

Margaret more than excused it, but she could not immediately answer. The tears trembled in her eyes, and her lip quivered when she would have spoken. Morris stroked her hair, and kissed her forehead, as if she had been still a child, and whispered that all things ended well in God's own time.

"Oh, yes! I know," said Margaret. "Has Hester told you how prosperous we are growing? I do not mean only about money. We are likely to have enough of that too, for my brother's old patients have almost all sent for him again: but we care the less about that from having discovered that we were as happy with little money as with much. But it is a satisfaction and pleasure to find my brother regarded more and more as he ought to be: and yet greater to see how nobly he deserves the best that can be thought of him."

"He forgives his enemies, no doubt, heaping coals of fire on their heads."

"You will witness it Morris. You will see him among them, and it will make your heart glow. Poor creatures! I have heard some of them own to him, from their sick beds, with dread and tears, that they broke his windows, and slandered his name. Then you should see him smile when he tells them that is all over now, and that they will not mistake him so much again."

"No, never. He has shown himself now what he is."

"He sat up two nights with one poor boy who is now likely to get through; and in the middle of the second night, the boy's father got up from his sick bed in the next room, and came to my brother, to say that he felt that ill luck would be upon them all, if he did not confess that he put that very boy behind the hedge, with stones in his hand, to throw at Edward, the day he was mobbed at the almshouses. He was deluded by the neighbours, he said, into thinking that my brother meant ill by the poor."

"They have learned to the contrary now, my dear. And what does Sir William Hunter say of my master, now-a-days? Do you know?"

"There is very little heard of Sir William and Lady Hunter at present—shut up at home as they are. But Dr Levitt, who loves to make peace, you know, and tell what is pleasant, declares that Sir William Hunter has certainly said that, after all, it does not so much signify which way a man votes at an election, if he shows a kind heart to his neighbours in troublesome times."

"Sir William Hunter has learned his lesson then, it seems, from this affliction. I suppose he sees that one who does his duty as my master does at a season like this, is just the one to vote according to his conscience at an election. But, my dear, what sort of a heart have these Hunters got, that they shut themselves up as you say?"

"They give their money freely: and that is all that we can expect from them. If they have always been brought up and accustomed to fear sickness, and danger, and death, we cannot expect that they should lose their fear at a time like this. We must be thankful for what they give; and their money has been of great service, though there is no doubt that their example would have been of more."

"One would like to look into their minds, and see how they regard my master there."

"They regard him, no doubt, so far rightly as to consider him quite a different sort of person from themselves, and no rule for them. So far they are right. They do not comprehend his satisfactions and ease of mind; and it is very likely that they have pleasures of their own which we do not understand."

"And they are quite welcome, I am sure, my dear, as long as they do not meddle with my master's name. That is, as he says, all over now. After this, however, the people in Deerbrook will be more ready to trust in my master's skill and kindness than in Sir William Hunter's grandeur and money, which can do little to save them in time of need."

Margaret explained how ignorantly the poor in the neighbourhood had relied on the fortune-tellers, who had only duped them; how that which would have been religion in them if they had been early taught, and which would have enabled them to rely on the only power which really can save, had been degraded by ignorance into a foolish and pernicious superstition.

Morris hoped that this also was over now. She had met some of these conjurors on the Blickley road; and seen others breaking up their establishment in the lanes, and turning their backs upon Deerbrook. Whether they were scared away by the mortality of the place, or had found the tide of fortune-telling beginning to turn, mattered nothing as long as they were gone.

The tea-table was cleared, and Morris and Margaret were admiring the baby as he slept, when Hester and her husband returned. Mrs Howell was very unwell, and likely to be worse. All attempts to bring Miss Miskin to reason, and induce her to enter her friend's room, were in vain. She bestowed abundance of tears, tremors, and foreboding on Mrs Howell's state and prospects, but shut herself up in a fumigated apartment, where she promised to pray for a good result, and to await it. The maid was a hearty lass, who would sit up willingly, under Hester's promise that she should be relieved in the morning. The girl's fear was of not being able to satisfy her mistress, whom it was not so easy to nurse as it might have been, from her insisting on having everything arranged precisely as it was in her poor dear Howell's last illness. As Miss Miskin had refused to enter the chamber, Hester had been obliged to search a chest of drawers for Mr Howell's last dressing-gown, which Miss Miskin had promised should be mended and aired, and ready for wear by the morning.

"Margaret!" cried Hester, as her sister was lighting her candle. The exclamation made Edward turn round, and brought back Morris into the parlour after saying 'Good-night.' "Margaret! your ring?"

There was as much joy as shame in Margaret's crimson blush. She let her sister examine the turquoise, and said:

"Yes, this is the boon of to-day."

"Edward's hundred pounds has come," said Hester: "but that is nothing to this."

Margaret's eyes thanked her. She just explained that poor Platt had been the thief, and had restored it to her before he died, and that she could get no explanation, no tidings of Hester's watch; and she was gone.

"Dr Levitt's early stir about this ring prevented its being disposed of, I have no doubt," said Edward. "If so, it is yet possible that we may recover your watch. I will speak to Dr Levitt in the morning."

"Dear Margaret!" said Hester. "She is now drinking in the hue of that turquoise, and blessing it for being unchanged. She regards this recovery of it as a good omen, I see; and far be it from us to mock at such a superstition!"

As usual, when she was upon this subject, Hester looked up into her husband's face: and as usual, when she spoke on this subject, he made no reply.

Chapter Forty Four

Late Religion.

A few days after Morris's return, she told Margaret that the tidings in the village of Miss Rowland's illness were not good. Mrs Rowland was quite as sure as ever that, if anybody could cure Matilda, it was Mr Walcot; but Mr Walcot himself looked anxious; and a bed had been put up for him in the room next to the sick child. Margaret wondered why Mr Rowland did not send to Blickley for further advice: but Morris thought that Mrs Rowland would not give up her perfect faith in Mr Walcot, if all her children should die before her face.

When Morris had left the room, Margaret was absorbed in speculations, as she played with her sister's infant—speculations on the little life of children, and on their death. Her memory followed Matilda through every circumstance in which she had seen her. The poor little girl's very attitude, voice, and words—words full, alas! of folly and vanity—rose again upon her eye and ear, in immediate contrast with the image of death, and the solemnity of the life to come. In the midst of these thoughts came tears of shame and self-reproach; for another thought (how low! how selfish!) thrust itself in among them—that she was secure for the present from Philip's departure—that he would not leave Deerbrook while Matilda was in a critical state. As these tears rolled down her cheeks, the baby looked full in her face, and caught the infection of grief.

He hung his little lip, and looked so woe-begone, that Margaret dashed away the signs of her sorrow, and spoke gaily to him; and, as the sun shone in at the moment upon the lustres on the mantelpiece, she set the glass-drops in motion, and let the baby try to catch the bright colours that danced upon the walls and ceiling. At this moment, Hester burst in with a countenance of dismay.

"Margaret, my husband has a headache!"

A headache was no trifle in these days.

"Anything more than a headache?" asked Margaret. "No other feeling of illness? There is nothing to wonder at in a mere headache. It is very surprising that he has not had it before, with all his toil and want of sleep."

"He declares it is a trifle," said Hester: "but I see he can hardly hold up. What shall I do?"

"Make him lie down and rest, and let me go to Mrs Howell instead of you. She will be a little disappointed; but that cannot be helped. She must put up with my services to-day. Now, do not frighten yourself, as if no one ever had a headache without having a fever."

"I shall desire Morris to let no one in; and to bring no messages to her master while his headache lasts."

"Very right. I will tell her as I go for my bonnet. One more kiss before I go, baby. Do not wait tea for me, Hester. I cannot say when I shall be back."

Margaret had been gone to Mrs Howell's about an hour and a half, when there was a loud and hasty knock at the door of the corner-house. It roused Hope from a doze into which he had just fallen, and provoked Hester accordingly. There was a parley between Morris and somebody in the hall; and presently a voice was heard calling loudly upon Mr Hope. Hester could not prevent her husband from springing from the bed, and going out upon the stairs. Mr Rowland was already half-way up, looking almost beside himself with grief.

"You must excuse me, Mr Hope—you must not judge me hardly;—if you are ill, I am sorry... sir; but sir, my child is dying. We fear she is dying, sir; and you must come, and see if anything can save her. I shall never forgive myself for going on as we have been doing. She has been sacrificed—fairly sacrificed, I fear."

"Nay, Mr Rowland, I must comfort you there," said Hope, as they walked rapidly along the street. "I have had occasion to see a great deal of Mr Walcot and his professional conduct, in the course of the last few weeks; and I am certain that he has a very competent knowledge of his business. I assure you he shows more talent, more power altogether, in his professional than his unprofessional conduct; and in this particular disease he has now had much experience."

"God bless you for saying so, my dear sir! It is like you—always generous, always just and kind! You must forgive us, Mr Hope. At a time like this, you must overlook all causes of offence. They are very great, I know; but you will not visit them upon us now."

"We have only to do with the present now," said Hope. "Not a word about the past, I entreat you."

Mrs Rowland, to-day reckless of everything but her child, was standing out on the steps, watching, as for the last hope for her Matilda.

"She is much worse, Mr Hope; suddenly and alarmingly worse. This way: follow me."

Hope would speak with Mr Walcot first. As he entered the study, to await Mr Walcot, Philip passed out. They did not speak.

"Oh, Philip! speak to Mr Hope!" cried Mrs Rowland. "For God's sake do not do anything to offend him now!"

"I will do everything in my power, madam, to save your child," said Hope. "Do not fear that the conduct of her relations will be allowed to injure her."

"My love," said Mr Rowland, "Mr Hope came from a sick bed to help us. Do not distrust him. Indeed he deserves better from us."

"Pray forgive me," said the miserable mother. "I do not well know what I am saying. But I will atone for all if you save my child."

"Priscilla!" cried her brother, from the doorway, against which he was leaning. His tone of wonder was lost as Walcot entered, and the study was left for the conference of the medical men.

As the gentlemen went upstairs to Matilda's room, they saw one child here, and another there, peeping about, in silence and dismay. As Hope put his hand on the head of one in passing, Mr Rowland said:

"There is a carriage coming for them presently, to take them away. Anna and George are now with Miss Young, and she will take them all away. She is very good: but I knew we might depend upon her—upon her heart, and her forgiveness. Ah! you hear the poor child's voice. That shows you the way."

Matilda was wandering, and, for the moment, talking very loud. Something about grandmamma seeing her dance, and "When I am married," struck the ear as Hope entered her chamber, and entirely overset the mother. Matilda was soon in a stupor again.

It was impossible to hold out much prospect of her recovery. It was painful to every one to hear how Mrs Rowland attempted to bribe Mr Hope, by promises of doing him justice, to exert himself to the utmost in Matilda's behalf. He turned away from her, again and again, with a disgust which his compassion could scarcely restrain. Philip was so far roused by the few words which had been let drop below-stairs, as to choose to hear what passed now, in the antechamber to the patient's room. It was he who decidedly interposed at last. He sent his brother-in-law to Matilda's bedside, dismissed Mr Walcot from the room, and then said—

"A very few minutes will suffice, I believe, sister, to relieve your mind: and they will be well spent. Tell us what you mean by what you have been saying so often within this quarter of an hour. As you hope in Heaven—as you dare to ask God to spare your child, tell us the extent to which you feel that you have injured Mr Hope."

Hope sank down into the window-seat by which he had been standing. He thought the whole story of his love was now coming out. He waited for the first words as for a thunderclap. The first words were—

"Oh, Philip! I am the most wretched woman living! I never saw it so strongly before; I believe I did it with an idea of good to you; but I burned a letter of Margaret's to you."

"What letter? When?"

"The day you left us last—the day you were in the shrubbery all the morning—the day the children found the shavings burnt."

"What was in the letter? Did you read it?"

"No; I dared not."

"What made you burn it?"

"I was afraid you would go to her, and that your engagement would come on again."

"Then what you told me—what made me break it off—could not have been true."

"No, it was not—not all true."

"What was true, and what was not?"

Mrs Rowland did not answer, but looked timidly at Mr Hope. Now was the moment for him to speak.

"It was true," said he, "that, at the very beginning of my acquaintance with Hester and Margaret, I preferred Margaret—and that my family discerned that I did—as true as that Hester has long been the beloved of my heart—beloved as—but I cannot speak of my wife, of my home, in the hearing of one who has endeavoured to profane both. All I need say is that neither Hester nor Margaret ever knew where my first transient fancy lighted, while they both know—know as they know their own hearts—where it has fixed. It is not true that Margaret ever loved any one but you, Enderby; and Mrs Rowland cannot truly say that she ever did."

"What was it then that Margaret confided to my mother?" asked Enderby, turning to his sister.

"I cannot tell what possessed me at the time to say so, but that I thought I was doing the best for your happiness—but—but, Philip, I really believe now, that Margaret never did love any one but you. I know nothing to the contrary."

"But my mother?"

"She knew very little of any troubles in Mr Hope's family; and—and what she did hear was all from me."

"Do you mean that all you told me of Margaret's confidences to my mother was false?"

There was no answer; but Mrs Rowland's pale cheeks grew paler.

"Oh God! what can Margaret have thought of me all this time?" cried Philip.

"I can tell you what she has thought, I believe," said Hope. "Her brother and sister have read her innocent mind, as you yourself might have done, if your faith in her had been what she deserved. She has believed that you loved her, and that you love her still. She has believed that some one—that Mrs Rowland traduced her to you: and in her generosity, she blames you for nothing but that you would not see and hear her—that you went away on the receipt of her letter—of that letter which it now appears you never saw."

"Where is she?" cried Enderby, striding to the door.

"She is not at home. You cannot find her at this moment: and if you could, you must hear me first. You remember the caution I gave you when we last conversed—in the abbey, and again in the meadows."

"I do; and I will observe it now."

"You remember that she is unaware—"

"That you ever—that that interview with Mrs Grey ever took place? She shall never learn it from me. It is one of those facts which have ceased to exist—which is absolutely dead, and should be buried in oblivion. You hear, Priscilla?"

She bowed her head.

"You believe that—."

"Say no more, brother. Do not humble me further. I will make what reparation I can—indeed I will—and then perhaps God will spare my child."

Hope's passing reflection was, "How alike is the superstition of the ignorant and of the wicked! My poor neighbours stealing to the conjuror's tent in the lane, and this wretched lady, hope alike to bribe Heaven in their extremity—they by gifts and rites, she by remorse and reparation.—How different from the faith which say; 'Not as I will, but as thou wilt!'"

"Where *is* Margaret? Will you tell me?" asked Enderby, impatiently. "But before I see her, I ought to ask forgiveness from you, Hope. You find how cruelly I have been deceived—by what incredible falsehood—. But," glancing at his pale sister, "we will speak no more of that. If, in the midst of all this error and wretchedness, I have hurt your feelings more than my false persuasions rendered necessary... I hope you will forgive me."

"And me! Will you forgive me?" asked Mrs Rowland, faintly.

"There is nothing to pardon in you," said Hope to Philip. "Your belief in what your own sister told you in so much detail can scarcely be called a weakness; and you did and said nothing to me that was not warranted by what you believed.—And I forgive you, madam. I will do what I can to relieve your present affliction; and, as long as you attempt no further injustice towards my family, no words shall be spoken by any of us to remind you of what is past."

"You are very good, Mr Hope."

"I tell you plainly," he resumed, "that you cannot injure us beyond a certain point. You cannot make it goodness in us to forget what is past. It is of far less consequence to us what you and others think of us than what we think of our neighbours. Our chief sorrow has been the spectacle of yourself in your dealings with us. We shall be thankful to be reminded of it no more. And now enough of this."

"Where *is* Margaret?" again asked Enderby, as if in despair of an answer.

"She is nursing Mrs Howell. As soon as I have seen this poor child again, I will go home, and take care that Margaret is prepared to see you. Remember how great the surprise, the mystery, must be to her."

"If the surprise were all—" said Philip.—"But will she hear me? Will she forgive me? Will she trust me?"

"Was there ever a woman who really loved who would not hear, would not forgive, would not trust?" said Hope, smiling. "I must not answer for Margaret; but I think I may answer for woman in the abstract."

"I will follow you in an hour, Hope."

"Do so. Now, madam."

And Hope followed Mrs Rowland again to the bedside of her dying child.

Chapter Forty Five

Rest of the Placable.

Margaret was not at Mrs Howell's at the moment that her brother believed and said she was. She had been there just in time to witness the poor woman's departure; and she was soon home again and relating the circumstances to Hester, by the fireside. Even the news that Edward was now in the same house with Philip, could not efface from her mind what she had seen; nor could Hester help listening, though full of anxiety about her husband.

"Miss Miskin was prevailed upon to leave her room at the last, I suppose?"

"Scarcely. Poor Nanny was supporting her mistress's head when I went in; and she said, with tears, that there was no depending on any one but us. They both looked glad enough to see me: but then, nothing would satisfy Mrs Howell but that I should warm myself, and be seated."

"To the last! and she offered you some cherry-bounce, I suppose."

"Yes; just as usual. Then she told me that it would be as well to mention now, in case she should grow worse, and be in any danger, that she should be gratified if you and I would select each a rug or screen pattern from her stock, and worsteds to work it with: and she gave a broad hint that there was one with a mausoleum and two weeping willows, which she hoped one of us would choose; and that perhaps her name might fill the space on the tomb. Poor Nanny began to cry; and this affected Mrs Howell; and she begged earnestly to see Miss Miskin."

"And then she came, I suppose."

"Not she! She would not come till her friend sent a message threatening to haunt her if she did not."

"Did you carry the message?"

"No; but Nanny did; and, I thought, with hearty good will; Miss Miskin came trembling, but too much frightened to cry. She would not approach nearer than the doorway, and there fell down on her knees, and so remained the whole time she was receiving directions about the shop and the stock,—'in case,' as the poor soul again said, 'of my getting worse, so as to be in any danger.' And yet Dr Levitt thought he had told her, plainly enough, what he thought of her state this morning."

"And was she aware at last? or did she go off unconsciously?"

"I think she was aware; I think so from her last words—'Oh, my poor dear Howell!' I sat behind the curtain while she was speaking to Miss Miskin—sometimes so faintly that Nanny had to repeat her words, to make them heard as far as the door."

"That selfish wretch—Miss Miskin!"

"It was very moving, I assure you, to hear not one word of reproach,— or even notice of Miss Miskin's desertion in this illness. What was said was common-place enough; but every word was kind. I have it all. I took it down with my pencil, behind the curtain; for I was sure Miss Miskin would never remember it. Mrs Howell went on till she came to directions about the bullfinch that her poor dear Howell used to laugh to see perched upon her nightcap of a morning; and then she grew unintelligible. I thought she was only fainting; but while we were trying to revive her, Nanny said she was going. Miss Miskin drew back into the passage, shut the door, and made her escape. Her friend looked that way once more, and said that we had all been very good to her. She mentioned her husband, as I told you, and then died very quietly."

"Miss Miskin knows, of course?"

"I told her, and did not pretend to feel much sympathy in her lamentations. I told her she had lost a friend who would have watched over her, I believed, till her last breath, if she had been the one attacked by the fever."

"What did she say?"

"She exclaimed a great deal about how good we all were, and wondered what Deerbrook would have done without us; and said she was sure I was too kind to think of leaving her in the house with the corpse, with only Nanny. When I declined passing the night there, she comforted herself with thinking aloud that her friend would not haunt her—certainly would not haunt her—as she *had* gone to her room at last. Her final question was, how soon I thought it likely that she should feel the fever coming on, in case of her having caught it, after all, by going into the room."

"What an end to a sentimental friendship of so many years!"

"I rather expect to hear in the morning that she has taken refuge in some neighbour's house, and left Nanny alone with the corpse to-night."

"My husband's knock!" cried Hester, starting up. "How is your headache, love?" asked she anxiously, as she met him at the room door.

"Gone, quite gone," he replied. "I must step down into the surgery for a minute, about this poor little girl's medicine; and then I have a great deal to tell you."

The sisters sat in perfect silence till his return.

"Matilda?" said Margaret, looking up at her brother.

"She is very ill;—not likely to be better."

"And poor Mrs Howell is gone," said Hester. "What a sweep it is! Did you hear, love? Mrs Howell is dead."

"I hear. It is a terrible destruction that we have witnessed. But I trust it is nearly over. I know of only one or two cases of danger now, besides this little girl's. Poor Matilda! But we have little thought to spare, even for her, to-night. If I did not know that Margaret is ready for whatever may betide," he continued, fixing his benevolent gaze upon her, "and if, moreover, I were not afraid that some one would be coming to tell my news if I do not get it out at once, I should hesitate about saying what I have to say."

"Philip has been explaining—He is coming," said Margaret, with such calmness as she could command.

"Enderby is coming; and some one else, whose explanations are more to the purpose, has been explaining. Mrs Rowland, alarmed and shaken by her misery, has been acknowledging the whole series of falsehoods by which she persuaded, convinced her brother that you did not love him— that you were, in fact, attached elsewhere. I see how angry you are, Hester. I see you asking in your own mind how Enderby could be thus deluded— how he could trust his sister rather than Margaret—how I can speak of him as deserving to have her after all this. Your questions are reasonable enough, love, and yet they cannot be answered. Your doubts of Enderby are reasonable enough; and yet I declare to you that he is in my eyes almost, if not quite, blameless."

"Thank you, brother!" said Margaret, looking up with swimming eyes.

"There is one great point to be settled," resumed Hope: "and that is, whether you will both be content to bury in silence the subject of this quarrel, from this hour, relying upon my testimony and Mrs Rowland's."

"Oh, Edward, do not put your name and hers together!"

"For Enderby's justification, and for Margaret's sake, my name shall be joined with the arch-fiend's, if necessary, my love. You must, as I was saying, rely upon the testimony of those who know the whole, that Enderby's conduct throughout has been, if not the very wisest and best, perfectly natural, and consistent with the love for Margaret which he has cherished to this hour."

"I knew it," murmured Margaret.

"He will himself disclose as much as he thinks proper, when he comes: but he comes full of fear and doubt about his reception."

Margaret hung her head, feeling that it was well she was reminded what reason there was for his coming with doubt and trembling in his heart.

"As he comes full of fear and doubt," resumed Hope, "I must tell you first that he never received your last letter, Margaret. He thought you would not answer his. He thought you took him at his word about not attempting explanation."

"What an unhappy accident!" cried Hester. "Who carried that letter? How did it happen?"

"It was no accident, my dear. Mrs Rowland burned that letter."

Margaret covered her face with her hands; then, suddenly looking up, she cried:

"Did she read it?"

"No. She says she dared not. Why, Margaret, you seem sorry that she did not! You think it would have cleared you. I have no doubt she thought so too; and that that was the reason why she averted her eyes from it. Yes, it was a cruel injury, Margaret. Can you forgive it, do you think?"

"Not to-night," said Hester. "Do not ask it of her to-night."

"I believe I may ask it at this very moment. The happy can forgive. Is it not so, Margaret?"

"For myself I could and I do, brother. I would go now and nurse her child, and comfort her. But—"

"But you cannot forgive the wretchedness she has caused to Philip. Well, if you each forgive her for your own part, there is a chance that she may yet lift up her humbled head."

"What possessed her to hate us so?" said Hester.

"Her hatred to us is the result of long habits of ill-will, of selfish pride, and of low pertinacity about small objects. That is the way in which I account for it all. She disliked you first for your connection with the Greys; and then she disliked me for my connection with you. She nourished up all her personal feelings into an opposition to us and our doings; and when she had done this, and found her own only brother going over to the enemy, as she regarded it, her dislike grew into a passion of hatred. Under the influence of this passion, she has been led on to say and to do more and more that would suit her purposes, till she has found herself sunk in an abyss of guilt. I really believe she was not fully aware of her situation, till her misery of to-day revealed it to her."

"Poor thing!" said Margaret. "Is there nothing we can do to help her?"

"We will ask Enderby. I take hers to be no uncommon case. The dislikes of low and selfish minds generally bear very much the character of hers, though they may not be pampered by circumstances into such a luxuriance as in this case. In a city, Mrs Rowland might have been an ordinary spiteful fine lady. In such a place as Deerbrook, and with a family of rivals' cousins incessantly before her eyes, to exercise her passions upon, she has ended in being—"

"What she is," said Margaret, as Hope stopped for a word.

"Margaret is less surprised than you expected, is she not?" said Hester. "You did not suppose that she would sit and listen as she does to your analysis of Mrs Rowland. But if the truth were known, she carries a prophecy about her on her finger. I have no doubt she has been expecting this very news ever since she recovered her ring. Yes or no, Margaret?"

"I should rather say she has carried a prophecy in her heart all these long months," said Hope, "of which that on her finger is only the symbol."

"However it may be," said Hester, "it has prepared a reception for Mr Enderby. There is no resisting a prophecy. What is written is written."

"I must hear him, you know," said Margaret, gently.

"You must; and you must hear him favourably," said her brother.

"I had forgotten," said Hester, ringing the bell. "Morris, a good fire in the breakfast-room, immediately."

Within the hour, Philip and Margaret were by that fireside, finally wedded in heart and soul. It was astonishing how little explanation was needed when Margaret had once been told, in addition to the fact of her letter having been destroyed, that she was declared to have made Mrs Enderby the depository of her confidence about a prior attachment. There was, however, as much to relate as there was little to explain. How Enderby's heart burned within him, when, in sporting with the idea of a prior attachment, it came out what Margaret had felt at the moment of his intrusion upon the conference with Hope, of which he had since, as at the time, been so jealous! the amusement on her own part, and the joy on Hester's, which she was trying to conceal by her downcast looks! How his soul melted within him when she owned her momentary regret at being saved from under the ice, and the consolation and stimulus she had derived from her brother's expression of affection for her on the spot! How clear, how true a refutation were these revealings of the imputations that had been cast upon her! and how strangely had the facts been distorted by a prejudiced imagination! How sweet in the telling was the story of the ring, so sad in the experience! and the recountings of the times that they had seen each other of late. Philip had caught more glimpses than she. He came down—he dared not say to watch over her in this time of sickness—but because he could not stay away when he heard of the condition of Deerbrook. But for this sickness would they have met—should they ever have understood each other again? This was a speculation on which they could not dwell—it led them too near the verge of the grave which was yawning for Matilda. Mrs Rowland would have been relieved, but the relief would have been not unmixed with humiliation, if she could have known how easily she was let off in this long conference. Not only can the happy easily forgive, but they are exceedingly apt to forget the causes and the history of their woes; and the wretched lady who, in the midst of her grief and terror for her child, trembled at home at the image of the lovers she had injured, was, to those lovers in their happiness, much as if she had never existed.

"Mrs Howell!" said Margaret, hearing her sister mention their departed neighbour, after Philip was gone. "Is it possible that it was this very afternoon that I saw that poor woman die?"

"Even so, dear. How many days, or months, or years, have you lived since? A whole age of bliss, Margaret!"

Margaret's blush said "Yes."

Chapter Forty Six

Deerbrook in Sunshine.

On the first news of the fever being gone, the Greys returned to Deerbrook, and Dr Levitt's family soon followed. The place wore a strange appearance to those who had been absent for some time. Large patches of grass overspread the main street, and cows might have pastured on the thatch of some of the cottages, while the once green churchyard looked brown and bare from the number of new graves crowded in among the old ones. In many a court were the spring-flowers running wild over the weedy borders, for want of hands to tend them; and the birds built in many a chimney from which the blue smoke had been wont to rise in the morning air. Sophia and her sisters noted these things as they walked through the place on the morning after their arrival, while their father was engaged in inspecting the parish register, to learn how many of his neighbours were gone, and their mother was paying her visit of condolence to Mrs Rowland.

Fanny and Mary were much impressed this day with Matilda's death. They had first wondered, and then wept, when they heard of it at a distance: and now, when once more on the spot where they had seen her daily, and had hourly criticised her looks, her sayings, and doings, they were under a strong sense of the meanness and frivolity of their talk, and the unkindness of their feelings about one whose faults could hardly be called her own, and who might now, they supposed, be living and moving in scenes and amidst circumstances whose solemnity and importance put to shame the petty intercourse they had carried on with her here. Both resolved in their hearts that if Anna Rowland should praise her own dancing, and flatten her back before she spoke, and talk often of the time when she should be married, they would let it all pass, and not tell mamma or Sophia, or exchange satirical looks with each other. They remembered now that Matilda had done good and kind things, which had been disregarded at the time when they were bent on ridiculing her. It was just hereabouts that she took off her worsted gloves, one bitter day in the winter, and put them on the hands of her little brother who was crying with cold; and it was by yonder corner that she directed a stranger gentleman into the right road so prettily that he looked after her as she walked away, and said she would be the pride of the place some day. Alas! there she lay—in the vault under the church; and she would be no one's pride in this world, except in her poor mother's heart.

"There is somebody not in mourning," cried Fanny; "the very first, besides my cousins, that we have seen to-day. Oh, it is Mrs James! Shall we not speak to her?"

Mrs James seemed warmed out of her usual indifference. She shook hands almost affectionately with Sophia. The meeting of acquaintances who find themselves alive after a pestilence is unlike any other kind of meeting: it animates the most indifferent, and almost makes friends of enemies. While Mrs James and Sophia were making mutual inquiries, Mary called Fanny's attention to what was to be seen opposite. There was a glittering row of large, freshly-gilt letters—"Miskin, late Howell, Haberdasher, etcetera." Miss Miskin, in the deepest mourning, with a countenance trained to melancholy, was peeping through the ribbons and handkerchiefs which veiled her window, to see whether the Miss Greys were on their way to her or not. Sophia would not have been able to resist going in, but that, on parting from Mrs James, she saw the true object of her morning walk approaching in the person of Mr Walcot. Her intention had been to meet him in his rounds; and here he was.

If Mrs James had been almost affectionate, what was Mr Walcot? He had really gone through a great deal of anxiety and suffering lately, and his heart was very soft and tender just now. He turned about, and walked with Sophia—walked a mile out into the country by her side, and neither seemed to have any thought of turning back, till Fanny reminded her sister how long mamma would have been kept waiting for her to go and call on the Levitts. The conversation had been in an under voice, all the way out and back; but, when the parting was to take place, when Mr Walcot was to leave them in the outskirts of the village, the little girls heard a few words which threw some light on what had been passing. They caught from Sophia, "I must consult my parents;" and as they hurried homewards with her, they ventured to cast up a glance of droll meaning into her face, which made her try to help smiling, and to speak sharply; and then they knew that they had guessed the truth.

Mr Grey made his call upon his cousins that evening. He requested some private conversation with Hope. His objects were, to learn Hope's opinion of Mr Walcot, as he had seen him of late under very trying circumstances; and, if this opinion should be sufficiently favourable to warrant the proposition, to open the subject of a partnership—a partnership in which, as was fair, Mr Walcot should have a small share at present of the income, and a large proportion of the labour—which was all that the young man, under the effect of his recent terrors, and of his veneration for Mr Hope, wished or desired. He had declared that if he could obtain his beloved Sophia, and be permitted to rely on Mr Hope as his partner and friend, he should be the happiest man alive; and he was confident that his parents would consider him a most fortunate youth, to be received, at his outset into life, into such a family as Mr Grey's, and under the professional guidance of such a practitioner and such a man as Mr Hope.

There seemed to be every probability of his becoming the happiest man alive for the Greys were clearly well disposed towards him, and Mr Hope had nothing to say of him which could hurt their feelings. He repeated what he had declared to Mr Rowland—that Mr Walcot's energies seemed to be concentrated in the practice of his profession, and that his professional knowledge appeared to be sufficient. There was no doubt of his kindness of heart; and, though it could not be expected of him that he would ever make a striking figure in the world, yet he might sustain a fair portion of respectability and usefulness in a country station. As to the partnership, no difficulty arose. Mr Grey frankly explained that present income was far less of an object than to have his daughter settled beside her parents, and his son-in-law usefully and honourably occupied. Sophia would have enough money to make Walcot's income an affair of inferior consideration. If he should deserve an increase by and by, it would be all very well. If not, the young people must get on without. Anything was better than sending the young man away to establish himself in a new place, with no happier prospects to Sophia's family than that of parting with her to a distance at last.

It did not require many days to complete the arrangements. Hester was at first a little vexed, but on the whole much more amused, at the idea of her husband having Mr Walcot for a partner: and she soon saw the advantage of his being spared many a long country ride, and many a visit at inconvenient seasons, by his junior being at hand. She made no substantial objection, and invited Mr Walcot to the house with all due cordiality. The young man's gratitude and devotion knew no bounds; and the only trouble Hope felt in the business was the awkwardness of checking his expressions of thankfulness.

When the announcement of the double arrangement was to be made, Mrs Grey could not resist going herself to Mrs Rowland; and Sophia was sorry that she could not be present too, to see how the lady would receive the news of a third gentleman marrying into the Greys' connection so decidedly. But Mr Grey took care to enlighten his partner on the matter some hours before; so that Mrs Rowland was prepared. She persuaded herself that she was very apathetic—that she had no feelings left for the affairs of life—that her interests were all buried in the tomb of her own Matilda. Mrs Grey had therefore nothing in particular to tell Sophia when she returned from paying the visit.

In exchange for the news, Sir William and Lady Hunter sent back their congratulations, and a very gracious and extensive invitation to dinner. Finding that Mrs Rowland's brother was really, with the approbation of his family, going to marry Mrs Hope's sister, and that Mrs Rowland's *protégé* was entering into partnership with Mr Hope himself, they thought it the right time to give their sanction to the reconciliations which were taking place, by being civil to all the parties round. So Lady Hunter came in state to Deerbrook, one fine day, made all due apologies, and invited to dinner the whole connection. Mrs Rowland could not go, of course; and Margaret declined: but all the rest went. Margaret was on the eve of her marriage, and she preferred one more day with Maria, to a visit of ceremony. She begged Philip to go, as his sister could not; and he obeyed with a good grace, grudging the loss of a sweet spring evening over Sir William Hunter's dinner-table the less, that he knew Margaret and Maria were making the best use of it together.

Once more the friends sat in the summer-house, by the window, whence they loved to look abroad upon meadow, wood, and stream. Here they had studied together, and cherished each other: here they had eagerly imparted a multitude of thoughts, and carefully concealed a few. Here they were now conversing together for the last time before their approaching separation. Maria sighed often, as she well might: and when Margaret looked abroad upon the bean-setters in the distant field, and listened to the bleat of the lambs which came up from the pastures, and was aware of the scent of the hyacinths occasionally wafted in from poor Matilda's neighbouring flower-plot, she sighed too.

"You must take some of our hyacinths with you to London, and see whether they will not blossom there," said Maria, answering to her friend's thought.

"I hardly know whether there would be most pain or pleasure in seeing plants sprout, and then wither, in the little balcony of a back drawing-room, which overlooks gables or stables, instead of these delicious green meadows."

"How fond you were, two years ago, of imagining the bliss of living always in sight of this very landscape! Yet it has yielded already to the back drawing-room, with a prospect of stables and gables."

"We shall come and look upon your woods sometimes, you know. I am not bidding good-bye to this place, or to you. God forbid!"

"Now tell me, Margaret," said Maria, after a pause, "tell me when you are to be married."

"That is what I was just about to do. We go on Tuesday."

"Indeed! in three days! But why should it not be so? It is a weary time since you promised first."

"A year ago, there were reasons, as Philip admits now, why I could not leave Hester and Edward. There are no such reasons now. They are prosperous: their days of struggle, when they wanted me—my head, my hands, my little income—are past. Edward's practice has come back to him, with increase for Mr Walcot. There is nothing more to fear for them."

"You have done your duty by them: now—"

"*My* duty! What has it been to theirs? Oh, Maria! what a spectacle has that been! When I think how they have 'overcome evil with good,' how they have endured, how forgiven, how toiled and watched on their enemies' behalf, till they have ruled all the minds, and touched all the hearts, of friends and foes for miles round, I think theirs the most gracious piece of tribulation that ever befell. At home,—Oh, even you do not know what a home it is!"

Nor was Margaret herself aware what that home was now. She saw how Edward had there, too, 'overcome evil with good' how he had permanently established Hester in her highest moods of mind, strengthened her to overcome the one unhappy tendency from which she had suffered through the whole of her life, and dispersed all storms from the dwelling wherein his child was to grow up: but she did not know half the extent of his victory, or the delight of its rewards. She knew nothing of the secret shudder with which he looked back upon the entanglement, the peril, the suffering he had gone through; or of the deep peace which had settled down upon his soul, now that the struggle was well past. She little imagined how, when all the world regarded him as an old married man, his was now, in truth, the soul of the lover: how, from having at one time pitied, feared, recoiled from her with whom he had connected himself for life, he had risen, by dint of a religious discharge of duty towards her, from self-reproach and mere compassion, to patience, to hope, to interest, to admiration, to love—love at last worthy of hers—love which satisfied even Hester's imperious affections, and set even her over-busy mind and heart at rest. Little did Margaret imagine all this. There was but one, beside Edward himself, who knew it; and that one was Morris, who daily thanked God that strength had been given according to the need.

"There is but one person in the world, Maria," said her friend, "on whose account I cannot help being anxious. I was faithless about Hester as long as it was possible to have an uneasy thought for her; and now I am afraid I shall sin in the same way about you."

"And why should you, Margaret? If I were without object, without hope, without experience, without the power of self-rule which such experience gives, you might well fear for me. But why now? It is not reasonable towards the Providence under which we live; it is not just to me."

"That is very true. But though it is not too much for your faith, that you are infirm and suffering in body, poor, solitary, living by toil, without love, without prospect—though all this may not be too much for your faith, Maria, I own it is at times for mine."

"Of all these evils, there is but one which is very hard to bear. I *am* solitary; and the suffering from the sense of this is great. But what has been borne may be borne; and this evil is precisely that which has been the peculiar trial of the greatest and best of their race—or of those who have been recognised as such. You will not suppose that I try to flatter my pride with this thought; or that the most insane pride could be a support under this kind of suffering. I mean only that there can be nothing morally fatal in a trial which many of the wisest and best have sustained."

"But it is painful—very painful."

"For the mere pain, let it pass; and for the other *désagrémens* of my lot, let us not dare to speak evil of them, lest we should be slandering my best friends. If infirmity, toil, poverty, and the foibles of people about us, all go to fortify us in self-reliance, God forbid that we should quarrel with them!"

"But are you sure, quite sure, that you can stand the discipline? that your nerves, as well as your soul, can endure?"

"Far from sure: but my peril is less than it was; and I have, therefore, every hope of victory at last. In my wilderness, some tempter or another comes, at times when my heart is hungry, and my faith is fainting, and shows me such a lot as yours—all the sunny kingdoms of love and hope given into your hand—and then the desert of my lot looks dreary enough for the moment; but then arises the very reasonable question, why we should demand that one lot should, in this exceedingly small section of our immortality, be as happy as another: why we cannot each husband our own life and means without wanting to be all equal. Let us bless Heaven for your lot, by all means; but why, in the name of Providence, should mine be like it? Nay, Margaret, why these tears? For their sake I will tell you—and then we shall have talked quite enough about me—that you are no fair judge of my lot. You see me often, generally, in the midst of annoyance, and you do not (because no one can) look with the eye of my mind upon the future. If you could, for one day and night, feel with my feelings, and see through my eyes—."

"Oh, that I could! I should be the holier for ever after?"

"Nay, nay! but if you could do this, you would know, from henceforth, that there are glimpses of heaven for me in solitude, as for you in love; and that it is almost as good to look forward without fear of chance or change, as with such a flutter of hope as is stirring in you now. So much for the solitaries of the earth, and because Providence should be justified of his children. Now, when is this family meeting to take place in the corner-house?"

"Frank hopes to land in August; and Anne, Mrs Gilchrist, will meet him as soon as she can hear, in her by-corner of the world, of his arrival. The other sister is still abroad, and cannot come. I hope Anne may be a friend to you—an intimate. Judging by her brothers, and her own letters, I think she must be worthy."

"Thank you; but you are, and ever will be, my intimate. There can be no other. We shall be often seeing you here."

"Sometimes; and we shall have you with us."

"No: I cannot come to London. I shall never leave this place again, I believe; but you will be often coming to it. When that crowd of new graves in the churchyard shall be waving with grass, and those old woods looking more ancient still, and the grown people of Deerbrook telling their little ones all about the pestilence that swept the place at the end of the great scarcity, when *they* were children, you and yours, and perhaps I, may sit, a knot of grey-headed friends, and hear over again about those good old days of ours, as we shall then call them."

"And tell how there was an aged man, who told us of his seeing the deer come down through the forest to drink at the brook. I should like to behold those future days."

"And to remember whose face you saw in the torchlight, at the time and place of your hearing the old man's tale. Whose horse do I hear stopping at the stable?"

"It is Philip's. He has galloped home before the rest," said Margaret, drawing back from the window with the smile still upon her face. "Now, Maria, before any one comes, tell me—would you like to be with me on Tuesday morning or not? Do as you like."

"I will come, to be sure," said Maria, smiling. "And now, while there is any twilight left, go and give Mr Enderby the walk in the shrubbery that he galloped home for."

Margaret kept Philip waiting while she lighted her friend's lamp; and its gleam shone from the window of the summer-house for long, while, talking of Maria, the lovers paced the shrubbery, and let the twilight go.

Printed in the USA
CPSIA information can be obtained
at www.ICGtesting.com
LVHW091817261223
767356LV00005B/273